Fate of the Warriors

by

Mike Johnson

Bloomington, IN Milton Keynes, UK

AuthorHouse™
1663 Liberty Drive, Suite 200
Bloomington, IN 47403
www.authorhouse.com
Phone: 1-800-839-8640

AuthorHouse™ UK Ltd.
500 Avebury Boulevard
Central Milton Keynes, MK9 2BE
www.authorhouse.co.uk
Phone: 08001974150

First published by AuthorHouse 3/1/2007

ISBN: 978-1-4259-7824-2 (sc)
ISBN: 978-1-4259-7825-9 (hc)

Printed in the United States of America
Bloomington, Indiana

This book is printed on acid-free paper.

For Lynne and Andy

Also by Mike Johnson:

Warrior Priest

PROLOGUE

Young Edward Lawrence watched in silent awe as his father, Henry, led four mammoth draft horses from the whitewashed barn. The brutes dwarfed Henry, a bronzed, tautly muscled man of medium height. Henry paused, drawing in deeply a breath of crisp morning air. He smiled at Edward. Expertly, Henry hitched the four horses to an iron plow. He gripped the reins lightly, issued a soft command, and the huge animals began lumbering toward a nearby field. Six-year-old Edward went skipping along behind. The year was 1906.

It was the horses' first time in the field that spring. Three were veterans and used to working together. The fourth was a young newcomer Henry had purchased from Amish farmers the previous fall.

"Can I help, Daddy?"

Henry glanced down at his son and smiled. "Maybe next year."

With steady hands and sure commands, Henry positioned the horses for their first, slow swath through the rich earth near Shelby, Ohio. They snorted excitedly and strained, their iron-shoed hoofs struggling for purchase, and the plow began to break and turn the crusted ground. They had not gone far, perhaps 20 yards, when something spooked the new horse. He reared up, panicked and broke, and the other three followed.

The reins freakishly looped and tightened around Henry's right hand. He pitched forward. The frightened team didn't drag Henry far, but during their run, a large, hard hoof hammered his head.

Dread spread instantly through Edward's small body. He went dashing toward his father. The team had stopped. The young horse snorted again, threw his head back and reared slightly. Edward knelt beside Henry, freed his hand from the reins and eased his limp body to the ground.

The boy blinked away the first tears but couldn't stem the flow. Gently, his small hands passed across his father's cheeks. He stood and began to trudge back to the house to tell his mother.

At age six, Edward soon would learn, he would be wearing the mantel of "the man of the house." His three older sisters, responsible all, would ease his burden and that of his mother.

Edward grieved, but the resilience of youth helped him cope with his loss. He went on to complete eight years of school, then quit to help support his mother. He found work in an auto assembly plant in Cleveland, 90 miles north of his native Shelby. He lived frugally in a boardinghouse owned by a professor and weekly sent home most of his meager earnings.

In 1918, over his mother's protestations, Edward enlisted in the Army and fought in Europe. Several small shards of shrapnel pierced his right thigh and hip, but he recovered. He returned to Shelby and went to work in a factory that made the renowned Shelby Flyer Bicycle.

CHAPTER 1

Shelby, a small community in north central Ohio, long was a model of serenity. At one time, the most hotly debated issue found residents contesting vigorously the retention or removal of parking meters on Main Street. The meter backers lost. For decades, the population hovered around 10,000. The town, founded in the early 1800s, first was known as Gamble's Mill. Beginning in the late 1800s, Shelby blended industry and agriculture in a way that enabled the town to prosper quietly. The tallest structure long has been the grain elevator, the largest employer a steel mill. A stream, the Blackfork, divides Main Street and the town into east and west but, except for occasional floods, is hardly noteworthy and divides the community in no other appreciable respect.

Early settlers bore such names as Gamble, Marvin, Lewis, Whitney and Smiley. Then came Metzgers, Yetzers, Yosicks and Friebels. Generations of Shelby youngsters grew up wrongly believing there existed an ordinance that required blacks to be out of town by sundown. For years, the Jewish community consisted of two old-maid schoolteachers whose specialty was Latin. Shelby, in a word, was white if not WASP; about 20 percent of the community was Roman Catholic.

In 1920, a pair of Shelbians, Edward Lawrence and Sarah Thomson, married. They were a striking couple. She was delicately boned and pretty. Her smile was white and even, her eyes blue and clear, her hair flaxen and short. She was generally reserved but with a sunny disposition. Edward's height – five feet nine inches – was a little above average for the era, and he was broad shouldered and deep chested. He possessed enormous strength, especially in his hands, which it seemed could squeeze sweat from a stone. His handsome face was sculptured as finely and cleanly as Michelangelo's David.

This union produced two sons, Dick in 1922, and Bill two years later. The boys were engaging and musically inclined. Dick started playing a clarinet in 1932, and Bill began piano lessons at the same time.

After more than 15 years of marriage, Edward and Sarah still were in love and still sensitive to each other's needs. Although Edward generally was a practical man, he occasionally lavished expensive gifts on Sarah, often over

1

her sincere but futile protests. To pay for them, she knew Edward had to put in hours of sweaty overtime in the machine shop of the bicycle factory.

On a steamy August evening in 1936, Edward and Sarah were in the kitchen doing dishes. Sarah was washing, using a rough cloth, Edward drying. They were chatting easily about nothing in particular, flitting from one topic to another. Dick, now 14, and Bill, 12, were playing catch in the backyard of the neat, two-story white frame house on Second Street.

"Edward," said Sarah with motherly concern, "you'd better call Bill in. I don't want him to get overheated in the damp night air and bring on his asthma."

"Okay," Edward answered with fatherly detachment, "just as soon as we finish these dishes."

"Whew." Sarah exhaled. "I feel a real headache coming on. Must have done too much today." In the last few days, several severe headaches had attacked Sarah. They were excruciating but brief. They passed within minutes, and she ascribed them to tension or possibly some womanly disorder.

"Let me finish," Edward offered. "You lie down."

"No, I'm just about done."

As Sarah was reaching for a dirty plate, the throbbing inside her skull quickened and sharpened. She never before had experienced pain like this. She paused, holding the plate just above the surface of the sudsy water. In the next moment, the plate slipped from her hand. The warm water splashed on Edward's bare arm. He turned with a smile, prepared to make a small, affectionate joke about her clumsiness. Instead, he saw Sarah beginning to slump. Her knees buckled and bumped against the cupboard door beneath the sink. Edward's hands grabbed for her shoulders, but her body was falling too quickly away from him. She dropped hard against the freshly waxed linoleum floor.

She's fainted, thought Edward. From the heat. I hope she didn't hurt herself falling. He knelt beside Sarah, who was lying on her back, knees slightly bent. "Sarah, are you all right?" Edward said softly. "Sarah, wake up," he commanded gently. He patted her lightly with his right palm against her left cheek. Her eyes opened and showed panic. Her body didn't move. Her breathing was shallow. Fear began snaking through Edward's body, first constricting his throat and then slinking downward into his chest and beyond. He knew something was horribly wrong.

2

At Memorial Hospital, Sarah died within the hour. A massive stroke had felled and killed this warm, vigorous woman. She was 35.

Sarah's death severely buffeted Edward, 36, shocking him into silence. At the hospital, he did not rage. Instead, he felt queasy, as though someone had kicked him hard in the groin. That she had not lingered and suffered was little solace. The days that followed and the funeral itself barely registered. His own will to live wavered. Yet, in the next few weeks, he rebounded well from the initial shock, revived in large part by the need to care for his two sons.

It was only when Dick and Bill began to recover from their shock that Edward started truly to grieve. As much as for Sarah, he sorrowed for himself. For help, he turned to bourbon. I only need a shot or two to help me sleep, he thought at first. I'm working as much overtime as possible, sometimes two straight shifts, more to fill my time than my wallet. Eventually, though, he needed several shots a night before sleep would come. Even then he sometimes slept fitfully. Finally, he no longer bothered going to the kitchen for his bourbon. After the boys were in bed, he brought the bottle into the living room and placed it on the floor beside his chair. Soon thereafter he stopped pouring shots into a glass, instead drinking from the bottle.

Each night dragged on interminably. Memories tormented him. Some nights he managed to stagger to bed. Others he spent dozing uncomfortably in an overstuffed chair that seemed to hold him prisoner. He would try to rise, but some unseen heavy hand overpowered him.

Before Sarah died, Edward Lawrence never needed an alarm clock. His own internal mechanism roused him unerringly. In the months following her death, the increasing quantities of bourbon dulled the workings of that internal clock. It became imprecise and unreliable. I guess I'd better get to the store and buy an alarm clock, he concluded. Just a cheap one should do. At the store, he was embarrassed to place it on the checkout counter. Cheap as it was, though, Edward came to rely on it.

His deterioration disgusted him. In the mornings, he meticulously brushed his teeth and tongue. But Dick and Bill knew their father was drinking, and Edward knew they knew. None of them said anything about it.

Dick and Bill still felt the void hewn by their mother's death. But their youth blessed them with resilience. Within months they were forging ahead,

3

taking on life toe to toe.   As they did so, the boys began to feel sorry for Edward. They loved and respected him, and they knew how deeply Edward had loved Sarah.   In an age when many men deigned to show affection, Edward had showered Sarah with playful squeezes and heartfelt hugs. Sarah had responded with girlish squeals and obvious delight.

In a way, Sarah's death had strengthened Dick and Bill. They were able to observe Edward's self-pity without avoiding or despising him. They were patient and hopeful.

Then came an epiphany. At 6:00 one morning early in July 1937, the alarm clock jolted Edward from a fitful sleep. The clock's firehouse bell lifted his upper body clear of the bed. Angrily, he slammed his left hand against the vibrating alarm pin. He silenced the alarm, but the blow sent the clock sliding off the edge of the night table and clattering across the cool linoleum floor. "Shit," Edward muttered, "the damn thing didn't break." Edward was relieved. He knew he would need the clock tomorrow morning.

He went shuffling to the bathroom. He stared at the mirror, set in a medicine chest door over the sink. What he saw angered him as the alarm clock had moments before. The brown hair was disheveled, but what disgusted him was realizing that it was oily and dirty. Before Sarah's death, Edward Lawrence had been peacock proud of his appearance. Something else angered him as well. His stubble looked longer than normal. Had he forgotten to shave yesterday?

"This has to change," he whispered to himself, "starting now." Determinedly, he ran warm water. He lathered his hands with Ivory soap. He jammed the suds into his mouth. Grimacing, he bent over the sink, cupped his hands to trap water, then quickly brought them upward. Straightening, he vigorously sloshed the sudsy water inside his mouth. He began to gag but forced himself to keep from spitting. He could feel the soap cutting through the stale taste left by the bourbon. After more than half a minute, he spat the suds from his cleansed mouth and rinsed twice.

Then he stepped across the room to the tub. He turned on the water, knelt on the floor and bent double over the side. Three times he lathered his hair with the same bar of Ivory used to cleanse his mouth. He rinsed for the third time and towel-dried his now squeaky hair. Then he lathered his face with the Ivory and shaved as closely and meticulously as the day he first went courting Sarah almost 20 years before.

4

At breakfast, Dick and Bill noticed the change but said nothing. Only when Edward smiled did they smile and say good morning. Still, Edward said little. After breakfast, he grasped the boys' shoulders. "Remember to check in at noon with Aunt Miriam," he instructed. She was Edward's widowed older sister, who lived on Third Street and who had been helping care for the boys.

Edward picked up his lunch pail and stepped outside onto the porch. It was now 7:30. The sun was beginning to climb into a sky that already was a radiant blue. High summer. Edward sucked in the air, which wasn't cool but still offered a hint of freshness. He stepped a few paces south along Second Street. Edward felt an urge to run. He trotted tentatively for a few strides, then quickened his pace. His stride lengthened and his knees began to churn like a pair of runaway pile drivers. Three quarters of a mile separated the Lawrence house from the Shelby Cycle Company, where Edward labored as a drill press operator. He went shooting past thick maple trees that lined the sidewalk on Second Street. He wheeled west onto Main Street, unmindful of the stares of passersby. Old Dan, the horse slowly pulling the milk wagon, shot Edward a glance and snorted derisively. At High School Avenue, Edward cut south, barely slowing to negotiate the corner. The Cycle Company, a three-story brick structure dating from the 1890s, lay ahead on the left. The hard run consumed just a few minutes.

As Edward came striding into the factory, sweat was dripping from his temples. Nonetheless, he felt clean. He had begun to purify his body and mind and he knew it. He had not dwelled on Sarah that morning, not in the bathroom, not at breakfast, not during his run. At work now, he thought of her. Though he still missed her dearly, depression and self-pity failed to clamp him in their familiar and painful grip.

That afternoon after work, the temperature was 84 degrees. Edward ran home. Hard, all the way. Again the sweat flowed freely. He felt purer still. And strong. The boys were not home. Edward ascended to the bathroom, filled the tub with a foot of tepid water and eased himself in. Once in the water, he relaxed, then luxuriated.

That night the bourbon stayed in the cupboard.

For Edward Lawrence, the period between mid-1937 and late 1941 sped by. He labored long hours at the factory, where he became machine shop foreman. More and more, Dick and Bill became his friends, although at times they were trying friends, especially the younger son, Bill.

Handsome as his father though resembling more his mother, Bill was a gifted young man who chose to apply his talents almost everywhere but in the classroom. Besides the piano, he now played trumpet. He played it well and was a standout in the high school band.

Bill caddied at the local country club. The money helped finance his active social life, and the opportunity to observe and practice uncovered a talent for golf. Bill was strong off the tee, confident and true from traps and roughs and supremely self-assured on the greens.

In the late 1930s, girls didn't pursue boys with the same overtness as young women of more recent vintage, but Bill was a popular target nonetheless. He was choosy about which girls caught him. Only the prettiest, most vivacious met with success.

Bill's nemesis was the classroom. For him a report card B was analogous to an early May snowfall – not unheard of but not expected. An A would have been cause for an investigation as much as a celebration. C's and D's were the norm. Not that Bill was lacking in gray matter. More than once a teacher would tell Edward, "Bill is very smart. He could do anything if only he would try."

Edward long ago had given up badgering Bill to try. Never had threatened him. Edward's own formal education had stopped after eighth grade. But he had read voraciously in many disciplines and was a learned man. In his wisdom, he knew with certainty the time would come when Bill would begin to try.

That time arrived in September 1940, shortly after Bill turned 16. He had learned to drive, with Edward as his instructor, in the summer of 1939. Now he was newly licensed. On a Thursday night after supper, Bill came ambling casually into the living room where, as on most nights, Edward was engrossed in a book. This night it was light reading, *The Last Trail*, a Zane Grey tale. Edward's feet were propped up on an ottoman. In front of the ottoman, Bill stood in tan beltless slacks, white t-shirt, white socks and brown and white saddle shoes. Carefree, thought Edward; he looks carefree.

"Dad," Bill said confidently, "I'd like to use the car on Saturday night. May I please?"

"You would?" Edward's response was non-emotional and non-committal.

"I have a date with Helen. We're going to a movie at the Castamba and we'd like to drive around for a while afterward."

"I see."

"Can I use it?" The slightest doubt had crept into Bill's voice. He had expected nothing more than a simple yes from his generous, loving father.

"Bill," Edward said calmly, "I'll tell you what. You can begin to use the car just as soon as you make the honor roll."

Bill was stunned. But in his remaining years in high school, he never again gave Edward cause to deny him use of the 1932 Ford V-8.

Dick presented fewer parental challenges. A practical-minded, serious student, he sailed through high school, charming teachers and fellow students alike. Like Bill, Dick was a talented musician. His specialty had shifted from clarinet to trombone, and he too played in the high school band. Dick more closely resembled Edward but was not as handsome. However, his height, an even six feet, his soft blue eyes, sparkling smile, sandy hair, bluff personality and resonant laugh made him as popular a target for girls as Bill.

If Edward harbored any regrets about Dick and Bill, it was their general disinterest in team sports. Golf, Bill's game, was not Edward's. Nor was Dick's tennis. They lacked the rough and tumble of football and baseball, which long had been passions for Edward. He longed to share his intense interest with his sons. At Friday night high school football games, Edward wished often that he just once could see Dick or Bill on a gridiron at some point besides halftime.

Not that Edward wasn't proud of his sons' musical accomplishments. He was. He watched them closely as they high-stepped their patterns every Friday night. Still, he thought it would be nice to have a son who wore a helmet instead of a hat.

In June 1940, Dick graduated second in his Shelby class. That autumn, with an academic scholarship as his ticket, he entrained for Evanston, Illinois, and Northwestern University. He did well his first year, achieving a 3.64 grade point average. Edward virtually popped his shirt buttons in July 1941, when he learned of Dick's final freshman grades.

In September 1941, Dick returned eagerly to Northwestern. He had decided to major in accounting, a wise, Dick-like choice, which Edward heartily endorsed.

Edward felt very different emotions when, on December 18, 1941, he received a letter from Dick.

December 15, 1941

Dear Dad,

You know me. Face up to a problem, think it through thoroughly – and then make a stupid decision.

Dad, I'm leaving school. I won't say quitting because I'm not a quitter and you know that. But I feel I have to enlist. I'm leaning toward the Navy, which certainly can use more men now. Don't write or send a telegram or even call. By the time you get this, I'll be on my way home.

See you soon.

Love, Dick

P.S. At least you won't have to send me money anymore.

Bill graduated from Shelby High School on June 4, 1942, and, despite Edward's urgings to follow Dick into the Navy, joined the Army on June 5. By the time Bill finished basic training at Fort Dix, New Jersey, Dick already was aboard a destroyer, the USS Corry.

Bill took to soldiering. He had outgrown his asthma. He had filled out and, with an appetite sharpened by daylong drilling, his six-foot one-inch frame now carried a hard 185 pounds.

When he enlisted, Bill left behind his father and Helen Wakefield, the dazzling, honey-haired girl who two years previously had been part of Bill's academic turnaround. That September Saturday night in 1940, Bill and Helen had gone to a movie, *Jesse James,* with Henry Fonda and Tyrone Power, but they had walked. After Bill had made the honor roll, he and Helen and the 1932 Ford V-8 were as much a threesome as Dumas' musketeers.

Before Bill left Shelby, Helen promised to wait.

"I'm going to marry you the day after I get back," Bill pledged.

"What about the blood tests and waiting period?" she laughed.

Helen held him fiercely and began crying when she heard the train approaching Shelby's Baltimore & Ohio station. Bill gripped her tightly. He felt tears welling but gritted his teeth and swallowed hard. "It won't be long," he whispered hoarsely. "You'll see. We'll have a lifetime together."

"Do you promise?" She was sobbing, her body heaving.

"I promise."

CHAPTER 2

This is crazy, Edward Lawrence chided himself. I'm 43 years old, two grown sons in a global war, and here I am trying to work up courage to ask a young woman out to dinner.

Young woman. That fact alone, mused Edward, probably explains why I've got so many butterflies fluttering around in my stomach. She's only 22. That's only a year older than Bill. And that makes her a year younger than Dick.

No self-respecting man dates a woman young enough to have been his son's playmate, Edward scolded himself halfheartedly. As he leaned against a hallway wall outside the door that led to the offices at the Shelby Cycle Company, the other half of his heart urged him to approach the young file clerk.

Harriet had started working at the factory in January 1943, just two months ago. Edward had noticed her right away on one of his frequent trips to the office of plant manager Gordon Davis. Once Edward needed to ask Harriet for some information to clear up a question one of his shop people had about overtime hours.

He knew nothing about this courteous, pleasant young woman who quickly and efficiently located and pulled the correct records. Yet he felt an immediate attraction to her. Harriet was the comely daughter and only child of sincere, hardworking parents. Her father Henry was a furnace man at the local steel mill, and her mother Abigail might have been called – if the term had been coined then – a workaholic. A slender, shy and deeply religious woman, Abigail was happiest when working. Which she did from dawn until after dark. Hers was an exhausting regimen of cooking, laundering, cleaning, gardening, canning, ironing and generally caring for Henry.

What more than anything drew Edward to Harriet was her open warmth and complete absence of pretense. When Harriet learned that Edward had two sons in the armed forces, she made a point of greeting him as he approached her desk and asking after his boys. That she was petite, five feet two inches, blonde and pretty with deep blue eyes, a soft yet sure voice, and a smile set off by brilliant white teeth, heightened Edward's desire to be in her company. Even if only for a few moments at a time.

As Edward stood nervously in the hallway trying to sort out his emotions on that March day in 1943, Dick and the USS Corry were cutting through the icy Atlantic, escorting troop transports and supply ships and watching for U-boats. Meanwhile, Bill was in North Africa with other infantrymen, plodding through the desert behind Patton's dashing tanks. Edward lived for their letters, written almost daily but generally delivered in batches. Combat and the vagaries of the postal service explained the irregularity. The letters provided the most minute detail of their daily lives. As a World War I veteran wounded at Chateau-Thierry, Edward could well understand their fears and frustrations. He missed them terribly and worried about them constantly, despite the boys' assurances that they were well fed, in good health and doing their level best to stay out of harm's way.

As one of Bill's letters read in part: *Got into a scrap with the Krauts yesterday. Found a nice sand dune and did my best to keep it between me and any Germans. More than happy to let Patton's tanks play leader to my follower. I won't win any Purple Hearts for sand burns, but then I really didn't bleed anyway, just baked a little.*

In the almost seven years since Sarah's death, Edward had hardly looked at women, much less dated. His female social contacts had been limited to visits by Helen Wakefield, who wanted to read the letters Bill wrote to Edward. That they generally contained the same information as the flood of missives that arrived at her house mattered little to Helen. Bill had written them with his own hand, and that counted for a lot. She devoured them hungrily, rereading each until it was virtually memorized. Besides, she enjoyed the bluff, witty company of Edward who kidded her unmercifully about virtually everything. This man, Helen told herself often, would make the ideal father-in-law and, in time, grandfather.

Suppose, Edward fretted, still standing outside the door to the office area, that I ask Harriet out and she says yes. Then what in God's name does she tell her parents? That a kindly old man asked her out? And if she says yes, what do I say to her parents when I pick her up? What would they say to me? Nice to meet you, young man? That's a laugh. Oh, hell, I might as well get my butt in there and give it a try. At least, she calls me Edward and not Mr. Lawrence.

Uneasily, Edward was approaching the steps of the Vogel home on Marvin Avenue. Theirs was a two-story white frame house quite like his own but 20 years newer. He sucked in the invigorating November night air. He needed its bracing effect. The night before, eight months after their first date, Edward has proposed to Harriet, who happily and without hesitation accepted. It helped that Edward had volunteered to convert from Presbyterianism to Catholicism and to raise any children as Catholics.

For Harriet, the 21-year age gap that had once seemed so cavernous and unbridgeable had shrunk into insignificance. Edward now was discounting it but couldn't totally ignore it. Someday, he knew, he would be an old man and a burden to a much younger woman. Unless illness or accident struck him down early. He pushed away such thoughts as far as possible.

Edward liked and respected Henry and Abigail Vogel, and they admired this father of two United States servicemen who were fighting the mad man who was destroying their Old World homeland and murdering millions in the insane process. Still, they too worried about the age gap, for the same reasons as Edward. They could foresee the possibility of a young widow with young children. But, given their feelings for Harriet and Edward, they said nothing.

"Good evening, Edward. Come in," Abigail greeted him warmly. "I'll call Harriet."

"No, wait," Edward said with a noticeable measure of abruptness. Nervously, he swished his tongue to promote moisture in his parched mouth. "I'm here to see you and Henry."

"Oh, what about?" A pause, then a blurted "Oh" and a becoming blush as understanding struck her. "Oh" she repeated, smiling. "I'll get him. He's upstairs. Please go into the living room and sit down."

"Thank you." In fact, Edward was too edgy to sit or to stand still. He paced back and forth, wondering briefly whether the modicum of courage he had mustered would desert him. He jammed his hands into his pockets and once again questioned the wisdom of his decision to ask Henry and Abigail for their daughter's hand.

Dick and Bill both were elated when letters from their father brought news of the wedding date. Bill was in Sicily when he received word about the big day, March 25, 1944. The letter arrived at a mid-morning mail call in late November 1943. He tore open the envelope bearing his father's return address. As he unfolded the paper, a snapshot dropped to the ground. When he saw it was a picture of a fetching woman, intuition told him what Edward's letter confirmed. A warm glow spread through him as he read the details. As always, he had to read slowly Edward's scrawling hand. He laughed aloud when he read Edward's account of his nervousness on the night he had sought Mr. and Mrs. Vogel's permission to marry Harriet. *I was as edgy as a cat on a high, thin limb,* Edward had written. *I felt like calling the fire department to rescue me. A net underneath me would have been a welcome sight.* Bill was delighted. He felt happiness – and love, too – for his father. He studied closely the picture of Harriet Vogel, a woman he only vaguely remembered, having been three classes behind her at Shelby High. She's as pretty as Helen, he mused. I wonder what she'll want me to call her. Judging by her looks, Mom doesn't fit. I can hardly wait to see them.

The wedding was everything Harriet had ever dreamed about or hoped for. The ceremony was conducted by Father Michael McFadden, whose stern demeanor masked kindliness and generosity. He had become pastor of Most Pure Heart of Mary parish in the summer of 1937. He had replaced Father Albert Fate, a dictatorial priest of enormous drive who had come to Shelby in April 1923 from St. Boniface parish in Oak Harbor. Father Fate decided that the parish needed a new church. Or more precisely, a small cathedral. When he first spoke of his plans from the pulpit of the existing church, a modest structure topped by a slender spire, the drooping eyelids of parishioners snapped open. Their opinions of his proposal were conceived, gestated and fully formed within minutes. What he was calling for amounted to excessive zeal at best and, at worst, outright lunacy. The magnificent structure he was describing would bankrupt the parish if it could ever raise enough money to lay a foundation. Parishioners pressured him to develop a more modest alternative. They failed.

On June 15, 1928, four years after ground had been broken, Father Fate's strong will was done and the new church was dedicated. Beige and red brick with red tile roof, it stretched half a block. Inside, the ornate, heavy-beamed ceiling peaked more than 50 feet from the floor. The interior was eye-popping. The mammoth center altar, the three side altars and the statues above them and the Communion rail were sculpted from Italian white marble. The floors of the three long aisles were pink and gray marble. Eight massive granite pillars, each with the girth of a mature maple tree, lined each side of the church's main body. Paintings were everywhere. All were done by European artists Father Fate had brought to the U.S. Along each wall were two banks of soaring stained glass windows.

To marry in this spectacular local residence of God had been a dream of Harriet's since childhood. Often she envisioned her father escorting her down the center aisle. Waiting calmly at the foot of the main altar was kindly Father McFadden. Standing off to the right by the side altar of the Little Flower was her handsome husband-to-be. For years, before she had met Edward, the groom had no name, but that dimmed neither the vividness nor beauty of the dream.

Back in 1920, Edward and Sarah had honeymooned at Niagara Falls, which had been the honeymoon destination in Harriet's girlish dreams. But Harriet sensed Edward's feelings when first she raised the subject. "Let's go to Florida." Their trip south was magnificent and memorable. During the days, Edward and Harriet happily reminisced about their wedding, discussed their plans for redoing Edward's home on Second Street and imagined the joyful prospect of the end of the war and the safe return of Dick and Bill. Harriet remembered the boys from high school, but they had moved in different circles. Before the wedding, both Dick and Bill had written Harriet warm, witty letters in which they wished her great and everlasting happiness as their father's wife.

13

The farther south Edward and Harriet drove, the more evidence of spring they observed. The still dull grass and barren trees of Ohio gradually gave way to signs of life renewed. When they arrived at West Palm Beach, it was Harriet's first view of the ocean, and she was captivated by its power and majesty. It was Edward's first view of the Atlantic since his return from France in 1919. He shared completely Harriet's awe. When they first stepped onto the white sand beach, they stood hand in hand and marveled at this most mysterious of nature's creations. The earth's tallest mountain would be scaled in a few years, but the sea's deepest canyon, harbor of the unknown, long would remain beyond man's daring or ability. Leisurely, Edward and Harriet padded toward the water. On this brilliantly sunny but windy day, the ocean was rough. A strong surf rolled toward shore, a three-to-four-foot wave pounding the beach every ten seconds or so. When the water first lapped their toes, Harriet squealed. "Oh," she said, shivering, "it's cold."

Edward laughed. "It's still early in the year."

"I don't think I want to go in," Harriet said timidly. "Are you?"

"Yes, I think I'll wade out a bit. You can wait here or find a spot to sit. Lay out the towels anywhere."

"Don't go out too far," Harriet, a weak swimmer, cautioned worriedly.

"Okay." Edward was a strong swimmer but unused to the power of the ocean's surf and a bit wary. As he eased tentatively into the water, he could feel its force as broken waves rapped against his knees. When the water receded, the strong undertow tried to suck him along. Were he to wade out farther, Edward knew he would have to time the arrival of each wave and jump to reduce the water's impact against his body. He eased out until the water was at shoulder level. He saw the next wave coming. It rose about two feet above his head. He prepared to jump. Too late. His feet still were planted on the ocean floor when the wave smacked him, sending Edward heels over head and to the bottom.

When the wave struck and buried Edward, Harriet stared wide-eyed in silent horror. She simply hadn't imagined the power of nature's colossus, simultaneously beauty and beast. A cold shiver of panic was descending through her when she saw Edward shakily arise from his hands and knees. He barely was on his feet when he saw the next wave bearing down on him. This time he jumped earlier, and the wave carried him harmlessly a couple feet nearer shore. He knew he would be swimming precious little that day. A few strokes and then prepare for the next wave would be about it. When his feet touched bottom again, he began walking slowly back toward the beach. He spat salt water from his mouth, but the taste would linger for hours afterward.

When he looked up, he noticed Harriet's worried eyes. Edward laughed in spite of himself. "You won't get rid of me that easily," he shouted above the surf. "And you can't get an annulment either; in the last three days, you shot your grounds for that."

During the two months following their wedding, Harriet showed herself to be a tireless and uncomplaining wife who rose with her husband to prepare his breakfast and who listened to broadcasts of boxing matches and baseball games with Edward on his prized Farnsworth console radio-record player. Often they put on 78 rpm recordings of Glen Miller and Tommy Dorsey and danced in the living room.

"I can hardly believe my luck," Edward reflected more than once. "First Sarah, now Harriet. That's more than any reasonable man could hope for."

CHAPTER 3

June 6, 1944, dawned gray, wet and cold in the English Channel. This 350-mile-long ribbon, so often shrouded by fog and whipped by storms, had not seen so many vessels and men since the evacuation of Dunkirk four years before. Among the Allied vessels firing on the five targeted beaches were six battleships, 22 cruisers and 63 destroyers. They supported a fleet of 5,000 transports, landing craft, mine sweepers and assorted other vessels.

Bill Lawrence was squatting, huddled against the penetrating, predawn dampness on the deck of a transport. Damn, he thought, let's get going. Nothing can be worse than this waiting and the damp chill. Wrong, he smiled ruefully. All I have to do is think for a second about Africa and Italy to remind myself that things could be plenty worse. Bill forced himself to shiver to relieve tension.

15

Next to him, his friend Warren Maxwell felt Bill's body quiver. "Anything wrong, buddy? I mean besides this liquid air – great for shrinking kidneys and busting bladders."

Bill's chuckle was barely audible. "You know what I could use? A weed. I'm out."

"Say no more." Warren's stiffening fingers fumbled inside his jacket and clumsily and slowly retrieved a pack of Camels from his shirt pocket. "Shit, if we don't get going soon, my goddamn icy fingers will slip right down the ropes into the Higgins."

Bill smiled and pulled a Camel from Warren's pack. Then Warren helped himself. Bill produced a match and the lights. He inhaled deeply and held the smoke in his lungs for long seconds before exhaling. Both men knew the cold they were feeling was resulting as much from nerves as from the damp sea air. "First," said Bill, "it's sand burns in North Africa, and now it's freezing fingers in Europe. Before this fucking war's over," he said matter-of-factly, "I'll probably get jungle rot on some Pacific island."

Warren sighed. "Ah, the Pacific. Think of all those lucky Joes over there. Warm. Sunny skies, Polynesian beauties, coconuts. What I wouldn't give right now for one Polynesian beauty. Doe-eyed, horny, hot-in-the-crotch."

"Right now," said Bill, grinning tightly, "I'd like to get off this bouncing tub and onto terra firma Europa."

Before they had finished their cigarettes, the order came. Stiffly, they straightened and rose, using the bulkhead for support. Bill's knees cracked when he stood. Shit, he thought wearily, either this wet cold has frozen all the fluids in my body or I'm aging prematurely. Probably the former, he concluded hopefully.

Moments later, Bill and Warren flicked their cigarettes into the water, heaved themselves over the side of the transport, down the ropes and into the bouncing Higgins landing craft. They had done it many times in training and in the amphibious landings in North Africa and Sicily. Behind them hundreds of guns, including the destroyer Corry's, were roaring their encouragement to the soldiers and their anger to the Germans. Bill and Warren hunkered down for the ride to a beach called Omaha. Bill's First Infantry Division, dubbed the Big Red 1 for the unit's arm patch insignia, had been bloodied in both North Africa and Sicily. They would lead the assault through the moderately heavy surf.

Aboard the Corry, Lieutenant Dick Lawrence, a gunnery officer, watched his crew feed a pair of five-inch guns, two of five aboard the 348-foot vessel. Three of the guns were aft; two were forward. Dick commanded the forward guns. He preferred to stand behind the second turret, positioned behind and above the first. His crew's precision always fascinated him. Rip open the breech, ram home a shell, slam shut the breech and fire. Then watch for the flash and shield the ears from the roar. Through his binoculars, Dick saw shells explode and hurl into the sky tons of earth and God knows what else. He shifted his glasses and refocused. Between the Corry and the ridges beyond the beaches, Dick watched the flotilla of landing craft tear away from their mother ships. The Higgins boats bobbed determinedly toward shore, looking more like children's toys in a tub than instruments of war ferrying young men to an earthly hell.

Dick's mind carried him back to his reunion with Bill three weeks earlier. Through their correspondence, Dick had learned that Bill was leaving Italy for England. In one letter he told Bill how to reach him by phone once he arrived.

Later, when they made connections over a faint, crackling line, Dick instructed Bill to meet him at the Duke's Head, a pub opened in 1583 in Romsey, a lovely market village a few miles north of Southampton – the port badly damaged early in the war and now serving as a major staging point for D-Day. It was approaching eight o'clock on a Saturday night when Bill entered the worn, warm pub. Dick saw him and leaped up, nearly knocking over his chair. He found himself mumbling " Sorry" as he bolted for the door. Startled patrons expected to see this robust Yankee naval officer crush some sweet English bird. Instead, they saw two very virile men embrace wildly and jump and dance in circles while simultaneously clinging to and slamming each other on the back and shoulders.

"Goddamn," boomed Dick's bass voice. "It is so absolutely good to see you. Christ, you look good too. I thought you would have shriveled up over there in the Sahara."

"I just about did," laughed Bill. "But all that Sicilian pasta fleshed me out again. And this pea soup that passes for British air has rehydrated me." He paused. "Is that a word, rehydrated? Tell me, college man."

17

"Who the hell cares," laughed Dick, his green eyes glistening with merriment. "No matter what word you use, it still comes out you're all wet." He again clapped his younger brother on the shoulder.

The next several hours passed swiftly. Together, they were laughing uproariously, swearing copiously, drinking profligately and reminiscing fondly. That night they enjoyed each other's company more perhaps than ever before.

"Any regrets about not joining the Navy?" Dick asked.

"Nah. I like to swim but not in the pools you play around in. They're too deep and wide. And besides, who would want U-boats for playmates?"

On March 17, 1944, the Corry had sunk German U-boat 801 and taken on 47 survivors as prisoners.

"Maybe so," said Dick quietly, "but there *is* something to be said for three hots and a cot."

"Hell," Bill said, smiling, "I made it across North Africa without getting a scratch, and there were damn few trees to hide behind. At least in Europe they got forests."

"Yes," said Dick, smiling softly. Then, speaking quieter still, he said, "But to get to the forests, you've got to cross the beaches."

"Well," cracked Bill, "at least the sand will look familiar."

"Look," said Dick, not trying to disguise his concern, "it could be rough when you guys land. Remember to keep your head and your ass down and keep moving."

"You sound a little like my old drill sergeant," Bill said, grinning. "But you sound a lot more like Mom. Worry, worry, worry."

"Just be careful. You won't have Patton's tanks to run interference for you."

"You guys on the ships will soften things up for us and keep the Germans occupied."

"Yeah," said Dick, "that's the idea. But depending on where you land, the Germans could be dug in but good."

"Maybe I'll be lucky and go in on the second wave. Or better yet, on a mop-up operation. Maybe I'll be able to pick flowers all the way to Berlin."

"Or push them up," Dick grumbled with brotherly concern. "I didn't really mean that."

"I know. Don't worry; you won't jinx me. I've got too much to live for. I don't plan to check out any time early. And one thing's for sure. Helen and I have a lot of loving and living to do. I'm not about to pass that up." He stopped, then added seriously, "Do you wish you had a girl back home?"

"Sometimes. But if I did," Dick mused, "it would just be someone to miss and someone who would be worrying herself sick. I guess I'm glad I'm unattached."

They were silent a moment. Then Dick asked, "How's Helen holding up?"

"Fine, I believe. At least that's what she says, and Dad too. 'Course, they probably wouldn't say anything else. They see each other a lot to compare notes. I hope Dad doesn't show her all my letters. I mean the ones where I've mentioned combat. She'd really worry herself sick."

"I'll bet Dad does too."

"Probably," said Bill. "But sometimes I feel like telling someone. And I figure he can handle it better, especially since he's been through it. But I've probably been kidding myself." Then Bill reached into a pocket and extracted a small thin booklet measuring four by six inches and containing 40 pages. Its title: *Instructions for American Servicemen in Britain 1942*. It was a catechism of sorts, instructing young Americans on British culture and what British regarded as appropriate – and inappropriate – words and behavior. "Guess I won't be needing this anymore."

Dick smiled. "Maybe they'll be giving you a French version."

"Or," Bill murmured, "a German one."

The night ended late and yet all too soon. It was a night to be cherished. Two men were never closer, never loved each other more, than the brothers Lawrence on that Saturday night.

Omaha Beach was defended by 12 strong points containing 60 artillery pieces and numerous machine guns protected by pillboxes. It was nearing 5 a.m. when the pitching Higgins landing craft approached the beach. Bill and Warren Maxwell and many other GI's nervously sucked in deep breaths. Several men in their craft were seasick. Their vomit splattered on each other and fouled the air. Leather combat boots slipped as the boat bounced in the choppy water. The men, so crowded in the tiny craft they could barely move, were silent.

"Get ready!" shouted a disembodied voice. "You all know what to do." The men had practiced amphibious landings several times, and Bill and Warren were veterans of those earlier combat landings. "Get through the water as fast as possible. Keep your weapons and ammunition high and dry. Hit the beach and keep moving. If you have to get down, keep your weapons out of the sand. Don't stay in one place too long. Keep moving forward."

Outside the landing craft, the men could see little but the smoke of battle. A hundred black thunderstorms seemed to be waging their own battle in the skies. Incredibly, as they neared shore, the naval barrage, already deafening, intensified. Bill and Warren looked at each other; they exchanged faint, rueful smiles. Warren rolled his eyeballs skyward in skepticism.

"When we get to Paris," yelled Warren over the roar, "what'll it be first? A bottle of French wine or a grateful and beautiful broad?"

"How about a bath," shouted Bill, "in wine and with a girl?"

"What about a song?"

"We'll sing to each other."

"What if she doesn't understand English?"

"Body English is a universal language."

"Right. To Paris."

"To Paris."

In the next moment, the Higgins slowed to a near stop. Winches spun, chains uncoiled in a metallic clatter and the landing craft gate dropped. Bill's stomach knotted tightly.

"Out, out!" screamed the disembodied voice. "Everybody out. Move! Move!"

Bill and Warren were in the middle of the pack. By the time they leaped into the cold sea, one of their buddies already was face down in the shallow surf, his blood reddening the gray water. At least for him, Bill thought fleetingly, death was swift.

He and Warren splashed by the corpse, holding their rifles high. Around them, bullets from German machine guns and carbines were pocking the water. They kept moving.

20

They reached the wet sand and began slogging up the beach. Ahead of Bill and Warren, another GI dropped his rifle and fell face down. Bill and Warren dropped beside him. They rolled him over. Two spreading ugly stains on the soldier's chest told them death had beaten life again.

They rose to continue their awkward dash across the sand to the sea wall and then to the brush at the base of bluffs that towered 100 feet above them. More than a hundred yards of open ground remained. They could see fire erupting from German guns. They took two more steps when Warren pirouetted jerkily and dropped to the ground. Bill dove to his side.

"Warren, you're hit."

"Sweet Jesus." Warren groaned and shivered.

"How bad?"

"Like a shaving nick, I think. Stings like hell."

"Where?"

"Just above my belt. On the right side." Blood already was staining his field jacket.

"Medic!" Bill screamed.

"No," said Warren. "I'm okay." He winced and Bill looked at him dubiously. "Really. The scar will probably excite the girls back home."

"Let's return fire and get moving again," said Bill. Both men sprawled in a prone position. Immediately Bill began to squeeze off rounds toward a German machine gun emplacement that was raking their section of the beach. Warren, still wincing from pain, squeezed his trigger once and then twice more. His rifle remained silent. "Shit," he hissed fiercely.

"What's wrong?" yelled Bill over the steady din.

"Fucking rifle's jammed. Probably wet sand."

Quickly Bill laid down his own rifle. He grabbed Warren's and yanked back the bolt. Out popped the jammed cartridge. He slammed the bolt closed. "Try again," he shouted, handing the freed weapon back to Warren.

Each fired several rounds, then Bill shouted, "Let's move."

Warren nodded and gritted his teeth. The two soldiers stumbled forward, bent double for the first few strides. As they straightened slightly, Bill felt a fiery pain tear through his left shoulder. His face contorted and his jaws clenched. He pitched forward and to his left.

Warren pulled up, then scrambled back to Bill. "How bad is it?"

"Worse than a shaving nick," Bill gasped. "Jesus. Let's keep moving. We've got to reach that brush."

Warren scampered around to Bill's left side. He helped Bill to his hands and knees, then slipped his right arm across Bill's back and under his right shoulder. Bill's blood began to stain Warren's field jacket that already was reddened on the other side from Warren's own wound. With his right hand, Bill planted his rifle stock in the sand for support. As they were struggling to their feet, Bill felt another stab of searing pain, this one in his upper right chest. He fell face down, pulling Warren with him.

"Goddammit," Warren muttered viciously. "Shit." He gently rolled Bill from his hands and knees onto his right side. Warren's chest heaved as he gulped air. His left fist angrily pounded the ground. Then he spun on his knees toward the water. "Medic!" he bellowed. "Medic!"

Dick had seen combat before but never on this scale. In November 1942, the Corry had supported the first landings in the North African invasion off Casablanca. In October 1943, the destroyer had escorted the carrier Ranger during an air raid on German-occupied Bodo, Norway. And in March 1944, it had sunk a German submarine. But most of the Corry's work had been escorting convoys. On several occasions the Corry and her 208 men had broken away from processions of Allied vessels to chase a marauding U-boat, much as a sheepdog would chase a coyote away from a flock. But that kind of fight hardly equated with the panorama of fire, smoke, metal and men that now was unfolding from one end of the horizon to the other.

Dick was not a prayerful man, but he found himself beseeching God to show mercy on all the young warriors who were trying to kill and not be killed. Through his powerful binoculars, he could see that his prayer was meeting with less than resounding success. But, hell, thought Dick, even God couldn't be expected to hear much over this unearthly racket.

That morning the Corry and the destroyer Fitch were the first two ships to fire on German-occupied France. It's about time, Dick thought, we start taking it to Hitler. Just as the first wave of landing craft was arriving at Omaha and Utah beaches, Dick's fascination with the precise, clocklike work of his gun crew and the spectacular sights and sounds of battle switched unexpectedly and suddenly to alarm.

At first he thought the two distant dots moving toward the Allied armada from the eastern sky were American and British planes. He watched, entranced as the small dots grew. Thankfully, he thought, more badly needed air support for the assault troops. As the dots neared the armada, they began to take shape. They swooped lower, like diving eagles, and seemed to accelerate. As yet, no markings were visible. Nor could Dick hear the roar of their engines over the battle below.

Hundreds of pairs of Navy binoculars on scores of ships joined Dick's in following the dive of the mechanical birds. So complete was Dick's concentration on the speeding planes that the battle seemed to momentarily abate. His mind blocked out all else. Now he could hear the distant rumble of the eagles' engines. Before he could see their markings, machine gun fire erupted from the wings of the oncoming planes and sprayed the beaches. Why the beaches? The same thought simultaneously struck him and scores of other gunnery officers. "Germans! Germans! Enemy planes!" he cried. The macabre swastikas were visible now. Young gunners on the Corry wheeled the ship's machine guns and began firing at the diving German planes that now flattened out and skimmed low over the water.

In the next instant terror struck sharply and quickly at Dick and his men and hundreds of other seamen and soldiers. With deceptive laziness, long cylindrical objects dropped from the underside of the German planes. When the cylinders struck the surface, they splashed and dove but did not sink. They began knifing rapidly toward the American vessels. Torpedoes.

A moment later, one of the deadly fishes, swimming an unerring course just under the surface, struck and lifted from the sea a landing craft. The explosion flung pieces of metal and men in every direction. An audience of thousands watched horrified.

At the same moment, German artillery shells began sending up geysers of water around the Corry. Lieutenant Commander George Hoffman, the Corry's skipper, immediately screamed instructions: "Evasive action! Figure eights! But stay in our zone! Those waters are damn crowded. No collisions!"

Dick was watching fire erupt from German artillery that quickly was zeroing in on the Corry. Two of the shells plopped into the sea just 100 yards to starboard. Sweet Jesus, Dick's mind raced. The Corry was capable of 35 knots. Now she was barely moving. Not enough time to evade, Commander Hoffman's order notwithstanding. Dick's initial terror quickly was supplanted by a grim, calm determination to do what he could. Which, he knew, wasn't much. "Shells coming closer!" he bellowed to his laboring, sweating gun crew. "Get ready. Brace yourself. Here they come." Dick tensed and waited.

A shell struck near the Corry's stern. It was a glancing blow that Dick hardly felt, although the deafening noise caused his hands to involuntarily loosen their grip on a rail and rise to cover his ears. An instant later, a second shell struck the Corry's bow. The explosion violently shook the destroyer and knocked Dick off his feet. Cold salt water splashed him. Pieces of sharp steel flew by him. Fire leaped toward his turrets. He scrambled to his feet.

Madly, the ship's klaxon shrieked, over and over. Moments later, before the command came to abandon ship, Dick knew the Corry was gone. An odd thought sped through his mind. Maybe Bill had been right about the pools I play in. Maybe they are too big and too deep. And German artillery shells and torpedoes, whether from U-boats or planes, make decidedly unpleasant playmates. At least, it occurred to Dick, rescue should come swiftly in the crowded channel.

In the next instant, in horror, Dick saw a shadow in the water. Mine. The Corry started to pass over it. Then came a thunderous explosion that opened a foot-wide crack across the destroyer's main deck. The Corry was splitting into halves, sagging amidships.

"Abandon ship," Commander Hoffman bellowed. "Abandon ship now!"

Life-jacketed men leaped from the foundering Corry into the water. Some threw rafts into the sea and jumped in after them. Just as Dick was preparing to leap, a secondary explosion rocked the crippled, dying ship. A piece of flying steel shot upward and hammered Dick's helmet near the left temple. He could feel himself blacking out and falling.

CHAPTER 4

Some 6,000 miles from Omaha Beach and 2,500 miles from the Lawrences of Shelby lived the Santiagos of Westwood. The contrast between Shelby and Westwood was as stark as the difference between poplar trees and palm groves. Westwood, home of UCLA, boasted academic dons and the football Bruins. Shelby, dotted by factories and water towers and surrounded by farms and one-room schoolhouses, took pride in its Whippet football teams and 4-H Clubs.

While wartime convulsions were threatening to dash old dreams of the Lawrences, the Santiagos were busy building a family and a future. While Bill Lawrence lay bleeding on Omaha Beach and Dick Lawrence bobbed unconscious in the English Channel, Maria and John Santiago stirred groggily in bed as six-month-old Kate loudly demanded her midnight meal. As Edward Lawrence fretted about the fate of his two sons, John and Maria lovingly nurtured their three young daughters and worried about the upcoming annual polio season. John and Maria lamented the devastating losses being visited on thousands of American families, but so far those tragedies were no closer than black-and-white headlines and Movietone News newsreels. They were lucky, they knew.

The Santiagos were thoughtful, caring parents. They doted on their daughters but not blindly. They wanted the girls to grow up warm, secure, sensitive and successful. John and Maria concluded early that meeting those specifications would require a very careful mix. They chose affection, discipline and stimulation. As the girls grew older, they intended to modify the mix, tossing in a dash of license balanced by accountability.

John was an aggressive building contractor who lived a life that would have exhausted most men. He thrived on it. Awake daily at six o'clock, he eased his lean body to a small rug on the bedroom floor. There he gritted his way through a strenuous session of pushups, sit-ups and leg lifts.

Before he finished, his oldest daughter, four-year-old Jeannie Marie, would toddle in to watch. Sometimes, two-year-old Ruth would traipse in. They would plop down on the floor and begin a predictable litany. "Daddy, how many pushups now? Are they hard? Is that why you make

those sounds? Can I feel your arms? Will you help me do some sit-ups?"
Maria would shush them, wearily reminding them for the umpteenth time
not to disturb their father while he exercised.

Where their daughters were concerned, John and Maria seldom
disagreed. When they did, they kept talking with the aim of reaching
common ground. Maria may not have been classically liberated in the
modern sense, but she was hardly subservient. Which was no surprise to
John. When they met, Maria already had enrolled at UCLA, and she made
it amply clear that she possessed a mind and will of her own. John found her
attitude refreshing. Sometimes, he reflected, it also was disconcerting.

The family Santiago was Catholic. Maria especially believed strongly
in God and his goodness. John willingly followed her lead, though not as
unquestioningly. Both, Maria in particular, worked hard to instill their faith
in the girls. As tots, they joined in prayers before each meal and at night. At
those tender ages, the rituals were meant more to build routine and discipline
than to inspire lofty religious thinking. When the girls were older, during
Lent the family gathered after supper each evening to pray the rosary. John,
though uncertain of its effect, brooked few absences from this ritual.

When Jeannie Marie reached school age, John and Maria enrolled
her at Warner Avenue Elementary. Maria had wanted her in St. Paul the
Apostle on Ohio Avenue. She agreed to the public school only after she
and John carefully checked the two schools, their curricula and facilities.
And only after John suggested and Maria concluded that she could use
her college-honed teaching skills to provide adequate religious training at
home. There she would emphasize the lessons to be learned from Bible
stories rather than the rote of the Baltimore Catechism. That sat well
with John. He stopped short of putting practicality on an even par with
religiosity, but he harbored nagging doubts about the inflexible dogma
unrelentingly hurled at young minds by overbearing nuns.

John prospered as World War II raged. Modestly successful as an
aggressive young contractor before the war ignited, his business began
to gather momentum as the United States prepared for war. After Pearl
Harbor, his construction crews ranged up and down the West Coast. As
military needs grew, so did John's bank account, a coincidence that would
keep troubling him. At installations from as far south as the sprawling naval
base in San Diego to the Army's Fort Lewis and McChord Air Base outside

Tacoma, Washington, Western Construction Company built warehouses, hangars, offices, barracks, mess halls, ordnance depots and chapels.

In one respect, this new prosperity arrived at an ideal time. When the Japanese devastated Pearl Harbor, the Santiagos were a small family that was destined to grow quickly. In later years John would tease his wife about how "busy" they had been in their youth, especially during one span barely longer than four years when all four Santiago daughters noisily greeted the world. As John and Maria grew older, they continued to love making love. Seldom did their love making conclude with quick drifts to dreamland. Generally they chatted about the day's events, John's at work, Maria's at home with her four rambunctious daughters. Other times they exchanged humor rather than goodnight hugs.

"Maria," John said dryly one night after they had made love, "you are a very thoughtful woman."

"How is that, Mr. Santiago?"

"Well, not only do you give me great pleasure, but you also save me time."

"Yes?" she said, right eyebrow raised in mock suspicion.

"That's right. After that workout, I won't have to do my pushups and sit-ups in the morning. Just bounce out of bed and hit the shower." John chuckled at his own joke and Maria giggled delightedly. Then John reached over and tickled Maria under her right arm.

She laughed and whispered, "John, you'll wake the babies."

"Me? Who's making the noise?"

"John, you-" Before she could finish, John playfully shot his right hand between her thighs and gently squeezed her crotch. Maria shivered and moaned.

"You were about to say?" John said, relaxing his hand.

"That busy minds and busy bodies make the best babies."

Both laughed quietly and rolled toward each other.

John was handsome. Years of outside work had deeply tanned his muscular upper body. Thick dark hair crowned a face that won admiring glances from countless women. High cheekbones and a square jaw and chin surrounded wide-set, intelligent eyes. He stood five feet nine inches, but broad shoulders, a hard, flat stomach, narrow waist and ramrod straight posture made him appear taller.

Maria was a brown-haired, brown-eyed beauty who stood five feet three inches. After the birth of each daughter, she worked assiduously to regain her form, a form that John remembered often to praise.

Maria was the second of four children, all daughters, whose parents traced their ancestry to California's early Spanish settlers. When sons and daughters were ready to marry, their parents influenced them to avoid any Mexican or non-Iberian matches.

When John arrived in California from New Mexico, Maria's family was comfortably ensconced in Santa Monica. Maria's father was a banker who invested profitably – very profitably – in real estate throughout Southern California.

John's family also traced its new world origins to early Spanish settlers. His bloodline, too, had remained largely European. For generations his family had ranched cattle in San Miguel County southeast of Santa Fe on the Pecos River. His childhood was lived under the sun and stars and it was happy. But by the time John reached his late teens, his eyes and his mind began to strain to see beyond the sunset. An inquisitive, energetic young man, John wanted to test himself. Precisely how, he wasn't sure. That was part of the test.

With his parents' reluctant blessing, he set off for California at age 18 in 1932. After arriving in Los Angeles in a battered Ford Model A, his sharp eye quickly saw a way to put food on the table in his small apartment. On his family's New Mexico ranch he had done more than a little carpentry. Building range shacks and corrals, repairing buildings and fences had taught him to handle deftly most hand tools.

He hired himself out to anyone he could find who needed able, willing hands. By working diligently and living frugally, John amassed a small bankroll. After a while, he decided that money earning two percent interest would only make others rich. He wasn't driven to accumulating staggering wealth but poverty held few attractions. The next time he walked into a bank it was not to deposit but to borrow. The bank he had chosen was owned by Maria's father.

Zeal, pluck and common sense were, as much as capital, the building blocks of Western Construction Company. The growth of John's company eventually put him in the office of Maria's father, who quickly took a liking to this young entrepreneur. When in the course of conversation he learned of John's Spanish heritage, a meeting with Maria was arranged. The results pleased everyone in both families. John's family journeyed to Santa Monica for the wedding in June 1938. John moved his young bride into a modest frame house in Westwood. Maria continued her teaching studies at UCLA, graduating in June 1940 when she was four months pregnant with Jeannie Marie, who was born on November 10, 1940.

John's war-based prosperity caused him some disturbing moments. When the Los Angeles Times' headlines trumpeted the destruction of Pearl Harbor, John was an eminently healthy young man of 27 – well under the draft-age ceiling of 36. Yes, I'm married. Yes, I'm a father. Yes, Maria is pregnant again. Yes, I can serve my country well by building necessary military facilities. I certainly don't relish the prospect of a long separation.

How to serve his country best was not an easy decision. Maria wanted him to stay home but didn't press him.

One evening in early January 1942, quiet had settled in the Santiago home. Maria was sitting at a small drop-top cherry desk in the corner of the living room. A few feet away a brass floor lamp with a plain beige shade illuminated the Los Angeles Times that lay on John's lap. He sat with his head tilted against the back of the rocker, which was heavily padded and upholstered in a bright, flowery print.

"Maria," he said, "I've made my decision."

She knew which decision he meant, so merely responded, "Yes, John. What is it?" A surge of anxiety shot through her as she turned sideways on the straight-backed, armless desk chair to await his next words. In truth, she did not know his choice.

"Maria, I love my country very much. She needs all the help she can get." He spoke quietly and slowly and chose his words carefully. "Certainly I want to help. You've heard me say that so often you're probably tired of it. I love you too. You know that. And Jeannie. You need my help now, and you will need it more after the baby comes. (Ruth would be born on March 11, 1942.) Nothing can take the place of going to fight our country's enemies, and yet I know that many contributions can be made, must be made, by people at home. I'm going to stay home. I'll land every government contract I can get, and at the lowest possible bid. I will not gouge my country ever. I will build everything I can for her and at the lowest possible price."

During the next three years John lived a frantic life, much of it away from home, negotiating contracts and checking progress at construction sites. When he was home, he and Maria stayed "busy." Kate, the most beautiful of their first three babies, was born on December 12, 1943.

On the night of February 9, 1945, John sat fidgeting in a waiting room at the UCLA Medical Center. As the hours crept by, the straight-backed hardwood chair became increasingly sticky and uncomfortable. When he rose to stretch and drink from the fountain, his pants clung momentarily to the chair.

At 2:00 in the morning, five hours after Maria had entered the hospital, Doctor William Moyer entered the waiting room. He had delivered Jeannie Marie, Ruth and Kate. He was obviously tired, but a smile of satisfaction foretold good news. Through the years, Bill Moyer and John Santiago had become, if not close friends, warm acquaintances. They were about the same age.

"John," said Doctor Moyer, "it's too bad you're not playing cards tonight."

"What?"

"Poker."

"I'm not sure I-"

"In poker, John, as you well know, four of a kind wins most hands."

Doctor Moyer left John grinning wanly but broadly. A few minutes later Doctor Moyer appeared, cradling in his large hairy hands one small but large-lunged Santiago. "What will you call this winning card?"

John stared fondly and, as he had on three such earlier occasions, with some incredulity at this tiny being he had helped create. "Unless Maria has a change of heart, we'll name her Natalie."

"I like that. Very much."

"How's Maria?"

"A little groggy. Otherwise, fine. Why not let her rest a bit before going in? Just another fifteen or twenty minutes."

John nodded. Then he extended his right hand. "Thanks, Doctor."

"Distinctly my pleasure." Doctor Moyer turned and left.

John plopped down on the same wooden chair. Four babies in 51 months. That's pushing "busy" awfully close to "buried," he thought, smiling slightly. I love our girls as much as Maria does, but I don't want her worn out before her time. Four's enough. I think Maria will agree. He then had another thought and it brought no smile. Any decision to end production would mean tussling with the tenets of Catholicism, which viewed the calendar as the only acceptable contraceptive. To John, the calendar was no more reliable as a preventative than locking the henhouse door after a coyote's visit. Maria, he hoped, would agree and put practicality before religious dogma.

Thoughts of war and daughters led to one reassurance. I won't have to worry about losing my girls to a bullet, mine or mortar shell. Some women serve as nurses and clerks, but they're generally in the rear and safe. And they aren't drafted. And unless I completely mismanage the company, the girls will have all the security they need. The Santiago daughters could anticipate fine educations, splendid weddings in resplendent gowns and impressive financial holdings. Following the war, California, by all reckoning, would boom, and John Santiago intended Western Construction to boom right along.

CHAPTER 5

Harriet was expectant. She couldn't help humming and smiling as she strolled the half mile from her home on Second Street to the office of Doctor Wilson Kingsboro on Mansfield Avenue. Frolicking children, fresh out of school, and chirping birds, newly out of their nests, added to her serenity. The air was still, no hint of a breeze. The temperature was a comfortable 66 degrees.

A week before, Harriet had told Edward that she might be pregnant. She had missed a period, and some mornings her stomach greeted her as though it was seeking revenge for having been forced to spend the night on some storm-tossed bucket of a boat. Now she was on her way, hopefully to confirm her suspicion. She very much wanted to be pregnant. A girl was her first choice. Though she could not drag from Edward a boy-girl preference, deep down she felt he would want a daughter after having fathered Dick and Bill. Fine sons they were, but Edward liked variety, and a daughter certainly would provide that. The thought tickled her.

Doctor Kingsboro's verdict elicited from Harriet an excited, unrehearsed response. "Oh, Doctor Kingsboro," she gushed, "thank you, thank you. Oh my, I don't know what else to say."

"Don't."

"Don't?"

"Say anything else." He smiled benevolently and walked her to the door. "You know, I delivered Dick and Bill. It will make me very happy to deliver your baby. I'm sure Ed will be just as thrilled as you are."

At home, she could hardly wait to tell Edward. "That's wonderful," his bass voice would rejoice at the news. He would hug her, long and lovingly. These things she knew. June 12, 1944, was turning out to be, next to her wedding not three months before, the most thrilling day of her life. To bear Edward's child was, to Harriet, a privilege of the highest order.

Harriet could barely contain herself. She daydreamed about the baby's birth, sex, name, hair and eye color, size, health and future. She wanted so much to share this great news with her family, Edward's family and all their friends.

She barely touched the egg salad sandwich she had fixed for lunch. She nibbled a few bites from an apple. She knew that she must eat well, if not for two. Her excitement would have to diminish before her appetite perked up.

About 1:30 that afternoon, Harriet, through the screen door, heard a car door close. When she looked through the living room window, an elderly man was approaching and   holding a small envelope. She recognized him as Mr. Kelly, the Western Union messenger.

He was walking slowly toward the porch steps. In the first moment, Harriet was puzzled. Why on earth, her mind raced, could he possibly be coming here? In the next moment, cold, unspeakable dread gripped and shook her. She glanced at the two blue stars on white shields with red borders in the living room front window. Tears began to cloud her blue eyes. When knuckles tapped gently against the screen door frame, her body stopped shaking and froze. Then, stiffly, she moved toward the door.

No words were spoken. With Mr. Kelly watching, Harriet opened the envelope. Those first tears quickly became a torrent. Mr. Kelly, uneasy but obviously not witnessing such an outpouring of grief for the first time, stayed to console her. He sat beside her on the couch, his arm tenderly about her shoulder.

After he left, Harriet wondered how she could tell Edward. First a wife and now a son. It's too much, too much for any man. Maybe I should call Mom. She didn't.

A little after 4:00 Harriet saw Edward springing up the walk. He saw her behind the screen door and his face lighted up. "Hi, honey." He bounded up the steps two at a time.

Edward had not wept since that August night in 1936. He had not forgotten how. When Harriet spoke the terrible, heartrending words, he stood dumbstruck. His head dropped forlornly to his chest, his hands hung limply at his sides. He felt a vast emptiness, as though his body had been plundered of its organs and then crudely stitched back together. Only a hollow, useless shell remained.

Harriet's small hands gently grasped Edward's strong upper arms. Slowly, tenderly, she guided him up the stairs to their room. She laid him on the bed, then nestled next to him and silently cradled him while he wept.

When at last the tears subsided, Edward whispered, "I can't talk about it yet. Sorry. I don't know what to say yet."

"I understand."

"Maybe later. Right now, I'd just like to lie here and think. If you don't mind, I'd like to be alone. I appreciate you telling me. I don't know if I could have stood learning it from a telegram. I love you but I need to be alone now."

Harriet descended the stairs. God in heaven, she implored, how can you make one man suffer so? Lord, you know I love you, and I know you work in mysterious ways. But it's such a loss for one man. A wife and a son. Please let it stop there. Please.

About 11:00, Edward descended the stairs. Harriet was dozing on the couch. Edward shuffled into the darkened kitchen. When he switched on the ceiling light, the small noise snapped Harriet from her light sleep. She listened but said nothing. Still, perhaps, Edward wanted to be alone. A

cupboard door opened. She heard the clink of glass against glass. Then the sound of the heavier container being plopped down on the counter. A cork popped and liquid gurgled from bottle to glass. Then nothing. Then the sound of liquid sloshing into the porcelain-lined sink.

Edward walked into the living room. "I had one drink. I needed it. I think I could have used more. But I couldn't put myself or anyone else through that hell again. Don't worry."

"I won't."

He walked to the old oak rolltop desk that had belonged to his father. He raised the top, then seated himself heavily. He reached for a writing tablet, pen and ink. He began:

Dear Dick,

I don't know how to begin. It's very difficult. I wish you were here. Letters are poor substitutes for words that should be heard and felt.

Bill is dead. I just found out today. He was killed on D-Day at Omaha. I don't think he suffered long. I hope and pray not.

I'm glad you two were able to see each other recently. I know from your letters that it meant a lot to each of you and it sure meant a lot to me.

I'll be okay. Nothing like the last time. Harriet has been a big help. She broke the news to me when I got home from work this afternoon.

Dick, I miss you and I love you. I wish I could be there to help you. If you need help, ask for it. Please. Don't make the mistake I made when your mother died. If I had talked to someone, I probably would have had an easier time. If you don't want to talk to your chaplain, talk to a friend.

This war will be over soon. Until then, until we are together again, take care.

As always,
Dad

CHAPTER 6

On September 8, 1945, Edward and Harriet stood expectantly on the wooden platform of the B&O station, a small frame structure painted yellow with black trim. With them was their seven-month-old son Ben, who was playing contentedly with the multicolored wooden beads on the front of his blue and white metal stroller.

"Edward, what time is it?" Harriet asked nervously.

"Ten thirty-two. Take it easy." Edward smiled. "We still have another twelve minutes."

"Oh, I won't know what to say. Or do. He's been through so much. I feel so stupid."

"And nervous."

"Especially." She tittered and squeezed Edward's arm.

Edward glanced around the busy platform. He didn't really expect to see Helen Wakefield. Edward had called the young woman, but she said only that she would think about coming to welcome Dick.

Helen had been devastated by Bill's death. It was as though someone had cruelly drained the sap from a healthy tree. She wilted, became dormant. She said little, saw virtually no one apart from her parents, who patiently but futilely tried to console her.

Edward had broken the news to Helen the day after learning of Bill's death. He went to her house early in the morning before she went to work at Ohio Steel Tube Company. Edward himself always coped better with bad news received early in the day.

It had been nearly 7:30 when he rapped at the Wakefield's front door. Rose Wakefield answered. "Oh, hello, Mr. Lawrence. How are you?"

"Fine, fine," said Edward distractedly. "May I see Helen?"

"Yes, certainly. Just a moment. She was about ready to leave for work. Come in, please."

Moments later, Helen, honey-colored hair shining and bouncing at the shoulder, half skipped into the living room. "Mr. Lawrence. Mom told me you were here. Did I miss a good letter from Bill? I couldn't come around yesterday after work. I'd promised Mom and Dad I'd weed the garden. When I was finished, I needed a bath."

Edward felt great affection for this lively, lovely young woman. He forced a swallow, then put his hands on her shoulders. "Come over here, Helen. Sit on the couch." He guided her across the room.

"What is it, Mr. Lawrence?" When Edward raised his eyes, hers stared intently in return. "Bill, uh..."

She began to tremble. "Oh, no, is he hurt?" Already her blue eyes were welling.

Edward cleared his throat. "No."

"Then what?" Her voice quavered.

"Helen, Bill is dead." Edward had written the same words to Dick the night before, but saying them aloud made it all sound so much more final, as though he were a mortician who had just closed the last clasp on a coffin. The job was finished.

For a long moment Helen's mind seemed to fend off the words she had just heard. She sat perfectly still, staring stonily at Edward. Then a huge sob began to build deep within in her. When it burst, it was the saddest sound Edward ever had heard, sadder even than Taps playing over a fallen soldier's grave, a sound he had heard often and which always moved him deeply. He clenched his teeth, pursed his lips.

Helen was sitting on the edge of the couch. Edward put his hands on her shoulders and gently eased her to the back of the couch. Then, tenderly, he placed his left arm across her back, moved his right arm to the back of her head and drew Helen's face to his shoulder.

Now, on the B&O platform, Harriet fretted. "Do I look all right?"

"On hot Sundays, do Father McFadden's sermons put me to sleep?" Edward grinned.

"You're terrible," she said with mock exasperation and punched him playfully on the shoulder. Harriet wore a pale blue dress with black patent belt and matching shoes. She carried a navy blue purse. She looked radiant.

Edward, standing ramrod straight as always, looked like a distinguished diplomat in his blue pin-striped wool suit, white shirt and blue regimental tie. He had spit-polished his black plain-toed shoes. Edward's thick, graying hair added to his stature.

Before they heard the train's whistle, they could see smoke billowing from its stack. Diesels soon would eclipse steam locomotives, and train watching would suffer from the transition. A few moments later, the huge black locomotive, its massive steel wheels slowing and struggling for purchase on the slick steel rails, eased toward the station. When the locomotive ground to a stop, uniformed porters hopped down to the platform. Before one of the hustling men could place steel portable steps at the end of one of the cars, a door flew open. Through it careened a sandy-haired young naval officer. "Dad! Dad!" he cried. "Hey, Dad!"

The startled porter looked up in surprise as the shouting sailor exuberantly leaped down from the train. Before Dick's feet touched the platform, Edward was dashing toward him. The two men collided in a crashing embrace. Tears welled in Edward's eyes. They held each other tightly, swaying from their impact.

"Dick, I'm so glad you're home. God, I'm glad. Welcome home, son."

"Dad, I missed you. More than you'll ever know."

After their long embrace, they drew apart to arm's length. They stared at each other, broad grins creasing their ecstatic faces. "Dick, come over and meet Harriet."

Dick recognized Harriet at once. The cracked, crumpled photo he still carried and the real thing were very much a match. No photographic generosity here. Dick left Edward behind and bounded to Harriet. He hugged and swung her into the air and then let out a mighty, joyful whoop. In quick succession, Harriet squealed, laughed and cried tears of happiness. "Oh, Dick, I'm so glad you're home. And that you're safe. Oh, you look so good." Dick's uninhibited greeting had obliterated Harriet's reservations about this long anticipated meeting.

"I feel good. Damn good." Dick cradled Harriet's face in his strong hands, then leaned forward and down and kissed her full on the mouth. "It's a good thing Dad discovered you first. You are terrific."

Edward was beaming. Warmth and pride were spreading through his every vein. He strode slowly toward Dick and Harriet, then wrapped his arms around both. All three then hugged each other simultaneously.

When they separated, Edward said, "Dick, meet your little brother, Ben."

Dick stepped back and looked down at the smiling youngster. In his straight brown hair and bright blue eyes, Dick could perceive the Lawrence line. Memories of Bill as a child flooded his mind. He inhaled deeply. Then Dick reached down and scooped Ben from the stroller. He held the boy in front of his eyes and studied his bright, baby-smooth features. Then Dick shot his strong arms skyward, extending them fully. Ben squealed. As Dick completed the upward thrust, he released his grip on Ben, sending the child another few inches skyward. When the child descended, Dick caught him neatly by the armpits. His eyes twinkled. Twice more Dick threw the child into the air, as effortlessly as an eagle glides higher on the current of an updraft. Each time the child's smile seemed to spread wider than before. Dick drew Ben to his breast and hugged him for a long moment. Then he handed him to Harriet, who shone as brightly as the North Star.

Ben had been born on January 11, 1945. His birth in no small measure helped to rekindle his father's vigor. Edward wrapped one arm around his wife and the other around his oldest son. Dick draped his arm across his father's shoulder. At peace with the world, they strolled happily away from the platform.

From the far corner of the station, at the other end of the platform, a lone young woman watched wistfully. She was dressed simply in a pleated navy blue skirt and white blouse and an off-white wool sweater. Honey-colored hair curled up slightly at her shoulders. Part of her wanted desperately to be part of the scene of loving reunion. If any of the Lawrences had noticed and hailed her, she would have come running. On her own, though, she couldn't bring herself to step forward. As close as she had been to Edward, her strongest link to the Lawrence family was conspicuously and painfully missing. Her presence, she felt, might convert a joyous reunion into a somber, sad remembrance of what might have been. At this moment, a vast emptiness left her devoid of hope. She felt a crushing loneliness. She waited until the Lawrences were in Edward's car and had pulled away from the station. Then slowly, head bowed, shoulders sagging, she shuffled away.

Days later, the postman delivered a letter to the Lawrences. It was written on the flimsy paper issued to servicemen, and it was addressed to Dick. Harriet handed the letter to him, and he looked closely at the return address before gently breaking the seal.

Dear Dick,

We've never met, and I don't even know if this letter will get to you. I'm sending it to your dad's address in Shelby.

Your brother was my best buddy and my hero. At Omaha when I was hit, he was right there with me. I was lucky. Just a scratch, really. When my rifle jammed, he grabbed it and cleared the chamber.

Then he got hit. Twice. There was nothing I could do. I felt so helpless. The medic gave him morphine. His last words were, "Thanks, buddy. Tell Dick and Dad, Helen, too." I don't have her address, but if you can get word to her, tell her Bill was just half-mad crazy about her.

I'm writing this letter in Paris. I'm sitting in a little bistro. It's – wait a minute, let me check. Okay, it's on Rue Cambon, which is a narrow street running off Rue de Rivoli which I guess is a main drag. You can see the Louvre, that famous art museum that I'd never heard of before. Don't know if I'll get into it. There's also a big nice park across the street. I'm not sure how to spell it. Something like Tooleerees Gardens. Looks like it could use sprucing up.

After VE-Day, I came from Germany back to Paris. I waited to get here to write this because when Bill and I were in the Higgins boat heading into Omaha, we toasted, "To Paris." I told myself I had to make it here – for Bill.

He was a great guy. The best. Never complained. Never. And brave. He was always talking about you and your dad and Helen. I hope she's doing okay.

If I make it through this war, I'd like to meet you, but I doubt it because I'm from California. Near Frisco. I'm going back there.

Well, I just had the barkeep pour two glasses of wine. I asked for his best. He asked why two glasses. When I told him, he said no charge. On the house, or something like that. My French is awful and I'm having some trouble understanding his English.

Well, Dick, I just clinked the two glasses. Here's to Bill.
Sincerely,
Warren Maxwell

CHAPTER 7

The muffled sounds suggested urgency and secrecy. Barely audible, they seemed determined not to penetrate beyond the room's walls.

Outside the closed door a silent figure was barely breathing. She had heard the mysterious sounds before. Not frequently or regularly but often enough for them to be familiar. There was a pattern to the sounds that drew her closer to the door.

For several indecisive moments she stood poised outside the room. Her left arm, seemingly detached from her body and moving of its own accord, slowly swung upward until her hand rested against the door just above the knob. Gently, the hand pressed. The door gave slightly. No squeaks.

The sounds continued.

As the arm and hand pressed again, the left foot tentatively followed, settling softly on the cool hardwood floor.

The face, a half step behind, showed caution, but the magnetic sounds continued to gently tug her closer.

The right foot brought itself even with the left. Another slight nudge against the relenting door, a second step forward, and she was in the room.

"Daddy, Mommy, whatcha doin'?" The toddler's small melodious voice exerted a powerful influence on the sounds; they stopped suddenly and completely. Shock and embarrassment froze the reddening faces of her parents. "Huh?" the little voice repeated.

To John and Maria, youngest daughter Natalie was la pistolita. Well before she lent new meaning to the term "terrible twos," evidence abounded that the youngest of the Santiago daughters harbored a strain that would forever spice the lives of her parents. Her luminous brown eyes radiated a mischievous gleam. Her probing fingers and grasping hands translated that gleam into continual chaos.

Before she was 12 months old, Natalie reached several conclusions. Lamp cords were meant to be pulled, not just from the socket end. Magazines were meant for ripping, vigorously and with unrestrained glee. Shelves were meant to be cleared; why, otherwise, would her mother carefully remove all items from a shelf before wiping it with a cloth? A strange ritual, the child concluded, and one to be emulated, although with less care and absent the white cloth. Two bare hands could do the job quite nicely. Cupboards were meant for emptying, and no one could call Natalie a laggard in that regard.

Once, after supper, the six Santiagos were gathered in the living room. John and Maria were both reading. The girls played on the floor. Jeannie and Ruth together built free-form structures with Tinker Toys. Kate happily stacked brightly colored wooden blocks. Natalie toddled about silently inspecting their progress.

After a while, Maria glanced away from the magazine she was perusing. Not to be seen was the youngest Santiago. "John, have you seen Natalie?"

John looked beside and behind his padded, upholstered rocker. No Natalie. "How long since you last saw her?"

"I'm not sure. Four or five minutes."

"That's too long." John arched an eyebrow. "Especially when she's silent."

John and Maria both grasped the sides of their chairs and straightened their arms to rise. Blades of anxiety, not unfamiliar to veteran parents, stabbed their abdomens. As they gained their feet, an ominous crash rumbled from the bedroom wing of the house. Infant wails, loud and terrified, quickly followed. Three little brown-haired heads pivoted toward the sounds. John and Maria, hearts suddenly pounding wildly, went racing by the girls.

At the door of their room, a frightening sight awaited them. Front down on the floor was a heavy, five-drawer chest. From underneath the second highest drawer protruded the soles of two small feet. Had it not been for the child's incessant wailing, John and Maria would have feared for Natalie's life. As it was, they were frightened nearly witless. What they would find when Natalie was pulled from underneath the chest they dared not imagine. After pausing from momentary shock, John and Maria, with the quickness of cats chasing quarry, bolted across the room. Quickly John dropped to his knees at the top of the chest and lifted, taking care to hold in the two top drawers. Maria reached under, grasped Natalie under the shoulders and plucked her out. They sat on the bedroom floor, breathing roughly, sweating freely, both from physical exertion and nervous release. They closely inspected the crying daughter whose three older sisters stood staring wide-eyed in the doorway.

"John, is she all right?"

"I don't see any blood. No obvious injuries." He passed his hands over her small, still body, gently pressing her bones and joints, feeling for any protrusion, alert for any involuntary retreat from his touch. "I don't think anything is broken. Thank God."

"Are you sure?"

"Reasonably. We'll have to watch her. Make sure she doesn't fall asleep for a while, in case she has a concussion. Which I doubt. She hasn't blacked out. Thank goodness babies are soft and resilient. They can take spills much better than older kids or adults."

Gradually Natalie's cries diminished to whimpers. She began to squirm.

"None of the other girls ever got into so many things." Exasperation and concern mingled in Maria's voice. "Sometimes I think she's more like a boy." She still cradled the shaken baby, who, in recovering from the shock, was becoming impatient.

"I assure you she's all girl, and beautiful to boot," said John. His voice lightened. "But it might take a miracle for her to survive infancy. One thing's sure. She's got spirit and spunk. When she puts her mind to something, it takes a lot to stop her. And then she comes right back for more." John tenderly placed his hand on Natalie's forehead, where he saw rising a small bump. He ran his fingers over and around the swelling mass. Natalie whimpered slightly but was straining harder against Maria's arms. "If you've got to take a knock on the head," said John, "the forehead's the safest place. I think she wants loose, honey. Let her go."

Natalie toddled off to her sisters, babbling unconcernedly. She was a trifle unsteady but determined. "For better or worse, Mrs. Santiago," said John dryly but lightly, "something tells me *your* youngest will lead a life more eventful than most."

CHAPTER 8

Dick Lawrence was troubled. A vaguely claustrophobic feeling was the cause. During the first few weeks after his homecoming, Dick was too tired and too glad to be out of uniform to notice much else. He passed the days lazily, enjoyed Harriet's company and her cooking. In the evenings, still balmy but with occasional touches of early autumn coolness, he and Edward frequently passed time lounging idly on the front porch, sometimes on the steps, other times on the wooden swing suspended by heavy chains from the porch ceiling. Some nights, they chatted amiably about virtually everything including, and not uncomfortably, Sarah, Bill and the past. Other nights, little was said; long silences dominated but did not unsettle.

During those first weeks back home, little Ben provided all the entertainment Dick craved. The youngster was taking his first tentative steps, along with some harrowing spills. Strangely, even apparently painful falls seldom produced tears. Typically, Ben lay still a moment, seemingly assessing the damage, before gamely regaining his feet. Sometimes Dick was unable to suppress his laughter in the wake of Ben's pratfalls. Dick's resonant laugh generally elicited from Ben a similar response, albeit at a decidedly higher pitch. "Ben, you're a stitch," Dick would say lovingly. Often the two wrestled on the floor.

Dick began to assess seriously his feelings the morning he first visited Shelby's Oakland Cemetery. When he arrived, dew still sparkled on the weedless, manicured grassy expanse. Bill's stone sat next to Sarah's. The inscription read simply: *William L. Lawrence, Born August 3, 1924, Died June 6, 1944, serving his country.* Bill had been buried under a white cross in Normandy, but Edward had wanted a memorial in Shelby.

As he read the simple words, Dick shed no tears, though an enduring sadness still gripped him. Standing before the headstone, he recalled their last night together in Romsey, with amazing clarity. He also recalled his own brush with death. The U.S. Navy lost only two destroyers on D-Day at Normandy. The Corry was one. When the steel fragment had hammered his helmet and knocked him unconscious, he had plunged from the foundering ship into the sea. Fortunately one of his gun crew saw him fall and quickly pulled him to safety.

The two stones, Sarah's and Bill's, signaled endings. Dick was starting to realize that he needed beginnings. At the end of October he started working as an accountant at the Shelby Cycle Company. He had taken the job at Edward's urging and after his intercession with plant manager Gordon Davis. Dick had been acquiescent, if not enthusiastic, about Edward's inquiring on his behalf.

One afternoon early in November as Edward and Dick were leaving work together, Dick asked when his father had last seen Helen Wakefield. "At Bill's memorial service," Edward responded.

That evening Dick picked up the phone and dialed.

"Hello."

"Helen?"

"Yes, who is this?"

"It's Dick Lawrence."

"Hello, Dick." Her voice was flat, devoid of the bubbly girlishness that Dick had remembered. Although he hadn't anticipated the change, it didn't surprise him. Indeed, sadly, the change seemed fitting. For their generation, the days of carefree play had been bludgeoned on the beaches and battlefields of a world bent on killing. Boys and girls had become men and women quickly.

Dick started to say, "How are you?" but checked himself. Instead, "Helen, if it's okay with you, I'd like to stop by for a visit."

A brief silence, then, "Okay."

"How about tomorrow evening? Say about seven?"

Dick arrived promptly. Helen greeted him at the door. When she opened it, Dick stepped inside. They faced each other silently. Then Dick cupped her left hand in his hands. "It's been a long time. It's very good to see you."

"It's good to see you, Dick." She was sincere and cordial, but there was only a trace of a smile. She was as pretty as Dick remembered but not as sunshine fresh. The scrubbed bobby-soxer had matured. She motioned toward a living room chair. "Please sit down."

Helen's parents were nowhere to be seen. The room was large and brightly lighted, but Dick felt ill at ease. He never had been here before and was no doubt sitting where Bill had sat many times with this beautiful woman, so suddenly and tragically forced to alter the course of her life.

"Helen, I wanted to talk with you, to see you, although I'm not exactly sure why. That bothers me. Now that I'm here, I still want to talk, but I feel uncomfortable. Could we get in the car, go somewhere else?"

Dick wanted privacy, as much for Helen as for himself. He drove to Mansfield, 12 miles southeast of Shelby on winding State Route 39. He found a parking spot on the city's square, and they walked to a quiet, respectable cocktail bar. Dick escorted her to a back corner booth in the dimly lit room. He ordered a scotch and soda for both of them.

After they had been served, Helen spoke first. "I saw you when you got home. At the station."

"You did? Dad said he'd called to tell you when I was coming home. He said he looked for you but didn't see you."

"I stayed out of the way. I wanted your father to see me, but I didn't want to intrude. I didn't want to upset your reunion."

"You wouldn't have." He was beginning to wonder now about his own feelings toward Helen. There was a pull toward her. He wanted to reach across the table and hold her hands in his. That feeling triggered guilt. "Helen, I want you to know...I know you know...but I want you to hear it. Bill loved you dearly. When I saw him in Romsey just a few weeks before..." His voice trailed off momentarily, his eyes lowered. "...before Omaha, he couldn't stop talking about you. I know it's been rough for you, and I certainly don't want to reopen old wounds. But I wanted to tell you this."

"I'm glad you did, Dick." Her voice had grown warmer, less wary. "It means a lot. Believe me. I loved Bill very much. I've missed him terribly."

"Helen, what will you do?"

"I don't know. I'm not sure. I've tried to think about my future, but each time it's more confusing. The future seems like it will never get here. Like it's empty and will never hold anything."

"Have you seen...Have other men called you?"

"A couple. I haven't been out with anyone since...until tonight. I'm glad you called."

As Dick watched and listened, it was all too obvious why Bill had loved this woman. She's beautiful and honest, he could see. Right now she's vulnerable, but I think she's a strong woman. I'd like to hold her. I'd - That's stupid. And selfish. Hell, I'm as confused and uncertain about the future as she is. She might need affection, but she also needs support, and I'd make a damned unstable crutch. But someday maybe...Oh, what the hell, she'll probably pull her life together before I do.

"Have you thought about leaving Shelby?" Dick asked.

"Yes, a little. But I'm not sure where I'd go. I haven't been many places. My family is here. I don't know anyone anywhere else. I'd feel lost in a bigger town." A hesitation. "Not that I don't feel lost now." Mild self-deprecation, not self-pity, tinged her remark. She permitted herself a small smile, which Dick reciprocated. They exchanged a long look.

"How about you, Dick? What will you do?"

"Dad, I know you'll be disappointed to hear this. It's not easy for me to say it." Edward tensed, sensing what his son was about to say. "But, Dad, I've thought a lot about it." Dick raised his downcast eyes to meet Edward's. "I'm leaving Shelby."

Edward merely nodded. His son's words were not unexpected. Harriet had noticed Dick's restlessness and had confided as much to Edward.

"I just don't feel Shelby can offer me what I want. Although, to be honest, I'm not sure what I want. But whatever it is, I don't think it's here. And believe me, I don't mean my decision to be a reflection on you or Harriet or any of the rest of the family. Or my friends. I just sort of feel trapped here. Knowing virtually everyone and...Do you know what I mean?"

Edward sighed. "Dick, I can't blame you for feeling that way. Shelby is a small town. Too small for some people. Not much variety. Not much spice. And you know that. You've seen a lot the past few years. Been a lot of places. I can understand why you'd feel confined here. Besides, with your mother and brother gone, well, maybe it would be healthier to try someplace else. Maybe you need to get away. At least for a while."

46

Dick was relieved. He hadn't expected Edward to object strenuously, but he hadn't expected him to understand so completely his feelings.

"Where do you plan to go?"

"I'm thinking about California."

Edward pursed his lips in resignation. "Whew. That's a long way. But I've heard it's beautiful. The Golden State."

"Some of my buddies sure made it sound that way. I know it's not the paradise they painted. Shoot, I used to tell the guys on the Corry that Shelby was paradise. I think a few of them started to believe me." Dick and Edward shared a relaxed chuckle. "For a long time I was convinced it was. But California sounds as good as any other place and better than most. And it's big and growing. I shouldn't have any trouble finding work and keeping my belly filled. Although I shudder to think of *how* I'll fill it. I'll miss Harriet's cooking."

"We'll miss you, Dick. *I'll* miss you."

"I'll miss you, Dad. And Harriet and Ben. You've got two real prizes there, but you know that."

"And Helen. Will you miss her?"

Dick wasn't surprised by his dad's question. "Yes, I will. The few times we've seen each other have been good ones. At least I think they were good for her. She talked out some of her feelings. I like her. Quite a bit. But right now I don't think either of us is ready for anything serious. It would be pointless to try that road now. Maybe later." A pause, then, "Besides, you know me. I like to keep the risks to a minimum." Edward smiled lovingly but thinly at his son's weak attempt at levity. Both knew he didn't genuinely feel like being funny. "Helen is a beautiful, intelligent girl. Time is healing her. Eventually she'll be fine." These last words conveyed hope as much as conviction, and both men knew it.

The train lurched as Dick turned for a last wave to Edward, Harriet and Ben. And to Helen Wakefield. At Dick's invitation, she had come to see him off, and this time she had not stayed half hidden in the background. In parting, they had kissed on the cheek and embraced warmly.

Now, on this early December day in 1945, as the train accelerated north toward Cleveland, Dick was beginning to feel free, as if his ankles had been released from hobbling shackles, his mind from a claustrophobic prison. He pushed his seat back into a reclining position, breathed deeply and settled in. His eyes closed to the passing farmland, Dick knew full well that he was escaping from as well as to, that what he found might satisfy him no more than what he was leaving. I might want to come back someday, he mused, but for now I need breathing room. My quarters on the Corry were suffocating, and Shelby was closing in on me. I need space.

For the 90-minute ride to Cleveland, Dick let his mind roam, from scattered reflections to speculations. The more distance the speeding train put between him and Shelby, the more he unwound.

At Union Station deep in the bowels of Cleveland's soaring Terminal Tower, Dick stepped down onto a concrete platform to wait for the east-west train. He lit a Chesterfield. The air in the cavernous station, well more than 700 feet below the Tower's pinnacle, was cold. Dick puffed the cigarette, mindful of little more than the chill that was beginning to penetrate him, and stuffed his hands into the pockets of his blue Navy pea coat. It was the only item of military clothing he had worn since returning home. Under it he wore a blue, black and red plaid flannel shirt. Blue dungarees, black belt and black penny loafers completed his outward appearance.

He paced slowly, waiting for the Lake Shore Limited that would carry him to Chicago, where he would switch to the Super Chief for the journey to Los Angeles. He finished the cigarette and flicked the butt to the tracks that lay some four feet below the soles of his shoes. He pulled another cigarette. As he lit it he noticed a lone female figure standing apart from the rest of the waiting crowd. She wore a gray coat of fine material and smart cut. Hanging down over the turned-up collar was a mass of rich reddish-gold hair. Between the hem of the coat and shining black shoes, a pair of exquisitely shaped calves and tapered ankles drew and held Dick's attention. He couldn't see the woman's face but silently wagered that its class would match that of the clothes, hair and legs, which was considerable.

The screeching sound of slowing steel wheels against steel rails and the sight of a lone headlamp rounding a bend in the track snapped him from this pleasant reverie. Minutes later a conductor briskly called, "All aboard." Dick waited for the other passengers to board. He was cold, but it would be a long ride and he was in no hurry.

Aboard the train, Dick walked slowly down the aisle, alert for an empty window seat. He knew the table-top flat land that stretched between Cleveland and Chicago offered few visual delights, but he was determined to see whatever might be of interest. As he neared the middle of the car, two rows in front of him, occupying a window seat was the head of magnificent reddish-gold hair. Curiosity defeated his preference for a window seat. Acting on impulse, an un-Dick-like reaction, he stepped forward and sat beside the gray-coated woman.

"Hello," he said.

"Hello," she answered, her expressionless face turning toward him.

Dick's silent wager was a winner. The face was no longer blossom fresh - Dick put her age at 30 or more years - but nonetheless was dazzling, full but finely featured, accentuated by sparkling green eyes and long, reddish-gold lashes. Cheekbones of perfect height and a strong chin added character. God, marveled Dick, she's a goddess. His mind clicked and recorded her face as would a camera.

"Nice day," said Dick, lamely. "Cold but nice."

"Yes, it is," she replied with a deep velvety voice and then turned away.

So much for brilliant conversation, mused Dick. Not exactly my strong point.

Neither said anything more.

About an hour out of Cleveland, Dick's eyelids again began to feel heavy. The gray-coated woman was paging through a magazine.

Sleepily, Dick glanced over. It was TIME. He reclined his seat, eased back and began to doze. In little time, he was sleeping deeply.

After a while the woman heard Dick begin to moan softly. The sound was distracting at first, then mildly disconcerting. She looked away from TIME toward him. Beads of sweat were forming on his forehead. His body twitched, slightly at first, then more violently.

The woman placed her right arm on his right shoulder and shook gently but firmly. "Young man, wake up. Young man."

Dick stirred. His eyes popped open. For brief moments he was disoriented.

"Are you all right?" she said. "I thought you were having a nightmare."

He shook his head to clear his mind. "I was. Thanks. Haven't had many. Very few since I got home."

"From the war?"

"Yes." Dick laced his fingers behind his neck and pulled forward. He exhaled.

"Where?"

"The Atlantic. The Mediterranean." Dick straightened.

"You were in the Navy?"

"Yes."

"Was it bad? I mean, did you see action?" She had not intended to talk with anyone on this trip, let alone a young man in a pea coat. But his pained, contorted face, tortured possibly by dreams of dangers past, aroused sympathy and curiosity. She could see that his face was far from matinee idol handsome but nonetheless good looking and strong. It seemed to reflect character and wisdom beyond its youth.

Dick stretched again and brought his seat back to the upright position. "Yes, I saw action. Several times."

"I'm curious. If I'm probing too much, tell me. I'll stop."

Dick turned toward her and smiled slightly. "No, I don't mind. Maybe talking about it would help."

"Have you talked about it with anyone?"

"Not really. I didn't want to burden anyone. Might have been a release for me but a burden for them." He smiled at the irony. "Maybe that's one reason I had to get away. At least for a while."

"What were you dreaming about?"

"My ship, the Corry. She was a destroyer."

"Was?"

"Went down. On D-Day."

The gray-coated woman shuddered. Her mind quickly conjured up raging flames and drowning men. Her sympathy for the young man was growing. In some indefinable way he was touching her as she had not been touched in a long time. Her throat constricted, and she spoke more softly. "How did it happen?"

"Artillery shells and a mine."

50

"It must have been very difficult. Watching your ship sink."

This brought from Dick a rueful smile and a brief, self-deprecating chuckle. "I didn't see her go down. A piece of something brained me and knocked me out. My exit from the Corry was decidedly ungraceful."

"How?"

"I fell into the sea. Lucky my gun crew were good fishermen."

A look of concern clouded her lovely face. She touched his arm lightly. "I'm sorry. I mean about your ship. I'm glad your friends were good fishermen too."

For a minute, there was silence. Each stared ahead and down. Then she turned toward him. "Do you have any family?"

"Yes, my father. And his wife and little boy, my half-brother."

"Your mother?"

"Died a long time ago. A stroke."

'I'm sorry. No brothers or sisters?"

"One brother. Younger. He's gone too."

"The war?"

"Yes. On D-Day. On the beach."

The gray-coated woman's emotions churned. Sadness was engulfing her. Both her hands moved to Dick's arm. This man, so young, had lost so much. And so tragically. She breathed deeply, then cleared her throat.

Dick put his hand on hers. "I didn't mean to upset you. Sorry. Like I said, my release is another's burden."

She shook her head twice. She cleared her throat again, regaining her composure. "No. You needn't be sorry. I'm glad you told me. Really. And you needn't stop. I'll be all right now."

"Sure?"

"Yes. Please continue."

"Well, there's not much else. My brother Bill was in the Army. First Division. Infantry. He was in the first wave at Omaha. He made it ashore but was shot before he got very far. That's really about all I know."

"It must have been a terrible shock for you. And your father."

"Yes. And for a girl Bill left behind."

"I'm very sorry. I wish there was more I could say."

After another momentary silence, the beautiful woman looked at her watch. "It's lunchtime." She brightened. "Would you like to join me in the club car?"

"Well..." Dick paused and then continued with a twinkle in his eyes, "we'd make a helluva pair. You're dressed up and look terrific. I look more like I should be on a hay ride."

"Not to mind," she said, her face brightening still more.

It was the longest and most enjoyable lunch Dick ever had eaten. The food was good, as was the dry white wine the woman had ordered. Dick found her company delightful in the extreme. She clearly was intelligent, curious and sensitive. For the gray-coated woman, too, this interlude had assumed a special dimension.

Usually the woman would have chosen to ride in the splendor of the Twentieth Century Limited, a New York-to-Chicago palace on steel wheels that stopped only to take on fuel. Travelers taking the magnificent train arrived at Manhattan's sprawling Grand Central Station at bustling Park Avenue and East 42nd Street. Shortly before the 6 p.m. departure, a red carpet was unrolled for the more celebrated passengers. About 8:00 the next morning, the train came rolling into Chicago's LaSalle Street Station. After a brief wait, passengers were transported to the posh Ambassador East Hotel, where they lunched sumptuously in the elegant and storied Pump Room. Then it was back to the station to board the splendid Super Chief at 3:30 p.m. for the two-night, one-day run to Los Angeles.

For this trip, however, the gray-coated woman had eschewed the plush Twentieth Century Limited for the less glamorous though still very respectable treatment and accommodations aboard the Lake Shore Limited. She had wanted nothing more than solitude. At this moment, however, thanks to utter chance, she wanted nothing so much as to share awhile this young veteran's company. They lingered over dessert, a fluffy chocolate mousse, and several cups of strong, rich coffee. The conversation, which had switched to a lighter vein, was punctuated often by smiles and laughter. The young man and the older woman had become comfortable in each other's company.

"You know," Dick said, "we've learned a fair bit about each other but not our names. Mine's Dick Lawrence. Yours?"

"Clara Louis."

"I've met a Clara or two along the way but none as beautiful or as nice as you."

She reddened. "Thank you."

"You are very welcome."

Only the train's arrival in Chicago terminated their time at the table. They left the Lake Shore Limited together to wait for the Super Chief. It was about 3:30 p.m. when they boarded. With neither speaking, they found seats together. For the most part, the next few hours were passed chatting amiably. Although Dick and Clara had been together for hours, they had not tired of each other's company. On the contrary, a pleasant, durable chemistry was prevailing. During one stretch of silence, Dick, satiated by the food and wine, dozed again. Clara Louis studied his face. In sleep, despite his 23 years, it still managed a mask of innocence. She continued to look at him as the train went rumbling westward.

Later, it was Dick who said, "Unless you've other plans or desires, would you join me for dinner? That is, if they will let me in dressed like this."

"They will."

"Are you sure?"

"Sure."

Dinner was, if anything, more pleasant than lunch. Crisp salad. Prime rib, medium rare. Fine wine. Delicious coffee. Delightful conversation. At one point, sharing laughter, their hands touched over the table. A special warmth flowed across the bridge through both of them.

Impulsively, Dick said what had crossed his mind several times. "Somehow, you look familiar. And that's tough to figure because I've never met anyone so beautiful. And you've probably heard that a hundred times."

"At least, but thank you."

"I don't know where I would have seen you anyway. And I sure as hell don't know how I could have forgotten."

"Well, the mind can play funny tricks."

"You haven't said much about the nature of your business in LA."

"No. It's not entirely pleasant. I have some things to straighten out. Please don't press me on that."

"I'll press no more."

Outside the dining car, darkness long ago had descended. The blackness, punctured only by isolated lights from passing farms and villages, soothed rather than threatened the woman and the man.

"Dick, I've been enjoying myself immensely. But if I sit in this chair any longer, I'm afraid it and I will become one."

"I know what you mean. I guess I just wasn't in any hurry for the evening to end."

"Well, will you come to my compartment for a nightcap? That will extend it a bit."

The invitation seemed natural enough, yet it surprised Dick. His initial awe had diminished, in large part because of her warmth and openness. But he still marveled at her beauty, her class. Why she had spent so many hours in his company was beyond him. He hesitated. He felt genuine affection for the woman. "Sure."

In her cramped compartment the niceties were as tasteful as the woman and her clothing. Still, Dick did not expect to see fresh flowers on a small table. Or a silver tea service. Or brandy in a crystal decanter. Dick sat. She poured, then handed a snifter to Dick. At first he sipped, then steadily drained the powerful liquid. A warm glow began coursing through him. He put the glass down. She stood sipping, peering down at him. She smiled. He reached for her hand and drew her down toward him. She was neither eager nor reluctant. They kissed lightly, then drew apart. She put the glass down, and awkwardly, with her bending down, they kissed again. Then she maneuvered to sit on his lap, her legs over the arm of the chair. They kissed again, tenderly at first, then with greater force. Their hands glided about each other's face and neck. Dick's hand moved down and gently circled her breasts, firm and full. She didn't flinch. Moments later, they lay naked between white sheets, which in the winter weather had been cold at first touch. They both had shivered and laughed. Their passionate kissing and foreplay warmed the sheets.

"The sheets on the Corry never heated up this fast," Dick said.

"They never had this kind of fuel," said the woman.

"Good morning." She was propped up on her right elbow. Her long, dazzling hair spilled to the pillow where it spread in all directions.

"Good morning," Dick said, his bass voice resonating with morning huskiness. After a moment he stretched his six feet luxuriantly. "I guess I really exploded the first time last night."

"It had been a long time."

"Too long."

"Well, *after* the first time, you were sensational."

"Thanks."

"I mean it."

"You were great too," said Dick. A pause. "What time is it? Where are we? Besides west of Chicago?"

"Does it matter?"

"No, but it must be late. I haven't felt so rested in months."

"It must have been the special treatment last night."

"It was an effective sedative."

"Actually, it serves equally well as a morning eye-opener."

"Maybe I should try another dose."

"It's perfect before breakfast."

Dick rolled from his back onto his left side. They kissed, then stretched their bodies taut so they touched from lips to where her toes pressed against the front of his ankles.

"Let's begin the treatment."

The rest of the journey was an idyll. Dining and drinking together. Talking about most everything. Sitting together, marveling at the spectacular passing scenery that was beautiful no matter the season or circumstances, but all the more so when two people who care for one another were watching and enjoying together, pointing out details. Making love, several times, at all hours.

As the Super Chief came rolling into Los Angeles, they sat together silently, watching the city slide into focus and take shape. When the train stopped, Dick, in the aisle seat, stood and extended a hand. Clara reached up. They walked to the end of the car, out onto the deck, down the stairs and onto the platform.

They studied each other, oblivious to the swarming crowd. Two pairs of sparkling eyes, both green, atop two satisfied smiles warmed them both. No sadness. They kissed, long and tenderly.

"You are a very special young man."

"And you are a very, very special woman. And I have a feeling that many people already know that...Oops." They both laughed. "I didn't mean it the way it sounded."

"I know."

"Chances are slim that we'll see each other again," Dick said.

"A seemingly safe bet. But then again, in case you haven't noticed, the world is shrinking. That may narrow the odds."

"Then I'll forego the bet."

"Good," Clara said. "Instead of goodbye, let's make it till whenever."

"Till whenever."

"In the meantime, Dick, have a hell of a good life."

"You too."

"I am. And the last two days were part of it."

"If this was a casual encounter, and I think it was much more than that, I won't forget it until I slip into senility – and maybe not then. It was one of the best things that ever happened to me."

"It wasn't casual," said Clara. "Not at all. And I'll remember it always. It was a good thing for me too."

They stepped back from each other, hands still touching, fingers still entwined. Then she turned and strode down the platform.

CHAPTER 9

In the post-war 1940s, California was volcanic. The state, especially its southern third, was busting out all over. Hey, it proclaimed, we've got it all and we feel darn good about it. The region was as buoyant as a skittish teenage boy who's just heard the prettiest girl in the class say yes to his stammered request for a date. He can't contain himself. He wants to run and skip and jump and, above all, he wants to shout to the world that he has arrived. Which he does with unrestrained glee. A goodly chunk of the world comes running to check out the commotion. They like what they see and hear. A vibrant youngster is making his mark, and it's a joy to behold.

Such was California after the war. Millions were enthralled by descriptions of this paradise with the Mediterranean climate, sweeping beaches, crystal sea and majestic mountains. California, a magnet for the adventurous, the restless and the shiftless, offered unmatched opportunities for striking out boldly and scoring big. The sun warmed spirits and cast long shadows, instilling in many the confidence to stretch higher and reach farther than they had in the less electric, less energized lands of their origins.

John Santiago had been thus affected. As much as the high skies of his New Mexico youth had dazzled with their clarity, they did not inspire in the manner of southern California's soaring sun. His Western Construction Company was helping to transform the area as it built everything from pioneer strip shopping centers and sprawling supermarkets to office towers that bumped against the 140-foot legislated ceiling on Los Angeles buildings. Earthquake worries had spawned the height restriction.

LA's rambunctious news media continually sought John out for interviews. What's next? what's new? they demanded to know. How much will it cost? John handled such encounters with aplomb and recognized clearly the value to his company of favorable exposure in the press. But it consumed more of his time than he liked, leading as it did to numerous civic awards, which in turn led to speeches and assorted requests to donate his time, talent and money to various civic and social causes. Had he not learned on occasion to say no, he felt he could have served on the board of every hospital and charitable foundation in Southern California.

Before the end of the decade, John hired a public relations agency, Bernard Young & Associates. A large part of Young's charter called for tactfully shielding John from the media and other potential intrusions on his time. John instructed his secretary, Phyllis Wilson, to carefully screen all calls. "If it's the media or a charity or civic group, call Young and let him figure out the motive. He can decide which ones deserve our time and attention."

John never felt totally comfortable with the screening arrangement. He preferred to answer all phone calls and to generally fend for himself. But he came to regard the arrangement as necessary to the preservation of a happy, healthy home life. Maria applauded the arrangement because it meant that she and the four girls saw more of her husband and their father.

John liked being a father. Had Jeannie, Ruth, Kate and Natalie been employed by Ringling Brothers, the circus would have been compelled to stretch the big top and add a fourth ring. Up at dawn or soon after, the girls quickly were hard and noisily at play. Kate and Natalie, the youngest, were the noisiest.

John, an early riser himself, found joy in this daily cacophony. Maria was less enthralled. After all, she needled John on this mid-December morning, she had to listen to it all day. At this verbal jab, John grimaced with mock pain and groaned, "One woman is all I can handle. I shudder to think what it will be like when the girls become young women. Davy Crockett had better odds at the Alamo."

On February 9, 1942, all U.S. automobile companies halted production of civilian passenger cars. Automobile rationing began on March 2. After the war, production of 1946 models began by mid-December 1945, but John still was making do with a collection of scrounged parts housed in a body that threatened to disintegrate whenever a bump or pothole jarred one of its well-worn tires and worn-out shock absorbers. When new, the 1941 Nash Ambassador had been the perfect car for a young family. For one thing, it contained a folding seat that formed a bed, ideal for the infant Jeannie.

Now John was reluctant to put his wife and daughters in the wheezing pre-war relic, never mind drive fast or far. He could have dealt for a better-conditioned car during the war, but nagging self-doubt about the worth of his contribution to the war effort had stopped him. He had seen photos of the new 1946 Packards and he meant to buy one as soon as he found time. He drove the decrepit Nash into a parking lot three blocks from his office on the 12th and top floor of Western Construction's headquarters on Wilshire Boulevard.

As usual, John strode purposefully down the nearly deserted sidewalk. It was early, barely past 7:30. He preferred arriving before the crush hit. He liked being able to work in solitude before his phone began buzzing and his door started swinging open. He regarded the hour before 8:30 as his most productive. Approaching in the opposite direction, from the east, was a lone figure. He was dressed neatly in a dark suit and tie. He walked slowly, occasionally glancing at a slip of paper in his hand. John could see the man was checking addresses. John watched with idle curiosity until he saw the man stop in front of his office building, pause and enter.

When John pushed through the heavy revolving door, he saw the man waiting for the elevator. The man looked up.

"Good morning," said John.

"Good morning. A beautiful day."

"Yes, it is."

The elevator door opened and they stepped inside.

"You're out early," said John.

"I want to be first in line."

"For what?"

"A job interview."

The man pushed the button for the 12th floor.

"At Western Construction?" said John.

"Yes," said the man. "I saw a classified in *The Times* for an accountant there."

"Oh, yes." John had forgotten about the slot that had opened up in his finance department. The elevator continued its lazy ascent.

"Do you work there?" said the man.

"Yes."

"What do you do?"

"Uh, I work in administration. Do you have any accounting experience?"

The elevator bumped to a stop and the door slid open. John and the man stepped into the hallway.

"No. Just one year of college, and that was a while ago. But I'm good with numbers and I learn quickly."

They walked a few paces and stopped before double-glazed doors with the lettering: *Western Construction Company, Room 1201.* John reached into his pocket for a key, inserted it into the lock and pushed open the heavy door.

"From California?" John asked casually as he flipped light switches.

"Ohio."

"Is that where you went to college?"

"No. Northwestern, in Chicago."

"I take it the war interrupted your education."

"Well, it would have," smiled the man. "I beat the draft by volunteering."

"Why did you come to California?"

"I needed a change of scenery. Some breathing room. My buddies told me there was plenty of that in California."

John was taking a liking to the candid, engaging young man. Their conversation caused him to recall his own decision 13 years earlier to traverse the mountains ringing his New Mexico ranch and set out for golden California.

"What's your name?"

"Dick Lawrence."

"Well, Dick, sit down and make yourself comfortable. Miss Green, our receptionist, will be in about eight. When the rest of the staff arrives, she'll get you started on your interviews. Good luck."

"Thanks."

In his office, John hung up his jacket on a coat tree in the corner. He sat in his swivel chair and lightly drummed a pencil eraser on his desk. Slowly he spun around and stood. He stepped to the window and looked out and down on the burgeoning city. Several minutes passed. He reflected on the past 13 years. They had begun on a very modest scale. With a little experience, a fair amount of talent and an excess of gumption, he had begun the climb that had led to here, a corner office, sparsely decorated but spacious and airy, reminiscent both of his childhood environment and the extra elbow room he had sought in coming to California.

He looked at his watch. It was just a minute past 8:00. He picked up his phone and dialed.

"Yes, sir," said the female voice.

"Miss Green, this is John Santiago. Just listen."

"Yes, sir," she answered quietly.

"You see the young man sitting across from your desk?"

"Yes."

"Has Fred Barker come in yet?"

"No."

"When he does, you wait until he gets to his office and then call and tell him to call me right away."

"Yes, sir."

"The same with Mike Ramirez."

"Yes, sir."

"Have any other job applicants come in yet?"

"No, sir. There's no one else out here."

"Okay. Offer the young man a cup of coffee, please."

"Yes, sir."

CHAPTER 10

"Dad, my head is bleeding." No fear or anxiety shook the voice of the five-year-old. He was standing calmly, arms at his sides, inside the house's front door.

Edward lay on the living room couch. It was a lazy, sunny Sunday afternoon, which he had idled away reading and dozing. Mostly dozing. He shifted his head toward his young son. "Are you sure, Ben? I don't see any blood."

"It's back here," said the blue-eyed boy, reaching behind his head. When he brought his arm down, blood ran between his fingers.

Edward, 50 now, nonetheless sprang from the couch with the quickness of a soldier snapping to attention when a general sweeps unexpectedly into a room. As he hurried to the door, he shouted, "Harriet, come here. Quick. Ben's hurt."

As Edward reached the boy, Harriet already was flying down the stairs. When she reached bottom, Edward was gingerly spreading bloody, matted hair on the back of Ben's head near the crown.

"What do you think?" she asked anxiously.

"I think you'd better get Susie and then let's head for the hospital. It's going to need stitches. I'll call Doctor Kingsboro." Then to his son, "How did it happen, Ben?"

"Playing football. I fell and hit my head on the sidewalk."

Edward merely shook his head. "Okay, let's get you fixed up."

"It's going to hurt, isn't it, Dad?"

"Yes, Ben."

"Are they going to put the long needle in my head before they sew it?"

"Yes, they are, Ben."

Fifteen minutes later on the emergency room table, a nurse trussed Ben in a strait jacket designed to still squirming children. Carefully, then, the nurse shaved the area around the wound. Ben flinched as the razor cut away matted hair.

"Remember, Ben, if you feel like crying, go ahead," said Edward. "Don't try to hold it in."

Moments later, Doctor Wilson Kingsboro, who had delivered, doctored and otherwise patched up all four of Edward's children, including Ben's two-year-old sister, Susie, strode into the room. "Ben, Ben," he said fondly. "This is getting to be an undesirable habit. Let's take a look." He winced at the ugly gash.

For the third time in a six-month span, Doctor Kingsboro stitched together Ben's torn flesh. First it was two stitches where nose meets forehead, opened when Ben ran and leaped from the top step of the Lawrence front porch. Awaiting his face at the bottom was the unforgiving edge of a cement walk. Then it was five stitches on his forehead, ripped when Ben, after having climbed onto a kitchen counter, jumped toward the table. He fell short, his head cracking against the table's edge.

"Four or five should do it this time, Ed."

As in the past, Ben whimpered but didn't cry. His eyes were fixed on Edward, who placed a hand on his son's chest. "You're a good boy, Ben. It'll be over in another minute." Ben's eyes misted but he choked back tears. His bravery deeply touched his father, who remembered clearly the same trait in his late son, Bill.

Doctor Kingsboro's skilled hands pinched together the flesh around the wound. Steadily, he pushed the hooked suturing needle through the flesh. Then, delicately, he tied and drew the knot and cut the thread. Three more times he repeated the procedure. "There. That does it. There will be a slight scar but his hair will grow back in and cover it nicely. But," he added wearily, "let's hope this is the last time. At least for a long time."

"If Ben knew any fear, I'd offer some assurance, Doc. But he still does everything hell-bent-for-leather."

"He's a gutsy boy."

At age five, Ben was the Keystone Cops and the Little Rascals rolled into one inquisitive, intelligent, impulsive and irrepressible boy. His derring-do reminded his parents of Harold Lloyd, the silent film star noted for hanging precariously from horizontal flagpoles atop tall buildings and other hair-raising antics. The difference so far was that Ben paid for his misadventures with blood and scar tissue.

Ben was fearless. The myriad spectacular spills he took when learning to ride his yellow and blue Donald Duck bicycle (a product of the Shelby Cycle Company where Edward still was machine shop foreman) rattled his parents but not the son. Indeed, before he learned to ride consistently well, he was practicing his self-described "tricks." Often, Harriet's heart leaped into her throat when Ben, bouncing on the bike's seat as he raced down the sidewalk, momentarily lost control and veered toward the street. Powerfully built and strong since birth, he always managed to regain control of the wayward bike before meeting with the ultimate disaster.

"Ben!" Harriet would shout in frustration and fear. "Be careful. Don't ride so fast. If you go into the street, you could get hit by a car and get hurt or killed. Do you understand? Do you? If you can't remember," she cried, "you'll have to put the bike away and come in the house. Do you hear me?"

To which Ben would inevitably and simply reply, "Yes." If he possessed contrition, it was suspect. Moments later he would be at it again.

Edward saw in Ben a miniature of Bill. Not a precise duplicate, but enough similarities to trigger memories that sometimes pressed hard. Facially, the resemblance rested on three specific features. Ben, like Bill, saw the world through alert blue eyes. Also, like Bill, Ben's left eye opened appreciably less than the right. The effect was dual. Whenever Ben concentrated or smiled, the left eye closed until it was barely visible, holding tightly the attention of onlookers. In contemplation, the eye peered intently; in merriment, it twinkled brightly. The third feature was the set of Ben's smile. Like Bill's, the left side of Ben's mouth rose a trifle higher than the right. The effect was a slightly roguish appearance.

Like Bill, young Ben was an extrovert. He perceived the world as his friend, his club, his private preserve. His open, warm greetings quickly converted strangers into friends.

On playgrounds, a swing was meant to be swung ever higher until the seat shot up past the crossbar, causing the chains to slacken momentarily before snapping taut and beginning a long, sweeping descent with the young boy whooping joyously. Wherever he found them, trees were meant to be climbed, with little regard for any link between altitude and safety.

Gradually, Edward acknowledged a truth: Ben was helping to fill a huge void hewn by Bill's tragic death and Dick's departure to California. Edward's acceptance of Ben both as a miniature of Bill and as a unique being eased considerably the burden of having had a son precede him in death.

To help shed the occasional melancholy induced by memories of Bill, Edward dreamed of the future that lay before his third son. He saw the swelling bud of a superior student and athlete. On Sunday afternoon drives before he was five years old, young Ben entertained his parents by reading roadside Burma Shave signs. By age six, he was throwing and catching baseballs and footballs with noteworthy skill.

Edward needed no special instruction in the art of motivation. Ben enthusiastically chased every carrot Edward dangled before him. When Edward bought Ben a small baseball bat and offered to help him learn the art of hitting, his invitation was accepted hungrily. Edward picked small green apples by the hundreds from a backyard tree. He then pitched them to Ben whose quick bat splattered them everywhere. To Edward, the juice that sprayed him was a small price to pay for his son's enjoyment and possible future success.

When Ben was five, Edward began taking him to high school football games. Before climbing to their seats, Edward positioned Ben by the gate where players poured onto the field. From the youngster's vantage point, the players, in their bulging pads and gleaming helmets, seemed nothing so much as storied knights come alive to joust on a modern field of contest. With marching bands blaring stirring school fight songs, a highly charged current of excitement coursed through the boy. Almost from the start, he began telling Edward about the years to come when he would play on the same field.

In the classroom, the boy – quite unlike Bill before he wanted use of Edward's car - excelled. As extra incentive, Edward offered Ben a dime for each A, a quarter for an A+, and a dollar bonus for straight A's. For the next eight years – Edward discontinued the practice when Ben started high school – the boy collected the bonus every six weeks without exception. Edward looked forward to paying up and did so cheerfully.

CHAPTER 11

By the late 1940s, Dick was a highly valued employee of Western Construction Company. He quickly had proved his worth, and John Santiago took great pleasure in promoting him, within five years naming the transplanted Ohioan vice president and controller. Dick parlayed his ability with numbers and his zest for learning and working into a financial apparatus far more sophisticated than John ever had envisioned.

Dick brought new order, detail and discipline to all financial aspects of the company. He consulted with lawyers on contracts, with purchasing people on materials acquisitions and, of course, with bankers on financing.

But more than that, Dick became a member of the Santiago family. To John, eight years Dick's senior, he became a cross between a close younger brother and the son he never had. To Maria he was an unpretentious, warm, wise and trusted friend in whom she could confide easily and confidently. To Jeannie Marie, Ruth, Kate and Natalie, he was Uncle Dick, a loving, lovable combination of daffy clown, hugger, tickler, baby-sitter, companion, playmate and spoiler. Frequently Dick accompanied the Santiago clan to the beach. He permitted the squealing girls to bury him in the sand. Patiently he helped them build sand castles. Whenever he sat the competition was spirited for space on his lap. Once as the girls clamored about him, vying for his attention and arguing about whose turn it was to perch on his lap, Dick joked, "I should have been born a hybrid octopus – four legs and four arms."

Although Dick was only seven years Maria's junior, he found himself the target of aroused motherly instincts. In short, Maria worried about him.

"You and John both work too hard – and too long under too much stress," she told Dick. "Your schedule is brutal. Endless meetings, reviewing construction plans and financing, checking building sites. Even when John manages to leave by 6 p.m., he gets home drained. You're young and strong, but how long do you two think you can keep this up before damaging your health?"

"You're right," Dick muttered lamely. "We should try to slow the pace."

Late one afternoon John rapped on the door frame of Dick's office and stepped inside. Dick, as usual, was poring over papers on his neatly kept desk. He looked up. "Hi, John. What's up?"

"Nothing. Just felt like getting away from my office and telephone for a few minutes."

"Park," said Dick, motioning toward one of the chairs across from his desk.

John plopped down. "I need a break."

"Advancing age."

"Thanks. Any other inspirational remarks?"

"Just making that one exhausted me," said Dick.

"Are you doing anything this evening?"

"Collapsing."

"Seriously."

"No, no plans," said Dick.

"Why don't you and I bach it this evening? I know that's no thrill for you, but it might be a good break for me."

Dick looked at his boss and friend with mock shock. "You? Bach it?"

"I admit it's been a while."

"Like forever."

"I don't like to exaggerate. Look, do you want to do it?"

"Sure. What do you have in mind?"

"Simple stuff," said John. "Nothing fancy. After work, let's stop someplace for a couple drinks. Then dinner, a couple steaks and salad. Then find a movie. An adventure, maybe a cowboy film. Then a couple more drinks. How does that sound?"

"Fine, now," said Dick. "I wonder what it will feel like tomorrow morning."

"Aah, you're young and strong," said John, smiling. "And a bachelor. You should be used to nightly carousing."

"I'm more used to nightly tranquility."

"Sure you are. Let me call Maria to see if there are any problems on her end. She'll probably think I've cracked."

"Have you?"

To John the evening proved thoroughly entertaining and relaxing. To Dick it proved something quite different. They started with drinks at a neighborhood bar, then moved on to a nearby restaurant for steak dinners.

When they left the restaurant, John spotted a theater marquee three blocks down the street. "Let's check it out."

As they neared the theater, they could see that the marquee read *I Was a Male War Bride* with Cary Grant and Ann Sheridan.

"Well," John sighed wearily, "it's not exactly a cowboy film, but I don't feel like looking around for one."

"Nor I."

"Good. Let's try it."

They arrived just before curtain time. The lights had dimmed. A uniformed usher, flashlight in hand, showed them to their seats. The theater was nearly filled. John and Dick settled back. They sat through two cartoons, a newsreel and previews, and then the feature started. Moments into the movie, Ann Sheridan appeared on screen. Dick stared for a moment, squinted in concentration, then straightened in his seat. His initial uncertainty vanished quickly, replaced by the concreteness of positive identification. "Sweet Jesus," he murmured.

Dick's abrupt change in posture and whisper of astonishment startled and alarmed John. "What's wrong, Dick? Are you all right?" No reply. John poked Dick on his upper arm. "Dick, are you all right?"

Dick blinked. His head shook slightly. He turned toward his friend. "Yes, I'm all right." His head swung back toward the screen. "Surprised but okay."

John was thoroughly perplexed. "What is it, Dick?"

"I'll tell you about it after the movie, over drinks. Okay?"

"Okay."

Dick settled back again in his seat. Amusement began to supplant the shock that moments before had frozen his face. Occasionally, during the rest of the film, he shook his head. Incredulity lingered. By the time the curtain closed, Dick knew he would get in touch with Ann Sheridan, a woman he had known only as Clara Louis.

The following day, Dick consumed much of his morning at the office persistently placing a series of phone calls. He listened as a phone rang several times. "Hello," said a familiar velvety voice.

"You were right," Dick began. "It is a small world."

"What? Who is this?"

"The sailor in the pea coat. From the U.S.S. Lake Shore Limited and the U.S.S. Super Chief."

Silence on the other end of the line. Then, "Dick. Dick Lawrence!"

"I'll be darned. You remember."

"Some things, some people are hard to forget." That familiar lilt had crept into her voice. "Besides, that treatment was highly effective. Long-lasting effects."

Dick laughed. "How have you been?"

"Fine. Much better since that cruise with you. When was that? Let's see. The war hadn't been over long. Late 1945. Just before Christmas. Right?"

"Impressive memory," said Dick. "That was four years ago."

"Must be that miracle tonic. Improved the health of my memory as well as my body." She laughed. "How did you find me? Why did you phone me?"

"As for the why, I wanted to. I stopped to see a movie last night and saw somebody familiar. An old friend. As for the how, well, I'm persistent and resourceful. Some well-placed phone calls, some words that apparently carried the right ring of authority."

"You should have been an actor."

"Sometimes I am, a bad one."

"I'm glad you called."

The restaurant was elegant. The food was superb, as was the service. The prices were high. By now, however, Dick could afford them. This evening was his treat. He had picked her up in his cream 1950 Studebaker. An expensive charcoal gray suit, white shirt, dark blue tie and black wing-tipped shoes contrasted with the dungarees and pea coat and made him appear older and far more distinguished. She noted the change. As aboard the Super Chief, she was stunning. A black velvet dress, high necked, sleeves to the elbows, complemented faultlessly her shining reddish-gold hair. A single strand of pearls perfectly highlighted her milky complexion.

"Beautiful…matchless," Dick had said when she appeared at the door of her house.

Now, in the restaurant, a waiter brought two scotches, both straight up. She sat to Dick's right at a small corner table, which Dick had requested. "Better for conversation," he had told her. "And privacy."

They raised and clinked their glasses. "To a thankfully small world," she said.

"May it keep shrinking," said Dick.

They each sipped the smooth scotch, which quickly warmed them.

"Dick, you look prosperous."

"I am. More so than I ever dreamed. I've had some good fortune."

"And you've worked hard."

"Yes." Then, "You look positively gorgeous."

"Thanks. Just four years older."

"No. Four years better."

"The makeup does wonders."

"You're the wonder."

"You haven't married yet?"

"Not yet."

"Soon perhaps?"

"I don't know."

The dinner proceeded. This time, unlike the episode aboard the Super Chief and without much urging, Dick learned quite a bit about Clara Louis. He learned that she had been born Clara Lou Sheridan in Denton, Texas, in 1915. That she had won local and regional beauty contests, gone to Hollywood as a winner in a studio *Search For Beauty* publicity extravaganza, and then been dubbed the Oomph Girl. That she had married and divorced actors Edward Norris and George Brent. That she had starred in comedies, dramas and musicals. Dick had liked her in 1945, without knowing much, and he liked her more now. She was witty and warm. As before, each felt comfortable in the other's company.

"The Santiagos sound like a lovely family," said Ann. "You were very lucky to find them. Do you live near them?"

"Yes. I have an apartment in Westwood. Besides being close to the Santiagos, I thought it would be handy for taking classes at UCLA. I never got around to that, though. Too busy at work and too tired afterward."

"Well, you're young. There's plenty of time for everything."

A waiter came by. Solicitously straightforward, he told them the restaurant was closing. Both Dick and Ann were surprised the hour was so late. Both had enjoyed immensely an evening that had passed swiftly.

"My twentieth century chariot awaits, my lady."

"Let us depart, Sir Pea Coat."

Maria worried about Dick in other respects too. She was convinced that a bachelor, especially a busy one, could not eat properly. She took it upon herself to overcome as much as possible Dick's nutritional deficiencies. She encouraged him to dine with the Santiagos at least once each weekend and once during the week.

Dick teased Maria about her concern for his well-being. In fact, both knew her concern was not without foundation. Maria was creative, and her culinary talents weren't wanting. The Santiagos and Dick ate from a menu that was nutritious, succulent and endlessly varied. French, Spanish, Chinese, Greek, Jewish, German and American dishes all graced the Santiago table and caressed their palates. Two of Dick's favorites were moussaka and cheese blintzes, both made from scratch. That Maria somehow remained trim and fetching in the face of all the delectable dishes she prepared and served amazed both her husband and her friend.

Maria was no fire-breathing apostle of God, but she also worried about Dick's religiosity. Or lack of it. That he wasn't Catholic didn't disturb her. That he attended no church did. On one Christmas Eve, she invited him to join the family at Mass. Dick politely declined, offering instead to babysit with Kate and Natalie. Maria accepted. She couldn't stand the thought of his being without family on Christmas Eve.

On another Christmas Eve, Dick was recalling his childhood holiday experiences, including church services. Maria asked him in which religion he had been raised.

"Presbyterian."

"When did you stop going to church?"

"High school, I guess. Dad and Bill and I kept going awhile after Mom died, but gradually we stopped. Later, Dad started going again but Bill and I didn't."

"Did your father pressure you to go?"

"No, never. We never really talked about it. Whether or not we went was our decision."

"Do you believe in God?"

"Yes, but probably not the same way you do."

"How so?"

Dick hesitated. "Maria, I'm not sure we should go into this. It would probably upset you. And maybe you too, John. I don't know if it's worth it, especially if it comes between us. And on Christmas Eve...I haven't met too many people who seem to be able to discuss religious differences calmly."

"It won't come between us," Maria said with quiet conviction. "From somebody else, it might. I admit that. But we're too close. Isn't that right, John?" Her husband smiled slightly and nodded his assent. "Besides, knowing you, I have a feeling you've thought it all through very rationally. Go ahead, please."

"You might even convert her to your way," John said dryly.

"All right," said Dick. "Let's see. For starters, I don't think it makes much difference how a person prays or worships. Whether it's in a church or a synagogue or a forest. I consider myself first and foremost a child of God. Then a Christian, but that's an accident of birth. I don't think Christians have anything over Jews or Buddhists or Moslems. Christ himself was a Jew. But honestly, I don't have much use for any organized religion. I think we all look to the same God, and I don't think he gives two hoots how. I certainly don't think he chooses sides in so-called holy wars. I can't believe he'd help one man kill another when they both believe in him." Dick paused. "Are you ready to throw me out yet?"

John and Maria both laughed. "Go on," she said.

"Well, I don't think God is a very active God. Oh, I concede that once in a while he might be. But by and large, I think he's passive. I think he lets us make our own decisions and lets us live with them. I don't think he intercedes much, no matter how much we pray."

"Why do you think that way?" Maria asked.

"Too much suffering. If God were truly active, I don't think he'd permit it. I'll tell you," Dick said, intensity now working its way into his voice, "it makes my blood pressure climb when something tragic happens and I hear somebody say, 'It was the will of God.' I think that's so much...I just don't believe it. I don't think God willed the death of thousands of Americans at Pearl Harbor, and I don't think he willed the deaths of thousands of Japanese at Hiroshima." Maria and John sat straight, listening intently as Dick was speaking. Dick breathed deeply and continued. "Too many people have suffered too much, died too early and too painfully for me to believe it's God's will. I still believe God is good, and I can't reconcile goodness with him actively permitting all that suffering. I'm not talking only about young men dying in war. Or innocent civilians. Although that too. I'm talking about day-in, day-out suffering. Kids getting hit by cars. People slowly starving to death. Or a person suffering a stroke and being imprisoned in his own body...alert but not able to speak or do anything for himself. I can't believe that's God's will. Not if he is compassionate, and I think he is."

"How do you think he is compassionate?" Maria asked quietly.

"I don't think many people go to hell. I'm not sure there is one. But if there is, I think it's reserved for the world's true bastards. Sorry, Maria. The Hitlers, the Stalins, the Capones. Others might have to wait or suffer before getting into heaven, but I have to think eternal punishment is reserved for the truly evil and unrepentant."

"Do you think he listens?" Maria asked.

"Oh, yes," said Dick with a touch of lightness. "He listens. I just don't think he reacts very often."

"I can't help wondering," Maria said barely audibly, "if your faith in God was ever very strong."

"It probably wasn't."

Maria didn't worry about Dick's status as a single man. But for his own happiness, she wished he'd meet and marry the right girl. She knew he dated. And being an attractive and healthy man in his late twenties, she assumed he slept with some of his dates. She didn't dwell on that thought, and it didn't overly trouble her. To Maria, Dick represented the finest in young men, and she wanted only the most complete happiness for him. To her, however active and pleasant Dick's social life, that meant marriage and children of his own. Sometimes, as with the subject of religion, she found herself on the brink of asking Dick why he hadn't selected from the pick of lovely young California women and wedded one. In the end, she couldn't bring herself to raise the subject. Quite simply, lovely, vivacious Maria didn't want Dick thinking of her as a nosy, nagging woman.

CHAPTER 12

For Helen Wakefield, time did help scab over the painful wounds inflicted by the sudden, violent death of Bill Lawrence on Omaha Beach. A turning point came when she no longer dreaded getting ready for work in the morning. She awakened feeling unburdened. Her body seemed appreciably lighter, as though she had lost many pounds. She found herself dwelling not on Edward's devastating announcement but on the conversations she and Dick had had about what lay ahead.

From California, Dick continued to help Helen's healing process. At Christmas of 1945, he surprised her with a card and a rambling, folksy letter that humorously recounted his first days in Southern California and the accompanying cultural and climatic shock. He ended the letter by encouraging her to step decisively forward, even if unseen potholes led to bruising stumbles. *If we're not pushing forward, we're standing still – or worse, going backward. Let's promise each other to keep pushing ahead.*

In June 1946, Dick Lawrence returned to Ohio for a vacation. During his 10-day stay, he and Helen saw much of each other. Primarily they talked and listened. Dick sensed a chemistry that he thought was mutual but which he suppressed. If I were to tell you how I really feel, Dick reflected, it could tear open old wounds, and I couldn't bear to see you suffer more. On their last evening together before his return to California, they embraced and kissed tenderly.

Dick had analyzed the chemistry correctly. It was mutual. Helen felt deeply about Dick. By the end of his vacation, she was wishing that romance would take root. From her position, two factors intervened. Proper young women didn't take the initiative in establishing male-female pairings, and she didn't want to push or pull Dick into a relationship that might cause him more heartache than happiness. I'm sure he still sees me as the woman who loved and mourned his brother. It's been two years since Bill died, she reflected, but memories of him still are powerful.

In September 1946, Helen enrolled at Ashland College, a small private school in Ashland, Ohio, which lay about 20 miles east of Shelby through rolling Amish farm country. One-horse carriages frequently slowed auto traffic on State Route 96, but Helen seldom minded the delays. Indeed, she enjoyed watching the rhythmic trot of carriage horses.

In the spring of 1947, Dick again returned to Shelby. This time he saw little of Helen who was busy studying for final exams. She had done well her first year and had decided to earn a degree in education and then teach in high school. History would be her major.

During the 1947-48 school year Helen bumped into Roger Hoerner, Shelby High School class of 1940, and a friend of Dick's. Roger, like Dick, was a strapping, good-looking young man who had served in World War II. Unlike Dick, he had joined the Army and spent the war years in the Pacific. On his return he had enrolled at Ashland, where he intended to major in physical education and then coach high school football, which as a halfback and linebacker, he had played well at Shelby. Helen and Roger began dating in the spring of 1948, when Roger was finishing his junior year.

When Dick learned that Helen was dating Roger, his reaction was mixed. I'm glad she's bounced back emotionally and feels like dating. I'm just sorry it's Roger and not me. In California, Dick had continued to date several women, but dazzling, honey-haired Helen Wakefield seldom was far from his thoughts.

In early May 1950, Dick received from Helen an invitation to attend her graduation from Ashland. Dick had been planning his annual trip to Shelby, so immediately scheduled his return to coincide with the ceremony to be held on Sunday, June 11.

Saturday, June 10, 1950

In the days before jets commanded the airways, a flight between the West Coast and Ohio served well to test a passenger's physical and mental mettle. The planes were as cramped as a crowded church on Christmas Eve and as noisy as a room full of rowdy kids on a rainy day. At the end of long flights, passengers emerged with both bottoms and brains benumbed. Nevertheless, Dick endured the rigors of air travel for one practical advantage: time.

Before dawn on June 10, John Santiago pulled up in front of Dick's apartment. Dick was waiting by the door. Before John could get out of the car to help, Dick had hoisted two large, heavy bags and begun lugging them to the car. Dick set the bags down at the rear of the car, and the two men shook hands.

"All set?" said John, half stifling a yawn. "Any more baggage?"

"This is it."

"Let's roll."

"You look like the only place you want to roll to is bed. You know I appreciate this."

"My pleasure," said John. "Well, at least I don't mind." John slapped his friend on the shoulder. "Besides, I wouldn't want to leave my car at the airport for a week or more either."

The two men rode in comfortable silence awhile before John spoke. "As usual, Maria's worried about you."

"Glad things are normal."

John bit off a yawn and chuckled. "Not just about the flight, although your cross-country flying scares the dickens out of her. She's afraid you and the Rocky Mountains might have a sudden, first and final meeting. What really worries her is that you might not come back from one of your visits to Ohio. She wouldn't feel that way if you'd marry a California girl. But with no ties here, she's worried you'll leave. She wouldn't blame you. In fact, she'd understand if you wanted to be back with your family. She'd just miss you terribly. So would the girls."

"No ties out here? Come on, John. That's a laugh. Of course I have my Ohio roots. I enjoy visiting my family and friends there. But you tell Maria that if she wants to make a safe bet, she should bet I'll be in California for a long time. And that's regardless of whether or not I marry a California girl. Or if I ever marry."

Sunday, June 11, 1950

It was late morning when Dick, Edward, Harriet, Ben and Susie Lawrence piled into Edward's new black Hudson for the half-hour drive to Ashland. Edward had suggested driving over in the morning so they could lunch leisurely in Ashland and not be rushed to make it to the 1 p.m. graduation exercise.

The morning was sunny, breezy and pleasant with the temperature climbing toward a high of 73 degrees. They lunched in a small restaurant on Main Street and then walked to the campus, just a few blocks north off winding Claremont. As the Lawrences were strolling across a shaded, grassy expanse to an area where chairs had been arranged for the ceremony, among the mingling people Dick eyed Roger Hoerner. "Roger, hey, Roger," he called.

Roger craned his neck, searching for the source of the hailed greeting, saw Dick, and went striding toward him. The two clasped hands firmly.

"Dick, great to see you. It's been a long time. Since our own high school graduation ten years ago. If you've changed, it's for the better."

"Thanks, Roger. You look great, too. Understand you got a coaching job in Mansfield."

"At Madison High. I teach phys ed and help coach the football and track teams. I had mixed feelings when we played Shelby last fall."

"I'm sure it seemed strange for Shelby to be the enemy."

Roger nodded. "I'm glad you could make it back for Helen's graduation. And it's nice of your family to come. It means a lot to Helen."

"It would have taken a lot for me to miss it. Dad too. Helen was through a lot, and she was very close to us."

By this time, Edward, Harriet, Ben and Susie had caught up with Dick. They exchanged warm greetings with Roger.

"Say," said Roger expansively, "I hope you'll all be able to come to the wedding. The invitations will be going out soon."

Dick looked blankly at his old friend. "Wedding?"

"Yes," said Roger, "I guess you haven't heard. Helen and I are to be married...in a couple months."

Dick looked at Edward, who slightly shrugged his shoulders. The news surprised the father as much as the son. "No. Well, uh, congratulations. That's wonderful."

It was nearing 1 p.m. The graduates were lining up to parade to their places. Somewhat awkwardly, Roger said, "I guess we'd better take our seats." He then turned to join his and Helen's parents. The Lawrences took seats near the rear.

When the graduates were marching up the center aisle, Dick had no difficulty spotting Helen among the advancing wave of billowing black and white gowns and bobbing caps and tassels. To Dick she appeared as beautiful as ever. What surprised him was her serenity. That was new. And becoming. Throughout the ceremony – the invocation, introductions, speeches, parade of graduates across a portable stage to accept their diplomas, closing remarks, benediction – Dick saw or heard little. He focused on the scene before him only when Helen's name was announced. He watched intently as she walked gracefully up the steps on one side of the stage, past the gowned and capped faculty and honored guests, down the steps at the other side and back to her seat. Turmoil brewed within Dick. Conflicting, confusing thoughts were rampaging through his mind.

At last the ceremony ended. The graduates walked to the rear, followed quickly by the throng of families and friends. In the commotion, Dick found Helen. When they saw each other, no words were spoken. They embraced, closely and warmly. They pulled back slightly and their eyes met. "Helen," Dick said softly but without hesitation, "may I call you? Tomorrow?"

Monday, June 12, 1950

Before Edward left for work, Dick asked if he could use his father's car. He knew the answer would be, "Yes, of course." It always was during Dick's annual retreats to Shelby.

Shortly before noon, Dick parked the gleaming Hudson in front of the Wakefield home. He paused for a long moment. Damn, he mused, there are times when I'd rather be a simpleton. Maybe I am. He looked at the white frame house, surrounded by neatly trimmed shrubs and colorful flowers. Then he stepped out and approached the door. He clenched his right hand to knock, but before his knuckles rapped the screen door frame, Helen appeared.

"I heard the car door slam," she said, smiling.

"Hi, Helen."

He stepped back, and she pushed open the screen door and walked onto the porch. Ravishing, thought Dick, absolutely ravishing.

"You look good too, Dick," she smiled, reading his mind. "What do you have in store for us?"

"I thought we'd take a spin through the countryside. Have lunch. Do some catching up."

"That sounds nice."

Little was said as Dick eased the car toward Shelby's south end. In silence, they passed the town's cemetery.

"A new chapter," mused Dick.

"What?"

"I'm not very literary minded, but if your life was a book, this would seem like the beginning of a new chapter. You've graduated from college and you're going to get married."

"Roger said he mentioned the wedding to you. Said you looked surprised."

"Pole-axed is more like it. But I guess I shouldn't have been. How long have you and Roger been dating?"

"Two years. Steadily for the last year or so. He gave me a ring at Christmas."

Dick admired the diamond. "Are you excited?"

"Yes. There's so much to do. We didn't want to get married until August so there would be plenty of time to plan the wedding and the reception after the school year ended. I didn't want to be worrying about wedding details while I studied for finals."

"You sound like me," Dick kidded.

"How so?"

"Very practical."

They spent lunch and the drive back to Shelby reminiscing. Dick learned about Helen's teaching plans. She had landed a job teaching American history at the high school in Plymouth, a sleepy village about eight miles north of Shelby. With Roger teaching and coaching at Mansfield Madison, which lay south of Shelby, the pair planned to buy a house in the town where the Wakefields, Hoerners and Lawrences all had sunk deep roots.

It was mid afternoon when they pulled to a stop in front of the Wakefield house.

"Dick, when do you have to go back?"

"On Sunday, the eighteenth."

"I see."

"Helen, today we pretty much covered the past. I'd very much like to see you again, to talk more about your new chapter."

"All right."

"Great. How about tomorrow? Lunchtime."

Tuesday, June 13, 1950

His lunch date with Helen couldn't come soon enough for Dick. During their conversation the day before, a familiar feeling began flickering. If she has the same feeling, Dick mused, I don't really want to think about the complications. Still, I have to know. What will I say? What will I tell her? He shook his head. The central question: How do I ask a beautiful woman who is going to get married in just two months if she truly loves the man she is about to marry? A man who also happens to be my friend? Only an insensitive lout, he scolded himself, could ask that question. I'll ask it anyway. Somehow. He mulled over several gambits. They all struck him as weak and ineffective, not to mention transparent and tasteless. In atypical Dick Lawrence fashion, he resigned himself to playing it by ear.

Which he did. During the first 15 minutes of their drive through the countryside, Dick and Helen made only the smallest of talk. It was awkward, and it was Helen who decided to elevate the dialogue. "Dick, I thought we were going to talk about new chapters. Today's weather," she kidded, "and the height of the corn don't seem to qualify."

"I'm not sure what does. This is like a game, and I don't know the rules. At least, I haven't played before and I'm not sure of the next move."

"What do you mean?"

"I'm curious about you and Roger, but I haven't been able to figure out how to ask."

"So ask."

Dick smiled, a trifle uneasily. "All right. What attracted you to Roger? I know he's a nice guy. A veteran. We were friends in school. But, well…"

"He asked me out. At the right time. After I started at Ashland, I studied hard. Being busy, and over time, I finally learned to accept that I'll never get over Bill. Not totally. But I also remembered your advice. Do you remember what you told me in that letter you wrote the first Christmas you were in California?"

"Vaguely."

"You encouraged me to take bold steps forward. That's one reason I decided to go to college. I knew I had to get my life moving. I didn't really want to leave Shelby. But I knew I needed to meet new people. Going to Ashland seemed like a good decision."

"And it was."

"Yes, it was. My freshman year I lived at home and commuted. At the start of my sophomore year, I decided to live on campus. It was good for me. I met Roger at a dorm mixer. We danced and talked. Gradually we saw more and more of each other."

"Does he know you're seeing me today? And yesterday?"

"Yes. He knew about Bill and me. That I loved him. And he knows you and I are good friends. I just told him you and I had some catch-up visiting to do. I borrowed your words."

"I envy him." The words slipped out, barely audible and unpremeditated. He glanced at Helen, who eyed him steadily. Since Dick couldn't retrieve the words, he decided to plunge ahead. "He's a very lucky man. I'm sure after you two started to date, other men asked you out."

"Yes," she smiled. "Word got around that I was a coin back in circulation."

"Wish I'd known."

A pause. "Me too, Dick. But, well, you were very far away."

"And Roger wasn't."

"No. I mean yes."

They laughed softly. Dick's throat had tightened with rising emotion. His eyes left the road and turned toward Helen. Her eyes were on him and were reflecting tenderness and perhaps regret. He reached for her hand, which she placed in his. They squeezed. Dick cleared his throat. "It's lunchtime, but I'll be darned if I'm hungry."

"Me either."

"Let's just keep driving a bit more and talk."

"Fine."

Dick released her hand. His emotions still were churning. His next words didn't come easily, but once uttered, an immense wave of relief languidly washed over him. "Helen, never have I said these words to anyone. I love you. Very, very much."

He turned to face her. Again their hands came together and held, locked in an extraordinarily strong yet tender emotional vise.

"Dick, I care very much for you."

"Not surprised I love you?"

"No."

"The only person I was fooling was me," said Dick. "You were too intelligent and perceptive not to know."

"I knew."

"So where do we go from here?"

"I don't know."

"I don't either. Except you haven't said it, but I think you love me too."

"Dick, please. I can't say anything now. I'm sorry. I just can't. Will you take me home? Please?"

Wednesday, June 14, 1950

For Dick and Helen, June 14 amounted to earthly purgatory. The day was interminable and virtually intolerable. Each wrestled, inconclusively, with slippery thoughts and emotions. Worse, each wrestled alone, no tag team matches, no seconds in the corners, no coaching.

Helen divided the day between distractedly cleaning her parents' house and mentally reviewing plans for her wedding and reception.

After breakfast, Dick tried reading a morning newspaper. When he'd read half a story without remembering a word, he tossed the paper aside and retreated to his old room. For the better part of the day, he stretched supine on the bed, stared at the cracks in the plaster ceiling and tried objectively to sort facts and feelings. He failed.

Thursday, June 15, 1950

Edward had remained an early riser. He liked to get up at six o'clock and perk coffee while awaiting the arrival of the *Cleveland Plain Dealer*, an out-of-town morning supplement to the afternoon *Shelby Daily Globe*, a paper especially skilled in satisfying those who craved knowledge of births, deaths, weddings, hospital admissions and discharges, traffic citations and the *Alley Oop* comic strip. *The Globe's* front page distilled wire service offerings on world and national news. The paper knew its niche and excelled at filling it. Everyone read it.

About 6:15, Edward was hunched over the kitchen table, propping up the *Plain Dealer* front section with his left hand. With his right, he hoisted to his lips a heavy mug brimming with home-ground, heavily scented coffee.

Dick came padding into the kitchen, the linoleum floor cool to his bare feet. He sighed audibly and cinched the cloth belt on his bathrobe. Edward looked up.

"Good morning."

"Morning, Dad." Dick's voice conveyed all the enthusiasm of a schoolboy trudging to the principal's office to serve an after-hours detention.

"Have some coffee."

"Thanks." Moving mechanically, Dick shuffled to a cupboard and retrieved a mug. He picked up the pot and poured. Instead of joining Edward at the table, he leaned against a counter.

Edward felt Dick's eyes upon him. "Sit down."

"No, thanks."

Edward studied his oldest son, normally the picture of vitality. He decided to ask a simple question that he felt certain would lead to a less simple dialogue. "Anything wrong?"

"Only everything." Dick sighed again.

"Hmmm. Let me guess."

"You're no wizard, Dad, but in this case I don't think you need to guess."

"Well?"

"Do you think you could take the day off and do some fishing?"

By 7:30, Edward and Dick had placed rods and tackle in the trunk of Edward's Hudson and bought a pail of minnows. They headed north out of Shelby on State Route 61 for a few miles, then cut east

over unpaved country roads. After a few minutes of bumpy, dusty driving, Edward eased the car to a stop. He and Dick collected their tackle and bait and waded through high weeds and thick brush to one of Edward's favorite fishing spots, a stretch of the Black Fork, the stream that divided Shelby's Main Street into east and west addresses. Here the water eddied around ancient, well-worn rocks. It was a good place to catch crappies, which Edward liked to clean and fry the same day they were hooked.

Thick trees shaded the banks from the rising sun. Father and son baited their hooks, cast their lines into the gently swirling water and dropped into semi reclining positions. Dick told his father everything there was to tell about him and Helen and their feelings. As he spoke, he looked toward the ground and over the water. When he finished, his eyes shifted to Edward. "Well, Dad, what do you think?"

"I think you've got a bite."

Instantly, Dick swiveled his head and shoulders and checked his line. His bobber lay motionless in the water. "Aw, come on, Dad. I've got a problem and feel lousy. Don't feel much like joking."

"Sometimes joking can ease the pain."

"Then you'd better make another joke because it still hurts."

"Dick, I don't know if I can solve your dilemma. You're the one in a fix, the one who's got his heart doing his thinking."

"You're not making this any easier for me."

"Sorry, son. I just know that I don't have all the answers. You know as well as I do that I've made my share of mistakes."

"Maybe, but-"

"No maybes."

"I'm still willing to take my chances with you," said Dick.

"You take chances?" Edward ribbed his son. "Are you sure you want to listen to cheap advice from an old geezer like me?"

"Especially from an old geezer like you."

Edward gazed out over the water, collecting his thoughts. He picked up a small stone and flipped it into the water. Then he looked at Dick. He spoke quietly and deliberately, with words glazed by experience. "The way I see it, Dick, life is a now-you-see-it, now-you-don't proposition. First it's here and then it's there. You're in between and if you don't keep your eyes open and move fast, you wonder where the blue blazes it went. And it's no place for chicken gamblers. You get a hand and you play it. You don't get too many second chances. I did. I was lucky to get Harriet after your mother died. Darned lucky. You go through life once, and it pays to make the most of it, to grab on and don't let go. Especially with people. You plan for the future but you don't shortchange today. Is this making any sense?" Dick nodded. "When you play to win, sometimes you can get pretty battered and bruised. I think you're learning that. Still, you make commitments and you try hard to keep them. Especially with friends. Be true to them and yourself. Most of us spend too much time lying to ourselves. That's because most people are afraid of life and play it safe. No risk, no loss, no pain. Not much heartache but not much love. Playing to win is a risk. Lots of time you're scared going in. You're afraid to say or do what you really want. Your stomach is all twisted. You've got to screw up your courage. It takes courage to go ahead because there is a chance you won't get it. Failure hurts. Rejection is tough to handle, darned tough. But when all is said and done, I guess I'd rather try and fail and suffer than let my chance slide by and regret it later."

Friday, June 16, 1950

Dick looked at the living room clock, just as he had done every few minutes for the last hour. It was now 8:00. Too early to call Helen. At least give her time to get out of bed. He tried reading the newspaper to no avail. He got up and walked out onto the front porch. A clutch of boys, young Ben among them, was gathered to discuss the first item on their day's heavy schedule of play. To them, serious business, thought Dick. He smiled.

By 9:00, he could wait no longer. He picked up the phone and dialed 32561. A ring, a second one.

"Hello?"

"Helen?"

"Yes."

"It's Dick. I want to see you."

"I don't know...When?"

"Now."

"I'm not dressed."

"I'll walk instead of drive. That'll give you time."

Fifteen minutes later, Dick and Helen were strolling a few doors down the street from the Wakefield house. As they walked, parts of Edward's homily were flitting across Dick's mind. He stopped and turned to face Helen. His hands grasped her upper arms. He breathed deeply. "I love you and I want to marry you." He drew her to him, her face to his shoulder. She didn't resist.

Helen whispered, "Dick, you mean very much to me. But I love Roger."

"Do you?" Dick asked softly.

"Yes."

Before Dick could further analyze, he said, "More than me?"

Her face still was nestling against his shoulder. "I don't know."

"Helen, I'm certain. I want to marry you. I want you to be the mother of my children. I'm holding you now and I want to keep on holding you. I love you and I want you."

"Dick, I do love you. But I need time."

"It's late," he murmured. "There isn't much."

"I know, I know," she said miserably. "Give me until tomorrow. Can you do that?"

"Yes. Of course."

Saturday, June 17, 1950

As Helen waited for Dick, questions were cramming her mind. What would I say to Roger? How would I say it? He would be devastated. And his parents? They have been so nice to me. They would be shocked and hurt. Would Dick be willing to live in Shelby or would he want me to move to California? Would I do that? Dad's not well, and I want to be close to Mom when she needs me. And what about my new teaching job?

Helen met Dick outside the Wakefield house. They reached for each other's hands.

"Helen, I've done some more thinking. A lot of it. I fly back tomorrow morning. The wedding is two months away. You probably feel like the world is spinning faster than a 78 rpm record, and you've got to run like the dickens just to keep from getting thrown off the turntable. Like I said, I'm certain. I love you. But I want you to be certain too, and you're not. I want you to think things over without me looking over your shoulder. Like the cavalry, I came riding over the ridge. But instead of coming to the rescue, I just made a lot of noise and stirred up a lot of dust."

"Dick, please. Nothing's your fault. If I didn't have some doubts about me and Roger, I guess I wouldn't have let us go this far."

"What kind of doubts?"

"Well, our love...We're comfortable together, and I think we'd be comfortable as man and wife. But maybe there should be more. I...Dick, if you and I did marry, when would we marry? And where would we live? And what about my parents?"

"I really managed to screw up your life, didn't I?"

"It *was* rather neat and orderly." She smiled weakly.

"Which, as you know, is the way I usually am. Maybe I'm becoming less that way. Maybe I'm a little more willing to risk a little. At least where you're concerned."

"Dick, I-"

"Just listen," he interrupted, gently but firmly. "My feelings about you aren't going to change. You need to sort things out. Talk to someone about all this. Your mom or dad or a friend. It'll help. Believe me. Then make your decision. I'll call you, and be holding my breath when I do."

Helen nodded. "When will you call?"

"On Friday, the thirtieth."

"The thirtieth? Why so long? That's almost two weeks."

"I know. You might not need that much time to decide. But I have to go on a business trip to Japan. That's why I have to go back to California tomorrow."

"Why Japan?"

"The Japanese are talking about constructing a trade center in Los Angeles. Our company wants a crack at building it. We've been told that we might improve our chances by going to Japan to get to know their trade officials and learn first hand what they're thinking."

"When do you leave?"

"On Tuesday. Next Tuesday. I'll be back on the twenty-ninth and call you the next day. At the crack of dawn, your time."

CHAPTER 13

Tuesday, June 20, 1950

At Los Angeles Airport, Dick and John and Maria and their four girls stood gawking in all directions in the ticketing area. Just as John had predicted, they had no difficulty spotting Brigadier General Henry Briggs, U.S. Army, retired. Fiftyish, General Briggs still was lean and hard. His hair, gray turning white, still was close-cut, but since retiring he had grown a luxuriant mustache that drooped at the ends. He was tall, over six feet, and even in a civilian suit, exuded command presence.

He and John greeted each other. "Here," John said to Dick, "is the man who says he can deliver the trade center contract to Western Construction – if we're as good as I've painted us."

Dick and Henry Briggs shook hands firmly. "Hello, General."

"Good to me you, Dick. And please make it Henry. The Army has more than enough generals."

Dick took an instant liking to the man who was to be his liaison in Japan. During the war, Henry had served with MacArthur, had tasted bitter defeat in the Philippines and then sweet victory. After the war, he had stayed on in Japan as part of the occupation force. As Japan struggled to regain its social, political and economic bearings, Henry observed carefully and gradually became an expert on Japan and its bureaucratic workings. Early in 1949, he retired from the Army with a plan. He would offer himself as a consultant to American businessmen seeking entree into the intricate workings of Japanese commerce and government, a delicately spun web that in later years would spawn a powerful world force known as Japan Inc.

When boarding was announced, Dick picked up, hugged and bussed on both cheeks all four girls. As usual, he played it safe, bestowing his affection first on Jeannie Marie, the oldest, and then in turn, on Ruth, Kate and the youngest, five-year-old Natalie. They all smothered him with hugs and kisses with, as usual, Natalie the most exuberant.

He embraced Maria closely and affectionately. When he released her, they traded kisses on the cheek. Dick and John shook hands and hugged manfully.

The flight to Japan, via Hawaii, would be long and boring. And to Maria, dangerous. No rugged mountains to traverse but endless expanses of water that easily could swallow a metallic bird without chewing or burping. When earlier she had voiced her concerns, first to John and then to Dick, each had sought to allay them, pointing out the airlines' safety records. Maria wasn't having any of it, they knew, but she refrained from further pressing the issue. Instead, she prayed.

Thursday, June 22, 1950

Flying west from Hawaii, Dick and Henry had crossed the international dateline and lost a day. By the time they deplaned at Tokyo's Haneda Airport, it was predawn on Thursday. The two men had done their best to sleep on the long flight but arrived far from fresh.

They cleared passport control, collected their baggage and cleared customs. Henry flagged a taxi that whisked them to the Imperial Hotel.

"We have until noon to snooze," said Henry. "Then we get rolling." Dick groaned. Henry laughed and cuffed him on the shoulder in sympathy.

Japan's burgeoning Ministry of International Trade and Industry already was labyrinthine. Throughout their punishing schedule, Henry invariably found the right office and said and did the right thing. Dick was impressed with this man who had invested wisely the time and effort to learn the language and customs of a people little understood – in fact, still mistrusted – by most Westerners.

Late Thursday night as they headed back to their hotel rooms after a lengthy, multi-course feast with several Trade Ministry officials, Dick voiced his admiration. "Henry, you're good. Damn good. I can see why John felt it crucial to come here and to retain you. I'd have been lost. Totally lost."

"Thanks, Dick, but save it. We still have much to do over the next few days. But let me tell you this. The Japanese are impressed with you. They-"

"Hold it," Dick interrupted. "I haven't done anything. You've carried the ball."

"You've watched and listened," said Henry. "And been polite. That impresses the Japanese. You haven't tried to be the typical American stud.

But as I was about to say, I also let it slip that you are a former naval officer who saw action and whose ship went down. They have only the highest regard for brave naval officers."

Friday, June 23, 1950

Shelby, Ohio

During the five days since Dick had left, Helen had thought much and decided little. She had tried to analyze and resolve her dilemma alone, and it hadn't worked. She moped around the house, only half listening when spoken to. Both her mother Rose and Roger sensed something was amiss. But she turned aside their inquiries. "Nothing's wrong," she insisted. "It's just all the wedding details." Every time she mouthed this lie, she despised herself. She finally acknowledged to herself that Dick's advice had been right; she had to share her problems. This day, she resolved, she would seek the counsel of her mother.

Tokyo

Friday ended none too soon for Dick. He was exhausted. He and Henry dined together at the Imperial. As they finished, Henry said, "Let's sack out early tonight."

"Those just might be the most welcome words I've heard since we got here," said Dick. "I'm bushed. Boy, it will be good to sleep in tomorrow. No more meetings until Monday. I need the break."

"And I've got in mind just the break you need."

"Such as?" Henry's tone – semi conspiratorial – caused Dick to eye him as a shrewd housewife does a door-to-door salesman. "If it's geishas and saki, forget it," said Dick. "Normally, I'd say Sure, but I'm just too pooped."

"Better than that."

"Henry, the tone of your voice suggests we might not see eye to eye on that. In fact, I don't think I want to know what you've got in mind."

Under his thick mustache, Henry smiled slyly but said nothing. He just kept peering at Dick.

"Okay, all right," Dick said with exasperation. His mounting curiosity had managed to momentarily shove aside his heavy fatigue. "Tell me."

Henry's grin grew wider. "Korea."

"Korea!" Dick cried in disbelief.

Henry was unperturbed. "Look, you don't want to spend the weekend lolling on your bed. So, instead, you'll spend it in Korea."

"Henry, I thought you were a paragon of sanity, but I was wrong. You're loony."

"Here's what we'll do."

"You mean here's what *you'll* do. This weekend, *I'll* do what I'm doing tonight. Sleeping. I'm not sure I'll eat, but I will sleep."

Henry continued to roundly ignore Dick's objections. "I have an old Army friend who recently transferred to Korea. He's with KMAG."

"What the hell's KMAG?" Dick snapped.

"Korea Military Advisory Group. It's a small advisory unit. Just established a year ago. July of '49, if I recall correctly. They're located in Seoul. With the communists running North Korea, KMAG's mission is to help stabilize the south by deterring the North."

"Henry-"

The former general brushed aside Dick's weak protest. "I have another friend at Yakota Air Base outside Tokyo. He's set it up so we can get on a cargo flight to Seoul. You might even find some bargain gifts for the Santiagos at the Yakota PX. My friend will get us in."

"Henry-"

"Dick, how many chances do you get to see another corner of the world? We'll fly over tomorrow morning, have a look around and fly back on Sunday afternoon. You're young and strong. You can catch up on your sleep when you get back to the States."

Saturday, June 24, 1950
Shelby, Ohio
Helen's talk with Rose helped. She had made her decision but would sit on it until she talked with Dick. She felt immense relief.

Over the Sea of Japan/East Sea
The long peninsula that is Korea juts southeasterly from Asia toward Japan's southern islands. Its rugged east coast is washed by the Sea of Japan (East Sea to Koreans) and its west coast by the Yellow Sea. China lies due west, and its Manchurian province shares the peninsula's northern border. The 120-mile-wide Korea Straits separate the southern tip from Japan. About 600 miles long and 130 to 200 miles wide, the peninsula is

about the size of Utah. The South Korean portion is virtually the same size as Indiana.

By mid morning, the lumbering four-engine Boeing C-97A Strato-Freighter neared Korea's east coast. Thousands of feet below, over the centuries, lashing tides had chopped the shoreline into sheer cliffs and rocky islets. Mountains arose abruptly from the sea. Dick looked down at the stark vista and shook his head. He would make the best of the weekend foray but longed to be back in his Tokyo hotel room, sleeping and dreaming about his phone call to Helen.

About noon the huge plane touched down smoothly at Kimpo airfield, 15 miles northwest of Seoul. Colonel Bruce Morrison, Henry's friend, greeted them. When they reached Morrison's jeep, Henry said, "Let me drive this buggy. It's been a long time since I wheeled one of these babies. You navigate."

Dick climbed onto the back seat with the light bag he and Henry had decided to share for the overnight trip. Over a combination of dirt and poorly paved roads, the jeep went bumping along for upward of 30 minutes before reaching Seoul's outskirts. Along the way they passed countless grimy storefronts, numerous ox-drawn carts and tiny women balancing outsized loads on their heads. During the jarring, noisy, windy ride, Colonel Morrison provided a running commentary. He twisted in his seat so Dick could hear his half-shouted descriptions of the passing scenes.

Henry thoroughly enjoyed handling the bucking jeep, which behaved like an unbroken colt burdened by its first rider and trying to shed him.

Once at KMAG headquarters in Yongsan Compound just east of downtown Seoul, the three men spent the balance of the afternoon reminiscing and drinking. Henry and Bruce did most of the talking. For a while Dick kept pace with the drinking. After an early dinner, Dick excused himself. He bedded down early and slept heavily.

Sunday, June 25, 1950

"Dick, wake up. Dick." Henry poked and prodded the sleeping hulk. "Come on. Up and at 'em."

Slowly, Dick pried open his right eye. "Jesus, Henry, it's still dark. What's the hurry?"

"Last night after you hit the hay, Bruce said I could borrow his jeep. See some of the country. I want to get started early so we'll have plenty of time. If we leave now, we can drive awhile and get back in time for some chow before we have to head out to Kimpo for our plane."

"You go." Dick groaned and rolled over on the narrow and lumpy bunk which last night had seemed like goose down to his exhausted body. "Don't you ever slow down?"

"No reason to. The world keeps spinning. Doesn't wait for anyone. I don't want to get left behind."

"Highly unlikely."

"Come on. Roll out. Splash some water on your face, grab a cup of coffee, and we'll be off."

"To where?"

"Wherever."

Dick plodded to the jeep in the predawn and stiffly climbed in. Henry vaulted in, grabbed the wheel and ignited the frisky machine.

The sun had yet to rise on Seoul, then a sprawling city of two million people ringed by treeless mountains that soared steeply to craggy summits. Henry's quarter-ton toy sped through Seoul's deserted streets. Within minutes he reached the city's north end and started northwest.

"Where are we headed?" asked Dick.

"Up toward Munsan, maybe a little beyond. Bruce said it makes for a scenic drive." Munsan was about two-thirds of the way along a dirt road that snaked to the 38th parallel.

"Yeah, if we could see anything."

"It'll be light soon."

Japan had annexed Korea in 1910 and occupied it ruthlessly until its defeat at the end of World War II. In 1945 at Yalta, the United States and the Soviet Union agreed to temporarily divide the peninsula at the 38th parallel. The U.S intended to restore independence to Korea, but the Soviets had other ideas. After Japan's surrender, Russia treated the 38th parallel as an international frontier. Between 1945 and 1947, the Soviets rejected several United Nations efforts to negotiate for a unified and independent Korea.

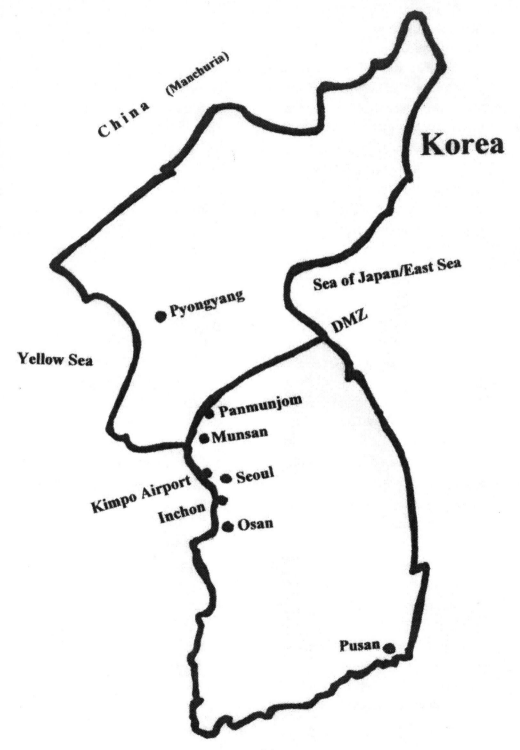

China   (Manchuria)

Korea

Sea of Japan/East Sea

DMZ

Pyongyang

Yellow Sea

Panmunjom

Munsan

Kimpo Airport

Seoul

Inchon

Osan

Pusan

In 1948, the area south of the 38th parallel became the Republic of Korea. Syngman Rhee was elected its first president. North of the 38th parallel, Russia established the Democratic People's Republic of Korea. It installed Kim Il Sung as dictator.

In December 1948, in a surprise action, the Soviets announced they had withdrawn their occupation troops from North Korea. The U.S. was obliged to follow suit in the south, and the evacuation of American troops was completed in June of 1949. A small consulting group, KMAG, stayed on at the new government's request.

The road north was rough, dusty, hard-packed and narrow. It wound through a sleepy Munsan, whose shops and dwellings hugged the primitive road. A few minutes farther the bucking jeep crossed a rickety bridge that spanned the Imjin River.

As darkness slowly surrendered to light, the only signs of life were farmers and their hulking oxen, girding for a day's labor in the rice paddies, and women bending under the weight of water they were carrying from nearby wells.

"Henry, pull up at the next service station with a clean men's room."

Henry laughed heartily. "Glad to see your sense of humor has cracked through the doldrums. I knew you couldn't bitch forever."

"Be that as it may, pull over. My bladder is about to burst."

Henry braked. Dick stepped to the side of the road to relieve himself. To the east, the sun was beginning to scale the sky.

"I guess I'll join you," said Henry, climbing out of the jeep. "Coffee on an empty stomach can pass through in a hurry."

"Yeah, especially when encouraged by a collection of ruts and bumps that a map depicts as a road."

As the two men stepped back toward the jeep, in the distance they heard low rumblings.

"What's that?" asked Henry.

"Listen."

The rumbling continued, growing more belligerent.

"Henry, it's been five years, but I don't think I've forgotten that sound."

"Now that you mention it, it does sound familiar."

"Artillery."

"Right," said Henry. "The ROK Army must be working out. Let's have a look. We could get our Fourth of July fireworks a bit early."

Henry twisted the key, and the jeep lurched north. Before long, the explosions increased in frequency and intensity.

"Must be more than target practice. Probably an exercise of some kind," Dick speculated.

"Surprised Bruce didn't say anything about it," said Henry. "Must have forgot."

The jeep drove on, soon coming to the top of a hill near the 38th parallel. By now the distant thunder had sharpened into clearly defined explosions. Not far off, Dick and Henry could see puffs of smoke. Then, perhaps half a mile to the north, they saw shattered earth flung into the air.

"Close enough?" Dick asked.

"I think so."

In the next minute, diving planes screamed over them. Bombs dropped from their bellies and ripped open the earth at the base of the hills.

"Dick..."

"Henry, I think we're thinking the same thing. During maneuvers they usually drop only smoke bombs."

"Just in case we're right, let's get the hell out of here."

Henry threw the jeep in reverse and spun the steering wheel. Then he jammed the gearshift into second. Wildly spinning tires fighting for purchase threw up a cloud of dust and dirt. As the perky jeep started its careening descent, the two men could hear one of the roaring planes growing ominously closer. They twisted their necks for a quick look back. At that moment, through the deafening roar, a salvo of machine gun fire sprayed the dirt road on either side of the jeep.

"Get down," Dick bellowed.

Henry braked the jeep. Both men leaped out and sprinted for cover at the side of the road.

"Somebody's mad at somebody," hollered Henry.

"Either that or they don't like olive drab vehicles."

"Let's get back in the jeep and skedaddle."

The two men ran for the jeep. As they were about to climb in, they could hear - then see - a second plane swiftly approaching. Neither said anything but pivoted and dashed back to the roadside. As they dove for cover, the plane's guns erupted. A second later, a sharp explosion lifted and overturned the jeep which instantly burst into flames.

"I don't like to swear, Dick, but goddammit, we're in some deep shit. That was not an American plane."

In the southern sky, Henry and Dick could see the second plane bank lazily to the east and start back toward them.

"Christ," spat Henry, "he's not satisfied with the jeep. Here he comes again."

"What now?" cried Dick. "I bow to the Army's experience on land."

Henry looked around quickly. Hills lined each side of the road. "We stay put and stay down. As low as possible. I don't think we could make the top of the hill in time, and we'd be ducks on a pond if he caught us in the open. Besides, we don't know if there's better cover on the other side."

"This grass is plenty green enough for me."

"You scared?" said Henry.

"Shitless."

"Makes two of us. I told you you'd be glad you came to Korea. You'll at least get your bowels cleaned out."

The plane came swooping in low, spitting rounds into the earth and underbrush where Dick and Henry lay concealed. Then it pulled up and sped away. Moments later it returned for a third run. As it roared toward them, both men lay motionless. Neither thought to pray.

The two planes that attacked Dick and Henry were among 100 Russian-built craft that were providing tactical air support for six reinforced divisions of the North Korean infantry, more than 60,000 men, who came driving down the historic invasion route to Seoul. Used by invaders of the peninsula since Genghis Khan in the 1200s, the route is a north-to-south valley running through mountainous terrain. Artillery and 100 Russian-built T-34 heavy tanks also were supporting the invasion.

Because of the time difference between Korea and the United States – 14 hours ahead of Ohio and 17 ahead of California – news of the invasion reached the Lawrences and the Santiagos on Saturday, June 24. Both families were upset by the prospect of another war, coming so soon after

World War II. Both families were relieved that Dick was no closer to Korea than Japan. Maria offered a prayer of thanks.

As the curtain of darkness descended on Korea that Sunday, Dick and Henry lay exhausted atop a ridge somewhere north of Seoul. They had spent the day scrambling south from rock to rock and tree to tree, staying low at all times, running in a painful crouch that exerted extra strain on their backs, lungs and knees. They hid at the slightest sign or sound of danger. The ordeal sapped physical strength but also exacted a stiff mental and emotional toll. Especially on Dick, whose mind alternated between thoughts of staying alive and of reaching Helen Wakefield. Two large, non-uniformed, non-Asians made conspicuous targets. Throughout the day the sights and sounds of battle grew ever closer. Around them, the ROK Army was in full retreat, no match for the bigger, Soviet-equipped North Korean juggernaut. So far they had escaped detection by soldiers in any uniform, which they had concluded was the only sure way to avoid the ultimate harm. Dick and Henry had analyzed their options. It was a ballot of unattractive choices.

"Maybe we can join a retreating ROK Army unit," Dick suggested.

"Not a particularly enticing proposition," Henry replied. "Those units are under heavy fire. We could be captured – and executed as spies. Not a very appealing prospect."

"Shit," Dick grumbled. "Somehow I need to get word to Helen within the next five days."

Henry shrugged. "That could be problematic. If we're detained…If we find someone who understands English, well, it would be asking a lot to expect them to believe a farfetched yarn…Two American civilians claiming to be trapped innocently at the beginning of a war while on a Sunday morning sightseeing excursion. Truth might be stranger than fiction," said Henry, "but this isn't the time or place to put that theory to the test." That seemed especially so during the first hours of a new war when chaos reigned and the unexpected was the rule. They decided to proceed on the assumption that Caucasians in civvies would be treated as spies and shot on sight – by either side. They continued to duck from tree to tree and rock to rock. Occasional bursting shells showered them with dirt and assorted debris. The crackle of rifle and machine gun fire became as commonplace as the buzz of houseflies on a hot summer day.

Monday, June 26, 1950

Sunday night, the fighting slowed but didn't stop. The shelling continued. Dick and Henry rested in a clump of trees. One catnapped while the other stood watch. During World War II both men had endured some long nights. This first night in a new war was as bad as any. Each sound was amplified by the knowledge that it could be the last they would hear.

As dawn broke it was clear that the second day would be no better than the first.

"Henry, I don't know what our chances are, but let's do our best to beat the North Koreans to Seoul. This will sound crazy, but if nothing else, I've got to find a way to make a phone call. And I've got to make it before the end of the week."

Henry studied the face of his young companion. "Dick," he smiled affectionately from beneath his grayish mustache, "you are crazy. If we get our butts out of this mess, I'll feed you enough dimes to call every girl in the states."

"One in Ohio will do."

"Why this week?"

"I'll explain later. Don't you suppose we should get moving?"

"The sooner the better."

They used the road to Seoul as their lifeline but didn't venture too close. Besides fleeing civilians, retreating ROK Army stragglers clogged the narrow dirt ribbon. It was slow going over rough terrain. They were hot, thirsty, tired and hungry. When they came to scattered farms, they stuck to the tree-lined fringes of rice paddies.

Their luck held until early afternoon. Perspiring heavily and gasping for breath, they had stopped to catch their wind in a cluster of trees. As they struggled to their feet to renew their flight, an artillery shell burst in the trees above them. Limbs and leaves showered them as they scrambled for cover.

"What now?" said Dick.

"We don't know which Army fired that shot, but it doesn't make much difference. If you're going to have any chance to make that phone call, we'd better keep moving."

They continued south, moving cautiously. A shell exploded ahead of them, then another. They dashed for the crater created by the first shell. They dove in and lay panting.

Through the sweat-sodden dirt that caked his face, Henry looked Dick in the eye. "If they ever give a prize for two guys being in the wrong place at the wrong time, we'll win hands down. I am really sorry."

Dick lowered his head and cupped his smudged face in his grimy hands. Then he drew his hands down his face and looked toward Henry. "Do you think we can make it?"

"I don't know."

"Are you still scared?"

"At the moment," said Henry, "I'm too tired to be scared."

"Same here."

They heaved themselves to their feet and climbed out of the crater. They had moved not a hundred yards when, fatigued though they were, fear gripped and shook them. Henry was in the lead. A small hillock lay in their path. They started around it. Suddenly, Henry froze. A second later, he dropped to the ground.

"What is it?" said Dick.

"Infantry. North Korean."

"Shit. How many?"

"A couple hundred. A company."

"Which way are they moving?"

"Southwest. Toward the road."

Dick crawled up to Henry. They lay prone against the ground and peered ahead. Then they crawled backward, their bellies flat against the earth.

"This is getting dicey," Henry whispered. "It's gotta be an advance unit. The fighting is getting damn close, but I don't think the North Korean main body is going to catch us for a while. Let's keep moving but be damned careful."

At nightfall, Dick and Henry again took refuge among a stand of trees. Anything to stay out of the open. For the second day, they had gone without food or drink. They had resisted the temptation to drink from streams or irrigation ditches. Neither man needed *Don't drink the water* signs to alert him to the unfortunate consequences those waters might carry. Again the fighting slackened. But this night was different; they heard voices, muffled and seemingly distant. But, they knew, too close to risk idle conversation. When they dozed, each man avoided lying on his back to reduce the chances of heavy breathing or snoring.

♠ ♥ ♣ ♦

Tuesday, June 27, 1950

The clank of heavy tanks roused Henry from light sleep. Dick, already awake, listened as the metallic crunch broke the morning calm. It was an ominous sound that did nothing for their sagging morale.

Close by, artillery began to limber up. By now they could differentiate between the sounds of the good guys and the bad guys. Most of the artillery and all the advancing tanks belonged to the bad guys.

Henry and Dick crawled laboriously to the top of a low ridge and looked west toward the road. T-34 tanks, flanked by plodding North Korean infantry, were rumbling south.

"Dick, I don't want to sound melodramatic, but I think we've been had. I don't know what stands between them and Seoul, but it can't be much."

"Agreed."

"Damn. I'm sorry."

"I know."

"I think we have to rule out getting to Kimpo. Too far west."

"Agreed."

A pair of bedraggled observers on a natural viewing stand, they watched the passing parade. Their flagging hopes dwindled still further.

"I'm no military genius," grumbled Henry, "but this invasion promises to be a bloody rout unless the South Koreans stiffen somewhere. I can see the Americans providing air support from Japan, but it will take time to get armor, artillery and infantry over here. If America sends any help at all."

"If?"

"Politics."

"What about the KMAG advisers?"

"If they don't make it out, we – the Americans – probably will try to evacuate them."

"And us?"

"Nothing's changed," Henry said wearily. "I think we have to keep moving south. Of course, if we don't get food and water damn soon, it won't make any difference. In that regard, I do have one thing in mind. A long shot."

The two Americans spent the afternoon trudging south under a searing sun. Progress was excruciatingly slow. There were more enemy troops to evade, and nagging hunger and acute thirst were punishing them. As evening neared, they could make out in the distance the peaks of the mountains that ring Seoul. A knoll rose before them. "Come on," whispered Henry.

They crawled to the top. To the southwest lay a farm. A thatched-roof, earthen-walled house was surrounded on three sides by rice paddies and on the fourth by a large vegetable garden. Chickens pecked unconcernedly in the clay yard, and an ox was tethered to a post beside a nearby outbuilding. No people were outside.

"That's our long shot," said Henry. "I don't think we can go another night without water. Let's go. Don't worry about staying low this time. If there's anybody in that house, I want them to have plenty of time to look us over."

The two men descended the knoll and approached the farm. They maneuvered to one of the raised earthen walkways separating the paddies and went walking slowly toward the house. When they were about 50 feet away, a stern-looking man appeared at the door. He was holding a pitchfork. The traditional apparel of rural males – a dark, woven, broad-rimmed conical-shaped hat, baggy white trousers, white shirt jacket covered by a white vest – contrasted with his bronzed, weathered skin. A flowing white mustache drooped farther below the sides of his mouth than did the luxuriant growth on Henry's face. When Dick and Henry continued to advance, the farmer stepped forward to confront them. The square jaw of his grim face was set defiantly. Henry raised his hands, and Dick followed his lead. When the farmer shifted upward the tines of the pitchfork, Dick and Henry stopped, no more than a dozen feet from the farm implement turned defensive weapon.

Slowly, Henry reached into his hip pocket and extracted a sheet of paper that had been folded into quarters. He unfolded the paper, studied it, then spoke: "Nah-nulm mee-gook sah-kahm ihm-nee-dah. Doh-wah djoo-sheep-sh' yo?"

Dick stared slack-jawed at his companion.

The gnarled farmer squinted and studied the two huge foreigners. They appeared to pose little threat. They carried no arms and despite their size, appeared tired and weak. He lowered the pitchfork, stepped backward and bowed slightly.

"What did you say?" asked Dick.

"I told him we are Americans and asked him to help us."

"When did you learn Korean?"

"I didn't."

"It sounded damn good. Where did you get the paper?"

"At KMAG. It covers basic communications needs. Call it the vestige of a knack for military preparedness."

Inside the house, Dick and Henry feasted on steamed rice and kimchi, a cabbage-based dish garnished with radishes and liberally laced with hot peppers, garlic and other seasonings. Both men gagged on their first bite of the fiery dish, prompting a quick chuckle from their Korean host. But their hunger overcame sensory reluctance. The farmer offered them more kimchi, a staple in Korean households and eaten at most meals. They slaked their parched mouths and throats with several cups of weak tea served by the farmer's wife.

When they'd finished, Henry and Dick stood and bowed. Henry looked again at the wrinkled sheet of paper. With utmost sincerity, he said *Kahm-sah-hahm-nee-dah*. Dick said the same thing, in English: "Thank you."

Henry and Dick retired to a corner, slumped against a wall and slid to the floor. Only then did the farmer eat. And only after he had finished did his wife eat. Both men remained silent while host and hostess ate. "Korean tradition," whispered Henry. "Their culture makes them a nation of male chauvinists."

"I'm glad you played your long shot," said Dick. "They seem like friendly folks, and Lord knows we needed to fill our bellies."

As the wife cleared away the last dishes and started to clean up, the farmer beckoned them to join him at the low table.

"What now?" murmured Dick, rising slowly from the floor.

"No idea."

After his guests had squatted, the man enunciated carefully in a language that obviously differed from the guttural Korean.

"Do you know what he said?" asked Dick.

An ironic smile creased Henry's grimy face, lifting the ends of his drooping mustache. "He wants to know if either of us speaks Japanese."

Wednesday, June 28, 1950

Seoul fell to the North Koreans. A six-year-old girl, Lee Chong Hee, was wedged with vats of cabbages and peppers in a cellar beneath her house by parents trying to protect her from marauding, rapacious invaders.

Friday, June 30, 1950

Helen awoke early. Had she possessed wings, she would have fluttered up to a tree limb and joined the birds in song. She sat in her room before the dresser mirror, brushing her hair, stroke after happy stroke. Satisfied with its sheen, she stood and walked to the window and basked amid the morning sun's first rays. She had awaited this day with the same anticipation a child feels in counting down the last days before Christmas. Her only plans were to stay close to the telephone. There would be no races to pick up the receiver. Her mother, Helen knew, would let her take all calls.

When by noon the phone hadn't rung, Helen merely assumed that Dick, exhausted after his trip to Japan and back, had slept in. Or perhaps had slept through his clock's alarm.

When by nightfall he still hadn't called, only the most minute element of doubt had edged into Helen's mind. Probably, she reasoned, his plane from Tokyo had been delayed. Dick was one of the world's reliable people. He would call as soon as he could get to a phone.

Saturday, July 1, 1950

During the night, Helen slept fitfully. She awakened early. All day she waited for Dick's call, growing more concerned as the clock ticked away. Rose watched her daughter's mounting anxiety but bit her tongue. She didn't want to begin consoling her daughter too early. That, she felt, would only further dent Helen's morale. Then a thought struck her. "Helen, it was a very important trip. Maybe Dick had to stay on a day or two longer. And maybe he has no way to get word back to you."

The thought assuaged Helen. It seemed a reasonable explanation. Indeed, it was the only one that she could accept as valid and that presaged no harm to Dick.

Sunday, July 2, 1950

By evening, Helen could wait no longer. With Rose standing by at a discreet distance, she dialed the operator and gave her Dick's apartment phone number. She let it ring a dozen times. As she replaced the receiver in the cradle, Helen began to shake. By the time Rose reached her, Helen had dissolved in tears.

Monday, July 3, 1950

At 1 p.m. Eastern time, 10 a.m. Pacific Coast time, with Rose standing beside her, Helen again asked an operator to help reach Western Construction Company on Wilshire Boulevard in Los Angeles. Person-to-person for Dick Lawrence.

Helen listened. After one ring, a female voice said, "Western Construction. Good morning."

"I have a person-to-person call for Dick Lawrence," said the operator.

"I'm sorry, Mr. Lawrence isn't in."

"When will he be?"

"I don't know."

"Thank you," said the operator.

Helen's throat constricted. Tears filmed her eyes. Her choked "Thank you" was barely audible.

Tuesday, July 4, 1950

Helen stayed home while Rose and Bert Wakefield left for the traditional parade that began at 10 a.m. Marching in the parade as a member of the local American Legion Post contingent was Edward. He took considerable pride in participating in holiday events, but this morning Edward's mind was more on his oldest son and Helen than on the old uniform he wore and the rifle he carried.

By now, he too had expected to hear from Dick. He wouldn't have been surprised to hear from Helen, if she and Dick had decided to marry. That he had heard from neither baffled him. Whatever their decision, it just wasn't like Dick to let something so important slide by without informing his father.

Edward thought about the possibility that Helen and Roger Hoerner would be marrying. If that happens and we get invited, we'll go. I was hoping that Dick and Helen would get married, but I guess the odds were long. Maybe Dick was just too late getting in the game. As Edward and his fellow legionnaires crossed the Black Fork bridge and tramped west on Main Street, he decided to phone Dick if no word came by Friday.

When Rose, watching the parade from the sidewalk, saw Edward go striding by, she reached up and brushed away a tear.

Wednesday, July 5, 1950

It was 3 a.m. when Helen descended the stairs and nervously walked to the telephone. She was desperate. It's midnight in Los Angeles, but if Dick was away on some holiday outing, he'd be home by now. I know he changed his mind, but I need to know why he didn't call. He seemed so certain. What happened to change that? Helen was dumbfounded and distraught. She dialed the operator, who placed the call. Helen waited for nearly 20 rings before giving up.

North of Seoul

Dick looked through the window of the small farmhouse and scanned the countryside. He looked toward the road, 200 yards away. No sign of North Koreans, a welcome change. He looked at Henry, who was napping on a mat in a corner of the room. Dick stepped to the curtained doorway and again surveyed the area. Laboring in the rice paddies were the farmer and his wife. The only other signs of life were the ever- present, ever-pecking chickens and the tethered ox. Nothing else disturbed the stillness. He stepped outside, the first time he had done so in daylight since taking refuge here 11 days ago. He shuffled only a few paces, then stopped. Amid the clucking hens, he placed his hands on his hips and breathed deeply. The inrush of air didn't help much. Uncertainty gnawed at his gut as painfully as an intestinal parasite. *If only I could have gotten word back to Helen. If only someone besides Henry's friend at Yakota and Bruce Morrison at KMAG knew about our trip. Morrison no doubt is on the run, or dead. The man at Yakota had no way of knowing my origins, unless he happened to think to check at the Imperial Hotel. If he even remembered the hotel's name. What about John? He has to be wondering why he hasn't heard from me. But it's not likely he's had time to trace my whereabouts, much less send word back to Ohio. That would require a full-scale investigation. And Helen. She must be baffled – and possibly crushed. This has to be the ultimate irony. Never before have two brothers managed so successfully to screw up so thoroughly the life of one woman.*

Hands still on his hips, Dick looked skyward and then slammed shut his eyes. With utter disgust and despair, he kicked the ground, sending up a small plume of dust and scattering the chickens. "Fuck!"

CHAPTER 14

The air inside the Shelby Cycle Company was stifling. The plant was a three-story brick, turn-of-the-century structure at the corner of Mack and Tucker Avenues. Open windows and whirring fans did little to relieve the oppressive summer heat. Normal conversation could not easily pierce the noise. Machines milled, cut, turned, drilled and bent stubborn steel. Foreman Edward Lawrence sat at his paint-chipped, scarred shop floor desk studying production schedules. Sweat was rolling freely down his face and neck and staining his blue shirt. The sticky heat made it difficult to concentrate.

Through the factory din, Edward heard his name called. He looked up. Walking rapidly toward him was plant manager Gordon Davis. "Ed," Gordon repeated loudly.

Edward smiled. "Slow down, Gordon. Don't work up a sweat unless you have to."

"Are you kidding? I've got two fans blowing in my office and I'm still dripping. Ed, you've got a phone call in my office. Long distance."

"Dick?" Edward pushed back his chair and rose quickly.

"I don't think so. Didn't sound like him. Come on, you can take it in my office."

"Hello?" said Edward, picking up the receiver.

"Mr. Lawrence?"

"Yes."

"Mr. Lawrence, this is John Santiago, Dick's friend."

A pause. Then recognition. "His boss at Western Construction?"

"Yes."

"Mr. Santiago, is Dick all right? I tried to reach him last weekend but couldn't."

"I don't know, Mr. Lawrence."

"Call me Ed, please."

"I'm John."

"Okay."

"Ed, I don't quite know how to tell you this. I called you at work because I just found out, and I wanted you to know first."

"Go on."

Entranced, yet hardly able to believe his ears, Edward listened as John retold what he had learned of Dick's actions and whereabouts. Back on June 25, like most others in Seoul, Colonel Bruce Morrison, the KMAG adviser, had at first linked the distant shelling to ROK Army maneuvers. When news of the invasion reached him, thoughts of Dick and Henry failed to squeeze into his harried mind. Morrison and the other KMAG advisers were scrambling to help organize resistance. Some grabbed rifles and rushed to join front-line ROK Army units. Morrison's first thoughts of Dick and Henry coincided with his first thoughts of his missing jeep. He was not alarmed. He merely assumed that Dick and Henry were out of harm's way and would be rolling back into Seoul at any moment. Later that day when they failed to appear, he began to worry. In the end, it was only hours before fleeing south in the face of the North Korean onslaught that Morrison had managed to get word back to Yakota. Henry Briggs' friend there tried desperately but could not remember the name of the hotel where Dick and Henry were registered. Amidst the frantic atmosphere at Yakota where men were working around the clock processing flights to beleaguered South Korea, it took him days to locate the hotel and then to reach John Santiago with the shocking news.

The end of John's story was greeted by silence. "Ed, are you all right? Is anyone with you?"

"I'm alone but, yes, I guess I'm all right."

"I'm very sorry. I wish there was more I could say now."

"Yes. There's no way...I mean, did anyone say when we might hear about Dick? I've followed the news. The communists seem to be overrunning the country."

"No one said."

"I see. And about his chances..."

"Nothing. I'm very sorry. If there is anything I can do, anything at all..." John's voice faltered, "please tell me."

"I don't know. Thank you."

The phone call hadn't been easy for John to make. He was very much aware of Edward's tragedy-scarred past. To regain control of his wavering voice, John twice inhaled deeply and forcefully blew out the breaths. "Ed, I'll call everyone I know in the military to learn something more. I won't stop. Dick means very much to me and my family. We love him. When I learn anything, I'll call right away."

Edward left the plant early and walked home slowly. To an observer he might have appeared dazed. He wasn't. A curious calm prevailed. Why, he didn't know. Edward's emotions at this moment were an enigma to him. He was worried about Dick but was neither distraught nor despondent. Shock might explain the absence of inner turmoil. In searching his mind for an explanation, never had Edward imagined anything so mind-boggling as a weekend side trip sweeping his son up into a war. There was another possible explanation for the calm Edward was feeling, but he hoped it was groundless: had the unexpected deaths of his father, Sarah and Bill buffeted him so severely as to render him incapable of grief or strong emotion?

At home, Harriet listened in the same stunned disbelief Edward had experienced. Afterward she wept softly and prayed.

To five-year-old Ben, the tale of his brother was at first incomprehensible. Dick had been caught in a war, no one knew where he was, but he might not be dead or even hurt.

"Did Dick shoot anyone?" asked the little boy.

"I don't know," answered his father.

"Does he have a gun?"

"I don't know."

"What if someone finds him and tries to kill him?"

"I don't know."

"Is he lost?"

"Yes."

"Maybe someone will find him and bring him back."

"I hope so."

It was different for Maria. She and John and the four girls had gone to the airport on June 29 to meet Dick's plane. She had been worried since, her anxiety mounting daily. She had become as jumpy as a child waiting for the first fright in a carnival horror house. Once, the strident ring of the telephone had led to the clatter of broken china.

After calling Edward, John Santiago had left work early. On the way home he had struggled to find a way to lessen on Maria the impact of the news. She'll take it hard, no question about that. I don't think a man and woman could not be married and be closer than Maria and Dick. They have a beautiful, strong friendship.

When John entered the house on Glenmont, Maria greeted him with her daily question, "Any news?"

Often, a husband and wife needn't speak to communicate. Eyes, gestures, unaccustomed silences often say more and say it more eloquently than the most carefully articulated words. When John looked lovingly at Maria but didn't reply, she knew the answer and she knew it was bad. Before his eyes, John saw his wife begin to crumble. Her head sagged and her chin began to quiver. He walked to Maria and held her closely. It would take time, John knew, for his loving wife to accept and live with the unrelenting torment of not knowing.

In the weeks that followed, though 2,500 miles apart, a bond began to grow between the Lawrences and Santiagos. John called Edward frequently. Their conversations sometimes were brief, but the talks told both men, so different in age, appearance, background and economic status, that a strong commonality existed.

Gradually Maria began to pull herself together. The support she received from John and her daughters helped immeasurably. The evening she first brought herself to talk on the phone with Edward was a turning point. Maria was amazed by Edward's cheerful words and buoyant tone. From John, Maria knew how much Edward loved and missed Dick. She also knew of his previous tragic losses. That he was able to stand up so well against this latest blow imbued Maria with strength. What Maria didn't know, had no way of knowing, was that Edward was a fair actor. In earlier conversations John had told him of Maria's friendship with Dick and how hard she had taken his disappearance. Edward was not about to complicate her life still further by sounding despondent. After they hung up the phone, Maria said to John, "He seems like a wonderful man. I wish I knew him…that we were closer and could see him."

"I know."

"It's no wonder Dick turned out to be like he is."

John merely nodded his assent. He couldn't help thinking about Dick in the past tense.

CHAPTER 15

Had Dick been of a mind to pray, he would have thanked God for his deliverance unto Yoon Chun Heum and his shy, gracious wife. Two people from another world – and to rural Koreans, Americans were from another world – could not have received warmer hospitality than had Dick and Henry. Mr. and Mrs. Yoon sincerely cared for their well-being and did all they could to help the two de facto prisoners.

As Korean farmers went, Yoon Chun Heum was prosperous. The average Korean farmer worked two-plus acres that yielded perhaps 70 bushels of rice plus vegetables. Only five percent of Korean farms in 1950 were more than five acres. With seven acres, Yoon Chun Heum was one of the fortunate few. And so, in a sense, were Dick and Henry. Many other farmers with less acreage would not have been able to feed the strapping Americans. The Yoons did so and with great enthusiasm.

The Yoons' house was typical of rural Korean homes. Two rooms, one for sleeping, one for everything else. Dick and Henry slept in the latter. The windows were small and fitted with cloudily transparent paper instead of glass. Inside, there was no electricity or running water. Mrs. Yoon carried the daily supply of drinking and cooking water from a nearby well. She did her laundry in a nearby rocky stream. Bodily wastes were expelled in a crude outhouse about 50 feet from the back door. The Americans learned to hold their noses and make do.

Since Dick and Henry had moved in, the Yoons' home had acquired a new and unconventional feature. As a precaution, in their hosts' sleeping quarters under a large, crude trunk, Dick, Henry and Mr. Yoon dug a deep hole, which they shored along the sides with scrounged planking. In an emergency, Dick and Henry were to shoehorn themselves in and hide. The hole was dug at night, and the excavated dirt was transported to and scattered in the rice paddies.

Mr. Yoon, 42 years old, had learned to speak Japanese in his youth. Japan, during its 35-year occupation of Korea, relentlessly tried to impose its culture and language on the peninsula's people. Koreans were forced to take Japanese names. Mr. Yoon had hated the Japanese. He had learned the language of his oppressors not as a concession but as a practicality, a means to know what the loathsome foreigners were saying and planning. The youngster had seen the wisdom in knowing as much as possible about his enemies.

Now, in the summer of 1950, the enemy was not from across the East Sea but from his own land. Koreans were attacking and butchering Koreans. To Yoon Chun Heum, it was unthinkable and incomprehensible. More than that, it was unutterably sad.

Like most rural Koreans, Chun was isolated from the currents and eddies of international affairs. He had never been farther from his home than Seoul, just a few miles to the south. There were no newspapers or radios. From the Japanese occupation, Chun could understand his country as the helpless pawn of ambitious foreign powers. Never, though, had he perceived his harsh but beautifully mountainous homeland as a key to international military strategy.

To Chun it was ironic that the language he had learned out of hatred now was being employed in friendship. When Dick and Henry, two mammoth Caucasians, had walked out of the woods into his life, they might well have been two beings from a distant planet. They were the first white men Mr. and Mrs. Yoon had seen. Never even had they seen photos of Westerners. But the bonds between the pair of aliens and the pair of natives quickly took hold. Henry and Chun spent hours conversing in Japanese. Henry put Korea into a perspective previously unknown to Chun. He explained its strategic global importance as a buffer between East and West in a world fast growing smaller and more dangerous to itself.

Chun began taking it upon himself to learn what he could about the war and keep Dick and Henry informed. The news was unrelentingly bad.

On June 30, President Harry Truman had authorized General Douglas MacArthur to use American ground forces in Korea. The order was vastly more impressive than the facts warranted. The troops would come from Japan, where the U.S. had four divisions that were at less than 70 percent of their authorized strength. Most of their men were young and untested soldiers who were about to receive some humiliating on-the-job training.

The first American contingent flown to Korea was dubbed Task Force Smith. Lieutenant Colonel Brad Smith and 540 hastily assembled men were flown overnight from Japan to Pusan on South Korea's southern coast. Immediately, they moved by train to a position just north of Osan, about

45 miles south of Seoul. They were equipped with small arms and five howitzers, only one of which was supplied with armor-piercing anti-tank shells – a scant six rounds.

Standing on a hilltop, Colonel Smith surveyed the countryside. Greeting his men were 33 T-34 Russian tanks and 10,000 crack North Korean troops. The encounter started at 8:16 a.m. on July 5. Colonel Smith was a realist. To his radioman he said acidly, "Get word to Tokyo somehow that Custer stood a better chance at Little Big Horn." In seven hours, Task Force Smith was out of ammunition and on the run. About 150 of its men were killed, wounded or reported missing.

The North Koreans continued slugging away to the south. The U.S. 24th Infantry Division arrived in South Korea but resisted feebly and could not check the communist drive.

Chun was the most discreet of correspondents. No one knew, or suspected, that his inquiries about the status of the war were meant to accomplish anything more than to satisfy his own curiosity. After all, talk of the war dominated the conversations of virtually every Korean. So far, only Chun and his wife knew they had houseguests. They intended to keep it that way.

With his news so invariably discouraging, Chun toyed with the idea of coloring his reports. He decided against it. Dick and Henry's morale, especially Dick's, could have used a boost. With each passing day and each account of the seemingly unstoppable North Korean advance, Dick's spirits drooped lower than Henry's mustache.

When Henry interpreted Chun's report of the fall of Osan and pinpointed its location on a map drawn in the dirt, Dick asked, "Do you think anyone can stop them?"

"Yes," said Henry, "but it will take time." Henry was not nearly as sure as his words. The former general was tempted but decided against distorting his interpretations of Chun's reports. However, for the benefit of Dick's morale, he offered optimistic assessments of the facts.

"There isn't much time left, is there?" said Dick.

"There's enough. Chun says the Americans are landing more and more troops and equipment at Pusan. They'll make a difference."

"The way things are going, they'll be in for an Asian version of Dunkirk," said Dick.

"Won't happen," Henry said firmly.

"If it does, we either figure out how to look Korean or spend the rest of our lives hiding here. I doubt if the North Koreans would operate a ferry service to Japan. Or let us on if we could pay the fare."

"Dick, there won't be a repeat of Dunkirk. We've got too much muscle to let that happen. Believe me."

Despite such assurances, Dick grew increasingly lethargic. His conversations with Henry grew infrequent and terse. To Dick their de facto incarceration was a pitch-black tunnel with no light in sight. Dick was a planner and a doer. Now there was nothing to plan or do. Only think. Dick dwelled daily on Helen, speculating endlessly on what might have been had he been able to phone her. And on what might have happened between her and Roger Hoerner. He knew these thoughts were slowly poisoning his mind and body but was powerless to shut them off.

Early one morning during the third week in July, Mr. and Mrs. Yoon and Dick and Henry finished breakfast. Chun and Henry stood and chatted idly while Mrs. Yoon began to clear the table. Dick excused himself to make his morning trek to the outhouse.

Mrs. Yoon was first to hear the voices. They were distant and faint. Curious, she wiped her hands on her apron and started toward the door. Chun and Henry, oblivious to the sounds, continued to talk in Japanese. Mrs. Yoon passed them. When she got to the doorway and looked out, she froze. Her hands flew up to her cheeks. She spun and whispered frantically, "Chun!"

Her husband glanced toward her.

"Chun," she repeated insistently, "come here."

Chun, totally unaccustomed to being addressed so abruptly by his wife, merely stared. In Korea, male dominance flourished. Wives treated husbands with the utmost deference. A culture 5,000 years old dictated that wives insisted on nothing at any time. Even their suggestions and requests were generally circuitous. Now, although she spoke in a whisper, Chun's wife was commanding him to come to her. Chun found his feet leading him to the door.

When he got there, a gestating rebuke for wifely disrespect quickly disintegrated. Mr. Yoon's jaw clenched. He twisted toward Henry. "North Korean soldiers. Coming from the road."

"How many?"

"Four."

Henry peeked through a small window, watched the approaching soldiers for a moment, then turned and half ran through the doorway to the rear room and to the back door. For another moment he was undecided. *If I call Dick, those troops might hear me. If I run to the outhouse...* Before he had time to act, the outhouse door swung open. When Dick emerged, the sight that greeted him shattered his black mood. There was Henry, eyes wide, crouching, right forefinger pressed against his lips, his left hand gesticulating wildly, beckoning Dick to come at once. Dick smiled and would have laughed but for Henry strenuously shaking his head and keeping his finger pressed against lips.

About 100 yards from the side of the Yoon's house, the four soldiers were approaching. They included an officer, a sergeant and two privates. The soldiers were laughing and joking loudly. They epitomized the all-conquering warrior full of rip-snorting confidence.

At the front door, fear for themselves and their guests took hold of the Yoons. During the first terrifying moments, they silently watched the swaggering soldiers slowly make their way. Then Chun dispatched his wife to the rear of the house to check on Dick and Henry. When Dick was about three feet from the back door, Henry reached out, grabbed Dick's right arm and dragged him roughly into the house.

"What's up?"

"North Koreans. Coming toward the house. You picked a fine time to shit. Get your butt in here."

When Mrs. Yoon saw that Dick was safely in the house, she gestured toward the hiding place under the trunk and then scurried back to her husband.

When the advancing troops were about 70 yards from the house, Chun started to step outside. At that moment, his wife's small hands clamped shut on his left arm like the jaws of a crocodile. "The dishes," she whispered in near panic, "the extra dishes."

Chun studied the source of his wife's terror. He pursed his lips and closed his eyes in thought. "Take the extra dishes to Dick and Henry," he ordered. "Tell them to take them in the hole with them."

Quickly, Mrs. Yoon gathered up the extra pairs of bowls, cups and spoons and hurried to the hiding place. Dick and Henry had shoved the trunk aside and were preparing to lower themselves into the hole.

Back at the front door, the initial rush of fear had deserted Chun, replaced by a quiet nervousness that he was able to cope with. Chun waited until the advancing North Koreans were about 50 yards from his home. Then he breathed deeply and stepped outside.

The soldiers saw him and continued swaggering serenely toward the house.

After Dick and Henry had eased themselves into the shoulder-squeezing space, Mrs. Yoon handed them the cups, bowls and spoons. The men bent their knees and ducked their heads. The tiny woman then strained mightily to slide the trunk over the hole.

Almost as soon as the trunk was in place, Dick's and Henry's adrenalin-charged bodies began to heat the cramped hole. Sweat popped out on their foreheads and over their upper lips and started to trickling down their faces and necks. Dick's tongue nervously lapped at the salty perspiration around his mouth. The back lip of the hole had been cut slightly lower than the other three sides to allow a slender shaft of light and a narrow stream of air to penetrate the sweltering darkness. The slender opening prevented them from suffocating but not from suffering. Their knees and lower back and neck muscles quickly started to stiffen. There was no room to move. They could barely shift their weight from foot to foot. Dick grunted lowly.

"Dick," Henry whispered urgently, "whatever you do, don't faint. I'm not worried about you falling because there's no place to fall. But don't drop the dishes."

"I'm afraid I might. Maybe I can lower them to the bottom."

"Try it."

Slowly, Dick extended his right arm downward. It could not reach the floor of the hole. His effort was futile, but the exertion revived him. He no longer felt faint. "Won't work," he murmured, "but I feel better."

"Good," said Henry. "I wasn't thinking. Hand your dishes to me. I can hold them in my other hand."

"Thanks anyway, but I'll be all right."

"That's good. Keep hanging in there. We'll be out soon."

The sergeant carried a submachine gun, and the two privates bore rifles swung across their backs. A holstered sidearm hung from the right side of the officer's belt. He carried a clipboard that secured a sheaf of papers. The soldiers' rollicking chatter subsided as they neared Mr. and Mrs. Yoon. All fell silent when the officer, a bright-faced young lieutenant in his mid-twenties, stopped about five feet from the Yoons.

He bowed slightly and smiled pleasantly. Perfectly aligned teeth gleamed behind pink, full lips. "I am a representative of the Democratic People's Republic of Korea. Lieutenant Paek. As you know, the two Koreas are now one." His tone was almost that of a friendly neighbor. "With one government, one leader, the great Kim Il Sung, and one army. That's as it should be. There should be but one Korea. I would like to ask you a few questions." Again, he smiled. "Do you mind?"

Chun knew full well there still were two armies, not just one, in Korea, although it appeared the North Korean's premature assertion soon would be true enough. Chun was a private person not given to answering openly the questions of complete strangers. Which is not to say he was by nature suspicious. Rather, he was far from guileless. A gut feeling told him that not far behind the lieutenant's smiling veneer lurked a sneer that would bode ill for the Yoons and their two guests-in-hiding. Perhaps he'd detected in the lieutenant's tone a tinge of condescension. In any event, common sense, a hallmark of hardened farmers the world over, signaled Chun not to chance arousing the officer's ire. He merely nodded.

"What is your name?"

"Yoon Chun Heum."

"Your age?"

"Forty-two."

"How long have you lived here?"

"Since I was a child."

As Lieutenant Paek posed his questions and recorded Chun's answers on the top sheet of paper, he barely noticed Mrs. Yoon. It was as though she were a lifeless, straw-filled scarecrow, which was quite in keeping with Korean convention. Given the lowly status of Korean women, it would have been thoroughly irregular for the officer to question or in some way to take undue notice of Mrs. Yoon.

"How much land do you own?"

"Seven acres."

"That's a lot. Very valuable. You are well off."

Chun did not want to debate the officer's assessment of his land holdings, nor did he want to toady up to the invader from the north. Again he nodded, sober faced and as noncommittally as he thought advisable.

"How many people live here?"

"My wife and I."

"Only two? And you have all this?"

No reply from Chun.

"May I look around? Inside too?"

Inwardly, Chun bridled at the lieutenant's brazenness. It was inexcusably rude for this stranger to invite himself into another man's house. Chun swallowed his rising bile. "Yes."

Lieutenant Paek dispatched one private to the outhouse and the other to the small outbuilding where Chun stabled his ox, cooped his chickens and stored his few tools. The officer and the sergeant stepped past the Yoons and into the house.

Dick and Henry, now fully awash in their own salty sweat and growing desperate to breathe fresh air and stretch their aching bodies, strained to catch even the faintest sound. As much as they longed to escape the thin, stale air of their subterranean sanctuary, they yearned to know what was happening. The uncertainty was as painful as their incessantly complaining muscles. They heard the officer speak, "Sergeant, check the back room."

Dick and Henry heard the sergeant's boots scuff the clay floor. They blinked; instinctively, it was the only movement they trusted themselves to make. It helped. Sweat continued to flow from their pores in torrents. Ironically, at this desperate moment, Dick and Henry resembled nothing so much as a pair of marauding, misbegotten swashbucklers in a Hollywood "B" pirate film. Each hand held a stubby musket – a cup and a bowl. Between their teeth were clenched menacing daggers – the metal spoons. Their painful crouch lent them the appearance of scowling buccaneers poised to pounce on hapless merchant seamen. Dick and Henry had so arranged the tableware to guard against an accidental, and potentially lethal, clinking of china against china or metal.

Above, they heard the sergeant flip up the metal latch of the trunk. Dick and Henry blinked hard again and tried desperately not to swallow. In the eerie quiet of the room, a throaty gurgle would have announced their presence as clearly as a flourish of trumpets. The sergeant rifled haphazardly through the trunk's eclectic contents. Scant inches separated his probing hand from Dick's and Henry's upturned eyes. Satisfied, the sergeant dropped the trunk lid. To Dick and Henry below, the slamming of the lid assaulted their ears like the roar of crashing rock. Had Dick not recently been to the outhouse, he was sure at this moment that his urine would be joining his sweat in a race down his legs. Henry's bushy mustache lay matted and lifeless.

They listened to the sergeant turn and tread from the room. They permitted themselves to inhale and swallow. The officer and the sergeant emerged from the house and momentarily were joined by the two privates. Mr. and Mrs. Yoon stood silent and motionless.

"You have a very nice farm," said Paek. "Others should be so fortunate."

"I am fortunate," Chun acknowledged soberly.

"Your new government wants a complete record of all its citizens. The information you have given will be very helpful."

Chun nodded.

"Good day, Mr. Yoon."

As the soldiers turned away toward the road, Chun sensed his wife beginning to move toward the house. He placed a restraining hand on her shoulder. She looked up at him. He shook his head slightly. Chun waited until the soldiers were halfway to the road, then murmured to his wife, "Walk slowly."

Chun stepped around his wife and entered the house first. As Mrs. Yoon stepped through the door, Chun was streaking to the rear room. Dick and Henry heard the running and tensed. Chun's strong hands gripped the trunk and began to wrestle it aside. Underneath, Dick and Henry held their breaths, unsure whether the next instant would bring freedom or execution. Their frightened eyes saw Chun and blinked in relief. Mr. and Mrs. Yoon removed the tableware from their mouths and hands. Dick and Henry were too tired to smile. They tried but were unable to climb unaided from the hole. Gently, yet firmly and steadily, Mr. and Mrs. Yoon pulled the big Americans out. Then the aftershock of the crisis ripped through their drained bodies and they began to tremble.

When the shaking abated, Dick looked at Henry, wearily shook his head and smiled ruefully. "I thought we were goners."

"Me too."

"I wasn't ready to die."

"And now?"

"Not now either."

Mr. and Mrs. Yoon hovered near the bedraggled men. They supported Dick and Henry as they went shuffling uncertainly into the front room. Chun and his wife helped ease them to the floor where they stretched the full length of their bodies, gradually unkinking muscles and joints. Mrs. Yoon hurriedly fetched water, which their parched mouths gulped and dumped into their arid bodies.

"This tastes as good as a cold beer," said Henry gratefully. "Thanks, Chun. For everything. I don't know what you and your wife said and did out there, but it must have been right."

"Thank you both," said Dick.

Mrs. Yoon brought them more water.

"That's all the water we have until my wife goes to the well."

"We've had plenty, Chun. Tell her to rest. We've put her through a lot."

Dick and Henry rolled onto their backs and breathed the deep breaths of newly liberated prisoners. Their freedom was illusory, both knew, but they savored it nonetheless. The 20 minutes endured in the underground furnace had steamed as much life from their bodies as had the three-day flight south at the start of the war.

"Henry, I don't know how long I can take this. Being penned up. I know there's nowhere to go but I'm about ready to try."

"It's rough, but we have to stick it out," said Henry. "I know it's hard to believe now but I can't imagine Uncle Sam will let a fourth-rate country like North Korea push us into the sea."

"Uncle Sam is taking his sweet time. You know we can't stay here forever. Sooner or later somebody will see us. Or somehow learn about us. It could be damn bad for the Yoons. They've already done more than anyone has a right to expect. I don't want them to suffer on our account."

"Nor do I. I've talked it over with Chun. He knows the risk. So does his wife. She's shy and doesn't say much but she's smart."

"And tough."

"And tough. Chun won't hear of our leaving. He insists we stay. For as long as necessary. And he knows it'll be necessary as long as the communists control the country."

"They're terrific people, Henry. If we ever get out of here, I'll repay them somehow."

"No. They wouldn't want that. It would hurt them."

"I'll never forget them."

"Nor I."

"There's something else I'll never forget. That hole. It saved our butts, but I won't go in again. I couldn't take it."

"We may have to."

"No. I'd make the wrong noise at the wrong time. Damn, I can't stand the thought of having some North Korean shove that trunk aside and pull the trigger from point-blank range. Talk about going out with your tail between your legs. All you could do is stare at the end of his barrel and then close your eyes at the last second."

"You know what I don't like about that hole?" said Henry. "It's close. Too close."

"Huh?"

"When you're as close as we were, you learn something about a person. Dick, my man, you need a bath." Henry playfully punched his young friend on the shoulder, and both men laughed. For a few moments at least, the pressure and the anxiety ebbed.

CHAPTER 16

Summers see children romp, squirrels scamper, ball players spit, students unwind, businesses slow, parks prosper, gasoline burn, beaches swarm, root beer fizz, cottonwoods snow, gardens grow, lovers glow.

For the Lawrences and the Santiagos the summer of 1950 wore on like a badly warped record; it seemed as though it would never end.

Maria had recovered from her initial shock. Still, she wavered between faith that Dick was alive and would one day return home and despair that he was dead or rotting in a North Korean prison. Some days she was strong and cheerful enough to keep house and mother the four girls with spirit that approached the verve that used to amaze her husband. On other days, though, she merely went through the motions. She was past tears but not prayer. Even on her good days she beseeched God to return safely the young man whose own faith in God was weak.

One summer evening, Maria and John were sitting on lawn chairs behind their house. "I'm thinking of putting my UCLA degree to work. Natalie is going to be starting kindergarten," she said. "I could arrange to have someone watch her for the couple hours before the older girls and I get home from school. How does that sound?"

"I'm a little surprised," said John, "but it sounds okay."

"I know I told you I had been planning to begin teaching when Natalie started first grade. But I'm feeling a need now to be working hard at something outside the house."

"I think it would be good for you," said John. "And for the family."

In Shelby young Ben and his friends passed the summer in traditional fashion. When they played baseball, the stars were Joe DiMaggio and Bob Feller. When they played cowboys and Indians, historical accuracy was not a consideration; the antagonists were Roy Rogers and Geronimo. Invariably, when they played war, the enemies were Germans and Japanese. Never were they North Koreans. That war was too new and too little understood to be enjoyed on boyhood battlefields. The Germans were evil, clumsy Krauts, and the Japanese were sinister, sneaky Japs. Krauts and Japs were fun to hate. The North Koreans were communists, whatever that meant.

Three summers had snatched from Edward his first family. In August 1936, a massive stroke felled his first wife, Sarah. In June 1944, German bullets snuffed the life of his second son, Bill. In June 1950, chance dealt a joker to his oldest son, Dick. Edward didn't know yet whether the joker had been part of a dead man's hand, but it wasn't the kind of draw that inspired reckless betting.

He still didn't know, perhaps never would, whether Dick and Helen had intended to marry. Regardless, he was sure that Helen would want to know about Dick's misadventure and disappearance. Edward did not relish serving once more as the bearer of grim tidings. The prospect chilled him as would a damp winter wind.

The decision to face Helen carried with it another discomfiting possibility. No matter how he phrased his request to see her, Helen might sense something was amiss. Edward wanted to be able to talk freely with her. He inhaled and began to dial the Wakefield number. As a teacher with weeks to go before school resumed, Helen likely would be at home. His right forefinger spun the dial. To his relief, Helen answered.

"Helen, this is Edward Lawrence. How are you?"

Helen was taken aback. Only the voice of Dick Lawrence would have surprised her more. "Fine, Mr. Lawrence," she said mechanically. "How are you?"

"Fine thanks, Helen...Helen, if you can make it, I'd like to see you. Just for a few minutes. There's something I'd like to tell you. It's about Dick." There was no hesitation in Edward's voice and not much emotion. He was striving to avoid a suggestion of urgency.

There was no reply.

"Helen, are you still there?"

"Yes."

"May I see you, please? Will you come over to my house?"

"Yes. When?"

"Whenever it's convenient for you."

"Tonight. About seven-thirty."

As Helen put down the receiver, her mind seesawed with ambivalence. I really like Mr. Lawrence and normally I'd welcome a chance to see him. But why did he call now and what could he want to tell me about Dick?

Throughout the day, no matter what Helen did, she speculated about Edward's news. Maybe Dick finally got in touch with Mr. Lawrence, explained why he hadn't called back on June 30. Or since then. Now he's leaving it to his dad to tell me. That doesn't sound a bit like Dick. Whatever it is, I need to know. Can I even understand him? I was ready to marry Dick, but since I decided to go ahead and marry Roger, I – this is so confusing.

Later in the day a disquieting thought struck her. What if Dick was sick or hurt in an accident? Worry and remorse for doubting his integrity set in immediately. On its heels came a growing sense of irony. Like Dick half a world away, she found herself speculating on what might have been. Despite Roger's loving nearness, Helen felt a vague sense of isolation.

Helen was extremely fond of Roger. Indeed, she loved him. He was one of the world's truly kind people. He made Helen feel secure and contented. But never did he ignite in her the breathless, leaping fire of consuming love. How important was that? she wondered.

In Edward's living room, Helen listened with incredulity. She had braced herself for anything, so she thought, but anything didn't include this. A welter of emotions went raging through her. If only she'd called Dick's office again. And not person-to-person. If only they had made their decision before he left for Japan. If only, years earlier, they had given free rein to their feelings for each other. If only she could know now whether Dick was alive or dead. When Edward finished, she sat silently, her right elbow propped on the chair's right arm, her thumb and forefinger forked above her brow, cradling her drooping head.

Disasters are the dues of life. Few people manage to escape some costly tragedy. Most people will suffer loss of health or wealth, or crippling injury, or the loss of home to fire or storm, or a child who follows the path of wrong, or the unexpected death of a loved one. A relative few find they must pay extra dues. For no apparent reason. Just the diabolical luck of the draw. Chance seeks them out, targets them as victims and mercilessly stomps on their dreams. Those unable to cope with these brutal attacks turn in their time card and check out. The rest, a stubborn, resilient lot, keep picking up the pieces. Their pain is the greatest. They heal, sometimes slowly and only partially, but they keep aspiring. When disaster exacts more dues, the pain is acute and deep. Two such people sat together in a ghostly silent living room on Second Street in Shelby, Ohio. Both could attest that dues once paid are never fully recovered. The residue is a hurt that might subside but occasionally surfaces with a painful memory. This latest hurt would gnaw at them until Dick's fate was known. If it ever was known.

Saturday, August 19, 1950
"Do you, Roger, take Helen to be your lawfully wedded wife?"
"I do."
"Do you, Helen, take Roger to be your lawfully wedded husband?"
Through cascading tears and in a voice that wavered, Helen whispered, "I do."

In Korea, the rainy season extends from June through August, a three-month period that drenches the peninsula with much of its annual 40-plus inches. In 1950, the summer rains did wonders for the rice crop. They did little for the morale of Dick and Henry.

The seasonal wringing out of the skies not only dampened their spirits but also seemed to saturate the news that Chun regularly reported. Gradually it became apparent that the North Korean advance was petering out along the Pusan Perimeter, a 150-mile line that fanned out to the north and west of the southeastern port city after which the defensive alignment was dubbed. The North Koreans were bogged down. The 16-country United Nations force was buying time as it grew and strengthened. Chun's accounts and disposition brightened as the invaders' punch weakened.

"I'd really like to believe the best," Dick told Henry. "But what Chun tells us about what's going on down at Pusan seems like nothing more than a holding action."

"Hang on to your faith in Uncle Sam," Henry replied soothingly.

"Uncle Sam is taking his sweet time. We could be stuck behind these walls indefinitely. Permanently."

In the United States, Labor Day arrived. Maria needed no psychiatric confirmation to buttress her conclusion that to begin teaching was essential therapy. Late at night lying next to John, wrenching thoughts of her missing friend continued to chase away sleep. John sensed Maria's pain and tried to comfort her. Finally, common sense had told Maria that she needed to shake this destructive pattern. "John," she whispered one night, "the school year can't start soon enough."

"You need something else to concentrate on. Something else to worry about."

"Exactly."

Maria launched her teaching career with a third grade class at Warner Avenue Elementary, the nearby school her daughters attended. A roomful of energetic eight-year-olds did not daunt Maria. The management and disciplinary skills honed in running a household rocked daily by the tumultuous tremors of four young earthquakes had prepared her well for this new assignment. The seismic rumblings in a classroom did not threaten her sure footing. She thrived on the fresh regimen, hectic and tiring as it was.

Her day began at 6:00 when she rose with John. Quickly she learned that the household's morning madness was calmed considerably if she and John both breakfasted and completed their toilet before rousing the girls. At 7:00 Maria awakened Jeannie Marie and Ruth in the room they shared. Then beautiful Kate and pretty, perky Natalie in their room. A few minutes before 8:00 the Santiago four burst through the front door and under the arch of the home at the crest of Glenmont. The four girls pranced and skipped down the tree-shaded sidewalk toward Le Conte Avenue. Maria serenely followed them for the short, pleasant walk to school. As her legs glided over the sidewalk sections, her mind ticked off the items to be covered during the coming day. Mathematics, English, geography, history, reading, science. As a third grade teacher, she smiled in reflection, my specialty is everything. Just the way I like it.

Maria had easily overcome the one major obstacle – care of Natalie – that lay between her and her new career. A young mother who lived farther down Glenmont also had a kindergarten daughter. She enthusiastically agreed to babysit for Natalie until Maria's return from school.

In Shelby, Ben also started kindergarten. That summer he had been excited about going off to school with "the big kids." During his first week in the classroom, however, Ben was distracted. He was thinking about football. Edward had promised to take him to his first football game, Shelby High School's season-opening contest against Fostoria High School. Ben thought and talked about little else. He could hardly wait for Friday, September 8. That first week in kindergarten he would race home each afternoon, perfunctorily greet his mother, swiftly change his clothes, grab his football and dash next door to his friend Pete Carson's house. They and other neighbor boys ran, tackled, passed and fumbled on backyard gridirons until hailed by parents for supper. At night young Ben closed his eyes with visions of Shelby halfbacks breaking loose for long, twisting runs.

Ben's magic Friday dawned sunny, warm and full of promise. In kindergarten he daydreamed. "Ben, Ben," said the endlessly patient teacher, Mrs. Charlotte Lingo, "please pay attention." After the session ended, his feet seemed to glide about six inches above the ground. He could barely contain himself. When he saw Edward returning home from work, Ben went bolting toward him. "Dad!" he shouted, hurling himself at Edward, striking and wrapping his arms around his father's knees with such force that he nearly knocked him to the ground.

Edward's arms flew up and out to maintain his balance. "Whoa," he laughed. "Take it easy. You wouldn't be excited, would you?"

Man and boy ate quickly, bid adieu to Harriet and little Susie and climbed into Edward's black Hudson for the 50-mile drive to Fostoria.

"Dad, do you think Shelby will win?"

"They were good last year and are supposed to be better this year."

"I can hardly wait. Will a lot of people be there?"

"Yes. Probably four or five thousand."

"Wow. And the bands?"

"Yes. Both schools."

"Let's hurry. I don't want to be late."

Edward and Ben arrived about an hour before the kickoff. Ben watched intently as the red-and-gray-clad Shelby Whippets drilled at one end of the field, the red-and-white Fostoria Redmen at the other. Throughout the game, Ben fired burst after burst of questions at his father.

"Are the helmets heavy? Who's playing quarterback for Shelby? Is he good? Where do the players get dressed? Do they get to keep the uniforms? Who's number forty-two? Is he good? What position does he play? What does a guard do? Does he ever get to catch the ball? What's that flag for? What does offsides mean? What's clipping?"

From the opening whistle, the game dazzled Ben. Darting, hurtling bodies, crunching pads, crashing helmets, frenzied cheerleaders, screaming fans, bellowing coaches, pumped-up bands. When Fostoria scored, Ben groaned. When in the fourth quarter Shelby quarterback Jerry Wilson connected with end Dave Gump for a touchdown to tie the score at 7-7, Ben leaped from his seat and cheered wildly. At game's end, the score remained 7-7. As Ben slowly made his way down the bleachers, he announced, with great solemnity, "Dad, when I'm big enough, I'm going to play quarterback for Shelby. And we'll beat Fostoria."

Edward had enjoyed the game and his son's company. But for him the athletic war between boys possessed another dimension. On this night, the adrenalin-primed players, knocking each other to the ground, storming up and down the field, gallantly implementing the strategies and tactics of sideline generals, served as a jolting reminder of real wars with real armies intent on fatally crushing real soldiers. In war, there's no lighted scoreboard, Edward mused. But then there's no need for one. Newspaper headlines serve that purpose. In one respect, football is like war. Good news is bad for someone. But there's one big difference. In war, even when you win, you lose. At Omaha Beach, the Allies lost some 2,000 men. One happened to be my son. The Allies won. Bill lost. Brave? A hero who died defending his country? Certainly. That's the way I have to remember Bill. If I didn't, it would be like an unframed picture curling up and rolling out of sight and out of mind.

Edward kept these feelings to himself. Dick and Bill and I all served our country in war, and I don't regret that. And we paid, me with my wounds, Bill with his life. Dick, he managed to escape with a headache and a dunking in the English Channel. Now he's a civilian, and another war has swept him up.

What about Ben? I can see him as a grown man, in uniform and defending his country. I hope that vision never becomes reality. If it does, I'll pray he doesn't die a hero.

Father and son made their way to the black Hudson. Edward opened the driver's door, and Ben climbed in and scrambled across the seat. Edward settled behind the wheel and inserted and twisted the key. The engine roared to life, and the gleaming car crawled out of the congested parking lot.

For Roger and Helen Hoerner, Labor Day meant the start of school and teaching and the end of lazy mornings when they often didn't arise until almost lunchtime. As newlyweds, the reasons for getting up were not nearly as pressing as those for staying in bed. Their appetite for food was unremarkable, but the same could not be said about their appetite – and capacity – for sex. They hungered for each other and dined endlessly on conjugal meals.

"We're spending so much time in bed," Helen joked, "that it doesn't make sense to fluff the pillows. At this rate, we'll have to reverse the mattress before I have a chance to change the sheets."

For Helen, the sex and the silliness satisfied pressing bodily and emotional urges. But they also did for her what teaching did for Maria Santiago. They provided much needed therapy. For what she nor Roger never joked about was Dick's fate. Indeed, inside the Hoerner household the subject went unspoken after Helen relayed to Roger Edward's incredible story. Helen's early remorse over not waiting longer to hear from or about Dick slowly diminished. She continued to think of him, but more and more, past-tense memories supplanted present-tense speculation. She had a husband to love and to satisfy and she was working hard to please him. Burying Dick's memory was a long, painful ordeal, one much less cathartic than a brief graveside ceremony. Like the others who loved him, Helen held out a fragile reed of hope for Dick's deliverance. But that slender strand couldn't support hope and heavy memories as well as peace of mind and the health of a new marriage. I can't keep clinging, she told herself. I have to let go.

CHAPTER 17

Normally, Yoon Chun Heum's gait was measured and deliberate. Now it was quick and choppy. His arms, instead of swinging easily and rhythmically, sharply sliced the warm late afternoon air. Chun was in a hurry. He longed to run but feared drawing unwanted attention. Middle-aged Korean farmers did not run, apart from an emergency. Chun's home was not ablaze. His livestock were not imperiled. His wife was safe and his fields unthreatened. Discipline. Control. I must not run, Chun commanded himself.

His self-restraint under the circumstances was remarkable. He had reason to run, to sprint until winded and laboring for air. Chun had left home soon after dawn, bound for a small market on the northern fringe of Seoul. The crisp early morning air had invigorated him. He strode purposefully to the cluttered tangle of shops and stalls where area farmers bought, sold and bartered produce, household necessities and sundry items. The bustling market also had become a major news exchange. Indeed, since the outbreak of the war, information was the commodity most traded. Some of it was groundless but a surprising lot proved largely accurate, save for details. Hardened farmers were not easily excited and not given to exaggeration. They wanted their news, however bleak, unadorned by baseless hearsay and fantasy.

Chun had intended to return home by noon. When he neared the market, perfumed by the heavy scent of garlic, the buzz of husky male voices filled the pungent air like a massive swarm of bees. The news that greeted him was electrifying. So much so that he was compelled to stay on, to check as many confirming sources as possible, to flesh out the core information with all available detail. Everyone told him the same basic story, which was reassuring. When he left the market, it was all he could do to refrain from serving as a Korean Paul Revere. Now, some 200 yards from his home, physically tired after the roundtrip hike but emotionally charged by the big news, it took consummate restraint to keep from loudly beckoning his wife and Dick and Henry.

Dick was stretched supine on a mat, fingers interwoven behind his head, in a corner of the front room. Henry and Mrs. Yoon sat across from each other at the low, rectangular table. Henry recently had coaxed the Yoons into teaching him Korean. Mrs. Yoon was giving him a lesson. Henry, with his facility for learning languages, was beginning to catch on.

"Nah-nun moke-go-ship-soom-nee-dah," said Henry with easy precision.

Mrs. Yoon lowered her eyes and laughed demurely and delightedly. She was turning out to be a superb teacher, which pleased and surprised her.

"What did you say?" Dick asked idly.

"I want to eat."

"Not a bad idea. Let's stroll down to the corner pub for kidney pie and stout."

"Wrong continent."

"Wrong world."

"Easy, mate," said Henry. "London is no farther than your imagination. Soothe yourself. Think of Big Ben, ticking away for centuries. In no hurry. Reliable. Protector of time."

Dick's eyes closed. A smile spread across his face.

"Working?" said Henry.

"Actually, I can't seem to see Big Ben," Dick said dryly. "The birds in Piccadilly keep getting in the way."

"You devil. That kind of thinking will only heat your blood."

"If I can't exercise my body or brain, then I'll exercise my blood. Keep the circulation up."

"Your tongue is still sharp," observed Henry.

"I've been sneaking out at night to strop it on rice straw."

Both men chuckled. Dick hadn't been laughing often, and Henry considered this banter effective therapy.

In the next instant, the doorway curtain blew aside, propelled by a bronzed, brawny arm. A tawny, sweaty body followed the arm into the house. "Henry, Henry," the winded, excited voice gasped. In rapid Japanese, "I have news. Big news."

"What is it?" said Henry, pushing away from the table and rising from the floor.

Dick looked on, bewildered, as two human submachine guns – one American, one Korean – fired quick bursts of staccato Japanese. Chun blazed away with a series of short assertive statements. Henry responded with abrupt, incisive questions. With each exchange, their excitement grew. When Henry punctuated the Japanese fusillade with an astonished "Goddamn," Dick broke in. "Would you please tell a prisoner of English just what the hell you two are talking about?"

Three faces pivoted toward Dick. Two, Mr. and Mrs. Yoon's, were blank question marks. Henry's bore a widening smile.

"Well?" pressed Dick. "Are you just going to gawk at me? What's that grin for? Did you just make a killing on Wall Street?"

"Better than that, Dick, my lad. Much better." Henry could hardly contain his mirth. "We are getting out of here. You are going home."

Dick's eyebrows arched and a look of skepticism sharpened his features. "What are you talking about?"

"MacArthur landed at Inchon."

"MacArthur? Inchon?"

"General I-Shall-Return-with-My-Corncob MacArthur."

"That was a different war."

"It's the same MacArthur."

"But what...I don't..."

"What your mind won't register your ears shall hear anyway," said Henry. "Two days ago General Douglas MacArthur led a landing at Inchon. That's about fifteen miles southwest of Seoul on the coast. Completely surprised the communists. Threatens to break their back one hundred fifty miles behind their front lines. My God, the magnitude of it."

Dick now had managed to untangle his tongue. "You're the general, Henry. Keep it simple for a simple salt."

"Just as you say, Dick, my man. If MacArthur's force is strong enough and if our troops that are trapped around Pusan can break out, we should be all right. This whole turn of events could throw the North Koreans into a panic. Their supply lines are overstretched as it is. Chun says MacArthur took Kimpo Airport the day after he took Inchon. That bodes well. Inchon is southwest of Seoul. Kimpo is northwest. That means MacArthur has enough muscle to move forward and fan out at the same time. Damned encouraging."

"I take it we continue to sit tight."

"Like an eagle on her egg. It's the only thing that makes sense. Chun will do his best to keep us on top of things. Whatever happens, I do think we're going to get out of here. If we're patient. If we don't do something rash. I don't think MacArthur would have landed if he didn't have the strength to keep pushing and if our troops down south weren't ready for a big push north."

"I hope you're right."

Henry was. MacArthur's surprise landing at Inchon, Seoul's port city at the mouth of the Han River, was exquisitely daring but well conceived. The principal hazard MacArthur faced was geography. Inchon's tide is the second highest in the world. It rises 35 feet in three hours. When the tide is out, broad mud flats convert the harbor into a treacherous quagmire. MacArthur's timing in those dangerous waters had to be as precise as the finest of navigational instruments. Confusion or delay would have spelled disaster for amphibious troops and equipment.

At dawn on September 15, a reinforced battalion of the 1st Marine Division brushed aside light resistance and captured Wolmi-do Island at the harbor entrance. At the next high tide, other elements of MacArthur's force used ladders and cargo nets to scale the 14-foot seawall and bulled into Inchon. Again they overwhelmed light resistance, took the city and swung north toward Kimpo. The Army's 7th Infantry Division waded ashore on September 18 and wheeled south. This spreading military fan soon had the North Koreans falling back in disarray.

Along the Pusan Perimeter in the south, MacArthur's stunning assault had been the signal for the freshly muscled 8th Army to begin slugging North Korean positions. Several American units quickly pierced communist lines. Parts of the 1st Cavalry Division sped more than 100 miles to link up with the advancing men of the 7th Infantry Division.

North Korean supply lines, stretched thin before the Inchon landing, snapped. By contrast, U.S. logistics were smoothly orchestrated. Reinforcements and supplies, flown from Japan and air-dropped to advancing American units, neatly supplemented troops and equipment already stockpiled behind U.S. lines and hauled ashore from ships standing off the coast.

On September 26, MacArthur announced the capture of Seoul. The news was heady, and when it reached Dick and Henry through Chun, they were jubilant. MacArthur's bulletin, however, was premature. His message was meant more to boost morale and achieve political ends than to accurately reflect military realism. In fact, three days of grim, gritty street fighting remained before Seoul was secured. Little Lee Chong Hee remained hidden under her parents' home amidst the vats of cabbages and peppers. When Seoul was finally taken, American forces had captured more than 100,000 North Korean soldiers.

When word of Seoul's capture reached Dick and Henry, they calculated they were no more than a day or two from liberation. They wanted to laugh and whoop and leap. They settled for exuberant bear hugs. When Henry impulsively wrapped his brawny arms around Mrs. Yoon, he was squeezing 5,000 years of culture. Mrs. Yoon shrieked, as shrilly as a firehouse siren. Korean women were conditioned to shun physical contact with men. Wives did not embrace men not their husbands. The unbridled spontaneity and heartfelt gratitude in Henry's hug were inspiring cultural bridges. Mrs. Yoon quickly recovered her composure. Her dark eyes twinkled merrily and her smile radiated monumental affection. Then her short, strong arms reached out, encircled Henry's waist and squeezed hard in return. The merriment and physical contact were contagious. In the next minute, the four friends all were sharing wildly cathartic embraces. Dick wanted to go outside and run and shout but checked the impulse. The threat of exposure remained ominously real. A few days before the Americans captured Seoul, retreating North Koreans began to trickle north on the road that ran some 200 yards west of the Yoon's house. Soon the trickle escalated to a steady but unhurried stream. As American soldiers continued to push north and east and finally shoved the last communists from Seoul, the quiescent stream transformed into a raging torrent.

"I'm surprised we haven't had any North Korean visitors," Dick observed.

"The North Koreans are in a panic," Henry replied. "They're too intent on saving their skins to take any diversionary side trips to farmhouses. Still, it would be utter folly for us to risk any daylight excursions. We need to stay cozy here in our little cocoon. The North Koreans have been routed, but it would be Custeresque to think them blind."

Days later with the Americans fast slicing the peninsula in half, the rush of backpedaling North Koreans began to subside. Within a month of the Inchon landing, American and United Nations forces would capture about 135,000 trapped North Koreans. As the northward flow of enemy troops ebbed, Dick's and Henry's morale surged.

Dick began plotting his homecoming. First, when we get back to Japan, I'll call Dad. He'll tell me if Helen married Roger. If she hasn't, I'll ask her to fly to California to meet me. If she agrees, we'll be married in the Wayfarers' Chapel. This Frank Lloyd Wright-designed redwood and glass edifice overlooked 33 miles of shimmering sea out to mountainous Santa Catalina Island. Dick knew nothing could come as close to righting all the wrongs fate had perpetrated against Helen than for him to be able to step off a plane at Los Angeles International and into her outstretched arms. Dick's next thought was sobering. If she's married Roger, I'll just spend a few days getting things in order in LA and then fly back to Shelby to see family.

No matter what, Dick thought, I can't wait to see the Santiagos. He envisioned the airport bedlam. The four girls would swarm him, smothering their long absent "uncle" with hugs and kisses, all the while squealing with unrestrained glee. Maria, tears of relief and happiness mingling, would wait patiently until the girls stood aside. Then she would fly forward to crush herself against Dick's chest. Last would come John. Perhaps he too would shed a tear of gratitude for Dick's deliverance. Doubtlessly, he would clasp Dick about the shoulders, then hook an arm around Dick's neck and draw his head to his shoulders.

In Ohio, as Dick envisioned it, the Lawrences would drive from Shelby to meet him at the Cleveland airport where he would receive the same emotion-charged reception. Of course, before I hug anyone in LA or Cleveland, I'll be bidding farewell to the Yoons. That won't be easy. Literally, they've been our saviors. I'll be thrilled to be heading home but damned sad to be leaving the Yoons.

His spirits were much brighter than the gray light outside. Leaden, threatening skies blocked the new day's sun. In the distance, faint rumbling interrupted his reverie. Slowly, he pulled himself up and walked to the door. The rain he expected to fall at any moment would not dampen his outlook. Chun already was at work, about 175 yards northwest of the house at the far edge of his property where the paddies met the forest. Inside, Henry lay on a mat, eyes closed, but awake. Dick heard Mrs. Yoon clear her throat. He turned and saw her smiling, waiting to go outside to work in the vegetable garden. Dick stepped aside and held back the curtain so she could pass.

The Yoons' house sat near the southeast corner of their seven-acre farm, a roughly rectangular plot about 170 yards from north to south and 200 yards from east to west. The north-south road marked the farm's western boundary. The front of the two-room house faced north. Beside the house, about 20 feet to the east at the base of a hill that formed the farm's eastern boundary, was the small outbuilding that served as stable, chicken coop and tool shed. Paddies separated by raised, winding walkways occupied most of the farm. Thin strips of forest and underbrush flanked the farm to the north and south.

Mrs. Yoon had been in the garden only moments when a drop of rain lightly tapped her hand. She paused to glance skyward, and a second drop bounced off her raised forehead. As she bent down, her eyes caught movement where the path from the house met the road. Four North Korean soldiers were stepping from the road onto the path. They stopped and looked in all directions. Then they began walking slowly toward the house. Mrs. Yoon glanced across the paddies toward her husband. Chun, his back to the path, hadn't spotted the soldiers. Cold fear began worming through Mrs. Yoon. The soldiers looked vaguely familiar. She breathed deeply and swallowed hard to get control of herself. Then, pretending not to have seen the intruders, she straightened, turned and forced herself to walk calmly back to the house. Once through the door, she whispered frantically the only English words she had mastered, "Henry! Dick!" She feverishly beckoned the two men to join her at a small window at the side of the house. They scrambled across the room and peered outside. Through the barely transparent window paper and the muggy, gray air, they stared hard at the approaching soldiers.

Mrs. Yoon tugged at Henry's sleeve, raised four fingers, nodded and pointed to the rear room.

Henry stared at her, baffled for a moment by her sign language, then looked back out the window. "Sweet Jesus," he whispered. "I see what you mean, Mrs. Yoon. I think those might be the same four who visited us here a couple months ago. The census boys."

"Are you sure?" asked Dick.

Henry watched them for a few moments more. Then he looked at Mrs. Yoon. Again, she nodded gravely, confirming his impression.

"I wonder what they want this time," said Dick.

"I don't know but I'll give you odds it's not to count heads. Considering the way the war's going, the only heads they should be worried about are their own."

The four soldiers, led by the young lieutenant, were in fact the same men who earlier had driven Dick and Henry into hiding in the hole under the trunk in the Yoons' sleeping quarters. This time, however, they constituted a far different portrait. Gone was the easy, arm-swinging jauntiness and light-hearted banter. The uniforms were the same but they were soiled. On their first visit, the sergeant and the two privates had borne their weapons slung across their backs. This time they carried them at the ready. Last time, the lieutenant carried only a holstered sidearm and a clipboard with a sheaf of papers. The sidearm still hung from his right hip but in the clipboard's place was a submachine gun. The foursome's brimming self-confidence had departed too. In its stead was a heavy-limbed, grim-visaged weariness. They looked tired, suspicious and mean.

About halfway to the house the four men stopped again. They surveyed furtively in all directions. They saw Chun. One of the privates pointed toward him, but he still gave no indication of having seen them. The light sprinkle continued to fall, a drop here, a drop there. The soldiers resumed their slow, silent walk toward the house.

"What do you think?" whispered Dick, anxiety beginning to creep into his voice.

"I think they're hungry. I think their supplies are gone and they've been reduced to living off the fat of the land, such as it is. I think they're here to fill their bellies. Or to order carryout."

"I don't really know those guys," said Dick, "but I'm building a strong hate."

"An honest and understandable reaction. But dangerous. We can't let our emotions get the better of us now. We're too close to blow it."

Mrs. Yoon, though plainly worried, had stood by patiently. Now she again tugged at Henry's sleeve. She gestured toward the rear room.

"She's right, Dick. We haven't much time. Let's get in the hole."

"Uh-uh. Sorry, Henry. I said it before and I meant it. Once was enough. Too much. I'd make the wrong noise at the wrong time. And if those guys stick around to eat, there's no telling how long we'd be in there.

138

Sorry. I'm the last one to want to foul things up but I'm taking my chances above ground."

Henry pursed his lips, looked pensively at Dick, then shifted his gaze toward Mrs. Yoon. "I think the young man's serious. Not necessarily smart, but serious," Henry grumbled. "Anyway, he'd no doubt smell up the hole something dreadful."

Henry motioned Dick toward the back room. Then he placed his hands on Mrs. Yoon's shoulders. In the elementary Korean she had been teaching him, Henry instructed, "Stay here." Then he followed Dick into the rear room.

"What now, Henry?"

"I was hoping," Henry said dryly, "you might have that doped out."

"No," Dick smiled lamely, "I just knew I couldn't take another round in that hole. I don't have an alternative."

"All right," Henry sighed. "We don't have much time. Our options are limited. Trying to get up over the hill would be too chancy. Let's sneak out the back door and duck over to the far side of Chun's shed. Stay close to the back of the house and then move fast to the shed. Walk fast but don't run. Running makes too much noise. Especially on sloppy ground. Then we stay low and close to the far wall. I'll watch the front corner, you watch the back."

"What if they see us?"

"Run like hell up the hill. That'll possibly give the Yoons a chance to run the other way. Otherwise they're doomed."

"We'd be better off in the hole, wouldn't we?" Dick said, contritely.

"No, not if you didn't think you could handle it. Hell, maybe I couldn't either. And I'll tell you, as bad as you smell, I wouldn't want to be in the hole alone."

"Thanks."

The four soldiers came to an awkward halt in front of the Yoons' house. They were milling around and again furtively studying the area. The intermittent drops of rain had accelerated to a light sprinkle. Henry, lying flat on the ground, squinting between the slats in the outbuilding, could see now that these were the same four troops who had paid the initial visit. Lieutenant Paek, his tone no longer cocky but solemn, ordered one of the privates to head toward Mr. Yoon, far off in the paddies. The private walked away slowly, without apparent enthusiasm. He carried his rifle, barrel down. Paek stationed the second private in front of the house. Then he and the sergeant, without bothering to announce their presence, stepped inside.

When they appeared, Mrs. Yoon was standing by the stove in the middle of the room, her arms folded. She did not feign surprise. She sensed danger but hoped she was appearing reasonably calm.

"Good morning," said Lieutenant Paek, with a smile somewhere between friendly and forced.

"Good morning."

"I'm sure you remember us."

"Yes."

"Good. Then we are no longer strangers."

To this Mrs. Yoon said nothing.

The lieutenant continued, "I saw you outside. You were smart to come in before the rain started. I think it will soon be raining hard. Your husband probably will get soaked."

Mrs. Yoon took a step toward the door. "I should call him."

"No need." Paek's smile gave way to pursed lips. His eyes hardened. "I've sent one of my men to get him."

"What do you want?" asked Mrs. Yoon. "If you seek shelter, you are welcome. If you are hungry, I'll feed you."

"Yes, we want shelter and food." A brief pause. His eyes hardened still more. His voice, already chilly, turned abrasive. "But we want more. You have much and we want some of it. Since we can't take it with us, we'll take it here."

Mrs. Yoon fought back the impulse to gulp and blink. Her arms, which had dropped to her sides, once again folded across her chest. "What do you want? We really have very little."

"I will tell you exactly what we want and why," said Paek. "Since the American capitalists sent their criminal dogs to sneak in the back door of our country, the war has gone badly for us. We wanted to unify Korea in the interests of lasting peace. For all Koreans. North and South. But the selfish cowards who run your illicit puppet government called in the filthy Yankees."

By now, Lieutenant Paek was snarling. His eyes were flashing evil intent. "Eventually we will defeat the imperialists. But for now we must fall back. Worse, your countrymen welcome and cheer the American dogs. I have seen them. Unbelievable. Traitors."

"We have not seen any Americans," Mrs. Yoon said meekly, hoping to assuage the flushed, raging officer.

"Shut up!" he snapped. "You are no better than the others. They vilify us, your fellow countrymen. We will not forget this despicable and traitorous treatment. We will make you pay, starting now."

The officer's anger had boiled over. He remained immobile, but Mrs. Yoon found herself involuntarily flinching and retreating. She now was fearing for her life.

"Sergeant, check the back room," Paek ordered.

The sergeant stepped quickly to the curtain separating the two rooms, drew it aside, and looked about. "Nothing, sir."

"Good. Stand watch out here." Then he barked at Mrs. Yoon, "Get in there."

Her heart pumped violently but she stood motionless. Her mouth going dry, her tongue flicked nervously across her lips. She shivered. Mrs. Yoon was terrified. She now expected to die, executed in her own home.

"In there," Paek snapped. "Now."

She took a tentative step toward the back room. Her dilated eyes still were locked on Paek. She took a second slow step, and then the lieutenant, impatient, strode quickly toward the startled woman. He extended his arm and pushed her roughly toward the door and through the flimsy curtain. She staggered into the back room.

Outside, the rain was falling harder. Mr. Yoon heard steps and looked up from his work as the soldier approached. "Hello," he said, forcing a cheerful tone. He did not recognize the dour-looking private, who said nothing.

On his belly, Henry scooted away from the front corner of the shed toward Dick. He placed his lips next to Dick's ear and whispered as softly as humanly possible. "Did you hear that?"

Dick nodded.

"It sounded bad," whispered Henry. "That bastard officer is up to something. Damn, I wish I understood more Korean."

Dick pivoted his head so he could whisper in Henry's ear. "If he's doing something to Mrs. Yoon, we've got to stop him. Or at least try. We might-"

"Shh."

Through the rain, which now had intensified to a drizzle, Henry's ear strained for a telling signal. He did not want to act unnecessarily and disastrously.

Inside the back room, Paek strode purposefully toward Mrs. Yoon. Her folded arms instinctively flew up in self-defense. The lieutenant batted them away. Mrs. Yoon half-stifled a scream.

"Quiet, woman," he growled. "Or you and your husband will both die."

Her eyes widened further. She bit her lip and whimpered.

Henry to Dick: "Did you hear that?"

Dick nodded.

"You were right. We've got to do something. Now."

The lieutenant pointed his submachine gun at her, then placed it on the floor. He grabbed Mrs. Yoon by the shoulder and spun her around so that her back was toward the middle of the room. His raging eyes remained locked on her panic-stricken features. Again she whimpered.

"Quiet," he growled. His strong hands grasped her white blouse at the throat. She began to sob silently. His hands jerked sharply apart and downward, ripping the material and baring her shoulders. Then he gripped her undergarment and pulled sharply downward, exposing Mrs. Yoon's small, firm breasts. Paek's determination and desire to take her surged from deep within and matched his unchecked anger. His heart pumped faster. His penis swelled.

Mrs. Yoon was terrified but also mortified. *This is the ultimate shame. To be violated by this hateful man. This stranger. I can never again face my* husband or friends. Chun loves and respects me but he cannot accept me after this. If I live. Had she been able to, Mrs. Yoon, at that very moment, would have willed her death. She rocked backward, still on her feet.

Dick to Henry: "He's raping her. Goddammit. I don't have to know Korean or any other language to know that."

Henry: "Listen up. Do as I say. Lie down on your belly. Then moan. Moan so that private in front of the house can hear you. Don't move. Just keep moaning."

"Now?"

"Now."

The second private spoke tersely to Chun, "Stand up. Let's go back to the house."

Chun chanced a question. "Why?"

"My orders."

"Your orders? I-" Then a flash of recognition as he placed the soldier's face. "Let me get my tools." Chun was holding a pitchfork. He fetched a hoe and then slowly started walking toward the house, about 170 yards distant on a straight line, considerably farther along the curving walkways. He could see the second private, doing his best to stay dry, standing against the front wall of the house. He assumed his wife and any other soldiers were in the house and that Dick and Henry were hiding in the hole under the trunk. Worry was nipping at Chun's thoughts.

Dick moaned softly.

"A little louder," whispered Henry. "Make him hear you."

"Unnhh. Unnhh. Ohhh."

The soldier in front of the house heard the eerie sounds and looked around as though he really preferred not to detect the source of the pathetic groans. Uncertainty and anxiety partly explained his reluctance, but there was another reason: where he was the drizzle wasn't.

"Unnhh. Ohhh."

Curiosity won out. He placed the sound and slowly began moving toward the shed.

Paek slapped Mrs. Yoon twice, hard across her cheeks. A mingled cry of misery and fear erupted.

"Get down," Paek hissed.

Instinctively she shook her head.

"Bitch, get down or I'll strangle you." Again he slapped her. She went stumbling backward until her back struck the wall.

Cautiously, the private moved toward the moaning. He wasn't sure whether the unnerving sound was human. But it was real and it was compelling. It drew the soldier onward. As the drizzle transformed into a downpour, Henry motioned Dick to crawl back around the corner to the rear of the shed. Henry squinted between slats and saw the soldier approaching the building's front. As he passed from sight, Henry began to circle around behind him to the front of the building. This is suicidal, Henry reflected, and then tried to shrug off the discouraging thought.

Through the heavy rain, Chun saw the soldier moving around the side of the shed. He was startled to see Henry sneaking up behind the unsuspecting soldier. Chun fought off the impulse to stop or to run to help. He was unsure of what was happening, but the specter of death, perhaps his own, jarred and sharpened his mind. Despite the imminent danger and the driving rain, he decided to stall for time. The private guarding Chun had yet to see the drama unfolding barely 100 yards away. He was more concerned with shielding his face from the rain. He had pulled his helmet down and watched, fascinated, as the rain dripped past his eyes in a watery curtain. Chun feigned slipping and dropped his tools as he struggled to keep his balance. The wet soldier muttered a curse but otherwise waited patiently, his eyes still directed groundward, while Chun slowly retrieved his tools and regained his footing.

The lieutenant forced Mrs. Yoon to the floor and knelt astride her legs. He began to pull her ankle-length skirt up. She resisted. Her small, strong hands pushed against Paek's offending fists. He released his grip on her skirt and slapped her hard again. The back of Mrs. Yoon's head rapped the clay floor, dazing her and slowing her reflexes. Paek raised one of his knees and shifted to Mrs. Yoon's left side. He unsnapped his holster and drew his sidearm. He pointed the weapon at her face, then reached behind her head and jerked Mrs. Yoon's knotted black bun. Once. Twice. A third time. Pain shot through her scalp. The bun loosened and fell. Her hair, normally brushed to a sparkling sheen, now damp and dirty, spilled on the floor. The lieutenant hissed, "Spread your legs." She hesitated. Deliberately, he pulled back the slide on the gun.

As the soldier neared the rear corner of the shed, Henry was just two paces behind. He swiftly closed the gap, like a stalking cat lunging for its prey. The soldier sensed a presence lurking behind him. Too late. Henry jammed his left knee into the rear of the soldier's left knee. Simultaneously, the retired general drove his left fist into the soldier's kidney and viciously coiled his right arm around his neck. Dick, by now soaked through to the skin, looked up. He saw the soldier's terror-stricken face. Henry, his right forearm locked under the hapless North Korean's chin, dropped quickly to the ground in a prone position. The soldier, unable to resist, dropped his rifle and collapsed to the ground on his back, his arms outstretched behind him in an effort to cushion his fall. Henry applied increasing pressure to his pinched throat. The soldier's eyes widened and teared. He saw death approaching. Henry jerked his powerful arm down and back. The soldier went limp. Henry released his grip. He saw Dick, now on his haunches, looking at him in wonderment. "An old lesson remembered," Henry whispered grimly.

The rain was dripping from Dick's matted hair and down his face. He swallowed hard. "What now?"

"Help me carry the body to the front of the shed." Henry rested the dead soldier's rifle against the side of the building. He and Dick lifted and lugged the body around to the front and unceremoniously dumped it on the wet ground.

Chun was baffled and disturbed by what he saw. His anxiety rose quickly. For Dick and Henry to be chancing such action, the danger must be great. His guard, still intent on protecting his face from the heavy rain, had seen nothing but Chun's footprints preceding him. Chun walked slowly forward, now about 40 yards from the front of the house.

Henry and Dick dashed back to the cover of the shed. Henry retrieved the soldier's rifle. He wiped his left sleeve across his eyes. Dick waited alongside the shed near the front corner. Henry returned, breathing hard, rain coursing down his face.

"What next?"

"Scream," panted Henry, still unrecovered from the exertion and tension of the last few moments. "A loud anguished scream. No intelligible words. Just loud and long. Stay hidden."

With his left hand, the lieutenant reached down and crudely fondled Mrs. Yoon. She shuddered in disgust and fear. His right hand still held the gun pointed at her face. He raised his left hand and clumsily began to unbuckle his belt. He had just undone the belt buckle when Dick's primal scream pierced the earthen walls of the Yoon's home. A second scream followed immediately.

All heard them. Chun's guard froze. His helmet jerked up as he peered through the driving rain for the source of the macabre howls. The sergeant in the front room stopped pacing. His ears strained like a radio direction finder trying to locate an enemy signal. The lieutenant's hand involuntarily tightened on his belt buckle. A momentary pause, then he barked, "Sergeant, what was that sound?"

"I don't know."

"Get outside and check it out."

As the sergeant started for the door, Paek rebuckled his belt and holstered his sidearm. Then he reached down, grabbed a fistful of Mrs. Yoon's hair and pulled her to her feet. He picked up his submachine gun and dragged her through the doorway into the front room. Halfway across, Mrs. Yoon stumbled. The lieutenant felt her starting to go down. He roughly pulled upward on her hair; another wave of pain went surging through her scalp. Precariously, she maintained her footing. Mrs. Yoon's left hand struggled to pull her torn blouse together over her breasts, but her shoulders remained exposed.

Outside, the sergeant first saw Chun and his guard. They stared back at him through the vertical gray curtain of rain. Then the sergeant saw the body of the first private lying on the sodden ground. He stared, simultaneously curious and disbelieving. As he began to advance toward the corpse, the lieutenant pushed aside the curtain at the front door. He stepped outside, still grasping Mrs. Yoon's hair. The strength of his grip forced Mrs. Yoon's head backward so that her face was turned up into the rain. She closed her eyes. She sensed death close by. Chun did not notice his wife. His eyes were riveted on the sergeant and Henry waiting around the corner of the shed.

Henry motioned Dick to slip to the back of the building. Instantly Dick obeyed the silent order. He had no plan but, with his moaning and screaming assignments completed, was of no further use beside the shed.

The sergeant raised the rifle to his shoulder and advanced four steps. As he started the fifth, Henry dove from beside the shed and flopped on the ground prone, steadiest of the firing positions. Simultaneously he brought the captured rifle to bear. Before the bewildered sergeant could aim and fire, Henry squeezed off a shot. The bullet slammed into the upper center of the sergeant's chest. The rifle flew from his hand. He staggered backward and fell, dead before he hit the ground. Henry watched dispassionately.

At the crack of Henry's shot, Dick scampered unseen through the downpour to the rear of the house. He stayed hidden a moment but couldn't stand being unable to see what was happening. He began inching along the side of the house nearest the road.

The lieutenant stepped farther away from the front of the house. He further tightened his hold on Mrs. Yoon's hair and pulled her between him and Henry. Paek could scarcely comprehend the scene before him. His brow furrowed. Who, or what, was this fair-skinned, mustachioed killer lying on the ground in soaked and tattered civilian clothes? "Stand up slowly," commanded Paek, "or I'll kill the woman now."

Henry didn't understand all of the Korean words but he easily grasped their meaning. Slowly, he rose to his feet, using the captured rifle as a prop.

"Drop the rifle." Again Henry understood the meaning of the command without understanding the words. Again he obeyed. Nobody had to tell him, in any language, that disobedience would mean an instant end to Mrs. Yoon's life. His, he figured, would end in the next few seconds.

Chun and his guard now were just 20 feet from his wife and the lieutenant. The scene that Chun focused on was enraging him. The sight of his bruised, bedraggled wife, clutching feebly at her torn blouse, her shoulders exposed, filled him with immediate, utter loathing for this fellow Korean who had violated her person and now threatened her life. His lips tightened and his jaws clenched until the veins in his neck strained like thick cable stretched to the breaking point. His right hand tightened its grip on the pitchfork.

Dick edged to the front of the house and chanced peeking around the corner. At the sight of Mrs. Yoon, Dick felt impotent, unarmed and unable to come to her aid. Henry stood helpless, less than 30 feet from Paek and Mrs. Yoon. Henry saw the rage in Chun's contorted face and the shocked, disbelieving eyes of the guard.

Lieutenant Paek studied Henry for a moment, still baffled by the presence and appearance of the burly foreigner. Then he shoved Mrs. Yoon to the wet ground. His left hand reached for the grip underneath the barrel of the submachine gun and his right forefinger poised on the trigger. His left hand raised the barrel toward Henry, who stood motionless. In the instant before Paek squeezed the trigger, Chun's powerful right arm swept up and back behind his right ear. Then the brawny arm shot forward. The pitchfork sailed toward the lieutenant on a straight, unwavering line. From the corner of his eye, Paek detected a blur approaching but had no time to react. Three of the pitchfork's four tines missed their target. The one that didn't pierced the left side of the lieutenant's neck and passed through, the first six inches of the tine emerging on the other side. Paek stumbled but stayed on his feet. Blood squirted immediately from the ruptured artery. Paek's eyes bulged in stunned disbelief. The long handle of the pitchfork bobbed and dangled from his neck. Dumbly, he watched it sway. He choked, and blood gurgled up from his throat into his mouth. It oozed between his lips and dripped down his chin. His hands loosened their grip, and the submachine gun clattered on the ground. As life spurted from his body in a stream of red, his hands reached up to the pitchfork. He tugged but, weakened and slipping into shock, lost the struggle to remove the offending tine. Chun watched expressionless as Paek choked again, buckled and fell face down in a heap beside Mrs. Yoon.

Chun's guard shook his head and gulped in horror. In a span of moments, his eyes had witnessed two unexpected, grisly deaths. His own life imperiled, he swiftly shook off revulsion and regained his composure. He raised the stock of his rifle and clubbed Chun, striking him high on the back near the base of his neck. The blow sent Chun reeling forward to the ground on the brink of unconsciousness. In that moment, Henry dropped to his knees to scoop up the rifle that lay before his feet. As he reached for the weapon, the North Korean hurriedly fired two rounds. Both missed but one bullet kicked up a small puddle that sprayed Henry's eyes. Half-blinded, he continued to grope for the rifle. As Henry's hands found and started to lift the weapon, a third shot sent him screaming and sprawling. The right side of his face pressed against the cool, muddy earth. He grimaced in pain, and mud smudged his lips. Blood began to pour from him, mixing with the rainwater on the ground. The North Korean soldier again took aim.

At that moment, through the driving rain, impulse sent Dick sprinting from the corner of the house and across the open ground. As he neared the unconscious, almost dead lieutenant, he dove for the submachine gun. Dick's desperate dash distracted the North Korean guard whose sense of survival had sharpened his reflexes. He spun away from Henry to confront Dick. Dick grabbed the submachine gun and rolled away from Paek and Mrs. Yoon. The North Korean fired twice at the rolling target but missed narrowly. Dick, face splotched with mud, eyes blinking away rain, steadied himself and squeezed the sensitive trigger. A crackling hail of bullets tore through the air at the North Korean. The soldier spun and crumpled, blood staining his uniform in four places.

Dick released his finger from the trigger, and the deafening racket stopped. The only sound to be heard was rain tattooing the ground. Dick knelt stock still, staring at the man he had just killed. At that moment, he was devoid of emotion.

With a groaning effort Henry had hoisted himself to his hands and knees. His muddy hands rubbed gingerly in an effort to clear his eyes.

He sucked in gulps of wet air, then elevated his head to blurrily survey the carnage. His chest heaved a sigh of relief.

Chun, dazed, his head ringing, struggled to his feet. Mrs. Yoon, her face drained of color, her arms, shoulders and clothes streaked with mud, rose shakily. Her long, black hair, soaked and soiled, clung to her cheeks and shoulders. In the aftershock of her ordeal, she began to shiver and sob.

Her first cry of misery snapped Dick's attention away from the fallen North Korean. He rose and through the unslackening rain, moved to Mrs. Yoon and supported her. Henry staggered forward, favoring his right leg. Blood continued running from the wound in his thigh. Gently, he cupped Mrs. Yoon's right elbow in his hand.

"Henry, do you think...?"

"No. I don't think he had time. Look at his clothes. I don't think he had his pants undone. I'm going to tell Chun that too. Right now. I don't know if they could bring themselves to talk about it. And I don't want something unsaid to drive them apart. They might have enough trouble as it is handling this."

"Goddammit," said Dick.

"I quite agree," Henry said grimly.

The two huge men, Henry dragging his injured leg, led the tiny woman to her husband.

"Thanks, Chun," said Henry in Japanese. "You're making a habit of saving our skins."

Chun nodded, and the slightest of smiles played on his lips. His normally ramrod straight back sagged wearily. He returned Henry's look, then directed his gaze to his wife. She was shaking but her sobbing was subsiding. Chun swallowed hard and closed his eyes. He winced in pain and his head drooped.

"Chun," Henry said compassionately but directly, "we stopped him before he could violate your wife. He manhandled her but he did not rape her. She resisted, fought hard. We could hear the scuffling."

Slowly Chun opened his eyes and lifted his head.

"Chun," Henry continued kindly in unhurried Japanese, "we come from different lands and different cultures, and I've no right to lecture you. No right. You are my friend. As your friend, I tell you that your wife loves you very much. And never has she needed you more than she does now. Don't shun her. Help her. Now."

Affection between a Korean husband and wife is a very private matter. Somehow, Henry's words managed to crack thousands of years of tradition. Chun's eyes closed and opened once more, and then he stepped forward and placed his hands on his wife's bare shoulders.

Mrs. Yoon's knees buckled at his touch. Chun and Dick and Henry reached out and caught her before she fell. The three men and the woman stood sopping under a dismal canopy of gray. The pouring rain and the spongy ground were dissipating and absorbing the red rivulets that trickled from the fallen soldiers and from Henry's leg. Chun, back straightening, moved nearer to his wife and held her closely. They said nothing. Dick and Henry stepped back, and Chun led Mrs. Yoon toward the house. Dick and Henry watched for a minute, then began to trudge after them. Henry limped painfully. Dick lent him a supporting arm.

Inside, Chun guided his wife to the rear room. He unrolled a sleeping mat and eased her down. He gathered clean water, a washcloth and a towel and blankets. Tenderly, he removed her rent, sodden garments and began to cleanse and dry her. She submitted willingly to his loving ministrations. From the trunk he removed clean clothing, dressed her, and then covered her exhausted body with warm, dry blankets. He soothed her with spare, soft words. Gently, he caressed her cheek and forehead. Then he rose and walked to the front room.

He found his two American friends slumped silently on the clay floor. Dick had used a cloth to tie a bandage tightly around Henry's thigh. Chun plopped down beside them, his back leaning against the edge of the low table, his elbows propped on top, his forearms dangling over the side. "Thank you. Thank you both. Henry," he said quietly, "you must tell Dick how grateful I am."

"I think he knows."

"Tell him."

Henry conveyed Chun's gratitude to Dick, who smiled and extended his hand. Chun took it and held it warmly.

"You saved our lives," said Chun. "You saved my wife's honor. I can never repay you."

"Let's consider our debts even," said Henry.

"Perhaps."

"We were lucky," Dick said quietly. "Damn lucky."

"Surprise," said Henry, "was our savior. Caucasians in civvies. Your moans and screams. The rain. Their training never anticipated a situation like this. And yes, we were lucky."

The three men rested silently for several minutes. Then Chun eased himself to his feet and went to check on his wife. When he parted the curtain separating the two rooms, the look of child-like innocence on Mrs. Yoon's face told Chun that merciful sleep had taken her to its bosom. He stepped into the room and affectionately studied the woman who had loved him for a quarter century. He was, he knew, a fortunate man.

When Chun returned, Henry asked, "How is she?"

"Resting, sleeping."

"Good. She needs it. She's a brave woman, Chun, a strong woman. But she'll need your help."

"I know."

"Well," sighed Henry, "I guess we have work to do. Outside."

"Yes." Chun extended a hand that Henry grasped. Chun pulled Henry to his feet. Then both men extended helping hands to Dick and hauled him up. Said Henry to Dick, "We'd better take advantage of the rain to dispose of the bodies. Are you up to it?"

"I'll manage. How about your leg? Can you manage?"

"I think so. No damage to my bones."

Together the three men shuffled outside into the unrelenting rain.

The next day dawned as bright and cheery as the day before had been drab and dismal. The sun's first rays barely had peeked into the house when the clank of tracked vehicles and the husky roar of heavy engines joined the rooster's incessant crowing. Dick and Henry both threw aside their blankets and scrambled to their feet, Henry still favoring his wounded leg. Before reaching the small window, intuition told both men to expect a welcome sight.

The convoy of American vehicles crunching north sent their spirits surging. The two men turned to each other, embraced and whooped the whoop they had suppressed since first learning of MacArthur's Inchon landing. Again they whooped.

In the rear room, Chun and his wife lay side by side, facing the curtained doorway. Chun caressed his wife's face. A tear formed in her eye. It was a happy moment tinged with regret. Their two American friends would be departing.

From the front room came new shouts. "Chun! Mrs. Yoon! Come here," Henry beckoned in Japanese. "Wait until you see this. Come on." The joyous calls had a child-like quality that was irresistible. Chun and his wife threw back the blankets and rose. More shouts. "Chun! Come on. Hurry up. The U.S. Army is here." The Yoons dressed. When they pushed aside the curtain, Henry and Dick were waiting to drag them to the front door.

The four friends stepped outside. The passing parade of American hardware filled Dick and Henry with a mixture of unbounded exultation and unimagined relief. They were going home. The two Americans flanked their Korean hosts and took their first steps back to the world from which they had come more than three months before. Their spirits were gliding skyward like an eagle after catching a canyon updraft. Their disintegrating shoes bounced with each buoyant stride. They made no effort to restrain their mirth.

When they exchanged glances with the Yoons, their gaiety subsided. Chun's sad eyes betrayed his small smile. His wife's lips curved downward under tears that were beginning to ease down her cheeks. She tried to smile. She couldn't sustain it. A wave of melancholy splashed over the two visitors. They were about to leave behind a world, two members of which had come to mean as much to them as life itself. The pain of imminent farewell stabbed their soaring spirits and sent them plummeting.

The four friends paused and faced each other. Tenderly they shared last, lasting embraces. Then they resumed their slow walk up the path to the road. Henry draped his arm across Mrs. Yoon's shoulders. This time there was no recoil at his touch. Instead, Mrs. Yoon unhesitatingly stretched her arm around the small of Henry's back. Dick placed his hand on Chun's shoulder and Chun reciprocated. Chun looked at his wife who stared straight ahead, tears still filming her eyes. He reached down and took her free hand. The convoy of jeeps, trucks and tanks continued to roll by.

One of the trucks slowed, and a young captain pushed open the passenger side door and jumped down. Hands on his hips, he looked at the foursome, smiled and shook his head. "I won't even guess who you are or why you're here."

"Just as well, Captain," Henry smiled, eyes twinkling merrily, "you'd no doubt come up empty. I'm Henry Briggs, this is Dick Lawrence and these are the Yoons."

The captain's right hand moved from his hip to his chin. "Dick Lawrence?"

Dick's eyes reflected mild curiosity, and he stepped forward and extended his right hand. "That's right." They shook hands.

"Man, this is going to be a long shot," the captain said, lowering his chin and pursing his lips. "You from Shelby, Ohio?"

Dick's eyes narrowed. "Originally, yes."

The captain again shook his head, this time his eyes showing astonishment. He then pointed to the name patch on his fatigue shirt.

"Maxwell," Dick read aloud.

The captain said nothing for a long moment. Then he murmured, "You're Bill's brother."

Recognition began to dawn for Dick. "Warren Maxwell?" The captain nodded. "Well, I'll be..." Dick said, barely above a whisper. "I never... This is too much. Way too much."

Henry's curiosity was spiking as was the Yoons'.

"This is what happened when I made the mistake of becoming an officer," Captain Maxwell smiled ruefully, pointing to the twin bars on his helmet.

"When?" Dick asked.

"Late '44. In the Alsace."

"Battlefield commission?"

"Right."

"So they called you back up for Korea," Dick said.

"Not exactly," Warren Maxwell said. "I volunteered."

"Mind if I break in?" Henry asked.

"Not at all, Henry," Dick replied. "General Henry Briggs, retired, meet Captain Warren Maxwell. He was with my brother Bill at Omaha Beach."

Henry's pursed lips, the set of his chin and a slight nod reflected immediate respect, and he extended his right hand. "My pleasure, Captain."

The two men shook hands, and then Warren Maxwell stepped toward the Yoons and shook their hands. To them he said, "I'll let Dick and Henry explain. Well, this is shaping up as one heck of a small-world story," Warren smiled, "and Bill would love it. I'd like to stick around to hear more, but..." and he gestured toward the advancing convoy.

"Go," said Dick. "But there will be a next time. A time when we can get properly acquainted."

"Suits me fine," said Warren, pivoting and jumping onto the running board of a passing truck. "Hope it's not too long."

CHAPTER 18

When Dick and Henry arrived at Los Angeles International Airport, their reception was all they had imagined and more. As they ducked through the doorway at the top of the plane's stairway, they could scarcely believe their eyes and ears. The four Santiago daughters, waiting excitedly at the foot of the stairs, let loose with an ear-splitting chorus of squeals and screams. Their eruption was the unrehearsed cue for a sizable crowd, including many of Dick's Western Construction colleagues, to break into enthusiastic and sustained applause. Still cameras began to click. Television and newsreel cameras began to grind away. The military had seen wisdom in celebrating their arrival and had paved the way for the crowd to be waiting on the tarmac.

It took the two men several moments to arrive at a startling conclusion. They were news. Big news. Somehow, breathless accounts of their harrowing adventure had preceded their homecoming.

It happened this way. Soon after they arrived at Kimpo Airfield to begin their homeward journey, a reporter for *Stars & Stripes*, the worldwide armed services newspaper, spotted them. Two civilians, newly scrubbed but still wearing clothes that obviously had seen better days, aroused the reporter's curiosity. His reportorial instincts were true. His story was the stuff from which instant celebrities, and sometimes heroes, emerge. Other newsmen shared his judgment. Associated Press, United Press and International News Service all picked up and moved the *Stars & Stripes* story.

Scarcely an American newspaper or magazine didn't run the dramatic tale, along with mug photographs of Dick and Henry snapped by the *Stars & Stripes* reporter. His account included the basics of their saga, but it lacked some of the more engrossing detail, including the full depth of their relationship with the Yoons. At the time of the Kimpo interview, Dick and Henry still were too drained to discuss all elements of their ordeal. To some of the reporter's questions – such as his request for an explanation of precisely how the North Korean soldiers were killed – the two Americans pleaded fatigue. Only a few, select persons would ever learn all they had done, felt and thought during their more than three months of confinement.

One of those people was standing at the rear of the crowd. As Dick was descending the airplane stairs he caught only a glimpse of her. It was enough. Her blazing reddish-gold hair, ivory complexion and stunning face and figure would have stood out in any mass. Dick continued down the stairs. He had yet to reach bottom when little Natalie lunged toward him. The other girls and Maria were quick to follow. A massive group hug. Dick loved it.

Then a crush of cheering, applauding people surged forward. They strained, fully extending their arms in attempts to pump the hands of the two Americans, to clap them on the shoulders and back, to ask questions that Dick and Henry tried politely to turn aside with, "Not now. Later, please. We'll talk to you later."

Again Dick glanced toward the rear of the throng. Through the sea of smiling, bobbing faces and clawing fingers, he saw the woman with the reddish-gold hair turn away and walk back inside the terminal. Dick turned to the Santiagos. "John, Maria," he said, nodding toward the rear of the crowd, "there's a friend back there I want to see. Please excuse me. You'll find me inside."

"Sure, Dick, go ahead," said John. "We'll catch up to you." John had not seen the friend but sensed who it might be. Maria, her cheeks glistening, hugged him once more. Then Dick extricated himself from the swarming Santiago daughters and began to wade through the pawing, fawning throng. Henry stayed behind, a dashing, mustachioed target of adulation. Never in the days when stars sparkled on his shirt collar was he saluted like this. He made an engaging idol.

After a couple minutes, Dick popped out of the crowd and into the gate area. He looked around. The woman had disappeared. He dashed to the concourse and looked toward the main terminal. He saw the crown of blazing hair striding away. "Ann. Ann Sheridan," he shouted. The woman stopped, turned and smiled. Dick bounded toward her. She started back toward him, slowly at first then faster. They slowed as they neared each other. There was a slight hesitation. Then he extended his arms, she did likewise, and they embraced warmly. After a long moment they released each other.

"You look wonderful," Dick said, beaming. "Better than that even. If you feel less than whole, it's because I'm devouring you with my eyes. Lord, it's good to see you."

"Dick," she smiled radiantly, "it's good to see you."

"Why did you come? Why did you start to leave?"

"I saw your story in the paper. I thought you might need a friend. But a lot of other people saw it too. I should have guessed that. You've got a lot of friends."

"Some of those people back there are friends, but most were just curious. Not that I blame them. Henry and I could show up in the next edition of *Ripley's Believe It or Not*."

"You two may be oddities," said Ann, "but you're also heroes. Who knows? Maybe someone will make a movie. If they do, what role could I play?"

"Certainly not Paek."

"Who's Paek?"

"I'll tell you later."

"You're too much."

"Not as much as I was three months ago." Dick pulled at his loosely hanging shirt. Despite the inactivity, he had lost some 15 pounds. "You haven't answered my second question. Why did you start to leave?"

"You didn't need me. The Santiagos and others were there. Besides, if I'd come closer, the spotlight might have been on me, not you and Henry. You two are the real stars. You deserve the spotlight today. I decided to call you later."

"I wouldn't have minded sharing center stage with you. I'm glad you came. We only get one walk across the planet, and it's nice to take it with friends."

"You're sweet."

"When will you call?"

"What are your plans?"

"I'm going to spend a few days here. Maybe a week. Then I'm going to fly back to Ohio for a week or so to see my family and then it's back here again."

"I'll call you then. In fact, I have an idea you might like."

"Do *you* like it?"

"Yes."

"Then I will."

The next two weeks were a whirlwind of acquaintances renewed and loose ends tied. When Dick reappeared at Western Construction's offices, ecstatic colleagues greeted him with a boisterous party that lasted for hours. Residents of Dick's apartment building strung a *Welcome Home, Dick* banner across the main entrance. Back in Shelby there had been a homecoming parade. Dick rode in a cream-colored convertible. Dick's father, Edward, and his wife, Harriet, shared the back seat. Their kids, Ben and Susie, rode in front. Al Bourgeois, owner of the local Pontiac dealership, drove. Helen Wakefield Hoerner called Dick. They met over coffee late one afternoon after school in the Coffee Shop on West Main Street. The conversation was strained.

"I tried several times to call you," she said in a hushed voice that started to crack but didn't. "I was frantic. I thought you'd changed your mind. I'm sorry."

Dick nodded. "I am too."

"When I found out what happened and…when so much time went by, I thought you were dead…I still can't believe I'm sitting here with you now. It's so unreal."

"I know."

When Dick returned from Ohio to California, he was exhausted. This time only John Santiago met him at the airport. They spoke few words during the drive north on meandering Sepulveda Boulevard to Wilshire Boulevard. At Dick's apartment, John helped him with the luggage and quickly left. Dick undressed and collapsed in bed. He slept undisturbed for 14 hours. The next day, it was nearly lunchtime when he arrived at his office. On his desk was a deep pile of letters, telegrams and message slips. One of the phone messages was from Ann Sheridan. He reached for his phone and dialed. She was out. He left his name and number. She returned the call early the next morning.

"You sound tired, Dick."

"I am."

"I thought you would be."

"Doctor Sheridan, do you have an anti-fatigue prescription?"

"Tested and proven."

"I'm game."

"Do you have any plans for the weekend?"

"Rest."

"Do you think you can get Friday off from work?"

"I reckon John would let me break back in with a four-day week."

"Good. I'll pick you up Friday morning. About nine. Pack enough for three days."

"No problem. I made one outfit last three months."

She laughed. "Casual clothes only. And bring your bathing suit."

The next morning, Ann pulled up in front of Dick's apartment almost precisely at 9:00. Dick, watching from his living room window, couldn't suppress a grin. How many men, he mused, had fantasized dating a movie actress? Here he was being picked up by a beautiful star driving a sleek black Austin-Healey. Dick hefted his bag and hurried to the door. He met Ann coming up the sidewalk. They kissed lightly and turned to walk to the car. He draped his free arm across her shoulders and squeezed.

"Nice car."

"It's fun."

Ann opened the small trunk, and Dick tossed his bag in. They eased into their seats and Ann ignited the powerful, responsive machine. She wound south to Wilshire Boulevard and turned right.

"Ready to tell me where we're headed?"

"West."

"Ah, yes. I thought I noticed the sun behind us. I'll bet the ocean's in front of us."

"Still as perceptive as ever."

Ann drove about five miles on Wilshire to its terminus at Ocean Avenue in Santa Monica. As they waited for a traffic light to change, Dick inhaled deeply and marveled at a sight that never failed to move him.

"Beautiful view, isn't it?" said Ann.

"Perfection."

In front of them, on the west side of Ocean Avenue, lay lovely Palisades Park with its magnificent vista.

"Are we in a hurry?" Dick asked.

"That's the one thing we aren't this weekend."

"Then could we stop for a few minutes?"

"As long as you like."

Ann eyed a parking space around the corner to the left. The light changed, she accelerated, expertly negotiated the turn and wheeled the car neatly into place.

They climbed out. Dick slipped a coin into the parking meter and cranked the handle. As he was crossing the sidewalk, he again inhaled deeply the exhilarating sea air. He held his breath for a long moment and then exhaled forcefully.

Palisades Park stretched from north to south for 14 blocks along the top of a steep precipice. Its lush 26 acres contained a dazzling variety of flora. Eucalyptus trees, date palms, windmill palms, coconut palms, rubber trees, bamboo clumps, and myriad other trees, flowers and bushes graced the enticing, color-splashed corridor. The park's centerpiece was a statue of Santa Monica. Dedicated in 1935, the eight-foot statue stood atop a six-foot pedestal with her back to the sea, watching over the city that bears her name. At the foot of the palisades, the fabled Pacific Coast Highway (Route 1) kept gawking motorists zipping along. Running to the northwest and southeast horizons and separating Route 1 from the sea was an expanse of wide, beckoning beach. This morning only the lifeguards and a handful or two of bathers and sun worshippers populated the sand and the surf. To the northwest, sweeping up and away from the ocean were the Santa Monica Mountains. To the southeast, stretching more than 2,000 feet from Ocean Avenue across the beach and into the sea was the colorful Santa Monica Pier. Erected in 1912, the pier daily lured thousands of visitors with its rollicking collection of arcades, games, souvenirs and eateries. To Dick the pier's most enchanting feature was a hippodrome. The two-story, barn-like structure housed a carousel with 46 hand-carved horses that pranced endlessly to spirited music. The hippodrome's red-trimmed, mustard-hued stucco façade bore the invitingly simple sign, *Merry Go-Round.* An octagonal cupola perched on each corner of the building, and an upside down funnel-shaped cupola crowned its tin-roofed center. The hippodrome's bright colors and lilting sounds beckoned the child that still resided inside Dick.

"Let's walk down to the pier," he said.

"All right."

Dick took her hand, and the two strolled leisurely for three blocks through the park to where they would turn right to descend to the pier.

"Maria's parents live here in Santa Monica," said Dick. "They've been trying to get Maria and John to move here for years."

"Why haven't they?"

"John and Maria like Westwood. They and the girls love the beach and water, but they like the nearness to their schools and UCLA. The campus atmosphere. And John likes the short drive to his office. Besides, they're only a few miles from the ocean and Maria's parents. And I think that's close enough for John."

"Probably smart," said Ann. "How about you?"

"I've considered moving here. I might some time. I guess inertia stops me. I'm comfortable where I am."

"You obviously like it here."

"Yep...Hey! Let's go in the hippodrome and ride the carousel."

"Oh, Dick, I-"

"No kid left in you? There should be. Come on."

He led Ann by the hand into the hippodrome. Cheery, calliope-like music pleasantly assaulted their ears. They stood waiting for the carousel to stop. Dick winked at Ann, who broke into a wide smile. The music and the horses wound down and stopped. They watched a platoon of beaming children alight from the proud horses. Ann stepped toward a gallant red steed. She inserted her left foot into the stirrup. As she raised her right leg to swing it over the saddle, Dick patted her bottom.

"Take it easy, cowboy."

"Just checkin' the stock, ma'am."

"Is it fit for the trail?"

"Seems firm enough for a long ride."

Dick mounted a glossy black stallion beside Ann's. The music started. The mute, wide-eyed horses glided along with the music. Dick and Ann both laughed. Up and down and around, over and over again.

After the carousel ride, they stopped for frosty root beers and small talk. Then they sauntered back to Ann's Austin-Healey. She pulled into traffic, descended the palisades and joined the traffic scooting northwest along scenic Route 1. The car cruised along, fresh sea air whipping Ann's reddish-gold tresses and Dick's sandy hair. Soon they reached Malibu. Ann slowed the car. She drove a short distance, then turned left into a driveway and braked in front of a sprawling clifftop house.

"Well?"

"It's…It's terrific," Dick stammered. "Is it yours? Is this where we're spending the weekend?"

"Well, it's not a cheap rental," Ann smiled. "Yes, it's mine. Come on, get out. The best part isn't the house at all."

"It could be and I wouldn't be disappointed."

Ann unlocked the house, which had been constructed in the late 1930s, about a decade after movie stars began to build seaside homes in Malibu. This glass, stucco and redwood cliffside dwelling seemed to wander in all directions at once. From the sunken central room, doors, steps and hallways scattered randomly. Ann led Dick across the room, up three steps and to the far side of a glass-walled eating area.

Dick gazed outside and shook his head in wonderment. "It's magnificent, inspiring."

Ann pulled back a sliding glass door. They walked through to an open deck outfitted with table, chairs, two chaise lounges, a pedestal umbrella and a grill. Below, cement stairs built into the cliff dropped sharply down the steep precipice. At its foot lay a wide beach. Beyond, the brilliant blue Pacific spawned the waves that created Malibu's famed surf, not as strong here as at some other points. A flawless Mediterranean-like sky and sun completed a vista that no canvas or film could capture as vividly as the naked eye.

"Just think. If Europe was west of here and Columbus had discovered America from the Pacific," Dick mused, "he never would've gone back to Spain to report his find."

"Maybe it should've happened that way."

"Maybe, maybe not. That's a fascinating thing about history. Much of it happens by chance. It can be downright ugly. But it can lead to some unforgettable experience that you wouldn't want to miss or trade."

"Like this one?"

"Precisely. Geez, I'm sounding philosophical. Must be the view. The one out there and," looking at Ann, "the one here."

She smiled, squeezed his arm and playfully pressed her cheek to his shoulder. "Sit down and relax, Sir Pea Coat. That's the whole point of this weekend. You need relaxation and rest. Solitude."

Dick arched a skeptical eyebrow.

"All right," she said, amending her prescription, "near solitude. I'll be around. But for the next three days, I want you to unwind. No agenda. Do only what you want. If that's nothing, terrific. Now, sit. That's a command, sailor."

Dick snapped to attention and saluted. "Aye, ma'am." He eased himself onto one of the lounges and lay back, face seaward. He sighed long and loudly. The warm sun, the salt air and the caressing breeze begat tranquility.

"I'll be back in a minute," said Ann.

"I'll be here. Even an earthquake couldn't move me."

When she returned, Dick was wearing only his beige slacks. He had removed his blue canvas shoes and socks and pastel blue shirt. "I decided to take you at your word about relaxing."

"Good." Ann was holding two gin and tonics. She handed one to Dick. He sipped, then loudly smacked and licked his lips. "Ahh, perfect. You may join me if you like, my lady."

"Oh, why, thank you, Sir Pea Coat."

Ann finished her drink first and then bounced up and went back inside. Not long after, she returned with two luscious tossed salads swimming in vinegar and oil and accompanied by a loaf of warm Italian bread.

Dick grinned. "I could swear we didn't stop at any grocery stores on the way up this morning."

"Stocked up during the week. How is it?"

"Fantastic, like you."

"You keep flattering me."

"You make it easy. In fact, it's fun. Besides, my lady," he grinned wickedly, "please don't tell me you don't like it."

She didn't tell him.

After lunch Ann carried the tableware inside. When she had finished cleaning up in the kitchen, she walked back outside onto the deck. Dick's chest was expanding and contracting rhythmically. She smiled and sat down and watched him. His breathing grew deeper. She was reminded of the time five years before when he had dozed off on the train. His face had matured and grown softer and more attractive. Experience showed in the lines that were beginning to etch around his eyes. She worried that the sun might burn him. As quietly as possible, she tiptoed across the deck to a corner where the large white pedestal umbrella stood closed. Slowly, carefully, she opened and maneuvered it so that it protected Dick's face and chest. She picked up his shirt and carefully draped it over his feet. Dick didn't stir. He slept for hours. It was late afternoon before he awakened. He opened his eyes, stretched and rotated his head to work the kinks from his neck.

"I guess I needed that." Dick stretched again and groaned pleasurably.

"How do you feel?"

"Lots better."

"Up to testing the water?"

"Sure. Let's get changed."

Dick and Ann strolled hand in hand across the spongy sand. Dick wore simple black trunks, Ann a daring, white two-piece suit that had Dick admiring her openly. About 50 feet from the sea, he tightened his grip on Ann's hand and broke into a gallop. He half-dragged her along, causing her to stumble. "Hey," she protested laughingly, "not so fast."

He accelerated. "Come on," he shouted, "don't be a laggard."

She recovered her balance, and they went speeding on. At the water's edge, Dick whooped, and they plunged full tilt into the surf. When they regained their footing, they laughed uproariously and hugged joyously.

For nearly half an hour they cavorted and swam in the clear, warm water. Then, tuckered out, they waded out and trudged back across the sand. Still breathing heavily, they started up the cliff. About halfway, chest heaving, Dick tapped Ann on the back. She turned around, and he motioned her to sit. She was happy to comply. They caught their wind and resumed their climb. Back at the house, Dick collapsed on a chaise lounge. Ann rested on the other lounge for a few minutes and then set about preparing steaks at a charcoal grill on the spacious deck. Dick was content to recline and watch the water and the woman. He couldn't remember when he'd last felt so at peace.

After their meal, still in their swim suits, they returned to the beach.

"Let's walk," suggested Dick.

Hand in hand they strolled ankle deep in the sudsy surf. An occasional, stronger wave broke at their knees. They were in no hurry and had no destination in mind. Neither felt compelled to support conversation. Each spoke only when the mood struck. As dusk approached, they turned around and started back. As they neared the stretch of beach in front of Ann's house, the sun was about 30 minutes from sliding beneath the horizon. It cast a breathtakingly majestic shaft of red across the water toward shore.

Dick and Ann shook out and spread their blankets and sat down close together to watch the day end. The air began cooling.

"I could be persuaded this is Shangri-la," said Dick, sighing.

Ann laughed. "I'm glad you're enjoying yourself."

"If I enjoyed myself anymore, you might have a permanent house guest."

"I wouldn't mind."

"Don't tempt me."

"Why not?"

"If I stayed permanently," said Dick, "I'd probably become a beach bum. But come to think of it, I've counted enough numbers. I'm tempted to switch to counting grains of sand. Or the strands of hair in your head."

"That wouldn't leave time for much else. Would you settle for brushing it for me?"

Dick had been leaning back on his elbows. He sat up and sifted some of Ann's dazzling hair through his fingers. "When do you want me to start?"

She turned toward him. "Not now," she said.

Their eyes, hers and his both green, locked on each other's and held. With his hand Dick cupped the back of Ann's head and drew it toward him. They kissed, tenderly at first, then harder. They lay back on the long beach towels. The sun cast its last glow upon the water. Darkness was descending swiftly.

"Do you think anyone will see us?" said Ann.

"Only the stars, and I don't think they'll complain."

The next morning, the sun already had completed a good chunk of its day's labor when Dick first pried open his eyelids. Before he focused on anything, his nostrils picked up the scent of freshly perked coffee. He struggled up, moaning, wrapped a bath towel around his nude body and padded into the kitchen. Ann was sitting outside on the deck, sipping coffee. A light breeze was playing with ends of her long hair. She wore a lightweight white dress adorned with multi-hued flowers. On her feet were white sandals.

Dick slid open the glass door. "Good morning." He breathed deeply and rubbed his hands through his tousled hair.

"Good morning." Ann smiled and held out her hand. "Even with your long nap yesterday, it's obvious you needed a lot more rest."

"Thanks in no small measure to you."

"I have certain talents."

"Which obviously aren't confined to the silver screen."

She laughed. "Sit down. I'll get you some coffee."

"No. Sit still. I'll help myself."

They spent the balance of the morning sitting, sunning and sipping coffee. Cup after cup. Ann took hers black, Dick with milk. Despite the caffeine, Dick could feel his metabolism continuing to slow. The lovely creature beside him, the sea, the sand, the sun and the wind gradually were wringing from him the stress that had accumulated during the last four months. He closed his eyes and breathed deeply.

"Drowsy?" asked Ann.

"No, just relaxing."

"Good."

After lunch they headed for the beach. In the water, Dick tickled Ann, tugged at her swimsuit and squeezed in spots that had her squealing and jumping in the surf. In retaliation she scored with a couple strategic squeezes as well as a probing poke to the posterior. Dick leaped, yelped and laughed. When at last they waded out of the water, they stretched out on their towels.

"Ann, you're one lady who knows how to treat a man."

"One I like."

"How about your husbands?" he said softly. "Or is that a sore subject?"

"Not really. The Hollywood marriages that last are the exceptions. There's too much pressure, too many absences, too much temptation. My husbands were good men and I loved them. I just wasn't ready to commit myself to them totally and permanently."

"Think you'll ever?"

"Perhaps."

"Ann, at this moment, I think I could spend the rest of my life here. Do nothing else. How about you?"

"The truth?"

"The truth."

"I don't think so. I bought it for times like this," she said pensively. "To get away. To hide. To rest. But not to live here. At least not yet. I need more. More to do. At least I tell myself I do. And I think I'm right. And I think the same is true for you. You're not cut out to be a bum. Ever."

"Probably, but I'm damn glad I'm here now. And there's no one I'd rather be with."

"No one?"

"Not here. Not now."

"Keep up that kind of talk and you may change my mind. I might get to thinking I could take your company on a permanent basis...But that..."

"That's not meant to be."

"I don't think so, Dick. We're good for each other. Maybe it's love. Or a very strong mutual affection. But I need the world I live in now, as imperfect as it is. I don't think you'd be happy in it. If you tried it and weren't happy, we'd both be miserable. And probably lose what we have between us now."

"Friendship."

"The very best kind. We give to each other. And without being asked. And we ask for nothing in return."

"It's more than strong affection," said Dick. "I love you. If I had any doubts before, I don't now."

"I know. I love you too."

"I also think you're right," said Dick. "We're great as friends. I don't know if we could make it as husband and wife. Our lives are different. Maybe too different. I guess I'd want my wife at home. Mothering my kids."

"And that's not me. At least not now. You know that. The bright lights still mean too much to me to give them up. I'm not ready for children. Maybe never."

"Damn, you're honest. But I'll take you as is, old honest Annie."

They rolled toward each other and embraced warmly. Dick pulled back slightly and gazed fondly into Ann's eyes. "You know," he said, "we are an exception."

"In what way?"

"It's difficult for men and women to be just friends. Especially close friends. Not impossible. But Mother Nature has a habit of getting in the way. One or the other usually wants more. It's natural. I think it's even rarer for a man and woman to stay friends, knowing they love each other."

"Something tells me we can," said Ann.

"We'll give it a good shot."

The weekend had proved to be an idyll as enjoyable and therapeutic to both Dick and Ann as their cross-country train trip in 1945. That night in bed with Ann's head nestled between his shoulder and neck, Dick began to tell her about his Korean ordeal. For the first time he felt at ease enough to share the story with all its detail. Ann lay virtually motionless throughout the long narrative. Occasionally she would quietly interject a question. When Dick was finished, she waited a minute and then asked, "Do you think you'll ever go back to see the Yoons?"

He lay staring at the ceiling. "I don't know. I guess if I did I'd need Henry with me. Or," he reflected, smiling in the darkness, "someone else who could speak Japanese or Korean."

"Something tells me words wouldn't be necessary. Just showing up would say it all."

"Are you trying to tell me I should?"

"Not at all," said Ann. "But I'll bet you'd be glad if you did."

"Are you ever wrong?"

"Even an accountant would get tired of counting my mistakes."

They chuckled and cuddled. Then Ann spoke softly. "Dick, I…I…"

"What?"

"Nothing."

"Yeah. Right. Nothing. Come on, what is it?"

"Forget it."

"Sure, like forgetting how to ride a bike. Look, if ever there was a time to ask me something, this is it. I've never felt closer to anyone than I do right now."

"It's personal…really personal."

"Fine."

"All right. When you…when you shot that North Korean, what did you feel? What do you feel now? About shooting him, I mean."

"Nothing," Dick said quietly but without hesitation. "Nothing at all. I've thought about it a lot. It's strange. When I was in the Navy firing guns at long range, it was easy. The enemy was some target in a far-off shooting gallery. If my guns killed anyone, I never saw them die. I used to wonder if I could shoot an enemy if I could see his eyes. I had my doubts. When I killed the North Korean, I wasn't thinking or feeling. Just acting. I didn't feel any remorse then, and I haven't felt any since. Of course I wish it hadn't happened. But I haven't had any nightmares, not like after Normandy. I actually felt more emotion when I saw the face of the soldier Henry killed with his hands. That soldier was absolutely terrified. I'd never seen such fear. Never. It was a shock."

"What about Henry?"

"Same for him, I'm sure. I don't think he felt anything. It was something he had to do to save a life, and he did it. There was no time for self-examination. Chun was different. He killed out of hatred and revenge. Oh, he was helping Henry when he threw the pitchfork, but more than that, he was killing the man who'd violated his wife. He wanted to kill Paek. No mercy. And I'm sure he has no regrets."

They fell silent. Dick caressed Ann's back. He let several minutes pass. "No more questions?"

She cuddled even closer to him. "Not tonight."

Sunday morning started for Dick when Ann placed a hand on his shoulder and shook him. He groaned. "What time is it?"

"Ten o'clock, sleepy head. Time to rise and shine."

"Rise, doubtfully; shine, never. What time did we get to sleep?"

"Probably about two or three?"

He groaned again. "Are you sure I have to get up, Mom? It's not a school day."

"Look, junior, it was your talking that kept us awake. But I got up to fix breakfast. Bacon, eggs, biscuits, coffee. Everything's almost ready. You're going to eat while it's hot, bub. Come on."

Ann jerked back the sheet. She threw Dick's legs over the side of the bed. "Take it easy," he pleaded, smiling. Then she grasped his upper arms and helped pull him up. He stood sagging while Ann fetched his robe and slipped his arms into the sleeves. "Should I cinch it for you too?" she said with mock motherly exasperation.

"I can manage. Barely." Clumsily he tied an uneven bowknot and shuffled after Ann into the kitchen.

"Go out on the deck and sit down. At the table. I'll serve out there."

Dick trudged outside and plopped down. He folded his arms on the table and cradled his head on them. Slowly, the aroma of bacon and coffee began to arouse his appetite. By the time Ann poured piping hot coffee, laid out strips of crisp bacon and served the still steaming eggs and biscuits, Dick had straightened up and was ready to dig in.

"Where did you learn to fix a breakfast like this? Especially these biscuits. They're fabulous."

"I did more than enter beauty contests back in good old Denton, Texas. Momma saw to it that I learned my way around the kitchen."

Neither wanted that Sunday to end. Dusk again found them sitting on the beach. They held hands and watched the sun cast its familiar red glow on the water.

"Ann, I can't thank you enough for inviting me up. I feel like a new man."

"That was the idea. This place will do that."

"This place and this woman." He squeezed her hand affectionately. "What happens tomorrow morning? I mean, what's next for you?"

"I'm supposed to be at the studio. We start shooting a new film. Dick, it's a little scary."

"What is? The new film?"

"Not exactly. It's...Well, I'm getting a little old for an actress."

"Oh, that's bull. You're beautiful. More beautiful than when I met you five years ago. And you were a knockout then. Besides, there are plenty of actresses lots older than you who still make movies. Good movies."

"No, there's not a lot of them. And the ones that do are exceptions. Producers like their women fresh and innocent. I'm thirty-five now. Hardly fresh and innocent. Thirty-five is getting up there for an actress. You get that old and the offers thin out. And most of the roles you do get aren't Oscar winners. To an actress, to me, that's scary."

"Ann, listen to me. You're a hell of a woman. Beautiful and bright. You'll be all right."

She shook her head slowly in uncertainty.

Dick, his protective instincts surfacing in a rush, coiled his arm around her shoulders and drew her closer. "Ann, if you ever need help of any kind, I'll be genuinely pissed off if you don't call. Got that? Hey, look at me. Agreed?"

She nodded and smiled weakly. Dick kissed her lightly on the lips and the tip of her nose. She put her head on his shoulder.

"How about you, Dick?" she said, barely audible. "What's next?"

"Back to the office. Back to work. Beyond that I don't see much change. I don't feel like I've been wasting my time. I've made an unfortunate decision or two, but that's history."

"Marriage?"

"You know how I feel about Helen. Not much left to say about that. Just a bunch of what-ifs that lead to nowhere. As for someone else, well, most people get married sooner or later. I suppose I will too. Are you sure an accountant and an actress wouldn't make a good match? Yes, yes,

I know. Seriously, it might be someone I've already dated or met. But I have no one in mind and I'm in no hurry."

"How old are you now, Dick?"

"Twenty-eight."

"You're right. You do have lots of time. And I have a feeling you'll make the most of it."

"Like this weekend."

"Yes, but more. And, Dick, what you said about help goes for me too. If you ever need someone, for anything, please call and ask."

"I already owe you," he said.

"Who's keeping score?"

"So far it's a shutout."

"Richard-"

"Okay, but numbers come naturally to an accountant."

"No ledger sheets."

"Okay, okay."

"Dick, what about Korea? I mean, how did it affect…"

"Affect or change my outlook?"

"Yes."

He sighed deeply and looked out to sea. "I guess I learned a basic lesson that most people would rather not learn. Things can be as bad as they seem – or worse. Things were bad from the start over there, but I never dreamed how much worse they'd get. And I guess that lesson's not all bad. It teaches you to brace for the worst. And as bad as things were, I made it through. With lots of help. I'm alive. I'm healthy. I've got my family and friends, including one very special friend."

"But you lost a bride."

"Yeah." His lips pursed. He reached down and scooped up a fistful of sand. Slowly he let it sift between his fingers.

"I'm sorry I brought it up."

"Don't be. It's not something I expect to laugh about, at least for a long time. But with someone close, I can talk about it. It might even help."

"I hope so."

Their conversation ran out of steam. They were content to let silence rule. They listened to the water lap soothingly at the shore. Darkness was descending and still they sat.

Dick to Ann: "Chilly?"

"A little."

"Want to go back?"

"Not yet."

"Good. That'll give me a chance to use the auxiliary heater."

"The what?"

"Aah," he grumped with mock derision, "you native Westerners know so little about keeping warm."

Dick stood up and lifted his large beach towel with him. He stepped away from Ann and shook it vigorously. "Scoot over on your towel and make room for me." Dick then eased himself down next to Ann on her towel. "Stretch out on your back." Still sitting, he carefully arranged the towel at their feet. Then he spread it over them as he reclined. He didn't need to tell Ann to roll toward him. He lay on his back, holding Ann closely, half on top of him. "I think this will keep us warm a while."

"For a long while."

In the night sky above, the stars winked their assent.

CHAPTER 19

By the time the Korean War truce was signed on July 27, 1953, Natalie Santiago already was blossoming into an Iberian beauty. Her Spanish genes were sculpting a creature who combined classic Old World features with a spirited Southern California psyche. The result was remarkable. Cascading dark brown hair framed a medium-complexioned, delicately boned face. When amused or delighted, her expressive brown eyes sparkled as merrily as candles on a cake. White, even teeth punctuated a captivating smile. Natalie was a knockout in the making.

One characteristic of Natalie's had remained unchanged since toddlerhood. She was a child of boundless curiosity and energy. In the late spring of 1954, she barely had turned nine. School was out, and she was visiting her paternal grandparents' ranch in New Mexico. From the crisp dawn hours onward, Natalie lived in a saddle. She became virtually one with a frisky little brown mare named Sweetwater. Natalie called her

Princess Sweetwater. The affectionate horse tirelessly carried the girl on her daily quests for adventure.

Sun-splashed craggy ridges circled the ranch. In the mornings, the rugged ridges blazed with color and tempted with majesty. In the evenings with the sun snuggling down behind them, they appeared sheathed in luxuriant black velvet, and their darkness signaled mystery.

One morning Natalie and Princess Sweetwater started their day's explorations earlier than usual. In the brisk air, girl and animal both could see their breaths. They exhaled with gusto. Princess Sweetwater snorted boldly. Natalie shook her head, flailing her long dark brown hair, and shouted joyously.

The horse cantered, high-stepping vigorously. From the corner of her eye Natalie saw something. Or thought she did. She reined in Princess Sweetwater, who fidgeted excitedly, and peered again to the west. With the sun at her back, she saw it again -- a thin wisp of white smoke curling from a low ridge. The excited girl immediately christened the ridge Mt. Smoky.

The thought, *What is it?* flashed through her mind but she didn't wait for an answer. Quickly she kicked her high-heeled brown leather boots against Princess Sweetwater's flanks. The mare responded, enthusiastically breaking into a gallop.

Natalie rode easily for more than a mile until the high range gave way to a steep, rocky slope. From here the smoke no longer was visible. The girl dismounted and began steadily ascending. On the narrow trail Princess Sweetwater's exuberance gave way to skittishness as loose stones squirted from beneath her skidding hoofs. Natalie alternately soothed the horse with soft words and coaxed her with sharp jerks on the reins.

A climb of 60 minutes brought the pair of explorers to the ridge's summit. Before her feet reached the peak, Natalie's eyes peered over the crest.

A man was squatting by a fire. Gingerly he sipped steaming coffee from a metal cup. The brew was strong and enticing, deliciously scenting the early morning air. For several moments the girl stared. As she parted her lips to speak, the man's head lifted slightly. His eyes pivoted upward under gray brows. He saw the girl – had heard her approach for some minutes before – but his expressionless face signaled nothing.

"Hello," said Natalie.

"Hello," said the man, his bass voice devoid of emotion. His copper face was the texture of a weathered satchel. His eyes were as black as the mountains at sunset. His pants were blue denim, his shirt blue and yellow plaid. He wore an aged brown leather vest. His copper hands were large and strong. Although squatting, he appeared tall.

"Are you an Indian?" Natalie asked.

A flat smile creased the man's lips. The lines in his face multiplied and deepened. "Yes."

"Why aren't you wearing feathers?"

"Feathers help a bird to fly. They do not help keep the sun from a man's eyes. An old man's eyes need protection." His brown flat-brimmed hat was tattered but obviously still suited the man.

Natalie stood watching but came no closer.

The Indian spoke again. "Are you afraid of me?"

"A little."

"That's good. You should be." His face softened. "A little fear means a little caution and everyone, especially one so young, should have a little caution." Again he raised the cup to his lips. "But I can see you also have spirit and that's good."

In Shelby, Ben Lawrence took one look, maybe two, at Natalie and was hooked. Fantasy mounted the throne of Ben's imagination, and thoughts of food, football, family and friends fled before images of the dark-haired, dark-eyed beauty who sang and danced for him five days a week. He picked indifferently at favorite desserts, daydreamed in school, moped around the house, ignored the biographies he typically devoured. Young Ben was smitten.

It began in the fall of 1955. Natalie flashed a first twinkling eye and Ben stared wide-eyed. Never mind that she was 2,500 miles away and didn't see him. Television was the cupid that shot an electronic arrow into Ben's heart. Cupid drew his bowstring shortly after 5:00 on Monday, October 3. By 6:00, Ben was bonkers over Natalie. Of course, so was a sizable chunk of the rest of pubescent male America. Not all the boys who watched Natalie flipped over her. Others succumbed to the blossom-fresh charms of Natalie's colleagues. Doreen and Darlene were favorites. So was Annette.

> *Who's the leader of the club*
> *That's made for you and me?*
> *M*I*C*K*E*Y M*O*U*S*E*
>
> Hey there hi there ho there
> You're as welcome as can be!
> M*I*C*K*E*Y M*O*U*S*E
> Mickey Mouse, Donald Duck!
> Mickey Mouse, Donald Duck!
> *Forever let us hold our banner high*
> *High, high, high.*
> *Now it's time to sing along*
> *And join the jamboree!*
> *M*I*C*K*E*Y M*O*U*S*E!*

On flickering black-and-white picture tubes across the country, a gaggle of precocious Californians exuberantly introduced themselves to the rest of juvenile America.

Darlene, Bobby, Doreen, Lonnie, Sharon, Tommy, Annette, Johnny, Natalie, Karen, Cubby.

From its ballyhooed debut the Mickey Mouse Club was an electronic powerhouse. The airways of the American Broadcasting Company transmitted images of 24 talented, wholesome, beaming Mouseketeers into millions of homes. Their impact was awesome. The show wrecked old routines and created new fads. Children stopped eating with their parents and started wearing black skullcaps ornamented with two oversized ears.

In the pre-Mickey Mouse Club days, Ben and his playmates devoted the late afternoon hours to kicking, passing, tackling, sliding, batting, running and arguing.

"I was safe!"

"You were out!"

"No, I wasn't!"

"You were too!"

They quit and returned home for supper only when hailed by hollering parents. In those days a clock was regarded largely as a sadistic apparatus that ticked along at a maddeningly slow pace while itchy school children fidgeted away the last minutes before afternoon dismissal. Otherwise, time was virtually irrelevant.

The Mickey Mouse Club changed all that. Ben and his friends became acutely aware of time's swift passage. In those autumns of the mid-1950s, fresh dialogue punctuated neighborhood football games.

"Fourth down. You guys gonna punt or gain?"

"What time is it?"

"Just a minute." A boy would dash to the sideline to check the hands of his Mickey Mouse Club watch. "Five till five."

"Already?"

"Well? Whatcha gonna do? Punt or gain?"

"Neither."

"Neither?"

"We're not gonna punt or gain. We're going home to watch Annette grow."

The Mickey Mouse Club did more than entertain the nation's youth with song and dance numbers, cutesy homilies from Clubmaster Jimmie Dodd, cartoons and serials such as *Corky and White Shadow* and *Spin and Marty*. It also forged new loyalties. Especially among boys. Most young males became ardent Annette advocates. Small minorities presented vigorous cases for others, notably Doreen, Darleen and Natalie. When Ben eventually learned from his older half-brother Dick that Natalie was one of his adopted "nieces," Ben's allegiance was fixed. His steadfastness spawned regular debates that Ben couldn't win but that he wouldn't concede.

Annette, her proponents argued, is the cutest.
Yeah, but Natalie, Ben retorted, is the prettiest.
Annette has great legs.
Natalie doesn't?
Annette's older.
So?
Look at Annette's hair.
Look at Natalie's smile.
Look at ALL of Annette.

The concept for the new show was born early in 1955. As one of his first steps Walt Disney ordered a search for "ordinary kids." He issued guidelines. The Mouseketeers would range from 9 to 13 years old. They would be able to dance, sing or both. They would be well groomed, bright and glow with "the All-American look." They would prove to be anything but ordinary.

Word that Disney would conduct open auditions spread like a California brush fire. Natalie and Kate heard about it from a friend whose cousin supplied dairy products to the Disney Studios commissary. Details were sketchy, but the possibility of appearing on a Walt Disney television program fired the imaginations of the two youngest Santiago daughters.

In the mid-1950s, the name Walt Disney possessed new magic. The country, adults and children alike, were agog over Disney's Davy Crockett character. Disneyland was abuilding and the nation waited breathlessly. Sunday evening family television viewing was given over to *Walt Disney Presents*; a highlight was a regular Disney-narrated progress report on Disneyland.

In the Santiago kitchen that same evening it was obvious that something besides food was cooking. As the family seated themselves at the table, Natalie and Kate began to giggle.

"What's up?" said John.

"Nothing, Daddy," Kate replied.

More giggles.

"Sure," John sighed dubiously, barely able to suppress a smile.

Jeannie Marie and Ruth looked at each other for some sign of comprehension or insight, but neither knew what was precipitating the silliness.

Maria, smiling: "Do you two think you could calm down while we say grace?"

They nodded. As she tried to control her mirth, Kate snorted. The grossly comical sound triggered giggles in Jeannie-Marie and Ruth. Then, in spite of himself, John started to laugh. He looked at Maria half apologetically.

"I can see this is going to be hopeless," Maria said sternly as she tried to mask a smile that threatened to crack her sober facade. "Let's just sit down and eat."

Nobody was eating much for all the giggling.

"Before someone chokes," grinned John, "would one of you please share the source of this silliness?"

Natalie and Kate looked at each other and half giggled, half snorted.

Natalie: "You tell them."

Kate: "No, you."

Natalie: "You're older."

Kate: "It was your idea."

Natalie: "Uh uhh."

John: "Okay, okay. One of you, come on."

Kate: "Oh, all right. Momma, Daddy, we..." Another uncontrolled eruption from Natalie caused Kate to giggle and falter. "We want to try out for a Walt Disney TV show."

The giggling subsided. Jeannie Marie and Ruth looked first at their younger sisters and then at their parents with disbelieving yet expectant expressions. Maria stared at her two youngest daughters in stony silence.

John was first to speak. "I get the distinct impression that you're serious. Despite the giggles. Or maybe because of the giggles. Are you?"

Natalie and Kate nodded.

"What TV show?" said Maria, curiosity worming its way into her studied nonchalance.

The two girls excitedly told their parents and sisters what little they knew about the show. They pleaded for a chance to audition. Promised to do their homework without being told. To help around the house without being asked. To keep their room clean. And not to squabble over what belonged to whom. Anything. Please?

"I don't know," Maria said guardedly.

Kate and Natalie groaned in despair.

John smiled. "Don't you suppose we should learn a little about it first? *I'd* like to learn a bit more about it. Okay? Let me check it out."

After the girls were in bed that night, John and Maria sat down together in the living room.

"Going to watch any television?" asked Maria.

"Is there a Walt Disney movie on?"

"I almost wish there was. I think I need some escape. Shall we talk instead?"

"I think we both have the same topic in mind," said John.

"What do you think?"

"The idea doesn't thrill me," said John. "Show business has a reputation that ranks somewhere below construction."

"John!" Maria spoke his name reprovingly.

"Facts are facts. Oh, I know there are good, honest people in the construction industry. But a lot of shady ones too. I'm sure show business has its morally upright people too. Like Disney."

"I'd be worried," Maria admitted.

"No kidding."

"Even with Walt Disney. It has to be such a different world, a different life. I'm sure it's not all glitter and glamour but I don't know what it's really like."

"Yeah," John said pensively. "But I'm of a mind to let them try. We always said we wanted our girls to strive. To have the confidence to try things. We don't want to clip their wings when they try to fly. Even if we're scared silly they'll fall out of the sky and break their beautiful necks."

"Or their hearts."

"Yes, but think of the odds. If they heard about it from a dance teacher, chances are hundreds of other kids did too. Talented kids. They probably wouldn't stand much of a chance."

"You know what really scares me?" said Maria.

"What?"

"That both will try out and only one will make it."

"I don't know how they'd handle that. Or how we would. At least," he smiled ruefully, "Jeannie and Ruth haven't decided they want to try."

"Maybe it would be better."

"How?"

"If all four tried and only one made it, the hurt might not be so bad."

"What if three out of four made it?"

"You're a big help." They both smiled, tiredly and affectionately.

"Look, I'm going to try to check into this show," said John.

"How?"

"Through Dick's friend."

"It's ironic, isn't it?" said Maria.

"How so?"

"We live so close to Hollywood and know so little about it."

The next day, John asked Dick to check with Ann Sheridan. He hoped her show business connections could supplement the girls' sketchy information. Dick dialed Ann. She promised nothing but said she'd gladly pass on anything she learned.

Her connections turned out to be excellent. Within 48 hours she was back to Dick with a detailed report. She reached Dick at his office. He called John in so he could hear first hand Ann's report.

That evening at the dinner table, John broached the subject. "Dick heard from Ann Sheridan today about the new Walt Disney show."

The five female Santiagos pivoted expectantly toward John.

"And?" said Maria.

"What, Daddy? What did she say?" blurted Kate.

"Was it good?" Natalie chimed in anxiously.

"I think so. They're planning a show for kids. No surprise there." Tittering and chuckles around the table. "It's supposed to run in the afternoons after school. Five days a week, an hour a day." All four girls and Maria were listening attentively. Kate and Natalie were leaning forward from the waist. "Lots of singing and dancing. That's where the kids come in. Boys *and* girls. Miss Sheridan says they're planning to hire a couple dozen. The show will also have cartoons, games and serials."

"Five days a week," Maria said pensively. "That's a lot of time."

Natalie and Kate looked apprehensively toward their mother. They sensed what was coming from a concerned parent who also was a concerned educator. "What about school? Would the girls have time for anything but work?"

"The state takes care of that," said John. "The law requires that child performers be educated during the day on the studio grounds. Miss Sheridan says that Disney hires fine teachers. Everything's fully accredited."

"I see." Maria's voice was noncommittal.

Natalie and Kate fully expected a strong objection from their mother. When this moment passed and none came, it seemed too good to be true.

"I know you girls are excited about this," John said lovingly. "But you know there will be many very talented children trying out. You might not make it."

"I know."

"I know."

"What if," Maria said softly, "you tried out and one of you made it but the other didn't?"

"We talked about that," answered Kate, barely able to control her excitement. "We agreed we'd feel bad, and the one that didn't make it would feel hurt. Maybe jealous. At least for a while. But we're going to try to remember we're trying out against other kids and not each other."

"That's right," Natalie confirmed hopefully.

"I don't know if you can do that," said Maria, "but I'm pleased you've talked it over." Actually, she was surprised that her youngest two had shown such maturity.

Silence.

Kate, softly, "Can we try? Please?"

John looked at Maria. Reservation showed plainly in her eyes, but she nodded her assent. John smiled. Natalie and Kate squealed in delight. Natalie excitedly clapped her hands. Jeannie and Ruth joined in the mounting uproar. During the next 30 minutes, much was spoken, little was eaten.

At Disney Studios in Burbank, plans for the new show were proceeding apace. By March 1955, the staff for *The Mickey Mouse Club* numbered 200. As master of ceremonies, or Clubmaster, Disney selected Jimmie Dodd, a warm, religious 45-year-old songwriter from Cincinnati who had been with the studio for less than a year. Roy Williams, who had joined Disney fresh out of high school in 1925, was teamed with Dodd to lead the group of youngsters. The portly Williams was dubbed, over his protestations, the Big Mouseketeer.

Dick offered to drive the girls to the audition. That was fine with Maria. It saved her missing a day at school and warded off the case of motherly butterflies she knew would accompany the trip to the studio. Not in any respect did Maria want to join the infamous ranks of stage mothers. John didn't object to Dick's driving, although he wouldn't have minded escorting the girls.

Natalie and Kate developed the butterflies that lost an opportunity to invade their mother. After breakfast they dressed. Both girls chose simple pastel yellow dresses that contrasted sharply with their lustrous dark hair and eyes and black tap shoes. They studied themselves in their dresser mirror. Both were satisfied.

When Dick arrived at the house on Glenmont, anticipation and anxiety had created a chemical mix that had the girls simmering like laboratory beakers ready to bubble over.

By the time they arrived at the main gate of Disney Studios on Buena Vista Street, the effervescent girls had thoroughly tested the seat springs in Dick's cream-colored 1955 Pontiac Catalina. During the drive, they had ceaselessly prattled and squirmed.

As they passed through the gate on Snow White Boulevard, lush manicured flowering grounds dazzled the threesome. They cruised by Mickey Mouse Boulevard and Dopey Drive. Dick stopped the car and asked a groundskeeper where *The Mickey Mouse Club* auditions were to be held.

When Dick and the girls entered cavernous Sound Stage 1, a sizable horde of chattering children and nattering parents already had gathered. Natalie studied the milling crowd. After a few minutes and well before the auditions began, she concluded that the sole determining factor would not be facial beauty. Natalie knew she was a beautiful child. She also knew she was outshone by Kate, a blossoming goddess. None of the other girls there outdazzled Kate, but several nearly matched her peerless features. None of the girls or boys was unattractive.

Jimmie Dodd, Roy Williams and Walt Disney himself presided over the auditions. From the start Natalie and Kate knew they were in fast company. They watched wide-eyed as 14-year-old Bobby Burgess danced up a storm to *Rock Around The Clock*. Burgess had taken dance lessons since he was three. Pert Doreen Tracy's parents both were dancers who ran a dance studio. They had passed on a generous dollop of talent to their daughter. Her uncle was comedian Ben Blue. Eight-year-old Carl "Cubby" O'Brien was an accomplished drummer who had appeared on *The Ray Bolger Show*. When he put sticks to skin, the rest of the hopefuls were captivated; pulsating vibrations tapped out tunes on their tingling spines. Darlene Gillespie stepped confidently to center stage and belted out the *Ballad of Davy Crockett*, and everyone knew she would be selected. Clearly, Disney's call for "ordinary kids" had brought forth an extraordinary assemblage. Along with Bobby Burgess, Sharon Baird was the best dancer. As early as age seven, she had danced with Eddie Cantor on the *Colgate Comedy Hour.* Lonnie Burr's mother was a theatrical agent who had landed her precocious son roles on *Ruggles, The Lone Ranger, Space Patrol* and *Father Knows Best.*

Then it was Kate's turn. She stepped tentatively out on stage. Natalie waved timidly and blew her a kiss. Kate smiled weakly. She breathed deeply. The music started. For more than two and a half minutes, Kate tapped in flawless synchrony to the bouncy rhythm of *Under The Bamboo Tree.* About half way through the tune the tempo accelerated. Kate, more relaxed now, confidently kept pace. When she finished, Natalie clapped, ran forward and hugged her. "You were great, Kate." Kate, breathing heavily, smiled and embraced Natalie. "Thanks," she said wearily.

"Natalie Santiago, your turn," said a disembodied voice. She unwrapped her arms from Kate and walked over to the technician who was running the record player to be sure he was ready to spin the right tune. Then Natalie returned to center stage, nervously smoothed her dress and scraped her taps on the stage. She looked at Kate who formed a circle with her right thumb and forefinger and reassuringly flashed the *Okay* sign. In the next moment the honky tonk sound of *Redwing* struck up. Rollicking, raucous piano backed by a toe-tapping drum and other plucky percussion instruments seemed to shake the fortress-like soundstage. Then hundreds of eyes saw a pair of frenzied legs explode into action and go ripping through nearly two minutes of wildly uninhibited taps, spins, kicks and assorted acrobatics. Natalie's long brown mane flew in all directions. Natalie might have been short on professional experience but she was far in front of the pack when it came to sustained sheer energy. The spectators were watching more than a dancer; they were watching a superb athlete. She was tapping as she never had before and she knew it. She concluded her number with a leap that would have impressed a Ukrainian folk dancer. At the zenith of her ascent, she split her legs, tapped them lightly with her fingers and folded her arms across her chest before executing a perfect landing. Kate led the cheers that erupted from the appreciative audience of highly competitive strivers. Natalie, adrenalin still pumping, leaped high in exulted self-satisfaction.

Despite her rousing performance, Natalie was genuinely astonished when she learned she had been picked as one of 24 Mouseketeers. Only one thing surprised her more. Incredibly, the last of the two dozen selected was the beautiful, dark-haired, doe-eyed Annette Funicello. Walt Disney had seen Annette dance *Swan Lake* at the Starlight Bowl in Burbank. Disney himself called the 12-year-old's teacher and asked her to send her star pupil to the auditions.

Kate didn't make it. She was disappointed but Natalie was hurt. She thought her sister superior to several of those selected. When they embraced, both were in tears, Kate out of happiness for her younger sister, Natalie out of sympathy for Kate. Kate became, along with the rest of the Santiagos and Dick, one of Natalie's most ardent fans.

Natalie reported for work on June 13, 1955. Her starting salary was $185 a week, which John banked. Natalie would continue to make do with the same allowance her sisters received. Five dollars a week.

From the start Natalie enjoyed the work and the company of her fellow Mouseketeers and the Disney production crew. Not all their time was spent preparing to launch the new TV program. They also readied for the grand opening of Disneyland. On July 17, 1955, the long-anticipated day arrived. The gates to Disney's Magic Kingdom swung open. As a part of the festivities the Mouseketeers staged an exuberant production number featuring a cleverly crafted rendition of *Old McDonald's Farm.* Afterward they visited Disneyland often to greet visitors. They also made many promotional stops at hospitals, toy stores and other sites likely to result in published photos.

That first TV season flew by. Monday of each week was *Fun With Music Day.* Tuesday was *Guest Star Day*, Wednesday *Anything Can Happen Day*, Thursday *Circus Day*, Friday *Talent Roundup Day.* And then the cycle repeated itself, week after week. As hectic as the schedule was, Natalie relished it. She grew close to the other Mouseketeers. When the triumphant season drew to a close, the Mouseketeers savored their success and looked forward to regrouping for a second season.

Late one afternoon soon after the first season's production had halted, Kate was approaching the bedroom she shared with Natalie. She heard low, muted sobs. She paused momentarily, then stepped to the doorway. Natalie was stretched prone on the bed, her head cradled in her arms. Her shoulders heaved with each mournful sob.

Kate walked quickly to the bed. "What's wrong, Nat?"

"Nothing," she said miserably.

"Hey, Nat, come on. It's me, Kate. You can tell me."

"Please just leave me alone. I don't want to talk to anybody."

"Is it something I said? Or did?"

"No. Nothing. It's not you. Please leave."

Kate laid her hands on her sister's shoulders, then turned and left the room. Moments later, Maria entered and sat on the edge of the bed. "What is it, Nat? Kate said you don't want to talk, but it's always better to talk something out."

"Not always."

"Sweetheart, what is it?"

"Oh, Momma, I feel terrible. They only invited ten of us back for next year. Just ten." She choked back a surging sob, an anguished sound that tugged at Maria's heart and pushed a lump into her throat.

Maria placed her hand at the base of her daughter's neck and rubbed gently. "Go ahead and cry if you want, sweetheart. Don't try to hold it in."

Natalie did just that. For three minutes, perhaps, Maria ached as her daughter poured out her grief. When the tears subsided, Natalie lifted and twisted her head toward her mother. With reddened eyes she painfully began to translate the hurt into words. "They were such good kids. They were so nice and they worked so hard. It's not fair."

"I know it seems that way," Maria said compassionately. "Don't you suppose Mr. Disney had a good reason?"

"No. Just ratings. They were starting to go down. He just decided to get some new kids. He really hurt their feelings. They were good. Really good. All of us were good. But he wanted new kids. He shouldn't have done it."

"Natalie, it's…I'm sure Mr. Disney likes all of you very much. I'm sure he didn't want to hurt anybody. But - and I know it's hard to understand - television is a business. Remember," she said gently, "it's even called show business. It's like any other business. Like your father's construction business. Mr. Disney can't keep everybody if they aren't doing well enough. I know your father has had to let people go that he liked but who weren't doing well enough. It's very hard for him. Those are very difficult decisions."

"That's different." Natalie's voice stiffened with righteousness. "Those are just kids and they did work hard."

"Natalie, Kate didn't even make the show, and she's a very good dancer."

"That's different too," she insisted, her voice melding hurt and anger. "I get to see her. I'll never get to see those kids again."

"Of course you will."

"No. I won't. I'll miss them. It's so sad. I hate to see someone hurt."

"I know, sweetheart. Who was invited back?"

"Annette, Karen, Cubby, Sharon, Bobby, Darlene, Tommy, Lonnie, Doreen. And me. Momma, Mr. Disney shouldn't have fired the other kids. He shouldn't have. It won't be the same."

"Are you going back?"

"I don't know."

Natalie went back for the second season, but she was right. It wasn't the same. The show's ratings had begun dipping from their lofty pinnacle before the end of the first season. The slide continued. The new Mouseketeers were Eileen Diamond, Sherry Allen, Larry Larsen, Jay-Jay Salari, Margene Storey and Cheryl Holdridge. The infusion of fresh faces failed to bolster *The Mickey Mouse Club's* sagging popularity.

In Shelby Ben's sizzling ardor for Natalie had cooled. In the fall, football again was king. Mickey Mouse was a prince who had fallen from favor.

Of the six newcomers, only blond, blue-eyed Cheryl Holdridge was retained after the second season. Joining Cheryl and the original 10 for the third year were Don Grady, Lynn Ready, Bonnie Lynn Fields and Linda Hughes.

The show was cut to 30 minutes for the 1957-58 season. It staggered through with plunging ratings that nearly sank from sight. ABC canceled the show at the season's close. It was not a shock for Natalie or the other Mouseketeeers. They knew the axe was poised to fall.

Of the remaining Mouseketeers, Walt Disney offered contract continuances to only four: Natalie, Annette, Karen and Cubby. Natalie was undecided whether to accept. She agonized over the pros and cons. Eventually, Dick offered to help. Indirectly, that is. Natalie was thrilled by his suggestion. Indeed, she was more excited by the prospect of being helped than by deciding.

Two days later just before 8 p.m., Dick's familiar Pontiac Catalina pulled to a stop in front of the Santiago home. Inside, Kate heard two car doors slam. She walked to the living room picture window. She stared wide-eyed. Accompanying Dick up the walk was a stunning woman with blazing reddish-gold hair. Kate pivoted away from the window. "Natalie!" she cried. "She's here! Momma, Dad. Dick's here with Miss Sheridan. Oh, my God, a movie star in our house! Oh, Geez! Hurry up, you guys."

Outside the door Dick heard Kate's cries. He turned to Ann and smiled. "Do you think they know we're here?"

The other three Santiago daughters converged on the living room like a herd of dust-dry cattle stampeding to a water hole. John and Maria followed a bit more sedately and moved to the door. The four girls, bunched close behind them in a tangle of legs, tripped over each other.

"Watch where you're walking," snapped Ruth.

"You watch, clumsy," Natalie retorted.

"You stepped on my heel," charged Kate.

Outside, Ann to Dick: "They sound normal."

"Calm down, all of you," Maria admonished.

John pushed open the screen door and extended his hand. "Hi, Dick. Come in."

"Hi, John. Maria, how are you?"

"Fine, Dick."

John offered his hand a second time. "Miss Sheridan, please come in."

"If you'll call me Ann."

"Done. It's a pleasure to meet you."

Said Dick, "I guess introductions are in order." He paused a moment and surveyed the four gawking girls. "You know," he teased, "I do believe this is a first. I don't think I've ever seen all four of you awake and this quiet."

The girls blushed. John and Maria smiled.

Dick introduced Ann to Maria, Jeannie Marie, Ruth, Kate and Natalie. She shook hands warmly with each one. "Dick," Ann said lightly, "you sure know how to pick your women." The girls tittered. Maria reddened.

"Come on," said John, "let's go in and sit down."

From the foyer, John escorted Ann to the couch at the far end of the living room. She stepped around the glass-topped coffee table, smoothed her lightweight, off-white dress and sat. John motioned Dick to sit beside her. John sat in his favorite chair, the twice-reupholstered padded rocker. Maria sat in a chair that faced John. Jeannie Marie, Ruth and Kate knelt beside their mom and dad. Natalie sat cross-legged on the far side of the coffee table away from the couch. She gazed unabashedly at their lovely, famous guest.

Maria: "Ann, Dick, can we get you something to drink?"

"Not now," said Dick.

"Maybe later," said Ann.

"I'm glad you came, Ann," said John. "It's always good to meet a friend of Dick's."

Ann smiled. "I can't tell you how good it is to be here. Dick's told me so much about all of you. I've wanted to meet you for a long time. In fact, that's really why I came. I don't know if I can help Natalie make her decision."

"Maybe you can't," said Maria. "But Dick thought – and we agreed – that perhaps you could offer extra insight, a different perspective."

"I'll try. You know, in a way it's funny. Natalie, when I was your age, I was only beginning to dream of being a movie actress. A star. And here you are...How old are you, Natalie?"

"Thirteen."

"Thirteen and you've been a TV star for three years."

"Not a star," Natalie protested shyly.

"Oh, don't take anything away from yourself, Natalie. You accomplished a lot. I saw you dance, more than once, on *The Mickey Mouse Club.* You are very good. And your personality comes through. You're alive and you want to do your best. The audience can tell that."

"Thank you," said Natalie, lowering her eyes.

"Was it fun, Natalie? Did you really enjoy the show?" Ann asked.

"Oh, yes. Very much. I especially enjoyed the other kids. They were great."

"That's wonderful. Was there any part you didn't like?"

"No. Well, nothing with the program itself. I felt very bad when other kids were fired. I felt sad. I didn't think it was fair. But Momma said it was business. She said show business is like any other business."

"Natalie, your mother is very smart. Television is a business. So are the movies. But I don't think it's like other businesses. Show business is the only business I've been in, so I can't be certain, but I think it's different."

"How?"

"I think show business is more cruel. In show business, I think people hurt each other's feelings more."

"Why?"

"I'm not exactly sure. But I think it's because so many people in show business are so self-centered. They care too much about how they look. How they do. How many cars and clothes they have. How much money they make. They forget about other people. And they forget about other people's feelings. Do you know the golden rule?"

"Yes."

"Do you try to live by it?"

"Yes."

"Lots of people in show business don't. They hurt other people to keep from getting hurt."

"Does it work?"

"Not very often."

"Do you?"

"Sometimes. When you grow up, do you want to get married and have a lovely family like yours?"

John and Maria were both coming to realize why this woman had come to mean so much to Dick. She obviously was special. She exuded warmth and concern. She was honest and candid. Maria, who had entertained doubts about the moral fiber and integrity of any movie star, fast was becoming a convert.

"Yes," answered Natalie.

"It's very difficult," said Ann, "to have a happy marriage and family in show business."

"Why?"

"Too many performers spend so much time trying to make themselves happy and secure they don't have much time left to make other people happy and secure."

"Is that why you're divorced?"

"Natalie-" Maria blurted, embarrassed.

"That's all right," Ann assured Maria. "It's an honest question. And the answer is yes. And it's also why I don't have any children. I always felt I wouldn't have time to love them the way children should be loved. Like your parents love you. There was another reason, too," she said gently but directly. "I didn't want to *take* the time."

"Are you sorry?"

"Sometimes...Yes. Natalie, how badly do you want to be in show business? Do you want it enough to maybe not have a happy marriage and a happy family?"

"No. I want to marry someone like Daddy. Or," she directed her eyes toward the man sitting beside Ann, "like Dick. And I want a family. A happy family."

"You're young."

"Yes," asserted Natalie, "but I'm sure about that."

"I think you are," Ann said with kindness and admiration.

"Well," said Maria, expelling a breath she had seemingly held for the duration of the dialogue. "Now, can I get somebody something to drink?"

"I'd love something," said Ann.

"Me too," piped up Kate.

"Let me get it, Momma," said Natalie. "Please."

"You'll need some help."

Dick sprang up. "I'll help. Come on, Nat. Let's take orders."

"I'll take a Pepsi," said Jeannie Marie.

"Me, too," chimed in Kate.

"Pepsi would be fine with me too," said Ann.

"Are you sure?" said Dick. "I know this kitchen well enough to know there are other choices."

"I'm sure."

"Well, I'd like a beer," said John. "Maria?"

"Mmm. I'll have a Pepsi too."

"Beer for me," said Dick.

"Come on," said Natalie, pulling Dick by the arm toward the kitchen.

In the kitchen, Natalie started fetching Pepsis from a carton on the floor beside the refrigerator. Dick opened the refrigerator door and retrieved two Miller High Lifes.

"I'll get the glasses," said Dick, opening a cupboard door over the counter beside the sink.

"I can reach the ice cubes," Natalie said excitedly.

Dick smiled at the bustling girl. Together they stood at the counter. Dick pulled an opener from a drawer and began popping bottle tops. Natalie began dropping cubes into the glasses.

"Dick," she said, her eyes not leaving the glasses and the cubes, "you like Ann." It was an assertion, not a question.

"Yes. She's a very nice woman."

"You like her very much."

"Yes."

"Do you love her?"

Dick looked down and found Natalie peering intently at him. "Yes."

"Does she love you?"

"Yes."

"Then why haven't you two got married?"

"For the reasons she said in the living room. We'd rather be friends and not get married and maybe have to get divorced."

"That's sad. I don't think I ever want to be a movie star."

Dick smiled but said nothing.

"Dick?"

"Yes."

"Do you think you'll ever get married? I mean to anyone?"

"I don't know."

"You date other women."

"Yes."

"And you like some of them very much."

"Yes."

"I don't understand."

"Sometimes I don't either."

ABC televised edited reruns of *The Mickey Mouse Club* for a fourth season in 1958-59. During its three-year production run, more than 1,000 children auditioned. Forty wore the uniform of the Mouseketeer, that rare strain of American youth incubated, if not hatched, in the laboratories of Walter Elias Disney. The 10 Mouseketeers who stayed through all three seasons each earned slightly more than $30,000.

Now it's time to say goodbye to
All our company,
M*I*C...
See you real soon
K*E*Y...
Why? Because we love you!
M*O*U*S*E
Good-bye!

CHAPTER 20

"I thought the boys might get it done tonight."

"I'm sorry, honey," Helen replied to Roger. "I know this is hard on you."

"We were doing okay until Larry got hurt. If we lose another boy to injury, I might have to ask the cheerleaders to put on helmets and pads," he smiled in a weak effort at levity.

Shelby was one of those small Ohio towns that deified high school football. Each autumn the red-and-gray-clad Shelby Whippets were placed reverentially on an athletic altar. Skiles Field was the community house of worship. Thousands of fervent followers flocked there for each home game in search of deliverance from the workaday world.

The Whippets, named after the breed of sleek racing dogs, were perennially successful. The team had last suffered a losing season in 1948. In the nine years since, the Whippets had compiled a record of 64 wins, 16 losses and a tie. In seven of those seasons the Whippets lost two or fewer games. They won Northern Ohio League championships in 1949, 1950, 1952, 1953, 1954 and 1956. They finished second the other three seasons.

In 1958, though, the usually swift Whippets were hobbled by a series of devastating injuries. This season they would limp to a record of one victory, eight defeats and a tie.

Each week the familiar buzz of pre-game excitement fizzled out like a spent sparkler on the Fourth of July. Traditionally, Shelby wins were celebrated noisily. Jubilant fans would exit from the stadium, climb into their cars and wear out their hands honking their horns. In 1958, the post-game silence was deafening.

The citizenry ached. Hurting most perhaps was Roger Hoerner. Since 1949, when he graduated from Ashland College, Roger had been an assistant football and track coach at Mansfield Madison High School. During his tenure there he longed to return to Shelby where he had starred as a hard-running halfback. In the spring of 1958, his dream was fulfilled. Shelby hired Roger as a mathematics teacher, assistant football coach and head track coach. Now he agonized as the proud Whippets lost, week after week.

Despite the losses Helen was happy about Roger's new job. It meant the end of commuting for both of them, and it meant the opportunity to sink even deeper roots into the community where both had lived since birth, save for Roger's World War II service. Since graduating from Ashland College, Helen had taught English at Plymouth High School, about nine miles from their Shelby home. In the summer of 1958, she heard about a vacancy in the English department at Shelby High. She applied and won the job.

The Hoerners had been living in an aged, two-story white-frame house on East Whitney Avenue. They decided to celebrate their new jobs by buying a new home. They knew precisely what they wanted. They eschewed the ranch-style houses that had grown popular in Shelby. They both preferred a house with a clearer demarcation between living and sleeping quarters. They bought a frame colonial with an attached two-car garage on Morningside Drive. The house had three bedrooms that they hoped one day would be filled by the children they had yet to have.

Helen and Roger wanted children badly. They were puzzled and frustrated by their inability to produce new Hoerners. Tests on both failed to detect any physiological deterrent.

On a brisk Saturday morning in early November 1958, an alarm clock jangled Helen and Roger awake at 7:00. Helen wanted to beat the Saturday morning crowd to Kroger's Super Market on Main Street. Roger wanted to get outside to clean leaves from the new house's gutters and rake the yard so he would be free to watch Big 10 college football on TV in the afternoon.

"Roger," said Helen as she dressed, "why don't you stay in bed? I'll help with the leaves when I return from the store."

"No." Roger shook his head. He rubbed his eyes, yawned widely and groaned. "It will do me good to get out in the air." Groggily, stiffly, he eased out of bed.

"You're stubborn," Helen admonished lightly.

Roger nodded in agreement, then yawned again. "If I get in plenty of physical work today, maybe I'll sleep better tonight."

Helen shook her head in exasperation. She left the room and descended the stairs. In the bright, cheery kitchen, decorated in yellow with white trim, she perked coffee while Roger washed, shaved and dressed. When he shuffled into the kitchen, he declined her offer to fix eggs. Coffee would suffice. They kissed and she left for Kroger's.

Roger sat at the kitchen table and slowly drained a large mug of coffee. Visions of last night's game - another loss - again invaded his mind. He pushed away from the table, crossed the kitchen and trudged to the garage. He plucked a pair of jersey work gloves from a high shelf and walked to the other side of the garage. He couldn't shake the stiffness and fatigue that had gripped him since rising from bed. A 20-foot wooden ladder hung flush against the wall from two L-shaped brackets. Roger breathed deeply, then reached up and jerked the ladder away from the wall. He carried it outside and lugged it to the rear of the house. Tired muscles straining, he stood it upright and leaned it against the house. He felt very tired. Again he breathed deeply. He gripped the ladder and leaned against it. The sluggishness persisted. He pulled the ladder away from the house and shoved up the extension until it rested against the gutters. Gingerly, he started up the ladder.

Shortly after 9:00, Helen emerged from Kroger's. In her left hand she carried a purse. Her right hand and arm cradled a large, heavy grocery bag. Behind her, a teenage boy carried two more. As she neared her car, a familiar-looking man and a strapping boy were approaching from the opposite direction. In his right hand the boy carried a packet of arrows. He and the man were kidding each other about something. The boy slapped the man on the back, and the man playfully punched the boy on the shoulder. Both laughed.

Helen's heart leaped. Years had passed since she had last seen the man. She couldn't remember how many. His hair had grayed and thinned. The lines in his face had deepened. Wire-rimmed glasses framed his eyes. He still was handsome, his shoulders still broad and unbent, his chest still thick and strong.

"Mr. Lawrence," she cried impulsively. "Mr. Lawrence."

Edward and his son looked toward the woman. Edward squinted but there was no glint of recognition. The woman was wearing dark blue slacks and a gray, belted car coat. Floppily crowning her head was a red and gray stocking cap with a script *Shelby* stitched across the front. The top of the large grocery bag partially obscured her face. Helen shifted the purse from her left hand to her right. Then she reached up and yanked off the stocking cap. A thick mass of honey-colored hair bobbed at her shoulders. "Mr. Lawrence, it's me, it's-"

"Helen!" Edward boomed. "Helen Hoerner." Edward walked rapidly toward her. Ben lagged behind, puzzled by his father's exuberant greeting of this stranger. Edward closed on Helen and placed his hands on her shoulders. "Here, let me take that bag." He removed it from her arm. "Where's your car?"

"Just behind you." She stepped toward the car and fished keys from her purse. She unlocked the car and opened the rear door. Edward placed the bag on the seat, then straightened up and backed away from the car. The bag boy stepped forward and placed the other two bags on the seat. Helen handed him a quarter. The boy mumbled a thank you, turned and left. Edward slammed shut the car door and turned to face Helen. His eyes met hers. A broad, affectionate smile lighted up his face. His eyes twinkled. Hers responded in kind. They stepped toward each other and embraced. Ben looked on dumbly. The only other woman he'd seen his father hug was his mother.

They parted. Edward planted his arms on his hips. "Let me look at you." A momentary pause and a grin. "You look wonderful."

"So do you."

"Thanks. How long has it been?"

"I'm not sure. Too long."

"Much too long," said Edward. "How've you been?"

"Fine. And you?"

"Good. Good. Say, I see that Shelby has a new coach this year name of Hoerner. Congratulations."

"Thank you."

"And you. I remember reading in the *Daily Globe* that you're teaching at Shelby High now. English."

"Yes. I like it very much."

"Maybe you'll get Ben next year. Which reminds me. Ben, come here. Ben, this is Helen Hoerner."

She extended a hand. "It's very nice to meet you, Ben."

He took her hand. "Nice to meet you, ma'am."

She studied his eyes and face for a moment before releasing his hand. A hint of melancholy momentarily clouded her eyes. "The last time I saw you," Helen said wistfully, "you couldn't have been more than five or six years old. Amazing. How old are you now, Ben?"

"Thirteen."

Ben was fast approaching the age when Helen had met and fallen in love with Bill Lawrence. The Bill in Ben was uncanny. The same blue eyes. The left eye that opened appreciably less than the right. The set of his smile. Not an exact duplicate of Bill, not quite as handsome, but an exceptional resemblance for two sons with different mothers. Helen smiled and shook her head. Ben, already five feet nine inches tall, looked uncertainly at the woman who was several inches shorter. Helen shifted her gaze to Edward. The unbridled joy in her eyes and voice had faded. "It's been very good seeing you. I guess I'd better-"

"The next time I talk or write to Dick," said Edward kindly, "I'll tell him I saw you." Edward sensed Helen was curious about Dick. He wanted to give her an opening and spare her any embarrassment about asking.

"Oh, please do," said Helen, brightening. "How is he?"

"Just fine. Still with Western Construction. Still single," added Edward, answering another question he felt Helen wanted to ask. "He's busy but he still manages to get back home about once a year."

Ben observed this exchange with growing curiosity.

"That's good," said Helen. "I'm glad he's doing well." She glanced at her wrist without seeing the watch that was concealed by her coat sleeve. "I have to get going." She forced a small smile. "I want to help Roger with some yard work. He was really tired this morning. And a little down."

Edward nodded in sympathy. "Too bad his first season with Shelby has to be so lousy. I'm sure it's been rough on him. Tell him we wish him well."

"I will. Mr. Lawrence, it was so good to see you. I'm really glad we bumped into each other."

"So am I, Helen."

She moved around the rear of her car to the driver's side. Edward followed closely. She gripped the door handle and pulled it open. Edward held the door while Helen slid in.

Edward bent down slightly. "Helen," he said quietly, out of Ben's earshot.

She looked up.

"You're lovelier than ever," Edward said softly. "I'm glad things are going well for you. You deserve it." He reached down and lightly touched her left hand, which rested on the steering wheel. "Take care."

"I will," she whispered hoarsely. "And thank you, Mr. Lawrence. You're sweet."

Edward smiled and closed the door. He twisted to check oncoming traffic and then stepped to the rear of the car and back onto the sidewalk. Helen started the car and pulled from her parking spot. Edward watched her drive away.

Ben stepped toward Edward. "Who is she, Dad? I don't remember her at all."

"She's an old friend."

"I never heard you mention her. How come?"

"No reason, I guess."

"Why did you mention Dick?"

"They were friends too."

"Dad," said Ben, smiling wryly, "I get the feeling there's something you don't want to tell me."

Edward sighed. "Not really."

"There is more to tell…"

"Yes."

"Well?"

Edward eyed his youngest son, already his match in height. He smiled and clapped him on the shoulder. "Tell you what. Let's take these new arrows home, get our bows, and go out and do some target shooting. Take a couple empty boxes, find a field and ask the farmer if we can practice. I'll tell you about it then. Okay?"

"Sure."

When Helen arrived home, Roger was raking the front lawn. He paused, using the rake handle for support, and watched Helen pull in the driveway and get out of the car.

"Hi, honey. How do you feel?"

"I think I'm ready for a nap now. Going up and down that ladder really bushed me."

"Well, why don't you go in and lie down. I'll finish."

"I can handle it," said Roger.

"I know you can," she said with mild exasperation. "But why should you do it all? You're pooped and you know it. Now don't be so stubborn."

"Okay…On one condition."

"That being?"

"Let me help you take the groceries in."

Roger passed the rest of the morning reading Paul Horgan's *A Distant Trumpet*. He was enjoying the sweeping tale set in the American Southwest of the 1880s. Thoughts of last night's football loss and this morning's immense fatigue gradually faded behind vivid images of stoic cavalrymen and treacherous Indians.

When Helen finished raking the leaves, she came inside, cleaned up and prepared lunch. Roger ate heartily. Early that afternoon he stretched out on the living room couch to watch Michigan play Michigan State. Sometime during the first half he dozed off. He napped for more than two hours. On awakening he felt far stronger. That night he slept soundly. The next morning he felt as fit as an Army recruit after basic training.

The next three weeks passed uneventfully. At 10:00 on Thanksgiving morning, Roger, three other coaches and a dozen Whippet footballers met outside the northeast gate of Skiles Field. The morning was brisk, breezy and dry. With a dismal 1958 season tucked into the record books, the group had gathered for a game of touch football. Everyone was in the mood for fun. Roger unlocked the gate. The four men and 12 boys stormed shouting onto the field. They flung three footballs around for a few minutes, then scattered to loosen up. All did calisthenics. Some jogged around the track that belted the field. Others ran wind sprints. Roger felt good. Then the group again tossed and kicked the footballs for several more minutes. Afterward, teams were chosen. Two coaches and six boys on each side.

The game was spirited. The men and boys ran hard and dove for errant passes with abandon. Good-natured banter and boisterous laughter ricocheted off the empty bleachers. Each breath expelled crystallized in the crisp late November air.

During the first 30 or so minutes, Roger snagged five passes, including one for a touchdown. On the scoring reception he whooped delightedly as he went gliding across the goal line. Moments later with his team again in possession of the ball, Roger raced downfield. Thirty yards beyond the line of scrimmage, a perfectly thrown pass floated toward him. He reached out to receive the ball. It struck his hands, slithered away from his frantically clawing fingers and fell to the ground. Roger pulled up, threw his face skyward, then raised his hands and clapped them in disgust. "Shit," he muttered.

"Hey, Coach," a young defender teased, "watch the language. You'll deflower our virgin ears."

Laughter broke out. Roger shrugged off the frustration and joined in the merriment. The next time he was in position to catch a pass, the ball again bounced off his usually sure hands. Twice more he flubbed catches. Roger jogged back to the team huddle. "I must not be concentrating. My fault."

"Shoot, Coach, we were dropping balls all season. We just set a bad example."

Laughter all around.

Roger muffed a fifth consecutive pass. When he stooped down to pick up the ball, he noticed a slight tingling, or numbness, in his right hand. He rubbed it. He attributed the feeling to the hard football stinging his cold hands. The numbness persisted. He sloughed it off.

The game ended a little after 11:00 with Roger's team behind by one touchdown. The winners ribbed the losers, who conceded only that the winners were luckier. Roger allowed that his dropped passes made the difference.

"It takes a big man to admit his faults," one of the players deadpanned, "and you did have plenty of faults to admit."

"I should have played blocking back," Roger said, with a self-deprecating smile.

"Or," one of the boys needled him, "blocking dummy."

"Hey, can that kind of talk," Roger admonished kiddingly. "Remember, I'm your elder and you know what elders deserve."

"Yeah, bedpans for their brains."

A chorus of guffaws.

Roger relished the riposte and the camaraderie. "When you guys are my age, you'll probably have beer bellies and fallen arches."

"Coach, when we get to be your age, *you'll* be dozing all day in a rocking chair."

Roger spun toward the source of this latest gibe and playfully hurled a football at the youngster. The boy, still chortling, danced out of the way, then twisted and went loping after the bouncing ball.

The group trudged from the stadium. Roger locked the gate behind them. Then they went plodding toward the locker room and hot showers. They had had fun and were enjoying the warm afterglow of strenuous physical activity. All except Roger. Absent was the familiar sense of accomplishment that tends to lighten fatigue and create a good tired feeling. Roger was exhausted.

It was noon when Roger opened the front door on Morningside. His overpowering fatigue showed plainly in his drawn face, sagging posture and heavy gait. He closed the door behind him and leaned against it. He sighed audibly.

Helen emerged from the kitchen. "I hope the game was better than you look," she kidded. "You look pooped."

"I am. My legs feel like a couple of dead tree trunks. Maybe I'm getting too old for this stuff."

"Well, you can relax awhile. We're not due at your parents for dinner till two."

"Good. What are you doing now?"

"I just put two pumpkin pies in the oven. I'm going to clean up in the kitchen. You just take it easy."

"I think I'll turn on the Lions-Packers game. Should be starting about now."

Leaden-legged, Roger shuffled across the living room. He turned on the TV. The annual Hudson's Department Store Thanksgiving Day parade was just ending. Roger walked to the couch and eased himself down.

Moments later he watched the Detroit Lions and Green Bay Packers line up to engage in their traditional Thanksgiving Day gridiron war. When the first half ended, Roger pulled himself up to go to the kitchen for a glass of water. As he turned on the spigot, he remembered the numbness in his hands. It had disappeared. He drained the glass and set it on the counter. At least, he mused, he hadn't dropped the glass.

CHAPTER 21

In the play that was Ben's life, Joyce Worthen was a supporting player. She made her presence felt, though, and her performance was memorable.

In the spring of 1959, Joyce was 41 years old. She was a pretty woman who had lavished care on her face and body, and the results were notable. She knew what became her – what colors and designs. Her black hair was cut in a pageboy. Her brown eyes were large, oval and expressive. They could also, when she chose, blankly mask her emotions. Her nose was small and slightly upturned. Her face was narrow and slightly angular but still conveyed softness. Joyce stood five-feet three inches. She was small-boned but far from frail. She was quietly proud of her small, firm breasts, tiny waist, narrow hips and finely contoured legs.

Joyce was a lifelong Shelbian. In high school she was a cheerleader and a good one. She zipped through her choreographed routines with high-octane energy, and her spontaneous leaps and whirls were athletically bold. A month after graduation, she became Mrs. Jerry Worthen. Twenty-three years later, she still was. Jerry Worthen, ex-high school basketball player, owned and operated a furniture store on Main Street. The Worthens had no children. They lived in a pre-World War II house on Glenwood Drive near the town's Seltzer Park. Joyce hadn't held a job since she worked part-time as a drug store soda jerk during high school. Jerry occasionally let her help out at the furniture store, but he was adamant about his wife not working full-time outside the home. He wanted Joyce to play golf, cook, clean and darn his socks.

Ben had begun delivering newspapers soon after his twelfth birthday in 1957. His 80 customers included several on Glenwood. From the start Joyce had taken uncommon interest in her paperboy. When Ben called to collect, Joyce always asked about his well-being. In cold weather she frequently asked Ben in for hot chocolate and cookies. Sometimes Ben accepted, especially when his fingers were frigid and stiff from repeatedly removing his gloves to make change. On weekday winter mornings after heavy snowfalls, Joyce made a point of greeting Ben at the door to tell him whether there had been any radio announcements about school closings. Ben appreciated that. On those occasions when snow-clogged streets and roads closed Shelby schools, Joyce would invite Ben inside to warm up. Her husband Jerry generally would mumble a hello as he readied himself to leave for the furniture store. Ben liked Joyce. She was easy and fun to talk with.

Ben, however, never felt entirely at ease with her. It had to do with the way she dressed. Not long after Ben began delivering papers, Joyce began appearing at the door in filmy negligees, whatever the weather. The negligees invariably were pastel pink or yellow. They dropped to the top of her knees. At the neck, they were cut wide and low, exposing the tops of her breasts. When she wore a robe, it was equally filmy and rarely cinched. With his height advantage, Ben found it difficult to avert his eyes from Joyce's smooth, pale flesh. When she bent over to serve him hot chocolate at the kitchen table, Ben got an unobstructed view of her nipples. He invariably was interested and aroused. Joyce knew it, and Ben sensed she knew it. Neither said anything about it. To anyone. Joyce kept showing and Ben kept looking.

What Ben did talk about was the upcoming baseball season. He looked forward eagerly to opening day 1959. That afternoon he would begin his second season in Pony League, a nationwide organization for boys ages 13 and 14. Ben figured his team, Mutual Insurance, had two of the league's best pitchers in Phil Schramel and Frank Barry. Both also were excellent batters and fielders. Ben, who threw right-handed but batted left, played center field.

Mutual Insurance's toughest competitor figured to be Tilden's Sohio Station. Tilden's was defending league champion and was returning a good nucleus of players.

Opening day came and went and so did Ben's pre-season calculations and confidence. Mutual Insurance lost its first game, won its second, then lost three more. The team's pitching was inauspicious, the fielding erratic and the batting feeble. Ben was no better; he had only three hits, all singles, in 17 at bats. Neither the boys nor Coach Wendell Klein had a ready remedy for the team's ills. Wendell preached practice and patience, and the boys followed his lead. The boys hadn't yet panicked, but their confidence ebbed with each loss.

Ben took failure hard. Beneath his placid exterior dwelled a fierce competitor with an explosive temper. It didn't erupt often but, once unloosed, was incendiary. Once, after striking out on a bad pitch, he disgustedly banged his bat on the ground and hurled it back toward the dugout and into the stands behind it. Fortunately, it hit no one. On another occasion he slid into third base well ahead of the ball and the tag applied by the third baseman. Still, the umpire called Ben out. Even the third baseman appeared stunned by the umpire's ruling. As swiftly as a snake strikes at unsuspecting prey, Ben leaped to his feet and whirled to face the umpire. Flames of anger flashed from Ben's eyes. Hot words followed. Little League rules prohibited arguing with umpires. The rule was so strictly enforced that it was seldom violated. The shocked umpire was slack-jawed in the face of the youngster's withering tirade.

"Out? Out? You're crazy!" Ben thrust his nose just inches from the umpire's chin. The umpire stepped back. "It wasn't even close. What were you looking at? You missed it! You blew it! Stupid!"

Ben's coach raced from the dugout to calm his furious young player, but Ben was beyond appeasement. His coach had to grasp him by the arm and lead him away. When the stunned umpire regained his composure, he immediately ejected Ben from the game.

"You have to apologize to the umpire," Edward said after the game. "Now, before he leaves."

Ben did. It wasn't easy.

The third Tuesday in June of 1959 dawned gray and misty. A steady, windless rain began falling about 8:oo and continued all morning. Mutual Insurance was scheduled to play Tilden's Sohio Station that evening at 6:00. All morning Ben moped around the house. He tried reading but his concentration wavered. He turned on the television, but the witless game shows and mindless laundry detergent commercials left him yawning and watery-eyed. If this rain keeps up, he reflected glumly, at least we can't lose.

The rain began to abate around noon. About 4:00 Ben went upstairs to his room. Mechanically he stripped and put on his white uniform with the royal blue lettering and number 9. At 4:45 Ben mounted his bike and pedaled 15 minutes to Conley Field. He and his teammates sat on the dugout bench and watched glassy-eyed as two adult groundskeepers used push brooms to sweep water from home plate, the bases and the foot of the pitcher's mound. Then the two men spread sand to soak up the remaining moisture.

In view of field conditions, both coaches agreed to forgo warm-up sessions and   the game started. Ben came to bat for the first time in the second inning. Pitching for Tilden's was Dirk Browne, one of the two or three hardest-throwing pitchers in the league. He also was wild. Opposing batters seldom dug in; they preferred to stay on their toes, ready to bail.

Ben stepped into the lefthander's batter's box. He took two practice swings and set himself.

Dirk's first pitch was low and outside. His second pitch was a scorching fastball that sailed low and inside. Ben tried to dance out of the way but his spiked shoes stuck stubbornly in the spongy ground. The ball caught Ben on his right calf. It stung but was a glancing blow that didn't seem an exorbitant fare for a trip to first base. Before the inning ended, Mutual Insurance had taken a 1-0 lead.

Ben's next at bat was in the fourth inning. By then, Tilden's had tied the score at 1-1. Ben readied himself in the batter's box. Dirk's first pitch missed inside. Ben backed out of the batter's box to try to tap gooey mud from his caked spikes. He stepped back in. Dirk rocked into his delivery and threw the ball. Ben saw it rocketing toward his head. Batters are taught to avoid such pitches by falling straight down. They are warned not to back away; a ball sailing inside is likely to keep tailing toward a retreating batter. Ben remembered the lesson. He tried to throw his feet from under him, but the gummy earth would not release its grip on his spikes. The speeding ball followed Ben's head like a heat-seeking missile zeroing in on a doomed jet fighter. The ball hammered Ben's head just above and behind his right ear. It struck with such force that it caromed off his red plastic wraparound protector and rolled across the infield grass and onto the dirt base path. The second baseman watched stunned as the ball rolled harmlessly to a stop at his feet. The explosive crack of the ball against the plastic reverberated across the field and into the stands.

At home plate Ben dropped as though shot. There was no grace to his fall. The blow ripped his spikes from the clawing earth and threw his feet into the air while his head and back struck the ground. The impact seemed to jar loose every bone in his skull but he felt no pain. He did feel consciousness slipping away. A strange, and strangely peaceful, sensation. He saw himself in a small, high-ceilinged room. It was dimly lit. The walls were black. Faint light filtered through the lone window, a tiny aperture near the ceiling. Then an unseen hand reached up and slowly pulled down an opaque shade. Impenetrable blackness.

A hush settled over the field, in the dugouts and in the bleachers. It lasted for perhaps five seconds. Then motion and sound resumed. The home plate umpire threw aside his mask and chest protector and bent down over the fallen batter. He placed a hand on Ben's shoulder and saw blood beginning to trickle from Ben's nose. Coach Klein flew up the dugout steps and raced pell-mell to home plate. He glanced at the blood dripping from Ben's nose and murmured, "Oh, my God." In the bleachers Harriet sat horrified. Susie went white and, more remarkable for the talkative girl, speechless. Edward went cold with fear. He sat stunned for a moment, then went scrambling down out of the bleachers. He vaulted over the restraining wall and dashed toward his youngest son. He expected the worst. On the pitcher's mound, Dirk Browne began to weep. One of his teammates, awestruck, had murmured, "I think he's dead." Frightened, Tilden's catcher backed away from home plate.

Ben was supine and spread-eagled. He lay motionless. The three men squatted around him. Edward spoke softly, "Ben, can you hear me? Ben...Ben..." No response. The blood continued trickling from his right nostril, past the corner of his mouth, over the edge of his jaw and down his neck. Coach Klein noticed that the head protector had cracked. He whispered, "Ben...Ben...Come on, Ben, wake up."

Time seemed to have stopped. Edward took Ben's left hand and rubbed gently. "Ben...Ben...Can you hear me?"

Ben was not dead. The men around home plate could see that. His chest was expanding and contracting steadily. He looked peacefully asleep. Another minute passed. Ben stirred and groaned lowly. Faint voices seemed to be floating toward him through a dense fog. He moaned again. Slowly his eyelids rose. His entire head was throbbing. Out-of-focus faces hovered over him. He closed his eyes, opened his mouth and swallowed.

"Watch his tongue," Klein cautioned. "Be sure it doesn't roll back."

Ben again opened his eyes. Tears welled. His senses were returning. He breathed deeply.

Edward: "Ben, can you hear me?"

"Yeah."

"Don't move. Take it easy."

"I'm okay."

"Just take it easy."

"Help me up."

Klein: "Don't move."

"I'm okay." Ben slowly drew his legs up and brought his arms into his sides. He started to struggle up.

Edward and Klein grasped his arms and began to ease him to his feet. From behind, the umpire supported his back.

Edward with relief: "How do you feel?"

"Okay."

"You sure?"

"Yeah."

The men released him. Immediately, his legs wobbled like a pair of fresh licorice sticks. As he began sinking to the ground, the three men grabbed and steadied him. Klein: "Let's get him to the hospital."

The diagnosis was a concussion. Painful but not serious. Rest was prescribed. The next morning Ben's head felt like a drum and bugle corps was drilling inside. What also hurt was learning that Mutual Insurance had gone down to its fifth loss in six games. Two days later the team played again, but Ben's doctor ordered him not to suit up. From the bleachers Ben watched glumly as the Insurers lost for the sixth time.

On Wednesday, the morning after Ben was beaned, and on Thursday and Friday as well, Edward delivered Ben's newspapers. By Saturday, though, Ben felt chipper enough to resume the route. His head no longer hurt when he walked or rode a bike. But when he went up and down stairs too quickly, his skull pounded as if a bowling ball were bouncing around inside.

He delayed his usual Saturday morning collections until the afternoon. On Glenwood, Joyce was sunbathing in her backyard. Ben was at a house next door from the Worthens. Joyce, wearing sunglasses, stood up to go inside for a Coca Cola. She saw Ben before he saw her. After making change, Ben mounted his bike and glided to the Worthens. He dismounted and started up the walk. As he bounded up the steps, pain shot through his head. He grimaced and stopped, cursing himself for moving too fast. From inside the front door Joyce saw his face contort in pain. A wave of affection surged through her. Gingerly, Ben continued up the steps onto the front porch. As he pushed his forefinger toward the doorbell, he saw Joyce's face behind the screen. She smiled and said hello. Ben tried to smile in return, but it was a feeble effort. His right hand swung up to rub his forehead.

"Come in," Joyce said, pushing open the door.

Ben stepped inside. His downcast, half-closed eyes suddenly snapped open like a pair of runaway window shades. He stared in utter amazement, completely unprepared for the sight before him. Joyce was not wearing her usual filmy negligee. Instead she wore almost nothing. A bright yellow bikini that scarcely qualified as apparel struggled to cover her nipples and genitals. Ben's face flushed crimson as fast as a traffic light changing from yellow to red. His mind forgot about the throbbing in his head. He tried to raise his eyes to meet Joyce's, but they seemed riveted to what lay partially hidden by the narrow bands of cloth.

"Ben, are you all right?" she said softly. He continued staring. "Ben?"

The red in his face deepened still further. He forced his eyes upward. "Yes." He couldn't see Joyce's eyes, still shaded by her sunglasses.

"I read about your accident in the paper. It must've been scary."

"No, not really. There wasn't time to be scared."

"Were you scared afterward?"

"No, ma'am."

"Are you going to play anymore this season?"

"Sure. I plan to play Wednesday. That's our next game."

"That's good. Can I get you something to drink?"

"No, thank you."

"Come on," Joyce said brightly, ignoring his polite refusal. "I'm having a Coke. I'll get you one too. You look like you need to rest a minute. Come on." Joyce turned and walked toward the kitchen.

Ben followed slowly, his eyes locked like a pair of vise grips on her small, swinging buttocks. Heat was spreading through his body and his pulse was quickening. Geez, Ben's mind raced, what I wouldn't give to reach out. To pull that suit down. To touch that tight little behind. Mrs. Worthen, Ben felt sure, knew precisely what he was thinking. She had to.

In the kitchen, Joyce opened the refrigerator and removed a Coca Cola. Ben pulled a chair back from the table and sat. His straining eyes didn't divert from Joyce's tight behind. Joyce found a glass and bottle opener, popped the cap and poured. Ben's vivid imagination continued to look beneath the scanty bikini. His body reacted predictably. He felt a certain pressure begin to build. It wasn't the pain inside his skull. No, no, he anguished silently. Underneath the table his penis was swelling and hardening. Immediately Ben willed it to shrink, but the bulge in his crotch continued to grow. Of all the lousy times. I wonder if she knows what's happening. This phenomenon wasn't new to him. For the past two years or more, unexpected and uncontrollable erections had plagued him. Often, as on this occasion, they occurred at precisely the wrong times, leading to acute embarrassment. He remembered it happening just before the ring of the school dismissal bell. Ben was uncharacteristically slow to rise from his desk. He feigned intense interest in some book or paper.

Joyce set the drink on the table then, sipping from her own bottle, leaned against the counter. "I'll bet a lot of boys would be scared to start playing again after being hit in the head. You're brave."

Geez, thought Ben wildly, what does she mean by brave? He sipped the Coke and again silently commanded his rock-hard penis to soften and shrivel. It remained insubordinate. "Not really. I just don't think about it. Maybe I'll be scared when I actually go up to bat next time."

"But you don't think so."

Leave it alone, lady, he pleaded silently. "No." Again he sipped the Coke. He was determined to nurse it until he could stand up without embarrassing himself. Given the independent nature of his organ, he concluded dejectedly, that might be an embarrassingly long wait.

"How old are you, Ben?"

"Fourteen. Last January."

"You look older."

Now what? Are you teasing me? Do you really know what's going on under the table? "People tell me that."

Joyce still stood leaning against the counter across the table from Ben. She removed her sunglasses. "You'll be starting high school this year."

"Yes. Ninth grade." Why, he wondered frustratedly, do you have to be so friendly? So curious? Why did you have to invite me in? Why are you dressed like that? Geez, you're beautiful. And sexy. How old are you? I have no idea. Too bad you don't have children. Then I could at least guess.

"High school should be fun," she said brightly.

"I hope so," Ben said somberly. He went on sipping the Coke.

"But you have to study too. Do you get good grades?"

"Yes, ma'am." He shifted in his chair. He forced himself to stare at his glass. He tried to think about baseball's charms instead of Joyce's.

"Are you going out for football?"

"Yes." He stared harder at the glass and squeezed his legs together. At last, the throbbing in his penis quelled. He tried to breathe deeply without being obvious. His penis began to shrink. Go down, Ben silently ordered, then pleaded. Keep going down.

"What position do you want to play?"

"Quarterback. Mrs. Worthen," he said quickly, "I'd better get going."

"You haven't finished your Coke."

"I know but I want to finish my collecting. Thanks for the Coke." Ben pushed away from the table and stood. He turned away and blew out a large breath. He wanted to escape before his penis decided again to emulate a baseball bat.

"You're welcome, Ben."

Joyce followed him to the door. Ben quickly descended the steps. Instantly, pain shot through his head. He grimaced and stopped. He breathed deeper, the pain subsided and he resumed his walk to the bike. Joyce watched him mount and ride away. Ben fought off the temptation to turn for a last look.

Harriet still was fretting over the beaning incident. She and Edward sat sipping coffee across from each other at the kitchen table.

"I'm worried, Ed."

"I know and I don't blame you."

"Are you?"

"Not like you."

"Right now I can't stand the thought of him playing again. At least not this year."

"I understand."

"Yes, but are you going to say anything to him?"

"Don't plan to," Edward said calmly. "Don't think you should either. He had an accident, a freak accident. Odds are it won't happen again. It's rare for a player to get hit in the head. It wouldn't have happened to Ben if the ground hadn't been so muddy."

"He got hit twice in that game," responded Harriet. "It could happen again."

"Yes, it could."

"And that doesn't worry you?" she said, her voice shrilling.

"I wish I could say it did. For your benefit."

"Don't patronize me," she bristled, as much from fear and frustration as anger.

"I didn't mean to," Edward said evenly. "Look, that kind of risk is part of growing up, of living."

"But he's so young," she protested dispiritedly.

"Harriet – and I'm not meaning to patronize you – it's natural to want to protect your child. Especially when he's been hurt. But they heal and you have to let them keep going. If you try to smother them with protection, that's worse. Their confidence crumbles like a stale cookie. They don't try as hard. And why should they? If they fall, you're there with a net. You have to let them fall and you have to let them pick themselves up."

"Do you think Ben's afraid to bat again?" she said, still plainly worried.

"He hasn't said anything. No, I don't think so. But if he is, we'll know. One way or another."

"What do you mean?"

"If he's scared at bat, he'll know and we'll know. He'll back away quickly from inside pitches that aren't anywhere near him. Or he'll pull his head back just as he swings. Or he won't swing as aggressively."

"So what if he does one of those things?" Harriet challenged. "Or all of them?"

"He won't hit the ball."

"And?"

"If he doesn't hit, he won't get to play. Not regularly anyway."

"Do you think he's ready to play? I mean physically."

"Not quite. But soon. He's young and the young may stumble and fall a lot, but they heal fast."

"I don't think I can watch him play again."

The following Wednesday evening Edward was in the stands to watch Mutual Insurance again play Tilden's. Harriet stayed home with Susie. As much as anything, Edward was curious. Dirk Browne was scheduled to pitch for Tilden's. Ben's courage would be tested quickly, and Edward felt that would be best.

The two teams and the fans stood while a scratchy recording of the Star Spangled Banner blared tinnily through a pair of cheap speakers. Minutes later Ben pulled on a head protector and walked toward the batter's box. When he stepped in, he felt relaxed. On the pitcher's mound Dirk appeared edgy. His face was drawn. He blinked repeatedly and nervously rubbed the ball. His first two pitches were blazers, but both were low and outside. In the bleachers Edward was thinking that Harriet might have been worried about the wrong boy being scared. Dirk's third pitch was headed for the middle of the plate, but it lacked sizzling speed. Ben whipped his bat around and stroked the ball on a low line to right field for a base hit. From the dugout Coach Klein and his teammates cheered: "Way go to, Ben. Nice hit. Let's go."

In the bleachers, Edward was pleased. He had watched Ben carefully. He had seen no hint of tentativeness. Ben had readied himself with confidence and swung with authority.

At first base, on the next pitch Ben broke for second. The pitch was a fastball strike. Tilden's catcher released the ball quickly and threw accurately to second base, but Ben's slide beat the tag. As Dirk unleashed the next pitch, Ben broke for third base. His dash caught Tilden's by surprise. The catcher's throw edged Ben's arrival but was high, and Ben slid in safely under a late tag on his shoulder.

Ben's electrifying base running ignited the Insurers. They sculpted two runs in the first inning and swept to an easy victory. The impressive win proved a turning point. Their confidence buoyed, during the next six weeks Ben and his teammates attacked the ball like a pack of fevered carpet cleaners. They hit the ball hard and seldom missed. Phil Schramel and Frank Barry mowed down opposing batters like a pair of well-sharpened farm combines at harvest time. The Insurers were unstoppable. They reeled off 13 consecutive wins. The last one lifted them into a first-place tie with Tilden's. A best two-of-three-games playoff series would determine the league champion.

About 1,500 Shelbians turned out for game one. In that era when televised baseball still was largely a Saturday afternoon happening, attendance at Pony League games was much more than a scattering of family members and friends. They expected a well-played, closely contested game by a pair of evenly matched, highly motivated teams. Instead, they saw the baseball equivalent of Custer's Last Stand. Tilden's was the 7th Cavalry. Ben was Crazy Horse. His teammates were a deadly swarm of Crow warriors. Crazy Horse led off the first inning with a ringing single to center field and raised two billowing clouds of dust when he promptly stole second and third base. The massacre was on. Crazy Horse ripped three more base hits, stole four more bases and the Indians slaughtered the soldiers 12 to 1.

If in the first game the two teams appeared to be waging war with spears and sabers, they competed in the second with palettes and paintbrushes. It was Pony League baseball at its artful epitome. Through seven regulation innings the Insurers and Tilden's played flawlessly to a 1-1 tie. On to extra innings. The two teams traded scoring opportunities in the eighth and ninth innings, but gritty pitching and tight defense by both teams shut down scratching and clawing offenses before either could score. In the bottom half of the tenth inning with one man out and nobody on base, Ben came to bat. He lashed a low line drive to right center field for a double. When the pitcher released his first pitch, Ben broke for third base. Tilden's catcher threw quickly and accurately but Ben's slide beat the tag. Two pitches later Phil Schramel slammed a single to leftfield, and Ben scampered home easily with the winning run.

Euphoria erupted. When Ben jumped on home plate with both feet, his exulting teammates already were swarming over him like a group of excited children leaping around a fallen piñata. They were jumping and shouting and waving their arms. From last place to first to the championship on the crest of a 15-game win streak. Coach Klein tried to sniff away tears of joy. He was proud of the way his boys had hung together. Edward's chest swelled and his eyes beamed.

"Congratulations."

Ben's brow wrinkled in momentary puzzlement.

"For winning the championship. I read about it in *The Daily Globe*." Joyce Worthen smiled kindly. "You were the hero."

Ben blushed. "Thank you." He found it hard to look Joyce in the eye as Edward long had instructed him when speaking to someone.

"Come on in. I'll get the money." Joyce pushed open the door and Ben stepped inside. It was the Saturday morning after the playoff series. As usual, Joyce wore a tantalizingly filmy negligee. Soft pink. Her feet were bare. Ben watched as her finely contoured body lightly ascended the stairs. "I'll be down in a minute," she said without looking back.

Ben sighed, pursed his lips and arched his eyebrows. He fiddled with the drawstring of his olive green moneybag and shifted his feet.

"Ben," Joyce shouted down the stairs, "do you have any change?"

"Yes," he hollered.

"Come up here for a second, please."

Ben shook his head in exasperation and trudged up the stairs. He paused and looked around.

"In here," said Joyce.

Ben followed the sound of the voice across the hall to a bedroom. He stopped at the door.

"In here," she repeated less loudly. "All I've got is this twenty. Can you change it?"

"Sure."

Joyce padded slowly toward Ben. She extended her hand and Ben reached for the $20 bill. It slipped from Joyce's hand and fluttered to the floor. "Oh, excuse me," she said, flustered. She started to bend down.

"I'll get it," offered Ben. He dropped easily into a squat and picked up the bill. He started to rise. As he straightened, he felt Joyce's hands on his shoulders, exerting slight downward pressure. Ben looked up. Joyce's face moved forward. Her brown eyes closed just before her lips kissed his. Ben's eyes remained open. He tensed. Joyce pulled away slightly and opened her eyes. She kept her hands on Ben's shoulders. He straightened and stared questioningly at the pretty woman who was gazing at him unwaveringly. She was searching for a sign of panic but found none. She rose up on her toes and pressed her lips to Ben's. Her body closed against his. She curled her arms behind Ben's back to the base of his neck. She kissed harder. More than her lips, Ben felt her breasts and legs pressing against him. He closed his eyes and tentatively encircled her with his arms. Ben felt a hardening and began to back away, but Joyce pulled downward and prolonged the kiss. Thoughts were racing through Ben's mind too fast to focus on. Everything was blurring.

Joyce pulled back again, and Ben involuntarily breathed in a great gulp of air. Joyce smiled and led him to the bed. She pulled him down with her.

215

He was hot, flushed and beginning to feel torn between guilt and desire. Ben couldn't quite believe this was happening.

They lay side by side. Joyce peppered his lips with light, quick kisses. Through her barrage, Ben lay stiffly, eyes wide, arms at his sides. He knew where this was leading and was embarrassed not to know the route. Joyce sensed the depth of his discomfort.

"Touch me," she whispered.

"I-"

"Shhh. Don't talk," Joyce murmured calmly.

"But-"

"Don't talk, don't think. Just do as I say."

During the next several minutes Ben proved an apt and willing student. Gradually their bodies slowed and their muscles began to relax. They caught their breaths. Ben was spent. He slid his hands higher on the bed and rested on his elbows. He lowered his head to the pillow beside Joyce's left cheek. "Whew," he exhaled.

Joyce chuckled. "You can say that again."

"Whew."

She laughed and hugged him.

Ben hoisted himself over Joyce's leg and rolled onto his back. He inhaled deeply and exhaled slowly. He was satisfied in a way he'd never imagined, not in his most vivid, titillating fantasies. Still, he had to satisfy himself in one more way. "Why, Mrs. Worthen?" he said softly. "Why?"

She lay still for a few moments, eyes shuttered. She opened them, sucked in a deep breath and stared at the ceiling. "A desert. I've been like a desert," Joyce said slowly, haltingly. "For a long time. For too long. Dry, dusty, hot. I felt like I was wrinkling and withering. I needed to feel rain on my face. To feel worth having."

"Why me?" Ben said quietly.

"It was getting late. I guess I needed to feel young. You're so young, so strong. I thought about this for a long time. I've never done anything like this."

"Did you plan this for today?"

"Yes. No. I mean I wanted to for a long time. I started thinking about doing it today when I read about you winning the baseball championship.

It meant the end of another season. A dry season. It meant fall would be coming soon. Then another year. Do you understand?"

"Maybe. I'm not sure." A momentary silence, then, "Mrs. Worthen, what about your husband?"

"We – he-"

"Do you love him?"

"I want to say no. That would make it all easier. We've had our ups and downs. We don't talk much. He's dry too. I care for him. But I guess it's not love, not real love."

"Do you feel guilty?"

"I feel wonderful." She turned to face Ben, smiled and brightened. "I don't feel dry. The drought ended. I feel whole." A pause. "How do you feel, Ben?"

"I feel sorry for you."

"You don't have to, but thank you."

They were quiet for a long moment, and then Joyce asked tenderly, "Ben, do you feel bad? Or guilty?"

"Yes and no. It's funny. I don't and I guess I should. It was wrong. At least everything I know says it's wrong. But I don't feel guilty."

"Maybe you will later."

"Maybe," he said pensively.

"You might want to tell someone about it. Talk about it."

"Does that scare you?" he asked matter-of-factly.

"Well, I...I wouldn't want other people to know what happened. I understand if you'd-"

"Just a minute," Ben interrupted. He reached down and hitched up his pants. "They weren't made to wear around my knees," he said dryly. Joyce smiled. Ben continued somberly. "I don't think I'd want other people to know either. We sinned. The church says so anyhow. But I hope I don't start to feel guilty either."

"Why?"

"Because it was so...so good. And you were so nice."

"I seduced you."

Ben chuckled. "Yes. I remember looking up that word in the dictionary once. That and some other words. It sounded dirty."

"And?"

"This wasn't. I'm glad I didn't run."

"Really?" Joyce faced him and smiled.

"Really."

"I'm glad. You might not believe this but I was afraid. I didn't want to take advantage of you, although I did. But I couldn't just ask you. I thought sure that would scare you away. I didn't want to scare you. Or hurt you."

"You didn't."

"Good." She was relieved.

"I wonder why…"

"Wonder what?" Joyce said.

"Why I didn't get scared and run."

"I don't know. Curiosity. Desire. I don't know."

"Will this happen again?" Ben said directly.

"Do you want it to?"

"I don't know. I think so. Yes."

CHAPTER 22

From upstairs Natalie shouted, "Here she comes, everybody! Here she comes!"

Downstairs in the living room, John, Dick, Ann Sheridan, and the two oldest Santiago daughters, Jeannie Marie and Ruth, stood and walked to the staircase.

At the top were poised Natalie and Kate. Both had grown to about five feet five inches and had been blessed with breathtakingly lissome bodies. Tonight, though, they cut unlikely figures and they knew it. This was an evening to remember in more ways than one. Broad, silly grins creased both their faces. Raven-haired Kate was resplendent in a sleeveless pastel yellow formal with a modestly low neckline. Natalie, her dark brown mane spilling below her shoulders, wore her cheerleader outfit, a short, blue-pleated skirt topped by an orange turtleneck sweater emblazoned with a blue "U" on the chest. Behind them stood Maria. She looked proud and anxious.

The girls prepared to descend the stairs. Le grande entrance was not their objective. They merely wanted to reach bottom safely. This evening that would be a challenge.   Natalie, standing to Kate's left, picked up her older sister's left arm and draped it across her shoulders. Kate grasped the stair rail to brace herself. The smile faded and her beautiful features locked in concentration. She lowered her right foot. The left foot gingerly followed. Natalie served as a crutch. The first step completed, the group at the foot of the stairs applauded, cheered lustily and laughed. Kate's concentration cracked; she and Natalie looked toward them and grinned widely.

Their father joshed them. "You two look more like battered football players than a homecoming queen and a cheerleader." Everyone, including the girls, laughed. John aimed his camera, activated the shutter, and the flashbulb popped. "Posterity," he noted dryly, "deserves this moment." More laughter.

Using Natalie for support, Kate started her second step. First the right foot, clad in a white pump. Then the left, encased in a white walking cast cluttered with graffiti and autographs scrawled by friends with a bent for raunchy humor. The cast covered her leg to just below the knee. Natalie looked almost as incongruous. In addition to the University High School cheerleader uniform, she sported two elastic bandages, one tightly wound around each wrist. As much as anyone the girls saw the humor in their ungainly appearance. They started to giggle. It was contagious. At the bottom Jeannie Marie and Ruth started to break up.

From behind, Maria's hands fluttered nervously toward them. "Calm down," she urged them. "All you need to do is fall down the steps."

"Right," John piped up dryly. "All we need is another trip to the hospital instead of a football game. A couple more casts and a couple more bandages and you two could pass for refugees from a comic strip."

The girls' giggling intensified.

"John," Maria pleaded with her husband, "spare us any jokes for now. And you two, stop giggling and watch your step." Maria might as well have whistled into a hurricane.

Amidst their own giggles the girls continued their slow, awkward descent. John, Dick and Ann chuckled, and even Maria couldn't resist a nervous smile.

When they reached bottom, John still was chuckling, but love and pride radiated from his dark eyes. He stepped forward and hugged Kate. "You look terrific, honey."

"Daddy, I feel like I'm dressed for a costume party," Kate smiled, "not a homecoming."

"Kate, you look absolutely beautiful, cast or no cast," smiled Ann.

"I'm so glad you came," Kate said, beaming.

"I wouldn't have missed it for anything." Ann stepped forward and kissed Kate's cheek.

Kate had acquired her plaster footwear following the kind of accident pioneered by young Californians and later emulated by thousands of youngsters across the country. Kate and Natalie, ever venturesome, were among the first customers for a fledgling product that resembled a stubby surfboard on wheels. It was called a skateboard. In the years to come it would prove a remarkably enduring vehicle, especially in light of its propensity for hurling riders into spectacular and painful spills. It was a quiet Saturday afternoon when Kate and Natalie first tested their new purchases. They got the feel of the skateboards in their driveway at the crest of Glenmont, then ventured into the street. On their fifth run down Glenmont the girls were reveling in their four-wheeled freedom. They were weaving easily back and forth across the street. Suddenly, about two thirds of the way down, a car backed out of a driveway. The athletic girls reacted immediately. Their reflexes and coordination were good. Their luck was bad. Kate veered toward the curb. When the skateboard struck, she went flying headlong across the tree lawn. A small tree stood in her flight path. Her head and torso cleared the obstacle but not her ankle. It was a glancing blow but sharp enough to crack a bone.

Natalie tried a different tack to evade the car. She kicked the board from underneath her. Her feet flew up over her head. Reflexively, her arms reached down to break her fall. They did. All her weight came crashing down on her hands. The result was two sprained wrists and an abraded bottom. Initially, the latter smarted more than the former. It also left a more colorful wound.

"Tonight, all I have to do is ride around the field in a convertible and then sit for the game," smiled Kate. "But tomorrow night I'll be the proverbial wallflower at the homecoming dance."

"Umm, I don't think so," smiled Dick. "I don't think your date will mind at all. I think he'll be proud just to be with you. Not many guys get to date a homecoming queen."

Kate hobbled to Dick and kissed his cheek. "Maybe I can manage a slow dance or two. A very slow dance."

Dick winked. "I'm sure your date will be more than glad to lend the necessary support."

"As for the rest of the time," Natalie smiled wryly, "just act queenly."

"And pray tell," Kate curtsied clumsily, "any tips on that?"

"Just smile a lot and say thank you and lots of other nice things," answered Natalie brightly.

"Sounds a lot like being an actress," said Ann with dry self-deprecation.

"You'll have another advantage," offered Natalie.

"That being?"

"If any klutzy guys ask you to dance, you'll have the perfect excuse."

"Ahh," intoned Dick with mock somberness, "the sisters Santiago, scourges of male hearts."

Kate and Natalie had taken University High School by storm. Their remarkable beauty only contributed to their sweeping conquest. They both plunged headlong into school life. They ran first for student council and then for class president, positions for which they campaigned energetically, imaginatively and successfully. They joined the Thespian Club. They played basketball and quickly became standouts. Both were on the staff of the school newspaper, *The Warrior.* They both became cheerleaders.

Now, in the fall of 1961, Kate had been elected homecoming queen. To no one's surprise Natalie had anointed herself Kate's adoring lady-in-waiting. Just as Jeannie Marie and Ruth had become best friends, Kate and Natalie had become as close as consecutive pages in a book. They were close in age. Both were generous, loving and largely without pretense. They enjoyed the same activities. They liked the same music. Both could dance up a storm to the likes of *The Twist, The Bristol Stomp* and *The Locomotion.* They confided in each other. One topic was the persistent advances of their steady boyfriends. Both girls dated intelligent, confident athletes who eventually tried to test their sporting skills in amorous wrestling matches. Neither girl considered herself a candidate for a convent, but neither was ready to become a football player's off-the-field touchdown. In a series of bedtime gab sessions the girls settled on a strategy: no hands allowed below the waist.

Jeannie Marie and Ruth both had chosen to attend college at nearby UCLA. Both also had chosen to live at home. Kate had other ideas about college. One afternoon toward the end of her junior year at University High, Kate wandered into the library. From a high shelf, she pulled down *Barron's College Guide,* a directory containing descriptions of the nation's colleges and universities. She sat at a long table and leisurely began leafing through the guide, scanning most of the pages, occasionally pausing to read a description. One entry in particular caught her eye. It read in part: *Ohio University. First institution of higher learning in the Northwest Territory. Founded 1804. Located in Athens, amidst the hills of southeastern Ohio. Small city environment and a friendly campus where newcomers are quickly made to feel welcome. Hocking River meanders through campus where Georgian architecture prevails...*

Kate's mind painted a picture of a quiet, bucolic campus, romantically set in a part of the country she had never seen. She thought also of Dick, the Ohioan who had become as much a part of the Santiago family as any blood relative. She was curious about Dick's origins, his family and hometown. Kate stared straight ahead, focusing on nothing inside the big book-lined room, but on the future outside the window. A small, wistful smile played on her lips. She was quite aware that for all she knew about Ohio, it might as well have been on another planet. That too was part of its allure.

A few days later after supper, Kate, Natalie, John and Maria sat in the living room. Jeannie Marie and Ruth had returned to campus to study at the UCLA library.

Kate spoke first. "I think I want to go away to school."

Natalie's brow wrinkled in uncertainty.

Maria's face tightened. John's remained expressionless. He sensed, correctly, that Kate already had made that decision. His question was to the point. "How far away?"

"Maybe Ohio."

"Ohio!" blurted Natalie.

"Oh, Kate, are you sure?" Maria said with obvious concern. "That's so far."

"No, I'm not sure. But I want to learn more about it."

"Have you talked to your counselor?" John asked calmly.

"Not yet. I plan to."

"I see. Have you thought about a particular school?" asked John.

"Ohio University."

Later that night when Kate returned from the bathroom to the bedroom she shared with her younger sister, she found Natalie sitting cross-legged on her bed, weeping softly.

"Nat, what's wrong?"

"Nothing." The hurt in Natalie's voice was painfully plain.

"Come on, Nat, I...Oh, oh, I think I know what it is. Do I, Nat? Do I know?"

Natalie looked up at her sister. "How could you?" she groaned miserably. "How could you?"

"Oh, Nat, I-"

"I thought you loved me," said Natalie in a quavering voice.

"Nat, you know I do," Kate replied gently. She sat beside her sister.

"Then how could you even think about going so far away? And for so long?"

"Oh, Nat, it's...I feel like I want to try something different. Jeannie and Ruth stayed home. That's not me. I want to try a different place. Someplace I haven't seen." Kate circled Natalie's shoulder with her arm. "Nat, I've always felt that way. You have too. That's one reason we tried out for the Mouseketeers. That's why we like going to Grandpa's ranch to ride horses. We've always wanted to try new things."

"But we've always done them together," Natalie protested in a still shaky voice. "You could do that at UCLA. Like Jeannie and Ruth." It was an undisguised plea.

"That wouldn't be the same," Kate said evenly. "You know that."

Natalie, in utter misery, moaned. "I'll miss you. I'll miss you so much." New tears welled up and spilled over.

"I'll miss you too. Very much."

"I'll follow you there – or wherever you go."

"If you want to." A pause. "You know, Nat, we can't be together forever. Not like we are now. Someday we'll get married. We could live anywhere."

Natalie pressed her face against Kate's shoulder and sniffled to stem the flow of tears. "We'll visit often, won't we?"

"Of course."

"I hate losing friends."

"You'll never lose me."

"But we'll be apart. I won't get to see you whenever I want. I can take most anything, but I can't stand to miss people. Sometimes I still miss my Mouse Club friends. I wonder where they are, what they're doing, if they're happy." She sniffled twice more and drew a deep breath. The tears had stopped. "I almost don't want to graduate from high school. I know that's silly, but I'll miss my closest friends and I might not ever see them again. I hate to be apart from people I love."

"Me too."

"I wonder if it changes."

"What?"

"I mean, when you get older, I wonder if you miss people less."

"I hope not."

A momentary silence.

"Kate?"

"What?"

"I think I'll always like California the best. Of anywhere. The sea. The sun. The trees and flowers. The mountains. I don't think I'll ever live anywhere else."

"Then maybe you better not follow me."

"Why not?"

"What if you fell in love with some boy from New York or Massachusetts? And what if he didn't want to live here?"

"I don't know. Darn, why does it all have to be so complicated, so confusing? Maybe I shouldn't get so close to people. Maybe I wouldn't miss them so much."

Kate smiled affectionately. "You're not the type, Nat. You're like a sponge. You'll always soak up new friends. And when it's time to part, you'll miss them. But you'll soak up more new friends."

Natalie stared blankly straight ahead. She sighed deeply. "I wonder if it's worth it."

"It is," Kate assured her, "and you know it."

224

Natalie faced Kate and they hugged. Outside, the warm glow of California sunshine was giving way to the cool darkness of night. "You won't mind if I follow you to college?"

Kate smiled fondly. "If you won't mind me graduating a year ahead of you."

CHAPTER 23

Get Mrs. Hoerner any time you can; she's neat. Among Shelby High School students, that was a common refrain.

Helen had become highly respected as a skilled, dedicated, energetic English teacher. Besides her classroom duties she served as adviser to the cheerleaders and Pep Club, a group of uniformed girls from grades 9 through 12 who cheered en masse and in unison at pep rallies and football and basketball games. The girls adored Helen, sensing correctly that she lavished them with unqualified affection.

Roger's career at SHS was on the upswing. Following Shelby's dismal 1958 football season, the Whippets got some bite back in their bark. In 1959, they streaked to nine wins in 10 games and the Northern Ohio League title. In 1960, with strapping sophomore Ben Lawrence taking over at quarterback, they repeated, losing only once in nine games. In 1961, Shelby finished with a respectable record of 7-2

Although childless, the Hoerners were content with their life. An occasional unwelcome intrusion was the infrequent appearance of Roger's mysterious symptoms. Not quite two years after Roger had experienced numbness in his right hand during and immediately after that 1958 touch football game, the sensation returned.

"Helen, I've got that tingling in my fingers again." This time Roger was sitting in the bedroom easy chair, reading. He rubbed his hands together. "Can't figure it out."

"Maybe you should see Doctor Kingsboro. Let him have a look."

"I don't know. It's more a nuisance than anything else. No pain. I don't want to trouble him over something trivial."

"Why don't you see him anyway?"

"Let's see if it lasts."

It didn't. Within hours, the sensation had passed.

A couple weeks later, Roger and Helen drove home from school. The day had not been particularly grueling, but he felt drained. Inside the house he stretched out on the living room couch to rest. Soon he had dozed off. When he awoke, the numbness had returned and with it a more disconcerting symptom. As Roger slowly eased himself to a sitting position, mindful of the numbness in his right hand, he noticed that the room seemed out of focus. He blinked and looked around. He saw two of everything. The dual images were on top of each other, not side by side. He blinked again and rubbed his eyes. The double vision persisted.

The dawning of the 1960s saw Edward facing new reality. He was becoming an old man. He felt fine and radiated robust health, but the lines in his face had become deep crevices and his white hair no longer shielded his scalp from the sun's rays. His hearing had dulled, no shock to Edward given his years in noisy machine shops. The lenses in his wire-rimmed frames now were bifocals. His posture still was militarily correct, and if his strength had waned, the slippage was indiscernible.

Family was his life's fulcrum. Harriet, soft and pretty at 37, had passed the age when his first wife Sarah had succumbed to a stroke. Susie, a pubescent teenager, was blooming. Edward doted on her. Ben, strong academically and athletically, was Edward's can't-miss bet for the college degree Dick had forsaken. His first son still occupied a special niche in Edward's heart. When he and Dick talked, it was more a conversation between old friends than father and son. Both had endured tragedy, coped and continued to carve out meaningful lives. They loved and respected each other and they remained close despite the vast stretch of America that had separated them for some 15 years.

The Shelby Cycle Company had closed. More modern and productive American plants and a growing tide of imports had underpriced and overwhelmed the once-famous Shelby Bicycle. After the fall Edward had signed on as a machine shop foreman with the Ohio Steel Tube Company. Soon thereafter, with mixed feelings, he left the factory floor for the front office, where he eventually was promoted to personnel manager. The change from sweat stains and time clocks to secretaries and paper clips was not without its adjustments. In particular he sometimes missed the manufacturing floor's ribald riposte. But at age 60, Edward reflected, I don't regret deciding to discard my green work uniforms and safety shoes for white shirts and wing tips.

With equally mixed feelings, Ben, late in the summer of 1961, quit delivering newspapers. During the 1961 football season, he dated a sophomore, Saundra Brunson, but without real passion. She was tall, thin, brown-haired, intelligent and willing to grant the occasional favors Ben had grown fond of receiving from Joyce Worthen.

Late in the season another girl entered Ben's life. It seemed that everywhere he walked, he encountered pretty, willowy Barbara Mason. Like Ben she was a junior. She was five feet six inches tall. Shoulder-length golden-tinged brown hair framed an expressive face highlighted by high cheekbones and incandescent blue eyes. Barbara's face also bore a thin, C-shaped scar. It began at the inside end of her right eyebrow, dipped inside the bridge of her nose, and curled back and ended just under the inside corner of her right eye. It was the product of stone throwing with a gang of neighborhood kids years before. Ben had noticed the scar when he first spotted Barbara as a freshman but had long since ceased taking note of it. Barbara was reserved, mature and academically near the top of their class. Now, when Ben and Barbara met, she inevitably greeted him with a quiet, friendly hello and semi-shy smile.

On the Saturday after Thanksgiving the cheerleaders and majorettes jointly staged a girl-ask-boy hayride. A few days before that, Ben saw Barbara, a cheerleader, approaching in a school corridor. She smiled and veered toward him. She said hello and blocked his path. Without any apparent nervousness she described the upcoming hayride and asked Ben to be her date.

The hayride was a rip-roaring success. Lots of laughter, some shouting and a variety of songs with Ben uninhibitedly singing off key. Barbara was fabulous company. She also exercised restraint. Late in the evening, closely and warmly nestled in the hay behind a droning tractor that allowed whispered conversations to go unheard by nearby couples, Ben's best gambits got no further than a couple innocuous cheek pecks and some harmless hugging. Somewhat to Ben's surprise he didn't resent her refusal to go further. He was impressed – and smitten.

In that fall of 1961, Ben, like most teenagers, was a whirling blend of emotions, a complex stew of high anxiety and unshakable confidence. A festering pimple could induce panic, but in the last seconds of a close football game, his team behind and driving desperately for the winning score, a familiar calm prevailed.

Barbara further complicated Ben's emotional mix. Soon after the hayride, Ben decided he wanted to ask Barbara to the Snowball. The Snowball had been a big deal in the small town since 1947. It was traditional, and tradition was revered. The dance was held the Saturday before Christmas, and it was open to all high school students, faculty and alumni. A first-rate regional band was brought in.

Ben's decision to ask Barbara led to an interesting self-discovery. Faced with the possibility of rejection, his confidence ebbed. The more he thought about asking Barbara, the more he vacillated. This uncertainty was new to Ben. In the past, he had wasted little thought before asking a girl for a date. The difference now was the way he felt about Barbara. She was more than merely another tempting target. Much more. She aroused in Ben very different and unfamiliar desires. The irony of his dilemma didn't escape him. He smiled and winced.

Barbara liked him, he knew. The looks, the smiles, the hayride all told him that. Besides, at least three or four fellow students told him the same thing. So why the uncertainty? No doubt, Ben concluded, because he so much wanted to ask her and wanted her to accept. He could not recall wanting anything nearly as much.

It was on an early December Thursday that Ben went striding to school, resolved to invite Barbara to be his Snowball date. Time, he knew, was awasting, and further delay could result in opportunity lost. At lunch hour the opportunity arose. Ben faltered. His tongue, ordinarily facile, lapsed into paralysis. On Friday he faltered again.

On Saturday morning Ben's thoughts turned early to Barbara, and before the impulse deserted him, he lurched for the telephone. His fingers were cold and stiff but followed his directions. This is ridiculous, he thought. I shouldn't be nervous.

The phone rang. "Hello?" It was a female voice but not Barbara's. Probably her mother or younger sister.

"Is Barb there?" He could hear the slight tremor in his voice. Was it detectable to others? Probably not, he hoped.

"Just a minute," replied the cheery voice, whose owner no doubt had heard *Is Barb there?* countless times.

Long moments passed. His mouth went dry. He felt the urge to urinate. Should he hang up and go to the bathroom? No, that would only make matters worse. When, if, he called back, someone surely would ask, "Did you call a few minutes ago?" That would require dreaming up a phony explanation. Or lying. He continued to hold the receiver by his ear and sucked in a deep breath.

"Hello," said Barbara.

"Hi, it's Ben."

"Oh, hi, Ben. How are you?"

"Oh, fine," he lied. The urge to pee was passing. Ben was grateful for that. What to say next? Someone else has probably asked her. Shoot, probably some senior or maybe even a college guy. What the hell, he decided, go ahead. "Barb, uh, there's something I want to ask you. Uh," he swallowed, "would you go to the Snowball with me?" The words were out and he felt immense relief. He almost didn't care if she said no.

"Oh, yes, Ben." Her enthusiastic response came so quickly that it killed the suspense as fast as a hiccup fractures the dignity of the most solemn occasion. "I was hoping you'd ask me."

A week later the sun was barely beginning to creep above the horizon when Edward pushed open the door to Ben's darkened room. He nudged him on the shoulder. "Ben, Ben. Time to hit the deck." His son stirred and groaned. "Sure you want to go out?" Edward asked.

"Yeah."

"It's cold out. A brass monkey would have trouble hanging onto his balls out there. Somewhere around fifteen or twenty degrees."

"You tryin' to give me second thoughts?"

"It's Saturday," said Edward, "and you could stay between the sheets."

Ben stretched. "Let's go."

"I'll see you downstairs."

"I'll be down in a few minutes."

Before Ben reached the bottom of the stairs, a mouth-watering blend of tempting aromas came wafting toward him on the staircase updraft. Edward was working at the stove when Ben entered the kitchen. He glanced over his shoulder and smiled affectionately. "Have a seat."

"You didn't have to go to all this trouble," said Ben.

"No trouble. Dressing warm is one thing, but you need something to stick to your ribs."

"This oughta do it."

Edward held Ben's plate over the stove. From two black cast-iron skillets he heaped scrambled eggs and fried potatoes on the plate. Then he plucked two pieces of browned bread from the toaster, buttered them and placed them on the plate. He set it before Ben.

"Boy, I hope this tastes as good as it smells."

"You have doubts?" Edward smiled in mock surprise.

"None." Ben sprinkled salt and pepper on both the eggs and potatoes.

Edward fixed a plate for himself and poured coffee for both.

"Think we'll have any luck?" Ben said.

"Maybe. At least it's dry and there's no wind yet."

Soon after 7:00 father and son were chatting idly as the four-door 1960 Pontiac cruised along a straight country road. Between them on the front seat was a thermos of coffee. On the back seat lay two 35-pound lemon wood bows and two quivers of arrows. Edward slowed the car and turned into an unpaved, snow-dusted, rutted lane. Ahead about a quarter mile was a stately, old red-brick two-story farmhouse with a covered porch that ran across the front and the length of one side. Nearer to the road was a huge white barn. Edward eased the car off the lane and parked in front of the barn.

He and Ben got out of the car and opened the rear doors. Each strapped on a quiver, then picked up and strung his bow. They walked across the lane to a wire fence. Ben separated the top two strands while Edward bent low and stepped through. He returned the favor for Ben. Father and son stood shoulder to shoulder and surveyed the immense field. Cornstalk stubble poked through the thin sheet of snow like a two-day growth of beard. This was familiar terrain to the Lawrences. Edward was an old friend of the man who owned this farm and had standing permission to hunt its fields and forests and to fish the stretch of the Blackfork River that flowed through it.

Slowly Edward and Ben began treading over the rough ground. Each breath crystallized in the sub-freezing December air. The dry snow squeaked beneath their boots. After about 30 minutes the cold and the coffee began to work on their kidneys.

"I'm going to take a leak," said Edward. "I'll be back in a minute." He walked to a nearby patch of woods, propped his bow against a tree and began to relieve himself. He felt a burning sensation and glanced down. He was passing blood. The stream of red startled him. Damn, he thought, I wonder what the hell caused that. He was disturbed but not overly alarmed. He would watch his urine carefully. Probably some infection, he surmised, that would soon run its course. He rejoined Ben, said nothing about the blood, and they continued their slow trek through the field.

A few minutes later, they paused again to survey the terrain. Edward, standing to Ben's right, tapped his son on the shoulder and pointed to the two o'clock position. About 30 feet away crouched a large brown-gray cottontail. It sat perfectly still, ears cocked to pick up sound, eyes wide and alert for any threatening movement. A wave of adrenalin swept through Ben and dissipated the cold that had been penetrating his mind and body. Slowly his gloved left hand raised the bow. His right hand, also gloved in fur-lined black leather, drew back the taut string until the arrow's tip protruded just beyond the bow. He aimed and steadied himself. Then his fingers smoothly released the string, and the feathered arrow went slicing through the cold, still air. The rabbit sprung as the arrow pierced its flesh about half way along its body.

Ben and Edward watched for some sign of life, saw none, then looked at each other, nodded and half smiled. A sense of accomplishment further warmed Ben. The rabbit's blood was spilling on the ground. They walked to the fallen animal. The arrow had skewered the rabbit. Ben knelt beside it. The rabbit still was breathing. Without hesitation Ben pulled out a

Remington hunting knife with a five-inch blade. His face expressionless Ben's left hand grasped the limp, pain-wracked animal on the back of its neck and lifted. From underneath, his right hand drove the knife into the rabbit's heart. It died instantly. Ben removed the knife, pulled a rag from his jacket pocket and wiped the blade. He then replaced it in the scabbard.

Edward had watched silently and intently as his son calmly killed the rabbit. Edward knew Ben had acted humanely. Edward had performed the same rite on numerous occasions on rabbits and other animals. But seldom had he been able to apply the death stroke with Ben's decisive detachment. For Edward there usually was a moment of revulsion. He neither saw nor sensed any of that in Ben.

Dick paused at the hospital room doorway. He had learned that Edward had continued to pass blood and that Harriet had persuaded him to seek medical advice. "This is a hell of a note," Dick said with feigned gruffness.

Edward, sitting in bed reading, looked toward his oldest son and smiled wryly. "Does sort of take the edge off the holiday season."

Dick smiled, walked to the bed and leaned over. The two men hugged and patted each other. They parted and Dick straightened. "I've heard of getting a lump of coal in a Christmas stocking, but this is stretching things."

"Glad you could make it, Dick."

"Did you think I wouldn't?"

"It's a lot warmer in California in December than it is here. And not quite as white."

"Yeah, well, I'll admit your timing could've been a little better. So, what do you think, Dad?" Dick said worriedly.

"Doesn't look good," sighed Edward, lips pursed. "They won't know for sure how bad it is until they open me up. But if you're looking for a safe bet, this isn't it."

"Shit." Dick spat the word disgustedly. Then he dragged a chair to his father's bedside and plopped into it. "Sorry, but that was the only word that came to mind."

"Not inappropriate. I've used it once or twice myself recently. It helps."

"I haven't prayed much for a long time," said Dick. "Maybe that'll help, too."

"Can't hurt."

Dick forced a small smile. "Dad, you're a tough old bird. You'll come through this in good shape. I know you will."

"If they caught it in time, and if they can clean it all out. That's what it comes down to."

"When…what time-"

"Tomorrow morning at seven-thirty."

At that moment, Harriet, Susie and Ben appeared in the doorway.

"Looks like standing room only," smiled Dick. "I'll leave."

"No. Stay," said Edward. "I don't think the hospital will mind if we bend the visitors rule a bit."

His second family gathered around the bed.

"Let me get a good look at you," said Edward to Ben.

Ben stood erect beside the bed. "Dad, I really don't feel like going to the Snowball tonight. I'd rather just visit with you and then go home."

"And," said Edward kindly but firmly, "I've already told you that's foolish. You go out and have a great time. I mean it. Besides, we bought you that new suit especially for the Snowball. Looks good too."

The new suit was dark gray with thin black pinstripes and narrow lapels. Edward and Ben had picked it out at Oscar's, a local men's store. Ben also wore a white shirt with button-down collar and narrow black, gray and blue regimental striped tie.

"Back up so I can get a good look at you," Edward instructed.

Ben stepped away from the bed.

"I think he looks wonderful," beamed Harriet.

"Me too," chirped Susie.

Edward studied his youngest son carefully and then turned to Dick. The two men exchanged wry smiles. "Ben, what time are you picking up the Mason girl?"

"About half an hour. Why?"

"Because that means you've got time to get home and change your socks."

"Huh? What's wrong with my socks?"

"Nothing if you were wearing blue jeans or gym shorts. But you do not wear white socks with a suit. Especially a dark suit."

Dick muffled a chuckle.

"Why not?" Ben said defensively, glancing at his older brother, then pivoting back to his father.

"Because," winced Edward, "you just don't. It looks dumb."

"But all the guys wear white socks."

"Not with suits."

"I'll bet plenty of guys will be there tonight with white socks."

"But not you."

"Dad-"

"Look, you don't want to embarrass yourself. Or the Mason girl. Or me."

"Aw, Dad, give me a break," groaned Ben.

"I'm *trying* to give you a break. Now go home and put on some black socks."

"I don't *have* any black socks. Only white ones."

"What? Well-"

"Wait," said Ben, "I have a pair of red socks."

Dick was struggling to suppress laughter. He covered his mouth but a rippling snicker leaked out.

"Red?" Edward rolled his eyes toward the ceiling.

"I got them to match a red shirt," Ben parried lamely.

"Look," Edward said with exasperation, "go home and borrow a pair of my black socks. You'll look better and I'll feel better. White socks, red socks, I don't need this," Edward muttered. "Git."

"Okay, okay, but I'll probably be the only guy there with black socks. I'll feel square."

"Maybe you'll start a new teenage fad – dressing right. Come here," Edward ordered his youngest son. Ben approached. Edward stuck out his hand. The two shook hands firmly. "You look great, Ben. You really do. Just believe your old man about the socks."

"Okay, Dad. But I'll let you know tomorrow if I was right."

"Or wrong."

Edward glanced at his watch. "Harriet, you and Susie might as well go with him. Visiting hours are nearly over. He won't have time to change and come back for you and still pick up the Mason girl on time."

Harriet, relieved that the father-son tiff had passed, stood and leaned over the bed. She and Edward kissed tenderly. She felt a lump growing in her throat. "I'll see you tomorrow," she whispered huskily. She straightened and made way for Susie. Daughter and father kissed and hugged. "I'll see you tomorrow too, Dad."

"Of course you will," murmured Edward.

"I guess I'd better get going too," said Dick.

"No, not yet," replied Edward. "Stick around a few more minutes."

"All right." Dick was puzzled but willing.

Harriet, Susie and Ben backed from the room. All waved from the doorway. Harriet blew a light kiss. Edward returned the gestures. After they had disappeared from view, the room was silent for a few moments. Edward stared straight ahead, grim-faced. Dick studied his father.

"You know," Edward said pensively, "this is my first time in a hospital as a patient since I was hit in France."

"Does it seem like yesterday?" smiled Dick.

Edward smiled through closed lips and shook his head. "No, Dick. Right now it seems every bit like 40 years."

"Dad, did you ask me to stay just to reminisce?"

"No, no, I didn't."

"What is it?"

Edward faced his son and sighed. "Dick, I don't have a lot of money. I, uh-"

"Hey, Dad, don't worry about that. Let me worry about the bills."

"It's not the hospital or the doctors. I should be able to swing that. But, uh, if I don't make it-"

"Dad-"

"Dick, listen, please."

"All right."

"If I don't make it, it could be rough on Harriet and the kids. You know Harriet hasn't worked for years. I didn't want her to while the kids were home. She-"

"Dad, listen to me. They won't want for anything. Understand? Please don't worry about that."

Edward's eyes began to redden. He dabbed at them. "I never..." His voice caught. "Damn, I just never thought about anything like this." He swallowed. "Guess I should've."

Dick clenched his teeth and breathed deeply. More than 25 years had passed since he'd last seen tears in his father's eyes. Those tears, and his father's quavering voice, hit Dick like a punch to the belly. Edward had been his rock, chipped and weathered but indomitable. He reached for his father's hand. "Nobody can think of everything. And you've thought of a lot. You've sure helped me through some rough spots. I owe you. Nothing I do for you will ever square our account. Now rest easy. Don't stay awake tonight worrying. You don't need that. I'll see you tomorrow."

Sunday morning at 7:00 two nurses helped Edward onto a gurney and strapped him down. He stared at the whitewashed walls and ceilings that conveyed an antiseptic coolness that offered little comfort. This is not where it should end, he told himself. If grit counts for anything, then maybe I've got a decent chance of pulling through. The two nurses made comforting small talk, and he forced himself to smile and kid them. They wheeled him into the operating room. At 7:30 Doctor Paul Krell looked for a last time at Edward's X-rays. Then he picked up a scalpel and prepared to make an incision in Edward's abdomen.

Roger Hoerner had scheduled an appointment with his long-time family physician, Doctor Wilson Kingsboro, for the week between Christmas and New Year's. He merely told Doctor Kingsboro that he wanted a thorough physical examination.

Doctor Kingsboro, in his early 60s, was lean and bespectacled. He seemed well suited to handling the myriad pressing demands on a small-town general practitioner. Each day he was as serene and solicitous with his last patient as with the first. He seldom laughed uproariously but smiled often and kindly. He was a community favorite.

Doctor Kingsboro greeted Roger warmly. They pumped hands, he asked after Helen and congratulated Roger on the football team's continuing success. Then he asked Roger to sit on a small wooden chair with a rounded back and cylindrical slats. The doctor seated himself on an ancient swivel chair with cracked leather upholstery and switched on a fluorescent desk lamp to illuminate Roger's file that already lay unopened on the desk pad. Doctor Kingsboro opened the file and studied it. "It's been a long time since you've been here."

"Nothing to complain about," said Roger. "Guess I've been lucky."

"It's the best way to be. Well," the doctor's voice rose and brightened, "what prompted you to call me?"

"I decided I should have a physical. Like you said, it's been a long time."

"Umm." Doctor Kingsboro shoved his glasses farther up the bridge of his nose. "Anything specific you've noticed? I should know if I'm going to examine you as best I can."

Slowly, haltingly at first, Roger told him about the episodes of numbness. And about the recent attack of double vision. And about the extreme fatigue he had experienced on several occasions during the last three years.

"Anything else?"

"No. No, I can't think of anything else." Roger felt relieved for having confided. He sucked in a deep breath.

"Okay, let's move to the examining table." At the conclusion of his questioning and probing, Doctor Kingsboro took a blood sample from Roger's right forefinger and asked him to step into a small john to provide a urine sample. Then he scheduled X-rays.

"Are the X-rays necessary?" said Roger.

"Umm, not necessary. But you said you wanted a complete physical and they should be part of one."

"I see. Did you find anything?"

"No." It was an honest reply.

"Then, what…Uh, do you have any idea what's caused these things?"

"The symptoms you described could mean almost anything, including tension." Not untrue. "And," he smiled warmly, "I sure don't like to speculate. I leave that to the gamblers. Let's wait for the test results and the X-rays."

Roger cleared and lowered his voice. "What else could it be? Besides tension?"

"Roger, I really don't like to speculate."

"I understand, but I don't think it's tension."

"Well, for another thing, it could be a vitamin deficiency. But that's as far as I want to go. Okay?"

"Okay." Roger's anxiety had ebbed. He still had no inkling as to the cause of his symptoms, and Doctor Kingsboro had said nothing to induce fear or dread.

At mid-week Doctor Kingsboro's nurse called Roger and asked him to come in the next morning. When Roger asked what she knew, she answered only that the doctor wanted to discuss the test findings.

"Is Doctor Kingsboro there?" Roger asked.

"Yes, but he's with a patient."

"Could I please talk with him?" Roger asked politely but firmly.

"Not now. Well, just a minute, please."

About three minutes later, Doctor Kingsboro picked up the phone.

"I'm sorry to interrupt, Doctor, but I wanted to know what the test results showed."

"That's quite all right. I understand. They were negative or normal."

"Oh. I guess we're back where we started."

"That's precisely why I want you to come in tomorrow, Roger. I know you're looking for answers, so I'd like to go over everything with you again. Maybe you'll remember something else. Or maybe I'll think to ask something else."

"Sure, Doctor, fine," Roger replied cheerily. "And thank you. I'll see you tomorrow."

Despite the unsolved mystery, Roger felt reassured. It probably was tension or a vitamin deficiency after all, he reasoned. Whatever it was, it didn't appear to be serious. Indeed, given the apparent robust state of his health at the moment, he felt a trifle foolish about the anxiety that had been festering. He would see Doctor Kingsboro, listen to whatever advice was forthcoming and go about the business of life as usual.

"I'm not sure I understand," Roger told Doctor Kingsboro in his office the next morning. "If you can't find anything wrong, why do you want me to undergo more tests? Besides, I feel fine. Really."

"Well, I'm as puzzled as you are, and incomplete puzzles bug the dickens out of me. The Cleveland Clinic has far more sophisticated facilities than we have here. Maybe they can find the missing piece...if there is one. If those symptoms show up again, I'd like to know the cause before trying to treat them."

"But," Roger protested weakly, "you said it probably-"

"Aah," smiled Doctor Kingsboro, "probabilities. Speculation. Gambling. Like I said, that's not for me. We should be sure, don't you agree? If the Clinic doesn't find anything, we'll forget it. That sounds reasonable, doesn't it? As a football coach, you know it's important to have a backup at every position. Just consider the Clinic as my backup. I'll certainly feel better if they examine you."

"Well, I...all right, if that's what you think is best."

"I do. I'll make the arrangements and send your file up ahead of time so the doctors there can study it before you arrive."

Even in the early 1960s, the Cleveland Clinic, near University Circle on Cleveland's east side, was a sprawling complex. Nearby were Case Institute of Technology, Western Reserve University, the Museum of Art, the Natural History Museum, the Western Reserve Historical Society Museum, the Frederick C. Crawford Auto-Aviation Museum, the Garden Center and stately Severance Hall, residence of the Cleveland Orchestra. Roger and Helen spent the weekend happily strolling from place to place, often stopping to gaze wondrously at some of man's and nature's most inspired works.

On Monday morning the late January air was cold, windy and damp. Roger and Helen had spent the previous two nights in a downtown hotel. Now, as they walked from their car to the Clinic entrance, they hunched their shoulders and pulled up their coat collars to ward off the penetrating chill.

Roger met first with a Doctor Clarkson. They discussed Roger's history and the puzzling symptoms. Doctor Clarkson was cordial but more businesslike than Doctor Kingsboro. Roger felt somewhat ill at ease. Despite the room's coolness, his armpits were perspiring.

"Let's get started," Doctor Clarkson said crisply.

"What's first?"

"It's called a myelogram."

"What's that?"

"It's a kind of X-ray. We use it to check out the spine. It can show us a lot about nerves."

In the laboratory a technician strapped Roger prone and spread-eagled on a high table. Then the technician inserted a syringe into Roger's spinal column. She withdrew some fluid and replaced it with colored liquid. The table tilted so the colored liquid could move up and down the spinal column that was photographed in sections. Then the colored liquid was moved back to the top of the spinal column and withdrawn. The test was not particularly painful, but it was lengthy, tiring and unpleasant.

About dawn that same Monday at Shelby Memorial Hospital, Dick Lawrence sat slumped in a padded, vinyl-upholstered armchair. He was lost in thought, nearly oblivious to the early morning hospital bustle, the rattling wheels of carts, the clopping of soft-soled shoes and pages over the public address system. Dick was sitting beside his father's bed. He rubbed his sleep-starved eyes and resumed staring through the window. Outside, dry, light, small-flaked snow fluttered lazily to the frozen earth.

Dick's gaze shifted to his father. The morning after surgery, Edward seemed like a much smaller man. Eyes closed, face pale and sunken, blankets pulled to his chin, he appeared to have shrunken overnight. The change was startling. I've never seen him look so vulnerable, Dick mused, so fragile. Not even right after Mom died. Makes me wonder about myself. My own health. Wonder if there's anything nasty eating away at me? Lord knows I'm not invincible. I've seen too much death to have any illusions. I was just plain lucky in the English Channel and Korea. It's a damn thin line separating death from life. Really thin.

Earlier in 1961, Dick had celebrated his 39th birthday. The Santiagos had marked it with a lavish party and gifts, and Ann Sheridan had invited Dick to spend a weekend at her clifftop Malibu hideaway. 39. Middle age? On most days, Dick felt young, strong, in charge. In truth, he reflected wryly that morning in the hospital, the actuarial tables said he was nearly two thirds of the way along life's path.

Dick's vigil had begun at 2 a.m. Harriet had preceded him. Late Sunday night, scant hours after his abdomen had been stitched closed, Edward had awakened once briefly. Harriet had spoken to him, but he had been too weak to answer or even smile. Now he stirred again. Quickly Dick straightened and edged forward on the squeaky vinyl. His eyes watered as his dulled senses snapped alive. He watched anxiously as Edward's eyes opened, blinked and tentatively scanned the room's ceiling.

"Dad?" Dick gulped. A cold chill ran down his spine.

Edward's head rolled slowly toward Dick and a smile flickered weakly. His eyes closed and reopened. His tongue pushed at his cheeks and lips. Edward whispered something.

Dick vaulted from the chair. "What, Dad? What?" His hands grasped the bed's side rail as he leaned close to Edward.

"Dry...dry." The words barely escaped Edward's parched mouth.

"Hold on, Dad. I don't know if I can give you water yet. I'll get a nurse. I'll be right back." Dick bolted from the room into the corridor. He looked both ways, saw no one, then went running to the nurse's station. Moments later, Dick stood by while a nurse raised Edward's head and maneuvered a water glass to his dust-dry lips.

"Better," murmured Edward.

"Good," smiled Dick, "that's good." Dick breathed deeply.

Edward lay quiet for a long moment. "What's the word?"

"Huh?"

"What's the doctor say?"

Dick blushed. "Dad, I...You should rest now. The doctor will be by later this morning."

Edward closed his eyes and slowly shook his head on the pillow. "Tell me."

"Dad, I...it's-"

"No bull, Dick. Tell me now."

Dick sucked in a breath. Seldom had words come so hard. "They took out part of your bladder."

"So it was cancer."

Dick nodded.

Edward grunted as he shifted slightly. "Did they take anything else out?"

Dick lowered his eyes and shook his head.

"Did they get it all?" said Edward.

"They think so. They couldn't see anything else."

Edward winced.

Dick leaned forward in alarm. "Dad, I told you to take it easy. Just be still."

Edward smiled weakly. "Only time will tell."

"Tell what?"

"About the cancer. Isn't that what the doctor said about it?"

Dick averted his eyes and nodded.

"If nothing else," said Edward, "I've bought some time. Too bad it didn't come a little cheaper."

Dick looked at his father in surprise. Edward was smiling wryly. "Never lose your sense of humor, Dick. It doesn't cost much to keep, and it might be your most valuable asset. How's that for accountant's lingo? Not bad for an old geezer, huh?"

"Not bad at all," Dick winked. "And I expect to hear lots more of that lingo from you."

"Time will tell."

Doctor Clarkson greeted Roger and Helen with a tight smile and a tentative handshake. "Good morning. Come in." His taut face and voice belied his greeting. He backed away and shifted his feet uncertainly. Roger sensed that something was amiss. The doctor, previously the essence of self-assurance, appeared distressed. Roger and Helen both tensed.

"Please sit down," said the doctor, motioning toward the only two visitors chairs in his cramped office. He eased into his swivel chair, opened Roger's file and appeared to study it intently. His right thumb and forefinger cradled his chin. The room was so quiet that a sharply drawn breath would have sounded like a gale force wind. It became painfully obvious that Doctor Clarkson's eyes were blind to the file's contents. Rather, his mind was searching for words.

Roger decided to break the ice. "You've found the missing piece to the puzzle," he said, somehow managing to sound casual at a time when his anxiety was rising as fast as mercury heated by flame.

Doctor Clarkson nodded in reply. "Yes."

"Well?"

Doctor Clarkson rubbed his eyes. It was, Roger knew, a nervous gesture. Roger found the fingers of his own hands interlocking and flexing. "I – It looks like multiple sclerosis."

Multiple sclerosis is insidious. Typically it strikes young adults between the ages of 20 and 40. It's a chronic, progressive disease in which myelin, the fatty sheath that surrounds nerve fibers, is destroyed and replaced by scar tissue. The nerve damage disrupts the flow of signals from the brain through the spinal cord and leads to a gradual degeneration of various body functions.

MS is difficult to detect. It may escape diagnosis for years. One reason is the frequently transient nature of the early symptoms. They come and go, sometimes barely noticed. The attacks may recur with increasing severity, but lapses of two to three years may separate them. Another reason is the symptoms themselves. Often they are as numerous and as seemingly unrelated as raindrops and rainbows. A partial list includes blurred or double vision, involuntary rapid eyeball movement, impaired coordination, dizziness, extreme fatigue, stiffness, weakness, speech impairment, false "euphoria," shortened attention span and muscle spasms. Symptoms may occur in isolation or in nearly any conceivable combination. In its later stages and in its most virulent form, MS may lead to loss of bladder control and speaking ability as well as mental deterioration.

Whatever its cause, there is no cure. Physicians try merely to subdue the symptoms. Among the more common treatments are anti-coagulants, blood vessel dilating drugs, vitamins and anti-muscle-spasm drugs. As with other autoimmune diseases, MS sometimes is fatal.

"Are you sure?" said Roger. He knew it was a foolish question. No doctor would announce the presence of a dread disease without being certain of his diagnosis.

"Yes. The myelogram…I'm sorry." Doctor Clarkson's right hand toyed nervously with the top button of his white physician's frock.

Roger, lips pressed together, blew out a short breath through his nose. His head dropped. Then he raised his eyes and looked toward Helen. Her face was glassy, as though she had been in a different room and had heard nothing. Then she shook her head slowly, silently. Roger reached out and took her hand, as much for his own comfort as hers. A look of crushing defeat momentarily clouded her eyes, then she forced a small smile and squeezed Roger's thumb.

Roger looked at Doctor Clarkson. "What's this mean to me?" His voice was flat, devoid of any discernible emotion. The verdict had been rendered and he was calmly asking his sentence.

"I don't know. I can't say for sure. You've probably had it for three years or more. It hasn't, uh, impaired your ability to function."

"Will it?"

"I can't be sure. MS comes in several forms. Four types, actually. Type one is very mild. The patient – and the doctor – may not suspect it and may not diagnose it. Type two is more severe, but the patient remains ambulatory." Doctor Clarkson was speaking clinically now, and he seemed to take refuge in the medical recitation. His voice strengthened. "Type three may immobilize the patient, at least intermittently."

"A wheelchair?" said Roger.

"Yes. Or crutches or a walker."

Roger again pursed his lips and blew out a short breath of resignation. "Does it get any worse?"

"It can. With type four the patient is bedridden."

Roger's upper teeth bared, pressed against the outside of his lower lip and slowly retracted. "What type do I have?"

"I don't know. I can't determine that. MS is progressive. The symptoms may never get any worse than they are now. I have one patient in his late fifties who has had it for years and still holds down a job in a steel mill. But you'll just have to wait and see. And there may be remissions, long ones. We just don't know much about it. I am sorry."

Roger and Helen trudged from the Clinic to the parking lot. It was a long cold trek. They held hands but didn't speak. At their car, Roger unlocked the door on the passenger's side and opened it for Helen. Mechanically she reached across and unlocked the other door. Roger walked around the car and got in. He inserted the key in the ignition but didn't turn it. "I didn't ask the doctor, but I guess it's okay for me to drive."

Unnoticed by Roger, who was staring glassy-eyed through the windshield, Helen's chin began to quiver. "You know," said Roger, "it's funny. All of a sudden my body seems foreign. I thought I knew it, but now it seems like a stranger, keeping secrets from me." It was a quiet soliloquy, but it shattered the silence as sharply as a solitary thunderclap on a still night. Helen dissolved in tears. She buried her face in her hands. Roger sighed and swallowed, then slid across the seat and draped his arm across her shoulders. She raised her head and pressed her face to Roger's chest.

"I don't know what to say," she sobbed miserably. "It's so unexpected. So sad. Oh, my God. I love you. I'll do everything I can to help. I promise. I promise."

Her outpouring touched Roger deeply. His throat constricted. He inhaled deeply and held his breath until his throat relaxed. "I know you will," he murmured huskily. "I love you too. Maybe it won't be so bad. Like the doctor said, I've already had it a long time, and it hasn't slowed me down. And I'll do what he said. I'll keep exercising to keep my muscles strong." He stroked Helen's hair for a few minutes while her sobbing subsided.

"Do you think we should tell anyone?" she asked softly.

"I don't know. I'll have to think about that. All this will take time to sink in. To sort out. It's too much to absorb so fast." Several moments passed. "Feel better?"

Helen sniffed and nodded. She faced Roger and they kissed tenderly. His left hand brushed her golden hair away from her damp face. Her eyes glistened with affection.

Roger smiled. "Let's go home."

CHAPTER 24

"Whew! My ears finally stopped popping."

"We should've brought some gum," said Dick. "I'll ask a stewardess for some before we start to land."

"It doesn't take long to reach the desert, does it?" said Kate. "When you live near the ocean, the only sand you think about is on the beach. It looks so empty down there, so beige and brown."

"Yes, but a few hours from now you'll see as much green as you've ever seen. The only sand there is in sandboxes and cement mixers."

"Geez, I'm excited, Dick. I can hardly wait to meet your family. To see Shelby. To see OU."

"Well, you know I think my family is special. And the brochures make OU look special. But as for Shelby, I've told you it's just a typical quiet small town."

"Aw, come on, Dick. Admit it. Shelby's special. At least to you."

"Okay, to me."

"Then it's special to me too."

"Okay, you win, Kate."

"I usually do." A momentary silence. "Dick?"

"Yes."

"I really *am* glad you suggested this trip. I mean, Mom or Dad will come with me in September when school starts. Maybe both of them. But I'm really glad to have a chance to see OU now. They wouldn't have let me come alone. Thank you."

Dick Lawrence faced his young friend, the second youngest of his four adopted "nieces." He smiled affectionately. "You are most welcome. But remember, I'm getting something out of this too. It's been over six months since I've seen my dad. He says he's doing fine, but that's exactly what I'd expect him to say. I want to see for myself."

"I'm sure he's fine."

"You know, Kate, it's funny. I do have a warm spot for Shelby. A lot of me is there. But California is my home. I've lived there for 17 years. Almost half my life. If it weren't for my dad, I doubt if I'd visit as often."

"What about Harriet and Ben and Susie?"

"They mean a lot to me. But it's not the same. I just doubt if I'd come back every year."

The nonstop flight was due to arrive in Cleveland at 4 p.m., Eastern time.

"I can hardly believe I'm out of high school," said Kate. "It went so fast. I'll miss my friends. And my family."

"Second thoughts?"

"About coming to OU?" Dick nodded. "No. None. I really do feel a need to see different places, experience different things. But that doesn't mean I won't feel homesick. At least sometimes. I'm sure I will."

As the plane began descending into Cleveland Hopkins Airport, Kate pressed her forehead to the window and gazed down. Below, as the plane made its last sweeping turn, Lake Erie was lapping at the shoreline in downtown Cleveland. Then she turned toward Dick and grinned excitedly.

The plane touched down smoothly and taxied to the gate. When they stepped inside the terminal, Edward, Harriet and Susie hailed them and waved. Dick took Kate by the arm and guided her to his family.

"Dad, Harriet, this is-"

"We *know* who this is," Edward said, winking. He took Kate's hand, then pulled her toward him and hugged her. He released her and Harriet hugged her and kissed her cheek.

Kate was touched. "I'm so happy to be here," she gushed.

"We're happy to have you here, dear," beamed Harriet. "Kate, this is Susie." The two girls exchanged warm smiles and clasped hands.

Dick and Edward sized each other up like a pair of jewelers scrutinizing polished stones. "You *do* look good," allowed Dick.

"You thought I was bulling you?" Edward stepped forward and the two men embraced. "Good to see you, Dick, damn good."

"Great to be here."

Dick then hugged Harriet and squeezed Susie about the shoulders and pecked her cheek. Then the group began strolling toward the baggage claim area.

"Where's Ben?" said Dick.

"Baseball," replied Edward. "He had an American Legion game this afternoon. I didn't want to force him to come since he'll be seeing you this evening."

"How's he doing?"

"Just fine. Had a good high school baseball season this spring, and he's doing well in Legion ball."

"School?"

"Near the top of his class. But enough about Ben. We want to hear about you and your family, Kate."

"Yes," chimed in Harriet, "we've heard about all of you for so long, it hardly seems possible that we're finally getting to meet one of you."

Shelby is about 90 miles southwest of Cleveland. The interstate highway system was far from completed, so the route to Shelby passed through numerous small towns.

Continuous conversation filled Edward's car as it cruised past white farmhouses, barns with red or white vertical siding, fields of swelling corn, golden wheat and green soybean plants, and herds of grazing Holstein dairy cows.

"What are your plans, Dick?" said Edward.

"We'll visit with you folks tonight and tomorrow. Monday morning we'll drive down to Athens. We figure Kate can spend Tuesday and Wednesday visiting the campus and meeting some OU staff. Then on Thursday morning we'll start back to Shelby. We fly back to LA on Saturday."

"It sounds like a full week with a lot of driving," said Edward. "I want you to use our car."

"Thanks, Dad, but I'll rent one."

"Hogwash. If you can't get along without a car for a few days in Shelby, then you're in sad shape."

"Nevertheless," said Dick, "I don't want you walking to work."

"No problem. I can get a ride with a friend. Who knows? I might even feel like walking. It's barely a mile from Second Street to the office. The weather's beautiful. Walking would do me good."

"Uh huh," Dick said dubiously. "And what about Harriet?"

"Oh, I've stocked up on groceries. I won't need the car, Dick. Really."

"I think I smell a well-orchestrated plot," Dick smiled. "What about Ben?"

"He's not too old to use his feet or his bike," Edward grumbled. "Although sometimes he acts like walking a mile is the supreme sacrifice. Crazy, isn't it? He wants to drive to the football field when he's going to run laps or run up and down the bleachers. Or to the ball field when he's going to play a doubleheader."

"Sounds pretty normal to me," said Dick.

"No matter," Edward said crisply, "he'll survive this week without the car."

When Edward's car pulled to a stop in front of the Lawrence house, Ben was lounging on the porch's top step nursing a Coke. His richly tanned body contrasted sharply with his white t-shirt, white denim cut-off shorts and white sneakers sans socks. He watched passively as the car doors opened. Then with a loose, unhurried, athletic grace, he stood and descended the steps.

The two half-brothers grinned broadly as they approached each other and shook hands. Dick mussed Ben's brown hair, which was unusually long at a time when many teenage boys sported crewcuts.

"How ya doin', little brother?" Dick smiled.

"Just fine, big brother."

"You win or lose today? And you'd better say win. I was deeply hurt that you didn't meet me at the airport."

"Oh, oh, I'd better get the first aid kit," said Ben.

"Make sure it's got lots of bandages."

"It *was* a close game. Four to three. We were behind from the start and couldn't catch up. Forgive me? Please?" Ben made a specious supplicant.

"If you're willing to do penance," said Dick.

"Such as?"

"Meet a friend of mine." Dick turned aside and Kate stepped forward. She had enjoyed the repartee between the half-brothers and was smiling widely.

"Hi, Ben." Her right hand thrust forward.

"Hi." Ben took her hand and shook it gently. Kate wore a simple lightweight pastel yellow dress and white pumps. Despite the long flight and the two-hour car ride, she looked fresh and fetching. In the sliver of time during which Ben's eyes rose and fell, he saw a breathtaking body topped by a dazzling face.

"It's really nice to meet you," she said.

"Same here."

"Dick's told me a lot about you."

Ben blushed and glanced toward Dick.

"All favorable, little brother. Or most of it anyway. You don't want to be thought of as Saint Ben."

Ben blushed anew and everyone else laughed.

"Come on," said Harriet. "Let's go inside and get something to eat and drink."

That Saturday evening in the Lawrence home was unusual for early 1960s America. The television remained mute. *Gunsmoke* and *Jackie Gleason* lost out to sprightly conversation that continued to near midnight. Only when Dick's jaws parted in a gaping yawn did the chatter begin to subside. Harriet proposed sleeping arrangements. Kate would share Susie's double bed. Dick opted for the living room couch over half of Ben's double bed.

The next morning Kate joined the Lawrences, save for Dick, in attending Mass. Home alone, Dick contentedly sipped coffee and read *The Cleveland Plain Dealer*. Once, when pouring more coffee, his thoughts turned to Helen Hoerner. More than a decade had passed since he had seen her. He smiled at her memory, thought briefly of calling her, then dismissed the notion. It would, he knew, serve no constructive purpose other than to satisfy his curiosity. She did not need to hear a curious, intrusive voice. Better to ask Edward or Ben about her.

That afternoon Kate and the Lawrences watched Shelby's O'Brien Post play Mansfield's McVey Post in an American Legion baseball game. The two teams played artful baseball although, at bat, Ben was swinging like a painter who had forgotten his brush. In his first three times at bat Ben popped out once and grounded out twice. Through eight innings both teams played errorless baseball as they scrapped to a 2-2 tie. In the bottom half of the ninth inning when Ben came to bat, the bases were loaded and two were out. The first pitch was a rising fastball. Ben swung and slightly undercut the ball, which skipped off the top of his bat back to the screen. The second pitch was a changeup. Ben was fooled and swung too early. He expected the next pitch to be a fastball, and it was. Ben swung and connected solidly. The ball shot off his bat on a low trajectory. Mansfield's center fielder took two steps back, then stopped and watched helplessly as the ball soared past him and over the fence in right center field.

Ben's teammates leaped from the bench with joy. The spectators, except for the handful from Mansfield, cheered lustily. As Ben touched third base, he heard one voice cheering louder than all the rest. The voice was unfamiliar. Ben looked around. It took him a moment to locate the source of the high-pitched screams. When he did, he smiled. Raven-haired Kate Santiago, dressed in a white cotton top, light blue shorts and white sneakers, was alternately clapping her hands and waving her fists. When Ben's eyes focused on hers, she threw her fists above her head and leaped into the air.

That evening in the Lawrences' back yard Edward grilled hamburgers. Harriet made potato salad. She and Susie, Ben and Kate drank Cokes. Edward and Dick slaked their thirst with Pfeiffer's beer. The mellow evening air, pungent with the aroma of fresh meat sizzling over a charcoal fire, proved a perfect elixir. Cares went floating skyward with the deliciously scented smoke.

As dusk began nudging aside the sun and shading the sky, Kate stood and stretched. "Ben had plenty of exercise today, but the rest of us sure didn't. Anybody for a walk?"

"Walk?" screeched Susie as though someone had ordered her to tread barefoot over a bed of nails. The group laughed.

"I think it'll take all my strength to make it from this lawn chair into the house," groaned Dick. "Jet lag is doing me in."

"I'll pass too," said Edward. "Sorry, Kate."

Harriet remained silent, but her somber face betrayed a certain lack of enthusiasm.

"I'll go," said Ben as he eased himself up from a chaise lounge.

"You?" said Edward incredulously. "When's the last time you willingly walked anywhere?"

"I didn't hear any other volunteers," Ben said dryly.

"There's hope for you yet," grinned Edward.

"You said that, not me."

"Come on, Ben, before you change your mind," said Kate.

"Which wouldn't take much," Edward kidded.

Kate and Ben went strolling leisurely down a street lined on both sides by thickly trunked, aged maple trees.

"The street lights will be coming on soon," said Ben. Absently he reached up and plucked a leaf from a low-hanging limb. He twirled its stem between his thumb and forefinger.

"Do you and your dad always tease each other?"

"Only when we're not arguing."

"You're teasing me now."

"Yeah, I suppose. But sometimes we do get into some dandy arguments. Drives Mom crazy. She can't stand it."

"I don't blame her."

"I guess I don't either. But the funny thing is, I think Dad and I both enjoy them. At least afterward. When they're over, they're over. No grudges. I think they help keep the air clear."

"What do you argue about?"

"Whatever's handy. Sports, politics, clothes, the car. You name it."

"You love your dad."

"Of course."

"He's neat."

"Yeah."

"Your whole family is," said Kate. "Don't ever take them for granted."

Ben looked thoughtfully at Kate. He found her eyes boring through his. He smiled. "Yes, ma'am."

Kate returned the smile. "Shelby's neat too. I knew it would be."

"Why?"

"Because of Dick. I just knew he'd come from a special place."

"Any special place you want to walk?"

"No. You?"

"Anybody drive you through Seltzer Park today?"

"No."

"Okay, then, let's head for Seltzer Park. I think you'll like it. A creek runs through it, and it's got two large ponds. One of the ponds has a little island. You cross over a white footbridge. And there's plenty of ducks and lots of trees. 'Course, by the time we get there, it may be too dark to see much."

"That's okay. It sounds nice. Let's go."

"It's sort of a long walk."

"That's all right. Remember, this was my idea."

"Do you think Shelby's as neat as California?"

"In many ways, yes. But the ocean is fantastic. Have you ever seen an ocean?"

"No."

"You should. The salt water, the surf, the beaches, the breeze, the cliffs, the blue sky. It's fantastic. It has a very special feel. You should come out to visit Dick."

"Someday maybe. He's offered to fly me out. All of us, for that matter. Someday I'll take him up."

"But you're happy here."

"Sure."

Seltzer Park matched Ben's description. He and Kate entered the park from Mansfield Avenue and began walking east along the bank of the creek. They stepped slowly and carefully as their eyes adjusted to the lowering light. Ben pointed to the much higher bank on the opposite side of the creek. "We call that the Indian Trail. Lots of kids play there."

"You?"

"When I was younger, yes. Davy Crockett, Daniel Boone. Want to sit for a minute?" said Ben.

"Okay."

They sat contentedly on grass beside the gurgling stream. They saw no one but in the distance heard a nocturnal chorus of laughter and shouting.

"Where are those voices coming from?" asked Kate.

"The municipal pool. It's in the park. If you look through the trees over there, you can see the lights. Want to walk up and take a look? The ponds and the pool are the closest we have to an ocean."

Kate laughed. "Let's go." They stood and resumed their stroll. "Have you thought about college, Ben?"

"Not much."

"Are you going?"

"Oh, sure. Dad wouldn't have it any other way. He's been talking to me about good grades and college for as long as I can remember. He wouldn't force me, but he'd be hurt if I didn't go."

"So?"

"So I'm hoping somebody offers me a ride."

"A ride?"

"A full ride. A scholarship."

"I heard your dad say you're near the top of your class."

"They don't give many full rides for straight A's."

"Football?"

"I hope. Without a scholarship it'll be touch and go."

"Money?"

"Dad doesn't have much. We could probably scrape by somehow, but a scholarship would make things a lot easier. He's had it rough enough without sacrificing more for me."

"Dick would help."

"I know. And he'd be glad to, but I don't think Dad would ask him. I know he doesn't want to. And he wouldn't want me to."

"Has he said so?"

"No, but I know Dad." Ben tossed a small twig into the water, but it was too dark to see it float away on the gentle current. "I think he asked Dick for help when he was in the hospital. I don't think he'll do it again. Pride."

It was just past 9:00 when they reached the pool. They stood with their fingers curled through the high, chain-link fence that surrounded the pool. Lifeguards were whistling the last swimmers from the water. As usual, they had to shoo some exuberant, mischievous youngsters into the bathhouse. Ben and Kate watched in amusement.

"I've never had to worry about money," Kate said quietly.

"I don't worry about it either," said Ben, smiling wryly. "It's just not always there. Come on."

They moved away from the fence and began to walk from the park. They had gone perhaps 20 yards when a voice called out, "Ben, Ben."

Ben, standing in the beam of a streetlight, peered into the gathering darkness but saw no one. "Who is it?"

"It's me," came the cheery reply. Into the light stepped Barbara Mason. She wore shorts, a t-shirt and sneakers. Her hair was wet and she carried a rolled-up towel.

"Oh, hi, Barb."

"Hi, Ben. How are you?"

"Fine. I want you to meet someone. Barb Mason, this is Kate Santiago." The girls exchanged greetings. "Kate's from California. She's a friend of my brother Dick. She's going to Ohio University in September, and she came out to look it over. She and Dick are spending a couple days with us before they drive down."

"That's nice," said Barb. "I hope you're enjoying your trip."

"Thanks, I am. Ben's family has been very kind."

"Have you ever been to Ohio before?"

"No, but I like it. It's very pretty."

"Have you always lived in California?"

"Yes."

"Sometime I'd like to visit there."

"That's terrific. I hope you get a chance to soon."

"How long are you going to be here?"

"Dick and I are leaving for Athens tomorrow morning. We'll be back later in the week for a day or so before we fly back to California."

"Do you like to fly?"

"Yes. It's neat."

"I've never flown. I envy you."

"Maybe you should go to school in California. Take care of both things at once."

Barb laughed cheerfully. "Not much chance of that. I plan to go to college in Columbus. But maybe I can get a job in California."

"I hope your plans work out."

"Thanks. Hey, I better let you two go. It's getting late."

"It was nice meeting you, Barb."

"Same here, Kate. I hope you like OU."

"See you around, Barb," said Ben.

"See you, Ben. Say hello to your family for me." Barbara stepped out of the circle of light and headed toward her home on nearby Roberts Drive.

Ben and Kate continued on their way back to the Lawrence house.

"She seems nice," said Kate.

"She is."

"Have you ever dated her?"

"Yes. Some."

"She's very pretty."

"Can't argue with that. She's a cheerleader like you."

"And you're a football player," Kate teased. "You two are probably destined for each other."

"That stuff only happens on bad TV shows."

"What kind of football team will you have this fall?"

"Pretty good."

"Pretty good? Don't be modest."

"Okay. Actually, we should be very good."

"Tell you what," said Kate. "If you're really good, I'll try to come up from OU to watch your big game."

"All right. That'll probably be Bellevue."

Kate and Dick both enjoyed the drive to Athens. The high hills of southeastern Ohio served as forested green backdrops to the picturesque hamlets that dozed serenely along winding Route 13. In Athens Kate fell in love with the campus. Stately three-story red-brick Cutler Hall, built in 1816, set the tone for much of the rest of the architecture. Georgian buildings sprouted everywhere on the vast, hilly grounds. Majestic oaks and maples gracefully spread long, leafy limbs to shade buildings, walks and lawns. The Hocking River meandered lazily through the campus. Now, in the summer, in some spots Kate could see the river's muddy bottom. It was hard to imagine this innocently gurgling stream as a raging torrent, spilling over its 17-foot banks – as it did nearly every spring, flooding roads and basements, forcing the evacuation of students from some dormitories and canceling classes.

Kate visited dormitories and settled on Jefferson Hall, a block-long three- and four-story Georgian structure with its own cafeteria and library. It sat at the base of a steep incline popularly known as Jeff Hill. The street that rose to its summit was so steep that, from the top, the bottom couldn't be seen until a person peered down from its crest.

Everywhere they went, Dick took photos. Snap: Kate on the brick walk in front of Cutler Hall. Snap: Kate on the steps in front of Jefferson Hall. Snap: Kate on the footbridge over the Hocking. Snap, snap, snap: high hills, protective trees, scampering squirrels.

When he and Kate returned to California, the Santiago family excitedly gathered in the living room to see slide pictures of Ohio University, Athens, Shelby and the Lawrence family. Kate's sisters all oohed when a picture of handsome, husky Ben standing with Kate filled the screen in the darkened room. All agreed too on the beauty of the school Kate had chosen. She basked in the glow of family approval. After seeing the slides, Natalie was surer than ever that she would follow Kate to Ohio.

By mid-September the Ben Lawrence-led Shelby Whippets were racing through another schedule of bewildered opponents. For their opener the Whippets bussed about 90 miles to Lakewood, a western suburb of Cleveland. Shelby played Lakewood St. Edward and triumphed 22-6. Then came wins over Ashland (24-6), Tiffin Columbian (32-0), Norwalk (42-0), Galion (46-0) and Willard (52-0).

The afternoon before the Willard game, results of the homecoming queen balloting were announced. Janice Redhill would reign over the festivities a week later when Shelby would host the Upper Sandusky Rams on Friday night and at the dance on Saturday night. Janice and three of the four members of her court already had dates for the dance. Barbara Mason didn't.

After the game at Willard, in the dank, dimly lighted visitors' locker room, Ben stepped from the shower, toweled off and tiredly shuffled to a worn, wooden bench in front of a beaten, paint-chipped gray locker. Pete Carson, his friend since childhood and favorite pass receiver, plopped down beside him. The two naked boys were an island of quiet in the tumultuous room where teammates laughed, shouted, teased and snapped towels at each other.

"You *are* going to the homecoming dance, aren't ya?" Pete said quietly, looking down at the floor.

"Yeah, I guess. You?"

"I'm takin' Nancy Werner."

"She's nice. Pretty too."

"Yeah. How about you?"

"I don't know."

"Gettin' kinda late."

"I know."

"Nobody's asked Barb Mason yet."

"So I've heard."

"You askin' her?"

"Don't know."

"Be damned embarrassing if nobody asks her."

"Yeah."

"People sort of expect you to ask her."

Ben slowly pivoted his head to face Pete. "What?" he asked, his left eye narrowing until it was nearly shut.

"You heard me."

"I don't understand. What people?"

"Kids around school."

"Why me?"

"Well, you two've dated. You like each other."

Ben shook his head and muttered wearily. "I'm not the only one who's dated her."

"I know, but, well, this is special and-"

"Hold on," Ben interrupted. Intensity was creeping into his voice. "I don't owe Barb anything. Hell, I've dated Saundra Brunson more recently than Barb."

"I know. At one point I thought you two – I mean you and Barb – would go steady."

"At one point, I wanted to."

"And Barb?"

"Her, too."

"What happened?"

"Nothing. I just decided I wanted to date other girls, too. No big deal."

Pete twisted on the bench and flipped his towel onto a pile in the middle of the floor. "There aren't many guys left."

"Huh?"

"Most of the guys in the senior class already have dates for homecoming, at least most of the guys who would even dream of asking Barb."

"Not my problem," Ben muttered. He twisted and flung his towel onto the pile. "Nobody's asked Saundra yet either."

"She's not on the homecoming court. Barb is."

"But she's not the queen."

"She still needs a date," said Pete. "Did you vote for her?"

Ben looked away from Pete toward the floor. Small puddles glistened on the gray concrete surface. Ben's jaws clenched. "It was a secret ballot."

Pete sighed. "Yeah, right."

The two boys stood and dressed slowly. They were last out of the dressing room and onto the yellow bus. They sat together in silence at the rear while teammates celebrated noisily during the 30-minute ride through the countryside back to Shelby.

The next morning Ben awoke about 9:00. The house was quiet. He walked to the living room window. Edward was in the front yard raking leaves. Ben ran his hands through his disheveled hair, scratched his scalp, stretched and groaned. His body was suffering the usual assortment of aches that followed the pounding he absorbed each Friday night. They would disappear by Monday morning. He assumed, correctly, that Harriet and Susie had gone grocery shopping. Ben watched his father for a minute, then turned away and walked to the kitchen. He stared at the black telephone on the counter, lifted the receiver, paused, reflected and dialed.

"Hello?" said a young female voice.

At school the following Monday morning after first-period classes, Pete Carson saw Ben ahead in the corridor. He caught up to him as Ben neared his locker. "Is it true?"

"What?"

"That you asked Saundra."

"Yeah."

"Shit."

"Hey, leave it alone," Ben muttered. "What's it to you? You've got a date."

"Aw, man, that's…Saundra's not even a senior."

"You got something against dating juniors?"

"No, no I don't. But still, why Saundra?"

"Because, damn it, I wanted to."

"Yeah, but why?"

"Because," Ben whispered coldly, "Saundra's more fun."

Pete scrutinized his friend's face. "You know, sometimes you're not easy to like."

During lunch hour that day Pete and four other members of the football team huddled outside school and hastily organized a Get-A-Date task force on behalf of, and unbeknownst to, Barbara. By the time afternoon classes commenced, they had settled on a list of targets. To their satisfaction and relief, their first candidate, a thoroughly likable senior, Terry Wilman, agreed to ask Barbara to the dance. He did so after last period, and Barbara accepted graciously.

Friday night before a large festive crowd and a radiant Janice Redhill and her four-girl court, Shelby thumped Upper Sandusky 34-0. Ben played superbly. The next night at the homecoming dance Ben and Saundra left early. Her parents had gone out to dinner at the Shelby Country Club and would be home late. In the darkened living room of the Brunson home Ben and Saundra made out on the couch.

At Ohio University, when Kate saw in Sunday's paper that Shelby had raised its record to 7-0, she phoned the Lawrences who were delighted by Kate's plan to attend Friday's big game with the undefeated Bellevue Redmen. Friday at noon Kate would board a bus to Mansfield, where

Harriet and Susie would pick her up. She would attend the game with the Lawrences and spend the weekend with them before bussing back to Athens late Sunday afternoon.

On Friday, more than three hours before the 8 p.m. kickoff, a crowd that would swell to more than 8,000 began to trickle into Skiles Field.

At 2:30 the Whippets gathered for a final skull session. At 3:30 they walked two blocks to The Coffee Shop on Main Street for a pre-game meal, courtesy of the restaurant. Most of the players and coaches chose roast beef. The rest, including the Catholics, selected Lake Erie perch.

At 5:00 back in the locker room, assistant coaches, Roger Hoerner among them, began to tape players' ankles. Student managers distributed game uniforms to the players who inserted their knee and thigh pads into the inside pants pockets.

Afterward the players, still in street clothes, walked in stockinged feet to the gym, where they scattered on large, thick mats that had been spread on the highly polished hardwood floor. Some lay down and catnapped. Others lounged and engaged in whispered conversations. There was no tomfoolery. There was plenty of mounting anxiety. Several players made repeated trips to the urinals and johns.

Once on the field, neither team was sharp in its drills. Both were tight and tentative. At 7:25 they trotted off the lush green turf and returned to their locker rooms. At 7:50 they re-entered the stadium. As the Shelby players and coaches gathered in a knot at the northeast entrance, the crowd noise came crashing down on them like a roaring avalanche. Ben was standing next to assistant coach Roger Hoerner. Roger tapped Ben on the shoulder and spoke.

"What?" Ben hollered through the din.

"This," shouted Roger, "should be a night to remember."

In the stands Kate stood with the Lawrences and thousands of others to greet the team. Among those cheering were Saundra Brunson and Joyce Worthen. Barbara Mason and the other cheerleaders stood, leaped and waved red and gray pompoms.

Shelby received the opening kickoff and moved well. Ben directed the team to two first downs. Then the drive bogged down and Shelby punted. Throughout the first quarter Shelby completely throttled Bellevue's vaunted offense.

Early in the second quarter Bellevue had the ball near midfield. Bellevue's quarterback pitched the ball back to a fleet halfback who bobbled the ball as he swept wide. Shelby defenders pursued perfectly and forced the ball carrier wider than intended. About two steps from the sideline he suddenly cut back against the grain of the pursuing defenders. Along the sideline Ben sensed impending disaster. On the field, Bellevue players, with unexpectedly opportune blocking angles, began to chop Shelby defenders to the ground. In another moment the ball carrier broke into the clear. Seconds later he scored untouched.

Shelby players, coaches and fans were stunned. Bellevue players and fans were jubilant. A broken play had resulted in six serendipitous points. Bellevue attempted and made a two-point conversion and led 8 -0.

In the Shelby locker room calm prevailed. There were no zealous exhortations from the coaching staff, merely some quiet instruction.

Throughout the third quarter and well into the fourth Ben repeatedly led the Shelby offense into Bellevue territory. But each time, Bellevue's defense stiffened and Shelby remained scoreless. With precisely three minutes left to play in the game, Ben led the offense onto the field once more. The ball was on Shelby's 33-yard line.

In the stands on both sides, hoarse fans, their emotional reservoirs nearly drained, summoned up another burst of enthusiasm and simultaneously exhorted Shelby's offense and Bellevue's defense.

On the field amidst the din, Ben thought he heard Kate's screaming voice. It wasn't the first time that a singular voice had somehow funneled itself through the deafening crowd noise and reached his ears on the field. In the huddle Ben eyed his teammates. "All right," he snapped, "we've pissed around long enough. Let's get some points on the board."

On first down Ben hurled a sideline pass to Pete Carson for a 15-yard gain to the 48. Quickly, he hit Pete again, this time over the middle for 18 yards to the Bellevue 34. On the next down Ben called a draw play. He retreated as if to pass but handed off to fullback Zach Clements, who bulled for 18 yards to the Bellevue 16.

Shelby fans were standing and roaring. Bellevue fans were sitting, nervously. Between each play the Shelby band played a few bars of the school fight song.

On the scoreboard clock, one minute and 46 seconds remained when Shelby again lined up. Ben took the snap from center, faded back and found Pete a step ahead of his defender in the middle of the field at the 10-yard line. Ben threw. Pete caught the ball at the five, was hit by the trailing defender at the three but stumbled into the end zone.

8-6.

Shelby fans went berserk. Bellevue fans went ashen.

Shelby would have to try a two-point conversion for a tie and a share of the Northern Ohio League championship. Two-point conversion attempts were low-percentage plays. During the first seven games of the 1962 season, Shelby, without a reliable place kicker, had tried a two-point conversion after every one of its 36 touchdowns. The potent Shelby offense had succeeded on only 18 attempts.

Ben wanted choices. He called a sprint-out option. He could choose between running himself, pitching out to a trailing halfback or passing into the end zone to Pete. At the line of scrimmage, Ben surveyed the edgy Bellevue defense. In the stands, now eerily quiet, everyone could hear Ben barking signals. He took the snap and sprinted to his right. High in the stadium Kate's clenched fists were tucked beneath her chin. Saundra bit her lower lip. Joyce Worthen's stomach knotted. Susie Lawrence covered her eyes. Harriet uttered a quick prayer. Edward gritted his teeth and pursed his lips. Along the sideline Barbara stood with hands at her sides and held her breath. Running right, Ben raised his arm to pass but saw an opening, straightened his shoulders so they were parallel with the goal line and drove forward. In the end zone a striped shirt official threw his hands skyward. A Shelby lineman saw the official and leaped ecstatically into the air. A deafening roar exploded from Shelby fans. Just as suddenly it died. A yard from the goal line a teammate's errant foot had protruded suddenly in Ben's path. In the next sliver of time, he tripped, faltered, righted himself and, still untouched by a defender, stumbled into the end zone. A second official had seen Ben's left knee brush the grass before he crossed the goal line and quickly and decisively signaled the play unsuccessful.

Bellevue players and fans let loose with a wild celebration.

Ben picked himself up, stood still a moment and then went stalking from the field. His despondent teammates trudged with him to the sideline.

Roger approached Ben, wrapped an arm around his shoulder, squeezed and walked away.

With one minute and 37 seconds to play Shelby lined up to kick off. Ben stood staring grim-faced into the banks of lights high above the field. Several of his teammates were choking back tears. In the stands, Edward felt flushed and weak. He agonized for his son. Harriet's heart ached. Kate, herself a fierce competitor, empathized with Ben.

Shelby tried an onside kick. It failed. Bellevue covered the ball on its 43-yard line. Shelby still had its three timeouts. Three times Bellevue called running plays. Shelby stopped all three cold and called time out after each.

Bellevue lined up to punt with 71 seconds to play. Bellevue's punter, feeling late-game pressure, shanked his kick that sailed out of bounds on the Shelby 33-yard line.

Shelby's offensive unit raced onto the field. "Listen up," Ben commanded. "The defense gave us one last shot. Now let's do it." In the huddle, to conserve time, Ben called two plays, both sideline passes. He completed both, the first to wingback Ray Burns, the second to Pete Carson. On both plays Ray and Pete stepped out of bounds, stopping the clock.

Ball on Bellevue's 45-yard line. 53 seconds to go.

In the huddle, Ben again called two plays, a crossing pattern and, if successful, another quick sideline pass to stop the clock. The first pass over the middle to Pete was deflected by a defender and fell incomplete. 47 seconds to go.

"Let's try the same sequence," Ben said in the huddle. "A crossing pattern and then a down and out."

For all practical purposes Shelby needed to score a touchdown to win. The Whippets simply did not have a reliable place kicker.

At the line of scrimmage Ben took the snap and dropped back quickly. Pete broke open at the 25-yard line. Ben fired. Pete's sure hands caught the ball and hung on as he was tackled hard.

39 seconds to go and the clock was running. The Whippets ran to the scrimmage line. 38 seconds. 37, 36. Bellevue players shuffled slowly to their side of the line. 35, 34, 33.

In the stands tense fans found one last reserve of vocal power and screamed what was left of their voices. "Go!" screamed Kate's raspy voice. "Go! Go! Go! Come on, Ben!"

32 seconds, 31. Ben took the snap and faded back. 30, 29, 28. His offensive line shielded him flawlessly from Bellevue's frantically rushing defensive linemen and a blitzing linebacker. Ray Burns broke to the sideline. 27 seconds, 26. Ben's pass was wide and sailed out of bounds.

"We've got to stick with sideline routes," Ben said in the huddle. "They know it, but that's our only choice." He glanced up at the clock. At the line Ben took the snap, and again the seconds began to flash away on the digital scoreboard clock. 25 seconds, 24, 23. Pete grabbed Ben's pass, but a smartly positioned Bellevue defender tackled Pete before he could get out of bounds at the 14-yard line. 22 seconds, 21, 20, 19, 18. Again, the Whippets scrambled to the scrimmage line and formed up. 17 seconds, 16, 15, 14. Again the wait while Bellevue players slowly crossed back to their side. 13 seconds, 12.

Ben crouched behind the center and screamed the play to his teammates. "304X. Black 20 on 2." A crossing pattern. 11 seconds, 10, 9, 8. Ben shouted signals. "Five four," 7 seconds, "ready set," 6 seconds, "git one, git two." 5 seconds. He took the snap and dropped back. 4 seconds, 3, 2. Patiently he watched Ray and Pete flash past each other in the end zone in front of the goal post. He fired. 1 second, then the clock read 00:00. The stadium hushed. The ball was high. Pete leaped. The ball sailed into his cushiony hands. Simultaneously, a Bellevue defender hammered Pete. Ben watched helplessly as the ball wriggled free from Pete's clutching fingers and tumbled down the back of the defender to the ground. Hands by his sides, Ben clenched his fists, squeezed shut his eyes, dropped his chin to his chest and muttered a barely audible "Shit."

After showering, Ben toweled off and trudged dispiritedly toward his locker. Sitting dejectedly on the bench was Pete, elbows on his knees, face buried in his hands. Ben sat beside his friend. "You look as rotten as I feel," Ben said tiredly.

"My fault," murmured Pete miserably. "All my fault."

Ben inhaled deeply and draped his arm around Pete's naked shoulders. "That's crap," he whispered sympathetically. "You played a great game."

"I should have had that last pass. It was in my hands. Damn, I blew it."

"Don't be silly. Christ, nobody could've held that one. Nobody."

"I really wanted to win that one, Ben. To win the NOL in our senior year. To go undefeated. I dreamed about it."

"Me too. But we played a great game against a great team."

"We're a better team. You and I both know that. One lousy busted play beat us. I'll bet we had twice their yardage, twice as many first downs."

"Probably. It *is* tough to swallow. Take a while to get over it. But you know, we did have three terrific seasons. One championship and two seconds ain't bad. And there's one other thing."

"What's that?"

"We won't have to be ashamed to look in the mirror. We gave it our best, all of us."

They were alone now in the locker room. Slowly, they dressed. Pete finished first.

"I'll give you a ride home," Pete offered.

"Thanks, but I feel like walking."

"Sure?"

"Yeah. See ya Sunday to look at film."

When Ben stepped outside the locker room, more than an hour had passed since the game had ended. He zipped his red and gray varsity letter jacket against the night chill. All was quiet. He looked toward the empty, darkened stadium, sighed and jammed his hands into his jacket pockets. He had walked only a few steps when he heard his name.

"Ben?"

"Who is it?"

"It's me." Saundra Brunson stepped from the shadows of the school.

"What are you doing here?"

"I've been waiting. I thought you might want a ride home."

Ben smiled thinly. "Thanks. Pete just made the same offer. I really feel like walking."

"Oh, I see." Saundra lowered her head and started to turn.

The hurt in her voice was plain. "Wait, wait. Okay, you can drive me home."

She brightened. "Good. My car's over in the student parking lot." She took Ben's arm and they strolled toward the car. "I'm sorry, Ben. I mean, you deserved to win. If only Pete hadn't dropped that pass."

"He didn't drop it," Ben said evenly. "My pass was too high."

Saundra unlocked the door on the passenger's side. Ben got in, reached across and unlocked the other door. Saundra got in and inserted the key in the ignition. She hesitated, then slid across the seat. Ben faced her and she pressed her lips to his. She kissed ardently. Ben was slow to respond.

"Do you want to go right home?" Saundra asked.

"I should. We have company."

"Who?"

"A friend of the family. From out of town."

She wriggled closer and kissed him again. "Can't they wait a little longer? Please?"

A few minutes later in the Lawrences' kitchen the phone rang.

"I'll get it," said Harriet. She left Edward, Susie and Kate in the living room. Harriet picked up the receiver. "The Lawrences."

"Hello, Mrs. Lawrence. Is Ben there?"

"He's not home yet. Who's this?"

"Barb Mason."

"Oh, Barb, dear. How are you?"

"Fine, Mrs. Lawrence. Just fine."

"That's good. Can I take a message?"

"Oh, I just wanted to tell Ben how sorry I am about the game. That…I thought he played a great game. That's all."

"That's very sweet of you. I'll tell Ben you called and tell him that."

"Thank you, Mrs. Lawrence."

"You're welcome, Barb."

"Good night."

"Good night."

Back in the living room Harriet told the others about the phone call.

"I met Barb when I was in Shelby during the summer," said Kate. "She seemed like a really nice girl."

"She is," said Edward.

"She's super neat," gushed Susie. "She's the best cheerleader we have. I wish Ben would've taken her to the homecoming dance. He should've," she said petulantly.

"Now, Susie," admonished Harriet.

"Well…" she muttered defensively. "I wonder what's taking him so long to get home."

"It was a tough loss," said Edward. "He probably isn't in a hurry to see anyone. Give him time."

CHAPTER 25

It was midmorning on an early April Saturday in 1963. The sun had yet to warm the wide beach at Santa Monica. Two people, the only signs of humanity on an otherwise deserted stretch of sand, were walking along the water's edge. Around them, hungry gulls soared and swooped and squawked. The man's gait was strong and loose-limbed, although his sandy hair was starting to gray at the temples.

The woman at his side was nearly a head shorter and had to walk quickly to stay abreast of her older companion. Her lustrous dark brown hair fell straight to a line about seven inches below her shoulders. Occasional gusts carried by a vigorous northwest wind whipped it away from her face and back. She removed her hands from the pockets of her orange and blue high school jacket, cupped them in front of her mouth and blew. Then her clear, smooth fingers zipped the jacket to her neck. She slipped her hands into the pockets and hunched her shoulders against the chill.

"You've been strangely silent," Dick observed. "In fact," he teased, "anytime you're silent, it's strange."

Natalie grinned widely but said nothing.

"Keep this up and we'll have an entry for Ripley's," Dick said dryly under an arched eyebrow.

"The only clams aren't in the water," she retorted with a sly smile.

"When you said you wanted to come with me, I thought you wanted to talk. How about a beaten-up penny for your thoughts?"

Their pace slowed. She faced him and smiled, a trifle self-consciously. "They're more like dreams than thoughts, and I'm not sure they're worth that old penny. They're kind of silly."

"Ah, now we're getting somewhere," said Dick. "You know, there's nothing silly at all about a dream." He paused and looked at her. She said nothing, so he continued. "If you think about it, there's no more powerful force than a dream. It can help see you through pain and loneliness and despair. Or it can inspire you. Dreams have inspired some of history's loftiest words and greatest deeds."

"That's neat, Dick," Natalie said enthusiastically.

Dick laughed and shook his head. "But probably not very original." A moment passed and his faced turned pensive.

"What's the matter?" she said.

"Nothing. Nothing. I just realized I was sounding a lot like my dad. Wise and knowing. I guess it's easier to sound like that when you get older."

"You're not old," she asserted.

"Old enough to be your father."

They both smiled.

"What do you dream about, Dick?"

"I think my dream tank might be empty."

"Oh, come on. I don't believe that. You're only forty-one."

"Well, maybe…"

They walked on, their shoes leaving slight indentations in the wet, packed sand.

"Well?" she pressed.

"Well, what?"

"You know."

Dick stopped. He reached under his beige jacket and removed a pack of Camels from his shirt pocket. He placed a cigarette between his lips, then searched his pockets for matches. He found none and slid the cigarette back into the pack. "Don't want to be a litterbug." They resumed walking. "Some people share their dreams, Nat. Sometimes they share them with a nation or the whole world. But some dreams are intensely personal and private. But that doesn't mean they're any less important. To someone else a dream might seem trivial or laughable or threatening or impossible. But to the dreamer it might be the only reason for drawing his next breath."

"Is your dream like that?"

"No," he smiled, "nothing that monumental."

"But it is private?"

"For the time being anyway. And yours?"

"I want to go to college and be a teacher. I want to meet the perfect man and fall in love and get married and have children and be happy. And live in California." The thought and words warmed her.

"That's a beautiful dream, Nat. But I'm not sure there's a perfect man."

"Except for you."

"Whoa," said Dick, staring at Natalie. A small, self-deprecating smile softened his face. "I haven't had nearly enough practice to be perfect. Tell you what. I'll give you a piece of unsolicited advice, the very kind teenagers hate. When you fall in love, look at your man through sunglasses. You don't want to be blinded by a shiny surface. That's if you want the rest of your dream to come true."

Some dreams form as fast as a light flickers. Some coalesce from scattered fragments over weeks or years. Some endure unaltered. Some change subtly; others transform dramatically. Some dreams represent an ultimate vision, or spawn another and another.

Later that April, Martin Luther King continued to give shape and substance to his civil rights dream. In Birmingham, Alabama, which he termed "the most segregated city in the United States," he launched a campaign of marches and sit-ins.

On May 29, 1963, another dreamer, John F. Kennedy, celebrated his 46th birthday. On that same day in Athens, Ohio, Kate Santiago was dreaming of rejoining her family for the summer. Her freshman year had been successful academically - a B+ average - and enjoyable socially - she had pledged Zeta Tau Alpha. Now, with May and the school year drawing to a close, she looked forward to three months of fun, riding on her grandparents' New Mexico ranch, sunning on California's beaches and swimming in blue Pacific waters.

In Shelby Ben's two-part dream was taking shape. Foremost in his thoughts were visions of playing college football. Four universities – Bowling Green, Iowa State, Ohio and Vanderbilt – had offered the full ride he had dreamed of. His work as editor of the school newspaper, *Whippet Tales*, and the yearbook, *The Scarlet S*, had aroused his interest in writing and editing. A college degree in journalism was the second part of his dream. Because Ohio University possessed a highly respected journalism school, he chose to punch his football ticket in Athens.

Barbara Mason was dreaming about teaching high schoolers, helping to fire their zeal for learning. She was eager to begin her studies at Ohio State University.

More than a month before the junior-senior prom, Ben asked Barbara to be his date. On prom night as Ben drove to pick her up, another couple were preparing for the evening. Roger and Helen Hoerner were in high spirits. They were to serve as faculty chaperones, and both were looking forward to the night.

"Roger," Helen called from the bedroom, "would you zip me up?"

"Just a second." In the bathroom he gargled with Listerine, spat in the sink and dried his lips. He came into the bedroom and stood behind Helen, who was standing in front of the dresser mirror. Roger grasped the zipper of the cream-colored evening gown, then slid his hands beneath the silky material around Helen's waist to the base of her bra. "I'd rather unsnap than zip up."

"Hey, lover boy." Helen giggled and twisted. "We'll be late. So cut that out."

"I'd rather put it in," he murmured with mock lasciviousness.

"Zip me up and finish getting dressed, buster."

"I'm closer to being undressed than dressed. That chaperoning can be absolutely grueling. Sure you don't want an extra dose of nourishment? It won't take long." Gently, he squeezed her breasts and kissed her neck.

Helen shivered. "Well, since you put it that way."

A warm bond held Ben and Barbara close all night. At the prom they held each other tightly as they danced to *Moon River*, *Come Softly To Me*, *16 Candles* and other romantic tunes. Afterward they held hands through a special midnight showing at the Castamba Theater of *The Great Escape* with Steve McQueen and James Garner. Then it was on to the Rhythm Bowl, where Ben and Barbara laughed to the point of tears as Ben demonstrated convincingly that he could fling a football far more accurately than he could roll a bowling ball. In two of three games Barbara outscored him.

Back in the car Ben drove to the parking lot of a small factory located a few miles west of Shelby. He and Barbara kissed, sometimes tenderly, occasionally with controlled passion. Mostly they sat and listened, to crickets chirping and to each other.

"It went fast, didn't it?" Ben said softly. "These last four years…"

"Yes," she said. "I remember that first day at school. It seemed so big. I almost panicked going from class to class. I didn't think four minutes would be nearly enough." They both chuckled at the memory.

"I remember the seniors," Ben reminisced. "They seemed like gods. They seemed so tall and so smart. So perfect."

"And now that you're a senior?"

Ben smiled wryly. "The gods have proved themselves extremely human."

"Which is good," said Barbara. "Gods command awe. Humans are easier to like."

Ben, subdued: "And to not like."

They kissed again, a tender kiss that they held for a long minute. When they drew apart, Ben sighed. Two pairs of glistening eyes beheld one another. Impulsively they hugged and held their cheeks together. When they released, Ben placed his hands on the steering wheel and rested his head against the back of the seat. "Any regrets?"

"Yes," said Barbara. "That we didn't see more of each other." The words were spoken directly but tinged with sadness.

"Me too," Ben murmured. "That was my fault. If I…Will-"

"That's all right," Barbara said comfortingly. "I understand. Believe me. You don't have to explain."

"I'm self-centered."

"We're all that sometimes."

"Yeah," Ben said dryly. "I just happen to be more than most and too often at the wrong time." A pause. "At school in Columbus, what do you plan to major in?"

"Biology. Miss Snyder made it come alive, and I want to do the same for other kids."

"Miss Snyder is a heckuva teacher," Ben agreed. "I wonder if anyone ever asked her why she spells her name H-a-r-r-y-e-t instead of with an i."

"Biology."

"Huh?"

"Her dad probably wanted a boy."

They both laughed.

Time ticked by on the dashboard clock. It was nearing 5 a.m.

"I guess we won't be seeing much of each other," Barbara said.

"No, I guess not. At least for a while."

"That might be good."

"How so?"

"From what I've heard," said Barbara, "it's not so good to be too close to someone when you first leave for college. You get homesick and you don't concentrate on your studies. One of my friends was going steady when she went and almost dropped out during first semester. Lovesick."

"Yeah, well, we should be able to see each other during vacations."

"I hope we do."

"Good."

"Well," said Barbara, "I guess we should get going. Carol's parents are expecting a gang of us for breakfast at six."

"I almost forgot," said Ben. "But my stomach would have reminded me sooner or later." Ben switched on the car's engine, backed up and turned around. In another moment he and Barbara were riding in comfortable silence along a darkened road. Soon they passed a sign reading: *Shelby Corporation Limit*. Ben turned to Barbara and smiled wryly, "I wonder when we'll see that sign again."

"Alone or together?"

"Mmm. Together."

"In that case," Barbara said lightly, "maybe we better stop now, back up and drive by again."

"Nah. It won't be that long."

"Never know."

"Well, hell, in that case..." Ben braked hard, much harder than his father would have approved, shoved the car into reverse and accelerated. The car shot backward on the otherwise deserted road.

"Ben!" shrieked Barbara. She began to laugh, nervously at first, then joyfully.

The car weaved as Ben steered with his left hand while his right gripped the top of the seatback. He passed the sign and braked sharply again. The tires squealed and the car rocked. "There," he pronounced with mock haughtiness. "So much for your predictions. It wasn't nearly as long as you thought it would be."

Barbara threw her head back and dissolved in helpless laughter. Ben watched a moment and joined in. When at last their laughter subsided, Ben's right hand held Barbara's chin. He leaned toward her and their eyes closed. They kissed tenderly.

"You're special," Ben whispered.

"And you're crazy," Barbara whispered in a voice thickening with emotion.

"Only about you." Ben gulped. Then he cleared his throat, smiled mischievously, winked, slammed the gearshift into forward and stomped the accelerator pedal to the floor. The car lurched forward and past the sign. Inside, two young voices laughed merrily.

CHAPTER 26

In late August 1963 in Washington, D.C., Martin Luther King articulated his vision in words that would be etched in history. "I have a dream that one day this nation will rise up and live out the true meaning of its creed: 'We hold these truths to be self-evident, that all men are created equal.' I have a dream that one day on the red hills of Georgia sons of former slaves and the sons of former slave owners will be able to sit down together at the table of brotherhood...I have a dream that my four little children will one day live in a nation where they will not be judged by the color of their skin but by the content of their character."

Two months later, just six weeks into his first semester at OU, Ben's dream was blurred and his character tested. Ben had arrived in Athens with an ample amount of self-confidence in his academic ability. He was, in a word, cocky. In high school he had constructed, without undue labor, a grade point average that topped 3.8 on a 4.0 scale. As college neared, he had dismissed as exaggerations grim predictions on the severity of the classroom challenges that awaited. In his experience nothing ever had been as difficult as people portrayed it.

During that first college semester his course load included geology, which Ben took to satisfy a natural sciences requirement. He learned quickly that the study of rocks did not stimulate his otherwise fertile mind. The subject matter did not seem extraordinarily difficult, although there was a lot of it. Class reading assignments, he quickly found, served as incomparable bedtime sedatives.

When Professor Stanley Fisher announced the first exam, the news barely managed to penetrate the glaze that coated Ben's watery eyes. The night before the test, physically tired as usual after a day of classes and football practice, he studied three hours. Then he rocked back on the rear legs of his desk chair and reflected: I've never studied more than three hours for any test. I must know it cold. He closed the book and went to sleep.

The next morning he strode confidently into Professor Fisher's room. He sat and waited patiently while the kindly professor methodically distributed the examination. The test was printed on four pages. The questions demanded a variety of answers – true/false, fill-in-the-blank, multiple choice, short essay. As Ben scanned the exam, he nearly dropped it. This test was unavoidable, unmitigated disaster in the making. Before he first put pencil to paper, Ben regretted profoundly the hours he had contentedly slept away. Glumly he completed the exam.

Days later the ax fell. When Professor Fisher returned the geology exams, Ben's bore a large, hastily scrawled 47 circled menacingly in red. That, Ben knew, was an F on the most generous of curves. He heard Professor Fisher murmuring to him, "You can do better than this."

Ben saw his dream going up in a smoking, choking, eye-smarting pall of F's. Scattered among the ashes were a scholarship, a chance to play college football and a professional career. The five-minute walk back to his room in Gamertsfelder Hall seemed endless. He was sinking into depression, and in a morbid way, it was comforting. A verdict had been rendered; he had now only to serve the sentence. By the time he shuffled into his room, he was ready to pack his bags, head for Shelby and a job in a local factory. He was an inglorious study of defeat.

To Ben's great good fortune, one person, his roommate, would have none of it. Jeff Zink and Ben had taken quickly to each other upon meeting in September.

"Putting us together," Jeff had joked on their first day as roommates, "must be part of some devious social experiment."

"If oil and water don't mix," Ben replied smiling, "how can they expect us to?"

Theirs was a tale of two cities, one a capital of culture and finance and the other of corn and cows. Perhaps that explained the fast affinity. Their upbringings intrigued each other as would colorful tales of some exotic land. They figured to learn as much, perhaps more, from each other than from textbooks and classroom lectures.

As much as Ben was a product of small-town mid-America, Jeff was a child of the city. *The City.* Manhattan. The 200-foot-tall grain elevator, Shelby's highest structure, would have appeared Lilliputian amid the towers and spires that crowded together from Central Park to the Battery.

Ben's father had been a factory worker, then a steel mill personnel manager. Jeff's father was a Wall Street corporate lawyer who was at ease with the titans of industry and who felt most comfortable in French-cut blue pinstripes in the narrow, winding canyons of Lower Manhattan. Ben's mother was a housewife. Jeff's mother edited books for a major publisher.

For Ben, a rare visit to a museum meant a long drive. For Jeff, it was a frequent diversion that meant only a short walk from his Upper East Side brownstone. Ben's weekend family drives through the rolling countryside were Jeff's Saturday afternoon cab rides to matinees at Radio City Music Hall. Ben's childhood pets included three dogs, two cats, a rabbit, two parakeets and three chickens that eventually became meals. Jeff had an aquarium. Ben's empty lots and open fields were Jeff's concrete playgrounds. Seltzer Park was no greener than the spacious private lawns that bordered it. Central Park was a cherished splash of color amidst foreboding gray and black towers. Ben was used to elbow room, Jeff to sharp elbows.

For all the cultural differences, the boys were far from dissimilar. Like Ben, Jeff was tall. His 170 pounds were draped on a lanky frame that was a hair taller than Ben's six feet two inches. They both were bright, confident and inquisitive and shared a budding interest in journalism.

Jeff was sandy-haired. His large blue eyes radiated kindness and amusement. He smiled widely and often. Like Ben, he was a sports nut. His high school had fielded neither football nor baseball teams; there was no acreage for fields. But it did boast fine basketball teams. Jeff had been skilled enough to make the team but had played little. He cheerily acknowledged that his basketball prowess was confined chiefly to his ability to impersonate the style, if not the performance, of opposing players during practices.

During his first 18 years Jeff, an only child, had not neglected to study himself. Nor had he come away without lessons learned. His body may have suffered a lack of hand-eye-foot coordination, but his mind was as synchronized as a schedule of TV commercials. His intellectual and emotional strength, he knew, counted for something. After all, it was no mean feat to fend off the oppressive maternal instincts of his strong-willed mother, Alice, and her smothering attempts to shelter him from uncertainty.

In the matter of education, for example, Alice applauded Jeff's interest in journalism. She pictured him not as a sleazy hack reporter but as an impeccably dressed, intellectually superior, nationally renowned *New York Times* columnist. What appalled her was his choice of schools.

"Ohio University? My Lord, Jeff, where is that?" she asked. "How does one get there? It sounds so…backwoodsian. Does it have an airport? What are the credentials of its faculty? Why would *anyone* want to teach there?"

Concededly, Jeff's high school guidance counselor had confirmed OU's high standing among journalism schools.

"But," countered Alice, "Columbia is so much closer and more esteemed. No one will question Columbia's standing in journalism – or any other major. And it is Ivy League. If you go to Columbia right here in Manhattan, you will meet students and alumni from Harvard, Yale, Princeton and Brown. But Ohio University. You tell me it's in a league with Kent State and Bowling Green and Western Michigan. Is there any comparison at all?"

Alice continued to reason, reproach, plead and rant. Jeff resisted passively. He absorbed like a pincushion her most impassioned thrusts. He wanted to test himself outside his Upper East Side incubator. His father, Raymond – to Alice's dismay and Jeff's gratitude – remained aloof from the struggle. Afterward father patted son on the back and confided that he admired Jeff's stand and supported his decision.

"Your mother is a good and well-intentioned woman," said Raymond. "Make no mistake about that. She just has this knack for suffocating the lives of those she loves."

Jeff also learned about courage. Or more precisely, that he had it. Situationally, anyway. Once, when he was 16, he had stood on a subway platform beneath Lexington Avenue in midtown. As he waited for the uptown train, he saw a man knock an elderly woman to the concrete floor, snatch her purse and begin to run in his direction. Jeff acted with dispatch. As the mugger came racing by, Jeff wrapped his arms around the assailant's shoulders and wrestled him to the floor. They grappled and grunted until shouts by the victim and onlookers brought a transit cop. When the officer frisked the mugger and extracted a snub-nosed pistol from his jacket pocket, a shiver of fear went rippling through Jeff. But simultaneously he was pleased with himself. It was reasonable to expect he would perform the same deed in the same or similar circumstance. Later, he politely declined a commendation from Mayor John Lindsay because he did not consider himself heroic. Instead, he saw himself as a responsible citizen who had acted responsibly.

Jeff disdained affectation. Instead, he embraced irreverence. Much of it was directed to himself, unusual in a teenager. To him, preeners were pariahs who first and foremost deserved their own accolades and those of others only much later. If then. He lived life with what he regarded as a healthy measure of skepticism.

Jeff liked to spectate but also participate. To him, the role of the journalist came as close as any to permitting both. Jeff saw life as a continuing test of his limits, and he expected occasionally to fail.

Ben did not expect to fail. At anything. And the shock of his failure in geology plunged him into a miasma. He was stretched out on his dormitory bed, hands clasped behind his head, staring empty-eyed at the ceiling when Jeff pushed open the door. He saw Ben, paused and closed the door. Then he plopped an armload of books on his desk and eased himself onto the desk chair. "More bad news?"

"A D on top of yesterday's flag," Ben muttered glumly, referring to second test result in another course, Greek Words in the English Language.

"You made it."

"By two lousy points."

"That's still an improvement."

"I don't know if I can make it."

Jeff shook his head in gentle denial. "That's crazy," he said calmly. "All you have to do is look around at all the half-wits who've made it. You see them in business and politics. College may be tough but you're up to it."

"I don't know."

"Look, the way I see it, high school was so easy for you that you just took all this for granted. You knuckle down and this place will be a cakewalk."

"Think so?"

"I know so. Put girls on hold. Think less about football. You can do it."

"It might be too late," said Ben.

"After just six or seven weeks? One third of one semester? Not hardly."

"You know, when I saw that 47, the first thing I saw wasn't an F. It was my scholarship flying out the window. Then I saw my dad's face. God, what a jolt. More than anything else he wants me to get a college degree. I don't think I could face him if I flunked out."

"I have an idea," said Jeff.

"What?"

"You'll see. Meet me here after dinner. Now, damn it, put on some music and cheer up."

"Yeah," Ben said morosely.

The Union Bar & Grill was much to Ben's liking. Jeff had been there twice previously and relished its air of intimate informality. A long, narrow room dimly lit. A low ceiling. A worn wooden bar. Brick walls. Cozy booths with pitted wooden tables and high-backed wooden benches. Friendly bartenders and waiters. Cold beer in frosted glasses.

Jeff and Ben slid into a booth near the middle of the room. A student-waiter approached. "Two beers," said Jeff. "Draft."

From bar stools and neighboring booths, hushed conversations punctuated by outbursts of shouted laughter mingled with the sounds of clinking bottles, pitchers and glasses and muffled music from the jukebox.

The clean-cut young waiter put two large glass mugs before them. Jeff and Ben hoisted them. "A toast," smiled Jeff. "To us and to success." They touched glasses.

Ben gulped a long draught of the cold golden liquid. He licked his lips. "God, that tastes good."

Jeff lowered his mug to the table. "Had a feeling it would. You're going to have to bear down and start booking it, but you might as well start with a clean slate. Obliterate the past so it won't bog down the future."

"In other words," grinned Ben, "get bombed."

"To sudsy smithereens."

Ben drank again and then looked around furtively. "This could be my ass."

"What?"

"Training rules. No boozing except on Saturday nights. If I got reported, the coach could have my butt in a sling."

"Ben, do you expect any other football players to be here tonight?"

"I don't know. I guess not. Our next freshman game isn't till Wednesday."

"No sweat then. Who's going to know? Besides, if you get caught, I'll cover for you."

"How?"

"A little journalistic license."

"Huh?"

"I'll lie like a rug."

As Ben and Jeff were hoisting their first beers at the Union Bar & Grill, less than a block away Kate and Natalie Santiago were shoehorning their way into the raucous mob that nightly packed Conti's Inferno. The Inferno was a tribute to the resiliency of the human ear. To an initiate the cacophony that shook the walls and teetered glasses seemed a certainty to shatter the best-constructed eardrum.

The Inferno lured students like New York sucks in aspiring artists and actors. Apart from dormitory mixers and fraternity and sorority parties, the Inferno was the place for dancing in Athens. Rock music amplified to levels more often found on exploding battlefields kept young bodies gyrating for hours.

Between dances patrons inhaled beer and soft drinks. The Inferno was as conducive to thirst as to dancing. Dim, red lights bathed dancers and spectators in a warm glow. Then there was the sweat. Bottled, the nightly flow was enough to stock a saltwater saloon. The Inferno may not have been hell on earth, but innocents who chanced in could be forgiven for thinking that they had stumbled into Lucifer's anteroom.

Kate and Natalie liked the Inferno. It was a frequent weekend haunt and an occasional study break. That night Natalie and Kate had yet to dance. They were standing side by side on the dance floor perimeter, a pair of dark-eyed, dark-haired beauties surveying the sea of arms and legs flailing to the frug. Both were smiling, their feet keeping time with the music's beat.

A man materialized before them. He was only two or three inches taller than the two girls. His dark hair was straight and cut stylishly long. The shadow on his longish face hinted at a thick beard, eager to sprout if given a morning's reprieve from a razor. He stood a bit uncertainly, hands clasped behind his back, head bowed slightly. He glanced first at Kate and then at Natalie. A small smile flickered behind pursed lips. Then he leaned toward Natalie and spoke in a voice just loud enough to penetrate the din: "Might I ask you to dance?" His words were precise, clipped and uttered in a bass voice.

Natalie nodded and he led her to the dance floor. Artistically it was a mismatch. Natalie was a superb dancer. He was not. His coordination, Natalie could see, was good. He lacked experience and polish. He saw her studying him. He smiled, and his eyes twinkled mischievously. Natalie eyed him soberly. The music wound down and stopped.

"Thank you," Natalie said pleasantly.

"My pleasure, I assure you. I could stand a smidgen of practice, couldn't I?" he smiled apologetically.

Natalie shrugged and half-smiled. "Are you a student?"

"Ho, ho, ho. Do I look too old to be here? An older man preying on young maidens?"

Natalie reddened and smiled uneasily. "Oh, no. Your accent. I haven't heard any like it here before. It somehow seems older."

"I dare say I'm not faculty."

"What year are you?"

"Freshman."

"Really?" She blushed again.

The music resumed - a slow, quiet ballad.

"Might we continue this conversation through this dance?"

"Yes" seemed Natalie's only acceptable reply.

He held her properly, not too close, right hand placed firmly at the small of her back, his left gently holding her right well to the side. "I've not seen you before – or your sister?" Natalie nodded confirmation. "Twins?"

"Kate's a sophomore. I'm a freshman."

"And your name is…"

"Natalie, Natalie Santiago…You?"

"Gerry Graham."

"You're dancing this dance very well."

"Ah, well," he smiled, "it's a trifle more familiar to me."

"How did you choose OU?"

"It's not that far from Cleveland."

"Cleveland? Ohio?"

"As we British are fond of saying, quite."

"You *are* British."

"Guilty." He smiled mischievously, an easy, small-toothed smile. "My father's with the British Consulate."

"In Cleveland?" Natalie said incredulously.

"For the past two years. Cleveland isn't exactly a colonial outpost." Natalie shook her head in wonderment. "And you?" said Gerry.

"Me?"

"Where is your home?"

"California."

"Of Spanish extraction, not Mexican."

"Yes, but how did you know?"

"My father was previously posted in Madrid." Natalie again shook her head. "How did you happen to enroll here?" said Gerry.

"I followed Kate – my sister – and, well, that's a long story."

"I've a suggestion."

"What?"

"Let me ask your sister to dance. Then let's the three of us adjourn to a quieter pub where we can compare notes on a land I've never seen and on one which, presumably, has not been graced by the Santiago sisters."

Natalie reddened. "All right. Let's check with Kate."

Back at the Union Bar & Grill Ben and Jeff were conversing convivially and drinking steadily. Initially their talk was hushed and serious. After several drained mugs it began to sink like a foundering freighter. First it lapsed into silliness, then into marginal coherence.

"Wha' timezit?" Ben groaned lowly.

"Looka your wash."

"Oh yeah, damn good idea." Ben's head nodded and his eyes narrowed as he tried to focus on the watch face. "Can't tell."

"Why not?"

"God damn hands are movin' too fasht."

"Lemme see. Sheesh, thas the sweep hand."

"Oh. Maybe we better go. Gotta get some shleep."

"Right. Good point. But le's have one more beer."

When the portal to the Inferno swung shut behind the trio, it was like closing the door on Niagara Falls; there was noise in the street, but in such mild contrast to the deafening roar inside that it was barely noticeable.

"Have you a favorite spot?" said Gerry.

"Not really," said Kate. "You?"

"As a matter of fact, yes."

"Lead the way."

They began a short, leisurely stroll. Auto headlights were illuminating the brick pavement on Court Street. Overhead, street lights and neon signs shown congenially and protectively.

"Have you selected a major?" said Gerry.

"Secondary education," said Kate. "I'd like to teach English lit."

"Same here," said Natalie. "Except I think I'd rather teach science – maybe biology or chemistry. How about you?"

"Psychology. I'd like to do research."

"Heavy," said Natalie.

"Perhaps," he smiled, "but I find it exciting."

"Do you miss England?" said Kate.

"Oh, yes, but I like it fine here. I'm adaptable. Do you miss the fabled sun and sea of California?"

"Sure," said Natalie, "but I think more than anything I'll miss being outside a lot once winter hits. Wish they had indoor tennis courts here."

"Do you both play?" said Gerry.

"Yes," said Kate. "You?"

"Yes, I like to play very much."

"Maybe we can get in some court time before winter."

"That would be lovely," said Gerry. "I take it you play very well."

The two girls faced each other, shrugged and smiled cutely under elevated eyebrows. "I guess so," said Kate. "And you?"

"Fairly well."

"Fairly?" Natalie said dubiously.

"Actually, quite well."

All three laughed.

"Ah, here we are," said Gerry. In the years before the state of Ohio raised the legal drinking age, bars proliferated on Athens' two main downtown streets, Court and Union. "Either of you been here?"

"No," said Kate, "lead on."

Gerry pulled open a heavy, wooden door, ushered the girls in and followed. Gerry then stepped in front of them. They paused and surveyed the narrow, brick-walled, dimly lit room. "There's an empty booth near the back," said Gerry. The threesome, with Gerry in the lead, began to file to the rear of the room. Along the way they passed several booths. In one, Ben and Jeff sat hunched over the table, babbling and giggling. Ben's back was to the front of the room. He and Jeff were oblivious to most everything, including passersby. At the empty booth, Gerry stood aside while Kate and Natalie seated themselves, their backs to the front of the room.

Ben and Jeff drained their mugs for the last time. "Ready?" said Jeff.

"Ready, set, gooo," Ben giggled.

Slowly they eased themselves from the booth and stood facing each other. They began to giggle anew. Ben, wobbly, placed his hands on Jeff's shoulders to steady himself.

Gerry, seated across from the girls, saw the pair teetering in the aisle. He smiled. Recognition flickered in Gerry's eyes, but he refrained from commenting and possibly diverting the girls' attention from their conversation.

"If this was New York," said Jeff, wavering, "we could get a cab."

"'S gonna be a long walk."

"Le's go."

"Where?"

"Wherever." Jeff giggled again. It proved contagious. Together, giggling helplessly, the two youths stumbled toward the exit. Outside, they weaved on the sidewalk up Union Street to Court Street.

"Am I drunk?" said Ben.

"Do proshtutes fuck?"

More giggling.

"Never been drunk before," said Ben.

"Thas good. Wouldn' be the same."

"Very, very true. Shpoken like shcholar."

"How many beers we drink?" Jeff mumbled.

"Don' know. But probly 'nough to clean the shlate."

That night in the Union Bar & Grill was the second time in recent weeks that Kate and Natalie narrowly had missed seeing Ben. The first was in early September when the girls had come to Ohio. Their parents and Dick had accompanied them. Instead of flying to Columbus, which was nearer to Athens, they flew to Cleveland so Dick could introduce John, Maria and Natalie to his Shelby family. Ben, however, already had departed for OU to begin football practice.

When the Santiagos left for Athens, Dick stayed on in Shelby to visit. During the two days John and Maria spent at OU with their daughters, Kate phoned Ben three times. On each occasion he was not in his room. Each time, she left word but none of the messages got through. Working against her were the confusion attending the start of a new school year and the vagaries of a telephone system that, in those years, had some 50 boys sharing each hallway phone. During the next week, Kate tried twice more without success. As time passed and as she and Natalie became caught up in the whirl of school, she thought less often of Ben. About a month after school started, Kate phoned him again. Her luck was no better.

CHAPTER 27

Ben stepped outside Shively Hall's cafeteria after lunch, stopped and placed his hands on his hips. He rotated his shoulders and breathed deeply. The air was crisp and invigorating. Ben reached up to the bridge of his nose and shoved up the eyeglasses he recently had begun wearing. The first inkling that his eyesight had dimmed had come the previous summer when his American Legion baseball batting average had dropped mysteriously. After an exam revealed slight myopia, he selected wire-rimmed lenses that made him appear older but that seemed to distort his facial features less.

Ben stretched his arms skyward and flexed his fingers. Then he lowered his arms and extended them behind his back. His stomach was full and his mind at ease. His freshman football season had been successful and his grades were on the upswing. His second geology test had just been returned, and he had scored an 84. Not the A he had been accustomed to in high school but reassuringly good.

Jauntily he crossed the street to Gamertsfelder Hall, named after former OU president Walter S., then 78 years old, still vibrant and engaging, still living in Athens, and still an occasional visitor to the dorm that bore his name. Ben bounded up the steps two at a time to his third-floor room. He pulled off a maize v-neck sweater with brown trim and flipped it on his bed. Then he broke out an ironing board, filled his steam iron with water and began to attack a pile of shirts and pants. He was just beginning to press a pair of blue slacks when Jeff Zink threw open the door.

"Did you hear?" Jeff gasped, winded from his race up the two long flights.

"Hear what?" said Ben unexcitedly.

"The President's been shot!"

"President who?"

"Kennedy!" Jeff cried exasperatedly.

"Sure, sure, what's the punchline?"

"It's no joke. Honest."

"Come on," Ben said skeptically, continuing to slide the hissing iron back and forth on the slacks. "You been listening to Vaughan Meder again?" Ben was referring to the comedian who had been making a name for himself with uncannily accurate impersonations of President Kennedy.

"Friend, I am not joking," said Jeff, regaining his breath and his calm. "President Kennedy's been shot. In Dallas. They say he's been injured seriously. Turn on the radio."

It was just 2 p.m., Eastern time, on Friday, November 22, 1963. President Kennedy had been shot in Dallas at 1:30, Eastern time. At 1:36 ABC Radio reported the shooting. At 1:40 CBS Television interrupted a soap opera, *As The World Turns*; a distraught Walter Cronkite reported that President Kennedy had been "seriously wounded." At 1:45 NBC Television cut away from another soaper, *Bachelor Father*, to newsman Chet Huntley.

Ben would never forget what he was doing at the moment he heard the stunning news. Nor would millions of other Americans. Kate knew something was amiss when she walked into the Zeta house and found a living room full of usually ebullient sorority sisters weeping softly.

Natalie was walking down Jeff Hill. In front of her a male student's transistor radio suddenly stopped blaring rock music and loudly announced a shocking bulletin.

In California Ann Sheridan was at her Malibu beach house, reclining on a chaise lounge on the sun deck, perusing a television script for a new

Hallmark Hall of Fame production. The kitchen phone rang. It was Dick calling with the terrible news. Together they would spend most of the weekend watching television coverage of the tragedy's depressing aftermath. TV sets that weekend were strangely magnetic. Stark images of grieving individuals, somber officials and stiffly erect, square-shouldered soldiers, sailors and airmen moved in seemingly slow motion before the dazed eyes of stunned countrymen. On Sunday with millions of other Americans, Ann and Dick would see live the murder of Kennedy's suspected assassin, Lee Harvey Oswald, by Dallas nightclub owner Jack Ruby.

Nothing can devastate more viciously than a shattered dream. In its rubble may lay plans, ambition, dedication and hope. The end of a cherished dream can induce terrible hurt, precipitate deep depression, ruin health. John F. Kennedy's assassination shattered the dream of Camelot and plunged a nation into mourning. It was as though a power failure had suddenly darkened a packed theater near the final curtain of an electrifying play on opening night. Eventually light would be restored, and the show would go on but never with the same verve, the same high drama. The remainder of the show, no matter how well played, would be performed before an audience still thinking about the unexpected blackout.

President Kennedy's death darkened the gray mood that slowly had been shrouding Roger Hoerner. The news reached him in Shelby High School's faculty lounge. He long had dreamed of becoming a head football coach. If the slot at Shelby, his first preference, failed to materialize in the near future, he had planned to apply for a head coaching spot at some nearby school. Beyond that, his dream focused on coaching college football. Now that dream was crumbling like an imploded building. Instead of anticipating the day when he would head a football program, Roger now anguished over the possibility that one day soon he would be forced to abandon coaching altogether. That bleak prospect lay before him like a psychological gallows.

The multiple sclerosis symptoms that had been frightening and frustrating but mercifully brief and intermittent had grown chronic and more severe. The change had begun in August, soon after the start of summer football practice. When the stiffness and weakness that had periodically sapped his legs failed to abate, Roger became worried. He monitored his diet carefully, exercised regularly although not strenuously and was sure to get ample rest. Each day he awakened, hoping for a familiar and reassuring remission. It didn't come.

The hearts of those closest to him – Helen, her parents and his, coaching colleagues and the players – went out to him. To watch this handsome, husky, dedicated man hobbled by an unseen but treacherous enemy pained them deeply. By now, all knew the identity of his disease. But they seldom discussed it and never with Roger unless he mentioned it first.

Helen was an exception. She knew Roger needed an occasional release from his torment, and she willingly served as the escape valve. When Roger talked about his MS, Helen listened attentively. In her responses she offered encouragement but avoided falsely optimistic pep talks. When he forlornly talked about his dwindling prospects for attaining a head coaching job, Helen reminded him of the satisfaction he had derived as an assistant and encouraged him to continue as long as possible. When he glumly discussed her future, she tenderly but firmly reminded him that it was *their* future.

As the season progressed, Roger's spirits slowly sank. When his fatigue slipped a notch into exhaustion, increasingly he turned crotchety and snappish. These too were MS symptoms. Roger knew that but could not help it, and his depression worsened. Now, slumped in the lounge, listening to the funereal tones of a network radio announcer, Roger knew he had coached his last football season. No use fooling myself. I'll have to tell the other coaches. My coaching days are gone. By next September, at this rate I'll need all my strength to teach and help with chores around the house. What a miserable trade, he reflected morosely, giving up coaching so I can still help with the cleaning. Helen, she won't see it that way. She'll tell me she can handle the home front herself. She knows how much coaching means to me. No denying that. I love helping boys learn and refine their skills. I relish the electricity of game nights. I take pride in helping kids like Ben and Pete earn scholarships. But I won't coach if I need favors, if others have to make concessions for me. He rubbed his eyes, then let his face rest against his hands. As usual, he felt tired. He also felt slightly feverish. What now? What symptom will hit me next – and how hard and for how long? What part of my body will betray me next? What physical activity do I have to give up next? He sighed and slowly pushed himself up from a cracked and faded leather armchair. He shuffled stiffly from the lounge and began a slow, graceless walk toward Room 305. Teaching was important and gratifying, but coaching had been the foremost chunk of his professional life. Now it was gone.

CHAPTER 28

Heavy rains had been falling for a week. More were expected.

Gamertsfelder Hall and nine neighboring dorms sat sturdily on a grassy shaded plain called East Green. Similar clusters of Georgian-styled dorms elsewhere on the sprawling, hilly campus were called West Green and South Green. To walk from the complex of intramural football fields behind East Green across campus to the far reaches of West Green on a steamy spring day consumed 30 sweaty minutes.

Gam Hall's exterior of red brick and white wood trim was warm and inviting. The same could not be said about the rooms where each semester dwelled some 400 young men. The best that could be said about these monastic cells was that they were virtually indestructible – a consideration no doubt accounting in large measure for the durable spartan interiors and furnishings. The room Ben and Jeff shared was typical. Its sidewalls were concrete block painted beige. The outside wall was plaster painted beige. There were two single beds with metal frames of the same bland hue. Two metal desks, both beige, sat in front of two desk chairs with beige metal frames and beige, vinyl-covered, foam-filled seats and backs. One thickly padded easy chair completed the furnishings; it had a beige metal frame and matching vinyl-covered seat and back.

The logic behind the décor was as plain as the label on a paint can. A single color meant the ability to benefit from economies of scale. One color meant lower maintenance and replacement costs. When OU called a furniture supplier, the specifications were monotonously and economically predictable. A paint distributor didn't have to ask which color to ship.

The unrelieved dullness stirred many Gam residents to flurries of do-it-yourself decorating. Whims and fancies were indulged. Jeff and Ben responded by papering their walls with travel posters, *Sports Illustrated* covers and *Playboy* magazine centerfolds.

"You know," said Ben, "all the *Playboy* stuff will have to come down before Mom's Weekend."

Jeff laughed. "My mom might be relieved to see it. She might think - or hope - that our paper women immunize me from addiction to the fleshly variety."

On a muggy March night in 1964, Ben was sitting at his beige desk, oblivious to the erotic wall coverings. At 9:00 he removed his wire-rimmed glasses and placed them upside down on top of his geology book.

Outside, a steady rain was pelting the room's solitary window. Ben opened the window a crack to let in air that barely qualified as fresh. Rain had been falling for most of the past week. It had left the air close, the ground spongy and the Hocking River rising. People were talking about the possibility of a flood. A little extra excitement, thought Ben, might be fun. Since the end of the football season in November, the extra free time he now had occasionally hung heavy.

The door opened and Jeff stepped in. Water was dripping steadily from his blue trench coat and black umbrella. "How's it goin'?"

"Okay. Been booking it. You?"

"Same here," said Jeff. "Been over at Jefferson Library, reading *The Scarlet Letter* for lit class." Jeff reopened the umbrella and placed it in a corner of the room and hung his coat on a hook on the back of the door. "I'm thinking of building an ark tomorrow. Wanna help?"

Ben laughed. "Nah, I'm not much good with a hammer and nails. But I'll be happy to round up some animals. Only two-footed ones allowed, I presume."

"Of course. And we'll only take two of them onboard, both females. This will be an intimate ark."

Ben chuckled. "Does seem like it's been raining for 40 days. Think it'll ever stop?"

"I hope so. I'm beginning to feel like a sponge that needs wringing out."

Ben moved to the window, peered down and whistled. "Christ!"

"What's wrong?"

"Look at that," said Ben. "The damn street's filling up like a bathtub."

"Probably a sinister plot by the hygiene dean." Jeff joined Ben at the window. "Maybe it's true."

"What?" said Ben.

"I heard a rumor that a dam broke upriver and a wall of water is heading toward Athens. Supposed to be 20 feet high. Be here about 9:30."

"When did you hear that?"

"Tonight. On the way back from Jeff Hall."

"Think it's true?"

"Who knows?"

"Son of a gun," said Ben, brightening. "Let's go see it."

"Aah, it's just a rumor. Probably nothing to it."

"Yeah, but what if it's true? You ever seen a wall of water?"

"No and I'm not sure I want to."

"Party pooper," Ben needled. "Come on."

"Hey, it's raining out there, remember? Perfect weather for pneumonia."

"Jesus," murmured Ben. "Look at that street. The water is almost over the curb. Sewers must be backing up. Come on, Jeff, this could be a once-in-a-lifetime thing. Besides, it's warm out. It won't kill you."

"No," Jeff said acidly, "just get soaked for the umpteenth time this week."

"You won't melt. Come on."

The two youths stripped to their underwear, then put on short-sleeved shirts, Bermuda shorts and sneakers sans socks.

"Should we take our umbrellas?" asked Jeff.

"Is it windy?"

"Not when I came in."

"Mmm. Yeah, I guess. Keep the rain off our glasses."

The Hocking River entered the campus from the west and ran adjacent to West Green, separating it from the rest of campus. On campus there were only two places to cross the river. One was the Richland Avenue Bridge, a stretch of paved roadway supported by high concrete pilings planted in the riverbed some 50 feet below the street's surface.

Back at Gam Hall Jeff and Ben stood on the sidewalk. Water was lapping at their shoes.

"Well, we knew we were gonna get wet feet," said Ben.

"It's not too late to go back inside," said Jeff. "You know, show we're sane after all." Jeff's sarcasm was as heavy as the rain.

Ben smiled appeasingly his slightly crooked smile and stepped into the flooded street. They crossed, then turned left, or south, and strode past Shively Hall. In the windows they saw numerous girls watching them trudge by. From under his umbrella Ben waved vigorously. Several of the girls waved back. At the intersection they turned right, or west, and plodded up the steep grade that was Mulberry Street, better known as Shively Hill. Their wet, rubber-soled shoes slapped the brick pavement. Riverlets rushed underneath and between their shoes to the flooded street below. At the top of the hill they crossed a street and continued west behind College Green. About 12 minutes after leaving Gam, they reached the crest of Richland Avenue. One hundred yards south was the bridge. Hundreds of students, mostly men, huddling under umbrellas stood expectantly on the bridge's west sidewalk.

"Looks like I'm not the only one curious about seeing a wall of water," grinned Ben.

"Looks like the campus has more mental deficients than I thought," said Jeff. "You should feel right at home."

"At least we won't feel conspicuous." Ben laughed and slapped Jeff on the shoulder. Jeff, in spite of himself, laughed too. Unhurried, under the pelting rain they crossed Richland Avenue to the west sidewalk and strolled down toward the bridge. "Those guys aren't crazy," Ben said lightly. "Most of them have umbrellas too."

"I don't know why. Most of their brains are already flooded."

They stepped onto the bridge and peered over the wide cement railing.

"Good God," murmured Jeff. "That couldn't be the lazy little old Hocking River we've all come to know and love."

Below them, black, churning, rising water was rushing under the bridge and nearing the top of the river's banks. In its speeding current, the Hocking carried all manner of debris. Underbrush, saplings, discarded tires, bottles and cans were among the river's inanimate passengers.

Inside the 10 West Green dorms lights burned in nearly every room. Students had been warned at the dinner hour that they might have to evacuate. They already had received contingency room assignments in dorms elsewhere on campus. Many were packed and ready to go. Some in the dorms closest to the river were watching the water tear by at ever-higher levels. More than a few were among the throng on the Richland Avenue Bridge.

The Hocking River isn't nearly long enough to qualify for mention in atlases and almanacs. It isn't wide enough or deep enough to be navigable except by canoe, and even that's frequently impossible along some shallow stretches. The Hocking's headwaters are a few miles southeast of Columbus. It then snakes southeast, where it empties into the Ohio River at a cartographic dot called Hockingport. As the crow flies, that's a distance of some 80 miles. As the river bends and bows through the high Appalachian foothills, it chugs along for some 200 miles. Each spring it carries away the runoff from those hills. The winter of 1963-64 had seen above-normal snowfalls, and spring rains also had been atypically heavy. Downstream, the swollen Ohio River was compounding the threat. Smaller rivers like the Hocking, unable to spill into the rapidly rising Ohio, were beginning to back up. Unless the rain abated quickly, OU officials feared the worst. Most students didn't share the anxiety of university administrators. Instead, they waited expectantly for Mother Nature to throw a watery party.

"A twenty-foot wall of water might collapse the bridge," Jeff said matter-of-factly.

"That would rid the campus of a lot us crazies," Ben said, nodding toward the river. "I don't think many of us would survive down in that."

"My point exactly," said Jeff. "I think I'd rather be somewhere else, even if it's just off to the side."

"What time is it?"

Jeff glanced at his wristwatch. "Five after ten."

"I don't think there's gonna be any wall of water. According to the rumor, it should've been here half an hour ago."

"You ready to head back?" said Jeff.

"Yeah. Wanna go via the Footbridge? We can see what's happening farther downstream."

"I guess so. Okay."

The Footbridge was the second place on campus to cross the river. The Footbridge spanned the Hocking about a quarter mile east of the Richland Avenue Bridge. Using it most were East and South Green students passing back and forth between their dorms and Porter Hall, the football stadium, the gym, the ice arena and the tennis courts.

The Footbridge was aptly named. Built in the late 1940s, it was meant to accommodate shoes, not tires. Its surface was wooden planking and only six feet wide. Its 280 feet were anchored to the river bottom by wooden pilings. Iron side rails removed any danger from traversing the narrow span. The approach at each end of the Footbridge's central span rose steeply from the riverbanks. The surface of the central span was about 30 feet above the river's frequently visible bottom.

On the Richland Avenue Bridge Jeff and Ben turned away from the west railing, checked for auto headlights through the steady rain and crossed to the bridge's east sidewalk. They strode downhill off the bridge's southern end, turned left and picked up the path that ran along the river's south bank to the Footbridge. Their sodden sneakers sank slightly in the spongy earth. The raging river, just inches away from their feet, was mesmerizing them. Occasionally one or the other shouted a comment, but mostly they watched the bucking river slowly continue its inexorable climb to the lips of its channel.

Flood stage for the Hocking in Athens was 17 feet. Before the river crested late the next afternoon, it would reach a record 24 feet. All of West Green would be evacuated, with students taking up temporary residence in dorms and Greek houses elsewhere on campus. The flooded Hocking and its network of gorged feeder streams would close all roads entering Athens. Access would be by helicopter only. On East and South Greens, Army engineers would quickly erect temporary footbridges to link dorms isolated by flooded basements and ground floors. Canoes and motorboats would navigate the streets in front of and behind Gam Hall. Classes would be canceled. Most students would enjoy the spectacle and the unprecedented break in academic routine. Many would photograph the scene for snapshot correspondence with families and friends.

At one point where the path dipped, water tugged at Ben and Jeff's ankles.

"Damn," said Ben, "feel the force of that water. I guess you don't appreciate how powerful water can be until you feel something like this."

"Anybody in that water tonight would probably be a headline in tomorrow's paper," concurred Jeff.

"If they found the body."

"There's the Footbridge."

The south bank approach came into view about 50 yards in front of them. It was barely visible through the watery curtain. They walked on, steadily but unhurried.

Behind them, back upstream and just to the west of the Richland Avenue Bridge, the punishing water dislodged an unused utility pole and sent it careening downstream. On the bridge observers watched in fascination as the pole shot beneath them and headed toward the Footbridge.

At the base of the steep approach to the Footbridge's center span, the young men paused.

"Think it's safe?" said Ben.

"Now you ask," replied Jeff with a cutting edge to his voice. Then he sighed. "Probably. The pilings are pretty thick, and I'm sure they go down pretty deep. Besides, I'm not in any mood to go back."

"Me either."

Ben stepped first onto the wet planking. "Slippery. Watch your step."

Slowly, they started up the steep incline to the center span. Some 200 yards back upstream the dislodged utility pole was coming hard. Ben and Jeff reached the top of the incline and stepped onto the center span. They stopped and looked down. The angry waters, fighting for release from confinement by the river's channel, were scarcely a dozen feet below their wet shoes.

"Nasty," said Jeff.

Ben nodded and they started across.

About 100 yards upstream from the Footbridge the charging utility pole struck a piece of debris and swung sideways. One end of it snagged on brush along the bank.

Midway along the center span Ben and Jeff stopped. They leaned against the iron side rail and looked back upstream.

"Looks kinda spooky, doesn't it?" said Jeff.

"Yeah, you can barely see the street lights on Richland Avenue. Hardly make out dorm lights on West Green at all."

"Wonder how much higher the river'll get?"

"No idea," said Ben.

At that moment the snagged utility pole was freed and resumed its heaving course. Now it was bouncing along nearly parallel with the Footbridge.

Ben and Jeff straightened and turned to continue across. They had walked only a couple paces when they heard a loud thud. Immediately, the bridge began to shake and shift. On the wet, slippery planking Ben and Jeff struggled to maintain their footing. Then there was a second thud and the bridge shook anew. Jeff's shoes slipped beneath him. As he toppled backward his right wrist struck the top rail, and the umbrella he was holding dropped from his right hand into the black torrent. As he fell, the back of his skull cracked against a vertical strut in the railing. Pain went surging through his arm and head. He moaned, and reflexively his left hand grabbed the injured wrist. As Jeff was going down, Ben bounced off a side rail and crumpled to the planking. His ribs ached. He still held his umbrella, although now it was offering little protection. His glasses quickly became rain covered. On the surface of the bridge the two youths lay dazed.

Below, the utility pole crashed against the pilings twice more. Briefly, through his pain, Jeff wondered what object was attacking the bridge. A tree, most likely. A fifth blow followed, and suddenly there was the macabre sound of wood splintering and metal twisting and tearing. The young men froze.

Beneath him, Ben began to feel the planking separate. As the splintering continued, the gap widened. Gotta move, Ben thought. As he began to roll away, there was an ominous crack and Ben felt himself begin to fall through the span. He released his umbrella and frantically reached out. Everything was wet and slippery.

Jeff expected the bridge to collapse any second into the merciless water. He was a good swimmer, but in the turbulent blackness below, he figured he might as well be Ahab in his final struggle with Moby Dick. Jeff's left hand probed his right wrist. Despite the acute pain nothing seemed broken. He rubbed tenderly at the back of his skull. A knot but no blood. He shook his head to clear his mind and started to rise. Again the pole pounded the pilings and Jeff slipped back to the planking. "Shit," he muttered. The warm, hard rain was beating steadily against his face, blurring his glasses. In a matter of moments his shirt and shorts had been drenched. He struggled up and looked around. He saw nothing. Nothing. It took a moment for the terrifying thought to penetrate his consciousness. "Ben!" he screamed. "Ben! Where are you?" As he shouted the question, he dreaded the answer. For a fleeting moment, he thought - hoped - that Ben somehow had escaped the bridge. In fact, he knew there hadn't been time. Panic began crawling into his stomach. "Ben! Ben! Can you hear me?" Nothing. Apprehensively, he dropped to his hands and knees and peered between iron struts into the blackness below. Nothing. He closed his eyes in an effort to blot out the tragedy that his mind was picturing. It was no use. His mind's eye saw Ben swept away, helpless in the swift, churning current.

Then a new sound crept into his consciousness. It was faint, so faint as to seem ghostly. It was his name. He was hearing his name. He froze, his head still protruding between the struts. Then he retreated and listened again. This time there was no doubt. It was faint but real. Jeff, still on all fours, looked behind him. A dozen feet away, in the darkness, he saw two hands grasping a strut where it joined the bottom rail. Simultaneously, to his horror, he saw the gulf in the Footbridge's planking. For a moment he could neither speak nor act. He rotated his tongue in his dry mouth and forced himself to swallow. "Ben! Ben!" he bellowed over the thundering water. He didn't wait for a reply. He scrambled to the break in the planking. He peered over the precipice. Ben was hanging in the abyss. "Hang on, Ben, hang on."

Ben raised his head. "Even with two hands I don't think I can hang on very long. Might have cracked some ribs."

Without diverting his gaze from Ben's face, Jeff tore at his belt buckle. "Just hang on." Fiercely he pulled the belt through the loops in his Bermuda shorts. Then he dropped on his belly and lay flat. He reached out over the precipice and knotted one end of the belt around Ben's left wrist. Quickly, he rose to his knees and tied the other end around the joint where a vertical strut met the lower of the horizontal rails.

"Is the bridge broken in two?" Ben asked.

"Just on your side. The railing's still in one piece on the other side."

"What now?"

"Okay, now listen, I want-"

At that instant the utility pole again hammered a piling. The force of the blow rocked Jeff forward on his knees toward the gap. He twisted his torso and lunged desperately for the railing. He grabbed and held. Then he looked for Ben's hands. They still gripped the strut. Below, Ben's dangling body twisted and rocked. In the water the pole continued to thump the pilings.

"Hurry," Ben yelled anxiously.

"Okay." Jeff dropped to his belly. "Listen. Pull up with your arms – like you were doing a pull-up – and raise your left leg as high as you can. I'll try to reach it and haul you up. Ready?"

"Yeah." Ben contracted his arms, gritted his teeth against the fiery pain and lifted the leg.

Jeff stretched into the abyss and grasped Ben's soaked shorts just above the knee. He tightened his grip. "Got it." Slowly he rose and backed away from the gap. "Don't try to help," he cautioned Ben. "Just let me pull."

In another few seconds, he had Ben's legs onto the split surface. He kept pulling until they were safely away from the gap. Then he crawled forward between Ben and the rail to unknot the belt from Ben's wrist. He decided not to bother with the other end and let the belt hang from the rail.

Ben crawled away from the gap and collapsed on his stomach.

"There's blood all over your arms," Jeff said worriedly.

"There is?" said Ben, surprised. "Must have scraped them when I fell. Christ," he coughed, "what the hell's banging this bridge?"

"I don't know, but let's get the fuck off."

Jeff helped Ben to his feet.

"Ouch."

"Whoops. Sorry."

The young men half ran, half stumbled across the rest of the central span. Then they scurried down the steep incline at the other end. From the north bank they looked back out onto the river. Both were breathing hard. Ben removed his glasses. They could see the utility pole still battering the pilings. The Footbridge had bent where the gap was created, and the two pilings nearest the gap had given and shifted but not fallen.

Ben began to shiver.

"You okay?" Jeff asked.

Ben nodded. "Close call. Whew. I guess it's just soaking in. No pun intended."

"Just take it easy."

"Yeah, right. Sorry you didn't listen to your mother and go to cosmopolitan Columbia instead of Harvard-on-the-Hocking?"

"You sorry you didn't take up knitting instead of football?"

"Columbia's got a great journalism school."

"Which would never produce a story like this."

"You gonna report this story to your mom?" Ben smiled wryly.

"You kidding? She'd shit her drawers. She'd come down here and beg me to leave this wilderness outpost for the civility of Manhattan."

"And?"

"And leave you to enjoy this place by yourself? No way."

Nervous release began to set in, and Ben started to laugh. Jeff joined him. Then stabbing pain forced Ben to stop and catch his breath. Jeff hovered, concerned. Ben tapped him on the shoulder and pointed to the river. They watched the pole gradually shift until it became parallel with the banks and shot underneath the bridge and on downstream.

"Hey," said Ben, "you gonna go back and get your belt?"

"Nah. Let it go. Give people something to talk about come daylight. They'll go nuts trying to figure out who was out there and what the hell happened."

"When they see the belt, they might think some couple decided to screw on the bridge."

"Or that some insane asshole tried to fix the bridge with it."

Again they laughed. Again Ben winced and caught his breath.

"What about your umbrella?" said Jeff. "It's still on the bridge."

"It'll add to the mystery. Let's get on back to Gam. I can hardly see through these glasses."

"Right."

Ben put his glasses back on.

They turned and began to walk away from the river. Ben put his hand on Jeff's shoulder and stopped.

"What's wrong?" said Jeff.

"Nothing. Here." Ben extended his right hand. "Thanks. I owe you one."

CHAPTER 29

Weeks later one mid afternoon Ben again was returning to Gam Hall via the Footbridge. It had been repaired, and the Hocking River had returned to somnambulating. The day was one of those glorious spring extravaganzas of color and sound that resuscitates life and renews purpose. The grass, fed and nourished by spring rains and warm solar rays, would never be greener. Wildflowers, blossoming everywhere, would never be more captivating. High in the distance, Ben could see the tails of two colorful kites flapping in the breeze.

It was a perfect day for walking. Unless one was walking under abnormal circumstances. Ben was walking slowly in the shade of the trees that lined the river, but he was sweating. And wincing.

Ben was not yet used to the rubber-tipped cane that helped support his right leg. As he neared the steep approach to the Footbridge, he stopped, pulled a handkerchief from his hip pocket and wiped his brow.

"May I help you?" The voice, husky as though it had come rumbling up from a large, empty barrel, came from behind Ben. "That bridge will not be easy to negotiate." The words were spoken with British-accented precision.

Ben looked back over his shoulder. He half expected to see a towering, thick-chested specimen outfitted in jeans and a sweatshirt. Instead, he saw a slightly built young man of middling height who was clothed in white – shorts, short-sleeved pullover shirt with all three buttons open, sneakers and sweat socks. He carried a tennis racket and a can of balls. The sleeves of a lightweight, white jacket were knotted at the front of his waist.

"Thanks, I could use a hand getting up the bridge. I'm getting the hang of this cane, but it's taking longer than I thought."

The stranger stepped to Ben's right side. "Give me your cane." He held the cane and the racket in his right hand and wrapped his left around the small of Ben's back. Ben draped his right arm across the smaller man's shoulders. "Shall we give it a go?"

Slowly, they started up the steep incline. Ben's left hand gripped the iron side rail for additional support and balance.

"Guess I should've gone up Richland Avenue and avoided the Footbridge."

"Painful?"

"Some. It's more like a dull ache now. When it happened, it hurt so bad I almost cried."

"Your knee?"

"Yeah."

"Football?"

"Yeah. In practice yesterday."

"What's the prognosis?"

"Not real sure yet. It could require surgery. Hope not."

Ben's breath was labored, and the young stranger was beginning to sweat from the exertion.

"Wanna rest a minute?" Ben asked.

"When we get to the top will be fine."

"You sure?"

"Quite."

When they reached the top of the incline and stepped onto the level center span, the two young men paused to catch their breaths.

"What's your name?"

"Gerry Graham."

"Nice to meet you, Gerry." They pumped hands. "I'm-"

"Ben Lawrence."

Ben's eyes widened in surprise. "That's right, but how did you know? Freshman football players aren't exactly campus celebrities."

"Very true," Gerry said pleasantly. "I know your name simply because you live in Gam. As I do."

"You live in Gam? I-"

"I know. I'm not altogether noticeable or noteworthy. And there are four hundred of us in Gam."

"Have you ever come to one of our freshman games?"

"No."

"That puts you in a large majority." Ben grinned self-deprecatingly. "If we were a national secret, there'd be no need to guard us."

"The adoring crowd awaits you."

"I hope."

"Your football career-"

"Could be over."

"The prospect doesn't seem to devastate you."

"I said *could*. But if it is, I'll still have my scholarship. They won't take that away unless I quit. Which I won't, except on doctor's orders, and that should keep my scholarship. And I do want to keep playing."

"I take it your scholarship is rather important to you."

"It's my ticket to the future outside of a factory. I respect the people who work there. I just don't want that kind of work."

"How about the chance to play professional football?"

Ben laughed. "There was a time in high school when I thought I was that good. Then I came here. The way I see it now, I'll be lucky to start here before I'm a senior. And if some young hotshot comes along behind me, my butt could wind up collecting splinters for the next three years. I've found out what great is and I'm not. But that's all right. The main thing is to get my education, and I need to keep my scholarship to get it. How about you?"

"Me?"

"Financially."

"Oh, my father has a good job, and my mother works too."

"Any brothers or sisters?"

"None," Gerry smiled. "I'm the sole heir."

They had resumed walking, had cleared the bridge and were nearing East Green.

"Where do you live in Gam?" asked Ben.

"Second floor in the back."

"That explains why I don't remember seeing you. I'm third floor front."

"I've seen you elsewhere – off campus."

"Off campus? Where?"

"At the Union Bar."

"I haven't been there often."

"Ah, but you were there one night I'll not soon forget. Nor you, I'll wager."

Ben scratched the side of his head. "When was that?"

"Last autumn. You and a friend, your roommate, I believe. Both of you were, shall we say, somewhat inebriated."

"Oh, my God, no," Ben half groaned. "You're right. We were flat-assed bombed. And it was intentional. I was trying to erase a rocky academic start."

"Did you succeed?"

"I'll say. We just about erased everything that night. How's school treating you?"

"Quite well."

"How well is that?"

"I had a 3.65 the first semester."

Ben whistled admiringly. "That's outstanding. Congratulations."

"Thank you."

"Do you play tennis equally well?"

"Well, but not that well," said Gerry. "I don't play often enough to become truly proficient. And you?"

"Never picked up a racket. Always too busy with football and baseball. But if my knee doesn't come around, I might be looking for another sport. One where you don't have to worry about spikes or cleats or shoulder pads."

"You should try it anyway."

"You a good teacher?"

"Yes, as a matter of fact, and my fees are quite reasonable…free for friends."

"If that's an offer, I accept."

"Done."

"Can we seal this contract with a beer? My treat."

"When?"

"This weekend."

"Where?"

"Your choice."

"Well, actually," said Gerry, "I'm partial to the Union Bar."

The chance meeting burgeoned into a great friendship. Ben's injury, a severe sprain, didn't require surgery. He continued to play football, second string, but took up tennis anyway. Gerry taught him to stroke tennis balls nearly as sharply as he'd once lined baseballs. They drank together, most often in the Union Bar & Grill. They listened to music together. Gerry's favorite performer was Marianne Faithful. Ben's was a group, The Lovin' Spoonful. Occasionally on weekends they played catch with a football to relax and, in large part, to help keep Ben's arm in tune. Gerry could sling a football with surprising authority. He was smallish but raw-boned and strong.

Each semester beginning with their sophomore year, Gerry and Ben wagered on grades. The payoff was a beer and cheese coney.

In the summers they corresponded. They compared notes on whose summer job was most boring. Gerry worked in shipping and receiving at TRW Valve Division, a Cleveland auto parts manufacturer; only the capriciousness of sharp steel crating bands that he had to maneuver and cut kept him from dozing off on the job. Ben worked at AMF, helping to assemble automatic pinspotting machines for shipment to bowling emporiums.

In the summer of 1964, Ben visited Gerry's home in Lakewood, a western Cleveland suburb. They saw a major league baseball game and explored Cleveland's Vincent Street, a block-long beacon for those bent on evading virtue. In the summer of 1965, Gerry visited Ben in Shelby, where the agenda was more pastoral than provocative.

At school the two young men never felt closer than when they conversed, which they did often and long. Their friendship stood the test of disagreement. On some subjects their views meshed about as smoothly as those of Cornelius Vanderbilt and Karl Marx. They used to joke that the more they disagreed, the more their friendship seemed to grow. There was truth in that. Perhaps it was because they felt so old-shoe comfortable with each other. Theirs was a friendship not weakened by pretension. The more they learned about each other, no matter how surprising the new knowledge, the more comfortable they felt.

Once they and Jeff Zink went to see Max Von Sydow in *The Greatest Story Ever Told*. Afterward they headed to the Union Bar & Grill for beer and banter.

"Different kind of flick," observed Ben. "It was interesting the way they gave Christ a personality."

"Mmm. I thought it was a bit much," said Gerry.

"How so?"

"Well, it was a trifle literal for me. As when the devil tempted Christ in the desert. Not a credible story to begin with."

"Uh-huh," Ben cleared his throat. "I say, old man, do I detect a note of skepticism?"

"Actually, you devil, you detect atheism."

Ben and Jeff chuckled. "Nice crafting of the king's English, clever chap," said Ben, barely grinning.

"'Twas a noble effort," Gerry smiled, eyes twinkling above the heavy shadow that twice-daily shaves could not erase.

"Never knew you were an atheist. I mean, you never said and I never asked, but still, it's-"

"Surprising."

"Yeah. How come?"

"No evidence," said Gerry. "A ripping tale at times but no compelling evidence of God."

"I see. How about Christ?"

"Oh, yes. I believe he existed. But as a man, not God or the son of God. The immaculate conception is a biological myth."

"How about the miracles?"

"I don't dismiss miracles. Nor do I doubt the power of the mind. With proper incentive the mind can manipulate the body to perform miraculous deeds. But not conceive life."

"How long have you been an atheist?" Ben asked.

"Years."

"I sort of go along with Gerry," Jeff interjected softly.

"What?"

"I wouldn't call myself an atheist, but I have my doubts."

Ben smiled incredulously. "Here I am with my two best friends. Drinking. Relaxing after a movie. And I learn that one doesn't believe in God and the other's on the fence. My illusions are crumbling."

"They're unhealthy anyway. How about you?" Jeff asked Ben. "Do you believe in God?"

"Too scared not to." Everybody chuckled. "Yes, I believe. Sometimes I can't figure him out, but I believe. Although I have changed my mind about some of the things the Catholic church teaches."

"Like what?" Jeff asked.

"Like confession. I've come to agree with the Protestants. You don't need a priest to get forgiveness."

"Anything else?"

"Yeah. Original sin. I don't buy that anymore. I can't see a compassionate God burdening a baby with sin. And denying him heaven if he dies before he's baptized. And Communion. I don't believe the bread and wine become the body and blood of Christ anymore. I think it's a symbol, a beautiful one, but that's all. When I think of some priests I've known, I can't believe that a mere mortal can have the power to transform bread and wine into body and blood."

"I believe you're beginning to read the map correctly," Gerry kidded.

"Maybe, but I doubt I'll ever take your road. Too many dangerous curves and cliffs. Like I said, I'd be afraid not to believe. Especially if I was dying."

"Do you believe in the devil and hell?"

"I'm not sure about the devil. Hell, yeah. But I've come to believe that hell must be reserved for the world's true low-lifes. The real bastards. The Hitlers and the Capones. I think you've got to commit a real bad one to get a ticket for hell. Eternity is a long time, and I don't think God would doom anyone to burn forever unless he killed or crippled someone."

"So what about me?" Gerry asked. "Am I a candidate for salvation?"

"A little heat might do you some good in the faith department." Grins all around. "But no, I don't think you'll burn forever," said Ben. "But I'll tell ya, if I had death knocking at my door, I think I'd like the man upstairs to count me as a loyalist."

"Nothing wrong with safe politics," said Gerry.

"How about some kind of life after death?" Ben asked Gerry.

"Some kind of myth."

"And you?" Ben asked Jeff.

"The same as with God. Still undecided. Not ready to cast my vote."

"How about another round of beers?" said Ben. "Can we find unanimity there?"

Before 1965, among Ben and his friends Vietnam was a matter of little concern and infrequent discussion. People still debated how to spell the country – Vietnam or Viet Nam. Then in February Viet Cong attacks on Pleiku and Quinhon infuriated Lyndon Baines Johnson. The president ordered bombing reprisals. Ben saw the headlines, and a gut feeling told him immediately that his future had been altered. Before those first bombing missions Ben thought he stood a good chance of avoiding military service. Draft calls had been low and not particularly threatening.

On March 8, 1965, 3,500 Marines went splashing ashore at Da Nang. On June 9, General William Westmoreland coined the term *search and destroy* mission. In the fall Ben, Jeff and Gerry returned to school two days before classes resumed. All had reserved single rooms in the third floor front section of Gam. On a sticky September evening the threesome strolled to the Union Bar & Grill. The talk was of war before the waiter brought the first round of beers.

"My mom wants me to go to grad school," said Jeff.

"Is she against the war?" Ben asked.

"She hasn't said. She just doesn't want me to be drafted."

"How do *you* feel about it?" said Ben.

"I hope the war's over by then," answered Jeff. "I'm not crazy about being drafted, but I'm not real hot to go to grad school. How about you?"

"Well," Ben said pensively, "I don't think the war'll be over by the time we graduate. It's just heating up. It's funny though. I'm getting some of the same stuff about grad school. My dad wants me to go. So does my brother. They both fought and they both believe in serving their country, but they don't want me to go if I can help it. They both pointed out very clearly that grad school means a deferment. And by then maybe the war will be over."

"So?" asked Jeff.

"So I'm not hot on going to grad school either. School's been fun. Hell, except for having to associate with you two reprobates, it's been great. But when I'm done here, I'd like a change. I'd like to get a job and make some money."

"Philosophically?" Jeff asked.

"I'm not against the war," said Ben. "Oh, I'm not sold on the domino theory. And I sure as hell don't believe the communists will storm California if Vietnam falls. But I do think the U.S. should honor its commitments. We promised to help Vietnam and I think we should. If that means I get drafted," Ben shrugged, "so be it."

"At least you don't have to worry about it," Jeff said to Gerry.

"What do you mean?"

"You're not a U.S. citizen."

"My friend," Gerry smiled ruefully, "I'm a resident alien, a class which is very much subject to fulfilling American military obligations."

"Oh. Well, you could always go back to England," said Jeff.

"I might. The prospect of being drafted is damned disturbing. The U.S. should not be there. I am opposed to the war. Unalterably. It's unmitigated madness." Gerry was speaking quietly but with an intensity that surprised his friends. He sensed their surprise, drew a breath and modulated his voice. "The war in Vietnam is a civil war. America has no business there. It's wrong and it's stupid. Vietnam was a disaster for the French, and it will be a disaster for America. Mark my words. There is no logical reason for America to keep any commitment to a government that is rife with corruption. It's a war that benefits only Vietnam's corrupt leaders and America's military-industrial complex. The directors of Dow and Dupont and General Motors and TRW are having a bloody field day. I want no part of that. None."

"Would you go if drafted?" Ben asked softly.

"I'm definitely planning to go to grad school. If it's still not over by then and if I'm not married – that's another deferment," Gerry smiled ruefully. "I don't know...I'm not a shirker. Look, the whole sordid affair smacks of colonialism, and that is the product of another age, another era."

"Which is pretty convenient," Ben noted dryly, "given Mother England's history."

"Touché, old chap."

In June of 1966, commencement Sunday at OU dawned sunny and humid. That afternoon heavy caps and gowns would bake the wearers in some 2,000 rayon ovens. Apart from graduating seniors and their families and friends, few students remained on campus. Ben and Gerry already were on their way to New York for a long-planned visit with Jeff. He would show them the sights and delights of his beloved Big Apple before they returned to their humdrum summer jobs.

In .the Zeta Tau Alpha house that morning in Athens a welter of emotions was buffeting Kate Santiago. She was bidding tearful farewells to sorority sisters with whom she had grown closer than she ever thought possible four fast years before. In the midst of clinging, emotion-charged embraces there were heartfelt pledges to stay in touch.

Through the pain of impending separation from beloved friends Kate also was excited and happy. Her parents, both sets of grandparents, her two older sisters and Dick Lawrence all had come to see her graduate. At that moment they all were breakfasting with Natalie at the Ohio University Inn on the southern fringe of campus. Besides her graduation, Kate's family had come for another reason. They were eager to meet the young man Kate would wed on the Sunday after commencement.

A year earlier in the spring of 1965, Kate's Athenian adventure had taken a dramatic turn during J-Prom, a week-long festival of float building, parades, costume skits, parties and other revelry. Preparations for the annual rite had begun a month earlier when the names of men's and women's dorms and Greek houses were tossed into two hats. In the drawing, each men's housing unit was paired with a women's unit. The women of Zeta Tau Alpha were matched with the men of Bush Hall, which sat adjacent to Gam on East Green.

During the early days of the hectic month, Kate found herself drawn like a moth to a flame to a stocky, bespectacled junior. He was helping build backdrops for the Zeta-Bush skit. Clearly he enjoyed the participation, but he went at it quietly and methodically. The endless horseplay among his Bush buddies and the Zetas amused him, but he concentrated on measuring, sawing and hammering. His thick forearms and hands, Kate could see, were used to tools and manual labor.

Kate had caught his eyes watching her on several occasions, but apart from friendly smiles he made no overtures. His detachment was frustrating her. She considered taking some kind of initiative, but he seemed shy and she didn't want to appear bold and threatening. The age of inhibition, if still not in flower, hadn't perished. Then one day a hand tapped her on the shoulder. She turned. Laconically, he asked her to steady a board while he sawed.

Jacob "Jake" Avery stood five feet nine inches. His sandy hair already was thinning and retreating up his forehead. His face was broad and round. Clear plastic framed the lenses of his glasses. His face and his foggy voice both seemed far older than his 21 years.

Jake Avery, Kate soon learned, was very accustomed to hard, solitary work. He was the product of three generations of Ohio farmers. His rural upbringing had been simple but satisfying. He took pleasure in planting seeds that were transformed into fields of golden grain. He had helped foal a colt, for him an unforgettably magic moment. He was a practical young man who could identify the causes of problems quickly and solve them smoothly. He rarely was ruffled.

Jake cherished his farm heritage, but he had decided on a future in which delicate instruments rather than bulky agricultural implements would occupy his hands. Jake was aiming for medical school. The eldest of two brothers and a sister, Jake enjoyed the unswerving backing of his parents. In high school he felt sure that his decision to pursue a college pre-med major would upset his mother and father. He was wrong. They were thrilled and proud. Farming was a hallowed family tradition, they explained, but not one they felt should shackle their children to the soil.

Jake had several choices. He was the kind of prize med schools drooled over. Exceptional student. Active in extracurriculars. Skilled athlete. Mature. Articulate. And not shy. Deliberate and somewhat taciturn but decisive and direct.

Kate had not gone to college in search of a husband. Certainly Jake wasn't stalking a potential wife. As a future med school student, Jake knew he would fare best without unnecessary distractions or complications.

Enter love. Not at first sight but not long after. When it hove into view, it rolled forward like a summer storm. Kate and Jake were swept up and thrown about by a tornado of emotions. At first it all seemed hopelessly complex. California woman, Midwest man. Medical school they didn't know where yet. Uncertain finances. Catholic and Methodist.

Then one night, standing under an ancient oak, Jake clasped his brawny fingers behind Kate's back. "We're going to get married," he announced, "and soon. I'll convert to Catholicism. Financially we'll make ends meet. Somehow. We're in love and that's that. We might have to scrape and scratch but we'll cope." Kate peered adoringly into his solemn hazel eyes and beamed. He was a calloused, kind pillar of strength set on a foundation of unshakable confidence. She was strong, too, and they would make it work. "Time's on our side," Jake figured. "We have better than a year to sort things out and that's time enough." He was proved right.

311

During their senior year resolutions arrived. Kate and Jake would be married in California right after graduation. Natalie would be the bridesmaid, Jake's younger brother Alex best man. The early June ceremony wouldn't give them much time to prepare for the wedding – indeed, Maria enthusiastically took on the bulk of that chore – but it would give them most of the summer to get settled before Jake started medical school classes back east at Columbia.

The newlyweds would honeymoon on Santa Catalina Island. On their wedding night Jake would make love to a virgin. Once in New York Kate would try to find a teaching job. That failing, she would take the best available opportunity. They were presented – and appreciated deeply – a substantial financial cushion. Both sets of parents would contribute to their support. In fact, both the Santiagos and the Averys insisted on helping. Jake and Kate accepted, but only on the condition that the assistance be regarded as a loan which eventually they would repay.

Natalie was thrilled by Kate's good fortune. Nevertheless, melancholy was nipping at her emotions. The curtain was dropping on the long-running Kate and Natalie show. No longer could the younger follow the older. From now on, Natalie's act would be solo.

CHAPTER 30

Dick watched an overweight pigeon flutter to a graceless landing on the ledge outside his office. The plucky bird eyed Dick, then strutted nonchalantly out of sight. Dick turned away, walked down the hall and rapped on John's door.

"Come in," came the reply.

When Dick opened the door, John was seated behind his mahogany desk, intently reviewing papers strewn on the highly polished surface. John looked up. "Morning, Dick. Sit down. Like some coffee?"

"Sounds good."

John stood and poured from a pot on the credenza behind his desk. Dick sipped.

"Well," sighed John, "had enough time to think about it?"

"I guess so." Dick shifted in the blue leather guest chair.

"Good offer, huh?"

"Very generous."

"If we sold, we'd be very rich men. Never have to work again."

"For sure," said Dick. "Of course, I already have more money than I ever dreamed of. I'm not sure I'd know what to do with anymore."

"I know how you feel. Sometimes it seems like yesterday that I went to see Maria's father at the bank."

"How long's it been?"

"Over thirty years now."

"You've come a long way," said Dick.

"No small thanks to you."

"Aah."

"Now don't slough it off. You're a big reason, maybe the biggest, why another company is offering to buy us out. The smartest move I made was making you my partner. The next smartest was listening when you said we should switch to a closely held corporation. In this day and age lawyers are looking for a lawsuit behind every falling brick and loose board. The sidewalk superintendent's been replaced by the sidewalk shyster. We could damn well be penniless if we were still a partnership and still personally liable for every foul-up. Incorporating was your idea, and I'll bet it's saved us a bundle."

"Maybe."

"No doubt. Besides, now that I'm getting along in years, being incorporated will make it a lot easier on everyone when I retire. Or if something happens to me."

"You thinking of retiring?"

"No...no. In fact, I still get a charge out of getting up and coming to work."

"Me too." Dick sipped his coffee. "Of course, if we did sell, we'd have plenty of money to start a new company."

"I said I enjoy coming to work," John smiled wryly. "I don't think I'm game to start over from scratch. Have you forgotten the headaches that go with building a good organization? Finding good people? The endless paperwork, the snags?"

Dick shook his head and smiled. "Not by any means. I guess I was just thinking out loud."

"And testing the waters?"

"Yeah. Actually, Mr. Santiago, I share your sentiments." He smiled.

"That's reassuring – or scary."

"So," said Dick, "I guess we've made our decision."

"Looks that way."

By the early 1960s, Western Construction ranked among the largest building firms in booming Southern California. Western's growth rate kept accelerating as John and Dick guided the firm through a diversification plan, with emphasis on acquiring and maintaining expertise in construction management and real estate management.

Previously Western's business was limited to building to others' specifications. Now as construction managers the firm helped formulate specifications by coordinating the thinking and work of clients, architects, interior designers, subcontractors and general contractors (which on most projects was Western itself.) Its real estate management capability enabled Western to reap the benefits of operating the choicest office buildings and shopping centers it built.

Dick enjoyed the luxuries his success permitted. His special pride was one of Westwood's loveliest homes. The house contained more rooms than Dick needed, but he had left his apartment because he had begun to feel boxed in. He wanted room to spread out. He liked having an office at home and a library and a den with a superb stereo system. He liked strolling from room to room.

During the Christmas holidays in 1965, he finally persuaded Edward and Harriet to let him fly them to California. They and Susie came for a delightful week in late January of 1966. Ben could have joined them during semester break but elected to stay on campus with Jeff and Gerry.

In recent years Dick had taken to treating himself to luxury vacations. Among his favorite destinations were London, Florence and Zurich.

Dick found little joy in traveling alone, so he didn't. Instead, he invited a woman to join him. He delighted in sharing his excitement with a lovely companion equally thrilled by medieval castles, spectacular museums and snow-shrouded mountains. He marveled at aged structures, at the engineering and craftsmanship that allowed them to withstand centuries of wear and tear.

Dick's traveling companions ranged in age from their mid 20s to early 40s. All were good-looking, intelligent, curious and spirited.

Most of his dating relationships endured at least several months. They started to unravel whenever the talk turned seriously to marriage – a subject never initiated by Dick. In other matters Dick was unafraid to make and keep commitments. A friend was a friend for life. A deal was a deal, a promise a promise. A question deserved an answer, not an evasion. The exception was marriage. It was a topic that discomfited him. When a girlfriend broached that subject, Dick was kind but clear; he wanted steady companionship but not contractual obligations.

That had not always been the case. Save for his Korean misadventure, he would have wed Helen Wakefield Hoerner. Save for Ann Sheridan's hardheaded assessment of Hollywood marriages, he gladly would have made her Ann Lawrence. He no longer felt a compulsion to marry. Besides, remaining single offered advantages. Foremost among them was his continuing friendship with Ann.

Ann's last movie was 1957's *Woman and the Hunter.* When film parts no longer came her way, it was Dick who helped persuade proud, stubborn Ann to try television. The glamour of TV, he told her, might never match the sheen of the wide screen, but TV would continue to grow in popularity and prestige. And TV advertising revenues, Dick predicted, would one day dwarf box office billings. For once in their long friendship, Dick joshed Ann, she should let him prevail.

She did and was glad. During the next few years Ann's TV credits included *The Perry Como Show, Playhouse 90, Climax, U.S. Steel Hour, Ford Theater, Lux Video Theater* and *Wagon Train.* Later she succumbed to the lure of series work and, in 1965-66, starred in an NBC soap opera, *Another World.* "It pays the bills," Ann said bluntly. Since that was daytime TV, Dick seldom saw her perform. "That's just as well," Ann told him. When Dick did happen to see the show, he saw that Ann had managed to rise above her material. He told her so, she demurred, he insisted, and she grudgingly conceded that she was giving it her all, which was obvious to Dick.

In June of 1966, Ann exchanged wedding vows a third time. As were the first two husbands, this groom was an actor. Ann had met Scott

McKay eight years before when they co-starred in the play *Kind Sir*. Dick was surprised when, days before the wedding, Ann had told him of her plans. More so, he was chagrined. He had to bite his tongue to keep from suggesting an alternative mate. Ann sensed his hurt and squeezed and held him. "Friends," she reminded him, "we're each other's best."

That same year she contracted to play Henrietta Hanks, a sassy grandmother, in *Pistols 'n' Petticoats*, a spoof of westerns produced by Universal Studios and CBS. Dick watched enthusiastically the early episodes. Ann's performances were vintage Sheridan - effervescent, spunky, sensitive, intelligent.

Soon after *Pistols 'n' Petticoats* debuted in September of 1966, Ann began to feel tired. She complained to no one. Her role on *Another World* had taught her that series work is draining. She tried to slow down and rest, but she couldn't pull herself back up to snuff. She felt perpetually fatigued, the way a person feels when running a low-grade fever that refuses to break. She plowed on, confident that whatever bug had bitten her soon would have its fill and move on to another meal. But the fatigue persisted, and although she couldn't be sure, she sensed it had worsened. Still she told no one. She didn't want to worry anyone. Finally, though, she decided to see her doctor.

When the phone rang early on a Saturday morning, Dick was still asleep. The first few rings seemed eerily like part of a dream. It took several rings to penetrate his consciousness. Then he stirred and reached for the phone.

"Dick, this is Ann. I'm sorry if I disturbed you."

"That's okay. Must be important."

"It is."

"Where are you?"

"At home."

"Oh, what's up?"

"Could you meet me at Malibu? Spend the night?"

"Uh, well…your husband…Scott…"

"It's important, Dick."

"Well…"

"Don't ask me to explain now. I know my timing might be bad. I know it's asking a lot. But I would really like to see you."

"A rough patch?"

"Yes."

"I'll be there."

A strong breeze was whipping their hair as they strolled along a favorite stretch of sand. Ann wore a light dress and sweater, Dick cotton slacks and a long-sleeved shirt. Ann wore leather sandals, Dick sneakers. The sand crunched under their feet. Ann's hands were clasped behind her back, Dick's jammed into his pants pockets.

"I thought it might have been marriage problems," Dick said. "I almost wish it was. Are you sure?"

"Yes. The doctor's sure."

Dick breathed deeply and clenched his jaws. He desperately did not want to say anything stupid. "Who else knows?"

"Just you."

"Not Scott?"

"I couldn't bring myself to tell him. Not yet. Which is rich, isn't it? Me, afraid to tell somebody something. After a lifetime of shooting off my mouth."

"I think I understand," Dick said quietly.

"I didn't want to tell you either. But I needed to tell someone. Keeping it inside made it more frightening. You're my best friend. A soulmate. And, well, you're tough. You've handled some tough times. I thought I could lean on you." She faced him, eyes seeking reassurance.

"I'm glad you picked me. Lean all you want." He smiled kindly. "I'll do anything for you, and gladly. You know that."

"I know."

"This weekend?"

"I just want you to be with me."

"I will. Every second. No naps on the balcony either." They both laughed at his recollection of their first shared weekend at her Malibu house, 16 years earlier.

"How long have we known each other, Dick?"

"Not long enough."

"Let's see. Since we first met…It's twenty-one years now. I guess our friendship has come of age." She smiled, briefly, sadly.

"Our friendship came of age ages ago," Dick declared. "I've never had a better friend. Never."

"Me either."

They walked on.

"Dick, any regrets?"

"About us?"

"Not necessarily, but...well, okay, about us."

"Just one thing," he said.

A long pause.

"Well, Sir Pea Coat, do I have to drag it out of you?"

"My lady, it's a shame that you have a head full of horse sense."

"What?"

"If you didn't have so damn much horse sense, we'd probably have gotten married. At least, I would have pushed a lot harder. We may have been damned unhappy, but the way I feel right now, I wish we'd have given it a try."

"You're sweet, Dick, but we were right. Don't regret that, please. Anything else?"

"Between us?"

"No. Just anything."

"I suppose, but nothing worth mentioning. Nothing we haven't talked about before."

"How about Korea?"

"You mean going back?"

"Yes."

"We talked about that. A long time ago. Our first weekend here, as I recall."

"I know..."

"Way back then," he said, "were you really trying to talk me into going back?"

"No. No, I wasn't."

"But now?"

"Not trying to talk you into it."

"But?"

"But," she smiled, "I guess I'd like to know that you were at least thinking about it."

Dick smiled affectionately. "I'll admit I've thought about it from time to time. But I don't even know if the Yoons are still alive. If they survived the war."

"You'll never know if you don't go," Ann said quietly.

"You're a hell of a woman."

"Then you'll think about it?"

"Yes."

"Promise?"

He crossed his heart and she smiled, satisfied.

Dick took Ann's hand and squeezed. He didn't let go. For the remainder of their walk he held it gently, occasionally squeezing. That night he didn't let go either. As she slept, he lay awake. The last two decades paraded slowly through Dick's thoughts in a long line of evocative floats. Some were decorated gaily and depicted treasured moments of love and affection and achievement and fun. Others, shaded in black and gray and blue, lumbered by heavily and portrayed times of disappointment and frustration and sadness. The night passed slowly, yet all too fast. All through it Dick held Ann gently, occasionally caressing her shoulders and back. He didn't let go until the stars faded before the early morning rays of the new day's sun.

CHAPTER 31

Colonel Presser lit a Winston cigarette, fingered the small knot of his black necktie and crossed his legs. Exhaled gray smoke streamed from his nostrils, and a wisp curled lazily from the cigarette's tip. Twenty Gam Hall seniors sat around him at one end of the dorm's lounge.

"We're glad you could come, Colonel," said Jeff Zink.

"My pleasure. I don't get many invitations to mix with civilians. We ROTC people are beginning to feel like campus outcasts." Friendly smiles all around. "Now how do you want me to begin?"

"With our options," said Jeff.

"Okay, fine…First of all, as I think you all know, it's too late for you to get into ROTC. Of course I doubt if many of you are sorry about that." More smiles from the seniors. "But you wouldn't have asked me here if you didn't realize one other thing. Namely, if you're healthy, it's likely you'll soon be wearing a uniform. That's not a pleasant prospect for some of you, probably most. But Vietnam is reality and so is the draft. You could dodge the draft – go underground or skip the country – but that's only for the dumb and the desperate. I'll assume you're neither.

"Now, let's talk about the most painless options," said Colonel Presser. "Grad school and marriage. Both of them get you a deferment. The war could be over before your deferment's up. Of course it may not be. And all of you should remember that a deferment is just that. It's a postponement, not a cancellation. It's like a baseball rainout; chances are you'll have to make up the game. And since I think this is going to be a long, long game, your postponement could be very, very brief. Especially if your local draft board needs healthy young men. Deferments are not guarantees.

"Personally," Colonel Presser went on, "I don't recommend deferments. Military service will disrupt your life, delay your career, no matter when you serve. By the way, it could also help your career. You'd be surprised how good military service looks to employers. But the longer you wait, the rougher it will be. Physically, too. You'd be surprised how much tougher basic training is at twenty-four or twenty-five than twenty-two. And remember, you're subject to the draft until your twenty-sixth birthday. For most of you, that's four or five more years down the road – a far piece."

"So what do you recommend?" asked Ben.

"You'll soon be college graduates. If you serve, you don't want to be taking orders from twenty-year-old second lieutenants – or eighteen-year-old corporals. You'd find that tough to swallow. It would grate on you. I think you should think about OCS – Officer Candidate School. Go that route and you serve as a second lieutenant. You could give some orders instead of just taking them, and you'd have a better choice of military occupations."

"What's that mean in terms of time?" said Ben.

"Well, you start with your basic two-year obligation. OCS means another six months or so. You may have to wait a few weeks after basic training to get in. Afterward, you may have to wait a few weeks for your assignment. Altogether, you should count on, say, two years and nine or ten months."

"Seems like a long time," said Ben.

"It depends," said Colonel Presser.

"On what?"

"Your assignment and your attitude. I won't kid you. Each day in the Army can seem like an eternity. Like a jail sentence. Or it can shoot by like a hot date."

"What about enlisting?" Jeff asked.

"Three years," said the colonel.

"Ugh," muttered Ben. "Is there anything else?"

"The National Guard. Just six months of active duty. But then there's six years of weekend meetings and summer camps."

"Now, that *does* sound like a jail sentence. What's the fastest way in and out?" Ben asked.

"Volunteer for the draft."

"How so?"

"Well, you can get in as soon as you want – literally," said Colonel Presser. "You go to your draft board and tell them when you want to volunteer for the draft. They'll accommodate you as long as you're asking to be drafted sooner than they think you would have been called. Then you serve two years. If you serve in Vietnam or Thailand or Korea, you can get out three months early."

"That doesn't sound too bad," said Jeff.

"Yeah, I think even I could handle twenty-one months," said Ben.

Colonel Presser smiled. "There is one thing to keep in mind about the draft. Even if you volunteer."

"That being?"

"You've no mastery over your fate. Enlist or go to OCS and you might wind up with a cushy job. Or at least one that's relatively safe and interesting. Go with the draft and you could end up toting an M-14. And slogging through bug-infested swamps. The draft is like poker; you ante up and you take your chances."

CHAPTER 32

A man in a gray suit and topcoat pounded a wooden stake through the snow and into the ground in the Hoerners' front yard. Roger and Helen watched silently from the living room picture window. It was a cold day and the man shivered and hunched his shoulders.

Roger felt empty, purposeless. The man with the hammer might as well have pounded the stake through Roger's chest. It would have offered less resistance than the frozen ground.

Nailed to the stake was a sign. It was simple and direct. The home on Morningside was *For Sale.*

The Hoerners weren't moving far, but neither were they moving because they wanted to. Roger still could climb stairs but not without embarrassingly slow, awkward exertion that left him gasping. At Shelby High School, three stories tall, Roger's classroom always had been on the third floor. The emotional sap that had previously risen at the onset of each school year lay congealed in his leaden feet.

Moving two floors down at school was upsetting. Moving from Morningside was painful to the point of depression. This home had been Roger and Helen's dream and later their sanctuary and pride. Inside, on the gloomiest, most frigid days, they felt as warm and comfortable as lovers in front of a crackling fireplace, which they often were. Friends repeatedly told them their home was bright and cheery and fun to visit. Today it was as cheerless and gloomy as the weather.

The house and the Hoerners were no longer compatible. With all the enthusiasm attendant shopping for socks or soap, they searched for and found on nearby Woodland Drive a ranch-style house built on a concrete slab. Only two steps from the front walk onto the porch. Just one from the garage into the house. Compact. Convenient.

The man in the yard inspected the *For Sale* sign and started back to the house. Helen hugged Roger and smiled. Helen took his arm and they walked to the door to greet the man. He was aware of their reason for selling and felt ill at ease. He assured them he would phone as soon as he received the first inquiry. Then he walked quickly to his car. Roger closed the door.

CHAPTER 33

Dick knew how he would spend the day. A force, unseen but powerful, would pull him along. About 10:00, he parked his car on Ocean Avenue in Santa Monica. Hands on the steering wheel, he straightened and locked his arms and rested the back of his head against the seat. He stared at the car's roof for a long moment, then got out. He walked across narrow Palisades Park, looked at the beach below and stared out to sea. He shifted his gaze northwest to the Santa Monica Mountains, then swung his head south to the long pier.

Slowly he descended the steep steps to the nearly deserted beach. He walked across the wide expanse of sand toward the blue Pacific. With each step he felt more alone. With the emerald water lapping at his shoes, he squatted and fingered the wet sand. It was an unplanned motion but not a meaningless gesture. In the past these waters symbolized a special companionship, extraordinary joy. Today as the sand and water slid between his fingers, tears trickled down his cheeks.

He stood and dabbed them with a kerchief. Then he turned and walked along the water's edge toward the pier. Behind him water seeped into a single trail of shoeprints. Slowly he climbed the wooden steps to the pier. This winter morning, except for screeching gulls, it was quiet.

Dick shuffled to the carousel. He remembered the time he had coaxed Ann Sheridan into riding one of the glossy wooden steeds. A red one, he recalled. He remembered the squealing children and the bouncy music. It seemed like yesterday. It had been 16 years. He remembered patting Ann's bottom as she mounted.

Dick left the pier, returned to his car and drove northwest to Malibu. He was responding to urges that he chose not to resist. At Malibu he again descended steep stairs and began walking a familiar stretch of beach that today seemed strange. It was his first time here alone. His shoulders sagged and his head bowed. The solitude was crushing Dick like a kernel of wheat beneath a ponderous millstone.

Ann died on Saturday, January 21, 1967, in her Oakley Drive house in the San Fernando Valley. The sultry *Oomph Girl* of the 1940s and the sassy Grandma Hanks of TV's *Pistols 'n' Petticoats* would have been 52 on February 21. She was buried after a private funeral service held late on Sunday, January 22, in North Hollywood. Only her closest friends attended.

When she died, Scott McKay, her husband of seven months, was at her bedside. She had kept her cancer a closely guarded secret until the very end. It hadn't been easy. Friends and colleagues on her TV show couldn't help noticing the recent sharp decline in her health. She had weakened and, in her last days on the set, at times could barely stand.

She still was plugging away at Christmas, just weeks after her last weekend with Dick at Malibu. When Ann returned to the set soon after New Year's, the sudden change was startling. The buxom golden-maned star had withered, grown frail and drawn. She managed to continue for a few days more. Then on January 11, she phoned her producer to say she couldn't make it to work. She apologized for the inconvenience.

Ann was one of 33 young girls Paramount Pictures brought to Hollywood in 1933 as part of a promotional campaign for a film called *Search for Beauty.* She was the only one to forge a career from the opportunity. She had moxie, was a hard worker and became a good actress. Most important, Dick knew, she was a friend who could be counted on. He would not forget her gifts, especially the lessons on how to live and love, on how to give without getting. In his grief, Dick counted himself lucky. Ann had enriched his life in a way that still bordered on the incredible. As a young man, their kind of friendship would have seemed impossible. Even now, Dick shook his head over the chance meeting that brought them together in 1945 and the even more bizarre circumstances that led to their unforgettable reunion in 1950.

Dick stopped and turned. He sucked in a great gulp of sea air, held it, then released it slowly. He obliterated the last prints made by his shoes in the sand. A gull swooped low and landed on the beach scant yards from Dick. The gull looked him over imperiously, then strutted away. A small smile flickered on Dick's lips. He looked up at the balcony where he and Ann had shared priceless moments - the talking and listening, joking and laughing, touching and holding, joy and sadness, the sunrises and sunsets.

CHAPTER 34

Seldom does reality match expectation. *History of the English Language* was stacking up as an exception, a rare instance when fact deliciously parallels fancy.

Ben and Jeff had been shopping for a sure-fire Mickey Mouse course. As their final semester approached, senioritis had drained most of their academic energies. The race had been run and won. Both wanted to coast to the finish line. *History of the English Language*, Gerry Graham had assured them, was all downhill.

"I took the course last year, just out of curiosity," said Gerry, "and I found it wholly unchallenging. The course material is lightweight, and Professor Jones telegraphs exams. He always – always – tells his class which questions he will ask on an exam. Also, early in the course, he likes to spring a snap quiz. Not to worry. The results won't count. It's merely his way of insuring that bored upperclassmen read assignments and occasionally deign to come to class."

"Sounds just what we're looking for," said Ben. "Anything else?"

"Yes," said Gerry. "When the good professor informs the class that their miserable quiz scores won't be recorded, he also warns them that there will be more snap quizzes that *will* count. No sweat. He never hit us with another snap quiz."

"Sounds like unadulterated Mickey Mouse," said Jeff.

One afternoon in late January 1967, about two weeks into the spring semester, Ben and Jeff eased into adjacent seats in the second last row in Room 115 in Ellis Hall, a stately edifice built in 1904, three stories high with a huge stone porch and twin winding stone staircases. Professor Jones, short, balding, spare and frumpy-looking in a worn gray tweed jacket, stood placidly at the front of the room. He waited for the pre-class buzz to subside. "Ladies and gentlemen, today, I want you to be sure there is at least one empty seat between any two of you. No exceptions. Spread out, please. We're having a little pop quiz."

Groans erupted. Except from Ben and Jeff. They faced each other and smiled knowingly. Ben winked as he rose and moved one seat farther from Jeff.

"When you've finished the quiz, you'll be free to leave. Now each of you put two sheets of paper on your desk and put all other books and paper under your seats."

Ben ripped two sheets of white, lined paper from a spiral notebook. As he closed the book, a hand tapped him on the shoulder from behind. Simultaneously, a soft voice asked, "May I borrow some paper? Please?"

Ben responded mechanically. He didn't bother to look back at the source of this request. He yanked two more sheets of paper from the notebook. Still without looking back, Ben passed the paper over his shoulder. The hand took them and the voice whispered, "Thank you."

About 30 minutes later, Ben finished. He was sure he had done poorly. He was unperturbed. Professor Jones' predictability, Gerry had convinced him, was eminently justified. Ben retrieved his books and notebooks from beneath his seat and looked at Jeff who still was writing. As Ben edged past him, he whispered, "See you later." Then, curious, Ben looked at the seat behind his. The occupant's head was bowed over her paper, and long dark brown hair further obscured her face. Ben moved to the aisle, walked to the front of the room and dropped his quiz on the professor's desk. He collected his coat and scarf from a hook on the far wall and left the room. First stop was the men's room. Better to take a leak now before going outside into the January cold. Back in the hallway he pulled on a pair of lined black leather gloves. He walked out the rear door of Ellis and started across College Green's brick walkways toward the intersection of Court and Union Streets.

About 100 feet ahead a young woman was walking slowly, playfully kicking at the snow piled at the edges of the walkway. She was in no hurry. She was wearing a brown cloth coat, brown woolen gloves and knee-high brown leather boots. A mass of lustrous dark brown hair bobbed near her waist. It looked very much like the hair that belonged to the woman who had asked for paper. Ben was curious. His pace quickened. With a child-like absence of pretension the woman continued kicking the snow. Ben watched, amused. When he'd closed to within a dozen feet, he spoke, "I always thought snow was made for throwing."

The woman stopped and turned. She was smiling widely. "Not always. If you ever saw me throw, you'd know why I'm kicking it."

As she spoke, a mask of disbelief clouded Ben's face. He stared, his eyes growing wider.

"What's wrong?" asked the woman.

A grin crept across Ben's face. "I don't believe it," he murmured. "I just don't believe it."

"Believe what?" she half-smiled, puzzled.

"My eyes."

The woman blushed.

"Incredible. Absolutely incredible. I know you. I mean, we haven't met, but I know you."

Not the most creative of lines, the woman was thinking, but spoken with seeming sincerity. Still, she was thinking, I'm not up to listening to any line. She decided on a direct and graceful exit. "Thank you for the paper." She pivoted and began to walk on.

327

"Oh, you're welcome, you're welcome," Ben began to laugh. His hand slapped his thigh.

The woman stopped and turned around. "I, uh-"

"I know," Ben laughed, "you must think I've popped my cork, but this *is* crazy. You don't know me, do you?"

"No."

Ben laughed again in pure delight. "But I know *you*. This is too much."

The woman started laughing in spite of herself. "I don't understand."

"If you're not Natalie Santiago," grinned Ben, "then I'm not Dick Lawrence's brother."

The woman's laughter trailed off. Now it was her turn for incredulity to rule facial features.

Immediately the two were swept into animated conversation. Before they knew it, half an hour had sped by. Natalie was beginning to chill. Ben noticed her discomfort.

"Hey, look," he said, "we'll have to continue this inside. God, you know, I worshipped you when you were a Mouseketeer. What a crush. I used to walk around dreaming about you. 'Course, I wasn't the only one. Whattaya say we get together for a Coke after class next Monday?"

"Terrific. Fine."

That first Coke date at the Baker Center student union led to a second Coke date that led Ben to ask Natalie to accompany him to see a student production of *Stop the World, I Want to Get Off.* The chemistry was right, and it was soon apparent that they both wanted to climb aboard the same world and stay on. Within a month they were seeing each other daily, exclusively. Their budding relationship led Ben to an act unprecedented for him.

Feb. 20, 1967

Dear Big Brother,

Hang on to your hat. Seeing as how I've never written to you, this letter must come as a great shock. Sort of like standing over the epicenter of a California earthquake. In fact, I'm kind of shocked that I'm writing it. But if the mere fact that I'm writing to you bowls you over, wait till you read why.

I met this girl. I know what you're thinking. So what else is new? Right? Ah ha, thought so. Except this particular girl is special. Yeah, yeah, she's good looking and smart and personable and all that. But what makes her really special is you. Gotcha, don't I?

You know her, Big Brother, you know her. Name's Natalie.

Have you picked yourself up off the floor? Damn, I hope you didn't hurt yourself falling.

I met her about a month ago and since then, shall we say, my outlook has been altered. You may see me in California sooner than you ever expected. That's if your old offer to fly me out still stands. Well, does it?

I guess I don't have to tell you she's special. In fact, I guess I can't tell you much about her at all.

My future's kind of up in the air right now, but after graduation I'd sure like to visit her in California. If I come I might even stop by to say hello to you.

Meanwhile, go get drunk and laugh yourself silly over this letter.

Love,

Your Little Brother, Ben

Ben's passion warmed with the temperature. So did Natalie's. They lived to be together, and when they were, their joy in touching each other led to long, clutching embraces. Natalie's teenage resolve not to let a boy's hands wander below her waist evaporated in a clump of trees on the outer fringes of the OU golf course. Only when Ben began tugging at her panties did Natalie regain enough composure to slap a restraining hand on his wrist.

Weeks later Ben and Natalie struck out on a long Saturday morning walk. They went strolling east from Athens and found an unpaved road. Its terminus was a mystery, but they chose to follow its dusty way. No cars or trucks passed them. The countryside that morning looked like the canvas of an Impressionist master. Wisps of white hung randomly in the azure sky. Tall grass waved in a light breeze that carried the scent of wildflowers blooming everywhere. Birds on the wing, especially cardinals and black and orange orioles, colorfully accented the green fields and hills. A narrow stream gurgled under a one-lane wooden bridge.

At one point a path led away from the roadside and across a field to the base of an immense flat rock that looked like a huge gray layer cake. Ben and Natalie left the road and followed the path. It wound around the base of the gray monolith to a pile of smaller flat rocks that climbed like an irregular staircase. They started up. At the top they stared in wonderment. Below them in postcard serenity lay the whole of Athens and the OU campus. A stunning vista. Why word of it had never spread around campus puzzled them. After all, somebody knew about it. The narrow, well-worn path across the field and around the huge stone testified persuasively to frequent traffic. In the distance everything was compressed. Buildings they knew to be hundreds of yards apart appeared to be next-door neighbors. No people could be seen, no sounds heard. They sat on one flat rock, their feet resting on another below. Ben's left arm circled Natalie's waist.

Ben was direct. "Natalie, I want to make love to you, and I want to do it now."

"I know."

"Here. This will be our spot, even if we never return."

Natalie's mind was racing. I've always wanted to remain a virgin until I marry, she thought. A lot has changed, but not that. I also want to give myself to this man. I love him. Deeply. Ben hasn't said he loves me, and I haven't said it to him because I think the man should say it first. That thought amused Natalie. Natalie Santiago, bright, mature, a believer in the sexual equality of women, was thinking very much like a sappy traditionalist. Screw tradition. She faced Ben, looked dreamily at him and whispered, "I love you."

They kissed tenderly. Then Ben pulled away. He unbuttoned his shirt, removed it, wadded it and placed it carefully on the rock behind them. "A pillow."

CHAPTER 35

This was their last night together in the Union Bar & Grill. Graduation was only two days away. Their families would be arriving tomorrow. Ben, Gerry and Jeff hoisted beer mugs and clinked them.

"Here's to you, you colonial buggers," Gerry toasted.

"And," Jeff grinned, "here's to you, you son of an ill-gotten empire."

They both looked at Ben. "Aw, shit, here's to three SOBs – who happen to be friends."

They drank.

"I guess you and Ella just about have everything ironed out," said Ben.

"Just about," said Gerry. "I'm buying her a ring next week. We're going to be married in late August, just before grad school starts."

"She going too?"

"Yes. Her parents and mine have agreed to support us while we get our masters. After that, they'll cut us loose. She'll support me while I get my Ph.D."

"You've got yourself a good woman," said Ben.

"A lucky catch, I assure you," said Gerry. "She's more than I deserve."

"I won't contest that."

Chuckles around the table.

"What about you, my friend?" asked Gerry.

"Me?" said Ben.

"You and Nat."

"Well, there's not much to say," said Ben. "I'm flying out to see her in a couple weeks. Spend at least some of the summer there, depending on when I get called by Uncle Sam for my physical."

"Still volunteering for the draft?" said Gerry.

"Right after graduation."

"You love her."

"Yeah."

"Told her?"

"Not in so many words."

"You should," said Gerry. "It's a grand feeling."

331

"I've wanted to. She's told me. But with the Army...I don't know."

"Having second thoughts?" asked Jeff.

"Not really."

"You could still get into somebody's grad school," said Jeff.

"I don't see *you* changing *your* mind," Ben smiled. "And I don't have a mother begging me to stay in school."

"And," Jeff smiled kindly, "I'm not in love."

"I'll concede there's a difference."

"Big one."

"Yeah, but I still want to get the Army behind me, just like you."

"Ah, Ben," Gerry chimed in brightly, "your two closest friends try to dissuade you from a potentially disastrous course of action and we fail. Fail miserably. The pain is too acute. Without further delay, I must now suggest a new anesthetic – one of unparalleled pain-killing proficiency."

Ben and Jeff exchanged quizzical glances and shrugged. They shifted their gaze to Gerry and eyed him warily. He placed three small white sugar cubes on the table. "An experiment, my friends. On this last night together, we owe ourselves a debt. We must repay it. In full. This shall be the final installment."

D-lysergic acid diethylamide is colorless, odorless and tasteless. The cube that each young man washed down with beer contained about 250 micrograms of LSD, an amount about the size of a grain of salt. By the time the three left the Union Bar & Grill, they were embarking on a trip Gerry had made once before but was unprecedented for Ben and Jeff. Gerry briefed his friends on the experience that awaited them. It would be memorable. Unpredictable but memorable.

Later, as they weaved across darkened College Green, whooping and laughing, growing sillier by the moment, they were experiencing sights and sounds of unmatched clarity. Wild, yet divine music exploded inside their skulls. Darkness notwithstanding, colors of indescribably magnificent hues dazzled their dilated eyes. Jeff stopped to pluck flowers from a carefully tended garden and studied them intently, seeing new detail. Gerry and Ben sank to their hands and knees and sniffed the fragrant nectar. They stood and staggered on.

"Hold it, hold it," Ben cried, standing at the foot of the broad concrete stairs that led to vast Memorial Auditorium on the eastern edge of College

Green. He led his friends up the steps. Clumsily he tugged at a door. It was locked. He tried a second, third and fourth. All were locked. The next one opened. "Come on," exulted Ben, "we're going to make our own commencement speeches."

Gerry and Jeff giggled and followed him inside. They stumbled down the long aisle toward the huge stage. Dim nightlights provided the only illumination. They mounted the stage. Ben staggered off to one wing. He returned, dragging a podium. "Gotta do this right," he giggled. "Who wants to be first?"

"As a big worm from the Big Apple," Jeff proclaimed, "I shall go first in order to avoid the early bird."

Ben and Gerry applauded with mock solemnity.

"First of all," intoned Jeff from behind the podium, "and last of all, there is no all. There is only some. And then some. And when you subtract some from the some, you ain't got much. That's what life is somewhat about. Not much. Some of us, but not all of us, should not always remember that. You dig?"

Ben and Gerry cheered and clapped. Jeff moved away from the podium, curtsied slowly and belched. "Best damn sugar cube I ever licked."

As Ben stumbled to the podium, he nearly tripped over his own feet. "Harrumph, harrumph." He squared his shoulders and raised his chin. "Roses are red, violets are blue, God is our savior, he created OU. Thank you, thank you. Please, please. Enough, please. I promised the president I'd be brief. Please be seated. I appreciate the spontaneous outpouring but - all right already, now that's enough. Mr. President, release the water balloons. Splish, splash, you're all takin' a bath. Hee, hee, hee. Sir, turn the water hoses on the ruffians." Ben stepped away from the podium. With a flourish he unzipped his pants and freed his penis. A torrent poured forth over the edge of the stage to the concrete floor. "Whoosh, whoosh. Back in your seats. Order, order."

Jeff and Gerry were laughing uproariously. Jeff was on his hands and knees, helpless with mirth. He rolled onto his side, then onto his back.

Gerry pitched behind Ben toward the podium. Laughing to the point of crying, he rubbed tears from his eyes. "My esteemed colleagues on this stage. My friends in the audience."

Ben continued spraying until his bladder was empty. "We have them under control now, Gerry. The floor is yours."

333

"Only flies would want it now," said Gerry, wrinkling his nose. "Ah, well, to the point. As you prepare to venture forth, don't forget your Johnson's Baby Powder. There is no reason to chafe the rest of your life. Peace, that is what we all must strive for." His bass voice echoed over the 3,000 empty seats. "Tranquility is society's balm. Remember, a farthing of fun is worth a kilo of carnage. It is more humane to play polo than to ride to the hounds. Death awaits us all, so cheat it as long as you can. It is the epitome of humanitarian behavior to outwit and outmaneuver fate. As you go forth, go quickly and cleverly. Heed the immortal words of that renowned philosopher, Satchel Paige, who cautioned us all: 'Don't look back because something may well be closing on you.'"

"*Gaining*," Ben half shouted, half laughed, "it's *gaining* on you."

"No matter," Gerry sniffed imperiously. "The race belongs to the runner. Living is the cornerstone of life, so live, live! May you live treble the years of Methuselah – and have a bloody fantastic time doing it."

CHAPTER 36

"Man, that shower felt good," said Ben, ambling onto the patio. He was cinching a lightweight beige robe over a green swimsuit. "I think I had about an inch of dust all over me."

"You probably did," smiled Dick. "Why don't you hit the pool for a few laps while I open a couple beers."

"Sounds great."

In mid-August Ben was beginning his seventh week in California. He saw Natalie daily. In the first week he finally brought himself to tell her, "I love you." It hadn't been easy. He wavered even as the words were forming on his lips. But Gerry Graham had been right. Saying it was grand. In the weeks since, Ben had said it often. He and Natalie also had made love as often as privacy allowed. Generally that was at Dick's house when Dick was away. Natalie had begun taking the pill.

Weekdays Ben was working as an all-purpose gofer and helper at a Western Construction building site near Anaheim where a new shopping center was displacing an orange grove. The labor was hard and dirty. The pay was good and would have been better had Dick not checked John Santiago's generous impulses. Dick convinced John that Ben deserved not a cent more than the going rate for a beginning laborer.

Dick and Ben had reveled in each other's company. They ate, drank and swam together. They walked the beach together. They talked about their father's latest setback. In early June, soon after Ben's graduation, Edward had suffered a heart attack. He was hospitalized two weeks, the first in intensive care. Ben had come to California as planned only because Edward had insisted. Now Edward was home resting, adamantly dismissing suggestions that he retire, eager to return to work. "I'm not ready to stay home with my slippers on, rocking in a chair and slowly rotting. I'd rather die working than gather moss on my butt."

Dick returned to the patio holding two cans of Michelob in one hand and two envelopes in the other. Ben saw his half-brother approaching and hauled himself from the chlorinated water.

"You might need both these beers plus a six-pack when you see this envelope," Dick smiled wryly.

"I think I know what you've got," Ben said. "Been expecting it." Ben toweled his hands and took one of the envelopes. The return address bore the stamp of the Richland County Draft Board. Unhurriedly Ben opened the envelope. "I have to be back in two weeks to take my physical. The little old lady at the draft board knew what she was talking about. When I stopped in the day after graduation to check my status, she looked in her files and told me I'd probably be inducted in November. I said I wanted the summer off but didn't want to wait around any longer. She asked if September would be okay. I said sure, and here's my notice right on schedule."

"You know," said Dick, "you're not exactly thrilling a lot of people by going ahead with the Army. Especially with Vietnam getting worse. Natalie wishes you'd do almost anything else. So do John and Maria. They think the world of you. Then there's Dad and his reservations. If what I read is true, most young men today are trying their darnedest to stay out of the service."

"I know," smiled Ben.

"It's still not too late to try for a deferment."

"Dick, I'm going to miss Natalie like crazy. Sometimes I ache just thinking about it. But, damn, it just doesn't make sense to put it off. I'm healthy. Sooner or later they'll get me. Then it's two years. You tell me, would it be any easier if we were married, maybe with a kid?"

"Probably not."

"There's something else. I feel I owe my country a duty. Now, I'm not crazy about Vietnam. I'm not even sure we should be there. But if that's the way I have to fulfill my duty, so be it. You understand that, don't you?"

"Only too well," Dick said, sighing. "And deep down, Dad does too. He just doesn't want to see you get hurt, or worse."

"Me either." Ben sighed and took a long pull on the beer. "What's the other letter?"

"Oh, sorry. Almost forgot. Here."

Ben eyed the envelope. It had been forwarded from Shelby. "From Gerry Graham." Ben put his beer down on a small round yellow patio table and opened the envelope. As he began to read, his brow furrowed. He eased onto a chair.

August 12, 1967

My dearest Benjamin,

Sorry not to have written but, hoo boy, have I got an excuse. If you haven't heard, I'm in a hospital in Cleveland and I've got cancer.

Unfortunately, this isn't a joke. Right after I got home from Athens I was plagued by strange pains in my groin. Well, the doctors opened me up and pulled out a tumor. It was malignant and now some has gotten into my lung. So now I'm in the hospital and some specialists in nuclear medicine are going to give me some treatments to stop this stuff.

What's really depressing is that Ella and I have had to postpone our wedding. What a bummer. We're going to tie the knot just as soon as I get out of this bloody place.

I really have no idea what you are doing these days, Benjamin. Nothing strenuous I hope, but then I'm sure you wouldn't do anything strenuous anyway. I hope you haven't gone into the service yet because I would like you to come to visit me in this place. I'm in Lutheran Hospital on Franklin Avenue on the west side of Cleveland.

Last weekend I had a brief parole and went to Athens with Ella to see some friends. Saw a lot of people. They haven't changed. I heard that old friend Jeff Zink got drafted. I'm sorry to hear that and hope old Jeff gets a good break. You, too, for that matter, you old buzzard.

336

The best part was being with Ella. It's a great feeling – being in love with her. Crazy man that I am, I bought a ring I couldn't afford. But the look on her face was worth it. What a groovy feeling. Never have I been so happy. I'm sure you must know all about this.

Look, I hope you're OK, old man. Write to me at my home in Lakewood. If you could come up here, I would like it much. And during the week, you could stay at my place. It would be OK with my folks. Visiting hours are from 2 PM till 8 PM.

I hope to get out of here by September but very little is certain with me anymore.

Your old friend,
Gerry
Keep in touch, Benjamin. I'll write when I can.

CHAPTER 37

Gerry Graham was home now, in his parents' living room. Ben scrutinized him carefully. His weight appeared normal. His color was good, his dark eyes as clear and penetrating as ever. Ben had been prepared for much worse. Gerry was wearing a blue-and-gray plaid bathrobe over a v-neck t-shirt and boxer shorts. He was pacing the floor like a newly caged cat. Ben slouched lazily on the couch but listened intently to his friend's words.

"The doctors think they have it all," said Gerry. "And, mind you, I am exceedingly grateful for that. But this whole sorry episode has thoroughly messed up my life. Delayed my wedding. Delayed grad school. At least they can't draft me in my condition." He was biting off the words savagely. "Apart from that, there's bloody little good to say about all this."

Ben sighed and spoke quietly. "Have you reset your wedding date? I'd like to make it if I can."

"That would be very nice, old man, but no, my parents, without saying it in so many words, don't think it would be prudent for us to get married until the doctors are sure about the cancer. Or at least, more sure. They're right, of course, but that doesn't make waiting much easier."

"How much longer?"

"They want me to undergo treatment for another month or so. If things look good, then we'll set a new wedding date. Which won't arrive soon enough to suit me."

"How do you feel?" Ben had wanted to ask that since he walked through the door. Until this moment, though, it had seemed like an entirely inappropriate question.

"Fine. I get tired pretty easily but, otherwise, fine."

"That pacing for exercise?" Ben asked softly through a half smile he didn't really expect would mask his concern.

Gerry chuckled. "You old buzzard. Since when did you become diplomatic? Why don't you just tell me to sit down?"

"Sit down."

"Thanks, I can't."

They laughed.

Ben had returned to Shelby after Labor Day. A week later he and a busload of other draftees had traveled to Columbus for their physicals. The next week he had visited Gerry. In parting they exchanged promises to write often and see each other when circumstances allowed, however infrequent that might be.

That same month Natalie started graduate school. She planned to pursue a master's in English at UCLA and live at home. She had no desire to live alone. John and Maria made it plain that they would be available for company and counsel but otherwise would not intrude on her thoughts or comings and goings. Natalie appreciated their sensitivity.

In school her mind tussled with Geoffrey Chaucer and Samuel Johnson while her heart transmitted messages of love and longing to Shelby. Ben's airport farewell had battered her emotional foundation. Tears had spilled in torrents from the saddest eyes Ben ever had seen. As he pulled away to board the jet, tears clouded his own eyes. He tried to speak but a constricting throat choked off his words. He finally managed a croaked "I love you." She pressed her face against his chest and whispered the same words. They parted silently.

Now she wrote Ben daily. Long, heartfelt letters that over and over told him how much she missed him and how she longed for the day when she would be Mrs. Ben Lawrence. Exclamation points, often in long series, dotted her letters like blades of grass in a newly seeded lawn.

What hurt Ben most was knowing that their separation could span 104 interminable weeks. He tried to console himself with frequent reminders that separation now was better than later. But are we fools, he thought, to think that our love can stand that kind of strain? His gut wrenched at the possible answer.

In mid-October Ben received word he'd passed his physical. He would be inducted November 9. During those last weeks at home he read, helped Edward with the household chores, wrote often to Natalie and phoned her weekly. Twice he went bow hunting with his dad. He also watched his Shelby Whippets race through a 10-0 season, part of a 35-game unbeaten streak that would not end until the opening game of 1970.

Ben's unstructured, unhurried interlude was shattered by an alarm clock at 5 a.m. At 6:00, Ben and Edward pulled up in front of the Richland County Draft Board. Father and son bid a warm, quick farewell. An hour later after receiving medical papers from a Board clerk and a sewing kit from the Red Cross and standing around for 45 minutes, Ben and some 30 other men boarded an aging green bus bound for the induction center at Fort Hayes, 70 miles south in Columbus.

At noon he got his first sampling of Army chow. It was served on paper plates with plastic utensils. The meal was long on balance and short on taste.

At 1:00 he was ushered into a small room. He was asked to take one step forward and to raise his right hand. Ironic, he thought, here I am swearing to uphold the United States Constitution and at the same moment surrendering my constitutional rights to freedom of speech and assembly. For the next two years I'll say, do, and go as ordered – or else. Inwardly he smiled, certain that other such ironies lurked, poised to pounce.

Later than day, Ben boarded a Delta Airlines twin-engine turboprop. The destination was Fort Jackson, outside Columbia, South Carolina. After stops at Cincinnati, Chattanooga and Atlanta, it was 9:00 when the plane plopped roughly onto the runway at Columbia. The night was wet, windy and cold. Outside the terminal Ben and fellow inductees – tired, hungry and shivering – boarded another ancient green bus. Ben was beginning to doubt the transportation capability of the modern Army.

Half an hour later the bus braked in front of an equally aging yellow frame structure that bore a large sign: *Welcome to the United States Army Reception Station.* Flags from all the states fluttered from poles anchored to the railing of a banistered porch. Ben did not feel welcome. Instead, he felt like an alien in a hostile land. He glanced at his watch. 10:00. He stepped off the bus. On the pavement in front of him were white footprints to guide the newly inducted. Geez, he thought derisively, just how stupid does the Army think we are?

After a few minutes a white-frocked young man appeared on the porch. He seemed friendly enough as he beckoned the recruits. Inside, he spoke authoritatively. "Take off your coats and roll up your shirt sleeves." During the next hour both of Ben's arms were peppered with air-powered inoculations. The rest of the night Ben watched sleepily and skeptically a movie that touted the glories of military service, filled out forms and sat on hard, wooden chairs. The hours ticked by slowly.

About 5 a.m., roughly 24 hours after Ben had awakened in Shelby, the recruits were hustled outside and herded into a two-and-a-half-ton truck, a deuce and a half, as Ben later would learn to call it. Minutes later Ben and his mates were deposited at a faded yellow splintered barracks that looked like an oversized derelict chicken coop. Inside, he deposited his personal belongings in a battered gray locker, then was directed back outside and aboard the truck.

Next came breakfast. Ben had five minutes to wolf down his first meal since lunch the previous day. Then it was on to a small nearby building, also yellow, aged and splintering. This was the moment Ben had been expecting and dreading. Inside was a row of barber chairs. Beside each slouched a white-frocked man with glazed eyes. Holy shit, thought Ben, a haircut at six in the morning. Those guys look like they just climbed out of a coffin. Each man held sinister-looking tools. The operation took about 30 seconds of Ben's time, 75 cents from his pocket and most of his hair. He avoided looking in a mirror. Outside he and other freshly shorn creatures were herded into a converted cattle truck.

The truck went bouncing along for 10 minutes, stopping in front of still another neglected yellow building. It bore a sign that proclaimed: *You will soon be the best-dressed soldier in the world.* At that moment, as short on spirit as on hair, Ben gladly would have become the best-dressed anything else.

For the next few hours he endured seemingly endless lines and uncountable unpleasant remarks from supply personnel. As he left the building another sign declared: *You are now the best-dressed soldier in the world.* With his civilian clothes and his morale crushed against the bottom of a stuffed duffle bag, Ben felt like he had been outfitted at a church rummage sale.

At 8 a.m. Wednesday, 51 hours after last awaking, Ben was told he could sleep. With the grace of a toppling stone statue he flopped onto an Army cot. He thought of Natalie a few moments, squeezed his eyes shut to bring her image more sharply into focus and then, too tired to be depressed, submitted to sleep.

On the fourth day, new recruits were given orders, telling them where they would undergo basic training. Some would remain at Fort Jackson for the seven-week course but most, including Ben, were ordered to Fort Gordon, Georgia.

During the last four days rarely had Natalie been absent from Ben's thoughts. As each hour of each day crept by, he missed her more and more. Once while on barracks fire watch in the dead of night, exhausted, alone, dwelling on Natalie and how much longer he would have to endure separation, tears came welling into his eyes. Never had he felt so godawful rotten.

CHAPTER 38

This time the surgeon removed part of Edward Lawrence's stomach. Through his hospital gown, Edward fingered the new scar. Five years, he mused, and you are supposed to feel safe. I never did. First it was part of my bladder, now my stomach. The doctors don't feel this is related to the first time. And they think they have it all again. Maybe I'm just prone to cancer. Like some people are prone to accidents or broken bones. If I am, what's next? A lung? Damned if I'll give up smoking. Not after all these years. If I do get it again, will they catch it in time? Could I beat it again? I can live with the pain. God, what pain. After they cut through your belly twice, what else can you expect? But the pain reminds me how good it feels to be alive. And it does feel good. Tomorrow I get out and go home. I can't wait.

Edward looked across the room. In a chair in front of the window Dick was napping. Wonder how long he's been there, thought Edward. Must have replaced Harriet while I was asleep. No wonder he's tired. Home for my surgery, then back to California. Then back here again to be sure everything's okay. Couldn't ask for a better son. Such a worrywart. Reminds me of me. Tomorrow I'm booting his rear end out of here and back to California, whether he likes it or not.

I wonder how much time I've got left, mused Edward. I'm 67. I've outlived Sarah by over 30 years, Bill by over 20. Who would have dreamed it? I've already lived longer than most men. What's the average? 65 maybe? Keeps getting higher but can't be much over 70. There can't be many years left.

But I'm not ready to die. First time I had cancer I wanted to live to see Ben graduate from college. Made that. I wanted to see Susie married. Made that too. I'd like to be a grandfather. That's my new goal. Hang on till I'm a grandfather. High time, anyway. A man 67 ought to be a grandfather. Susie's my best bet. Ironic. My youngest could be the first to make me Grandpa Lawrence. She's been married now, what? seven, eight months? Shouldn't have to wait much longer. Hmph. I hope they aren't delaying on purpose. 'Course, that might not be all that bad. The longer she and Bruce take the longer I'll have to hang on. Take your sweet time, kids.

Edward shifted in his bed and groaned. Dick stirred. Dammit, Edward reproached himself, keep it down. Dick needs sleep. Damn pain. Maybe I'll ring for a nurse. Take something to help. No, no. Gotta get used to it. Besides, it'll get better. Always be some pain, but it'll ease.

Truth be told, I'm afraid to die. Silly, an old man and afraid to die. Funny, this is really the first time I've ever admitted it to myself. I've known it; I've just never owned up to it like this. I'm not sure I could ever tell anyone else. Who would understand? Or if they did understand, it would probably make them feel uncomfortable. Queasy. An old man who's going to die, and probably soon, and he's telling me he's afraid. Change the subject, old man. Why should I be afraid? I tell myself I'm a good man and have lived a good life. But how good? Just how forgiving is God? That's the problem. Death is final but it's also very uncertain. What's on the other side of the gate? If I get through the gate. I don't know. No one knows. That's why I'm afraid. Huh, admitting it to myself helps a little. At least for now.

I want to be a grandfather but I don't want to outlive another wife or child. Don't know if I could take that and I don't want to find out. If Ben makes it through the Army, I shouldn't have to find out. God keep him.

Cancer, it sure doesn't care what chicken it plucks. I get it twice as an old man. Ben's friend Gerry gets it as a young man. Hope he makes it. God keep him, too.

Well, Edward, you old fart. What's next? Maybe I should slow down. Retire. Put myself out to pasture. Just walk out of the barn and have someone lock the door behind me. Now that's enough to scare anyone.

CHAPTER 39

Strange, Ben ruminated, but I'm not the least bit nervous. But then why should I be? Vietnam has been a foregone conclusion since I was inducted. Ben sat calmly while a sergeant first class riffled through a stack of papers on a clipboard. Ben and his classmates at the Defense Information School had been told to report to the dayroom to receive their permanent assignments. The school at Fort Benjamin Harrison just north of Indianapolis graduated a class of new Army correspondents every week. Every man in the last five classes had been ordered to Vietnam.

Ben's assignment to the school had surprised him. I mean, he had thought, the Army is actually taking into account my OU journalism degree. Imagine that.

Eighteen men were in Ben's class. They had graduated and were gathered now to receive travel orders. The sergeant read 12 names and told those men they were heading for Vietnam. Ben's name had not been read. Not Vietnam, he thought dully, I'm not going to Vietnam? Then where? The answer for Ben was Korea. The last lucky five received assignments in Germany and at U.S. posts.

Korea, thought Ben, I don't believe it. No one ever mentioned Korea. What are we still doing in Korea? The war ended, what? fourteen, fifteen years ago? How many troops are there? What are they doing there? What will I be doing there? Korea! Dick was trapped there when the war broke out in 1950. And Eisenhower went there after becoming president. I remember seeing Ike on TV from Korea. But what else?

In a way, Ben thought, it's a relief. It must be safer in Korea than Vietnam. No swamps, no snipers, no snakes, no scorpions. Not so bad. I'm either living right or I'm just plain lucky. I guess this must be the lucky break Gerry wished for me. Wonder how he's doing?

Ben had five days to report to Fort Lewis, Washington, some 40 miles south of Seattle-Tacoma Airport. He wasted little time. From Indianapolis he drove a rental car to Shelby for family farewells. The next morning he flew from Cleveland to Los Angeles. Dick, Natalie and the Santiagos greeted him at Los Angeles International. The next four days were an emotional roller coaster. He and Natalie were very much in love and they held nothing back. They talked little about the next year. The pain of the last six months' separation told them how much they would hurt during the next 13 months.

"It's such a long time," Natalie moaned on their last night together. "You'll be so far away. Oh, Ben, I miss you already and you're not even gone. Why did you have to volunteer? Why?"

Ben held her but remained silent. Debate at this point would make no difference except probably to worsen the hurt. Besides, he had nothing new to say.

"I know, I know," she whispered miserably, "we've already been through all that. But it's so hard. These last six months have been just awful. I missed you so."

"I missed you, too, more than you'll ever know."

"I'll write every day and we'll get married just as soon as you get back. I'll start making plans just as soon as you leave."

"We're not even engaged," Ben smiled.

"Oh, who needs a ring? Engagements are passé."

"Are they?"

"Well, they should be," Natalie declared. "In our case anyway. What more is there to know? We love each other. We've known each other more than a year. We've been apart for six months and our love is stronger than ever. But I'll tell you what, Mr. Lawrence. I'll compromise. I'll wait until you have only six months to go in Korea, then we'll set a wedding date.

You're coming back in June. We'll be married in July. That way you'll have time to buy a ring and we can be engaged officially."

"That's a thoughtful, generous compromise, Miss Santiago. I accept your terms."

"I knew you'd see it my way. I love you so very much. You know that?"

"I know."

"You better. Thirteen months. That's an eternity. I won't stop missing you for a minute. For a second. Thank God, you're not going to Vietnam. It's not dangerous in Korea, is it?"

As the Boeing 707 went sweeping up the Pacific Coast from Los Angeles to Seattle, Ben wondered what lay ahead. Besides time, that is. Where would he be stationed? In a forward camp? At a headquarters? Will I live in a tent or a barracks? What's the weather like? What's the terrain like? He half wished he'd taken some time to learn something about Korea. But that would have meant less precious time with Natalie and there was no question about his priorities.

He also was thinking about Dick. On their way to the airport with Natalie on the front seat between them, Dick had asked Ben a favor.

"Sure, I'll try," Ben responded.

"Thanks. That's all you can do," smiled Dick. "It may not be possible or practical. And if it's not, don't worry."

"I won't but I'll try."

The request surprised Ben. It was the last thing he expected to hear from Dick. He thought it would be something like *Please write to your parents at least once a week.* For all Dick's predictability, thought Ben, I guess he's capable of springing an occasional surprise. Or maybe his reputation just doesn't fit him anymore.

Ben logged barely a day and a half at Fort Lewis. Most of his time was spent processing records and orders and loafing. At the Fort Lewis Replacements Station goldbricking was de rigueur. Soldiers didn't worry about hiding and getting caught. After all, what could Uncle Sam do? Send you to Vietnam or Korea?

At midnight on a Saturday Ben's journey regained momentum. He turned in the bed sheets he had used only one night. Two hours later, baggage was checked. At 5:00, he boarded a bus for nearby McChord Air Base. Minutes later in the early morning haze he walked across the tarmac to a Northwest Orient 707. The cabin lights stared eerily through the murky morning. Strangely, Ben felt thoroughly at ease, more like he was embarking on a Sunday afternoon ride through the Ohio countryside than an 8,000-mile, year-long journey to the unknown.

Flight 287 roared off the runway at 6:00. As the hours ticked by, Ben dozed for long stretches. When a stewardess gently prodded him and offered a hot meal, Ben accepted gratefully.

A few of the younger men, infantrymen in particular, wondered aloud where they would be stationed. Some seemed apprehensive. Maybe they know more about Korea than I do, Ben reflected. Which isn't saying much, he smiled ruefully.

An hour and twenty minutes east of Japan, the lone stop en route, the pilot announced they had crossed the international dateline. It was now Monday, a day ahead. Fascinating, Ben thought, drowsily. By the time the stewardess removed his coffee cup, he was asleep again.

As the plane taxied to a stop at Yakota Air Base near Tokyo, soft music began to waft through the cabin. Ben's mind switched to Natalie. Melancholy descended on him. Thousands of miles in a few hours. So far, so fast, and for so long. Lord, I miss her.

The pilot asked the troops to deplane and wait inside the terminal while the jet was serviced and crews changed. A steady rain pelted Ben as he descended the stairs. The cool wetness refreshed him. Ben surveyed the base. Parked in the grayness were numerous camouflaged jet fighters and freighters. Wonder where they're headed, he mused.

To the other side of the world in a matter of hours. From Seattle to Seoul. From the American rat race to "The Land of the Morning Calm."

As Ben, weary but slept out, passed well-wishing stewardesses and descended the portable stairs at Kimpo Airport, his mind began to register impressions. A pinkish sun hovered in a hazy noon sky. The temperature rested comfortably in the 60s. In every direction, no matter where he looked, mountains rose to meet the heavens. Some of the peaks bore a few trees, others none. Even at the lower elevations trees were scarce. A result of the war? Probably not, Ben concluded. If there had been trees before, they would be growing back by now.

He moved inside a building near the terminal. Army medics waited to plunge a needle into each hip. He exchanged dollars for military scrip. Then he hoisted the clumsy duffle bag and trudged to a waiting bus.

The barrenness of the airport landscape quickly gave way to lush paddies and fields worked by bronzed farmers and massive oxen. The air was unpleasantly scented.

On a half-paved road, buses, trucks, cars and carts, bikes and motorbikes, and scurrying pedestrians vied for space among gaping potholes. Repeatedly Ben's bus lurched violently as the driver, devoid of visible emotion, jerked the wheel to avoid collisions. If they keep traffic fatality statistics, mused Ben, the everyday tally must look like a U.S. holiday highway death toll – with pedestrian casualties outnumbering the vehicular variety.

The bus passed through several hamlets that crowded the snaking road. Most of the homes were earthen walled with thatched roofs. A few were cement block with gray or red tile roofs. The communities were cramped and poverty-ridden, but the people seemed remarkably serene. Low expectations, Ben conjectured.

Ben hadn't thought about what to expect in the way of native dress, but what he saw surprised him. Tailored business suits and daring miniskirts mingled with pajama-like pants and brocade ankle-length dresses. The traditional garb was predominantly white.

Twelve miles and 45 grueling minutes from Kimpo the bus slammed to a halt. Ben winced as pain surged through his tender hips. Ascom City was a replacement station, even less inviting than Fort Lewis. Faded corrugated metal Quonset huts squatted inside a barbed wire-protected enclosure. Once more Ben hoisted the bulky duffle bag. It swung against his hip and again he winced in pain. Inside one of the huts a captain greeted them. His remarks were mercifully brief. There was some additional processing, then Ben was assigned a bunk for the night. The time difference – 17 hours – between the West Coast and Korea disoriented Ben. He was sure only that he was tired. Quickly sleep pushed aside jet lag.

CHAPTER 40

It was morning of Ben's first day at Yongsan Compound on the southeastern fringe of Seoul and headquarters for all 60,000 U.S. forces stationed in Korea. The compound also housed HQ for United Nations Command, a largely paper vestige of the Korean War that existed chiefly for ceremonial and political purposes. Besides Americans the only non-Korean troops in the UN Command were one company of Thais, a dozen British who rotated in every three months from Hong Kong and four Turks. The British, Turks and four men from the Thai company, along with some Americans and Koreans chosen carefully for their imposing height and bearing, formed the United Nations Honor Guard.

Yongsan was a sprawling complex of Quonset huts and brick and cement block buildings. Forested Namsan Mountain to the north hovered over the compound. Japan had constructed the camp during its 35-year occupation of Korea, which ended with the close of World War II. Ben's living quarters were in a 50-yard-long two-story red brick building that the Japanese had built for cavalry. Horses had been stabled on the ground floor, troops quartered above. Now American soldiers lived on both floors.

Three other soldiers shared Ben's ground-level bay. One houseboy, 37-year-old Pak, made their bunks, polished boots and low-cuts, laundered uniforms, dusted and mopped floors. He did likewise for four other soldiers in the adjoining bay. Each GI paid Pak $10 a month plus an occasional six-pack of American beer or carton of stateside cigarettes. By Korean standards Pak was on the high side of the middle class. To keep up appearances – few houseboys were willing to disclose to family and friends that they were GI liveries – Pak arrived and departed each day in a business suit. Inside the barracks he changed into old fatigues. Pak stood five feet five inches. He was slight but handsome and trimly muscled. His black eyes were clear, and his perfectly aligned white teeth contrasted sharply with a head of thick coal-black hair. He was hardworking, friendly and spoke passable English. He said little unless addressed but, when asked, spoke openly of himself and his circumstances. When Ben arrived, Pak had been a houseboy at Yongsan for 14 years.

The night before, Ben had slept little. Nonetheless, he felt buoyant. Correspondent. It had a satisfying ring. As he strode to his first day of work, Ben happily reviewed the job as the staff at Fort Benjamin Harrison had described it. He would research and write news releases, get clearances up the chain of command and with Korean government ministries and plan their distribution. There would be releases on humdrum matters such as soldiers earning ribbons. Those releases amounted to military propaganda that went only to military publications and hometown newspapers and, in the case of college graduates, alumni magazines. There would be occasional releases on weapons shipments and the deaths of GI's killed in firefights that, 15 years after a truce was declared, still flared daily along the DMZ. Those releases were distributed more widely, commonly going to the Korean press and sometimes to Associated Press and Reuters. He also would research and write feature stories for distribution both locally and worldwide.

He regularly would cover the truce talks at Panmunjom in the DMZ. Formal hostilities had ended in 1953, but the meetings still droned on. Once every week or 10 days. At most sessions the two sides traded vitriolic broadsides, the polemics usually concerning armed incursions and firefights. Each accusation was routinely denied. These days, though, some meetings were much more substantive, although no less volatile. On January 23, 1968, the intelligence ship USS Pueblo had been attacked and captured by North Korean torpedo boats and a submarine chaser in the Sea of Japan. Since then, Commander Lloyd Bucher and the Pueblo's crew had been imprisoned in North Korea. One member of the 83-man crew had died during the seizure. The two sides had been negotiating the crew's release for four months with negligible progress. Other duties would have Ben preparing predawn world news summaries for visiting military and civilian dignitaries and covering military maneuvers.

The job meant variety, travel and the opportunity to write. Of all the incredible luck, Ben mused. Here I am a lowly draftee, and I'm actually getting a chance to do what I went to college for. I wonder how Jeff is doing and where he's at. Vietnam, probably. And Gerry, I hope he pulls through. And Natalie. Jesus, I miss her. I haven't had time to write since I got off the plane.

Ben reported to the office of Drew LeBeau, a civilian and second in command to Colonel Frank Baumgarten. About 45 people worked in Public Affairs. There were 18 Army officers and men, two Navy lieutenants and an Air Force major. The rest were civilians, about evenly divided between Americans and Koreans.

LeBeau escorted Ben down the hall to a large office and introduced him to Sergeant First Class Harry Taber. Then LeBeau introduced Ben to Dave Bedford, a 30-year-old, pudgy, wavy-haired civilian who coordinated the correspondents' assignments and edited their copy. "Ben," LeBeau said next, "this is Specialist Four Clarence McDermott."

McDermott stood. "Nice to meet you."

"Same here," smiled Ben.

"And," said LeBeau, moving to another gray metal desk where a young man was rising, "this is Specialist Four Dan Cohen."

They shook hands.

LeBeau looked at an empty desk chair. Before he could say anything, Ben spotted the nameplate on the desk. He did an involuntary double take, his head whipsawing right and back to the left.

"Something wrong?" asked LeBeau.

"No. Nothing. Tell me, Mr. LeBeau-"

"Drew."

"Okay, Drew, what do you know about that correspondent?" Ben motioned to the empty chair.

Drew shrugged. "Well, he hasn't been here long. Arrived about the same time as Clarence. Good man. Tall. A college graduate. Journalism major."

"From Ohio University?"

"Yes. Say, that's where you're from."

Ben picked up the nameplate. It read: SP4 Zink. He smiled.

"Do you know Jeff Zink?" asked LeBeau.

"We were roommates."

"Lord, love a duck. Well, I guess you two should know how to work together closely. Which is good because you'll be doing a lot of that here. Oh, by the way, if you like, Sergeant Taber can get you a change of quarters so you can room with Dan and Clarence and your old roomie. It'll just mean switching with one other soldier next door. Should have put you there from the get-go. Would you like that?"

"Very much."

350

"Good. Makes things work a lot easier. There are no phones in the barracks, so it's easier to find a body when you need it. Saves chasing around."

Dan Cohen, like Jeff Zink, was from New York. Otherwise, differences dwarfed that common ground. Dan had grown up in Queens, the son of a middleclass haberdashery owner. He stood five feet ten inches with slightly stooped shoulders and weighed 155 pounds. Black hair crowned a round face that was perpetually shadowed by a heavy beard. Dan saw the world through deep-set brown eyes that somehow looked sad even above a broad smile. He was a chronic worrier and a perfectionist. He also was considerate and dependable. He was not notably religious but, in the absence of a rabbi, conducted services for the few Jewish GI's at Yongsan. He read rapidly and with remarkable retention. He loved to spend Sunday mornings in the compound's small library, plowing through novels as he sipped cup after cup of freshly brewed coffee. Dan played Scrabble well and was nearly unbeatable at gin. He had graduated from Columbia University with a journalism degree, been drafted and, after basic training, sent to Fort Benjamin Harrison. He was a good reporter and writer.

Dan had no wife or girlfriend at home, yet after three months in Korea had remained celibate except for one dalliance. On that night he had bedded a beautiful silken-skinned Korean prostitute and had contracted a urinary infection. Further such exploits, Dan concluded, although tempting, weren't worth the risk. So he stayed away from the busy bars and streets in the Vill just up the hill from the compound. But he did frequent Yongsan's NCO Club. He stopped regularly for a drink or two after work. Whenever his passion for feminine flesh was at its fieriest, he would arrive at the club on a Friday or Saturday night and settle in at a small corner table. He would watch Armed Forces Network TV, regretfully fend off the advances of prostitutes and get tangle-tongued, blurry-eyed plowed. Later he would stumble semiconscious back to the barracks, weave to the latrine and retch, return moaning to his bay, collapse on his bunk and quickly lose his mind to dreamless sleep. Dan called these occasional binges relative therapy. Relative to a comely piece of tail, pretty sorry. Relative to a burning cock, pretty good.

Dan had adjusted. If he suffered from homesickness, it didn't show. Unlike most GI's, he talked little about what he was going to do "when I get out."

Clarence McDermott was the only one of the four correspondents with a nickname. The others called him Casey. They insisted it was because he was the office engineer, the driving force. He wanted to believe them but didn't. In fact, Casey was short for Kind Clarence, a biting allusion to his righteous intolerance for imperfect examples of humanity. In other words, almost everyone else.

Casey was a Missourian who read and cited scriptures, interpreted them literally and showed scant tolerance for sinners. He didn't smoke, drink, swear or whore, and he heaped pointed, unrelenting criticism and threats of heavenly retribution on those who did. Casey was newly married and childless. He masturbated frequently and furtively.

Casey's piety made him a handy target for GI's in need of a human pincushion. They verbally pricked his thin skin, more to salve military irritants than to inflict pain. He had attended Oral Roberts University for two years before being drafted. Like Jeff and Dan he had attended Fort Harrison's Defense Information School. He too had been at Yongsan about a month. He spent most of his spare time reading the Bible, writing letters to his wife and longing for a good fuck. He was a pedestrian reporter and writer who got saddled with more than his share of the office drudgery. That suited him well, for he tried to isolate himself as much as possible from Koreans, whom he saw as slant-eyed, bad-breathed gooks for whom he had little use and less affection. An exception was Miss Lee, the 24-year-old office secretary who had spent much of the Korean War in a hole under her parents' house, hiding from marauding North Korean and Chinese soldiers. Casey granted her a modicum of civility and respect.

CHAPTER 41

"Lawrence, get up," whispered Pak, the correspondents' houseboy. "Lawrence, you get up now. Go to Panmunjom, remember?" Pak jostled Ben lightly, then moved to the other bunks and awakened Jeff, Dan and Casey.

The correspondents showered, shaved and breakfasted heartily. It would be a long day. Then they walked across the compound to a green military bus. Ben, Dan and Jeff, along with Sergeant Taber, climbed aboard. Jeff slid behind the steering wheel, started the engine and began steering the bus across Seoul.

"I'm looking forward to this," Ben said to Dan.

"First time's always exciting. After that..." Dan shrugged. "This meeting should be typical. Both sides will accuse the other of all sorts of evil. Both sides will accuse the other of flimflammery. Nothing will be accomplished. Nothing will change. There will still be firefights every day. People will get shot. The Pueblo crew will still be prisoners. I shudder to think what prison must be like in North Korea."

"How come we wear Khakis or dress greens instead of fatigues to Panmunjom?" Ben asked.

"Protocol. Everyone's supposed to look strack there. It's ironic," said Dan. "If you get north of the Imjin River five days during a month, you get combat pay for that month. We can earn combat pay in dress uniform."

"I take it that protocol is why we don't take any weapons with us."

"Oh, but we do take weapons," Dan grinned, eyelids crinkling. "They're in here." He reached into a bulging leather briefcase and extracted two blue elastic armbands with white lettering. In both English and Korean the armbands read *Press*.

"Are we supposed to put stones in this and use it as a slingshot?" Ben asked.

"That, or use it to slap a communist in the face."

"Sure won't stop many bullets."

"There shouldn't be any," said Dan. "Despite all the firefights and the North Korean intrusions into South Korean territory, there's never been any shooting at Panmunjom itself. The only guys who carry guns there are the American and North Korean honor guards and MPs. And they're limited to side arms. I have to admit, we really play it safe at PMJ. We don't allow any South Koreans to serve in the Honor Guard there. Too much bad blood with the North Koreans to take a chance."

"Is it necessary for four of us to go?"

Dan lighted a cigarette, inhaled deeply and wrinkled his nose. "Nah. Typical Army overkill. We need Jeff to drive. He's the only one of us with a license to drive this crate. You can write the news release and dictate it back to Seoul over the field phone. I'll show you how to get set up for that. We all know how to do it. I'll keep an eye on the South Korean news people. Make sure they don't cause a ruckus. As for Sergeant Taber," Dan winked at Ben and raised his voice, "he'll be in charge of eating cake and drinking coffee."

"Somebody's got to babysit you," the sergeant retorted with mock derision. "The Army needs experience in the DMZ."

"Razor-sharp wit," Dan whispered to Ben below the rumble of the motor and the squeaks and creaks of the bus's complaining body. "But a good man – for a lifer."

After about 15 minutes Jeff swung the bus onto the grounds of the South Korean capitol. Waiting were 20 reporters from Korean newspapers and Dongwha, the national news wire service. Two were women, middle-aged and hardened. The group was high-spirited. Some spoke English, mostly reporters for the two English-language dailies, the Korea Times and Korea Herald. Dan introduced Ben to regulars on the PMJ run. Then Dan passed out a sheet of rules governing behavior at Panmunjom. The don'ts included consuming or transporting alcoholic beverages, presenting gifts to North Koreans without prior approval, entering communist buildings and photographing communist personnel who expressed disapproval. Otherwise it was okay to take pictures and cross into certain areas on the North Korean side of the demarcation line.

Dan reached into his briefcase and began passing out American cigarettes, two packs to each reporter. "You can give these to North Korean personnel if you want and accept theirs in return if offered. But no giving or trading anything else. Okay?"

Dan sat down beside Ben. "They never have any trouble getting North Koreans to accept our cigarettes. They're infinitely better than the malodorous weeds they smoke." Dan lighted another cigarette.

"How far to Panmunjom?" Ben asked.

"In miles or minutes?"

"Both."

"About 35 miles as the crow flies," said Dan. "It takes about two and a half hours. This road makes the Coney Island roller coaster seem like a sleigh ride. You're in for a real bladder-busting treat."

From Seoul the road north was winding but fairly well paved. About an hour later there was an explosion. Ben jumped, startled. Flat tire. Jeff stopped the bus and everyone filed out. Seconds later there was a second explosion, far louder and more jarring than the first, and then another. Ben looked east. About a mile off across the rice paddies he saw smoke rising from an artillery range.

"That," Dan joked to Ben, "is likely to be the most action you'll ever get here."

"I'm not looking for a Purple Heart."

Minutes later, the tire changed, the bus again headed north.

About two-thirds the distance to Panmunjom a town hove into view. Almost simultaneously the paved road gave way to a rutted, dusty, narrow neck of land that curled among undulating rice paddies.

"What's this place?" Ben asked.

"Munsan," Dan answered.

The name rang a faint bell in Ben's memory. He strained to remember. Oh, yeah, Munsan. Dick was north of here when the war broke out. Eighteen years ago this month. Seems like ancient history. To me anyway. Not to Dick though. He remembers it plenty clearly. The road to Panmunjom was Munsan's main street. It coiled through the town as unpredictably as it had through the countryside. Merchants in tiny stalls waited patiently for customers. Ox carts were hauling produce and scrap lumber. Housewives swept the steps of homes with pagoda-like red-tile roofs. At a small, weatherworn station, passengers lugging all manner of inanimate and animate baggage jammed into a red and white rusting bus pointed south. In Munsan Ben saw no grass and few trees. Land was too precious for anything but homes, shops, gardens and livestock.

Minutes later the bus lurched onto a bridge that spanned the Imjin River.

"How often does one of us make it up here five days a month?" Ben asked Dan.

"Not often. Jeff has the best shot because of his driver's license. He makes all the trips. It's worth an extra sixty-five dollars if you do."

About five miles north of the Imjin the bus approached a gate with a sign marked *Joint Security Area*. Jeff braked the bus and opened the door. An American corporal stepped aboard.

"Raise your left arm," Dan instructed. "Show him the blue armband. Without that you don't go any farther on a meeting day."

Just forward of the Joint Security checkpoint was a sign that read *Mines, Danger.* Then another sign: *Warning, Demilitarized Zone—300 yards ahead.* Seconds later the bus passed under another sign that arched over the road: *Southern Boundary—Demilitarized Zone.*

Moments later Jeff wheeled the bus into Panmunjom. Before the war Panmunjom had been an honest-to-goodness village. Now it was a collection of specially built structures populated only on days when the Military Armistice Commission or their secretaries convened. The motley collection of buildings was located in the center of the 151-mile-long, two-and-a-half-mile-wide DMZ.

Jeff stopped the bus. Dan and Ben got off first and stood by to lend a supporting hand to the Korean journalists as they alighted.

Ben stretched inside his khaki uniform and wriggled the toes inside his black low-cuts. "You were right about the effect of this ride on the bladder. Does things to other parts of the anatomy, too."

Dan chuckled. "You'll never get used to it."

Ben surveyed the area. "Not like I thought it would be, although I'm not sure what I expected."

"I had the same reaction my first time."

Panmunjom, translated, means *Inn of the Wooden Gate.* There was no gate of any material to be seen. The first building Ben saw, to the north and built on a small rise, was an architectural mutation dubbed Freedom House. Built by South Korea, Freedom House tried unsuccessfully to combine Eastern and Western design. A pair of two-level rectangular wings, about 30 feet by 15 feet, flanked a three-level circular center section. The second level of one wing contained toilets and a rest area. The other was furnished with tables, metal folding chairs, field telephones and typewriters for the reporters. On meeting days one table always bore two large sheet coffee cakes and a huge coffee urn.

The circular center section rose in sharp contrast to the boxy wings. It enclosed a spiral staircase. The third level, a round observation deck, was crowned with a red-tiled pagoda roof supported by colorful and intricately painted circular columns and capitals. To Ben the contrast between the Oriental and Occidental, the monochromatic white and the deep, dazzling hues, was unconventional and unappealing.

On top of the rise and about 25 yards north of Freedom House was a row of 10 corrugated sheet metal buildings anchored to cement pads. The communists' were painted green, the United Nations' blue. They were rectangular, about 40 feet long, and looked better suited to a waterfront warehouse complex.

The conference building sat in the middle of the row. The main negotiating table cut the conference room in half. A white ribbon – the demarcation line – partitioned the green-clothed table and the two Koreas. The building's exterior was undistinguished except in two respects. It had two entrances, one at each end, so that neither side's representatives had to step foot on the other's territory. It was also flanked on each side by a raised boardwalk that allowed spectators to peer in through high, narrow windows to watch the proceedings.

"Come on," said Dan, "let's get some coffee. The meeting doesn't start until eleven. We've got fifteen minutes."

As they sipped coffee, Ben motioned to the typewriters. "This where I work?"

"Uh-uh," mumbled Dan, chewing cake. "Over there." He pointed to the blue building adjacent to the conference building. "You set up in there."

"How does it work?"

"Easy. After the American negotiator makes his prepared statement in English, it's translated into Korean. I bring you a copy. Then the North Koreans make their opening statement and it's translated into English and Chinese. We don't translate our statements into Chinese because we don't recognize Red China as a country. Anyway, you don't get a copy of the North Korean statements, but it's easy enough to pick up on the key points from the oral translation." Dan put his coffee cup down. "Come on."

They walked to the blue building. Dan opened the door. He pointed to a typewriter and field phone on a metal folding table. "That's for you." Then he pointed to a speaker near the ceiling. "That's so you can hear all

357

the statements and translations. First thing you do is call Yongsan to be sure the phone is working."

"Should I try it now?"

"Why not?"

The meeting started. After the lengthy opening statements, Dan invited Ben outside. "Let's look around. You've got plenty of time during the translations."

They stepped onto the boardwalk on the east side of the conference building. "These meetings are funny," said Dan. "At the Secretaries meetings they're supposed to discuss administrative matters. At the Military Armistice Commission meetings they're supposed to discuss diplomatic issues. Inevitably they all boil down to political haranguing. Shoot, they could just about use the same script every time."

"Even when the subject is the Pueblo crew?"

"No. You're right. For those," Dan said sarcastically, " they have to edit the script to accommodate current events."

They peered inside. On one side of the main table sat two North Korean officers, a senior colonel and a colonel. Behind them at a half dozen other tables sat more North Korean officers and three Chinese officers. Before them on the tables were ashtrays and glasses, the latter containing yellowish liquid which they seldom touched. Considering what it looked like, Ben mused, their abstention was understandable.

An American general always headed the United Nations delegation. This time it was an Air Force brigadier.

At each end of the main speakers' table were two small flags. One was the blue and white UN banner. The other was the North Korean flag that, ironically, was red, white and blue with stripes and a star.

"Those flags are a sterling example of how ludicrous things can get here," observed Dan. "Some time ago at one of the meetings, the North Koreans produced two flags with staffs about three inches higher than the UN flags. You can guess what happened. One-upmanship took on a literal meaning. Before long each side had flags brushing against the ceiling. One of the few agreements ever reached here was to return the flags to their original height."

Ben shook his head. "How long do these meetings last?"

"As long as bladders and lungs hold out," said Dan. "They never take any piss breaks. That would be a sign of weakness. So sometimes you see a lot of fidgeting. And teasing. If somebody on one side sees somebody on the other side beginning to fidget, the first guy will begin to drink water like a fish. They always run at least two hours. I was here for one that went close to seven. That whole meeting was like a broken record. Everyone kept repeating the same darn things."

"Can we take a look around now?"

"Sure."

The grounds around the buildings were gravel covered. But everywhere else was a continuous covering of thick, lush greenery.

"I think this is the most trees I've seen anywhere in Korea," said Ben.

"With no one living or working in the DMZ," said Dan, "it's become the garden spot of Korea."

"I'll bet there's a lot of game in here," said Ben. "Great for hunting."

"There's hunting every day, but the prey is human. Let's walk over to North Korea," said Dan.

They walked between the metal buildings and onto enemy soil.

"Seems strange," Ben said softly. "I can walk back and forth from North Korea at my leisure and just a few miles from here are eighty-two Americans who aren't going anywhere."

"I know," sighed Dan. "But we'll get them back. I really believe that."

To the north of the conference building was North Korea's response to Freedom House. Peace Pagoda was much smaller but more graceful and unmistakably Oriental. It was surrounded by carefully tended trees, bushes, flowers and green park benches.

Each side had guards and military police at Panmunjom. Some manned specific posts while others milled about. Between the two sides was a stiff silence. The armistice rules forbade fraternizing between communist and UN soldiers.

That, however, was not true between soldiers and civilians. The South Korean journalists were particularly garrulous. Many of their conversational gambits to North Korean troops were met by sullen silence.

359

Occasionally, however, they could induce a communist to converse, though usually briefly.

A South Korean reporter beckoned Dan to the boardwalk outside the conference room. Ben followed. The South Korean grinned naughtily. "We have fun." He scribbled something in Korean and tore the page from his notebook. "It say, 'You do not truly seek peace, only war, but if you fight you will be trampled.'" He reached through an open window and handed the note to a junior North Korean officer, who seemed as bored as most by the head table hyperbole. The North Korean read the note and his eyes began blazing. He turned the paper over and scribbled fiercely. He passed the note out. The South Korean reporter translated: "You are imperialistic scum, and one day I shall grind you under my heel." The reporter giggled and began to pen a rejoinder.

"Better stop it there," Dan cautioned him. "He doesn't think your joke is very funny."

"He has no sense of humor," the reporter giggled again.

Dan arched an eyebrow.

"But, okay, no more."

Dan and Ben walked away.

"Will he mind you?" Ben asked.

"Yeah. Without our approval, he gets no press credentials."

They watched while a fresh squad of North Korean guards goose stepped onto the grounds. They halted, saluted smartly, then began milling about. The uniforms of the two sides differed markedly. The American MPs wore form-fitting, sharply creased beige uniforms. The North Koreans' uniforms were dull green, ill-fitting and bulky.

"The North Koreans have an explanation for those god-awful uniforms," Dan smiled. "They say we wear tight-fitting uniforms because there is a shortage of material in the South. They say they have an abundance of material, so it's only reasonable that their uniforms are large and loose fitting. If you look closely, you'll see that their uniforms fall into the category of one-size-fits-all."

Ben chuckled, then turned and walked inside the blue communications building. He sat down, organized his notes and began to compose a news release. I suppose Dan's right, he thought. After a while, these trips to Panmunjom will get boring.

CHAPTER 42

"Mail call."

As usual, Casey McDermott received a letter from his bride. She wrote him daily or nearly so. When she missed a day, Casey seemed more surprised than distressed. "Is that all?" he would ask as Sergeant Taber handed out the last envelope. Nothing more. No sign of inner turmoil. On all those days when he sliced open a letter from his wife, seldom did he show more than smug satisfaction.

Most of the other soldiers, draftees and lifers alike, responded rawly to news from home. Sergeant Taber, fewer than two years from his 20 and out, grimaced and grumbled every time he read a letter in which his wife complained about the long separations and the troubles she had coping. Sometimes he shredded the letters angrily. Taber was into his second marriage, and he desperately wanted this one to survive. He was 36 but looked 50. Stress and chain smoking and a sustained reliance on bourbon and beer had added pounds, lines and years and had smudged the sparkle in his eyes.

Jeff received a message slip telling him to pick up a package at the Yongsan mail room. "It's another care package from my mother." Alice Zink had sent him tins of tuna and sardines, jars of cheese spread, boxes of Ritz crackers and cartons of chocolate chip cookies. She had packed it all in popcorn. That night Jeff shared the loot with the correspondents, but what excited them most was the one nonedible item. Alice Zink had sent a paperback copy of *The Voyeur*, a novel whose pages smoked unrelentingly with sex. In the care packages, Alice consistently enclosed a sex-drenched tale. Her message was clear. Read this to get your rocks off, but whatever you do, stay away from those disease-ridden prostitutes. Jeff, Ben and Dan laughed heartily at Alice's protective measures. Casey chided them. "I don't approve of those trashy books and I certainly wouldn't read them, but I admire your mother's motives." To taunt Casey, the others sometimes would read aloud the steamier passages.

For Ben the news from California was good. There was the daily pledge of love and longing from Natalie. Ben depended on them as heavily as an addict on his daily fix.   When she wrote *I love you and I want to hold you and hug and kiss you and touch you for the rest of my days and nights and forever after*, his spirits soared.   When she described graphically how much she missed him, his heart ached.

The news from Shelby was equally good. Edward was back in harness. He had retired but scarcely slowed down. He was tramping the fields, hunting at least weekly. He fished just as often. When at home he worked feverishly to trim a list of chores that he made sure grew just as fast. He hired no help, not even for the most strenuous jobs.   To Edward, Ben wrote,

Dear Dad,

Are you ever going to slow down? Keep it up and when your time comes, I'll give any odds that you'll be on a ladder or pushing a lawnmower. Or tracking a deer through brush up a hill or wading into a fast-moving stream. But, hey, you and I both know that's better than slowly fading. It's better to aim the camera, snap the shutter, take that last picture and be done with the roll of film.

The news from suburban Cleveland further shored up Ben's morale. In early January Gerry Graham had married Ella and started graduate school later the same month. Gerry wrote,

Old Man, sorry I'm so late in bringing you up to speed but I have been, shall we say, otherwise occupied. This wedded state is blissful indeed. And lawful no less. I'm four-square for it.

You might have guessed. The doctors gave me the green light and I stomped on the gas. Am feeling better than bloody ever. Ella, of course, played no small part in my recovery. When you read this, it will probably be daylight in Korea and night time here. Night time. A time for slumber, which is time lost, but the prelude is pure pleasure.

I promise more details soon. Meanwhile, I hope you are doing all that is possible to remain out of harm's way. Take care, Old Man.

Your faithful friend,

Gerry

Ben grinned widely. Gerry's news was fantastic. Father and friend – the old man and the young lion - had whipped cancer. How's that for kicking death in the teeth?

The news in Korea was good too. Just weeks after he arrived at Yongsan, the Army announced a new regulation. Any GI who stayed in

Vietnam, Korea or Thailand until he had 150 days remaining on his hitch could rotate home and be separated immediately. The old regulation had stipulated 90 days. Ben was ecstatic. Just 19 months of active duty instead of 24. No boring, putting-in-time stateside assignment to fill out the two-year commitment. Home and out. Natalie, Sweetheart, he thought excitedly, hang on!

CHAPTER 43

"You seem a little preoccupied this morning," Maria said as she poured coffee for Natalie.

"I guess I am."

"Thinking of Ben?"

"No, not this morning. I have an appointment with Professor Sloane today, and I'm a little nervous."

"Why is that?"

"I'm late with a term paper and I'm going to ask for an extension."

"I don't think you've ever been late with anything," Maria said, concern elevating slightly the pitch of her voice.

"I know. But don't *you* worry about it. I either get an extension or I don't. I just couldn't seem to get started. And when I did, it was next to impossible to concentrate."

"Ben?"

"Yes. It seems like every time I went to the library to do research, I'd sit there and think of him. I'd try to force his face out of my mind, but it just wouldn't leave. Sometimes," she shook her head in mild self-reproach, "I'd give up and write him a letter."

"It's been difficult, Nat, I know. I'm so glad your dad and I never had to go through a long separation."

"I miss him so much and it's been so long since we've had any time together. I worry that he might be changing or I might be changing, or" Natalie's voice caught. "Better stop before I ruin my eye shadow."

Maria's heart went out to her youngest daughter. None of her other three daughters had had to endure this kind of punishing test. She tried to veer the conversation to a less distressing topic. "What will you tell Professor Sloane?"

Natalie cleared her throat. "I'm not sure. I don't want to lie but I don't want to get into Ben and me."

"You've been a good student. Perhaps you could just cite personal problems and let it go at that."

Professor Sloane tapped a ballpoint pen against his left hand. Momentarily his eyes closed. He opened them and smiled kindly. "In all honesty this comes as a surprise, Natalie. Oh, from time to time I could see you were distracted. Daydreaming perhaps." Natalie reddened. "But I never expected you to be late with your work. Why are you late?"

"Personal problems – which I haven't handled as well as I should."

"I see." Natalie expected Professor Sloane to press for more details and was relieved when he didn't. "How much time do you think you'll need?"

"About two weeks."

"Mmm. Are you sure that's enough time?"

"Yes, I think so."

"Have you finished your research?"

"No. But almost."

"Do you know where your paper is going? Have you outlined it?"

"No, I, uh-"

"Perhaps we could meet to discuss it. To facilitate matters for you. Would you like that?"

"That's very kind of you. I-"

"Shall we do it later today or tomorrow?"

"Yes."

"Over dinner? Tonight or tomorrow night? I think we should get started soon."

"Dinner?" Natalie replied vacantly.

"Yes."

This is all happening too fast, Natalie thought. She struggled to clear her mind and stave off a vague sense of panic. Is he talking about a date or just dinner to talk about the paper? I should say no but how? I came here to ask a favor and he's been so nice. "Maybe we should meet here again," Natalie stammered, blushing anew. "I have a boyfriend." Oh, she groaned inwardly, that sounds so corny.

Professor Sloane discerned her discomfort but wasn't ruffled. He refrained from smiling. "Here will be fine. I saw no ring on your finger, and I've never seen you with anyone. Is he a student here? At UCLA?"

The threat had diminished. Natalie's face began to drain and her pulse slowed. "No, no. He's a soldier. In Korea."

"I see. Has he been there long?"

"Yes - well no. About a month."

"But it seems longer."

"Yes, we…Never mind."

"No, go ahead."

"Well, we haven't seen much of each other for several months."

"Ah, yes, there would have been training before he went to Korea."

She nodded.

"Separations, long ones, can rend the fabric of the strongest relationship. You'll know a lot about yourself when it's over."

"Yes, I suppose."

"I'm sorry that your boyfriend is so far away. And I didn't mean to embarrass you when I asked you to join me for dinner. You are a very intelligent and very attractive young woman."

"Thank you."

Professor Sloane flipped a page on his desk calendar. "Shall we discuss your research and your outline tomorrow? At three? Here?"

"Yes. Fine. Thank you."

That's the first time a teacher ever asked me out, Natalie mused as she went striding across campus toward the library. I know I must have looked and sounded like a blubbering teenager. But he didn't let on. He was so nice. No condescension. I don't know anything about him. Except he's tall, about six-three. A little taller than Ben. His hair is long and brown and dry and sort of unkempt. The eyes are friendly. So is his smile. The voice is…smoky. He speaks sort of slowly, like his voice box always is just waking up from a nap. He's very cool, in the classroom and today in his office. He has some small lines around his eyes. I didn't notice any others. I'd guess he's in his early thirties, maybe…or forty. It's so hard to tell with a man.

Professor Sloane is right, Mom is right, everybody's right about long separations. No love should have to survive them. A year and a half will go by, and Ben and I will've seen each other for five days. Five days out of five hundred. It's so painful, so depressing. I wish we were engaged. The ring might help. Not just to warn other men but to bond us. To make us stronger. Oh, who am I kidding? A ring wouldn't do that. Love doesn't need a ring as a reminder.

I wonder if Professor Sloane is married. I don't remember a ring on his finger. He must be single or else he wouldn't ask me to dinner. Lunch, maybe, but not dinner. Or would he? I really don't know him at all.

CHAPTER 44

"How's the newest smutty tome from Mrs. Zink?" Dan Cohen asked Ben from his bunk. No chairs graced the barracks, so the GI's spent a lot of time reclining on their bunks.

"My kind of book," Ben replied lazily. "You can open it anywhere and you'll be within a page or two of a fucking or a sucking."

"Keep that filthy tongue in your mouth, Lawrence," Casey McDermott snapped. "We don't need that."

Ben ignored Casey and winked at Dan. "It's getting late, Dan. Would you like a bedtime story? I can read two or three pages out loud. Just enough to give you the gist."

"Don't you dare," Casey warned. "That's smut, dirty smut."

"Better not," Dan told Ben. "It might give you the wrong kind of dreams."

"You're gross, too, Cohen," Casey barked under a wrinkled nose.

"Of course," Dan reasoned unflappably, "a wet dream is vastly preferable to a burning dick. I speak from experience. Aah, but I'm down to my last pair of olive drab boxer shorts."

"Pak can do laundry first thing in the morning," Ben suggested.

"Yeah, but he's got no electric dryer."

"True, we couldn't have you in the office with wet boxers," Ben said dryly. " I guess that means your virtuous ears are safe for tonight, Casey."

"Just keep a lid on it, Lawrence."

"Casey," said Dan, "have you seen Jeff?"

"Not since after chow. Went out somewhere."

"Did he say where?"

"Not to me."

"What time is it?" Ben asked.

"Ten-thirty," said Dan.

"He should be back soon."

But he wasn't. Dan and Casey already were asleep when Ben turned off the lights soon after midnight. He was worried. Ben hoped his friend wasn't out on the streets. The nightly curfew ran from midnight until 5 a.m. and was strictly enforced by Korean police who were under standing orders to shoot first and ask questions later. Security in Seoul, always tight, had been cinched still tighter after 30 North Korean agents had tried unsuccessfully to assassinate President Park in early 1968. They had penetrated to within blocks of the Blue House, the presidential residence, before being intercepted. If Jeff was outside Yongsan, where was he? Ben conjured up the worst. He visualized his friend lying dead or dying in an alley, shot by suspicious Korean police. Damn it all, Jeff, why didn't you say where you were going?

Ben awoke to the clip-clop of rubber shower sandals slapping the cement floor of the barracks. He rolled over and sat up in a single motion. Jeff was kicking off the sandals and reaching for clean underwear.

"Damn it," Ben whispered, trying not to waken Dan or Casey, "where the hell were you last night?"

"Aah, you wouldn't believe it."

"Try us," Dan said groggily, head against the pillow and eyes still closed.

"You guys worried about me?"

"Not me," lied Dan.

"The thought did cross my mind," Ben said sarcastically, "that you might have gone bump into trouble. It's not like you've made a habit of staying out all night. Tell me, do you plan to make it a habit?"

"Look, I'm sorry if you were worried. But I'm a big boy."

"Yeah," Casey grumbled suspiciously, "but where were you?"

"I got to drinking with a couple GI's in The Vill. At the King Club."

"That vile place," Casey sniffed.

"You've been there?" Dan asked.

"Oh, get off my case, Cohen. I've heard about it."

"Your entire body of knowledge is second hand."

"Can it, Cohen."

"So what happened then?" Ben asked.

"We got bombed," Jeff shrugged. "Next thing we know it's after midnight. We didn't want to chance being caught out after curfew, so we looked for a place in the Vill."

"And?" said Ben.

"We wound up at the Village Hotel. Three of us. In the same room. Dead drunk. We took the mattress off the bed and put it on the floor and slept there. That was it."

"Jeff, my lad," said Dan, "that sounds just bizarre enough to be true."

"Sounds fishy to me," Casey grumbled.

"Did you have a pass?" Ben asked.

"No. You know the MPs never ask to see one when you leave or return to the compound during the day. Today I found out they don't ask to see it even when you come in before dawn."

That night again Jeff's bunk remained empty. This time Ben worried less. Jeff, he felt, could take care of himself, even with too much booze behind his belt. The next morning Jeff returned as the correspondents were pulling on their fatigues.

"Well," Casey said sarcastically, "I suppose you're going to tell us that you got drunk again at the King Club."

"It was the 7 Club this time," Jeff said evenly.

"Sure, sure. Why don't you tell the truth, Zink? You were probably out with some moose."

Jeff's eyes flashed anger. "Watch it, McDermott. Don't let your bigotry get in the way of the facts."

"Who's a bigot?" Casey growled defensively. "A hooker is a hooker. In Korea they just happen to call 'em a moose. And up in the Vill everybody knows half the gook women are mooses."

"Casey," Ben bit off each word, "if you were Abraham Lincoln, Martin Luther King would have died a slave."

"That's not true," Casey whined. "Everybody calls the Koreans gooks and their prostitutes mooses."

"Not everybody," Ben sighed.

"Look, let's get to work," said Dan.

Jeff was in his bunk that night but not the next. Before he returned in the morning, Ben and Dan both warned Casey to keep quiet. No snide remarks, no accusations, they cautioned him.

When Jeff walked in, they limited the dialogue to strained small talk. Casey muttered, "Morning, Zink." Threatening stares from Ben and Dan froze Casey's lips that begged his mind for permission to say more. Permission denied. On pain of pain.

Jeff had expected a probing examination. The reprieve offered only partial relief. A barracks skirmish would have vented emotions.

The hours at the office that day passed uneventfully. Then late in the afternoon Ben invited Jeff to stop by the NCO Club for an after-work drink. Jeff accepted.

"What'll you have?" Ben asked Jeff. "My treat."

"Beer."

"Same here," Ben told the pretty Korean barmaid.

"Busy day at the office, huh?" Jeff asked.

"Yeah, real busy." A pause. "I hope she's not a moose," Ben said softly.

"Huh?"

"Or if she is that she's clean. And that you're taking precautions. I assume you've been out with the same girl each night."

"Hold it, hold it," protested Jeff. "I told you-"

"For somebody who was bombed, your eyes were pretty clear. And you didn't seem to be suffering much. You must be able to handle your booze remarkably well. Now, when Dan gets bombed, you can see the rockets going off. If you were getting bombed, the explosives were damned clean. Casey was right. There's something fishy. Of course, you don't have to tell me a damn thing. Or any of us. It's your own life. I just thought you might feel like talking about it."

"Guess it wasn't a very convincing story." Ben nodded his agreement. Jeff inhaled deeply. "She's no moose. In fact, you know her."

"What?"

"Her name is Kim Soon Yi."

Ben searched his mind. "The name doesn't ring a bell. You sure I know her?"

"She works at Protocol."

"Miss Kim?"

"Yeah."

"Whew. I mean-"

"We're in love."

Ben opened his mouth to speak but checked himself. "You're kidding" would have been a supremely stupid response. He removed his wire-rimmed glasses and rubbed his eyes. "For how long now?"

"About three weeks. We've been out several times. The first few times it was strictly dinner or a movie or tea. Shoot, I had to ask her four times before she even agreed to a date. Then she made me promise not to tell anyone. And she made me meet her at a neutral site. The district post office." Ben shrugged. "It's not that far from the compound. Anyway, one thing led to another and the another was love."

"Friend, I don't envy you. She's very nice, but envy you I do not."

"Me either. Damn, I've done some checking, and the red tape is endless if you want to marry a Korean. Uncle Sam does his best to protect his innocent charges from the wiles of cunning Oriental women."

"Have you talked marriage with her?"

"No."

"Does she know you love her?"

"Oh, yeah. She wouldn't...uh, well, she wouldn't until that was clear."

"Smart woman. You shacking up with her?"

Jeff reddened. "I wouldn't put it quite that way."

"I know."

"But the answer is yes. She has an apartment in Yeongdeungpo. Overlooks the Han River."

"Sounds nice."

"It is. At night when the bridge is lit, it's beautiful."

"Miss Kim is very attractive."

"She sure is," agreed Jeff, eyes lighting. "And she's bright. Her English is very good. And she's teaching me Korean. At least enough to tell a cab driver where I'm going. She's a college graduate. Graduated last year from Ewha University. That's Korea's Bryn Mawr."

"I'm impressed. Seriously. You told anybody else about her?"

"No."

"I wouldn't."

"I know. It could make it rough for her at Protocol. But I needed to tell someone. Someone I can trust."

"Thanks."

"It's hell being in love and not being able to talk about it."

"Agreed."

"I'm thinking of telling Dan too."

"Wouldn't hurt. He's concerned and you can trust him, too."

"But not Casey."

"Not unless you want the entire Eighth Army to know all the gory details by sunrise. If not sooner."

Jeff chuckled emptily.

"What's next?" Ben asked.

"I don't know. The red tape alone is enough to gag a whale."

"You can cut through the red tape. You've got plenty of time before you go back home."

"I know."

"It's not really the red tape, is it?"

"Not really."

"Is it your mother? And how she'll react?"

"Yes," Jeff grimaced. "Shit. I hate myself for even thinking like that."

"It's only human."

"That's a phony excuse. I've never let my mother stop me before. Now I'm in love, really in love, my mother is ten thousand miles away and she's stopping me without even knowing it. Shit, shit, shit."

"You can't be sure she wouldn't accept Miss Kim. Especially for your sake."

"Don't kid yourself, Ben. There's no way I want to take Suni – that's what her friends call her and so do I – back to a scene like that. It would be positively ugly."

"You don't have to go back to New York. The States are roomy. But even if you did go home, you could avoid your mother. It's not like New York is a two-street hamlet. Except you love your mother too and you don't want to hurt her."

Jeff nodded agreement. "Shit," he muttered miserably, "shit."

"Maybe you should break off with Suni. Now, before it gets any deeper. And more complicated."

"I can't."

Jeff nodded. "I don't know what else I can say."

"You can't. Look, would you tell Dan for me? I really don't feel like going through this again. Not right now."

"Sorry. You're going to have to deal with this by yourself. You might as well get used to it."

"Yeah. Yeah. You know, this is the first time I ever really flipped for anyone. I never expected it to happen here."

"Who ever expects it to happen anywhere?"

CHAPTER 45

The library was closing for the night. Good timing because Natalie had just completed the research for her paper. She flipped shut Evelyn Waugh's *Men At Arms* and leaned against the chair's wood back. She luxuriated in a wave of relief. Then she scooped up *Men At Arms* plus Waugh's *Officers and Gentlemen* and *The End of the Battle*. Together the three books had provided her with rich materials on ethics, values and leadership. As she collected her notes and prepared to leave, a smoky voice whispered her name. She turned and saw a familiar face, softened by the beginnings of a smile.

"Professor Sloane. How are you?"

"Fine, Natalie. How goes the research?"

"I just finished it."

"Great. I'll bet that's a load off your mind."

"Absolutely. I want to thank you again for the extension."

"No problem."

"What are you doing here tonight? With school out, I'd think you'd want to forget about books and term papers. Especially late term papers."

"I'm an academiaholic," he smiled. "Driven compulsively by my work. It's the only pleasure I have." He winked. "Only kidding. Actually, I was here to pick up some light reading." He held up a copy of Richard Bradford's *Red Sky at Morning*.

"It's a terrific book. I read it last month." Natalie blushed. "Yes, I know, when I should have been working on my paper. I thought it was really neat. It was so funny and so sad. I especially liked - oops." She smiled self-consciously. "I don't want to spoil it for you."

"You won't. That much I know from reading the reviews and faculty bull sessions." A pause. "Come on, they'll be chasing us out of here in a couple minutes."

They walked toward the exit. Sloane checked out the novel. They stepped outside.

"Can I give you a lift?" he asked.

"Oh, no, thanks. I live just a few blocks away. It's a beautiful evening. I was planning to walk."

"That sounds fine. If you don't mind, I'll accompany you home. Besides, the exercise will do me good."

"Well, all right."

They began striding east toward Glenmont. With the spring term concluded, the campus and surrounding neighborhood were eerily subdued.

"What," said Sloane, "are *you* going to do this summer?"

"Not much. Work at my dad's company. He's chairman of Western Construction."

"I'm impressed," said Sloane.

"I'll fill in for people on vacation. Probably be a combination secretary-clerk-receptionist-gofer."

"Sounds pretty dull for one I'm guessing isn't at all dull."

Natalie smiled. "Oh, I'll spend some time at the beach, but that's about all."

"Do you like the ocean?"

"I love it."

"Do you sail?"

"Not really. I have once in a while, but mainly I go to swim and sun. And to walk. I love to walk along the beach."

"But do you like to sail?"

"Sure."

"When do you think you'll finish your term paper?"

"It shouldn't be long. With the research done, umm, I should have it written before the end of the week."

"You have the outline done?"

"Yes."

"Tell you what," Sloane said brightly, yet in a way that left little room for negotiating, "you finish writing your paper by Friday night. Then I'll come by Saturday morning and we'll go sailing."

As when he had invited her to dinner, Sloane caught Natalie off balance. He had switched abruptly from talk of sailing to her paper and back to sailing. And his invitation was more an assurance than a request. Which put Natalie at a disadvantage. It was so much more difficult to say no to an assertion than to a question. She would try anyway. "Oh, I appreciate the offer, but-"

"No buts. A summer's not a summer without sailing. Now you don't want to lose an entire summer, do you?" His eyes were affectionately mischievous. "Summers are far too precious to squander."

"Professor, I-"

"Do you have plans for Saturday? Besides mine, I mean?"

"No."

"Good. That's settled. We'll salvage your summer in a single day."

The sea was nearly perfect. A steady southwest wind billowed and snapped the sails and carried the frisky craft across rolling swells. The boat was about three miles from shore and running against the wind. Its white canvas was the only relief on a serene and seamless expanse of rich blue.

Natalie was seated near the front of the 22-foot boat's cockpit. She was working the jib. Sloane sat at the rear, one hand on the tiller. He glanced up at the taut main sail.

Natalie leaned back over the gunnel and ran her free hand through the sparkling sea. She tossed her long dark brown hair and breathed deeply of the exhilarating ocean air. Spray splashed over the bow. The wetter she got, the more she smiled and laughed. Natalie felt like champagne in a bottle. The sea was the corkscrew that was slowly extracting the cork and relieving the pressure. Then, pop! The cork was out and Natalie was alive, more alive than at any time during the two months since Ben had flown out of her life. Then abruptly her mood shifted. She felt a surge of guilt. Then by sheer force of will she wrenched her mind back to this moment.

"Natalie." No reply. A little louder. "Natalie."

"Oh." She faced Sloane and blushed. "I'm sorry. I...My mind was just off somewhere. It's so beautiful out here."

Sloane smiled warmly. "Let's prepare to come about."

"Okay." Natalie readied herself. "Prepared to come about."

She and Sloane both crouched low. "Come about," he said.

They slid to the other side of the cockpit and shifted the mainsail and jib. The boat arced around and picked up speed as it skimmed over the swells with the wind.

"Well done," Sloane congratulated her.

"Thank you. This is great! Super!"

"I'm glad you came."

"Me too." Natalie again tossed her lustrous hair that now was damp and becoming tangled. Her blue blouse with button-down collar also was spotted with spray. So were her yellow shorts and white sneakers. "Professor-"

"Call me Evan, please. You're no longer an undergrad, and I don't consider myself an ivory tower godling. I know in your eyes I'm probably a weathered relic of antiquity, but I'm not quite a member of the geriatric set."

"I guess that's just one of the many things I don't know about you."

"I'll spare your asking. I'm thirty-five."

"You were right," grinned Natalie, eyes merry. "You're not an ancient mariner."

He laughed. "Nor as callow as a cabin boy. More?"

"More?"

"About me."

"Yes," she said puckishly.

"I'm divorced. Have been for two and a half years. I have two daughters. My wife – ex-wife – has custody."

"Do you see them often?"

"Not as often as I'd like. It was not…a particularly amicable parting."

"I'm sorry."

"More?"

"Umm, not now. Not unless you feel like it."

"I do. I'm one of those perpetual students. Or perpetual hangers-on. Anyway, I couldn't tear myself away from Dear Alma Mater. UCLA has been my womb since I was 18. I got my B.A., M.A. and Ph. D. there. All in English. I wasn't the world's greatest husband but I wasn't the world's worst father. I have a passion for living and I do my best to satisfy that passion. This," he swept his arm out and to his side, "is one of my passions. Tell me, what did your parents think about your sailing with me?"

"They were curious…and concerned."

"And disturbed?"

"I don't know. Oh, maybe because I knew so little about you. But, no, more curious and concerned."

"I don't blame them. In fact, I understand perfectly. If an older man, a stranger, were taking out one of my daughters – they're thirteen and eleven – I'd be concerned."

A pair of gulls glided parallel to the boat and to port. Then one peeled away and dove to the water.

"Natalie?"

"Yes?"

"Slide this way."

She sensed what was coming and hesitated. Her emotions were beginning to churn as she edged toward him on the seat. She wanted to be held, to belong. She gripped the gunnel with one hand and reached for his shoulder with the other. He slid toward her. With one hand on the tiller he cupped her chin with the other and drew her lips to his.

CHAPTER 46

Ben's assignment was covering military maneuvers. He packed his field and personal gear in a jeep and rode midway in a long convoy over 40 dusty miles that wound like a tangled ribbon through valleys and atop ridges. When he arrived at the campsite southeast of Seoul, he helped Dan, Jeff and Sergeant Taber set up.

On the second day he began filing reports back to Yongsan Compound. They included ones on the construction of a pontoon bridge, the planned temporary evacuation of a village in anticipation of an air drop of men and equipment, the evacuation itself, the air drop and a story on the aged, ornamentally clothed matriarch of the evacuated village.

On the seventh night, weary of mess tent chow, Ben and Taber decided to go scrounging. Heavy cloud cover blackened the countryside and enabled them to move like a pair of olive-drab-clad phantoms. They returned to their tent with ground beef, eggs, onions, celery, salt, pepper and bread. Using a helmet for a pot, they whipped up a semicircular meatloaf. After

Ben, Taber, Jeff and Dan wolfed down every bite of the loaf, Dan pulled a bottle of scotch from his duffel bag. The four of them slept contentedly.

On the eighth night Ben showered for the first time since leaving Yongsan. Quartermaster troops had erected a shower tent on the banks of a nearby stream. Ben could hardly wait to shed his uniform. His skin was crawling, or something was crawling on it or both. When he entered the tent, a sign over the showerhead warned: *Danger – keep this water out of your mouth.* Ben was not surprised or perturbed. He knew the nearby stream served several villages as bathtub, sink, laundromat and sewer. The water might have been pestilence-laden, but aided by strong detergent soap, it washed away the accumulated crud that only grudgingly loosened its grip.

The tenth day, he arrived back at Yongsan. He was stiff, sore and bone tired. In his room he stripped and snapped open a clean towel to evict any cockroaches that might have taken up residence in the folds. He wrapped it around his waist and trudged wearily down the long hallway to the showers. He stood under the cascading water for 15 minutes.

Back in his room he opened his gray locker, where Casey had deposited his accumulated mail. He collapsed on his bunk and placed the envelopes on his belly. He was too tired to read and quickly fell asleep.

Hours later he awoke. He removed his glasses and rubbed his eyes. He ran his tongue around the inside of his mouth. It felt like sandpaper and tasted like rotting sawdust. Christ, he thought, what I wouldn't give for mouthwash and a cup of coffee. He had none of the former and the mess hall was closed.

He picked up the envelopes. He had expected 10 letters from Natalie. One for each day in the field. There were three. Plus a letter from his parents that he read first. It was full of family and hometown chitchat. A sentence in which Edward told of climbing a ladder to replace storm-damaged roof shingles caused Ben to smile.

He checked the postmarks on the letters from Natalie and opened the envelope bearing the earliest date. From the first paragraph this letter was different. Natalie had dispensed with the usual exuberant greeting. She launched immediately into a graphic description of her misery. Ben kept waiting for, expecting, *The Big But* that would bridge the gap between Natalie's account of her suffering and her reaffirmation of perpetual love.

It wasn't there. Natalie's black mood dominated from start to finish. The "I love you!" with a single exclamation point at the end seemed perfunctory.

Ben opened the second envelope. It contained more of the same. Damn, she's really down in the dumps. And I can't do a damn thing about it except write another letter. He kept on reading. His stomach knotted as Natalie hinted that the long separation was more than either of them could endure alone.

In the third letter she told of going sailing and how it had lifted her spirits. She did not say when and with whom she had sailed, but when she suggested that further such outings might bolster her morale, Ben sensed that the crew had been a small one. Otherwise, he reasoned, she would have named names. Or at least mentioned that they were old friends he hadn't met during his time in California. He dropped the letter on his chest.

From across the room Dan thought he could read worry in Ben's eyes. "Anything wrong back home?"

"What? No."

"I think I napped as long as you did," said Dan. "The only way I'll get back to sleep tonight is with a couple good stiff belts. What do you say we drag our butts over to the NCO Club?"

"Nah, I don't think." A pause. "Aah, what the hell. Let's go."

"That's more like it. How about you, Jeff?"

"Okay."

"Casey?"

"No, thanks. I'll just stay here and read."

In the NCO Club, Dan ordered double scotches on the rocks for all three. "My round."

"Good to be back at Yongsan, huh?" said Jeff. "Never thought I'd say that when I first saw the place. Of course, that's before I knew about ten-day field ops."

Dan smiled. "Actually, we're damn lucky. If we were in Nam, Yongsan would look like Shangri-la."

"I'm thinking of taking sick leave tomorrow," said Jeff. "I'd love to spend the day in my bunk, just reading and relaxing."

"Not a bad idea," said Dan. "I thought you'd be over at Suni's tonight. After all, ten days is a long dry spell."

"Too pooped."

"Isn't that supposed to be a woman's excuse?" Dan ribbed Jeff.

"Someone should tell Suni."

Dan laughed. "You mean our shy and proper Miss Kim is a real bundle of energy?"

"High octane."

"You've been awfully quiet," Dan said to Ben.

"Too tired to talk."

The barmaid brought the drinks.

"A toast," Dan said cheerfully.

"Do I have to raise my glass?" Ben smiled tiredly.

"Do kittens like to play with twine?"

"I feel like the loser in a cat fight."

"Hoist your glass. Here," Dan said solemnly, "is to daily showers and reasonably clean sheets."

Before swallowing, Ben swished the scotch around in his mouth. He ran his tongue around his teeth and stared emptily past Dan's shoulder.

"Bad letters?" Dan asked gently.

Ben lowered his head and looked at the ice in the glass. He peered over the top of his wire-rimmed frames. "You don't miss much, do you?"

"My best talent."

Ben's lips creased in a small smile. "Not exactly bad but not exactly good." He described the letters to Dan and Jeff and felt better for doing so. Two more rounds of double scotches didn't hurt either. "When we get back, I'll write her. It's been over a week."

"I wouldn't," advised Dan. "Wait till tomorrow. You'll be fresher. You'll write with a clearer mind and a lighter heart."

The next morning Jeff chose to stay in bed. Dan covered for him, telling Sergeant Taber that Jeff must have picked up a bug in the field. Jeff planned to go to Suni's apartment that evening and spend the next day and night there. Jeff expected he could persuade Suni to take a sick day too. Dan would cover for him the second day as well. Even if Sergeant Taber was skeptical, Dan was confident he wouldn't probe. Taber understood things.

At his desk Ben wrote to Natalie. *I've been drinking more than I should – or will when I get back to the states. I understand your need for companionship, but I'm not so sure about sailing. It could be dangerous.* Ben wasn't about to bless an activity that could sink their love. *Your days will go by faster when school starts in September. When you get your master's next June, I'll be there to watch you walk across the stage. Or if I miss that by a few days, I'll be there to help you frame your diploma.* He ended with a pledge of love so powerful that the words were almost physical.

Later that morning at mail call there was no letter from Natalie.

CHAPTER 47

The ocean was glass smooth. Evan Sloane's boat sailed gracefully about a mile off shore. He had one hand on the tiller, the other resting on Natalie's shoulder. The sun was within moments of sliding below the horizon.

"It's gorgeous," Natalie said softly. "Poetic. I've never seen a sunset so peaceful, so magnificent."

"It's the sea," said Evan. "The sea and the sun at nightfall. You're right, it is poetic. I take it you're glad you came."

"Yes." Natalie was feeling pangs of guilt but was glad to be at sea with Evan.

"The first sail salvaged your summer. This one should make it something special."

Natalie shifted her gaze from the western horizon to his eyes. They were magnetic. She and Evan kissed, and she caressed his cheeks.

"Umm." He pulled back. "Better look the other way. There she goes."

Like an omnipotent god retiring for the night, the awesome orb reclined slowly and majestically and slipped from view.

"Fantastic," murmured Natalie, "just fantastic."

"The day is gone," he murmured, "but the night is only beginning."

Two days later Natalie wrote Ben another joyless letter. It contained not a single exclamation point. She described dispassionately the second sailing outing and started to tell him that the romantic sunset had made her want to reach across the vast sea and snatch him back. But she couldn't bring herself to lie. She did miss him, but the distance, his prolonged absence and Evan's powerful presence were driving a wedge between her and Ben. This time Natalie identified her sailing companion. She characterized him merely as *one of my professors* and described him no further.

What she really wanted to write was:

Dear Ben,

I can't stand it any longer. I've tried but it's no use. We've seen so little of each other, we're almost strangers. It's destructive. Only these letters keep us together. And what are they but pieces of paper with ink. They say things but what do they feel or do? Ben, darling, you were the light of my life, but that light has dimmed. Maybe we should turn it off for now. When you get back, we could turn it on again and see how brightly it shines. Could we do that, sweetheart? Please? I know it would hurt you. It would hurt me. But I really think it would be better for both of us.

That's what Natalie wanted to write but couldn't. Not yet. So she wrote again of her dejection. When she wrote sketchily about sailing with Evan, she knew Ben would read between the lines and stew, that he would sense this letter was a prelude for more unsettling news. She mailed the letter as she and her father left Western Construction.

Natalie despised herself for her weakness but felt powerless to shore herself up. That night at home on Glenmont she cried into her pillow. Ben, she grieved, why don't you just tell me it's all over. That we're through. That we loved and lost. Oh, no, don't do that, please. Stay with me. God, how I miss you.

Downstairs in the living room Maria looked up from her reading. John was sipping brandy, meditating.

"What are you thinking about?" Maria asked.

"Our youngest daughter."

"It's hard not to."

"True enough," John smiled ruefully. "She's in such a funk. It tears at my gut. I'm wondering what's going on between her and Professor Sloane. And how it will affect her and Ben. I wonder how much she misses Ben?"

"More than either of us will ever know."

"You know," said John, "in a way I wish Nat weren't living with us. It might make it easier for her to share with us, to open up."

"And I don't want to pry."

"Agreed. I wonder if Ben suspects there's any trouble."

"I don't know."

"Sloane seems like a nice enough fellow," said John.

"Yes," Maria agreed without any enthusiasm.

"Too old perhaps."

"Perhaps."

"Do you think Nat and Ben can stick it out?" John asked. "Wait for each other?"

"Honestly?"

"Honestly."

"I'd like to say yes. Or even that I think so. But the truth is, I don't know."

CHAPTER 48

Hubert H. Humphrey, vice president of the United States, didn't know it but he had Ben Lawrence's butt dragging. For the second consecutive morning Ben had had to roll out of his bunk at 4:30. This morning sternly tested resilience of body and soul, since last night he had stayed up late to drink and play gin with Dan. He resolved to hit the sack early tonight.

Humphrey was in Korea. The Democrat's leading candidate for the presidential nomination at the party's convention later that summer was out to score political points and get a first-hand feel for the tinder box that was the Korean peninsula in the summer of 1968. As with other visiting VIPs, Ben's role was to prepare pre-dawn news summaries.

He switched off the alarm on the pocketsize travel clock. Dan and Casey didn't stir. As usual, Jeff's bunk was empty. Ben slipped into his fatigues and laced up his boots. He would wash and shave after completing his early morning chore.

He walked across the dark compound. In a small room next to the correspondents' office Ben ripped news copy from the Associated Press and Reuters clacking wire machines that had been spewing world news all night.

At his desk he quickly culled the most important stories. He fed yellow copy paper into his Royal typewriter and distilled the stories into two- and three-paragraph capsules.

He reviewed his work. Satisfied, he hiked to the VIP quarters, arriving at 6:30, right on time. A military guard and a Secret Service agent both nodded as he came up the walk. Ben made no attempt to cover a gaping yawn, then handed the news summary to the agent.

During the long walk back across Yongsan Compound his mind flitted randomly to Natalie (her disturbing letters with continued references to Professor Sloane were germinating his own seeds of doubt), breakfast (he was famished), Gerry Graham (he hoped all was well with him and Ella), work (he dreaded tomorrow's 4:30 wakeup but was grateful it would be the last, at least for a while), and Jeff (he was now spending virtually every night with Kim Soon Yi but was saying nothing about marrying her).

384

As he was nearing the barracks, Ben saw Jeff approaching from the direction of Yongsan's south gate. He stopped and waited.

"I should recommend *you* for this duty," Ben teased. "Keep you off the streets at night." He yawned widely.

"It's so reassuring to have an altruist for a friend," Jeff answered dryly. "How much longer will Humphrey be here?"

"He leaves tomorrow, which won't be soon enough for me."

"Shoot, a young stud like you can hack one more early wakeup."

As Ben reached for the barracks door, Dan emerged.

"You're getting an early start," Ben said.

"I have to catch a flight out at Kimpo at eight. Here comes my transportation now." A jeep driven by an American-uniformed young Korean KATUSA (Korean Attached To The U.S. Army) pulled up beside them. Dan's assignment was to fly via Korean Air Lines to Pusan, the major port city on the southeast coast. He would cover the arrival of a mammoth cargo of trucks, jeeps, tanks, armored personnel carriers and M-14 rifles. The resultant news release would amount to propaganda meant to help dissuade North Korean ruler Kim Il Sung from acting on any whimsical war notions.

Ben and Jeff showered, shaved and breakfasted. On entering their office, Miss Lee, the silken-voiced secretary, said Colonel Baumgarten wanted to see them.

"Now?" said Ben.

"Mr. LeBeau said right away," she answered.

Ben and Jeff walked down the hall. They compared notes and found that neither had the slightest inkling about the early morning summons. Ben rapped on the Colonel's door.

"Come in."

Ben and Jeff entered.

"Good morning, specialists." said Baumgarten, a tall, slender officer with thinning gray hair.

"Good morning, sir."

"Morning, sir."

Ben and Jeff also exchanged greetings with Drew LeBeau, Dave Bedford and Sergeant Taber. The other man in the office was a stranger and a civilian.

"Specialist Lawrence and Specialist Zink," said the colonel, "I'd like you to meet Agent Ray Bigelow. Agent Bigelow is with the Secret Service."

Ben and Jeff shook hands with the agent, an impressive physical specimen about age 40.

"We have a special assignment for you," Colonel Baumgarten said gravely. "As you know, the vice president is here to assess for himself the military and political situation in Korea. He's met with top military people as well as ROK government officials, starting with President Park. Last night, he – the vice president – sprung a surprise on us. He was supposed to rest today before heading back to the States tomorrow. Instead, he said he wanted to spend the day visiting troops. On a very low-key basis. No reporters. No entourage. No trooping the line before honor guards."

"And we're to be his tour guides," Ben stated with detachment.

"Right," said the colonel. "I hope you recognize the honor – and responsibility."

"We do," said Ben.

"We've tried to talk him out of this," sighed Agent Bigelow. "But the vice president can be rather strong willed."

Ben and Jeff smiled ever so slightly.

"We need someone who knows his way around," said the colonel. "Who knows how to handle himself and is responsible. And who's licensed to drive a jeep. He wants to go in a jeep."

"Why me?" said Ben. "Jeff's the one with a driver's license."

"That's all the vice president wanted," said Bigelow. "A driver. But no way would we let him go with just one military escort. We explained you correspondents work in pairs."

"He bought *that*?" said Ben.

"It's true, isn't it?" said Bigelow.

"Sometimes. Of course, there's Dan flying down to Pusan today by himself."

"That's good enough," Agent Bigelow smiled benignly. "If he asks, don't make a liar out of me."

"What's the itinerary?" Jeff asked.

"Down to Osan Air Base," said Colonel Baumgarten. "Then back through Seoul and up north to I Corps at Uijongbu. Then up to the Joint Security Camp and Panmunjom. And then back to Yongsan."

Jeff's eyebrow arched skeptically.

"I know," said the colonel with a hint of sympathy. "It's a lot of driving."

"And not exactly on smooth interstate highways," Jeff observed.

The colonel shrugged helplessly.

"If we leave now," said Jeff, "we'll be lucky to be back before dark."

"We *are* leaving now," said Bigelow. "There's a jeep waiting outside for us. We're to go to the VIP quarters right now and pick him up."

"Is that it?" said Ben.

"One more thing," said Bigelow. "We've put a radio in your jeep. The vice president wouldn't like the idea – he'd accuse us of mother henning – but there's no way we'd let him ride around the countryside without some ability to contact him. And of course I'll be with you."

Jeff and Ben looked at each other dubiously. "Neither of us," said Ben, "knows how to operate a radio."

"I do," said Bigelow, "and you are about to get a quick lesson."

"Anything else?" said Jeff.

"One final item," said Colonel Baumgarten. "You'll wear side arms. Sergeant Taber."

The sergeant produced two loaded, holstered Colt 45-caliber pistols, standard Army issue since 1911.

Jeff swerved but couldn't dodge the nasty bump. The jeep bucked and rattled, and Vice President Humphrey grabbed the edge of the windshield. Ben and Agent Bigelow rode in back.

"Sorry about that, Sir," Jeff half-shouted above the rumbling engine and rushing air.

"Quite all right," Humphrey smiled broadly. "This ride has been much more, shall we say, exhilarating than a cruise in the back of a cushy sedan. I'm glad we're doing it."

"I'd go slower," said Jeff, "but I don't want to waste any daylight. We'll need all we can get."

"You're doing fine."

The day was proving thoroughly enjoyable and memorable for all four. Humphrey's warm charm and disarming informality quickly had put Ben and Jeff at ease. They were barely out of Seoul when he asked them their first names. From that point on he dispensed with references to military rank and last names.

Ben and Jeff quickly won favor with Humphrey by demonstrating a solid grasp of current events. When he questioned them about their political preferences, he found a supporter in Jeff and an opponent in Ben. He asked them whether they planned to vote by absentee ballot – they did – and joked that "at least I'm starting even with Nixon."

During the visits at Osan and Uijongbu, Ben and Jeff stood in the background and watched entranced as Humphrey skillfully and energetically mingled with troops from generals to privates. Clearly, the vice president was enjoying the encounters at least as much as his hosts.

It was late afternoon when Jeff wheeled the jeep into the Joint Security Camp just south of the DMZ. "Sir, we're not going to be able to stay here long if we want to get up to Panmunjom and back to Seoul before dark."

"Fine, fine," said the vice president, "we'll be brief."

"They're planning to serve us dinner," said Ben.

"We'll eat fast and then apologize for running."

Hardly, thought Jeff and Ben. During the course of the day, they had learned enough about the gregarious vice president to conclude that he wasn't likely to rush away from good soldiers who might soon be good constituents. They turned out to be right.

At Panmunjom Humphrey stood on the hard-packed barren earth between the garish Freedom House and the row of corrugated metal buildings. Pensively he surveyed the ghostly conference site.

"It's so sad, so very sad," said Humphrey. "So much death and destruction and suffering. And still it goes on. Still." He breathed deeply and slowly. "Where's the Bridge of No Return?"

Jeff pointed north. They walked toward the unprepossessing span and stopped. A North Korean guard shack stood on the far side.

"I hope the Pueblo crew crosses it very soon," Humphrey said somberly. "They've been prisoners more than half a year. They must be suffering terribly." His jowly jaws clenched and his head shook slightly. He straightened. "I've seen enough. Let's go."

They got into the jeep and Jeff started south. Behind them was a second jeep. The Joint Security Camp commanding officer had insisted on providing an escort for Humphrey to Panmunjom. The CO dispatched Captain Sam Corporra, and he and three troopers rode in the second jeep. They were still inside the DMZ when the vice president spoke. "Hold it, Jeff. Stop here."

"What is it, sir? Are you all right?"

"Yes, I'm fine. I want to see the fence."

"The fence?"

"*The* fence. The DMZ fence." Humphrey was referring to a high barbed-wire-topped chain link fence that ran the length of the DMZ's southern border except for a gap at the Joint Security Area. The barrier was little more than a symbol of tension. Although patrolled continuously by American and South Korean soldiers, it served as a sorry deterrent to North Koreans determined to penetrate south.

Jeff rubbed the stubble on his chin and glanced over his shoulder. Ben's eyes narrowed and his head shook. Agent Ray Bigelow watched silently.

"Is that impossible?" Humphrey asked.

"Not impossible, sir, but," said Ben, "it's not on the agenda."

"Fiddle faddle, we can't be bound by an agenda," he said, brightening. "Not today. Right, Ray?"

"Sir," said Jeff, "that area is off limits, except by prior clearance."

Humphrey raised his right arm and waved. "Captain Corporra, please come here."

Corporra jumped out of his jeep and hurried forward to the vice president. "Yes, sir?"

"I want to take a look at the fence. Specialist Zink says I need prior clearance. Do I have prior clearance?"

"Well, sir...Permission to speak frankly, sir?"

"Go ahead," said Humphrey.

"Sir, there would be hell to pay for me and my men if anybody found out."

"Must anyone find out?" said Humphrey.

"Not necessarily," said Captain Corporra, glancing at both Jeff and Ben. They nodded their understanding.

"Good," said Humphrey with an air of genial conspiracy, "but even if someone does find out, I dare say you wouldn't get much heat if the vice president says he ordered you."

Neither Jeff nor Ben nor Agent Bigelow cracked a smile.

"I'm not ordering you, but don't be a spoilsport," Humphrey wheedled.

"It could be dangerous, sir," said Jeff. "You never know what's going to happen in the DMZ. Or when."

"This close to Panmunjom?" Humphrey said skeptically.

"There have been incidents uncomfortably close to PMJ," said Ben.

"Be that as it may," he cajoled them, "we could use a little adventure to spice up the end of our day."

"Sir," Jeff said, "we're going to be lucky to make it back to Seoul by dark as it is."

"We don't have to stop for long," said Humphrey. "Besides, the road gets better closer to Seoul, and this jeep has headlights. And you're an excellent driver."

"They'll be worrying about you back at Yongsan."

"No doubt. But if we are running late, you can tell them on that radio back there." Humphrey smiled slyly. Ben and Jeff looked at each other and at Agent Bigelow in semi-surprise. "You do have a radio in this jeep, don't you?" said Humphrey.

They nodded.

"Let's go," he said excitedly. "We're wasting time."

Jeff started the jeep and drove to just south of the DMZ's southern border. The second jeep followed. Then Jeff swung the jeep off the main road onto an even narrower and bumpier side road that ran east. Captain Corporra and his men stayed close behind. Jeff drove about a minute, then braked. He leaned forward and folded his arms against the steering wheel.

Humphrey sat pensively and stared at the fence. He eased out of the jeep and walked to the fence. A well-worn trail ran along its base. He gripped the chain links, looked up and gave the fence a sharp pull. "Come on," he called. "Let's walk along it a bit."

Jeff looked anxiously back over his shoulder. The sun was well into the last stages of its westerly descent. "Damn, I wish we could talk him out of this," he whispered to Ben and Bigelow.

"We have about as much chance of that as talking a bear out of a beehive," muttered Bigelow. "We either go with him or he goes alone."

"Sir," Jeff spoke, "let's keep it short. I'd at least like to make it back to Munsan before dark so we can make the rest of the drive on a paved road."

"Fine, fine."

Humphrey's chunky body was tireless. They had been on the go all day and his spunk and verve were undiminished. To Ben and Jeff's dismay the short stroll lengthened appreciably.

Jeff was in the lead. Then came Humphrey and Bigelow and Ben. Captain Corporra and two of his men brought up the rear. The third soldier remained with the jeeps. The vice president tramped along in his scuffed black wingtips as though they were comfortable hiking boots. He was oblivious to the dust that coated his wrinkled blue suit.

The sun slid beneath the treetops that cast foreboding shadows. Jeff looked again over his shoulder to recommend to Humphrey that they turn back. Before the first word escaped his mouth, Jeff stumbled and fell. Instantly, two dull whumps startled them. Reflexively, Humphrey extended a helping hand. As Jeff began to mentally curse his clumsiness, the sky exploded in a shower of light. The men stared dumbly upward at the aerial fireworks. Jeff had stumbled over the tripwire for a pair of flares.

He was mortified. "Geez, I'm sorry, sir," he murmured abjectly.

"That's all right."

In the next instant, shots rang out. Ben could hear bullets ricocheting off the chain link fence. He stepped forward and pulled Humphrey to the ground. Bigelow and Captain Corporra rushed to his side.

Sweat popped out on the vice president's forehead. "Who's shooting at us?" he asked, anxiety raising the pitch of his voice.

"Sir," Captain Corporra said coolly, "I don't know whether those are our guys or their guys and I don't much care. Whoever they are, they sure think we're the wrong guys. Move, sir, now."

Humphrey nodded and began to stand.

Ben tugged at his shoulders. "Stay low."

The firing stopped. In a low crouch, the men scurried quickly back to the jeeps. Another burst of fire rent the gathering dusk. Humphrey, Bigelow, Ben, Jeff, Captain Corporra and his men all flattened against the dusty trail.

"That was behind us," said Ben. "Let's keep moving."

There were no more shots. They arrived at the jeeps. Humphrey was sweating and breathing hard. He brushed dust from his clothing. Ben and Jeff did likewise, although Jeff's mind was more on his massive embarrassment than on dusty fatigues. Humphrey sensed his acute discomfort and broke the strained silence.

"Jeff," said Humphrey, smiling, "I was scared stiff back there, and I'm a little too old for pyrotechnic hijinks." Jeff reddened anew. "But, by gosh, this is the most fun and adventure I've had in ages." He thrust out his hand and pumped Jeff's. "Thank you. Thank you both. This is one day I'll remember forever. I owe you one."

CHAPTER 49

Just before leaving Los Angeles for Fort Lewis and Korea, Ben had promised Dick a favor. Now he decided it was time to make good. Or try. To proceed, however, Ben himself needed some favors.

From Sergeant Taber, he needed the use of a jeep. For next Saturday. Ben explained his request. Favor granted.

From Jeff, Ben asked for his services as a driver. Again he explained his request. Favor granted.

Then he approached the office secretary, Miss Lee. "I would like to ask you a favor."

Her expressive, large brown eyes, more oval than most Koreans', peered curiously at the tall American standing in front of her desk. "Yes, Specialist Lawrence?"

Again Ben explained his request.

"I go with you and Specialist Zink?"

"Yes."

"In a jeep." When speaking Korean, words skipped from her small mouth allegro con spirito. In English her rhythm was more allegretto - slower, more precise, but with an added note of sweetness.

"Yes. And that reminds me; you should wear slacks."

"Slacks?"

"Pants." Ben crimsoned.

"I have only dresses and skirts."

"Oh, I-"

"Do not worry, please. I will get slacks and I will ride in your jeep."

"You don't have to," Ben said quickly. "I can find someone else."

"It will be my honor to go." Her smile was small but sincere, as attested by the warm glow of her eyes.

"Are you sure?" Ben hoped she was sure.

"Yes, very sure. What time do we go?"

"Eight o'clock in the morning. Is that all right?"

"Yes."

"We can pick you up at your home."

"No. I will come here."

"Are you sure?"

"I prefer it." Two GI's arriving at her home in a jeep would be cmbarrassing.

"Okay, if that's what you want. Thank you, Miss Lee. I appreciate it." Ben smiled, bowed slightly, and turned to leave.

"Specialist Lawrence."

"Yes?"

"Thank you for asking me."

Saturday morning dawned sunny and promising. When Jeff and Ben braked outside Yongsan's Public Affairs Building, Miss Lee was standing there.

"Good morning, Miss Lee," they greeted her.

"Good morning, Specialists."

A pair of navy cotton slacks covered Miss Lee's shapely legs. She wore a long-sleeved white blouse and carried a yellow wool sweater. A white scarf covered her black hair, which she kept stylishly cut to shoulder length. Somehow she looked frail, which Ben knew she assuredly was not. As a child during the Korean War, Miss Lee had forever stamped herself as a survivor. She had subsisted on scraps of food under intermittent threat of rape and death. She had matured into a compassionate but tough-minded woman. She was single, had lived alone since the early deaths of her parents and had had no serious romances. Not that she avoided them. Rather, as an employee of American soldiers, Korean men shunned her. Koreans generally were pro-American, except where their women labored in too close proximity to the whoring young Yanks. Miss Lee was fully aware of - and regretted - the cultural clash and rejection. But she was pragmatic. Her job as a secretary for the U.S. Army paid much better than any job she could expect to find in Korean commerce or government. And it was secure. That was important, for she had vowed to avoid returning to the grinding poverty of her childhood.

Ben and Jeff wore their fatigues, including olive drab baseball-type caps. Ben hopped out of the jeep. Miss Lee walked to meet him. He helped her into the front seat beside Jeff and climbed into the rear.

"Before now, I have never been in a jeep," Miss Lee said as the machine scooted north through Seoul.

"And what's your verdict?" Ben smiled.

"Verdict?"

"What do you think about it, about riding in the jeep?"

"It is fun. When I was a little girl, in the war, I saw many GI's in jeeps. I waved. They waved at me. It looked like fun. More than once I wanted to ask GI for ride in a jeep, but I was so shy."

"Ah," Ben teased, "so that's why you agreed to come this morning. Just so you could ride with handsome GI's in a jeep."

"No, no," Miss Lee protested. "You know that is not true, Specialist Lawrence."

North of Seoul the jeep approached an ox cart. Ben leaned forward and tapped Miss Lee on the shoulder. He pointed to the farmer walking beside the massive, slow-moving beast. "Maybe you should ask him."

Miss Lee nodded. "Stop the jeep, Specialist Zink."

Ben bounded from the jeep and helped Miss Lee down. She faced the farmer and bowed slightly. The farmer, a broad-shouldered young man, eyed her Western garb and companions with heavy-lidded curiosity.

She spoke softly and rapidly and the farmer relaxed and lifted his lids, revealing friendly eyes. In reply to her questions he nodded three times and spoke in the rough, guttural staccato of rural males.

Miss Lee thanked him, bowed and got back into the jeep. Ben followed. "You start the jeep, Specialist Zink. Keep going the same way."

Two miles farther she again alighted from the jeep to question another farmer, this one at work in a roadside paddy. Again she got back into the jeep and told Jeff to proceed. "Drive slow," she instructed.

Miss Lee watched the passing countryside with meticulous care.

"Drive very slow." A quarter mile slid by, a half mile. "Stop," she commanded softly, the single word betraying a sense of anticipation. She sat still and looked east. She watched a woman resolutely carrying two buckets of water from a well. One bucket hung heavily from each end of a pole balanced behind her neck across her shoulders. The woman stopped in front a thatched-roof house and lowered the buckets.

In front of the house a man squatted. He was smoking a long-stemmed pipe. He smiled, said something to the woman and puffed the pipe. She carried the two buckets inside.

Miss Lee turned to Ben and nodded. He looked at her questioningly. She nodded again, pursing her lips authoritatively.

Ben jumped down from the jeep. He sucked in a huge breath, blew it out forcefully and began striding toward the house, about 200 yards distant.

The man rose slowly. He said something under his breath, and the woman emerged from the house. She stood beside him, tiny, straight, gray-haired. They watched the strapping American approach.

About six feet from them Ben stopped. He towered above the pair. His hands came to rest on his hips and he smiled tentatively. He felt excitement swelling in his chest. Ben looked into the narrow, wizened eyes of a white-haired man, aging but unbowed. "Yoon Chun Heum?"

The man nodded.

CHAPTER 50

Evan's 1964 Volkswagen Beetle rattled to a stop. He bounced out, skipped around to the passenger's side and opened the door for Natalie.

"Ahem, Professor Sloane," she said as he took her arm and guided her up the walk, "this looks like something other a restaurant."

"I believe," he smirked with mock wickedness, "that I invited you to dinner. I don't recall saying anything about a restaurant."

"One makes certain not unreasonable assumptions."

"Which as often as not turn out to be unfounded."

Evan's apartment was small and furnished in a utilitarian mode. Alimony and child support payments ruled out nonessentials. Except his boat, which he deemed more a necessity than a luxury.

While Evan labored in the kitchen, Natalie sipped chablis and browsed the titles on jammed shelves that all but hid the living room walls.

After seating Natalie, Evan lighted two candles and switched off the lights.

"Dinner by candlelight," Natalie cooed suspiciously. "Could this be a prelude?"

"It could be a means to an end," Evan acknowledged with seeming detachment. "Or an end in itself. Candlelight does create an otherwise unachievable ambience."

Evan proved that his talents extended beyond lecturing and sailing. He served an eminently respectable Caesar salad, warm bread and lobster newburg. And lots of wine.

They had a grand time. Between bites and even during mouthfuls, laughter flickered the candle flames and ricocheted off the book spines.

When they had finished, Evan stood and helped Natalie to her feet. The laughter ceased. Hands on her shoulders he brought their lips together. His tongue forced its way between her lips and into her mouth.

Natalie pulled back and managed a nervous smile. "Shouldn't we," she whispered hoarsely, "clear the table?"

"The candles will burn only so long," he said. "We shouldn't waste the wicks on dirty dishes."

They kissed again and he led her to the couch. Down they went in a tangle of limbs and emotions. Evan groped single-mindedly. Natalie gradually gave way amidst an uncertainty that surprised her. Wasn't this what I wanted? I knew it was coming. Evan's goal has been clear: wrench me from one set of loyalties to another. Sloane's lips and hands were all over her. Natalie shook her head. Memories of Ben flashed by like automated slides on a screen. She bit her lip.

Ben was sure that Natalie had slept with Professor Sloane. Well, as sure as he could be without really knowing. Each time he opened one of her letters, his gut knotted and sank at the prospect of reading a sorrowful confession of infidelity. In time, he half hoped for one. It would halt the uncertainty and release him. He wanted to be released yet remain bound. He believed that Natalie's love had wavered and shifted directions. Should he maintain faith in his love and its power to win her back once reunited? Or should he release her and look ahead to new love? Time was against him. So was Sloane, a foe of unknown but apparently impressive force. What gnawed at Ben was the grim prospect of Natalie giving herself to Sloane in body and spirit. And name. Natalie Sloane. The thought nauseated him.

Ben concluded he needed release, however illusory or temporary. One Friday after work he headed for the Vill, intent on alcoholic oblivion. Grimly, he entered the King Club and made for a small corner table in the dimly lit room.

It was early, and GI patrons were few. A jukebox blared an occasional rock melody. By the time the club began to perk, Ben had lost count of his beers. But oblivion was still a long way off. He ordered another beer. A solitary bender, he reflected morosely, was hardly a joyous undertaking.

Minutes later a GI with a Korean woman on each arm entered the club. The GI and one woman moved to a table on the far side of the room. The other surveyed the club, then moved across the floor toward Ben. He saw her casual approach, knew what was coming. He sipped his beer.

"You lonesome?" she said, standing calmly in front of the table.

Ben wasn't surprised. He had observed and heard often the directness of mooses, including those who regularly infiltrated the compound and frequented the NCO Club. He hesitated.

"I make good love. I please very much." She smiled prettily. "We go to my place." She offered a hand. Ben took it.

"Well, well, Lawrence," Casey McDermott sneered, "I suppose you're going to give us some kind of ridiculous alibi like Zink did the first time he stayed out all night."

"I don't feel like entertaining you," Ben said dryly. He unbuttoned his civilian shirt and sat on his bunk.

"Oh, how the mighty do fall. You should be ashamed of yourself, Lawrence. You've got a girl back home. Waiting for you. Faithfully. You should be faithful to her. I thought you'd make it. But you're like the rest."

"Drop it, Casey." Ben slipped out of his civvie loafers.

"Drop it? Forget it? You'd like that, wouldn't you? You're weak. You get a little horny and you go looking for a moose. No discipline. You need flesh, and filthy flesh."

"Look, Casey," Ben said wearily, "I know you like to hear yourself preach. But go find another pulpit." Ben flopped onto his bunk. "Let's keep church and state separate."

"The message is needed right here the most," said Casey with a goodly measure of righteousness. "And speaking of pulpits-"

"Look, I'll surrender my soul to God if you'll nail your lips together."

"As I was starting to say, Lawrence, you should try going to church. You might find real help there. I certainly hope your girl doesn't find out about this. Just think how hurt she would be. You're very disappointing. I expected more from you. What you need to do..."

Ben squeezed shut his eyes and tuned out the gospel according to Casey. He had lain awake most of the night, content to hold and stroke the young woman sleeping beside him. Now he was sleepy. Casey's droning sermon served as a sedative.

Saturday and Sunday nights Ben made love with the woman-child. Sunday and Monday mornings he again endured Casey's moralizing.

Jeff had left Yongsan Friday evening to spend the weekend with Kim Soon Yi. Monday morning at work he asked Ben to lunch with him.

"Sounds like I missed some action this weekend," said Jeff after they had put their mess trays on the red and white-checkered vinyl tablecloth.

"You mean Casey's show of concern for my wayward soul?"

Jeff smiled. "Let me put it to you the same way you put it to me a couple months ago. Is she a moose?"

Ben grinned wryly. "Sharp memory. Yeah, she's a moose. But," he muttered with a poker face, "obviously a discriminating one."

"She clean?"

"She says so, but who knows?"

"Does that bother you?"

"Yeah, a little."

"But she was worth the price."

"Yeah. She knew what I needed and she knows how to give it."

"You planning to shack up with her?"

"I could do a hell of a lot worse, but no." Ben was thinking that the last thing he wanted was the kind of dilemma Jeff was struggling with. Shacking up could lead to an attachment that would be traumatic to break, the kind Jeff had forged with Suni.

"How do you feel about her?"

"Do you mean am I smitten?" Jeff nodded. "She's cute," Ben went on, "and fun. And she's a hell of a lay. But mainly I was fucking away frustration."

"You seeing her again tonight?"

"Nope."

"You plan to see her again?"

"Only if I need her."

"Hmm. Look," Jeff said, "the next time you feel like you need her, hold off." Ben eyed his friend skeptically. "I know, I know, that's easy for me to say. But let me finish. You don't want the clap or syph if you can avoid it. I don't mean hold off forever. When you need her, let me know. Maybe I can help."

"How?"

"Suni has a friend."

"Do I know her?"

"Hell, *I* don't know her. She doesn't work at Yongsan."

"I appreciate the offer. But how do you know this friend would be willing to see me?"

"Suni and I have talked," Jeff reddened, "about you and Natalie."

"I see. I guess my private life has gone public."

"Look, I just told her how, uh, rough you've had it. About the letters. She was worried. She doesn't want you taking any unnecessary chances with a moose. She thought you might like a date."

Ben smiled gratefully. "Tell her I said thanks for her concern. What *do* you know about the friend?"

"She and Suni went to college together. She works in a bank. She's pretty, or so Suni swears. And she thinks she might be willing to date an American."

"Well, I'll keep her in mind."

"You never know."

"You sure don't."

CHAPTER 51

Guilt was swamping Natalie. She tried futilely to shrug it off. Ben and I weren't engaged, she thought, but who am I kidding anyway? I love him, I promised to wait. I'm the one who wanted to get married as soon as possible. That might not make for an official engagement, but it's real enough to me. God, why couldn't I wait? I'm supposed to be mature and strong. What do I do now? I'd like to blame Evan but I can't. He was the hunter, but I could have been more elusive prey. If there's blame to pin, it's on me.

She studied herself in the mirror. Her beautiful face was drawn. Defeat dulled her dark brown eyes. Her long hair was unbrushed. What a mess, she thought miserably. Who would've dreamed it would come to this? God, I can hardly stand the sight of myself. The feckless female, in living, lurid color.

She sat heavily on the edge of the bed. A compulsion to confess began to grip her. But confess to whom? Ben? She was depressed but not panic-stricken. Common sense told her that would be the surest way to permanently shatter their relationship. But maybe that's the thing to do. End it now. If I don't and he finds out later, it could destroy us. My parents? They would sympathize, but how could they understand? How could I expect them to? A priest? I haven't been to confession in so long I can't remember the last time. And I've never confessed anything more serious than a fib. Besides, a priest would just give out some silly penance. What good would that do? Dick? Dick would sympathize and I think he would understand. But would he forgive me? For being unfaithful to his brother? That would be asking too much. If only Kate were here instead of in New York. She would listen and understand and not judge. I'm home in my old room, and my parents are just down the hall and I've never felt so alone. Maybe Ben would be better off without me. But, I do love him.

Natalie brushed hair away from her face. She opened the drawer of her night table and removed a pad of writing paper and a cheap ballpoint pen. In the gray light she began to write Ben her dreariest letter yet. She stopped short of explicitly confessing her infidelity. She hoped that Ben would somehow discern the awful truth and somehow empathize and forgive without being asked.

CHAPTER 52

"Busy?"

John Santiago looked up from his desk. "Come on in."

"You sure?"

"Yeah, I was just giving a last look at these specs."

Dick walked to one of the matching visitor chairs and sat. "I've been running something through my mind. I'd like to send up a trial balloon."

"It's a good thing I'm not afraid of heights," John said dryly. "You've sent up a lot of those balloons over the years."

"I guess I have. Well, hang on. This one might set an altitude record. I think it's time we do something new with the business."

"Oh, oh."

Dick smiled. "We're one of the biggest construction management firms on the coast. Which makes us one of the biggest anywhere."

"Mmm-hmm."

"I think we can be more than that. Not that we aren't already substantial. But I remember how much the business grew when we expanded from construction to construction management."

"Granted. It grew a heck of a lot."

"And it was more challenging and more fun."

"Uh-huh."

"And it meant more money."

"Agreed. More than enough."

"Right," said Dick. "We don't want for more money. But I think we can stand a little more challenge and a little more fun. I think it's time we spread our wings and become some sort of a super construction company."

"Okay, how do you propose we do that?"

"Diversification. We broaden into new but closely related areas."

"Such as?"

"Architecture. Interior design. Exterior landscaping."

"Whew. That's one heck of a wingspan."

"It makes sense. I don't have to tell you how much time we spend refereeing differences between the architects, the designers, and the landscapers, not to mention the subcontractors. They're like a bunch of hockey players scrapping for a loose puck. It would be nice to write the rules instead of just enforcing them."

"How do we go about diversifying?"

"Where we can, by acquisition. Otherwise, we recruit and build our own capability."

"You know," John observed, "just about the time I think we've gone as far as we're going to go, you push back the horizon and spring a surprise."

"I'm worried you'll get bored and retire."

"Sure."

"Well, do you think it's worth thinking about?"

John rocked back in his chair, clasped his hands and stared toward the ceiling. "Yeah. Yeah."

"Ah, that's wonderful. Take all the time you need. There's no urgency."

"I have a surprise for *you.*"

"What?"

"Let's do it."

"Huh?"

"I don't see any reason to mull it over. You've thought it out. None of your balloons have crashed before. There's no reason to believe this one will. Let's just go ahead and get started."

"Well, I'll be. That *is* a surprise," Dick teased. He leaned forward and the two partners shook hands.

"Well," John said jokingly, "now that that's settled, is there anything else on your mind? Any new ventures to keep me from getting bored?"

"As a matter of fact, I have been thinking about doing something else. Only it doesn't involve you." A pause.

"Well," John said, "don't keep me in suspense."

"It involves travel."

CHAPTER 53

Ben was slouched at his desk. He felt like he'd been punched in the gut. He had just read Natalie's latest letter. It was devoid of life or any of its vital signs. It was a far cry from her early letters that were peppered with I love yous and I miss yous and long parades of jaunty exclamation points.

Ben was uncertain how to respond. For two days he moped. The second night, in the barracks, he lay on his bunk, hands clasped behind his head, staring at the ceiling.

Casey was writing his wife, Jeff had left for Suni's, Dan was reading a novel.

"Dan," said Ben, "you feel like playing some gin?"

Dan looked across the room. "Mmm. Why not? The usual? A tenth of a cent a point?"

"Sure. But I get the home bunk advantage." Ben shuffled the cards and dealt. "You have any plans for the weekend?"

"I was thinking of jetting to Paris and strolling the Left Bank. Checking out some bistros. But other than that, no big plans. You have something in mind?"

"I could use a change of scenery."

"Mmm. Any particular scenery?"

"Nope, I just feel like I have to get away from this place. It's closing in on me."

"I know what you mean."

"Any suggestions?" Ben asked.

"As a matter of fact, yes. There's something I've wanted to do for quite a while now."

Saturday began as a cold and clear early December morning. Dan and Ben pulled their field jackets over their fatigues and walked to the mess hall where they ate heartily. Dan downed sausage with no qualms about Jewish tenets. Afterward, they struck out on foot across Yongsan and passed through the compound's north gate. They headed for the base of nearby Namsan Mountain. At the foot of the mountain Ben and Dan stared up the steep slope toward the summit with its crown of radio and television transmission towers.

Namsan was unusual in that its slopes were heavily wooded, in emerald contrast to the rocky starkness of the peaks that ringed Seoul.

"We could take the easy way up," Dan said, nodding toward the red cable car waiting to make its next ascent to the mountaintop park.

"We could," said Ben, "but let's don't. I feel like walking."

"Me too."

They started up the serpentine hiking trail. The path was thick with Koreans of all ages, out for weekend exercise and sightseeing. Dan and Ben were the only Americans. Trees were barren of leaves, affording a virtually unimpeded view of the sprawling city below. About two thirds of the way up they paused to rest. They sat on a gray rock that looked like a huge loaf of bread. Despite the cold they were breathing hard and perspiring.

"And to think," smiled Ben, "we were in good shape when we left basic."

"Riding in jeeps and pounding a typewriter doesn't do much for the lungs and legs."

"I'm surprised I haven't put on much weight. But then Betty Crocker would condemn our chow hall," said Ben. "Jesus, what I wouldn't give for some fresh fish."

"Or cannelloni. Or moussaka. Or cheese blintzes. Or-"

"A cheeseburger and onion rings," Ben said dreamily.

"We better get up and get going before our deprived taste buds drive us to something suicidal."

During the remainder of the ascent they reminisced fondly about families and friends and hometowns and homecooking. At the top they stood silent and panting.

"My God," marveled Dan, "what a fabulous view."

Below them the sun-drenched city of four million stretched to and part way up the sides of the surrounding craggy peaks. They had a hawk's-eye view of Yongsan, which like everything else, looked Lilliputian. They walked the perimeter of the summit, then found a comfortable vantage point that faced north. They sat and talked.

"I guess this qualifies as a change of scenery," smiled Dan under his dark, twinkling eyes and crinkly eyelids.

"Easily," murmured Ben.

"Let's change subjects. More problems with Natalie?"

"Not really more, just more of the same. She's confused. That's about the only thing that's clear. In her letters she raises a lot more questions than she answers. Funny. She's the one who was so sure of everything when I left. She had no doubt about us."

"Rough."

"Yeah. I'm tempted to write and just call the whole thing off. I know I'd feel a damn sight better."

"For how long?"

"Beats the hell out of me."

"Her? How do you think she would react?"

"I really don't know."

"Well, talk is cheap and advice can be worthless or worse," said Dan, "but I wouldn't be too hasty about writing off your relationship."

"It wouldn't be hasty. I've been thinking about it for some time."

"The future is a long time. You can give it a while longer."

"Yes, sir, Chaplain Cohen," Ben smiled wryly.

"Just my nature, Soldier Lawrence."

It was mid-afternoon before they descended and returned to Yongsan. Ben felt tired. Tired but better. They flopped on their bunks.

"Hold it," said Dan.

"Huh?"

"You've had a change of scenery, but there's still a lot of today left. Let's wipe it off the calendar."

"With alcohol as the miracle cleaner?"

"Right. We'll do it with a giant economy size binge."

And they did. At the compound's NCO club. They became incoherently soused. Not one of the bevy of savvy prostitutes approached them. Something told the business girls that on this night anyway the two soldiers were far more interested in pink elephants than pieces of tail.

By midweek Ben still had not written Natalie. Despite the weekend retreat he again was feeling hurt, betrayed, resentful. Natalie had made a fistful of promises that she apparently had broken. I'm the one in uniform, with tough responsibilities and little control over my time. Natalie, you have choices I can only reminisce about. You don't have to follow orders or abide by dress codes or haircut regulations. You have room to breathe. You have the better of it. You're no doubt sleeping with that professor. Goddammit, Natalie, how can you do this? To me? To us? I love you and I miss you so much. I've told you that, over and over. Maybe I should just cut bait. Go my own way. Let you go yours.

When Ben did answer her letter, he could bring himself to say none of that. Instead, he told her what he always did. That he loved, missed and wanted her. He sealed and stamped the envelope. Then he threw the letter into the office mailbox. The letter would change nothing, he knew, not a damn thing. The thought further depressed him.

That afternoon he asked Jeff to learn whether Suni's friend still would consider a date with him.

Jeff's answer came the next day. "How about Saturday night?"

Saturday afternoon Ben was nervous. At first the anxiety puzzled him. Then it made sense. A blind date. Never been on one. What does she look like? What's she like? Will she like me? No wonder I'm feeling butterflies. Then there's Natalie.

About 6:00 Ben and Jeff, in their civvies, walked outside the compound and hailed a cab. They squeezed into the back seat of the tiny rattling, wheezing vehicle belching black exhaust.

"Bando Hotel," Jeff told the driver.

The cabbie was young, square-jawed, hard-eyed. He was wearing worn black leather gloves. He hurtled the taxi through traffic like a police car racing to a murder scene. It weaved from lane to lane, aggressively competing with other cabs, refusing to yield to lumbering buses. The driver held nothing back. Except his passengers' stomachs that seemed to be bouncing repeatedly off their spines. Ten harrowing minutes later the cab screeched to a halt in front of the Bando.

Two smartly dressed young women were standing huddled against the cold on the sidewalk outside the main entrance. Ben recognized one as Suni. She hadn't exaggerated. Her companion was very good looking. She was tall by Korean standards, about five feet six inches. She was medium-breasted, small-waisted, with sleek legs. Her cheekbones were exceptionally high. The tip of her nose hooked slightly to the left; the imperfection was barely noticeable except when seen straight on. Her black hair was thick and bobbed in a way that complimented her features.

Jeff paid the cab driver, then made introductions. "Ben Lawrence," he said formally, "this is Won Kyong Pok."

Ben extended his hand. "Nice to meet you."

She placed her hand in his and smiled shyly, revealing white, even teeth. "I am happy to meet you." Her voice was low-pitched and slightly smoky.

Ben turned to Suni and shook her hand. "How've you been?"

"Very fine, Ben. And you?"

"Fine," he lied. It was a lie he knew had fooled no one.

"Everybody ready?" said Jeff, smiling widely. They started off on foot, Jeff and Suni in the lead, holding hands. Ben and Won Kyong Pok followed, hands at their sides. They headed for Myongdong, Seoul's glittering strip of shops, theaters, restaurants, tearooms and nightclubs.

"Jeff said people call you Kyong," Ben said.

"That is right."

"Did I say it right?"

"Yes. Kee-ong."

"And you work in a bank."

"Yes."

The dialogue faltered. Ben's mind raced, searching frantically for a conversational line. One that she could follow with a limited knowledge of English. This isn't going to be easy, Ben thought. She knows why I asked Jeff to arrange this. This is stupid. Damn, I feel awkward. And guilty. I should've gone to the Vill and picked up a moose. Maybe the one I had before. Damn, that would've been so much easier.

"Do you like Korea?"

Ben was startled. The last thing he expected was her posing a question. "Uh, yes. Yes."

"What do you like most?"

"The mountains. I never get tired of looking at them. I see them every day and they always look different. Majestic. Oh, I'm sorry, I-"

"I know what means majestic," she said reassuringly. Ben smiled. "Are there mountains in Ohio?"

"No. Some high hills but no mountains. Hey, how did you know I was from Ohio? Oh, Suni."

"Yes. Jeff told her and she told me. Ohio is by Lake Erie," she smiled widely, eyes sparkling.

"That's right," Ben said, warming to her.

"I looked on the globe at the bank."

Ben laughed. "You do your homework."

"Please?"

"Oh, I mean you studied. You prepared yourself."

She laughed. "I was always a good student."

"I'll bet."

"You bet?" she asked.

"I agree."

"Oh."

"Were you born in Seoul?"

"Yes."

"Do you have any brothers or sisters?"

"Yes. I have two brothers. They are younger."

"We're almost there," said Jeff, looking back over his shoulder. "Suni says this is a good restaurant."

"Tonight you will eat like kings," laughed Suni.

The evening was young, but Myongdong already was swarming with chattering, laughing multitudes in pursuit of entertainment. The two GI's towered over most of the pedestrians. With their two Korean companions they drew endless curious stares.

"Here we are," said Suni.

A hostess led them to a small private dining room. They removed their shoes and knelt around a small, low table. Suni and Kyong conferred and ordered.

The first dish was a watery, rather bland soup. Ben and Jeff both professed to finding it delicious. Suni and Kyong, the former college classmates, eyed them skeptically, looked at each other, murmured and giggled.

"What kind of soup is this?" Ben asked.

"It does not matter," said Suni. "Just eat and enjoy." She and Kyong giggled again.

"Octopus," Jeff whispered to Ben.

"What?"

"I think we just ate octopus soup."

Ben rolled his eyes and forced the thought from his mind.

The waiter brought a cold dish that looked and tasted very much like potato salad. Jeff and Ben refrained from asking about it.

Next was a dish that looked akin to tossed salad. Artlessly, Ben maneuvered his chopsticks and managed to pick up a respectable amount. He leaned forward and took a bite. Instantly his mouth flamed and his eyes watered. He flushed and pitched forward, gagging. When Jeff saw Ben's distress, he discreetly lowered his chopsticks to the bowl. Suni and Kyong struggled to contain their mirth. Ben tried to swallow but could not. With as much dignity as he could manage, he let the searing salad out of his mouth and back into the bowl. His tongue still aflame, his eyes awash in tears, he reached for a tiny glass of perfectly clear liquid. Suni and Kyong watched expectantly as Ben tipped the glass to his mouth and sipped. It was like pouring gasoline on smoldering coals. The conflagration in his mouth erupted anew. He managed to swallow but was rendered speechless as the burning liquid singed his throat and esophagus. The women could no longer contain their laughter. Jeff snickered, tried mightily to restrain himself, then surrendered to waves of thunderous laughter. Mercifully, Kyong handed Ben another, larger glass. He hesitated. "Water," she said. He gulped it down.

"What was that?" he finally managed to gasp.

"Kimchi," smiled Kyong, sniffling to clear tears of laughter.

"What's in it?"

"Cabbage, onions, peppers, garlic."

"Does anybody actually eat that?"

"Oh, yes," said Kyong. "Koreans eat kimchi every day."

"Geez, I don't know how."

"We are used to it."

"Your mouths and throats and stomachs must be lined with lead."

"All kimchi is not so hot," said Kyong. "But we are used to it." She and Suni looked at each other, smiled demurely, then gracefully lifted large bites to their mouths. Ben and Jeff watched with awe as the young women delicately, unhurriedly chewed and swallowed the fiery salad. The Americans shook their heads in wonderment.

"What was in that small glass?" Ben asked.

"Soju," said Kyong. "It's very powerful."

"That might be the understatement of recorded history."

"What?"

"You bet."

"Oh," she smiled.

"What?" asked Suni, baffled.

"Ben agrees," said Kyong.

"Oh."

The waiter reappeared and began to prepare a brazier. He lighted the charcoal. Then, on the brazier's perforated metal dome, he began to array celery, onions, seaweed and thin strips of meat.

"What's that?" asked Ben.

"Vegetables and pulgogi," said Kyong. "You will like it very much."

"I'm sure," Ben said under narrowed eyes.

"You bet," Kyong said wryly.

Ben laughed. He was feeling better, more spirited, than he had in months.

The pulgogi turned out to be exquisite. Thin strips of beef, carefully marinated, chewy but not tough. The vegetables were no less delectable. Their juices had mingled with the beef broth, producing the equivalent of culinary nirvana.

When they left the restaurant, Ben took Kyong's hand. There was no hesitation on his part and no attempt by her to withdraw. They chatted easily, unexpectedly comfortable with each other.

Jeff led them to a theater nearby. Outside, a long line was slowly filing into the lobby. The marquis proclaimed: *Teahouse of the August Moon – Marlon Brando.* Inside, a huge throng – upward of 3,000 – buzzed excitedly. Ben and Jeff and Suni and Kyong climbed to the crowded balcony.

When the curtain parted, Ben was surprised. He had expected Korean dubbing, possibly with English subtitles. Instead, the film was in English with Korean subtitles.

In the darkened theater Ben held Kyong's hand. He was thoroughly enjoying Brando's performance but took at least as much delight in Kyong's touch and laughter.

"Can you understand many of the words?" he whispered to Kyong.

"No. They speak too fast. And too much slang. But I enjoy anyway."

The movie rolled on.

Outside the theater Ben asked, "Now what?"

"We'll go back to the Vill for a nightcap."

"Don't forget the midnight curfew," said Ben.

"You're talking to a human clock. It's only ten-thirty."

"Then what?"

"I'm not sure, but we'll find out."

"Meaning?"

"Meaning what?"

"What's the arrangement for the night?" Ben asked.

"I take that to mean you wouldn't mind bedding Kyong."

"Who wouldn't?"

"She *is* nice."

"She's terrific."

Ben opened the rear door of the cab. Suni and Kyong climbed in. Ben followed. The three back seat occupants wedged themselves into the tiny vehicle. To ease the congestion Ben sat tilted on his left hip and draped his left arm across the back of the seat. Jeff sat in front and directed the driver.

On the way to the Vill, Suni and Kyong chattered continuously in Korean. Occasionally the two long-time friends succumbed to giggles. Once Kyong patted Ben on the thigh as if to assure him they were plotting no conspiracy.

"Any idea what they're talking about?" Ben asked.

"Well, I wouldn't be surprised if it's what happens later."

They looked at the women. Suni and Kyong sensed they were being stared at, paused, eyed the two soldiers with great amusement, giggled and resumed their animated chattering.

"Well, I'm glad they're having a good time," Ben observed dryly.

In the Vill, Suni and Kyong led the way to a small hotel. "Wait here," Suni instructed. She and Kyong went inside.

"What do you think?" Ben said edgily.

"I think Suni is inspecting the accommodations."

"Oh."

"She's got the mother hen streak in her."

"I guess you'd recognize that."

"An allusion to my mother?"

"The singular Alice Zink."

"The quintessential mother hen."

"She should see you now," said Ben. "Her adorable son, pimping."

"She'd lay a double grade A large egg."

"Might do her good."

"Once she got over the pain of giving birth," said Jeff.

"It would be more like cutting the umbilical cord."

"Somehow the doctors overlooked that step."

"Over twenty-three years ago."

"That's what I meant."

The women emerged. "You come on, Ben," said Suni. "Jeff, you stay here."

Ben faced Jeff and shrugged. He passed Suni and followed Kyong inside. A tiny woman with gray hair knotted in a tight bun silently led them up a flight of narrow stairs. She led them down a narrow hallway and opened a door.

"How much?" said Ben.

"Seven hundred won," replied the woman.

Ben paid.

"Take off your shoes," murmured Kyong.

The miniature innkeeper departed as Ben and Kyong slipped off their shoes. The cramped room was no larger than a walk-in closet. Virtually no room to move. Ben closed the door. He and Kyong stood facing each other. They kissed heatedly. Ben's glasses fogged quickly. After the kiss they stood embracing each other.

"You undress first," Kyong whispered. She turned her back. Ben smiled. He stripped and piled his clothes on top of the bureau. "Get in bed and turn your back," she instructed.

Kyong opened her purse and removed a yellow short nightie. She pulled on the string of a dangling light bulb, and the room went black.

Ben lay on his side, listening to the sounds of rustling clothes. He gritted his teeth to keep from shivering between the cold sheets.

Kyong crawled over him, lay on her back and pulled up the top sheet and a single blanket. She shivered. Ben moved closer and put his arm across her shoulders. She lay still, arms at her sides. The shivering subsided.

To Ben their lovemaking seemed strangely awkward. When it was over, they held each other tightly. He kissed her forehead, eyelids, nose, cheeks, neck. Kyong nuzzled against Ben's hairy chest. She caressed his shoulders, chest and thigh. Ben faced her. Their eyes had adjusted to the darkness. They could make out each other's features. They smiled, with obvious affection.

"Is it always like that?" Kyong's low-pitched voice whispered.

"What do you mean?"

"I mean, does the man always, uh, get so big? Please forgive my not so good English. I have studied English since middle school but not hear many Americans speak."

"You should hear some Americans. Then you would know how well you speak English."

"Thank you. Is love always like that?"

"It depends. I-"

"You are my first man."

"You mean first American."

"No, first man."

"Oh, I can't believe that." She had not demonstrated any lovemaking expertise. Maybe it's true, Ben thought. But if it is, I'm not sure I want to believe it. I needed a woman but a virgin...

"It is true."

Ben hesitated, then sat up. He looked between her legs.

"No blood," said Kyong, smiling. "I took care of that before."

Ben looked at her quizzically.

She shrugged. "It is true."

"I don't understand. Why me? You don't even know me. Why not a Korean?"

"Not so easy with Korean man. He will not respect me if I do not marry him. Both lose face. But I wanted to know how love is. Suni told me about she and Jeff. She says making love is very, uh, romantic." Ben smiled affectionately. "I want to know for myself. Suni say you are very nice. Tonight I think so, too. So..."

"Unreal," Ben muttered.

"What?"

"Unreal."

"What means unreal?"

"Unreal means you and me. Tonight. In this place. Together. You a virgin. Understand?"

"Yes." And she did. "You miss girlfriend back in the States?"

"Yes, I do. Did Suni tell you all about that?"

"Yes, but I know anyway. I can see in you."

Ben studied her dark eyes. They were calm, wise. She was right, Ben knew; she could see in him.

"Will you and she get married?"

"I don't know."

"Do you want to?"

"Anymore, I'm not sure. It's confusing. I'm not sure what I want and I don't know what she wants."

"What is her name?"

"Natalie. Natalie Santiago."

"Very pretty name...Ben, do you want to see me again?"

"Yes." Ben caressed her cheeks. "May I?"

"Yes."

"You and Suni are very good friends."

"Yes. Long-time friends."

"Does Suni love Jeff?"

"Yes, very much love."

"Do you think she would like to marry him?"

"Yes."

"And go to the States?"

"She loves him. Yes, she would go."

"Has she ever said anything about marriage to Jeff?"

"Oh, no," Kyong said, as though Ben had suggested the unthinkable.

"Maybe you could, uh-"

"No, I not tell her."

"Oh."

"Do you think Jeff will ask Suni to marry?"

Ben sighed. "I hope so."

"But not sure."

"Not sure."

"Ben?"

"Mmm."

"I remember this night a very long time."

"I will, too, Kyong. It was very special."

"You bet."

Early the next morning Ben was still asleep, breathing heavily. Kyong was awake. She propped herself on an elbow and reflected on the American who lay beside her. I do not envy you, Ben Lawrence. So far from home and loved ones. Poor thing. And your girlfriend. She is probably very pretty and very sweet. I cannot see you falling in love with someone who is not. Yes, I can see in you. You say your girlfriend is confused, but are you not confused as well? When a person is lonesome, it is easy to be confused. It is so tragic. When you return to America, I hope you and she will join together and be as one. It will not be easy for either of you. I am touched by your concern for Jeff and Suni. You have your own problems with your Natalie, and yet you worry about another couple. That is sweet. You have many worries and can do so little about them. That is why I will help you, if you want. I will try to be good to you and good for you. But I do not think I will let myself take our relationship any further than that. I do not think you will either. I think both of us see us for what we are at this moment. Sources of comfort and warmth and understanding. We both can learn and benefit from this. I will help you whenever you want, as long as you are here. After you leave Korea, I will try to find a nice Korean man. And if I do, I will make him a good Korean wife. Kyong ran her fingers lightly over Ben's hair and then reclined again on the pillow.

Chapter 54

In Pyongyang, capital of North Korea, Premier Kim Il Sung listened attentively while a general detailed another mission of terror in Kim's increasingly vigorous campaign to undermine South Korea's political stability.

The general's pointer jabbed at a map. "Finally," he concluded confidently, "landing here will allow us to achieve complete and utter surprise."

"This is a large-scale operation," Kim pointed out, "the largest yet in terms of men. Should it succeed, how do you assess the possibility of retaliation by the United States?"

"Very slim, Sir, as long as we hold the crew of the Pueblo."

"Mmm. And how about the South Koreans? Their generals almost assuredly would press for retaliatory measures. Harsh ones."

"Yes, Sir, they would. But the American General Bonesteel rules and he would forbid it."

"Major General Charles Bonesteel...a solid military man. It seems a risky operation," observed Kim. "Many men may perish."

"There is an element of risk," conceded the general.

The premier arched a skeptical eyebrow.

"High risk," the general quickly amended his concession. "But the men will be volunteers, and they will know the risk. They also know that, if successful, the mission could induce further unrest in the South and facilitate our effort to unify the country."

"Yes. All right. Very good," Kim said soberly. "You have my approval to proceed."

The first Siberian winds blew the last warmth of autumn from the Korean peninsula. As 1968 tiptoed into December, the Pueblo crew still was imprisoned. In Southern California the onset of winter found Dick progressing nicely in his efforts to transform Western Construction into a diversified powerhouse. Natalie's coolness puzzled and frustrated Evan. He had sought her company frequently but with scant success. Natalie had agreed to see him just once – on neutral ground – since the night they had loved in his apartment.

Natalie's first winter missive was as barren as a denuded oak tree. It baffled Ben. The letter contained no mention of Sloane. That was a change. It contained neither a smidgen of cheer nor a hint of promise. That was not a change. It did, however, contain something new – and unsettling. For the first time, Natalie openly questioned whether she and Ben should stick it out. More unsettling was the apparent detachment with which she had penned the words. Natalie wrote: *So much time has passed without seeing each other. So much has changed. Maybe we should let it rest for now. We could get together when you return. See what we still have in common. What do you think, Ben? Do you agree or not? Whatever you want is okay with me. There's no hurry to decide. You still have another six months to go.* With this letter, Ben asked himself, is Natalie handing me the key to the door to emotional freedom?

After work that day, Ben, Jeff and Dan stepped outside into the gray, windy cold. They turned up the collars of their field jackets, now containing warm liners. They pulled on wool-lined leather gloves and began walking to the barracks.

"Can you send a telegram from here?" asked Ben.

"I suppose so," said Dan. "Where to?"

"Stateside."

"Did you forget somebody's birthday?" Jeff kidded.

A grimace creased Ben's face. "Something like that. Where do you suppose you can send one?"

"I'd try the mail room," said Dan.

That night Ben composed the telegram. He saw it as a way out of an emotional blizzard. The words came easily. Surprisingly so. He planned to send it the next day during lunch hour.

Early the next morning, in the gray predawn off Korea's rocky east coast, three North Korean gunboats edged near the perilous shore. About 120 crack soldiers clambered out of the boats and onto the rocks. The empty boats departed immediately, heading due east far out to sea before swinging north.

Not quite a year before, North Korean Premier Kim Il Sung had ordered 30 agents to infiltrate through the DMZ in an attempt to assassinate South Korea's president, Park Chung Hee. Soon after, North Korean naval vessels had fired on the Pueblo and captured and incarcerated her crew. During the summer, a dozen North Korean commandos had landed on Pusan's beach; South Korean troops, alerted by intelligence that the commandos were coming, set up machine guns and waited. They killed all the intruders before they could move off the beach. Almost daily over the past two years, North Korean patrols had probed American and South Korean defenses along the DMZ in a series of deadly firefights.

On this cold, damp morning, a ruddy-faced North Korean Army captain stood on a rock high above the pounding surf and gathered the company of infiltrators. He reviewed their mission. They would strike hard and fast and then work their way north to the DMZ, creating more panic as they progressed. They were confident of reaching the DMZ and breaking through to their own lines but were prepared to fail. The ultimate price of death was not too high a cost for creating more havoc and political unrest in the poisonous South where Koreans were willing lackeys to the imperialistic Yankee pigs. The price looked even more like a bargain should they succeed in killing American and South Korean troops during the mission. They were ready, more than ready.

A half mile farther north, a fishing village was beginning to stir. Wives were boiling water for tea and preparing breakfasts of kimchi and rice. Husbands were readying themselves and their nets and boats for a day at sea. Blurry-eyed children rolled up the sleeping mats and shivered as they shed their nightclothes and hurriedly dressed.

The North Koreans positioned themselves in a half-moon around the village. They waited patiently behind rocks and trees. Most of the village men and some of the children were outside the thatched-roof houses now. A boy, about 12, in a teasing mood, pinched his younger sister. She squealed. He ran and she went chasing him toward the surrounding forest. The boy was laughing. Suddenly, he saw something and pulled up, startled. He paused, then started to call to his sister. A North Korean soldier squeezed the trigger on his automatic rifle, and the boy and his sister were thrown backward and fell dead. The other soldiers opened fire. Ruthlessly, they sprayed automatic weapons fire and lobbed grenades among the bewildered villagers. Men, women and children were screaming in shock and terror as bullets and grenade fragments ripped unsuspecting flesh, and homes blew apart in flames.

Minutes later, the butchery ended. The only sound was the agitated surf.

The correspondents were pulling on their fatigues when Sergeant Taber burst into their quarters. He was breathing hard. He looked around the room. "Lawrence, Cohen. Finish dressing and come with me. Hurry."

"What's wrong?" Dan asked. They all were flabbergasted by Taber's unprecedented early-morning appearance.

"Some North Koreans came ashore over on the east coast this morning. They massacred a village. Seventh Division is sending troops to go after them."

"Holy shit," spat Ben.

"Those poor souls," said Dan.

"I've got a jeep waiting outside," said Taber.

"Chow?" said Ben.

"No time," said Taber. "We want you guys out there as soon as possible. General Bonesteel wants a detailed report."

"And," Dan observed dryly, "it occurred to him to send people accustomed to making professionally detailed reports."

"You'll go far, Cohen," said Taber.

"How do we get there?" Ben asked.

"Chopper. One's revving up for you at the pad."

Ben pulled on his field jacket and jammed a piece of paper into a pocket. Then he put on his cap.

"Leave the caps," said Taber. "Bring your steel pots. And don't bother bringing your blue armbands. I've got your pistols, rifles and ammunition in the jeep."

"Not that we'll need them," said Dan. "I hope."

"Just a precaution," said Taber. "Standard procedure."

"You mean there's procedure to cover this?" Ben asked caustically as he knotted a bootlace.

"You guys never stop, do you?" said Taber.

"Maybe there's been a mistake, Sarge," said Ben. "Didn't I read where a truce was signed in Korea fifteen years ago?"

"I think the North Koreans could stand a reminder," said Dan. "A polite memo, maybe."

In the jeep Ben sat beside Taber. Dan was in the rear.

"How did word get back here so fast?" Ben asked.

"A few villagers managed to sneak away," said Taber. "They ran into a South Korean patrol. Word was radioed back to Yongsan."

"Any word on casualties?" asked Dan.

"Not that I know," said Taber. "HQ just called it a massacre."

The jeep pulled away from the barracks and headed for the helicopter pad.

"Sarge," said Ben, "could you swing by the mail room?"

"Are you kidding?"

"No, I'm not," Ben said grimly. "I have to send a telegram back home. It's in my pocket. It won't take long. Just a minute or two."

"Lawrence, the chopper is waiting."

"Aw, come on, Sarge. Please. It *is* important."

"All right, but make it snappy."

"Thanks."

"Don't mention it. To anybody."

Ben grinned.

At the mailroom Ben bounced out of the jeep and ran to the door of the corrugated metal Quonset hut. He paused a moment to reread the message. Then he banged on the door. When it opened, he handed the paper to the soldier-clerk. Ben pointed to the address, asked the cost of sending it, paid and dashed back to the jeep.

Moments later at the pad, Ben and Dan and Taber walked briskly to the helicopter. They crouched low under the whirling blades. Ben and Dan climbed inside. Taber stood at the doorway and bellowed, recapping their instructions. "Warrant Officer Strickland will fly you to the village. You'll hook up with our troops from Seventh Division. Their job is to flush out the North Koreans. You find the commanding officer and get his radioman to make contact with Yongsan. They are expecting you. File your first report right away. Then stay with the troops and keep us up to date. And," shouted Taber, "be careful."

Ben and Dan nodded. Taber backed away. The chopper floated skyward and shot east. An hour later the rocky coast hove into view. Through the din of the chopper's engine and blades, Ben shouted to Dan, "It doesn't look any more hospitable than it did when I first came into the country."

"Assuming they landed by sea," replied Dan, "it must have been a pretty hairy operation. That surf and those rocks don't look very forgiving."

Strickland dipped lower, then angled southeast. He spotted a cluster of houses and smoking ruins. He handed Dan a pair of binoculars. Dan looked and passed the glasses to Ben. Ben surveyed the village. He lowered the glasses and shook his head sadly.

"That it?" shouted Strickland.

Dan nodded.

Strickland circled, searching for a reasonably flat open area, one not littered with corpses. He found one a quarter mile south of the village near the sea. Gingerly he put the chopper down. "Good luck," he yelled to Dan and Ben. "Thanks," they answered. They eased out, ducked and went scurrying inland to the cover of nearby trees. Strickland signaled thumbs up and lifted off. Ben and Dan waited for the racket to dissipate, then stepped into the open. They adjusted their ammunition belts and slung their rifles over their shoulders. Their helmet chinstraps dangled loose.

"I guess we'd better not waste any time finding our men," said Dan.

"I didn't see anybody coming in."

"Neither did I. Must be scouting the woods."

"Let's stay out in the open and close to the shore," said Ben. "I'd rather not have a case of mistaken identity."

"Good thinking."

They began walking north. The ground was frozen. The cold air, driven by a cutting sea wind, quickly chilled them. Unconsciously they hunched their shoulders. Ben pushed his glasses farther up his nose. They saw no one.

Moments later the village lay before them. They sucked in deep breaths and girded themselves. The first bodies they saw were of a young boy and girl. Except for an ugly red stain on his chest, the boy lay in peaceful repose, eyes closed. The girl's limbs were twisted grotesquely. Her right arm was nearly severed at the elbow. Her eyes were open. Ben knelt to close the lids but couldn't. The cold had frozen them.

Ben stood and shivered. "Those fucking animals," he hissed.

"God have mercy," murmured Dan.

"It's the least he can do," Ben muttered.

More bodies were scattered about. At the sight of a faceless woman, Dan retched and vomited what little remained in his stomach from last night.

The roofs of two houses had caved in. In others, mud walls had crumbled. Ben and Dan counted 81 bodies. They stood together amidst the carnage.

"I'll never forget this sight," said Dan. "Nobody has to tell me how cruel man can be to man. As a Jew, I'm keenly aware of that. But actually seeing…seeing this. It's almost beyond comprehension. Innocent people. Children. Why? Why on earth why?"

"Wish I knew," Ben murmured sadly.

"They never had a chance. They probably had no idea why-" Dan's voice caught. He removed his wool-lined leather gloves. He pulled a handkerchief from a hip pocket and dabbed at his eyes and nose.

"Have you noticed how quiet it is?" Ben asked.

"No," Dan sniffed, "but now that you mention it..."

"Not even any seagulls."

"Maybe they shot them too," Dan said bitterly.

"I don't think we're going to accomplish anything here," said Ben. "Our troops will return to bury the dead, but who knows when."

"I'm surprised they didn't start burying them right away."

"Yeah," said Ben. "Could be they didn't want to spare the time now. Or use combat troops. Maybe they've radioed for support personnel to clean up here."

"Hard to figure."

"I think we should try to find our men," said Ben. "It's the only way we'll radio back a report anytime soon."

"I suppose. To tell you the truth, I'm more than ready to get out of here."

"Let's head north," said Ben. "We didn't see or hear anything when we came in from the south. We'll go maybe a half mile, then sweep around to the west in an arc."

"If we don't make contact?"

"We come back here. If we go any farther, we'll just get ourselves lost."

"Agreed."

It was slow going. They picked their way north along the rough coastline. In some places they had to hop from rock to rock. The exertion warmed them. When they started inland, they encountered thick forest. It was preternaturally quiet.

Dan stopped. "Did you hear something?"

Ben shook his head.

"I feel like shouting, Is anybody home?" Dan whispered.

"You don't holler when you hunt."

"Yeah. My Queens upbringing didn't prepare me for this."

A few more steps.

"Hold it," Ben whispered.

They froze.

"What is it?" whispered Dan. "Can you-"

A burst of machine gun fire cracked the stillness and ripped the bark off surrounding trees. One bullet pierced Ben's canteen, and a second nicked his helmet, a glancing blow but forceful enough to hurl him to the ground. A third grazed Dan's thigh, purpling his green fatigues. He half fell, half dove to the ground.

"Ouch," gritted Dan. "Goddamn, it smarts."

"Let me look," said Ben. He separated the torn cloth and inspected Dan's leg. "A scrape."

"You sure?"

"Yeah. You'll be all right."

"Who the fuck's shooting at us anyway?"

"I'm gonna find out. Hey!" Ben cried. "We're Americans. Seventh Division, hold your fire. Did you hear me? We're Americans. Correspondents from-"

The response cut him off. It was another, longer burst of fire. A shower of bark and twigs and pine needles fell on them.

"Hey, goddamn it," shouted Ben. "Get your goddamn act together out there. Listen up. We're Americans."

A grenade detonated near them. The ground shook.

"Either those bastards are deaf," Dan muttered, "or we have a serious problem. And I don't think they're deaf. I think we beat our guys here. I think those are their guys."

Two more grenades exploded, raining dirt and more debris on them.

"I have the sinking feeling you're right," said Ben.

"What do we do?"

Ben didn't answer.

"Well," Dan persisted, "what do you think?"

"To tell you the truth," Ben murmured, "I'm thinking about words I wish I could take back."

"What the flying fuck are you talking about?" Dan whispered furiously, blood still oozing from his thigh wound.

"That telegram. I wish I hadn't sent it."

"This isn't exactly the ideal time for second guessing."

"If we don't get out of here, what a lousy-"

"We'll get out. I wasn't bar mitzva'd for this kind of end."

"I'd feel a little better if we knew what the hell we're supposed to do in this kind of situation," said Ben. "Kinda makes me wish I'd gone to advanced infantry training instead of the correspondents school. We can't see them but they can see us. Or at least they could. They sure as hell know where we are. If nothing else they can probably see our breath rising."

"I forgot about the cold."

"Let's try to get back to the village. We can get cover there or among the rocks. And at least see who the hell is after us."

Another barrage of bullets and grenades rattled the forest around them. They hugged the ground.

"Before we retreat," suggested Dan, "maybe we should fire a few rounds in their direction. Keep them honest."

"For an urban Jew, you make a decent grunt."

As they readied their rifles and prepared to fire, a presence loomed over them. Dan sensed it first. He swung his head left. Fear swept through him. Two North Koreans, automatic rifles lowered, edged closer, scanning the ground. They saw Dan and Ben an instant after Dan saw them. Dan jerked his rifle around and roughly pulled the trigger. Gunfire and screams erupted almost simultaneously. Ben was startled. He shifted, began to speak, then saw the North Koreans crumpling.

"You okay?" Ben whispered anxiously.

Dan nodded. "Let's get moving."

"We were damn lucky. Those guys-"

"Shhh."

A voice called out something in Korean.

"I don't think I killed them," said Dan.

Ben and Dan lay still a moment. Then, crouching low, they began to retreat toward the village. Behind them was more shouting and gunfire. Grenades exploded to the rear. They hit the ground and crawled on. Later, they stood and hustled seaward. At the edge of the village, they heard the drone of approaching engines. They looked up. Troop-carrying helicopters were swooping in low. Dan and Ben removed their helmets, ran to the center of the village and began waving wildly.

Maria handed the envelope to Natalie who opened it. The message was brief:

Dear Natalie, You are right. This is not going to work. It is too hard on both of us. I will never forget you. I wish you the very best. Ben

Natalie's eyes blinked. It was so unexpected she was slow to comprehend. She read the telegram again. Her hands began to tremble, her chin to quiver.

Maria took the message from Natalie and read it. She understood immediately. Instinctively she knew this message was the culmination of seeds planted in a long line of correspondence. Her heart and her arms went out to her daughter.

"If you want him," said John Santiago, grim-visaged, "I think you should tell him now. No procrastinating."

Natalie looked glumly at her father through grief-reddened eyes.

"I think your father is right," said Maria. "If you wait to reply, you're confirming the uncertainty and confusion he's sensed in you. Your message should be prompt and leave no doubt."

"You've both been under a lot of pressure," said John. "It's hard to think logically when you're stressed. You're prone to making bad judgments. If you want things fixed, you'll have to move fast to fix them. Don't let the situation fester."

"What if...what if he won't take me back?"

"There's no guarantee," John said gently. "But do you want him to be able to make that choice?"

"Yes."

Early the next morning, Natalie drove to the Western Union office on Wilshire Boulevard. Her message was concise and clear:

My Dearest Ben, I love you. I miss you. I want you more than anything. I will wait for you. I am so sorry for everything. Please forgive me. I love you with all my heart. And I always will. Natalie.

Ben had been in the field three days when Natalie's telegram arrived at Yongsan. He and Dan had been traipsing after a battalion from the 7th Infantry Division. The Americans were methodically hunting down the scattered North Koreans. Their orders: take no prisoners; send a clear message to Kim Il Sung. The GI's pursued the North Koreans relentlessly over ridges and through wooded valleys. They pinned them down in caves and among rocks. It was cold, hard, dangerous work. Not one of the North Koreans had surrendered. No prisoners were taken. One by one, the intruders were killed.

Twice each day, Dan and Ben radioed reports to Yongsan. From there they were distributed to the Korean government and news media.

Dan and Ben had grown inured to fresh death. At least in the case of these North Koreans. They viewed each corpse dispassionately. In some instances they were surprised to experience fleeting feelings of satisfaction.

Casey McDermott picked up the ringing telephone in the correspondents' office.

"I've got a telegram for Specialist Benjamin Lawrence," said the mailroom clerk.

"He's not here," Casey replied.

"When'll he be back?"

"I'm not sure. He's in the field."

"Well, I guess I'll hold it for him. I'll send a note over to remind him to pick it up. When he gets back."

"Is it important?"

"Who's to say?"

"Can I pick it up for him?"

"It's okay by me."

At lunch time Casey walked to the mailroom. The clerk handed him the telegram, and Casey signed for it. Outside in the cold air, Casey hesitated. Should I open it? It might be really important, but it might be very personal. Maybe I could just get it choppered to him. Or radio it to him. Maybe it's bad news. Someone in his family might be sick. Or maybe there's been a death in his family. Geez, if it's bad news, he really doesn't need that now. He would be really upset if it was bad news and he couldn't get back to do anything about it. Should I or shouldn't I?

Casey opened the envelope. It's from his girlfriend, Casey saw. This is no emergency. It's a love note. Casey read it again carefully. What does she have to be sorry for? Lawrence is the one who's been unfaithful. He's the one who's been screwing mooses. He's probably twisted it all around to make his girlfriend feel guilty. His morals belong in a garbage dump. He's unfaithful and he shows no sign of contrition. He tries to shift blame for his weakness on his girl back home. It's not fair. Not fair at all. But it's typical of him. She's probably a great girl who has no feel for what Lawrence is really like. He doesn't deserve a loyal girl. He's disgusting. Sleeping with those slant-eyed gooks. If anybody should be asking for forgiveness, it should be him. But he won't. He's admitted he never reads the Bible. Typical Catholic.

Casey folded the message and put it in a field jacket pocket. He walked to the mess hall. After lunch he sat at his desk, pondering. He got up and walked to the coat rack. He removed the telegram from his field jacket pocket and returned to his desk. He contemplated for another minute. Furtively he surveyed the office. Then he shredded the telegram and dropped the pieces into the wastebasket under his desk.

CHAPTER 55

The long wait was nearly over. The seemingly endless, at times apparently fruitless, negotiations had at last been concluded. Final details had been settled. It was about time, thought Ben. Today was way past due. For so many months this day had lain tantalizingly just beyond the horizon. North Korean insincerity and intransigence, combined with the communists' desire to prolong America's embarrassment, had repeatedly raised and dashed hopes.

Ben stood outside the unpretentious guard shack at the south end of The Bridge of No Return. The December air bit sharply, but no overcoat covered Ben's dress greens. He preferred the chill to the bake oven inside his heavy green greatcoat. The blue United Nations *Press* armband circled his left arm. Absentmindedly he blew his breath upward; his glasses fogged and cleared quickly. He reflected on the last few days.

On December 17, 1968, at the 26th Panmunjom meeting on the Pueblo, Ben had watched as agreement was reached on the release terms. Major General Gilbert H. Woodward, head of the U.S. negotiating team, would sign a document prepared by the North Koreans and simultaneously denounce it to try to save American face.

On December 19, Major General Pak Chun Kuk, North Korea's chief negotiator, impassively announced, "Now we have reached agreement."

Earlier this morning of December 22, a stony-faced General Woodward sat at the Panmunjom negotiating table. As he signed the document, he said, "The position of the U.S. has been that the ship was not engaged in illegal activities, that there is no convincing evidence that the ship intruded into territorial waters claimed by North Korea, and that we could not apologize for actions we did not believe took place. My signature will not and cannot alter the facts. I will sign the document to free the crew and only to free the crew."

In fact, the document admitted wrongdoing, apologized for it and acknowledged the crew's confession. It read:

TO THE GOVERNMENT OF THE DEMOCRATIC PEOPLE'S REPUBLIC OF KOREA

The Government of the United States of America,

Acknowledging the validity of the confessions of the crew of the USS Pueblo and of the documents of evidence produced by the representative of the Government of the Democratic People's Republic of Korea to the effect that the ship, which was seized by the self-defense measures of the naval vessels of the Korean People's Army in the territorial waters of the Democratic People's Republic of Korea on January 23, 1968, had illegally intruded into the territorial waters of the Democratic People's Republic of Korea on many occasions and conducted espionage activities of spying on important military and state secrets of the Democratic People's Republic of Korea.

Shoulders full responsibility and solemnly apologizes for the grave acts of espionage committed by the U.S. ship against the Democratic People's Republic of Korea after having intruded into the territorial waters of the Democratic People's Republic of Korea.

And gives firm assurance that no U.S. ships will intrude again in future into the territorial waters of the Democratic People's Republic of Korea.

Meanwhile, the Government of the United States of America earnestly requests the Government of the Democratic People's Republic of Korea to deal leniently with the former crew members of the USS Pueblo confiscated by the Democratic People's Republic of Korea side, taking into consideration the fact that these crew members have confessed honestly their crimes and petitioned the Government of the Democratic People's Republic of Korea for leniency.

Simultaneously with the signing of this document, the undersigned acknowledges receipt of 82 former crew members of the Pueblo and one corpse.

On behalf of the Government of

429

The United States of America
Gilbert H. Woodward,
Major General, United States Army
December 22, 1968

A folded copy of the document was in Ben's pocket. It was, he thought, as clear and damning a piece of evidence as any of America's diminished power and stature. Not since the North Koreans captured the Pueblo had they feared retaliation. Nor would they after the prisoners' release. In a politically complex and fragile world, America's hands would remain tied. Ben wanted retribution. At the very least, a bombing raid on a North Korean harbor facility or military complex. It would not happen, and he knew it.

A distant vehicular rumble switched Ben's train of thought. He looked across The Bridge of No Return, which got its name during the Korean War when it served as a major prisoner of war exchange site. The 250-foot span rested on nine pairs of concrete-sheathed pilings. Another guard shack sat at the north end. Ben forgot about the cold. He stood still as the vehicles stopped at the opposite end and slowly unloaded a large gathering of Americans and their guards. He was relieved that the end of the crew's ordeal was at hand.

He watched the Americans organize for their trek to freedom. They shuffled stiffly. Their faces were drawn and expressionless.

Commander Lloyd Bucher emerged at the head of the group. He looked haggard, a decade older than his 41 years. At a signal from one of his captors, he started across. A lump formed in Ben's throat as Bucher neared the south end. He completed the walk across the snow-whitened bridge.

"Welcome back, Commander," Ben murmured.

"Thank you," Bucher replied, unsmiling. He then turned to face his crew as they waited to start across the bridge.

"Your men will be well taken care of, sir."

Bucher sucked in a breath and let it out slowly. "They've had a rough time."

"You, too, sir," Ben replied.

Bucher nodded, almost imperceptibly. Then he looked at Ben's arm patch. "A correspondent."

"Yes, sir."

"Write it so they're heroes."

"Will do."

An American ambulance backed onto the bridge. It moved slowly to the midpoint and stopped. North Korean troops carried the body of Fireman Duane Hodges to the ambulance, which then drove slowly to the south end. Then the rest of the survivors began to cross slowly at 10-to-20-foot intervals. All were clothed in quilted blue coats, gray shirts, flannel trousers and white-soled black sneakers.

All the men were gaunt. They had subsisted on a diet of kimchi and soup. Pounds had fallen from their frames. As they completed the crossing, Ben and other Americans stepped forward and began helping the crew up the steps into three olive-drab U.S. Army buses. Ben followed the last man into the third bus. Slowly the convoy started south toward the Joint Security Area advance camp. Ben looked out the rear window. The Bridge of No Return was disappearing from view. Ben placed a hand on the shoulder of a Pueblo crewman and squeezed affectionately.

CHAPTER 56

The doorbell rang. Edward put down the brandy he was sipping. "Harriet," he called as he rose.

"I heard," she responded excitedly from the kitchen. "I'll be there in a second."

Edward walked quickly to the front door, decorated with a colorful holiday wreath, and pulled it open. Then he pushed open the storm door.

"Merry Christmas!"

"Merry Christmas!"

Edward and Dick embraced on the porch.

"It's good to see you, son."

"It's very good to see you, Dad."

"Dick!" cried Harriet, still drying her hands on an apron as she rushed to the door. As she stepped onto the porch, she and Dick threw their arms around each other and hugged tightly.

"Harriet, you look wonderful. Merry Christmas."

"I feel wonderful. Merry Christmas to you."

Edward was beaming. "It's a little warmer inside."

"I don't know about that," smiled Dick. "This kind of reception is enough to warm the air for a block around." He squeezed Harriet again and she reciprocated. "I almost forgot how good this kind of air can feel."

Dick hoisted two heavy suitcases.

"Here, let me help you with those," said Edward.

"There are two more behind me."

Harriet held open the storm door while father and son carried the luggage inside.

"I wish you'd have let us pick you up," said Edward.

"If I'd done that," said Dick as he slipped out of his coat, "Harriet couldn't have been here concocting whatever is producing that terrific smell."

"Peach cobbler," Harriet smiled.

"Ummm. See what I mean?"

Harriet hung Dick's coat.

"How about some brandy?" said Edward.

"Sounds great. But let's get my luggage stowed away first."

"Nah," Edward dismissed that suggestion. "Let it sit for now."

"Well, at least let me open the ones with the gifts so I can put them under the tree. After all, it is Christmas Eve." Dick squatted and snapped open two of the bags, removed several brightly wrapped packages and placed them under the tree.

"Looks like you outdid yourself," said Edward.

"Don't get the idea they're all for you."

"Wouldn't dream of it."

Edward poured another brandy and handed it to Dick, who eased into a large chair. Harriet removed her apron, took it to the kitchen and rejoined the men.

Dick sipped. "Man, that hits the spot."

"Thought it might."

"The tree looks great," said Dick.

"Your dad's had the lights on since dusk. He wanted to be sure they were on when you arrived."

Edward blushed.

Dick laughed at his father's embarrassment. "How's Susie?"

432

"Just fine," said Harriet.

"And Bruce and the baby?"

"They're fine too," answered Harriet. "They'll all be coming round in the morning. She can hardly wait to see you. And to show off little Bill."

"I like the choice of name."

"She thought you would."

"Well, old man," Dick needled, "how does it feel to finally be a grandfather?"

"Damn good. Except everyone's accusing me of spoiling the little guy."

"Which no doubt you are. And I'll bet the baby's enjoying it."

"I don't know about that."

"I do," piped up Harriet. "And you're absolutely right. That little boy's eyes light up every time he sees his grandpa."

"Same with his grandma," said Edward.

"Looks like retirement is agreeing with you," observed Dick.

"I guess, but it took a fair bit of adjusting."

"He still gets fidgety once in a while," said Harriet. "In fact, more than once in awhile."

They all laughed.

"You heard from Ben?" Dick asked.

"Yes," said Harriet. "We received a card and letter last week. And a couple days ago we received those." She pointed to a pair of gray, stone-carved bookends, depicting a Korean warrior and a scholar. "Aren't they lovely?"

"That they are."

"Have you heard from him?" asked Edward.

"Yes," said Dick, "but it's been awhile."

"How are he and Natalie handling their separation?" Harriet asked with motherly concern.

"Not too well, I'm afraid."

"That's what I was afraid of," Harriet said sadly. "Ben hasn't said much about her lately, nothing in his last couple letters. He used to mention her all the time."

"I don't know the details," said Dick, "but it doesn't look good for them. I think it's a case of too much distance and too much time."

"That's a shame," said Harriet. "Natalie's such a lovely girl."

433

"I couldn't agree more," said Dick. "But I don't blame either of them. That kind of separation is hard for anyone, especially young people. They've got a lot more to learn about themselves, and sometimes the lessons come hard."

Dick sipped the brandy and sighed. "Well, Dad, I've been doing a lot of thinking. I guess I've reached the age when I want to take a look backward. Not to recapture the past or even pretend it's possible. I just want to touch it again. Before it's too late. It's funny. I think when you're young you're afraid to look back for fear you'll get sidetracked. I've reached the point where I'm not afraid that'll happen."

"What do you have in mind?" Edward asked quietly.

"Before Ben went to Korea," answered Dick, "I asked him to try to find the Yoons. He did. They're still alive and well. Still on the same farm. I want to see them again. Before it's too late."

"Anything else?"

"Yeah. I'd like to see Helen and Roger."

"I think that's wonderful," said Harriet. "I think you're doing the right thing."

"You know about Roger," said Edward.

"Yes. Although it's been a long time since I heard anything. How's he doing?"

"It's been a long time since I heard anything too," said Edward. "But the news then wasn't very encouraging."

"I see."

"When are you going to Korea, Dick?" asked Harriet.

"February."

"Do the Yoons know you're coming?" she asked.

"Not yet. And I may not warn them at all. I think I'd like to surprise them."

"You mean shock them to death," laughed Edward.

"They survived Ben's visit. He didn't say I was coming. I didn't tell him that. But at least they know I was curious."

"And," said Harriet, "that you care."

"Hello, Dick."

"Hello, Helen."

434

"Come in."

"Thank you."

It was the Saturday evening after Christmas. Dick had waited until the day after Christmas before phoning.

"Let me take your coat."

"Thanks."

"Where's Roger?"

"In the den. He's very excited about your visit. I'm glad you called."

"Me too. But I have to admit," Dick smiled, "that I had a little trouble finding your place. This street was a field when we were kids."

"I should've told you. Most of this development has been built in the last ten years or so."

Helen led Dick toward the den at the rear of the house. He couldn't help noticing that Helen Wakefield Hoerner, at age 44, still cut an enviable figure. Her legs and bottom were as shapely as ever. In taking care of Roger, she hadn't let herself go. Dick was glad about that.

As they entered the den, Roger broke into a wide smile. He planted his canes on the carpet and struggled to stand.

"Don't get up on my account," Dick said hurriedly.

"Are you kidding? After all these years, you don't think I'm going to sit when I shake your hand?" Roger stood and steadied himself. He hung the cane on his left wrist and extended his right hand.

Dick gripped it firmly and shook warmly. "Roger, it's great to see you."

"Same here," said Roger. "You could've knocked me over with a feather when you called. But we were sure pleased that you did."

"I decided it was high time to see a couple of old friends."

"Sit down," said Helen. "Make yourself comfortable."

"Thanks." Dick chose the chair closest to Roger, who eased himself back into his chair.

"Can I get you a drink?" asked Helen.

"That would be nice."

"What would you like?"

"Anything, really."

"Scotch?"

"That's my idea of anything."

"Roger?"

"Sure, honey, make it two."

"I'll make it three."

"Good," said Roger.

Helen fixed the drinks at a small bar in the den. She handed glasses to Roger and Dick and returned with hers.

"May I offer a toast?" Dick asked.

"Please do," said Helen.

"To old and very dear friends." Dick leaned toward Roger, who held out his glass. Helen lowered hers, and the three clinked glasses.

"To old and very dear friends," she repeated.

They sipped.

The conversation started slowly, gradually becoming as animated and cheery as the flames dancing in the fireplace. The talk centered on reminiscences going back to high school and beyond. It never was strained despite its skirting Roger's illness. There was too much else to recall and cherish. For Roger, those memories did not include any suspicion of romance between Dick and Helen. Roger always had linked Dick and Helen's friendship to her romance with Bill Lawrence, dead now for nearly a quarter century.

Some two hours had passed when Dick noticed Roger beginning to tire.

"It's getting late," Dick said. "I'd better be going."

"There's no need to rush off," Roger protested.

Dick laughed. "Who's rushing? If I stayed any longer and drank any more scotch, you might have an overnight guest."

"That's not a bad idea," said Roger.

"I appreciate the hospitality," smiled Dick, "but..."

He put down his glass and rose. So did Roger, slowly and with effort. Dick started to tell him it wasn't necessary but decided not to. They all walked slowly to the front door. Helen got Dick's coat.

"Let me walk you to your car," said Helen.

"All right."

"I'll be back in a moment, Roger."

"Fine."

Dick and Roger clasped hands.

"It was great to see you again," said Dick. "It was a great evening."

"Let's not wait so long to do it again," replied Roger. "You'll have to come back from California more often."

"You're absolutely right."

Helen opened the storm door, and Dick followed her onto the small stoop of the neat ranch style house. They moved slowly toward Dick's car, parked at the end of the driveway. Helen raised the collar of her coat.

"You don't know how much this meant to Roger. He's been depressed a lot. It's been very difficult for him."

"And for you."

"Sometimes. But whenever I feel that way, I think of Roger's hurts. They never end."

"You're a hell of a woman," Dick murmured. "Roger's lucky to have you."

"And vice versa."

"I didn't call just because of Roger."

"I know."

"I was curious. But it was more than that. I just wanted you to know that I hadn't forgotten."

"If I ever doubted that, I never will again."

As they neared his car door, Dick glanced back toward the house. Roger still was standing at the door. Dick waved, and Roger waved back. Dick took Helen's hands.

"You'll always be very special to me, Helen. Always."

"I feel the same way about you. Good night, Dick."

Their hands squeezed and released.

"Good night."

CHAPTER 57

It was a sunny Saturday morning early in January 1969. Natalie was seated in UCLA's main library. She had come for a change of scenery and to escape the black thoughts that had shrouded her mind for the past month. Natalie had been surprised and hurt deeply by Ben's failure to respond to her telegram of reconciliation. *It's not like the Ben I know* not *to dignify my telegram with a reply. I guess I should quit hoping for one.*

Natalie tried to concentrate on her books, but her thoughts kept shifting to Ben and Evan. Sloane had phoned her the previous week to invite her to a New Year's Eve party. She had declined, not curtly but not cordially. She was continuing to try to reestablish fidelity to Ben. Now she was second-guessing herself. *Am I hurting Evan the same way I hurt Ben? Am I on the verge of making a second huge mistake? Maybe not, but should I take that risk? Maybe I should give Evan and me another chance. And what's wrong with now? Right now?*

She pushed away from the library desk. *I'll go to Evan's office. He often comes in on Saturday mornings, but even if he isn't in today, I could slip a note under his door. I'll do it,* she thought, *before I chicken out.*

Sloane heard a timid tap on his office door.

"Come in," he called distractedly. He did not stand.

The door opened. A pretty, blond young woman stepped into his office. "Good morning, Professor Sloane."

"Good morning," Evan said mechanically. "Do you have an appointment?"

"Yes, sir. I asked to see you to discuss my paper."

"You did?"

"Yes, sir."

Sloane glanced at his calendar. There was no Saturday morning appointment listed. "Are you sure?"

"Yes, sir, I asked you after our last class."

Sloane didn't remember and didn't want to bother trying. He was out of sorts this morning and in no mood for unexpected intrusions. "Umm, I must have forgotten to put it on my calendar. Well, sit down."

Brenda Paxon sat uneasily on Sloane's wood, unpadded guest chair.

As Natalie strolled across campus toward Sloane's office, her mood began to brighten. She began to mentally compose the note she would leave if Evan weren't in. She wouldn't be coy. She would tell him straightforwardly that she wanted him to phone her to discuss some things. If by chance he was in, so much the better.

When Brenda Paxon first entered his office, Evan hadn't intended to be harsh. But the first words from his mouth were cold, and almost immediately he began deriving pleasure from her obvious discomfort. He knew why. He had failed miserably to make further headway with Natalie. He was feeling the need to vent his mounting frustration. Brenda Paxon, a supplicant on the defensive, was making a handy, vulnerable target.

"You're putting me on the spot, Miss Paxon. You're a senior. By now you should have learned to manage your time. Obviously you haven't and you're asking me to bail you out."

She flushed. "Sir, I've been a good student. Conscientious. But-"

"Miss Paxon," Sloane cut her off, "if I started granting extensions to every student with an excuse, the word would get around soon enough. And then what? Nobody would take my deadlines seriously. I'd have an administrative headache. I won't have that." Sloane remembered the extension he had granted Natalie. He had used that to gain favor. He wished Natalie needed a favor now. At least it would force her to talk with him, and maybe that's all he needed to rekindle their relationship.

Brenda Paxon shifted in the chair. "Sir, I need this course to graduate on time. If you give me an extension, I wouldn't tell anyone."

Evan stared at her silently. A new thought flashed through his mind. "I could say no, Miss Paxon. Very easily." She blinked. "And I'm tempted to. It's a lesson you might benefit from in the long run."

"Professor, please, I wouldn't need much time. Just a couple weeks. I've been-"

"Have you ever received an F, Miss Paxon?"

She shook her head.

He tapped a pen on his desk.

"Please, Sir." She was near tears. "Let me explain."

"If I let you explain, if I gave you an extension, what would I gain? It would be a one-way deal. Nothing more. On the other hand, you might learn something from failure." He hesitated, then stood slowly and walked around his desk and stood behind the young woman. "Stand up, Miss Paxon."

She obeyed dispiritedly. She expected to be shown the door. Evan put his hands on her shoulders and turned her around. He sensed complete domination. "I could be persuaded to change my mind," he murmured, "but it's up to you."

She blinked back tears. "Up to me?"

Sloane leaned forward and kissed her lips. She flinched, a frightened animal cornered. "Professor-"

"Entirely up to you. An F or..." He shrugged.

Natalie's spirits were rising as she entered the large red brick building. Lightly she skipped up the stairs to the second floor. As she rounded a corner, her spirits rose higher when she saw a woman close the door to Sloane's office. He's in, thought Natalie. That's wonderful. No need for a note.

"Good morning," Natalie greeted the young woman as they neared each other. The woman averted her eyes and scurried past. Natalie paused, glanced over her shoulder at the fleeing woman, shrugged in puzzlement and continued to Sloane's office.

CHAPTER 58

It was early afternoon on a Thursday. Ben was hunched over his Royal Standard typewriter. Furiously his fingers were thumping the keyboard.

"Hey, Ben," Dan Cohen needled him, "your typewriter's beginning to smoke."

Ben grunted.

"Ease up," Jeff Zink razzed him, "or you'll drive your knuckles into your wrists."

"Can the kibitzing," grumbled Ben, his eyes fixed on the yellow copy paper in his typewriter. "I gotta finish this press release before I go to Kimpo. If I'm late meeting my brother's flight because of you guys, there'll be harsh retribution."

"Oh, my goodness," Dan said impishly, his crinkly eyelids almost shut, "do you suppose Specialist Lawrence might tattle on us?"

"Or," asked Jeff with mock concern, "have Pak starch our boxers?"

"Come on, dammit," Ben pleaded, "I'm trying to concentrate."

"Huh?"

"Duh, what?"

"You guys won't quit, will ya?"

"Get out of here," Dan said kindly. "Now."

"I told you, I-"

"I'll finish the release. Just leave your notes there. You get yourself out to Kimpo."

Dick Lawrence stepped outside the Northwest Orient Boeing 707. He gathered his shoulders against the cold swirling wind. Inside the terminal Ben watched excitedly as his brother descended the truck-mounted stairs and came striding across the tarmac in a line of other passengers. Dick entered the terminal, quickly cleared passport control and collected his luggage. Ben stepped forward to meet him. They shook hands and clasped each other's shoulders.

"Damn," said Ben, "it's good to see you. I might be the only GI with a brother foolish enough to visit him in Korea."

"I don't know about foolish, but I *am* beginning to think I should've waited until the weather warmed up a mite."

"Aah, this isn't so cold," said Ben. "No worse than a Shelby winter."

"Which can be plenty cold – as I was reminded at Christmas. My aged bones must be leaking marrow."

"How are Mom and Dad?"

"Fine. Your mom wishes you'd write more, but what mother doesn't?"

"And Dad?"

"Looked really good when I saw him at Christmas. But doesn't he always? Even when he's just been sick. He's amazing. Hard to believe he's had cancer twice and a heart attack."

"I'm really glad you came," said Ben. "I didn't think you would."

"For a long time, neither did I." Dick eyed his surroundings. "You wouldn't believe how this place has changed. Now it actually looks something like an airport. Nineteen years ago it looked like anything but."

"A lot's changed since then. But on the other hand I think you'll find a lot hasn't."

They hefted Dick's luggage and walked outside. "Your limousine awaits," Ben said, nodding to a nearby jeep.

"Not much chrome, but at least it's covered."

"It even throws out a semblance of heat."

As Ben whipped the jeep southeast along the Han River toward Seoul, Dick scrutinized carefully the mud-walled huts, hulking oxen, rickety bikes and buses, small women balancing outsized loads on their heads. It all looked hauntingly familiar. Add shell craters and burned out buildings and the scenes would have been nearly perfect duplicates of images that Dick had stored for almost two decades.

"You were right," Dick observed pensively. "A lot hasn't changed."

"Well, as the cliché goes, you ain't seen nothing yet."

Minutes later, as the jeep went roaring across the Second Han River Bridge, Dick saw what Ben meant. The war-leveled city of his memories had risen from its ashes and grown up a throbbing metropolis. Dick was most impressed by the heavy, hectic traffic and the tall buildings, not soaring towers by American standards, but proud pokes in the sky that symbolized the city's get-up-and-go.

"I got you a room at the Bando. It's right in the middle of town."

"I remember the Bando."

"It's still a nice place."

"As long as my room has a long bed with a firm mattress, I'll be okay."

"Bushed?"

"Hardly slept on the way over. Too much to think about."

"Well, just take it easy today."

"What do you have in store for me? I mean, besides visiting the Yoons?"

"Tomorrow I thought I'd take you to Yongsan to meet my friends and co-workers. If that's okay with you."

"Sure. I'd like that."

"We can do that in the afternoon. In the morning I'll let you sleep in."

"I'm all for that."

"Friday night, if you're up to it, I thought you could have dinner with me and Miss Lee. She's our office secretary, the one I told you about. She'll be serving as interpreter again, so I thought you might like to get to know her a little."

"Good idea. Sounds like you've got everything mapped out."

"Pretty much."

"We visit the Yoons on Sunday?"

"Right," said Ben. "Saturday is open."

"Let's leave it that way. I want to do some shopping."

Friday, Dick awoke about 7:00, much earlier than he had expected. Jet lag had rendered him restless, and he had slept fitfully. He craved coffee. He dressed and went downstairs to the restaurant. He drank two steaming cups, savoring each sip.

At a lobby newsstand he bought a map of Seoul, then went outside and began prowling nearby streets. The sidewalks were jammed with Koreans walking briskly to work. Dick found the walking and the cold air invigorating. And he got more exercise than he bargained for. At major intersections, merely walking across the street was now prohibited. He either had to climb stairs to pedestrian bridges or descend into pedestrian tunnels. Generally he chose the tunnels since there were fewer steps to negotiate at either end. He marveled at tiny, aged women with heavy loads who climbed the stairs with a grace and energy that put him to shame. At the moment, he was feeling every one of his 46 years.

By late morning he was back at the Bando. He lunched, then waited in the lobby for Ben. Dick saw his olive-drab clad younger half-brother enter the hotel about 2:00. They jeeped to Yongsan, where Ben delighted in introducing Dick to his colleagues.

About 5:30 Dick, Ben and Miss Lee left the building. Dick helped Miss Lee into the covered jeep and then climbed into the back. Ben slid behind the steering wheel.

"Where we headed, little brother?"

"I know a place where they serve a decent steak. Not great, but decent. It's not too far from the Bando. That sound okay?"

"Fine," answered Dick. "Is that all right with you, Miss Lee?"

"Yes."

In its menu and décor the restaurant was passably American. The food was a little better than mediocre.

"Miss Lee," said Dick, "I want to thank you for agreeing to interpret for us."

"You are welcome."

"I hear it's going to be very cold the next couple days. I would understand if you would rather not go."

"I am happy to go."

"Good. I appreciate your help very much."

"How long will you be in Korea, Mr. Lawrence?"

"I'm here until Wednesday. And please call me Dick."

"I hope your stay is more pleasant than your first visit to Korea."

"Thank you. I'm sure it will be."

"That reminds me," said Ben. "I have to go to Panmunjom on Monday for a meeting. Want to go?"

"The last time I got near the DMZ didn't turn out so well."

"Entirely up to you. It's just another military armistice commission meeting. The two sides will be content to harangue each other. But I thought you might enjoy the experience. It's a funny feeling to be able to step into North Korea and step back again. And the scenery is pretty."

"Well, why not?"

"Glad to see you've still got a sense of adventure," said Ben, "especially in light of your advanced age."

Miss Lee giggled.

"He's disappointing, isn't he, Miss Lee? He sure doesn't show much respect for his older brother."

"You can't deny the turning pages of the calendar, older brother."

"As you will learn soon enough, younger brother."

Miss Lee giggled again, and Dick and Ben laughed.

"Will there be any trouble with me getting up there?"

"Nah, I'll just get Colonel Baumgarten to clear you as a visitor."

"Have you ever been to Panmunjom, Miss Lee?" Dick asked.

"No. I have lived all my life in Seoul."

"You must know Seoul very well."

"Yes."

An idea popped into Dick's mind. "Miss Lee, I...Oh, never mind." He dismissed the thought as inappropriate and impractical.

"What is it? Please say."

"Well, I was wondering if you might be free to show me around Seoul tomorrow. Help me with some shopping."

"I would be most happy to."

"I don't want to impose. Saturday is your day off, and you may have plans."

"No, I insist. I will be very pleased to be your guide."

Miss Lee arrived by cab at the Bando on Saturday about 10:00. Last night she had politely declined offers by Dick and Ben to pick her up. Dick had invited Ben to join them, but he had had to refuse. The CINCPAC (Commander-in-Chief Pacific) was in Seoul, and Ben had been assigned to prepare daily news summaries.

In the lobby Dick and Miss Lee shook hands. She outlined the itinerary she had planned and asked for Dick's opinion. "It sounds fine," he said warmly, "let's get started."

The black-haired, almond-eyed Korean and the American, 21 years her senior and with sandy hair fast surrendering to gray, were a study in East-West physical contrasts. But they felt comfortable with each other. Lee Chong Hee did not feel threatened by the big Yankee. Indeed, she thought him decent, considerate, protective. For his part, Dick discerned in Miss Lee experience, wisdom and calm. Her soft voice was soothing.

With Miss Lee serving as interpreter-haggler, Dick hired a cab – 5,000 won, just under $20 at the prevailing exchange rate – for the entire day.

They began by riding the cable car to the top of Namsan. Later, in the bustling South Gate market and at the Bando Arcade, Dick shopped for gifts for the Yoons. He bought two colorful wool blankets, a shawl, tea, a pipe and tobacco, a pipe lighter with extra flints and fluid and fur-lined mittens. The Ronson lighter, flints and fluid and the mittens were black market American goods that had been diverted from their intended destination, the Yongsan PX. Dick considered giving cash to the Yoons but knew that gesture would injure their pride and cloud the reunion. He thoroughly enjoyed the sightseeing and the shopping, especially the haggling with wizened merchants. But most of all he enjoyed Miss Lee's company. He was enchanted by her increasingly animated chatter and laughter, tempered by Oriental reserve.

As darkness fell, Dick asked her to join him for dinner. She hesitated only momentarily before accepting. He asked her to pick a restaurant.

"Last night we ate American food," she said. "Would you like to try Korean food?"

"Sure. Remember, I ate a lot of it twenty years ago."

The restaurant was small and the tables cramped, but there were few patrons so it was quiet. The proprietor seated them at a Western-style table for two in a corner.

"I already like this place," Dick smiled.

"Why? You have not eaten anything."

"It's warm, and I was getting cold."

Miss Lee smiled broadly. "I was also."

A waiter appeared. Miss Lee ordered for them. She described each course as it was served. Dick found everything delicious, including the kimchi; Miss Lee had ordered the mildest variety.

"You are so much older than Ben," she observed. Dick playfully arched an eyebrow. Miss Lee blushed. "Oh, I did not mean that you are old man." Dick chuckled. "I mean, for brothers, you are wide in age."

"We're half-brothers." She looked puzzled. "We have the same father but different mothers. My mother died many years ago. My father married Ben's mother."

"I understand."

"Ben said your parents are dead."

"Yes."

"And you have no brothers or sisters."

"That is true also."

"Do you enjoy working at Yongsan?"

"Oh, yes. Very much. I also like Ben very much. I have worked at Yongsan for a long time, and he is one of very nice GI's."

"I'm sure glad he's here and not in Vietnam."

"Yes, that must be terrible. Do you know that Korean soldiers also fight in Vietnam?"

"Yes, I do. Two divisions, the White Horse and the Tiger. I understand they are excellent soldiers and that the North Vietnamese fear them very much."

"Yes, they hate communists. We all hate communists."

"Do you remember the Korean War? I mean, are you old enough to?"

"I was born in 1944. January. Yes, I remember. Very much. I will never forget. The communists were very cruel."

"For me," Dick said pensively, "the Korean War was very private. Very small. It was just me and Henry Briggs and Mr. and Mrs. Yoon. Do you understand?" She nodded. "Even when I got back to the United States and read about all the death and suffering in Korea, I still thought mostly about the Yoons and me and Henry. And the four North Korean soldiers who came there."

"I understand."

Dick sighed. "What was the war like for you? I mean, how did you live?"

"It was very hard. We were hungry and cold. There was very little food. Some days, nothing. And there was very little - uh, what is the word? - fuel. We were frightened. The communist soldiers did terrible things. They hurt many people."

"You?"

"No. My mother and father hid me."

"Hid you?"

"They dig - dug a hole under our house."

"You're kidding. I'm sorry. I know you're not kidding. It's just that...Do you know that I hid in a hole in Korea during the war?"

"Yes. Your brother told me."

"Well," Dick said sheepishly, "I hid in it only once. I couldn't stand it after that."

She smiled. "I understand. I hid in our hole often. Sometimes I stayed in it for a long time, with cabbages and peppers."

"It must have been very frightening for a child."

"Yes. It was very dark and cold. It made my dear father and mother very sad."

"Are you afraid now?" Dick asked quietly.

"Sometimes. I am afraid the communists will start another war. It would be too sad. My heart would die."

"I hope you are never that sad again." Dick was feeling a rush of affection for Lee Chong Hee. Her warmth and candor and the tales of wartime suffering were touching him deeply. "You know, I came to see the Yoons, but I'm glad I had the chance to meet you."

Her eyes lowered. "Thank you."

"Miss Lee, it's-"

"You may call me Miss Lee. But if I am to call you Dick, then I would like you to call me Chong."

"Chong it is." Their eyes met and held, and Dick searched them for a hint of the affection he was feeling for her. It was not hard to find. He hesitated, then slowly moved his hand across the table and touched hers. She did not recoil.

"It is not late," she said. "Would you like to take a small walk?"

"That's a wonderful idea."

"I will tell the taxi driver to meet us at the Bando. It is near. He can wait for us there. Then he can drive me home."

Dick did not want to see the night end in front of the Bando, but he decided to accept her proposal without protest. "All right."

Outside, as they walked, he took her hand. She allowed him to keep it.

"Seoul's a lively town," Dick observed.

"Lively?"

"Busy, exciting."

"Is Los Angeles not lively also?"

"Los Angeles is very nice. In some ways it's like Seoul. There are mountains all around, and it's near the sea. It's also sunny almost all the time, and warm."

"It sounds very beautiful."

"Would you like to visit America someday?"

"That will not happen."

"But would you like to?"

"It would be nice."

"Maybe some day you will."

"I do not think so."

The Bando's main entrance came into view.

On Sunday, Ben met Dick for breakfast at the Bando. At 11:00 Miss Lee arrived. They gathered up the gifts Dick had purchased for the Yoons and carried them to the jeep. Miss Lee told Dick to sit in front so he could better see the scenery. He objected, she insisted, he protested more strongly, she stood firm, and he rode in front.

During the ride north, there was little conversation. Dick was content to gaze on the mountains and rice paddies and lose himself in memories. He tried to imagine meeting the Yoons. How had they changed? Would they recognize him?

After they had driven awhile, Miss Lee leaned forward and spoke quietly to Ben. "Do you think you remember the Yoons' farm?"

"I think I'll recognize it."

Dick shifted sideways to face them. "I think I might remember it."

"That would not surprise me," said Miss Lee. "Some things stay forever in our mind."

Ben slowed the jeep. "I think that's it."

"I think you are right," said Miss Lee. "Is it how you remember, Dick?"

He nodded. 19 years. A lump had formed in his throat. He was thinking not only of the Yoons but also of Ann Sheridan. He wished mightily that she could be here with him. To share this moment she had encouraged him to capture. He swallowed and rubbed thumb and forefinger against his throat.

Some chickens were scratching near the Yoons' house. Gray smoke curled from the chimney.

Dick eased out of the jeep and helped Miss Lee out. She reached back inside and collected the gifts. Dick reached to take some. "No," she said, "you go first. Ben and I will bring the gifts."

Dick nodded and started down the path. Every step seemed as familiar as yesterday. He walked slowly. Old memories jostled anew for space. His mind pictured Yoon Chun Heum, drooping white mustache, pitchfork in hand, watching stoically as he and Henry Briggs straggled through rice paddies in search of a haven. He saw Mrs. Yoon feeding a pair of Occidental strangers. He saw the wrenching farewell.

Dick stopped in front of the windowless front door. He inhaled deeply, then knocked. The door opened. A tiny white-haired, weathered woman stared upward. Her eyes widened in disbelief. She began to tremble. Her hands cupped together in front of her bosom. Dick stepped forward, his arms outstretched, and drew her to his chest. She began to sob.

"Dick" she murmured, "Dick."

"Who is it?" A rough, rural voice called in Korean from the back room. Mrs.Yoon tried to reply but could manage only a choked whisper as her tears stained Dick's coat. Mr. Yoon walked toward the door. He saw Dick's smiling face above his wife's head, and he stopped short. Then he went rushing forward, and there was an ecstatic three-way embrace, punctuated by joyous moaning.

Ben and Miss Lee watched the reunion with rising emotion. When the hugging stopped, the Yoons saw Ben, and there was another three-way hug, with Ben a trifle self-consciously in the middle.

Dick beckoned Miss Lee, who bowed to the Yoons. They remembered her from Ben's earlier visit and welcomed her warmly. Mrs. Yoon invited everyone inside. They sat on floor cushions around a small table, the same one from 1950. Mrs. Yoon set about boiling water and preparing tea. As the water slowly heated, Dick began presenting the gifts.

"Twenty years ago I said thank you," Dick said, with Miss Lee translating, "and I know in your eyes that was enough. But when someone comes visiting after so many years, it is only appropriate to bring gifts, especially when the people mean so much to him."

As the Yoons opened the gifts, their faces conveyed gratitude and love to the man whose life they had saved and who forever had enriched their own lives. Mr. Yoon's eyes softened to the point of tears as Dick demonstrated how to insert flints into the lighter and fuel it. New tears trickled down Mrs. Yoon's face as she admired the shawl and the blankets and mittens.

She stood to serve the tea. "Dick," she said with concern, "how is Henry?"

"I told him I was coming and he wanted to join me. But he is recuperating from surgery for kidney stones and is still too weak for travel." Deep concern showed on the Yoons' faces as Miss Lee translated, and Dick hastened to add, "But there is no cause for alarm. Soon he will be well again. Besides the kidney stone problem, Henry is a very healthy man."

"That is good news," said Mrs. Yoon. "When you return, will you please tell him we asked about him and hope he is his old self very soon?"

"Of course. Your concern will please him very much. And help him recover even faster."

The Yoons sighed, and their visages brightened. They began to relax.

"Have you both been well?" Dick asked.

"Oh, yes," said Mrs. Yoon. "With age we are a little stiffer and we move a little slower, but that is all."

"Speak for yourself," Mr. Yoon growled with mock displeasure. He winked at Dick. "I am as strong and quick as ever."

Laughter all around.

"Why didn't you warn us you were coming?" Mrs. Yoon asked.

"I wanted to surprise you. But I was also afraid if I told you, something would happen to prevent it. And then we would all be disappointed."

"Your life has gone well, Dick?" Mr. Yoon asked.

"I've been very fortunate."

"Have you ever married?" Mrs.Yoon asked softly.

"No."

She sighed. "That's too bad. I had hoped you would."

"Things just didn't work out."

"Sometimes they don't."

The afternoon passed pleasantly, as Dick and the Yoons slowly filled in the details of the past two decades. Ben took photos and promised to send copies to all. He asked whether anyone objected to his writing a story about the reunion. None did. He would send it to *Stars & Stripes*.

The visit ended with warm embraces and a sincere promise by Dick to return again, and soon.

At the Bando, Ben offered to drive Miss Lee home. She declined, saying she would get a taxi.

"Well," said Ben, "I'll see you early in the morning, older brother. We leave for Panmunjom at eight."

"I'll be ready."

Dick and Miss Lee watched Ben leave the lobby.

"Chong," said Dick, "would you dine with me tomorrow night after I get back from Panmunjom?"

"Okay."

"Great. You know, Wednesday is beginning to seem too soon."

"Please?"

"So much has happened so fast."

"Yes, you have been busy."

"Busy...and thinking."

"Thinking?"

"About you."

She blushed and lowered her eyes. "You flatter me."

"Only with the best of intentions."

452

"Please think no more about me. I am only...uh...a ship passing in your night." Dick grinned affectionately. "I did not say it right."

"You said it fine. Am I only a ship passing in your night?"

"I think so."

"Is that the way you want it?"

"It is the way it must be."

"Why?"

"This is my home. Korea. Your home is in California. You should go home and remember the Yoons. Forget about me."

"Will you forget about me?"

She hesitated, then averted her eyes. "No." And, really, how could she forget this man who had come back to say thank you to her countrymen who had saved his life? This act alone had been causing Miss Lee to regard Dick Lawrence as a special man.

It was 7 p.m. when Ben returned to his Yongsan barracks. Only Casey McDermott was in the room.

"Where's Dan?"

"Don't know. Probably getting smashed."

"On Sunday night? Before a trip to PMJ? Of course, now that I think about it," Ben mumbled to himself, "that's probably the best time." Ben sat on his bunk. He stared blankly at the opposite wall. Natalie's image slipped into his mind. He tried to force it out but couldn't. He was finding memories of love can be difficult to evict. He felt an emptiness. He needed to fill it with companionship, with someone who cared. He stood and started for the door.

"Where're you going?" Casey asked.

"Out."

Ben walked quickly to his office, unlocked the door, picked up the telephone and dialed. He heard two tinny rings and then a soft "Hello."

"Kyong?" Ben said.

"Yes."

"It's Ben."

"Ben! How are you?"

"Fine. Kyong, I know it's Sunday and it's late, but could I come over?"

"Yes, if you want."

Jeff, hands clasped behind his head, lay in bed staring at the ceiling. Kim Soon Yi lay sleeping beside him. They had made love, and Suni had fallen asleep quickly. Only two months remained before Jeff's return to the States and his separation from Korea and the Army. And from Suni unless he stopped vacillating and made the decision he feared. The image of a menacing Alice Zink hovered above him in the darkened room like a fearsome black cloud poised to impale him on a lightning bolt of outrage and rejection. His gut tightened. He breathed deeply and pursed his lips. He would sleep little that night, and he knew it.

Monday's dawn had just broken when Dan Cohen began to awaken. He straightened his lean 70 inches and wiggled his toes. He had gone out Sunday after dinner to look for company in the form of a beer pitcher. The NCO Club was closed, so he had headed for a bar in the Vill. A good-looking young woman had approached him and offered her services. "No thanks," said Dan. After more time and beer, the woman again offered herself. I'm tempted, he admitted to himself. She has a fine face and body. But don't be stupid. I laid one moose and wound up with a urinary infection. The moose sensed his indecision and confidently zeroed in. "You like my cunt. You come with me now. I make you feel better."

Dan had reddened, not out of embarrassment but from desire. She's got me and she knows it. Who knows? Maybe she's clean. He shrugged and stood. They went to a nearby hotel. She turned out to be very good. No false advertising, Dan mused. He drifted off to sleep.

Now, emerging from deep, delicious slumber, he placed his right arm where the woman had lain, expecting the touch of smooth flesh. Instead, his fingers found a cold sheet. His face still buried in the pillow, Dan's hand searched the other side of the bed. Nothing. He rolled over. No sign of her in the room. Maybe she went out to piss, Dan thought. I wonder what time it is. He groaned as he sat up and swung his legs over the side of the bed. He shivered as his feet touched the frigid linoleum floor. Gingerly, he stepped to the chest of drawers to look at his watch. It wasn't there. His hands pushed back through his coal black hair. *Wonder where I put it? Maybe in my pants pocket.* He turned toward a small stool where he had piled his civilian clothes. They weren't there. He looked around the room. No sign of them. Nor of his watch. *My wallet,* he thought amid a growing sense of panic. No sign of that either. Then it all came crashing down on his morning-fogged mind. *Shit,* he silently cursed the moose, *you cleaned me out. Stupid, stupid, stupid. Damn, why didn't I listen to my better judgment? Damn. God, I've gotta go to Panmunjom today. Shit. Now what? It's a good thing I slept in my underwear, or the bitch would've taken that too.*

Dan pulled back the unraveling brown curtain covering the room's one small window. Three inches of fresh snow were on the ground and more was falling. *Just what I need,* he moaned. He looked around the room. He pulled a dark green wool blanket from the bed and wrapped himself. He tiptoed down the hall to the front door. *How could I be so stupid? Damn.* He screwed up his round face, squinted his deep-set brown eyes and stepped into the snow.

Casey McDermott was pulling on his fatigues, and Jeff, back from Suni's apartment, was changing into his dress greens for the trip to Panmunjom when Ben came through the door.

"Where's Dan?" Ben asked.

"More to the point," sniffed Casey, "where were you, Lawrence? I see you didn't come in last night."

"Keen eyesight."

"What were you doing, Lawrence? Laying some diseased moose?"

Ben bridled. "Getting my rocks off – and mentally fucking your wife."

Casey's eyes widened in shock. "Lawrence!" he shrieked. "You're gross. Take that back."

"Her tail really wags."

"Take that back!" Casey screeched. "Take it back or I'll-"

"You'll what?" Ben hissed. "I've had all of your poisoned mind I can take. Maybe you oughta learn to keep your fucking lips zipped."

Dan was approaching the military police shack at Yongsan's south gate. Snow covered his hair and clung to the wool blanket. Inside, the MP shook his head in disbelief.

"You say anything," Dan growled through chattering lips, "and I'll come in there and piss all over your spit-shined boots."

The MP dissolved in helpless laughter.

Casey left for the office in an impotent huff.

"That was hitting below the belt," Jeff murmured.

Ben blew out a breath. "I know, I know. I just get so damned tired of his accusations and holier-than-thou attitude."

"I grant you it can be pretty tiresome."

"How have you managed to keep from blowing up at him?"

"I did, sort of."

"You did? When?"

"Long time ago. You and Dan were out. I didn't exactly blow up. I did tell him in no uncertain terms that if he didn't cease and desist, his face would wind up looking like an overripe tomato."

"I wish you'd told me that. I might have said something sooner myself."

"You said plenty just now."

"Yeah. It wasn't fair-" The words died in Ben's mouth as his stunned eyes looked on a figure at once pathetic and comic.

Dan, snow-covered, teeth clattering, toes nearly frozen, padded barefoot and sniffling into the room. Again, his appearance was greeted by incredulity and gales of raucous laughter.

Jeff guided the lumbering olive-drab bus toward the Bando Hotel. It was slow going, with the unplowed snow further congesting the rush-hour traffic. He and Ben and Dan were the only ones aboard.

"This is shaping up as a thoroughly disastrous day," Dan observed dourly.

"It should be memorable," Ben responded wryly.

"It's already that," said Dan. "First I lay a moose who lands me in the infirmary, then one who robs me."

"Were the flesh not so weak," Jeff said over his shoulder.

"I thought my feet would drop off on the way to the compound. They've never been so cold. She probably gave me the clap to boot." A pause. "Geez, I'm hungry. Wish I'd gotten back in time for chow."

"You'll just have to eat more of the coffee cake at PMJ."

"The way my luck's going today, the cook at the Advance Camp probably ran out of flour."

Ben chuckled.

"I take it you were out with Kyong last night," Dan murmured. "It's been quite a while, hasn't it?"

Ben nodded. "I needed company. After I said goodnight to my brother and Miss Lee, I couldn't get the reunion with the Yoons out of my mind, and I started thinking about Natalie. I felt like I was a million miles away from everyone and everything."

"Only a million?" said Dan. "There've been times when I felt like I was standing alone on another planet. This ain't Queens, you know."

Jeff braked the bus in front of the Bando. Dick had been watching from inside the hotel doors and came out immediately. Jeff opened the door, and Dick bounded up the steps. "Morning, troops. All set?"

"I wish we could dress like you today," said Jeff.

Dick smiled. "I'm too old to look good in a uniform anymore." He wore a blue stocking cap, a brown hip-length parka with a fur-lined hood, brown corduroy pants and waterproofed hiking boots over thick wool socks. As usual for meetings at Panmunjom, the correspondents wore their dress greens sans overcoats, low-cut black shoes and cunt caps. And on their left arms were the blue United Nations *Press* armbands.

Jeff wheeled the bus some six blocks north to the capitol, which during the Japanese occupation was the headquarters of the governor-general. There they picked up a score of Korean journalists who clambered up the steps to escape the driving snow. Ben waited until they all were seated and then, as was customary, distributed complimentary packs of American cigarettes, two to each reporter. He returned to the front of the bus and delivered the customary lecture on PMJ behavior: "Remember, you can give these cigarettes to North Korean personnel if you want and accept theirs if offered. But no giving or trading anything else. There'll be no teasing or taunting. Stay out of unauthorized buildings and areas. Clear? Okay."

"Do they cause much trouble?" Dick asked as Ben sat beside him.

"No, they love to tease the North Koreans about how much better they have it in the South. You can imagine how that sits with the communists. I've seen a little pushing and shoving when tempers rise, but nothing serious. Today I don't expect any trouble. Not with this weather. They'll probably be content to stay in the pressroom and drink coffee and eat cake. These trips are as much social gatherings for them as anything else. They seldom get a meaningful story but they wouldn't pass up a chance to get free American cigarettes."

Jeff drove north. The snow, large wet flakes, still fell steadily. Near Seoul, where traffic was heavier, the road was slushy. The farther north they got, however, the more the temperature fell and the worse the road became.

"Dick?"

"Yeah?"

"Seen Natalie lately?"

"Couple times."

"How's she doing?"

"Okay, I guess. Miss her?"

"Sometimes. I try not to think about her. Which isn't easy. It's been confusing...and painful. I know I'll never forget her. But it couldn't go on the way it was. It was hell for both of us. My stomach was jumping all the time."

"I'm sorry, Ben, really sorry that it didn't work out."

At a camp north of the DMZ a second military bus, this one beige, started south through the snow toward Panmunjom. It carried a lieutenant, a sergeant, a corporal and 20 North Korean privates who would serve as honor guardsmen at today's meeting. Like their American counterparts, under armistice rules they were armed only with handguns. One of the North Koreans, Corporal Anh, was sitting in the back row of the bus, old and in need of fresh paint. Anh was in a foul mood. "These meetings are a waste of time," he muttered to his seatmate, Private Ryu. "I'd rather be on patrol, hunting South Koreans or Americans."

"What's eating you?" asked Ryu.

"Are *you* looking forward to this trip?" Anh whispered angrily.

"No," Ryu murmured defensively, "but-"

"But nothing," Anh hissed. "The only thing we'll do today is freeze our asses."

Jeff slowed as the bus entered Munsan. The narrow, winding road was snow clogged. Fresh snow continued piling up.

"From here on," Ben said, "it really ought to be interesting. The road from here is bad under good conditions."

"I thought after twenty years this road would've been paved," said Dick.

"No such luck."

The bus crossed the Imjin River and came to the crest of a steep hill. Jeff braked. "Holy shit," he murmured.

"What's up?" asked Ben.

"What's down is a better question."

Dan, Ben and Dick strained to peer through the wet windshield and its sweeping wipers. Ahead, at the bottom of the hill, two tracked armored personnel carriers lay in the deep ditches that bordered the road.

"If those babies couldn't make it down this hill," said Jeff, "this old crate never will."

"What are you going to do?" asked Dan.

"Give it a try," Jeff answered mechanically.

"I take it," Dick noted dryly, "that the brass has another mode of transportation to Panmunjom."

"Choppers," said Ben.

Jeff centered the bus on the road at the top of the incline and shifted gears. The bus began crawling ahead, the speedometer needle barely moving. About 50 feet down, the bus began to fishtail. Jeff tried to steer in the direction of the skid. It was futile. "Hang on," he warned, "here we go."

The slippery surface and the bus's weight increased its momentum. The skidding worsened. At one point the bus was sliding nearly sideways down the hill. Ben and Dick leaned forward, gripped the rail in front of them and braced. The bus righted itself briefly and then nosed off the road to the right. Its passengers held their breaths. The front end dropped into a deep ditch. The passenger door wedged against a hill that rose from the ditch. The ass end of the bus was still over the road, but the rear tires were about two feet off the ground.

Jeff looked back. "Everyone all right?"

There were no injuries.

"Nicely done," Ben told Jeff, "especially given the circumstances. No shit. You handled this old buggy beautifully."

"I'll second that," said Dick.

"Thanks, guys, but we haven't exactly made it to PMJ. And I don't know where we go from here."

"Don't sweat it," said Ben. "This is the perfect excuse for being late - or not showing up at all."

There was a knock on the driver's window. Jeff slid it open. It was a sergeant from the Joint Security Area Advance Camp. "If you can get your people out of there," he said, "there's a heated guard shack about a quarter mile up the road."

"Sounds better than the bus," answered Ben. "We'll have to use the rear door."

"I'll have a couple men help you out."

"Thanks."

Jeff stood. "Come on," he said to Ben and Dan. "We'll get out first and help the others."

"I'll lend a hand too," Dick offered.

The four headed to the rear. Jeff opened the door. Some five feet separated his shoes from the snowy road. A corporal and a private first class stood by, arms upraised.

"Here goes," said Jeff. He crouched and jumped. The waiting GI's grabbed his arms but his smooth-soled low-cuts slipped from under him and he went down, pulling one of the soldiers with him. "Sorry," said Jeff. He stood and brushed snow from his uniform. He looked at Ben. "Still as graceful as ever."

The others jumped without mishap. The sergeant led the snowy procession toward the guard shack. Within moments driving snow splattered against Ben's and Jeff's eyeglasses.

Jeff left his on. "I'm blind either way," he shrugged.

By the time they reached the guard shack, their uniforms were white. Everyone crowded inside. They brushed off snow. Ben and Jeff used handkerchiefs to wipe their glasses.

"What now?" said Dan.

"Who knows?" said Jeff.

"Not to worry," said the sergeant. "You'll get there."

"The question," Ben mumbled dryly, "is when."

"There comes the answer," said the sergeant. He pointed through the south window. Slowly descending the hill was the ungainliest vehicle any of the shack's occupants, save the sergeant and his two men, had ever seen. The machine looked like a monster created by a Hollywood special effects department. Edging down the slick road was a towering crane perched atop a platform that rode above four huge snow tires.

"I'll bite," said Dan, "what is it?"

"A tank retriever," replied the sergeant.

"Never heard of it."

"Not surprised. Not much call for one at Yongsan."

"Touché."

"Can it do the trick?" asked Ben.

"Piece of cake," said the sergeant. "She'll handle the bus first, then the APCs."

They watched in awe as the gargantuan machine maneuvered near the bus. Its crew fastened four huge, hooked cables to the bus. Then, seemingly effortlessly, the machine lifted the bus from the ditch and positioned it in the center of the road.

"Damn," whispered Ben. "I'll never forget that."

"Like you said earlier," Dan observed, "this should be a memorable day."

Moments later all were back on board. "We shouldn't have any more trouble," Ben told Dick. "There are no more hills like that one."

"You know," said Dick, "I think that was the hill where Henry and I first saw the war starting."

"Really?"

"I think so. I can still see the puffs of smoke. We thought they were part of maneuvers. Then we saw the dirt flying and we knew they were using live shells. And then the two jets came down on us. Whew," he shivered at the memory. "Never forget *that*."

"I think this driver is aiming for every pothole in the road," growled Corporal Anh.

"Hey, take it easy," Ryu said, trying to calm him. "With all this snow, he can barely see the road."

"I don't think he's even trying."

"What's really bothering you? It's not the weather or the bus driver."

"Sergeant Noh," Corporal Anh whispered furiously, jabbing a menacing thumb from a closed fist toward the back of the sergeant sitting at the front of the bus. "Sergeant Noh. He has it in for me," Anh complained under his breath. "He's on my back all the time."

"He's rough on everybody," whispered Ryu.

"But not like with me. Yesterday he assigned me to this detail, and then he had me walking guard early this morning. Ask me how much sleep I got."

"I admit that wasn't fair."

"He's been riding me hard for months, and I don't know what I did to deserve it. I've had just about all I can take."

At Panmunjom, Jeff braked near Freedom House, the architectural curiosity that served as pressroom and canteen for visiting journalists from the South. The snow had stopped and the sky had cleared. Panmunjom lay cloaked by a thick cape of unsullied white.

"It seems a shame to walk across the snow," said Dick.

"If it'll make you feel any better, " Ben kidded, "I'll go first."

"Hold it, I'm going first," Dan asserted. "And I'm heading straight for the coffee and cake."

The bus emptied quickly, Dan in the lead, the score of journalists close behind.

Resentfully, Corporal Anh watched the procession to Freedom House. "Why don't they have coffee and cake for us?" he grumbled to Ryu. "We don't even get a cup of tea."

"Take it easy," said Ryu. "This day will end soon enough, and then you can catch up on your sleep."

"I doubt it. That fucking sergeant will probably have me walking guard again tonight."

Ben, Dick, Jeff and Dan had moved from Freedom House to the communications building that sat immediately east of the conference building. Ben tested the field phone connection by calling Seoul.

Dan sipped coffee from a styrofoam cup he had carried from Freedom House. "That cake was really good today. Really hit the spot. Coffee's good, too."

The meeting began. The chief U.S. negotiator, a lieutenant general, read his opening statement, a salvo of truce-breaking allegations that was translated into Korean.

The chief North Korean representative responded with his opening remarks, a high-voltage diatribe against supposed U.S. misdeeds and scurrilous intentions. It was translated into both Chinese and English.

Ben typed a lead for his story, then sat back to wait for the next round of accusations. He noticed Jeff sitting on the edge of a table in a corner of the room. His eyes stared blankly at the far wall.

"You decided about Suni yet?" Ben asked.

"I've decided – and undecided – about ten million times." There was unmistakable disgust in his voice. "About a million times last night alone."

"And today?"

"About a thousand more."

"Time's running out."

"Don't I know it."

Corporal Anh was standing at the south end of the conference building. Now he was not only tired and disgruntled, but hungry and cold as well.

A South Korean reporter sidled up to Anh. "You look miserable," the journalist said sympathetically.

"You *are* miserable," Anh muttered darkly.

"My, my, aren't we touchy today?"

"Go write something nice about the imperialist Yankees. You're nothing but a shill for them anyway."

Anger began forming in the journalist. "Really? Well," the reporter responded caustically, "if I'm a shill, you're nothing but a puppet for the Chinese. They pull the strings and you dance."

"You've got a lot of nerve calling *me* a puppet," Corporal Anh bristled, eyes smoldering. "Your country hasn't done anything for itself in twenty-five years."

"Listen you communist twit..."

"I'm going for a cup of coffee," said Jeff. "Can I get one for someone else?"

"I'll take another one," said Dan. He drained his styrofoam cup and handed it to Jeff.

"I could use a cup," said Dick. "But I'll get it myself."

"Nah, I can handle three," said Jeff.

"Sure?"

"No sweat."

Jeff, holding three cups, left the communications building.

"You're a fat swine who feeds on the scraps thrown by the Yankees," Corporal Anh whispered heatedly.

"You," the reporter retorted angrily, barely able to keep his voice low, "would rape your mother to appease your Mongolian masters."

Anh's crimson face contorted in rage. The veins in his neck bulged. That was the ultimate insult, a lackey South Korean besmirching his mother. His right hand moved toward the handle of his holstered, Russian-made gun. At that moment, Jeff strode by, oblivious to the brewing tempest. He was thinking of coffee – and Suni and Alice Zink.

Inside the communications building Ben was batting out copy. Dick looked over his shoulder. "Not bad, little brother. I'd say you're worth the two hundred forty bucks a month they're paying you."

"I'll count that as a compliment."

"You should. You can-"

A sharp, solitary crack shattered the snowy stillness and seemed to quick-freeze the people at Panmunjom. A North Korean accusation was halted in mid sentence; the speaker's mouth was agape but silent. Many of the soldiers and reporters who had been milling about stood stock still in awkward positions, as though captured unaware by a roving camera.

Corporal Anh looked dumbstruck at his smoking gun, as if it had discharged of its own volition.

The South Korean reporter, on one knee, had slipped as he knocked Anh's arm aside, sending the bullet away from him and toward Freedom House. He started to rise.

"What was that?" Dan asked.

"Not the Fourth of July," Ben replied dryly.

"Could've been a backfire," Dan speculated.

"Don't think so," said Dick.

"I'm taking a look," said Ben, rising and moving toward the door. Dick was one step behind. They stepped outside into the cold. Ben looked between the buildings toward Freedom House. He saw a mound of green lying motionless in the snow. The mound was leaking, staining the green an ugly black and the snow a bright red. "Good Christ," Ben whispered anxiously. Then he went dashing toward the green mound through the ankle-deep snow. Dick went pounding after him.

As Corporal Anh's shot rang out at snow-shrouded Panmunjom, a heavy white blanket was covering Shelby, Ohio. Because of the 14-hour time difference, it was about ten o'clock the previous night in Shelby.

Edward Lawrence looked out his living room window. In the glare of a streetlight he could see the snow falling steadily. About four fresh inches lay on the ground. He pushed his glasses farther up his nose. "Think I'll go out and shovel."

"Why?" asked Harriet. "It's still snowing."

"If I don't do it now," Edward said laconically, "it's liable to be really deep in the morning. And heavy. It's not that cold out, so the snow is probably wet."

"It's so late," Harriet protested. "Let it go and we'll hire someone to do it in the morning."

"I've been cooped up since we went to church this morning. The air will do me good."

"You are so bullheaded," Harriet complained with mild exasperation.

"After all these years, would you want me to change?"

"Not really." She conceded an affectionate smile.

Edward bundled up, stepped onto the porch, hefted the shovel, descended the steps and began attacking the snow. It was tough going. The snow was wet and heavy.

Edward had been shoveling only a few minutes when his chest began to tighten. He straightened and paused. He forced himself to breath deeply and continued shoveling. The tightening worsened. Oh, brother, it's a real doozey. The pain emanating from his chest went shooting down his left arm. He started to fall. He tried to support himself with the shovel handle but lost his grip. Edward collapsed on his back in the snow. Heart attack, he thought instinctively. He tried to call for help but couldn't get the word past his lips. The wet snow fell on his face and glasses. He tried to raise his right arm to shield his face. God, he pleaded silently, please don't let me linger.

Snow was falling on Cleveland's west side, too. In a room in Lutheran Hospital Gerry Graham was lingering. The cancer symptoms had returned soon after his wedding with Ella and his matriculation at graduate school. The symptoms had worsened quickly.

Ella was at his side now. Gerry had remained spunky, but no one had to post the odds for him. He knew they were long. This night he felt weaker than he ever had before the first round of surgery and treatment. He doubted whether there was any use for more surgery.

He held Ella's hand and squeezed. "Not much of a grip, huh, wife?" His husky voice sounded weary.

Ella's eyes welled. "It's plenty strong for me, husband."

"I really wanted us to visit England. To see Petworth together."

"We will. You'll see."

"It was the right thing, wasn't it? I mean getting married."

"It was the rightest thing we've ever done."

"I'm glad you're here with me now. I would hate-" pain shot through him and he winced – "hate to be going through this without you. I do wish Ben could visit. Wonder what the old buzzard is up to."

Ben and Dick dropped to their knees on either side of Jeff.

"Jeff," Ben said urgently, "are you all right?"

"I'm hurting," he grunted, "but I think I'm more embarrassed than hurt."

"Embarrassed?"

"You can see where I'm hit. I won't be sitting on an unpadded chair for awhile."

Near the row of metal buildings an American honor guardsman drew his .45 caliber pistol. He hesitated, then fired at Corporal Anh but missed. Private Ryu watched, drew and fired at the American, but missed. In the next sliver of time, American and North Korean soldiers were drawing and firing and scrambling for cover. The South Korean reporter who had taunted and tussled with Corporal Anh gasped and threw himself frantically into the doorway of the conference building.

At the second shot Dan had walked to the door. "What the hell's going on?" He stepped outside and started toward the south end of the communications building. He stopped when he saw Ben and Dick bent over Jeff. By now Panmunjom was ringing with gunfire. "What the hell's happening?" Dan shouted to Ben and Dick.

Dan's call drew Corporal Anh's attention. Dan was standing no more than 20 feet away. Anh raised his gun and took aim.

Dick saw Anh poised to fire. "Dan!" he bellowed. "Look out!"

Anh fired. The bullet slammed Dan against the communications building. The metal siding reverberated from the impact. Dan crumpled, blood streaming down his face.

Instinctively Dick leaped to his feet, snow falling from his parka and pants, and went racing to aid Dan. Again, Anh took aim. Dick knew he was Anh's target, but there was no place to hide. He kept running toward Dan. Better to be a moving target. Ben and Jeff watched transfixed. As Anh squeezed the trigger, Dick feinted right, but the bullet smashed his left leg high above the knee. Fewer than 10 feet from Dan, Dick fell face down in the snow, writhing, moaning and grabbing his leg. Again, Anh took aim at Dick.

Ben left Jeff and went sprinting toward Anh. Through the falling snow Anh saw him charging and whirled to face him. Ben kept coming. Dick shouted to divert Anh, who momentarily froze. Then Anh fired quickly at Ben and missed. Before he could fire a second time, Ben slammed his shoulder into Anh's chest and kept driving his feet. Anh crashed into the metal conference building. His gun fell free. Ben wrestled Anh to the ground. Two strong, desperate young soldiers scrambled frantically for the loose gun. Ben slugged Anh on the jaw, grabbed the gun and rammed it flush against Anh's chest. He pulled the trigger. Anh's body jerked and went limp.

"Ben!" Dick shouted. "Behind you!"

Breathing heavily Ben rolled onto his back and fired twice without really targeting. Both shots missed Private Ryu. He returned Ben's fire but missed. Still on his back, Ben steadied himself, held the gun with both hands, and squeezed. Ryu stumbled back, holding his abdomen. Ben rolled over, leaped up and went lunging through the snow after him. He fell on the dying soldier, shoved the snout of the gun against the side of Ryu's chest and fired.

"Cease fire! Cease fire!" boomed the loudspeakers. The urgent command was sounded in both English and Korean. More shots rang out. "Cease fire now! That is an order!"

Miss Lee sat in the infirmary at Yongsan. Anxiously she watched Dick's closed eyes and even breathing. She glanced uneasily at his bandaged leg, elevated on a pillow. Another hour passed before Dick awoke.

"How long have you been here?"

"A while."

"How long have I been here?"

"You have slept many hours."

"I guess they really doped me up. Last thing I remember was being loaded on the chopper."

"You were in much pain. Does your leg hurt now?"

"A little." The truth.

"Your leg bone was splintered. But not too bad. The doctors say they have fixed it well."

"That's good news."

"There is bad news."

"Dan?"

She nodded.

"Is he dead?"

She nodded again, eyes misting.

"God…" Dick's voice trailed off. His jaws tightened. "How's Jeff?"

"He is not injured seriously. He is in the next room. He will leave hospital soon."

"That's good. How is Ben handling, uh - have you talked to him about Dan?"

"He is very sad. He cried. He was here with you. I told him to go and rest."

"Good…Chong?"

"Yes?"

"It looks like I won't be going home Wednesday after all."

CHAPTER 59

"I am so sad about Dan," Kyong whispered.

"They don't make people any better," Ben murmured dejectedly. "He was honest, honest to a fault. Not a selfish bone in his body. Not one. I keep asking myself, Why? There's no good answer. It was one of the most stupid, senseless deaths ever."

Kyong shifted under the blankets that covered them. She caressed Ben's cheek. "You are lucky to have such good friend. It is terrible sad he die. But you will have wonderful memory."

"A memory. That doesn't seem like very much."

"This is sad time for you. You lose friend, you lose father, your brother is hurt. It is natural you feel bad."

"It's almost impossible to imagine my father dead. He was always so strong. I really feel sorry for Dick. He's lost everyone."

"He still has you."

"Yeah, I'm a helluva prize. He comes to Korea to visit old friends, and I almost get him killed."

"Not your fault."

"Yeah, I know. But it's ironic."

"Ironic?"

"Crazy. Twice he comes to Korea. For pleasure. And twice he almost gets killed."

"Maybe he will come back again and have good time."

"Maybe."

Ben held Won Kyong Pok close, her head on his shoulder. He stroked her back. "You've been a lifesaver, Kyong."

"What? Not me," she said derisively.

"Yes, you. I don't know what I'd've done without you. You've been here whenever I needed you. And you've never asked for anything."

"There is no need to ask. You give to me also. We are friends..."

"Very, very good friends. Kyong, I, uh...I-"

"No," she interjected firmly.

"Huh?"

"Do not say anything more now. If you remain silent, you will not be sorry for your words."

"But-"

"Shhh."

"You cannot go," said Lee Chong Hee. "You are hurt very bad. You need to stay in hospital."

"I have to leave. I have no choice."

"But why? You said you would be here longer."

Dick held up a small piece of yellow paper.

"What is that?" Miss Lee asked.

"A telegram."

"What does it say?"

"That my father has died."

Miss Lee was stunned. "Your father. When?"

"When I was at Panmunjom."

"Oh." A great wave of sadness engulfed Chong. She knew what the news meant. Dick would go back and he would not return. "I am so sorry for you. Does Ben know?"

"Yes."

"When must you go?"

"The funeral is in two days. They're delaying it for me. I'll leave in the morning."

Miss Lee struggled to suppress her sadness. It would not be fair to Dick to become upset, she told herself. I must remain composed. "It will be a difficult trip. You will suffer much pain of the heart and body."

"The doctors will give me pills."

Miss Lee lowered her head. A tear began to trickle down her face. Quickly, she dabbed it. "I not cry in a long time." Her voice quavered. "Since a young girl."

"Sometimes it's better to cry."

"Sometimes cannot help it."

"I'm coming back."

Now her tears were flowing freely. She sniffled. "No, it is as I say before. My life is always here. Your life is in California."

Dick's eyes began to mist, his throat to thicken. "Chong, I won't say when, but I will come back. I don't make promises lightly." Dick cleared his eyes. He smiled warmly and took her hand. "I mean what I say. You mean very much to me. So do the Yoons."

"You are a very good man. I believe you. But, we know each other only six days."

"You've been counting," he said, smiling.

She smiled. "Six days is not a long time."

"These six days have been full of tragedy. Dan. My dad. But in some respects, they have been six good and memorable days."

"Ah, good." She forced a wide smile. "You remember them always that way, the six days."

CHAPTER 60

"My dad was a great man, although I don't think he ever believed that. I'm sure he would wince and blush if he heard me saying that now. I guess it has to do with the way you measure greatness. I remember once when Dad was belittling himself. He said he regretted not making more out of his life. Said he felt like a failure. I could hardly believe what I was hearing."

On the long flight back from Seoul, Dick had decided to ask Harriet and the parish priest whether they minded his delivering a eulogy for Edward. Harriet couldn't have been more pleased, and the priest did not object.

Now Dick leaned on his crutches behind a podium in the sanctuary of cavernous, ornate Most Pure Heart of Mary Church where Edward and Harriet had been married a quarter century ago. Some 200 of Edward's family and friends were there. Helen Hoerner was one. She sat about mid-way back.

Dick used no text. He was relying merely on notes he had penned in cramped letters on the backs of five of his business cards. "My dad was measuring success by the jobs he held, the money he made and by what he could do for his family. I guess that's sort of natural. But I remember telling him, 'Dad, if you believe you're a failure, then you're not nearly as smart as I've always given you credit for.' I reminded him that he had served his country proudly as a soldier. That he had married two wonderful women and always treated them like royalty. I reminded him that he had done a pretty fair job of raising his kids. He was always ready to play catch with a little boy. I reminded him he had friends, lots of them. And if he could be here today, he'd know that. When I reminded him of all that, I think he was somewhat comforted. But not entirely. To his last day I think he felt like he had somehow fallen short of some mark. He was wrong. My dad was great. He did the right things in the right way. And he paid his dues. Well, enough of this. I could go on for a long time, but you know my dad couldn't sit still long for what he called mush. He probably thinks I've gone too far already. Too bad, Dad. You'll just have to get used to that, at least for today, because I have a feeling a lot of people will be saying lots of nice things about you. You deserve it."

At the snowy gravesite Dick saw Helen Hoerner on the fringe of the crowd – just as she was back in 1945 when Dick returned from Europe. She was dressed in black. Her eyes were red and puffy and sad. Incredibly sad. She had loved the father and had fallen in love with his two sons. Three headstones for Sarah, Bill, Edward. In a way, Helen thought, I've been part of this family. Never in it, but part of it. I've watched it grow and change and die. God, I haven't asked for much, but please don't let me live to see any more of this family die. These men have meant so much to me. Don't take the last one away. Not before…not before my time.

The service over, the crowd thinned, the mourners slowly making their way through the snow to their cars. Dick paused and looked back. Helen still was standing by the grave. He told Harriet and Susie to go on, that he would be along in a minute. He swung around on his crutches and hobbled back to the grave. Helen looked up, with eyes as bereft of hope as any he had ever seen.

"Thank you for coming," he whispered.

She nodded, almost imperceptibly.

"Could we meet?" he asked. "Later?"

"You look much better. I hope you're feeling better too."

"I am. A little. Your father meant so much to me. He was one of the kindest men I ever met. He always thought of others first. He was so sweet."

473

"I think it's safe to say he felt the same way about you."

She smiled slightly, her grief still very much in evidence.

It was the Saturday after the funeral, and Dick and Helen were seated across from each other in a booth in the Coffee Shop on Main Street. Dick's crutches hung from a coat hook.

"In fact," Dick went on, "We all felt that way about you. I still do."

"Oh, Dick, please..."

"It's true." A pause, and then he smiled wryly. "It's a good thing my life never depended on my ability as a prophet."

"I know what you mean. When I think back, I never dreamed it would all turn out like this. But who does? How is Harriet?"

"Good. Better than I expected. She was totally devoted to Dad. I'm glad she's got Susie. And Susie's hubby Bruce and their little Bill. It gives her someone to worry about. And to lean on. It won't be easy for her, but she'll make it. What about you?"

"I'm doing okay. Still teaching. Still enjoying the kids. They help keep me young."

"I'd say they're doing a darned fine job."

She smiled. "Thanks."

"How's Roger?"

She slowly sucked in a deep breath. "Not very well. He spends - you don't want to hear that."

"Yes, I do. Please go on." Dick did want to hear. He also sensed that Helen needed to tell someone.

"He's no longer teaching at all. He always needs crutches, and more often now, he needs a wheelchair. Do you remember the last time you saw him?"

"Of course."

"He's...not the same. I don't mean just physically. He's so depressed now."

"He was very chipper that night."

"Yes, he was. He's hardly ever that way now. Once in a while, but not often. It's never been easy for him to accept the MS. I don't think it would be easy for anyone. But he was so full of life. He was so active. He was so proud of his physical abilities. He was a strong man. Now he's so blue.

I try to perk him up but…I can't blame him. Sometimes I think he would rather…" Her throat thickened and her voice faded.

"It hasn't been easy for you, has it? Any of it?"

Eyes closed, she shook her head.

"It's cold out," Dick said, "but let's leave. We can drive around awhile. That sound okay?"

She nodded.

"We'll take my car," said Dick as he maneuvered his crutches and tried to open the restaurant door for her. "We can come back and pick up your car."

"Are you sure? Your leg…"

"No problem. I don't need my left leg to drive."

Dick drove east from Shelby. They cruised through rolling Amish farm country. In the distance a horse-drawn carriage approached. As they passed, a bearded farmer, garbed in black, gave a short wave. Dick waved back.

"Thanks, Dick. I think I needed to get out."

"You're entirely welcome."

"How about you?"

"Me?"

"What are your plans?"

"I guess I'll stay here another week or so. Help Harriet straighten things out. I don't want her to worry about money or legal problems. Then, I guess it's time I get back to work."

"How about some time off to recuperate? I'd say you deserve that. That leg of yours isn't going to heal without proper rest."

Dick laughed. "Well, when I get back to California, I'm sure the Santiagos will insist I take it easy for a spell."

"Do you think you'll be coming back to Shelby soon?"

"I don't know. It's always nice to visit family and friends." In truth, Dick was thinking that his trips to Shelby would be fewer. With Edward gone, Shelby wouldn't exert the same pull. He expected to return to Korea before he came back to Shelby. "There is one thing that would bring me back on a moment's notice."

"What's that?"

"You."

"Oh, Dick…" She smiled widely, her eyes brightening.

"I'm not kidding. If you ever need help, I want to know about it. In fact, I'd feel terrible if I ever learned you needed help and didn't tell me."

"That's very kind."

"That, Helen Hoerner, is the truth. So, will you tell me? If you need help?"

"I've become pretty self-sufficient, you know. I've had to."

"I'm sure you have, but that doesn't mean you might not need help sometime. Even the strongest do."

"Dick, I don't-"

"Okay, okay. I won't ask you to promise anything. But if you ever need a hand, I want you to grab mine."

Chapter 61

Natalie was propped up in bed, studying. She put down the book and reached for the ringing telephone. "Hello"

"Nat?"

"Kate!" she squealed gleefully.

"How are you?"

"Fine, just fine. Are you okay? Is Jake all right? Is anything wrong?"

"Slow down, sis, take it easy. Everything is fine here."

"That's good. I was worried. You don't call all that often."

"I know. We try to watch the phone bills. Mom and Dad and Jake's parents have been so good about helping us out, so we try to keep our expenses down. But everything's okay, really."

"How's Jake doing?"

"Fantastic. He's near the top of his class. Just one more year of med school and then he starts his internship."

"That's neat. Almost a doctor. Dr. Jake Avery has a nice ring. How are *you* doing?"

"Terrif. Busy. I like it here a lot better now that I'm teaching."

"I'm glad you like it," said Natalie. "I hope I do."

"You will, I know you will. Gee, you almost have your master's."

"I can hardly wait to get that sheepskin."

"How's everything else?" Kate asked.

"Good, really good." Natalie wasn't quite convincing. Good was not a typical Natalie word. The familiar effervescence was missing. "Are you and Jake going to be able to make it back for my graduation?"

"We wouldn't miss it. Dad told us at Christmas he would send money for the airline tickets."

"That's wonderful."

"Natalie?"

"Yeah."

"Have you heard from Ben?"

"No. Not since early December."

"He never answered your telegram?"

"No."

"I'm sorry. I don't understand."

"Do you know I've been dating one of my professors?"

"Yes, Mom told me. Evan Sloane. What's he like?"

"He's nice. You know he's divorced? And has two children?"

"Um-hmm."

"Oh, and he's persistent. And, uh-"

"What?"

"Oh, nothing. Well, sometimes, he wants to move faster than I do. But what the heck. I know he's interested."

"That's something. But, Nat, don't move too fast. You've always had your head screwed on right. Try to keep it that way."

"Don't worry. I appreciate your concern."

"That's the least I can offer. Hey! You know what?"

"What?"

"You should come visit us."

"In New York?"

"No, Silly, in Timbuktu. Of course, New York."

"Oh, I can't."

"Why not?"

"School. I haven't finished yet."

"I didn't mean now. I meant this summer. After graduation."

"That would be so nice," Natalie said wistfully. "But I just don't know. I have to look for a teaching job. I don't know how long that will take."

"Think it over. I'd love for you to come." Kate was suggesting the visit because she missed her younger sister. She also sensed that a change of scenery might give Natalie some breathing space and lift her spirits. She also worried that Natalie could stumble into a doomed marriage with Sloane. She wanted to put some distance and time between her sister and the professor. "And if you can't come early in the summer, come later. We've got plenty of room for you. Well, a studio bed."

"Thanks, Kate. I appreciate it. Really."

"It's been too long since we've had a really good, long talk. Just you and me. Like the old days in high school and college. Up all night talking about positively everything."

"That seems so long ago."

"Promise me you'll come soon. As soon as you can."

"I promise."

CHAPTER 62

Evan was brimming with contentment. He skipped down the porch steps of the home he had once shared with his ex-wife Karen and two daughters, now ages 12 and 14. Jauntily he walked down the sidewalk to his faded yellow Volkswagen Beetle. He looked back to the house and waved. The two girls, beaming, returned his farewell. He eased his lanky frame into the small car. He smiled in paternal satisfaction. He had just finished a rollicking game of Monopoly with the girls. Tiny red and green plastic houses and hotels had been purchased with high humor and used as weapons of merriment. Sloane had gone bankrupt amid a tumult of girlish squeals and screams. He loved his daughters.

He was satisfied for another reason. The previous night he had persuaded his former spouse to have intercourse with him. Actually, the persuasion had been more like coercion. He had planned to leave Saturday evening and return to pick up the girls for a Sunday outing. But by the time he and the girls had completed a second game of Scrabble, it was late. He had accepted his ex-wife's offer of a nightcap, drank that and a second, then smoothly wangled an invitation to sleep over. He had bedded down on the living room couch. Soon after, he rose and walked softly into her room.

"Are you awake?"

There was a long pause before she answered. "Yes."

He sat on the edge of the bed and put his hand on her shoulder. She stiffened. "I couldn't sleep," he whispered. "We had such a good day together. There's something left between us. You know that, Karen."

"It's gone," she whispered flatly.

"I don't think so. Not all of it." His hand gently massaged her shoulder. "Tonight, at least tonight, there is still something between us. We need each other."

"No, Evan, we-"

"Shh," he commanded softly. He stretched on the bed. She lay with her back to him. His hand moved down her back.

"Don't. I mean it."

Do you really? Sloane thought. "No, you don't. It's been a long time. Too long. We've had our problems, God knows. But a divorce doesn't erase all feelings, all the memories. You need to feel love. We all do. You weren't asleep and we both know why." He forced her onto her back and kissed her. "I'm right and we both know it."

The next morning, back in his apartment, Sloane's mind replayed the night. Their lovemaking had been fiery. Karen needed a man and I seized the opportunity. She was aloof this morning, but that was to be expected. I satisfied her, and I can see more such nights. She's not thinking of remarrying, and I know she won't enter into any casual affairs. She'll still have her needs.

Monday morning Sloane was humming as he dressed. At his office the mail was on his desk. He flipped through the stack. One return address froze his attention. The envelope bore the imprint of *The Kenyon Review.* Sloane's pulse quickened. He fumbled excitedly for his letter opener. Inside the envelope was a verdict he coveted and feared.

Sloane had written and submitted to *The Kenyon Review* a daring article that argued Hemingway's major novels would not withstand the test of time, that they would fade, sliding from the ranks of classics into the less exalted category of important period works. In time, Sloane postulated, the ghost of novelist Hemingway would hold candles to illuminate the works of Hawthorne and Melville and even his contemporary, Fitzgerald. Their ghosts would not return the honor.

Sloane had thrown much of himself into the article. He had researched it meticulously, organized it smoothly, reasoned intelligently, citing numerous examples of Hemingway's unrealistic, redundant dialogue and sketchy narrative, and had written clearly and concisely. Or so he thought. He had submitted the article with high hopes. An article in this prestigious publication, he reasoned sensibly, would amount to a brilliant feather in his academic headdress.

He sliced open the envelope and pulled out the single sheet of stationery. It was a rejection letter. A form letter. Polite but brief and devoid of detailed criticism.

Sloane exhaled and slumped in his chair. His hands pushed back through his thick shock of unruly brown hair. Again he read the letter. It was a judgment from which there was no appeal. The letter didn't state that his article was inferior, rather it had failed to meet the magazine's "current editorial needs." A polite euphemism for sorry but no cigar. Sloane had struck a match that had been blown out by a cold wind.

There was a knock on his door.

"Come in," he answered dispiritedly, his smoky voice barely audible.

A young woman entered. One of his students. "Good morning, Professor."

"Morning."

"I have an appointment."

"You do? Oh, yes. Uh, well…" He shook his head to clear his mind and shake loose the heavy emotional yoke. "Sit down."

"Is there something wrong?"

He sighed. "It's nothing."

"Are you sure?" The young woman really cared. She liked Sloane. Most of his students did. To the men he was unpretentious, witty, an occasional Friday afternoon comrade at a Westwood beer emporium. To the women he was like a giant teddy bear. Oversized, mildly disheveled, huggable, nice. Many fantasized about having an opportunity to tidy him up, iron his wrinkles, brush his hair. "If something's wrong, we could meet later."

"You wouldn't mind?"

"Really, I don't mind."

"That's very nice of you. I'd like a little time to myself."

"Of course. If I can help later…"

"No. Thanks anyway. Let's set up a time."

"Anytime, really."

Sloane looked at his schedule. His afternoon was booked full. He glanced at his watch. It was 10:30. "Hmm. Things look pretty tight today."

"That's all right. Tomorrow would be fine with me."

"We need to get you going on your paper. I'm free at lunch. Are you doing anything? About twelve-thirty?"

"No. That would be okay," said the woman.

"Do you want to meet then?"

"Sure." She felt a swelling in her breast. She was relishing that unexpected prospect. Lunch with Professor Teddy Bear. "Where will we meet?" A slight quaver in her voice, which Sloane detected.

"I have a class at eleven," he replied pensively. "Then a short department meeting. Well," he noted in dry parentheses, "it had better be short. How about my apartment? Out front. There are a couple places nearby. We'll pick one."

"Fine." She swallowed.

Sloane scratched out his address on a memo slip. "It's near campus." As he handed her the paper, his spirits began to lift. An idea was forming, a strategy. If he maneuvered skillfully, as with his boat in a strong sea, this lunch meeting could lead to more than a discussion of 19th century British novelists. And something far tastier than soup and salad. From under his heavy lids, Evan eyed the woman with heightened awareness. She was pretty. Small features enhanced her aura of innocence. A petite, firm figure nicely complemented her face. A noon seduction of a student princess would go a long way toward easing the pain of a morning rejection from an editorial godling. And what if the young woman resisted? Or refused? Sloane long ago had assayed correctly his charms. What devoted student could deny Professor Teddy Bear a squeeze in his time of need? As the young woman rose to leave, Sloane looked up at her and smiled sadly.

On Friday evening Evan dined with Natalie in a Chinese restaurant. Afterward, they returned to his book-filled apartment where they made love. Evan tried mightily to persuade Natalie to stay the night.

She refused, as she had right along. "Evan, I've told you, as long as I live at home, I won't embarrass my parents, make them feel uncomfortable, by staying out all night. You can call me silly or old-fashioned, but I won't give in on that."

"Then move in with me. That's certainly an alternative. You'd have more privacy than living under your parents' roof. You know how much I love you."

"That's not what I want," she asserted, "and you know that."

"Then for crying out loud, let's get married."

"Not yet. Not before I get my master's. That's only a couple months."

"That's why I love you," he said under a wickedly arched eyebrow.

"Why? What do you mean?"

"You're so disgustingly easy to manipulate."

They laughed.

When Evan dropped Natalie off at her parents' home, he walked her to the front door.

"I'm sorry about your article."

"Aah," Evan shrugged, "the editor probably has a leather-bound collection of Hemingway for his personal altar."

Natalie never had envisioned Evan as a teddy bear, but she wanted to hug and squeeze him. She did. They kissed warmly. Natalie went inside. As Evan returned to his car, frustrated by Natalie's resolve, he was beginning to wonder whether he could finagle an unplanned extra weekend visit with his daughters and another sleepover with his ex-wife.

CHAPTER 63

Spring sunlight filtered through the grimy window of the barracks room. Houseboy Pak gently roused Ben. Groggily he swung his legs over and sat on the bunk's edge. He scratched his scalp and groaned. As he stood, he was surprised to see only one bunk empty instead of the customary two. Pak was waking Casey McDermott. Dan's bunk remained empty; his replacement had not yet arrived. What surprised Ben this morning was Jeff's bunk. Most unusually, it was occupied. Since shacking up with Kim Soon Yi, Jeff's bunk seldom needed making. When Pak changed Jeff's sheets, it was more formality than necessity. This morning, though, Jeff was beneath the covers and sleeping soundly. Pak approached to wake him. Ben signaled Pak and whispered, "Let him sleep. I'll cover for him at the office."

"You tell boss he sick?" Pak asked, eyes twinkling atop a small conspiratorial smile.

Ben nodded.

After breakfast in the mess hall Ben and Casey started for the office. Ben checked his watch. 8:12. Outside the Protocol office building, Ben halted. "I have to check something here," Ben told Casey. "I'll see you at the office."

From just inside Protocol's front door Ben surveyed the office. A corporal was sitting at his desk reviewing the schedule for a parade ground ceremony which later that day would honor a visiting Royal Canadian Air Force colonel. A female Korean clerk was working at a file cabinet. One other familiar face was missing. Kim Soon Yi, the office receptionist-secretary and Jeff's love, was nowhere to be seen. The clerk turned, saw Ben and greeted him. "Good morning, Specialist Lawrence. Can I help you?"

"I left something with Miss Kim yesterday," he lied. "I stopped by to pick it up."

"She is not here."

"Has she come in this morning?"

"No. Not yet. Do you wish me to tell her to call you?"

"Please."

Ben was not surprised by Suni's absence. With Jeff in his bunk, instinct told Ben that Suni would not be in her office. He had hoped Jeff would summon the courage to decide to marry Suni. Instead, he worried now that Jeff had abandoned their love, leaving it to rot along with other GI-Korean loves. Countless thousands of GI's had met and loved countless thousands of Korean women. And left them behind. Chiefly from fear of ostracism back home. And despised themselves for doing so. The evidence of these jettisoned loves could be seen in the Occidental-Oriental faces of children, spanning toddlers to teenagers. I wonder if Suni's pregnant, Ben mused. I hope not. If she is, I'll bet she won't tell Jeff. She's never asked him for anything, never pressured him. She wouldn't corner him with a swelling belly.

Jeff's return to the States and separation from the Army was imminent. In about two weeks he would be swapping olive-drab fatigues in Seoul for pinstripes in Manhattan. Korea and Kim Soon Yi soon would be a memory, never forgotten, but remembered less often and eventually with less clarity. A shame, thought Ben, a tragedy really. And yet Jeff and Suni as husband and wife in New York could be a disaster. Alice Zink could make life intolerable for Jeff and Suni. But only if Jeff chose to live in New York. He doesn't have to but probably will. Ben found himself judging Jeff harshly and tried not to. As far as he knew, Jeff had made no explicit promise to Suni or even hinted at one.

Jeff did not come into the Public Affairs office that day. Instead, on awakening, he pulled on his fatigues and went to the mess hall. Not hungry, he drank coffee, lingering until one of the Korean staff politely asked him to leave so she could clean up his table and begin preparing for lunch. He passed the remainder of the morning and afternoon walking and lying on his bunk. At 5:00 he headed for the NCO Club.

Ben found him there. "Mind if I join you?"

"No," Jeff answered morosely.

"Hungry?"

"No."

"Eat anything today?"

"No."

"Better eat something."

"This is only my first drink."

"It won't be your last."

"I couldn't swallow the garbage in the mess hall."

"We'll get a couple hamburgers here. My treat. Okay?"

"I guess so."

Ben signaled the waitress and ordered.

"I stopped at Protocol this morning."

Jeff's face tightened in anguish. "Was Suni there?"

Ben shook his head. "Not this afternoon either. I called."

Jeff sighed, removed his glasses, laid them on the red-and-white checked tablecloth and rubbed his eyes. "I had to make a decision. A final one." Jeff wasn't whispering, but his voice was barely audible. "God, it was awful. I went over to her place last night. I think she knew what I was going to say when she opened the door. Christ," he said wearily, "who am I kidding? I think she knew a long time ago. God, if I only had her courage." A tear trickled down Jeff's cheek. He made no effort to wipe it. "She hugged me and..." Jeff swallowed hard. "I tried to speak but she wouldn't let me. We sat down on her settee." Jeff sniffed as another tear escaped. "I never thought I'd be crying in my beer," he croaked through a swollen throat.

"You don't have to tell me this."

Jeff shook his head. He knew he had to tell someone. "She tried to comfort me. She told me it had to be this way. She told me I'd made the right decision. Can you believe it? I go to tell her it's over and *she* comforts *me*. Doesn't let me say anything. God, she should despise me. I sure do. She said we were both young and should try to find happiness. She said if we got married there would be more pain than happiness. She said we would be happier if we married our own kind in our own countries. She said it was better for us to part now and have some happy memories..."

"And then?"

"Nothing. We just sat there holding each other. Every time I started to say something, she put her finger against my lips. I never felt so helpless. I wanted to say, 'You're wrong, Suni. We love each other and we're going to get married and move to the States and that's that.' God, it was so easy to say it in my mind. I just couldn't say it out loud. And she knew it." He sighed deeply. "She stood up and led me to the door. I looked at those eyes, those beautiful, beautiful eyes…" Jeff's fingers flicked at the tears on his face. "We hugged and I left. God," he muttered abjectly, "I hate myself. A real fucking study in courage."

Ben sat watching his friend, face buried in his hands, weeping softly. What a waste, Ben thought, what a fucking waste.

"What do you think?" Jeff asked, eyes still closed.

"I feel sorry. Sorry that things didn't work out like you wanted."

"That's all? You don't hate my guts? Or lack of them?"

"Be serious."

Jeff's hands clasped and squeezed. "Do you think…" Jeff said in a cracking voice. "Do you think she'll quit her job at Protocol?"

"No."

"God, I hope not. She could never get a job as good off the compound."

"She's too sensible to quit."

"Christ, I hope so."

"Did she cry last night?"

"No, not a tear. Just me."

"She probably needed today for that," Ben said without malice. "She's got some grieving to do too."

Jeff nodded. "Do you think she was right? About us? About everything?" His voice pleaded for assurance.

"Yes, yes, I do."

"Are you sure?"

"I'm sure." But Ben wasn't. I have no idea what will happen to Suni. I can see her possibly falling apart, quitting her job, damning Americans and taking refuge among Koreans. Or I can see her staying on at Protocol but never marrying. Or marrying another GI. Or perhaps a Korean, but only if she quits her job at Protocol. Who knows? Who the hell knows?

"I've heard Dan's replacement is due in tomorrow," said Ben, not knowing what else to say. "And yours is arriving late next week."

"Oh?"

"Word came in today."

"Guess I'm really a short-timer now. Casey will be leaving soon too. I guess you'll have to get used to a new crew."

"Fortunately not for long. Remember, I'll be gone a couple months after you."

"I guess there's not much left for me to do. Show the new man the ropes. Finish up out-processing."

"What are you going to do tonight?" Ben asked.

"Sit here. Drink. Start forgetting. Or trying to."

CHAPTER 64

Maria Santiago was 51 years old. She had reached middle age with grace. Her hair was streaked with gray that she disdained hiding. Her eyes remained bright, her skin soft, her voice spirited, her figure trim. She made no bones about the benefits of Oil of Olay and exercise. They kept her skin moist and her muscles toned.

Maria treated her mind the same way. I can't lubricate it with Oil of Olay, she reflected, but I can give it plenty of exercise. The last thing I'll do is slide into a matronly vacuum. I've seen too many women allow affluence and comfort become their fulfillment. I'll continue to teach. I'm now sort of the dean at Warner Avenue Elementary, she smiled inwardly. Third graders for 18 years.

In the autumn of 1967, a new catalyst exercised Maria's mind. Politics. More precisely, the politics of Senator Robert F. Kennedy. Maria, like husband John, was an independent who tended to vote Republican. She had voted for Richard Nixon in 1960 and Barry Goldwater in 1964. There was something about Robert Kennedy, though, that captivated, stimulated, resonated. Nixon was running again, but his candidacy stirred in Maria nothing more than feelings that under his guidance the economic and social status quo would be defended fiercely. Which, Maria conceded in discussions with John, had certain merits. But Kennedy promised adventure. Maria wanted to campaign for him. She didn't seek John's permission or blessing, but she did want him to understand her choice. He surprised her by encouraging her participation in the Kennedy campaign.

Maria campaigned hard for Kennedy. She did trench work. Phone calls, solicitations, literature preparation and distribution, organizational meetings. She was in the Los Angeles Hilton that night in June 1968, when Kennedy and his supporters were celebrating his California primary triumph. She had shaken Kennedy's hand and wished him well only moments before a bullet fired by Sirhan B. Sirhan ended the quest.

Now, on a Friday evening in May 1969, Maria was sitting in the living room of the home atop Glenmont. With her was Dick. They were sipping drinks, Maria a glass of Robert Mondavi merlot, Dick a Chivas Regal on the rocks.

Dick had left his office early, gone home, showered and changed from his gray pinstripes into muted leisure wear. When he arrived at the Santiago's, John had not yet come home. John, Maria explained, had phoned from the office to say he had a couple items to clear up, then would stop on the way home to buy cigars. John allowed himself one H. Upmann each evening, along with an after-dinner drink. Besides giving him great pleasure, his nightly indulgence helped dissipate accumulated stress.

Maria was telling Dick about her most recent civic endeavor, helping a group of senior citizens complete and equip a newly built golden age meeting center. "I'm buying them a stereo. And not just for listening. A couple widows – darling little women – have told me if they had music they think they could get some of the men to dance. Their eyes positively twinkle when they talk about it."

"I'd be more than happy to help."

"I know. And I appreciate it, and you can be sure I'll let you."

Dick glanced at his watch. It was a little after 6:00. "I wonder what's keeping John."

"I don't know. Maybe he found something else to do at the office. If he doesn't come soon, I'll call."

"Well, we're in no hurry." That wasn't entirely true. Maria may not have felt hurried, but Dick was itching to report his own news. He sipped his drink and squeezed and jiggled the glass.

Maria sensed his restlessness. "Why don't you tell me what's on your mind? There is *something* you want to say."

"I can wait for John."

"Oh, come on, I want to know. You can repeat it for him. He won't mind."

"You don't think so?"

"Of course not. Besides, if you don't let it out soon, you're going to crush that glass in your hand. And I don't want blood on my carpet."

Dick chuckled. "Guess I'm a little edgy. It shows, huh?"

"Just a teensy bit."

Dick cleared his voice. Again, he jiggled the glass. He breathed deeply. "I'm going back to Korea."

Maria said nothing but worry began clouding her eyes.

"No," Dick grinned wryly and shook his head. "I'm not planning another trip to Panmunjom. Or anywhere near it." He then told Maria about Lee Chong Hee. About her war-torn childhood, her wisdom, her help as an interpreter. About their admittedly brief time together and the unusual depth of his feelings for her. About the pain and longing that had eaten away at him since he had returned from his father's funeral.

"How does she feel about you?"

"Right now I'm not sure. That's what I want to find out. I know we were strongly attracted. Boy, that sounds stilted and corny. But it's also true."

"And if you still feel that way about each other?"

"I'll ask her to marry me and bring her back." Dick looked at Maria expectantly. Silly as it seemed to him, he wanted Maria's approval. And John's.

Slowly Maria's pensive expression gave way to a wide, delighted smile. "That's wonderful, Dick, absolutely wonderful. I'm thrilled. I hope it works out."

He blew out a great breath of relief. "I can't tell you how glad I am you feel that way."

"How else did you think I might feel?" Maria teased.

"I don't know. I guess when you're happy you want your friends to be happy for you. And, well, to be honest, it's been a long time since I've fallen in love. And the thought of getting married...I think I might be getting ahead of myself."

Maria stood and walked to Dick. "Stand up." He put down his glass and stood. Maria threw her arms around him, pinning Dick's arms to his sides. She put her head against his chest, then pulled back and looked up into his eyes. "I love you, Dick Lawrence," she said spunkily, "and the only thing I want for you is complete and utter happiness. So there."

Dick freed his arms and drew Maria toward him. No words came but none were necessary. After a long embrace, they disengaged.

"John will be thrilled," she smiled. "And I have a suspicion you won't mind repeating your story for him one little bit."

Dick smiled and shook his head. "Are you ever wrong?"

"Not often," she smiled slyly, "just ask John." She glanced at her watch. 6:32. "I think I'll call the office now."

As her hand gripped the receiver, the phone rang. She was momentarily startled. "It's probably him." She lifted the receiver. "Hello."

A couple moments of silence, then Maria: "Yes. Yes, right." More silence, then Maria: "What?" Another silent moment, then, "Oh, no."

John lay unconscious in an oxygen tent. Maria could see him through the small window in the door. She shivered. Natalie and Dick supported her. From inside, a nurse opened the door. Maria and Natalie stepped inside. Maria's knees weakened. The nurse guided her to a chair.

John's heart attack had been severe, but he was expected to survive. He had been felled as he left the tobacconist shop. As consciousness faded, John had thought he was dying. Fast medical help saved him.

During the next few days, Maria, Natalie, Jeannie Marie, Ruth and Dick took turns watching over John. At her mother's urging, Kate, assured that her father would pull through, remained in New York. She and Jake would visit during his spring medical school break.

John, weakened, slept much and spoke little during the first week. The following Saturday he was awake when Dick entered the room. John extended his hand and they shook hands.

"Thanks," John said.

"For what?"

"For a lot, starting with all the hours you've sat here this week."

"Aah."

"And for watching over Maria."

"Aah, it was nothing."

"I've done a lot of thinking this week. Not much talking, but lots of thinking."

"Take it easy on the talking. Just rest."

"Oh, I'll rest. My body tells me I need plenty of that. But I can feel my strength beginning to come back. I don't think I'll be rolling out of bed to do pushups today or tomorrow, but one of these days…My morale is coming back too. Now, if you don't mind, I'd like to exercise my jaws a little."

Dick smiled. "No, I don't mind. Limber them up."

"I'm not one for second-guessing. Not often and especially myself. But maybe we should have sold the business. Maybe I could have avoided this."

"Maybe. Are you ready to sell now?"

"No. No. In fact, I'm itching to get back in the saddle."

"That'll be a while."

"I know. But I've decided I need the business. Although I'm not sure it needs me."

"I think the heart attack weakened your mind."

"Far from it. You could run the business without any help from me. We both know that."

"And," Dick kidded, "wind up sharing this room with you?"

John chuckled. "You could be right about that."

"Damn right. We're too big and diversified to be a one-man show. If anything, we should consider reorganizing to spread the worry."

"You've given it some thought?"

"Are you up to listening? It can wait," said Dick.

"I want to hear it now."

"I've been thinking about decentralizing the company. Dividing it into different operating units, each with profit responsibility. And unit managers with lots of authority."

"Each man would be like a president?"

"Sort of. Maybe we could call each unit a group or a division and put a vice president in charge."

"Any models?"

Dick nodded. "I've been studying General Electric's organization. Fred Borch is the CEO. He has it decentralized, and it seems to work. Of course, we're a lot smaller, but I think it could work for us. We – you and I – could concentrate more on planning and worry less about day-to-day details."

"Sounds interesting. And healthy."

"I think it's worth more study, but let's table the idea for now. You get better, stronger, think about it yourself, and then we'll sort things out. Maybe give it a try. Okay?"

"Okay. But I think there's one other matter we should discuss."

"What's that?"

"Maria tells me you're returning to Korea."

"That can wait."

"Can it? Should it?"

"Now, John," Dick smiled, "you said a few minutes ago you aren't a second-guesser. Don't start now."

"I said I don't do it often," he said stubbornly. "Look, Maria didn't go into details, but I have a feeling this trip was very important to you."

"Not as important as seeing you through this. I'll go back in due time."

"Mr. Lawrence, I will personally see to that."

"Mr. Santiago, no doubt you will."

CHAPTER 65

Ben was a short-timer. He sat at his desk looking at the short-timer calendar he had fashioned from a yellow sheet of paper. It contained 49 squares, each numbered and designating one of his remaining days in the Army. The square in the middle contained no number; it read *Go Home.* Today was Wednesday; he was going home Friday.

He thought about Natalie. She had graduated from UCLA with a master's degree the previous weekend. It had been two turbulent years since they had graduated from Ohio University. Never, mused Ben, not in a million years, would I have guessed it all would turn out like this. It's enough to make you give up planning for the future or worrying about what might happen, because it probably won't, not the way you think. In just two days I'll be flying back to the States. I'll visit Dick in LA on the way to Shelby. There could be awkward moments. Especially if Natalie's parents want to see me. There's no telling what they heard about our breakup. They might see me as a class-one jerk. I wonder if she'll avoid seeing me. She might still be seeing her professor. Even if she's not, she hasn't shown any desire to see me. She might hate my guts. That telegram could have turned her against me. The handwriting was on the wall, but she might resent *me* for doing the breaking up. Maybe that's what she wanted to do. Who knows?

"Mail call."

There was one envelope addressed to Ben. When he looked at it, dread instantly sent a cold shiver through him. It was from Ella Graham. With stiff, cold fingers, he opened the envelope. He wanted – and didn't want – to read its contents. He removed two items – his most recent letter to Gerry, still sealed in its envelope, and the letter from Ella.

Dear Ben,

This is one letter I never ever wanted to write. Even now it's almost an impossible task. I'd like to put it off forever, but Gerry asked me to write it, so I must.

Gerry died on Memorial Day. It all happened so fast. At first, the surgery and the treatment seemed to work. He seemed fine for a while. Then it just consumed him. It really hurt him to drop out of school, but he had no choice. He was too weak and in too much pain to continue.

The pain was awful. The medication helped but he wanted to be conscious and alert, so they couldn't give him enough to wipe out the pain.

Through his pain, the day before he died he joked about how ironic it would be if he died on Memorial Day. He, the arch pacifist, dying on the day meant to remember those who died in uniform. The thought brought that mischievous grin, that cute smile, to his lips. Through the pain, his eyes even managed to twinkle.

Oh, Ben, I cannot believe he is gone. I loved him so. He was so gentle and kind and caring. And he had so much to contribute. And he was brave. So brave. When he went back in the hospital, I think he knew he was dying. But he fought. He took those awful treatments, and he made black jokes about them.

He was only 23 years old. 23. That's so young. So very young. There are so many things he won't be able to do. One of Gerry's great regrets was not being able to visit England with you. To show you Petworth, his birthplace. He wanted that so much.

I didn't open your last letter to him. It came on the day of his

493

funeral. It was something meant for him, between you and him, and I didn't have the right to read it. And to be honest, maybe I couldn't have. Not then anyway. Someday maybe you'll want to read it again.

I'm not sure what I'll do. There's nothing for me in Cleveland. Or if there is, I don't want it, not now, not here. I've been staying with Gerry's parents since he dropped out of school. They have been very kind, very supportive. But this has devastated them too, especially Gerry's mother. I just can't stay here any longer. I may be gone before you read this letter. Maybe I'll just go home for a while, to my parents, the nest and safety. I don't know.

Ben, I'm glad, really glad, that you and Gerry were friends. You meant so much to him, and that means a lot to me. Maybe we'll see each other again sometime. I hope so.

If Gerry were writing this letter, he would say, 'So long, you old buzzard.' I guess I can say it for him. So long, you old buzzard.

Love, Ella

Tears were streaming down Ben's face. Trying to stem the flow, he gritted his teeth and blinked and swallowed. He knew it wasn't going to help.

"What's wrong, Ben?" asked Dave Bedford, Ben's civilian boss.

Ben shook his head and stood. He walked to Bedford's desk. "I need to get outside," he said, nearly choking on the words.

Then he walked past Miss Lee, who looked at him with deep concern.

Ben headed immediately for the compound's nearest gate. He managed to check the tears until he had passed through the gate, then let them flow again. He walked slowly, aimlessly and didn't return until mid-afternoon. At his desk again, he picked up the phone and dialed. "Won Kyong Pok, please."

"Hello?"

"Kyong? It's Ben."

"Ben! How are you?"

"In need of a friend."

"I am your friend. How can I help?"

"Are you busy tonight?"

"Yes, but-"

"If you're busy, don't change your plans. I understand."

"You are near to going home. I want to see you."

"There's still tomorrow night," said Ben.

"No, we meet today."

"When? What time?"

"Now," said Kyong.

"Now?"

"You can leave office early?"

"Anytime. My work is finished. I'm just clearing out my desk, killing time."

"Good. I leave, too. I tell my boss I not feel well. I say woman's problem and he not ask questions."

Ben smiled. "I need time to go back to the barracks and get out of my uniform."

"We meet in front of the Bando Hotel. In thirty minutes. Okay?"

Ben paid the cab driver and strode across the sidewalk. He and Kyong embraced warmly.

"I was hoping you would call," she said.

"Why?"

"We are good friends. I want to say goodbye."

"I'm not very good at goodbyes."

"That is true for most people. But goodbyes are important. They say many things. They say love and respect."

"Would you have called me if I hadn't called you?" Ben asked.

"Yes, tomorrow."

"Do you care what we do?"

"Anything you want."

"Let's get a cab and go to Namsan and take the cable car to the top," said Ben. Kyong smiled, puzzled, but said nothing. "I feel like a prisoner," Ben said. "I need to feel free. To get where the air is clear, where I can see a long way."

"Something is wrong?"

Ben began telling Kyong about Gerry. About their friendship, about its genesis on the Footbridge at OU. About the cancer and the death. It took him a long time to tell her everything. She listened attentively. Atop Namsan, Ben looked down on the bustling city and beyond to the ring of craggy peaks. One of Kyong's hands squeezed his arm and the other circled his back.

Near evening they descended. Ben invited Kyong to an early dinner. She accepted. Afterward, a taxi carried them to her apartment building. "Wait here," Ben instructed the driver.

"Why?" asked Kyong.

"Well, I guess this is it."

"It?"

"Well, I mean, you had plans for tonight and-"

"This is not good way for friends to say goodbye. You come inside."

"Are you sure?"

"You bet."

Her skin was smooth and cool. She nestled close to him.

"This," Kyong whispered, "is much better way for friends to say goodbye."

"You bet," Ben said, smiling in the darkness.

"I will miss you, Ben." It was an honest statement, said matter-of-factly.

Ben blinked back tears. He squeezed her shoulder. "I'll miss you too," he whispered.

"I want you to miss me," she stated. "Do you know that? If you do, it means we were very good friends."

"You don't have to worry about that. I'll always be grateful that Jeff and Suni brought us together."

"Good."

"You're going to make someone a hell of a wife."

"Yes, I hope so."

"Have you seen Suni?"

"Yes. Often."

"How is she?"

"Very sad. She misses Jeff very much. She will hold him dear to her heart always. You do not see her?"

"No. I stopped at Protocol a couple times, but she wasn't there."

"She not go to work many days. Now she does. I tell her she must, but it is hard for her."

"Does she say anything about Jeff?"

"She does not have to say anything. She loves him and he is gone."

"She hasn't heard from him? No letters?"

"No."

"Piss."

"Why you say that?"

"Because it's the way I feel. I'm losing everyone, everything. Dan, my dad, Gerry. Natalie. Jeff and Suni. You."

"Me?"

"You know we'll…" His voice caught. "Never see each other again." The words were barely audible. "I miss you already." He felt a tear drop onto his shoulder. Then another. They weren't his. "Kyong, I…"

Through streaming tears, she kissed his cheek. "You love me."

"You know that?"

"I am glad you love me. That is all. That is everything. You understand?"

The next afternoon, Thursday, Ben said his goodbyes at Public Affairs. He shook hands with Colonel Baumgarten, Sergeant Taber, Dave Bedford and Miss Lee. Early Friday morning Ben shook hands with Pak and gave the houseboy a carton of cigarettes, a six-pack of beer and the liner from his field jacket – the one item Pak said he would like when Ben asked him if there was anything he wanted. One of the new correspondents drove Ben to Kimpo Airport. On the way, memories flooded his mind as the scenery flashed past. One last time. This is it. Thirteen months. In a perverse way, I'll miss this place. Not the Army but the people. And the mountains. Shelby will seem different.

At Kimpo Ben completed processing and then got in a long line to board the Northwest Orient Boeing 707.

"Ben!" a voice called. "Ben!"

He turned and saw a hand waving, then a woman running toward him, the hand still waving. Other soldiers, curious, turned to watch.

It was Kyong. Breathless, she stopped in front of Ben. Her eyes beamed atop a wide smile and the slightly crooked nose. Ben found himself chuckling.

"Well," she demanded, hands on hips. "You do not hug me?"

They hugged. And kissed. Then hugged again, joyously.

"I thought we already said goodbye," Ben teased.

"Yes," Kyong said spunkily, her smile widening further, "but I think you should have happy memory of last morning in my country, so I come."

CHAPTER 66

"Not much of a dancer, am I?" Evan said, grinning self-consciously.

"You're doing just fine," answered Natalie.

"I was cut out for a lot of things, but when it comes to dancing, I might as well have stilts for legs and snowshoes for feet."

"Oh, you're exaggerating, really. Come on. Relax and enjoy the music."

Even when life's course seems clear, persistent memories and capricious emotions, the thickets of human existence, slow progress. Ben was trying to hack his way through thickets during his last long hours in the Army. The long transpacific flight was allowing plenty of time for meditation. He tried to concentrate on the future. The past kept intruding.

On this mid-June evening Natalie and Evan were celebrating her master's degree. In style. Dinner overlooking the ocean. Dancing – the first time Sloane had taken her – at a posh nightclub. Natalie had expected to be carefree. She was distracted. Thickets. Her cheek against Sloane's chest, her mind kept picturing a soldier in a plane in the dark skies over the vast Pacific. She could see him, restless, squirming to get comfortable in a cramped seat. Is he thinking about me? If he is, what is he thinking?

It was about 3 a.m. at Fort Lewis, Washington, the same post through which Ben had passed on his way to Korea. He was bushed. He had slept little during the flight. Too many thorny thickets had kept him awake. At Fort Lewis out-processing had begun. The procedure was very Army.

Lots of forms to fill out, lots of time to pass, lots of boring instructions from bored GI administrators. Ben collected his last pay.

After a brief visit with his brother Dick in LA and a reunion in Shelby with his mother and family, Ben would head to New York to search for a public relations job. His friend Jeff had gone home to New York and landed a job with Burson-Marsteller, a leading agency. Jeff's father, Raymond, a corporate lawyer with a web of contacts had, unknown to Jeff, smoothed the way with a phone call to Harold Burson, the firm's co-founder. "If your son is half the man you are, Raymond," Harold had said, "he'll do fine here. I really like the combination of his OU degree and Army correspondent experience." In ebullient letters to Ben in Korea, Jeff had persuaded him that New York was public relations mecca. Ben wanted to work in public relations. While majoring in journalism, he had taken several public relations courses. A sizable chunk of his army correspondent's assignment had amounted to public relations or, as the Army preferred to call it, public affairs. He would go to New York, share Jeff's apartment until he found a job (Jeff had moved out of his parents' apartment, to his mother Alice's consternation and his father Raymond's approval), work hard and enjoy life. Or would he? Damn those thickets.

Thickets were keeping Natalie awake. Evan had remained attentive, and his invitation to go dining and dancing as a final celebration of her graduation from UCLA had delighted her. But she remained uncertain and undecided about becoming the second Mrs. Sloane. Evan still pressed for mating at every opportunity, but Natalie no longer saw that as quite so objectionable.

At home that night, the thickets causing insomnia were memories of her and Ben, together and unimaginably happy. Those days are gone, she reflected. I'm not even sure if I'll see Ben again. I wonder if his plane has landed yet, what he's doing. Maybe I should wait to get married. I'm only twenty-four. It seems like I always end up hurting someone. I hurt Ben. I've hurt Evan. I'm hurting myself. I want to make someone happy. I really do.

About 4 a.m. a bus approached the main gate of Fort Lewis. Ben smiled wryly. He still was in uniform but again was a civilian. He needed to be in uniform to qualify for military air travel discounts. But he was free. It felt good. So why wasn't he elated? Well, he was tired. It had been a long, nearly sleepless journey. There also were those enervating thickets. Slowly, wearily, he hefted the heavy duffel bag.

"Dick will be here in a few minutes to pick me up," Maria said softly. "You know you're welcome to go to the airport with us."

"I know, Mom," Natalie answered. "Thanks." She was in her room, propped up in bed, absently scanning a teachers' association magazine. She had won a teaching job in Redondo Beach – high school English literature – and she was prepping herself for the start of classes in September.

"Sweetheart, I don't want to meddle. You haven't really said yes or no about going, and I just wanted you to know it's almost time."

Natalie lowered the magazine to her lap. Her lips pursed. Her eyes, showing pain, shifted toward her mother. "I'd like to see him, but I can't believe he'd want to see me. I don't want to ruin his homecoming. Maybe I…Oh, never mind."

Maria felt her stomach tightening at her daughter's pain. "I don't want to press you. You know that. But I don't think Ben would mind. Coming would tell him something. It would tell him you care. You do care?"

"Of course. But I don't want to ruin everything again. I mean, there's Evan, and I just - maybe I could-"

The doorbell rang.

"I'll get it," called John from downstairs. He was home from the hospital and recuperating nicely but still was too weak, or so Maria had insisted, for a trip to congested Los Angeles International Airport.

"That must be Dick," said Maria.

"You and Dick go ahead," said Natalie. "Tell Ben I said hello and that maybe we can get together before he leaves."

After Maria and Dick had left for the airport, Natalie remained on her bed, thinking. After a few minutes she reached for the bedside phone and dialed.

A smoky voice answered.

"Evan?"

"Hi, Natalie."

"Hi. Could we get together?"

"Sure. When?"

"Now."

"Now? I've got a class in another twenty minutes."

"Afterward."

Natalie intercepted Evan between his classroom and his office. Her face was incandescent as she half ran, half skipped up to him. Beaming, she slipped her arm inside his and squeezed.

"You look like you just answered the sixty-four thousand dollar question," Evan said, grinning widely.

"I have, in a way," Natalie replied, smiling impishly.

"What do you mean?"

Natalie stopped and faced Evan. Mildly curious students, gawking, passed by. Natalie was oblivious to them. "I've made up my mind. I've kept you on a string long enough. Too long. We, Evan Sloane, are going to get married. And further, Professor, we are going to wed soon. How do ya' like them apples?"

"Uh, well..." He cleared his throat. "This is, uh, unexpected. I mean-"

"I know, I know," she cooed, eyes aglitter. "Every time you've brought it up, I've ducked. I must have seemed like a moving target. Most other women in my position would have grabbed you and run to the altar at the first chance. Now I want to make up for lost time. I don't want any long engagement. I don't want any elaborate plans. We can just pick a date – why not the middle of next month? – reserve the church and do the deed. Well? Well? Have I made the professor speechless?"

"Just about," Evan said, smiling thinly. "When did you make this decision?"

"This morning. Just before I called you."

"I see. Isn't Ben Lawrence due back about now?"

"Yes." The brightness in Natalie's eyes dimmed momentarily.

"Is he coming back today?" Evan asked gently.

"Yes."

"Who's meeting him?"

"My mom and his brother."

Evan caressed Natalie's cheek and spoke softly, his smoky voice inaudible to passersby. "Natalie, I want to marry you. You know that. In fact, you'd put me off so often that I was almost ready to give up. But as much as I want to marry you, I want it to be only when you are ready. Really ready. Maybe you think you are. And maybe you are. But those are maybes, large ones, and they don't make a great foundation for a marriage. Believe me, I know."

"Evan," she pleaded, "please. I didn't make this decision lightly."

"Of course not. But you made it under highly stressful circumstances. Look, we don't have to wait long. But give yourself a chance to calm down. I'm not saying you'll change your mind. Hell," he grinned, "I sure hope you don't. But I want you to decide when you're not under so much stress. Hey, I'll bet you were invited to go to the airport to meet Ben. Am I right?" Eyes lowered, Natalie nodded. "Come on," said Evan. "We'll drop my books off at my office and go over to my place awhile. We'll have a drink. We can talk about your new teaching job. Okay?" His hand raised her chin. "Okay?"

She forced a small smile. "Okay."

CHAPTER 67

The lithe figure loped along gracefully. The legs had spring. The stride was long and light. A breeze mussed the hair, and perspiration stained the gray sweatsuit.

In Shelby in the summer of 1969, Barbara Mason was viewed as an oddity, something of an eccentric. She was 24, beautiful as ever and single. What had much of the town's populace murmuring was Barbara's unfathomable penchant: she jogged.

In the late 1960s in Shelby, virtually no one jogged. The mania for long-distance running still was a few years away. Certainly no women could be seen plodding through the streets. Except for one. It was unseemly. It was unthinkable. To Barbara it was neither. She had taken up jogging in graduate school at Ohio State. To her the decision was decidedly practical.

After four years of running women's track in undergraduate school – four years during which she felt wonderfully fit – the ensuing inactivity left her feeling sluggish.

She had become used to gawkers. On her jogs through Ohio State's sprawling campus, around the huge football stadium and along the Olentangy River, men and women alike stared as the lovely, solitary creature with the serene countenance loped lightly by. Jogging lacked the stimulation of a competitive track meet or a fiercely contested tennis match, but she could jog anytime, and it purged her body of lethargy and freed her mind from daily worries. It firmed her muscles and put color in her cheeks. In short, jogging made her feel good – about herself, about school, about life. What else mattered?

Now back in Shelby after getting her master's in secondary education, she was waiting for September and her first teaching assignment, biology at nearby Plymouth High School. And she was jogging, nearly every day. Shelbians clucked, scratched their heads, rubbed their chins, pointed their fingers and speculated. Is she training for the Olympics? Is she showing off? Running isn't good for women, you know. It can ruin the, uh, bosom. Do you suppose she's, uh, queer? No one asked her why she ran. It was none of their business, and it was more fun to guess.

On this day as she loped along, her route was taking her toward Seltzer Park. She came to the west entrance and turned in. She slowed as she descended a grade, cut off the road and picked up speed as she crossed a grassy expanse toward a creek that ran into a pond up ahead. As she jogged near the water's edge, the resident ducks paid her no mind. Their inattentiveness caused her to smile. At least, she thought, not everybody quacks when they see me jogging. Ahead, she saw a solitary figure skipping small stones across the pond. In profile the figure sparked an uncertain memory. She slowed so her eyes could focus better. It can't be, she thought. Her heart beat faster. Calm down, she admonished herself, I must be mistaken. She stopped completely, about 50 yards away, and stared. The figure sensed a presence and turned to face Barbara. No hint of recognition. He shifted his gaze away and stooped to pick up another stone. It is, Barbara thought excitedly. I don't believe it. She broke into a gallop and sped toward the figure. About 20 yards ahead, the figure heard her shoes slapping the grass and faced her again. Barbara halted. "Ben! Ben!"

He stared uncomprehendingly, then, "Barb! Hey, Barb!"

They skipped toward each other, quickly closing the gap, and hugged. Ben lifted Barbara and spun her around. They eyed each other, broke into helpless smiles, and hugged again and held on.

"I don't believe it," said Ben. "I just don't believe it. I mean, you're the last person I expected to run into. You look great, absolutely great."

"Thanks. You do too."

Ben laughed. "I'm surprised you recognized me."

"Why?"

"Well, you never saw my hair this short. It's still got some growing to do before I can shake the GI look. And I don't think you ever saw me in glasses."

"You're right. But I don't think you ever saw me in this either," she said, fingering the shoulder of her sweatsuit.

Ben laughed. "That's true. Besides, uh, regular clothes, I guess I've only seen you in swimsuits and a cheerleader's outfit. But, hey, I think you'd look good in a gunnysack."

Barbara blushed. "How long have you been in town?"

"Just a few days. I got out of the Army and spent a little time in California. Visiting my brother. How about you?"

"I've been here since graduation. I'm going to be teaching at Plymouth High."

"Plymouth?" Ben asked dubiously. "No desire to live in a city?"

"No. Columbus was okay, but I had enough of it while I was in school."

"Well, I'll admit there's something about Shelby roots," said Ben. "They seem to really put a grip on us. And nothing wrong with that."

"So how about you?" said Barbara. "Are those roots going to keep you here?"

"No. Not because I want to leave. But Shelby can't offer me what I want."

"Which is?"

"Well, I want to work in public relations. And you won't find a whole lot of PR jobs around here."

"I guess not, but then I don't know much about it – public relations."

"I've got to learn a little about it myself. But what I learned in college and the Army makes me think I'll be good at it."

"Where do you think you'll go?"

"New York."

"Oh, wow! That sounds exciting. And scary. Have you ever been there?"

"Once. To visit a college friend. It's big, but I didn't find it scary. As long as you didn't try to cross Broadway against a red light."

They laughed.

"Do you have a job lined up?"

"No. I figure to do some pavement pounding."

"Where will you live? How will you get by?"

"I'll live with that same friend till I get a job. And I've got a little money saved. I won't starve. My friend works in PR, and it didn't take him long to find a job. It's funny. He says my Army experience should help and not just the fact that I worked in public affairs. These days when you think of GI's and uniforms you usually think of antiwar demonstrations. But when I look for a job, my friend says I'll be interviewed mainly by men who served in World War Two or the Korean War. He says they all aren't gung-ho about our involvement in Vietnam but they respect guys who didn't dodge the draft."

"Your friend sounds perceptive."

"He's a good guy. I roomed with him at OU and we wound up working together in Korea."

"How long are you going to be in Shelby?"

"A couple more weeks. I can use the time to unwind."

"I remember reading about the incident at Panmunjom. It sounded horrible."

"Yeah." Ben's eyes glazed slightly.

Barbara sensed she had said the wrong thing. "I'm sorry for mentioning it," she apologized with obvious concern.

"Aah, that's all right." Ben sighed. He looked at her ringless left hand. He thought, why not? "Do you think we could get together? For dinner maybe? We could do some catching up."

She brightened. "I'd love to."

"Great."

"How about tonight?" said Barb.

"Tonight? Sure, if that's not too soon."

"It was my pick."

Ben smiled. "Tell me. How often do you run?"

"Almost every day. Only I call it jogging. I don't go fast enough to call it running."

"You enjoy it?"

"I love it."

"Do you think you could stand some company?"

"Jogging?" Ben nodded. "Sure." Barbara smiled, surprised. "That would be super."

The two sweatsuited figures were trotting along Smiley Road. Nearly two weeks had passed since they had first jogged together. Ben looked forward eagerly to the daily runs. So did Barbara. For Ben the jogs were proving to be the tonic that Barbara had described.

Today they were running west into a descending sun. On either side of them, fields of thigh-high corn rustled in the breeze. Intermittently they chatted. Barbara, in better condition than Ben, found it easier to talk while jogging. They cut south on Funk Road. For a mile they ran between green fields and whitewashed barns, silos, sheds and houses. They turned east back toward town. After another mile they approached the city limits. Ben stopped and placed a restraining hand on Barbara. He pointed toward a *Shelby Corporation Limit* sign. "Remember," he panted, sweat streaming down his face, "the last time we saw that together?"

"Yes."

"It was a little over six years ago. We sure weren't dressed like this."

Barbara smiled fondly at the memory. "Prom night. I think we talked all night. Remember how we talked about our plans? The future seemed so clear then."

"We were confident."

"You were positively cocky," she teased.

"I had a right to be," he teased back.

"I think we even managed to be profound."

"Or just naive."

During the past week they had discussed much. During and after their jogs, over dinners, during evening walks, they caught up.

Barbara told Ben about her college years. About her success as a miler on the college track team. About her broken engagement – a mutual parting. The young man had wanted a full-time housewife and mother for their children. She wanted children, but she also wanted her teaching career. She had foreseen – and persuaded him – that their difference of opinion on that issue could be fatal to marital happiness.

Ben told Barbara about Gerry Graham and Dan Cohen. About Jeff Zink and Kim Soon Yi. About Miss Lee and the Yoons and their reunion with Dick. About his breaking up with Natalie he glossed over details and ascribed their parting to the stresses of time and distance. He said nothing about any romantic link between Miss Lee and Dick nor did he say anything about Kyong.

At the end of their second week of jogging and catching up, they were walking back to Barbara's parents' house on Roberts Drive. Sweat was pouring from them. They were breathing hard after a strong finishing sprint.

"Boy," Ben gasped, "we must be a sight."

"No doubt," Barbara wheezed, "we are spurring additional gossip."

Ben chuckled. "People probably think we're a couple masochists."

"At least," Barbara smiled, "seeing me with you might put a stop to speculation that I'm a lesbian."

"What?"

"Oh, yeah. I've heard that's been a favorite explanation for this indisputably masculine preference of mine."

Ben laughed uproariously. Then, poker-faced, with one eyebrow raised, he looked Barbara in the eye. "You're not, are you?"

"You should be utterly ashamed," Barbara said with mock reproach.

Ben wiped away tears of laughter and cleared his throat. He raised his right hand and used his forefinger to trace the thin, C-shaped scar that wrapped around the inside edge of Barbara's right eye. "Look," he said, "since you're not a homo, let's get married. Will you marry me?"

She paused before answering. "Well, look yourself," she said with mock haughtiness. "Since I am indisputably hetero, as you appear to be, and since I have fallen madly in love with you, yes."

They embraced, a pair of sweating targets of gossip.

"You realize this is the only reason I started jogging with you," said Ben. "To get you to fall in love with me."

"Ben!"

"Seriously," he whispered, his arms still around her back, "there are some things to work out."

"Like whether I will leave Shelby and live in New York?"

"Like exactly that."

"I've thought about it."

"And?"

"If you don't mind my getting a teaching job in New York, then I'll live in New York. *And* if you don't mind my teaching after we have children."

"Agreed. But there is something else to consider. New York is big and crowded."

"Do you think New York is ready for a woman jogger?"

"In New York," Ben deadpanned, "they won't even notice. The streets are full of weirdos."

"You're terrible," she said, her fists playfully pounding his shoulders.

CHAPTER 68

Natalie felt thoroughly awful. Her stomach rose and fell like a small boat bobbing in gale force seas. Moaning, hands clasping her abdomen, she staggered to the bathroom and vomited.

Eyes watering in relief, she shuffled back to her room and eased onto her bed. Nerves, she thought. School was starting in two days. The prospect of facing her first class of high school freshmen was enough to unsettle anyone. The thought caused her to smile wanly. She wondered how many other novice teachers were experiencing the same anxiety.

The morning bouts with nausea persisted past the first day of school. Why? After a couple days she no longer felt nervous before her students. It didn't make sense. She tried to shrug it off.

When the second week of school began and brought no relief, she phoned Doctor William Moyer, the long-time family physician who had delivered Natalie and her three older sisters. He saw her the same day, after school. After the examination his diagnosis was quick and sure. "You're pregnant, Natalie."

Natalie was stunned but not surprised. For the past few days she had half-suspected pregnancy. She had hoped it was anything but. Indeed, she had tried to blot the fearsome notion. Her period had been late, but that was not without precedent, particularly during stressful times. Still, Doctor Moyer's verdict was like a cell door slamming shut. It was a life sentence. She shuddered.

She imagined her parents' reaction. They'll be hurt, but they'll support me. I'll tell them first. Then I'll tell Evan. We'll be married soon. Our wedding won't be big, but I'll wear white. I want it that way, and I think Evan and Mom and Dad will too. Ben.   I'm glad we didn't talk during his visit here. I know what he would think about this. No strength. Fickle. Knocked up by my professor. How could I blame him? How could I explain?

Dick. I feel ashamed. But I know he loves me, and he'll offer to help. He'll be like Mom and Dad. He'll be hurt, but he won't show it. He doesn't want to hurt anyone.

A child. There's a baby inside me. I'm going to be a mother. I'm scared. Is it a boy or a girl? Evan will be shocked. Why weren't we more careful?

"I see," Evan said. He and Natalie were sitting on the couch in his small apartment. His arm circled her shoulder.

"We'll get married as soon as possible," Natalie said decisively. "I'd like to do it in two weeks, if that's okay with you. Mom says we can get the church for a small wedding. She said she'll take care of it."

Evan removed his arm, rubbed his eyes and blew out his breath. He cleared his throat. "Are you sure you want to rush this?"

"What choice do we have? I know this is a shock, but we knew we'd be getting married sometime anyway." She forced a weak smile. "It's not like we just met last month."

"I know. But, this, well, it certainly doesn't make for the strongest foundation for a marriage."

"I know that, but we owe it to the baby to be married as soon as possible."

"Yes, the baby." He sighed. "You know, you're not that far along. I know...I have a friend who can take care of you. He's a doctor, a very good one, and he's discreet."

"What do you mean?"

"Do you really want this baby? I mean, think what a baby would do to your teaching career."

Natalie's jaw dropped. Evan's allusion was beginning to sink in. Natalie was incredulous. The color drained from her face. The very thought was repugnant. Natalie's next words were a barely audible whisper: "You want me to get an abortion?"

"I'm only suggesting," Evan lied. "It's your decision. But it makes sense. Rushing into a marriage this way, well, we know what the divorce statistics are like. I'm one myself. This kind of situation doesn't help the odds for a successful marriage."

"It makes sense?" Natalie said dully. "Divorce statistics?" Natalie's shock at Evan's words was giving way to hurt, followed quickly by the seeds of anger. "Evan," she said, regaining control, "I'm carrying a baby. Our baby. How can...I thought you wanted to marry me."

"I do." He placed his arm across her shoulder. She tensed. "It's just that I never thought of doing it under these circumstances."

"Do you think *I* did?" she said, ice forming on her words. "Do you think I wanted it this way? Do you think I want a birth certificate for this child that's less than nine months younger than the wedding license? I don't think I understand this at all. Or maybe I do. Yes, on second thought, maybe I do."

"Natalie, listen," he said placatingly. "I love you. And someday I want us to have a baby. But, now, well, this just isn't a very suitable time. Aah, dammit, I'm not choosing the right words."

"You certainly aren't," Natalie said coldly. "But I understand what you're saying perfectly. And I don't like what I'm understanding. But that doesn't matter. Evan," she said resolutely, "we are going to get married, and we are going to have our baby. I won't consider anything else."

"Natalie, think of my situation." The pitch in his smoky voice was rising, betraying anxiety. He recognized this sign of weakness and willed it away. "I pay alimony and child support. Remember, I have two daughters. I'm hardly in a position to be a father again now."

"Evan, you *are* a father again."

His lips pursed and his jaws tightened. "Not yet." The smoke was back in his voice. "It doesn't have to be that way."

Another realization, cold and frightening, was beginning to dawn on Natalie. "You don't want to marry me, do you? Not really."

"Of course I do."

"No. No, you don't. Not really. I think you did at one time, but not anymore. You've got an ex-wife, two daughters and a pregnant lover. You don't want the lover to be your wife, and you don't want the lover to be pregnant. Not now, not later."

"Natalie, calm down. You're just upsetting yourself."

"No, I am *not* upsetting myself. *You* are upsetting *me*. You don't want to marry me and you won't admit it, and you want me to get an abortion. *That's* what's upsetting me. That's enough to upset anyone, don't you think?"

"Natalie, please let me explain."

"Explain what? How you've lied to me? How I should kill our baby? You've already explained all that."

"You're not being fair. I do love you, and I want to marry you. But I'm just not ready to be a father again. At least not yet."

"But you are, Evan. I will *not* get an abortion."

"Think about it. Sleep on it."

"I've made my decision."

"You may regret it."

"I have plenty of regrets, believe me, but having this baby won't be one of them."

CHAPTER 69

Barbara Mason was standing in the vestibule of the First Presbyterian Church with her father, Harmon. Her left arm encircled his right arm. Images, all of them happy, were parading through her mind. She shook her head remembering the chance meeting that had brought her and Ben together again. A jog through a park. Of all things. Then there was Ben's decision to marry outside the Catholic Church. Barbara had been prepared to convert, but Ben had dissuaded her. "You can convert if you want to," he had said, "but don't do it on my account. I can worship in any church."

Ben stood at the side of the sanctuary. He was having a hard time suppressing a smile himself. The last few weeks had been hectic but exhilarating. He had landed a job at Burson-Marsteller where Jeff worked. He had much to learn but liked his early experience working with a consumer account (cameras) and an industrial account (stainless steel). He watched Jeff, serving as head usher, guide family and friends to the pews.

Ben counted himself lucky to be marrying Barbara. Beautiful, effervescent, independent, brilliant, generous. She looked like a goddess, swathed in white, holding a bouquet of magnificently hued flowers, countenance radiating ecstasy. On this day Ben's mind had no room for memories. At this moment he could not have imagined wanting to be anywhere else doing anything else.

Standing at Ben's side was his best man, brother Dick. Dick had been surprised but felt honored when Ben had phoned to extend the invitation. Now Dick's eyes widened in surprise once more. He saw Helen Hoerner,

512

alone, being escorted down the aisle. Ben and Barbara had invited Helen and Harryet Snyder, their favorite high school teachers. Dick felt a pang of sorrow and a familiar wave of affection. He forced himself to stop staring and looked away. Dick did think of Natalie. She and Evan had not married, she had not aborted and she had been visibly stunned and wounded when Dick told her he was flying to Ohio for Ben's wedding. After Natalie asked who the bride was, the subject was dropped.

The reception at the Shelby Country Club was a rousing occasion. Barbara's father had spared no expense. Filet mignon. Champagne – plenty of it. A small orchestra.

"Would you like to dance?" Dick asked Helen. As the music ended, Dick murmured, "Could we talk? Later."

"All right."

After the crowd, in high spirits, had boisterously sent Ben and Barbara off, Dick and Helen got in his rented car and drove through the countryside.

"I'd suggest stopping somewhere for coffee," Dick said, smiling wryly, "but in this tux, we'd be the center of attention."

"That's all right. I'd just as soon ride anyway."

"Good. How's Roger?"

"Not very well."

"I'm sorry to hear that."

Helen sighed and let her head rock backward against the headrest. "His condition keeps getting gradually worse, and he's more depressed. He has to be in a wheelchair most of the time now. His remissions have disappeared. Do you have a cigarette?"

"Huh? Oh sure. Just open the glove box. Lighter there too."

She removed a Camel from the pack and lit it. She inhaled deeply and let the smoke out slowly. "Thanks. I know what you're thinking. You didn't know I smoked. I have for a year or so now. It's not a habit. Not yet anyway. It helps to unwind."

"I know."

"It's become harder. I'm not complaining. If it sounds like that, I don't mean it. It's been over six years now. It wears you down. I feel older."

"You look smashing."

"Thanks. I wanted to today. It was sweet of them to remember me and Miss Snyder."

"Says something, doesn't it?"

"I guess so."

"You guess? Hah, that's rich. I'm not the only one who thinks you're special, and that's obvious."

She blushed. A tear trickled down her cheek. "I'm sorry. I didn't mean to do this."

"Oh, for...You don't have to apologize for anything." Dick slowed the car and pulled into the entrance of rural Crestview High School between Shelby and Ashland. He handed her his handkerchief. "Take a deep breath. Finish your cigarette in peace."

She dabbed at her eyes. "It's been so long since I talked about it. I just didn't expect I would act this way."

"Are you in a hurry?"

"No. Well, I don't have a lot of time, but-"

"Look at that," Dick said, pointing to the sun. It was dipping to the tops of the trees that surrounded the school grounds. A red glow was beginning to spread across the horizon.

"It's beautiful." Helen took a last drag on the cigarette and crushed the butt in the ashtray.

"And made for talking. At least awhile longer."

She sniffled and smiled. "You've always been good for me."

"You haven't exactly been bad for me."

They smiled. Dick took her hand between his and squeezed. He studied her eyes. They were large and unblinking. He leaned toward her and she toward him. Their eyes closed and their lips met, tentatively, tenderly. They parted and her head fell to this shoulder. She began sobbing. "I feel so guilty."

"There's nothing to be ashamed of." He raised her head and dabbed her cheeks. He smiled kindly and kissed away the last tears.

CHAPTER 70

Senator Hubert Humphrey's administrative assistant knocked on his office door. She opened it tentatively. The senator was meeting with legislative staffers. "I'm sorry to disturb you, Senator. There's a man outside. He doesn't have an appointment. I told him he can't see you without one, but," she shrugged apologetically, "he says it's an emergency and he insists you'll want to see him."

"How does he know that?"

"I don't know. He said I should remind you of the flares in Korea."

The senator's round face reflected momentary bafflement, then it lighted in recollection. "Send him in." He was grinning widely. "Gentlemen," he said to his staffers, "please excuse me. The man was right. I do want to see him. We'll finish later."

Jeff and Senator Humphrey shook hands exuberantly. The senator clasped Jeff's forearm.

"It's good to see you, Mr...."

"Zink. Jeff Zink."

"Oh, yes, forgive me, Jeff. Usually I'm very good with names."

"I'm hardly offended, sir. I couldn't blame you for wanting to forget my name."

"Nonsense. That was one heck of an adventure. I'll never forget it. It wasn't your everyday jeep ride." He laughed. "Sit down, Jeff. You look prosperous. Not quite as, shall we say, disarrayed and dusty as when we parted. But," the senator teased, "what made you think I'd want to see you?"

"Unquenchable curiosity."

Senator Humphrey chuckled. "Nicely put. Well, what brings you to my door? For that matter, where are you coming from? D.C.? Are you looking for a job?"

"I need help."

The senator smiled. "Why didn't you call beforehand?"

"I'm not a constituent. You're a very busy man. I didn't know if I could get an appointment."

"So you flew down here."

"Right."

"I like moxie. How can I help?"

"By cutting some red tape."

"A specialty of mine."

"I was hoping it would be."

"What kind of tape?"

"Immigration. I want to go back to Korea. There's a woman there, Korean. I want to marry her and bring her back. I want to do that very soon, soonest. The Immigration and Naturalization Service has procedures which they say must be followed and which consume considerable time."

"I see."

"I'm trying to correct one of the biggest – no, make that *the* biggest – mistake I ever made." Jeff sighed and pursed his lips. "I mean that, sir."

"I meant what I said, too. Cutting red tape is a Humphrey specialty. And one I roundly enjoy. I also happen to believe that mistakes should be corrected. Too often they aren't. Besides, I still owe you one."

"Whew." Jeff felt an immense wave of relief. "Thanks, sir. Thank you very much. I guess I don't have to tell you I'm totally grateful and relieved."

"No, you don't, but it's nice to hear nevertheless."

"Where do we start?"

"With plane reservations. Why don't you make some?"

CHAPTER 71

"Happy New Year!"

"You've already said that," Helen answered, smiling widely. "Several times, in fact."

"Can't hurt to say it again," Roger said lightly.

"True. And it's nice hearing you say it. But I think I could use another day to get ready to face the horde again."

It was January 1970, the first day of school after Christmas vacation. Helen and Roger were in their bedroom, she dressing, he watching from his wheelchair.

"You're more than ready. It's been a nice vacation."

"One of the nicest." She bent down and they kissed. She finished dressing, humming as she buttoned her blouse and zipped her skirt. "The cheerleaders are going to do the new routine I choreographed for them at the game tomorrow night. Would you like to come?"

"Sure."

"Great! Central Gym should be jammed."

Helen was happy. Unexpectedly, Roger had been in high spirits during the holiday break. His cheery mood contrasted sharply with the moroseness in which he had wallowed in recent months. During that time, Helen had had to come home from school every lunch hour to help him in the bathroom. It was the severest blow yet to his dignity. Helen had become as much a mother as a wife. For Roger it was degrading and demoralizing.

But things had changed remarkably during the last two weeks. Roger had shown renewed interest in Helen's work. He had asked how she was progressing with a dyslexic student in one of her English classes. He also had asked about his former teaching and coaching colleagues. When Helen had suggested a couple of them might like to visit, he welcomed the idea.

Roger's surprising turnabout had elevated Helen's morale to its highest level in months. It felt good to feel good.

Helen left the bedroom and walked across the living room to the coat closet. Roger followed in his wheelchair. As she slipped into her coat, he held the right sleeve.

"Thanks, honey," she smiled.

"You're welcome."

"Is there anything I can get you today?"

"Umm, no, I don't think so."

"Okay, I'll see you at lunch. Okay?"

"I'll be looking for you."

They kissed and smiled. Helen walked through the kitchen and out into the attached garage. Roger wheeled himself to the living room picture window. He watched as Helen backed into the street. She waved lovingly and Roger waved back. Her car passed from sight.

Roger sighed shallowly and slumped forward, catching his forehead in his hands. He tried to breathe deeply; it was difficult. He was exhausted and felt empty.

Slowly, laboriously, he pivoted and wheeled the chair across the living room. He steered toward the hallway that led to the bedrooms. At the end of the hallway he carefully guided the chair into the bathroom.

The last two weeks had been an unprecedented strain. His forced gaiety had sapped him. He felt he had owed it to Helen. She had uncomplainingly tolerated his crankiness and pettiness. Somehow she always had managed to swallow her hurt or bite off her anger before it burst forth. She deserved so much more than he could give her.

He sighed. I cannot – will not – put Helen in a position to blame herself. After all, none of this was her fault. MS. Was it a stroke of genetic bad luck or a freak viral mishap? Who knows? Who cares? What difference does it make?

To Roger everything now seemed so heavy yet so empty, impossible but unimportant. He straightened in the chair and stretched upward. He opened the medicine cabinet above the sink. He reached for a bottle.

I want Helen's last memories of us to be happy ones, Roger thought sadly. If they are, maybe she won't blame herself so much. I don't want that. The trouble is, there's nothing else I want. And why should I? I can't do anything. I'm a prisoner in my own body. It's like a dungeon. This chair is a prison cell. There are no bars but there's no way out. Nobody can say I didn't try. Try for years. But now I'm so tired. I'm so tired of fighting, of not giving in.

Roger looked at the bottle in his hand. She'll be upset, he knew. She'll cry. Maybe she'll be angry. But if she is, she'll get over it. If there's one thing for sure about Helen, she can't hold a grudge. Roger's melancholy had generated a comforting warmth. The sensation encouraged reverie. I'm making an old woman out of her. She doesn't deserve that. She's too young, and she's still so pretty. And loyal. She's stayed with me all the way. She deserves to be free. That's all I can give her now, freedom. She won't have to bathe me and dress me and help me in the bathroom. She won't have to worry about me. She'll be free of all that. Love. If it means giving as well as receiving, I don't have anything left to give. Nothing except freedom.

Roger opened the bottle and poured some of the pills into his hand. He paused, then emptied the bottle into his cupped palm. I'll need water, he thought. I could never take all these dry. I'd choke. He smiled sadly at the irony. He turned on the water and filled a plastic cup. He swallowed all the pills, filling the cup a second time, then backed out of the bathroom and wheeled into the bedroom. With every remaining ounce of strength he could muster, Roger struggled from the chair and lay on the bed. He sighed and closed his eyes.

CHAPTER 72

The baby opened its eyes. They were dark brown, bright and clear. Natalie, in her maternity ward bed, smiled as she cradled the newborn girl. She maneuvered so the infant could nurse from her breast. The tiny being nuzzled her mother and began to suck ravenously. Natalie beamed. "There'll be time enough," she whispered tenderly, "for you to learn not to rush through your meals."

Natalie had named the baby Victoria because she liked the name and it made sense. Victoria was her triumph. Yes, she had conceived and carried Victoria outside wedlock, and that was nothing to be proud of. A bastard. The word shook her. But she had forsaken an abortion and she was proud of that. And grateful. It would have been so quick and so easy to destroy this beautiful being. A brief visit to a doctor.

Evan's name was on the birth certificate as the father, but the baby was recorded as Victoria Santiago. The idea that Victoria might bear the name of the man who first fathered and then wanted to destroy her repulsed Natalie. She considered the complications her decision might someday pose for Victoria but dismissed them as distant and manageable.

The door to her room opened slowly. Dick Lawrence eased his way in. "Oh," he said, startled to see Natalie nursing her baby. "I'll wait outside."

"No, you will not," Natalie objected, a teasing smile betraying her deep affection for this visitor. "I am now a mother, Mr. Lawrence, and what I am doing is nothing to be ashamed of or for you to be embarrassed by. So there."

"Uh-huh," Dick mumbled dubiously.

"Granted, I would not do this in a classroom in front of my students. But I will do it now and you will watch and not be embarrassed and you will talk to me."

Dick chuckled. "I guess there's no need to ask if mother and child are doing well."

"Indisputably, Mr. Lawrence." Natalie smiled and sighed joyfully. She eyed Dick. A puckish smile played on her lips. "*Are* you embarrassed?"

"No, not now. In fact, I'm...entranced. You and the baby make a beautiful picture."

"Is that why you brought the camera?"

"You two make a photogenic pair." A pause. "I have news."

"What?"

"Promise you won't say anything to your mom and dad?"

Natalie's brow wrinkled in puzzlement. "Sure. What is it?"

"Well, I'm thinking again of going back to Korea."

"To see Miss Lee?" He nodded. "Wow, that's terrific. I mean, absolutely marvelous. You should, you really should. But why keep it a secret?"

"I don't want your folks to worry. Your dad's not back at full strength. Close, but not quite. If I told them, they'd pester me to go now. I want to wait until your dad's fully recovered, and that shouldn't be much longer. So will you keep it between us?"

"Sure, but it won't be easy." Natalie felt pleased and privileged that this man she had idolized for much of her life had confided in her. "I want you to go back as much as they do. But," she pressed her fingers to her lips, holding them there as she mumbled playfully, "your secret is safe."

Victoria seemed to slurp her concurrence. Dick and Natalie smiled as they watched the baby resume sucking, then grow drowsy and drift toward sleep.

Miss Lee stopped typing. She smiled demurely as the new correspondent was introduced to her. They shook hands politely. Later, she surveyed the large office. They keep changing, she reflected. Every year we get a new sergeant and four new correspondents. We have a new group now. They are gentlemen.

Sometimes Miss Lee wondered about the ones who had departed. She liked to speculate on their circumstances, and she liked to think they were prosperous and happy.

When the current sergeant was newly arrived, he had asked Miss Lee for a date. Long ago she had decided never to date someone from the office. It would be awkward and could be messy. There was no future in it. Further, the sergeant was married. He didn't try to hide the fact. Nor did he portray himself as unhappily married. He simply was lonely and longing for female companionship. Miss Lee understood that and sympathized. He seemed a nice man, and she declined as gently as possible.

Miss Lee breathed deeply. Little in her life had changed, and she didn't expect it to. She resumed typing.

"Geez, are you sure you want to jog tonight?" Ben asked.

"Why not?" Barbara answered cheerfully.

"One good reason is that there's three inches of white stuff out there. And it's still coming down."

"Oh, don't be a sissy. It's barely freezing and there's no wind."

"My glasses'll get wet. I'll be the city's first jogger in need of a seeing eye dog."

"Wear a baseball cap," Barbara said. "The bill will keep your glasses dry."

"You really want to go out, don't you?"

"You can't stay in shape just being a fair-weather runner."

"I can if I just want to be in fair shape."

"Funneee. Look, if you get chilled running, I'll see that you get plenty warm when we get back. Get my drift?"

"As clearly as a snowball in the face. Let's start picking 'em up and laying 'em down."

They left their apartment and headed north and west toward Central Park. The fluffy snow scattered beneath their shoes. After a while, Ben began to feel sweat forming on his chest. They were chatting comfortably as they went loping through the park.

"You know," said Barbara, "I'm glad we went jogging tonight. I may not be able to much longer."

"What do you mean?"

"I went to the doctor today."

"Doctor? What for? What's wrong?" Alarm had formed quickly.

"Nothing. Nothing at all," Barbara said expressionlessly.

"I don't get it."

"I went to see a gynecologist. You're going to be a father."

Ben braked. "You're kidding? No, you're not kidding. My God, why are you jogging? You shouldn't be doing that. Should you?"

Barbara was beginning to laugh. Ben was looking intently at her. "You're a stitch," she smiled widely. "I'm barely along. I've got a while before I have to slow down. All I have to do is use a little common sense. I won't do anything foolish. Don't worry."

"Whew. How about that? Me, a father. You, a mother. Father and Mother Lawrence. Hot damn." He hugged Barbara, and as he did so the bill of his cap struck her forehead. He swiveled the cap sideways, stuck out his tongue in a silly face and embraced her. They laughed.

"Hey," she said, "you better turn your hat back or your glasses *will* get wet."

"Who cares? Hey, we'll have to think about names. We'll have to get furniture. We'll – hey, why didn't you tell me you were going to the doctor?"

"Simple. I wanted to be sure before I said anything, and I wanted to surprise you."

"Mission accomplished. Hah, what a night to remember. Think about it. This is probably a first, a certifiable first."

"Why?"

"I can't imagine another husband ever learning he was a father while jogging through the snow with his pregnant wife."

"I told you jogging was wonderful."

"It is," Ben said, affection pouring from his eyes. "And so are you."

Dick was silently shaking his head. His lips were pursed and his eyes closed. I'm beginning to think I should've been a doctor, he mused. I could never count the hours or the days I've spent in hospitals. Dad, Ann, John, Natalie, myself. And here I am again. I'll probably be in a hospital when my time comes. I hope John's tests are all negative.

John Santiago had felt chest pains the day before at work. Not debilitating pains, but sharp enough to cause alarm, especially with memories of his heart attack a year ago so clear and frightening.

The tests, in fact, did prove negative. No new heart attack. At least none that was detectable. Stress, the doctors said, was a likely diagnosis. Perhaps stress induced by worrying about recovering from his heart attack.

The negative test results brought immense relief to everyone. But the episode did mean disappointment for Dick. Once again he had delayed his return to Korea. Maybe, Dick reflected, Miss Lee had been right. Maybe we were just ships passing in the night. Maybe I should just forget about it. Hell, it's been over a year since I saw her anyway. And I'm tired of thinking about lost loves.

CHAPTER 73

The doorbell roused Dick from a nap. He rose quickly and hurried across his living room. He pulled open the door. Natalie was holding Victoria to her chest and precariously grasping an umbrella that shielded them from a pelting rain.

"Come in, come in," said Dick. "Here, let me take that." He took the umbrella and collapsed it as Natalie stepped inside.

"Thanks."

"Let me hold Vickie while you get out of your coat. Just hang it in the closet."

"It's dripping wet."

"Aah, that's all right. Of all days for it to rain. Just when two of my favorite ladies come calling." As Dick spoke his eyes were riveted on the tiny, smiling visage peering up at him from the cradle of his own arms. "A few drops of water won't matter. How many times did you ring before I answered? I was dozing."

"Just a couple. I hope you don't mind that I invited myself over. I mean, I hope I didn't ruin any of your plans."

"What plans? I wasn't going anywhere in this rain. Want some coffee?"

"No, thanks. Sure you don't want me to take Vickie?"

"I'll hold her and listen. You talk."

"Okay...except I'm not quite sure how to begin."

"Anywhere's fine. Even if you start at the end, we'll eventually get around to the beginning."

"Okay, here goes." A pause. "This won't be easy."

"No one's grading you."

"Dick, I need a change of scenery..."

"Uh-huh. Go on."

"I feel like I need to get away. I guess I need to be just another face in the crowd. You know what I mean?" He nodded. "Here in LA I feel like I'm on a stage and the whole audience is looking at me. There's nowhere to hide. Do you understand?"

"Do I? Do I ever." A knowing smile. "You're feeling the same thing I felt when I got back to Shelby after World War II. It's what drove me to California."

"Yes, but Shelby was so small. It seems silly to feel like this in LA. It's so big anybody should be able to hide. And don't get me wrong. I love California."

"I loved Shelby. Still do."

"But you had to get away."

"Exactly. I felt caged. And I don't think the size of the town has much to do with it."

Natalie heaved a palpable sigh of relief. She had come hoping for understanding but not expecting empathy. "I don't know how long I need to be away. I just need to be where I won't be noticed. Where people won't ask me questions."

"Where would you go?"

"New York. Kate has been after me to visit for a long time. I know I'd be welcome. And Vickie too, of course."

Victoria was sleeping beatifically in Dick's arms.

"And after you get there? Do you have plans?"

"Sort of. I'd like to find a teaching job, either in high school or college. I don't want to be a leech on Kate and Jake, and I don't want Dad to go on supporting me forever."

Dick had been speaking quietly and calmly. His next words were nearly a whisper. "Have you seen Evan?"

"No. Not once. He hasn't even called." A glint of anger began to flash in her eyes. "I just don't-"

"He called me at the office."

Natalie's eyes widened. "When? How many times?"

"Once. Soon after you went home from the hospital."

"What did he say?" Anger still was tightening her face, but curiosity was beginning to soften her features.

"He wanted to know how you and Vickie were doing."

"That's all? Nothing else?"

"No. It was a very brief conversation. Just a few questions."

"What did you tell him?"

"Not much. I just answered his questions."

"I still don't believe what's happened. Oh, that's not true. But it was all such a shock. I never dreamed he would be so dishonorable. I thought I knew him better than that. For a while it made me think I couldn't trust anyone."

"Sometimes you know someone for a long time and never know them at all," said Dick. "Perhaps because they lie to you or omit something or maybe because they just never open up. It hurts."

"In a way, maybe I was lucky. I mean that I learned about him before we married."

"Agreed."

"You really haven't said what you think about me going to New York."

"You haven't talked to your mom and dad about this, have you?"

"Not yet. I guess I wanted to hear someone say it was a good idea before I told Mom and Dad. You still haven't told me how you feel."

"I know."

"And you won't."

"You've got to make the decision. When I left Shelby, it seemed like the right decision."

"And now?"

"Still does."

"Mom and Dad have been wonderful. Through this whole mess. I certainly don't want to hurt them. Especially Dad with his heart. I could never forgive myself if...This is my home and I love it. I used to say I'd never leave. I certainly never thought I'd *want* to leave."

"There's no mystery about it. You have a lovely child and loving parents and lots of friends. But, let's face it, you've had a lousy experience. Lots of stress. A change of scenery may be just what you need. Now, if you *do* leave, that's not the same as saying you'll never come back. Frankly, I hope you would. I'd miss you – and Vickie."

"I'd miss you too. Everybody. Do you think Mom and Dad will feel that way? The way you put it?"

"You tell them everything you've told me, and I think they'll understand. And it'll help for them to know you'll be with Kate and Jake."

"I'm glad I came over."

"Me too. Just remember, this *is* your home. You'll always be welcome."

Natalie spoke softly, almost sadly. "Tom Wolfe said you can't go home again."

"Bullshit."

CHAPTER 74

In September 1970, Sarah Lawrence was born. Ben and Barbara named her after Edward's first wife. Although she had died in 1936, nine years before Ben was born, she had not been forgotten.

The desire to name their first daughter Sarah caused Ben some anxiety. He was concerned that the choice might hurt Harriet. Barbara urged him to call Harriet and sound her out. He did – to his great relief and delight. Harriet thought Sarah the perfect choice. Edward, she told Ben, would have been proud and touched beyond words.

Little Sarah was a beacon of joy and contentment, but Barbara had not changed her mind about wanting to be more than a full-time mother. As soon as I'm strong enough and confident that Sarah can be left with a babysitter, she told Ben, I'll begin searching for work.

In the matter of finding a babysitter, the Lawrences were lucky. One found them. Mrs. Anne Stock, age 60 and a widow for three years, offered her services. Even luckier for the Lawrences, they knew Mrs. Stock; she lived on the same floor in their apartment building. She was intelligent, vibrant, tall, gray and striking. Although comfortable financially, she worked part-time as a clerk at Bloomingdale's, her first job ever. She was convinced that working helped keep her young in attitude, she joked, if not in appearance. "It's a good thing wrinkles don't cause pain," she was fond of saying.

To babysit for Sarah, she would not give up her job at Bloomingdale's; she would rearrange her schedule, working evenings and weekends. She was sure the store would accommodate her. After all, she was reliable and a good sales clerk. Only with great reluctance did Mrs. Stock agree to accept payment for the babysitting.

Within six weeks after Sarah's birth, life was settling into a pleasant routine. Each morning Ben left the apartment for Burson-Marsteller at 83rd and Third Avenue. Each evening he hurried home, eager to see wife and daughter. Later in the evenings Ben and Barbara jogged - together when Mrs. Stock was available to watch Sarah, otherwise separately. Within two months after Sarah's birth, Barbara was looking and feeling as fit as ever. The Lawrences were a happy family.

By now, Natalie and Vickie had their own apartment. They had lived with Kate and Jake until Natalie had found a job teaching freshman English at New York University. Kate and Jake had been more than happy to house Natalie and Vickie in their small apartment, but all were relieved when Natalie moved to her own place.

Natalie also had found an older woman, Mrs. Anita Coyle, to babysit for Vickie during the day. When Natalie had to get out by herself at night or on weekends, she could count on Kate to watch Vickie. Kate lived just two blocks away and adored her little niece.

Natalie's move to New York had been as therapeutic as she had hoped. She reveled in her anonymity and independence. She enjoyed living in her own small apartment. Still, Natalie didn't view New York as a permanent home. One day I'll return to California. I'm not sure when but I will. I want Vickie to grow up there. It doesn't matter now, but when Vickie is older, I want her to grow up with the same sunshine, mountains and beaches that meant so much to me. I also want her to grow up near her grandparents. For now, though, I feel content.

CHAPTER 75

By mid afternoon the sun was disappearing behind the walls of Manhattan's canyons. Christmas 1970 was only a week away. New York glittered with decorations. Skaters glided over – and sometimes fell on – the ice at the Central Park and Rockefeller Center rinks. Happy crowds thronged to holiday shows at Radio City Music Hall. Shoppers with colorful, bulging bags scurried from store to store. Often they paused to ogle enchanting window displays. It was a time of anticipation, planning and partying.

Ben was naked and Barbara wore only panties. They were in their bedroom.

"I'm sure glad our Christmas shopping is done," Ben said, pulling on a jock strap. "I'll bet the stores are jammed tonight." It was Friday, December 18.

"We still have all the gifts to wrap," Barbara responded, pulling on sweat pants over white tube socks. "We can get started when we get back."

"Okay," Ben said agreeably, pulling a navy blue sweatshirt down over his head. "But you know I won't be much help. I never could wrap a package that didn't look like it had fallen off a truck."

Barbara smiled. "You can put your finger on the ribbon while I tie the knots."

"That's about all-"

The phone rang. Barbara picked up the bedroom extension. "The Lawrences."

"It's me," said Mrs. Stock.

"Oh, hi."

"Hello, dear. I'm not feeling well and I don't think I should come over tonight. It might be nothing, but I don't want to expose little Sarah, especially just before the holidays. I wouldn't forgive myself if she caught something from me and it ruined your holiday season. I'm very sorry."

"Oh, don't worry, Mrs. Stock. We'll just jog separately. The important thing is, are you okay?"

"My throat is scratchy and I feel a bit feverish. Perhaps I'm just over-tired."

"You need to take care of yourself. Your children and grandchildren want you healthy for the holidays. Is there anything I can do for you?"

"No, dear, I don't think so. Thank you."

"You're welcome. I'll call you in the morning to see how you're doing."

"Thank you, dear."

"Good night."

"Good night."

Barbara put the phone down. "I guess you got the gist of that."

"Yeah. What's the matter?"

"Fever and sore throat. She's worried she'll expose Sarah to something serious."

"No one's more thoughtful than Mrs. Stock."

"For sure. Well," said Barbara, "who goes first?"

"Doesn't matter to me."

"In that case, I will. That way I can shower and get the paper and ribbon and stuff out while you're out."

"Sounds good."

That same evening, nearby, Natalie was bundling up Vickie. She would drop her off at Kate and Jake's and go Christmas shopping. She had been woefully late getting started, and now she would have to rush to complete the task. She was fretting that pickings would be slim in shopped-out stores.

She looked at the small artificial Christmas tree she had bought and decorated. Already under it were packages mailed early from California by her sisters, Jeannie Marie and Ruth. Nothing from Evan. Not even a card. A twinge of hurt and longing started to invade. She forced it down by concentrating on happier thoughts. John and Maria were flying to NewYork early next week. They would stay through Christmas Eve with Kate, Jake, Natalie and Vickie and then fly home Christmas Day to be with

Jeannie Marie and Ruth and their families. Natalie put on her boots, coat, hat and gloves, scooped up Vickie and hurried out.

In the darkness Barbara was smiling. As she jogged west along the south shore of the large pond in Central Park, she let her mind drift to the upcoming visit to Shelby. She thought of her parents and how happy they would be to hold Sarah for the first time.

Now Barbara was jogging north along the pond's west shore. A lone jogger, a man, passed, heading south. They nodded to each other. It would be so good, Barbara thought exultantly, to be with family and friends. I can't wait to show off Sarah. And the simple things, helping mom in the kitchen, sitting up late at night, sipping steaming coffee, talking about old times.

Barbara turned east. She was approaching the halfway point along the north shore. Then, in the narrowest shred of time, her world turned upside down. Her attacker had been crouching behind a bush. He sprang at her from her left and slightly to her rear. Lost in blissful reverie, Barbara neither saw nor heard his lunge. She felt a massive blow against her shoulder and back. Her legs collapsed. Strong arms pinned her own arms as she went crashing to the earth.

In those first bewildering milliseconds she was aware only of the arms around her and the frozen ground. She felt neither pain nor fear. Then, as the initial shock dissipated, Barbara realized she was in danger. Paralyzing fear went rippling outward from the pit of her stomach. She tried to ward off encroaching panic, commanding herself to think, think, think. In an attempt to shed her clinging attacker, Barbara drew up her knees and rolled fast and hard from her side to her stomach. She felt the foreign arms loosen and slip away. Without so much as a glance at the attacker, she began rising to her feet. A hand grabbed the hood of her heavy sweat jacket and jerked her down. As Barbara spun to free herself, a fist slammed into her left jaw, snapping her head against the frozen earth and dazing her.

Natalie was entering Saks Fifth Avenue. The gaily decorated store was jammed. Natalie smiled faintly. I'm late getting started but hardly alone. She pulled off her gloves and stuffed them into her coat pockets. She fished in her purse for her shopping list. It seemed dismayingly long. In the packed aisles and near cash registers, progress would be slow. Natalie pursed her lips and shrugged. She had run out of time. Besides, Vickie was staying the night with Kate and Jake, so she didn't have to hurry. She plunged into the crowd and headed toward women's apparel.

As Barbara regained her senses, her eyes were focusing on the blade of a long knife. The point was only inches from her nose. The night was dark, but her eyes had adjusted and she had no difficulty making out the assailant's features. A dimpled chin. Light eyes. A bushy mustache. Thin eyebrows. Thin nose. An unblemished complexion. His teeth were not visible behind clamped lips. A brown stocking cap hid much of his forehead and the tops of his ears. He wore a faded Army field jacket.

"You say anything, you even think of saying anything, and I'll cut your fucking throat." The voice was a controlled, thick growl. The words were enunciated precisely. "Understand?"

Barbara blinked and nodded. She was terrified. Her escape attempt had failed. Her mouth was dry. The first thought to take shape in Barbara's mind was a question: Why me? I don't have any money on me. He should know joggers don't carry money. Rape. Stabbed. My warm blood running onto frozen ground. She heard herself whimper, and the pathetic sound magnified her dread.

"Shut up," the voice rasped. "I said I'd cut your throat and I mean it. You whoring slut. Lay still and don't move."

Where were they? Barbara wondered frantically. The darkness here was deeper than along the path. Instinctively she knew she dared not let her eyes wander. There must be no indication that her mind was again beginning to function. He's pulled me off the path, she realized. Into a grove of trees and shrubs.

The man was astride her knees. His left hand was groping the elastic waistband of the gym shorts Barbara wore over the sweat pants. He began to tug. The knife still was poised over her face.

In the next instant, inexplicably, all trace of panic dissipated. Her helpless dread was supplanted by an unprecedented calm. Never had she more control over her thoughts. Never had she seen things more clearly. Barbara knew she wanted to live. For Ben, for Sarah, for herself.

Moreover, she knew she wanted to live without the haunting memory of having been defiled. Barbara knew she had to act.

Natalie was looking at sweaters, hunting for one for Kate. A few feet away a man and a woman were discussing a sweater. Something about them caught and held Natalie's attention. Mere fascination? Unfounded curiosity? At first she didn't know. She could see little of the man's face. He was tall. His hair was sandy. He wore glasses. Even wearing a winter coat, Natalie could see he was slender. The woman wasn't facing Natalie, but more of her profile was visible. Her hair was black and her skin darker hued than the man's. As the woman turned to replace the sweater on the shelf, Natalie could see she was Asian. "How about this one," the woman said, picking up a second sweater. The man turned.

Natalie's heart fluttered. Her eyes narrowed. Could it be? I don't want to say anything unless I'm sure. Maybe I should just walk away. It would be awfully embarrassing if I'm wrong. Aware she was staring, Natalie averted her eyes. This is terrible. What if I'm right? I might never have this opportunity again. The couple turned away, once more studying a sweater. Slowly Natalie edged toward them. Lightly, she tapped the man on the back.

"Jeff?" she said softly.

The man turned. Momentarily, his face was blank. Then the dawn of recognition. In the middle of the crowded store, he cried, "Nat! Nat!"

"Jeff!" she squealed. "Jeff!"

With nearby shoppers gawking at them, Natalie and Jeff hugged and patted each other's backs.

"I don't believe it," Jeff said. "What are you doing here? I mean, I know you're shopping. But what are you doing in New York?"

Natalie told him, after being introduced to Jeff's Korean wife, Suni. They talked quietly but animatedly for several minutes and then both agreed they had better continue with their shopping.

"Give me your phone number," Jeff said. "I'll give you a call and we'll get together."

"Okay," Natalie said. "That would be nice." She wrote her phone number on the back of one of Jeff's business cards. As she handed it to him, she doubted whether she ever again would hear from him. Not that she doubted

Jeff's sincerity. It's just that sincerity so often is transitory, the product of unforeseen emotional waves instead of steadfast resolve. Even so, she was glad she had acted on her impulse. It had been a precious moment she would long remember. It was one more benefit of her move to New York.

"It's been so nice to meet you," Suni said, smiling warmly.

"Same here," said Natalie.

"Have a Merry Christmas," Jeff said, still grinning happily, "and we'll see you soon."

Barbara's eyes and her attacker's still were locked on each other's. When he shifted his gaze to where he was tugging at the gym shorts and maneuvered to give himself more space to pull, Barbara acted. With all the force she could generate, Barbara drove her right knee upward and into the attacker's genitals. He bellowed and began toppling forward and to her right side. Nausea was spreading through his lower abdomen. Before his torso struck the ground, Barbara was rolling quickly the opposite way. She scrambled to her feet. Her eyes darted, searching for an escape route through the surrounding trees and shrubs. She could hear the attacker moaning and cursing her. She saw an opening and dashed through. The attacker suppressed the throbbing ache in his testicles, rose unsteadily and stumbled in chase. At the path, Barbara hesitated. Which way? Then decision. What does it matter? She began sprinting down the path. She could hear the footfalls of her pursuer. She glanced over her shoulder. In the dim light she could see blasts of frozen breath rhythmically obscuring his face. He was 30 yards behind Barbara. I'm probably not as fast as he is, she thought, but maybe I can outdistance him. She glanced back again. No, she reconsidered, he's too fast. I have to keep sprinting and hope someone sees us or I make it out of the park before he catches me. She dug deep within herself for extra speed, and momentarily the gap widened. Barbara now had her bearings. She was running east toward Fifth Avenue.

Then the gap began to close. She could hear his labored breathing. Her own lungs were on fire. Her legs were getting heavy. Both runners had slowed, but still he came closer.

Then hope. Barbara could see the lights of Fifth Avenue. Surely now the attacker would give up his hateful pursuit. He didn't. Barbara had been sprinting for about a quarter mile. Her lungs ached until she was on the verge of tears. Her legs were turning rubbery. God, she pleaded, give me strength. Please. Now she could see the street. Keep going, she commanded herself, keep going. The assailant had closed to just 10 feet. Barbara reached the sidewalk. The attacker knew now he couldn't catch her without being seen or possibly apprehended. In all-consuming anger and frustration he lunged and screamed "Bitch!"

His scream startled Barbara. Was he throwing the knife? She didn't dare look back. He was too close. Across the sidewalk Barbara lunged between a parked car and a beige rusting van. Headlights blinded her. She threw up her arms against the glare.

Her fleeting thought was of hope, hope that she had escaped her pursuer and hope that if he had thrown the knife it would miss. Then everything went black. Her body went hurtling through the air like a rag doll and then went rolling across the pavement.

CHAPTER 76

The phone was ringing when Natalie entered the apartment. It was early afternoon on New Year's Eve, a Thursday. She was just returning from Kate's place where they had lunched together and reminisced about their parents' recent visit. Natalie, still clutching Vickie, threw her keys on a small table and hurried to the phone.

"Hello," she said.

"You sound out of breath."

"Who is this?"

"Jeff."

"Jeff?"

"You've bruised my ego. Jeff Zink."

"Oh, Jeff! I'm sorry." Her apology was genuine. "I wasn't expecting to hear from you. I mean, you said you'd call, but I didn't think it would be so soon."

"Yeah, well, it seemed like a good time to call. Listen, what are you doing for dinner tomorrow night?"

"Tomorrow? Tomorrow's New Year's."

"Very good, Natalie," the voice teased. "You've looked at the calendar. But no matter what day it is, you've got to eat."

Natalie laughed. "I'm not doing anything."

"Now you are. Can you make it at seven?"

"Yes. Yes, I'd love to make it at seven."

"Bring your daughter if you'd like. Suni and I would like to meet her."

"Okay."

Natalie pressed the buzzer in the lobby of the apartment building at 135 East 71st Street. Jeff's voice crackled through the speaker. "Natalie?"

"And Vickie."

"Great! Come on up."

The meal was exquisite. Suni had labored long to prepare a multi-course Korean feast. The dinner conversation had been tentative at first, focusing on Vickie, then grew more candid. Jeff talked openly about meeting Suni, leaving her behind, seeking Senator Humphrey's help and returning for her. The saga thrilled and uplifted Natalie and heightened immeasurably her regard for Jeff.

Eventually Natalie felt comfortable enough to sketch her relationship with Evan, her pregnancy, her decision to come to New York. At first, she skipped over Evan's urging her to get an abortion, saying merely that their relationship had soured. But later in the conversation she decided to tell Jeff and Suni. When Natalie concluded, Jeff smiled. "It's obvious to me you made the right choice. In fact, I can't imagine you making any other one." Then he gazed affectionately at Vickie, who was sleeping on the living room floor on a makeshift pallet of sheets and blankets.

"I agree," Suni said quietly. "Vickie is your treasure."

Natalie smiled her agreement. "Suni," she said, "you cooked a terrific dinner. It was absolutely delectable."

"Thank you. I was going to cook American food, but Jeff said this was a special night and I should cook something special."

Jeff blushed.

"It was certainly special, Suni. It's obvious to me that Jeff is a lucky man."

"Oh, geez," Jeff moaned, the red in his cheeks burning brighter, "spare me. Please."

"I'm surprised you called me," said Natalie. "You know what they say about the best of intentions."

"Don't I though? I'm truly an expert. People all the time are saying I'll call you and don't. They mean well. They just don't mean deeply enough. I was that way once. Believe me. Now I try not to skip opportunities that might never come around again."

"I know what you mean. Last week in Saks I almost didn't say hi to you. But I knew I might never have another chance."

Jeff decided this was the time to change subjects. He girded himself. "Do you know Ben lives here in New York? And that we work at the same place?"

"Yes. His brother told me."

"Right. Dick. Do you know Ben lives on this street? Just two blocks down?"

"No. No, I didn't."

"Did you know he was married?"

"Yes. My sister Kate once met his wife in Shelby."

Jeff was silent a moment. "Did you know that his wife is in the hospital?"

"No." Concern immediately compressed Natalie's brow. "What's wrong?"

"She – Barbara – was out jogging," said Jeff. "A few days before Christmas. She was hit by a bus."

"Oh, my God. The poor thing." Her head bowed and shook. "Oh, and Ben."

"They have a baby."

"Oh, no," Natalie whispered.

For a moment, no one said anything. Then Jeff spoke. "Nobody's sure how it happened. The bus driver said that all of a sudden she was coming at him. He didn't have time to swerve or stop. Passengers verified his story. It's

537

a mystery. She had been jogging for a long time. Fortunately the bus was just pulling away from a stop, and she ran into the side of it. She's in a coma."

"How's Ben?" Natalie whispered.

"He's holding together. It hasn't been easy. Dick came in. He's still here."

"Oh, God. Why didn't I hear?" said Natalie. "I mean, from Dick or my parents?"

Jeff nodded. "Dick decided not to say anything to your parents or anyone else before Christmas ended. Didn't want to upset them. Your parents know now. Dick phoned them back in California. He told them he would tell you, but then I asked him if I could."

Natalie whispered, "Thank you."

Jeff shrugged.

"What's Ben doing now? Who's caring for the baby? What's her name?"

"Sarah," said Jeff. "Beautiful baby. Dick is with Ben now. After Dick leaves, a neighbor lady will see that Sarah is well cared for. Her name is Mrs. Stock. She's very close to Ben and Barb and already was watching Sarah a lot."

"Kate met Barb once in Shelby and said she's really nice."

"Does Ben know you're in New York?" said Jeff.

"I think so. Maybe Dick has told him."

"Do you want him to know I've seen you?"

Natalie's eyes closed. Her head lowered. Her right hand rubbed her forehead and cheek. "I don't think so. Not now. I don't think it would do any good." She looked up, eyes seeking confirmation. "Do you understand?"

Jeff nodded.

Natalie reached for a tissue and dabbed at her eyes. "I'm glad you told me."

CHAPTER 77

Ben hung up the telephone in his office. He blew out a deep breath and rotated his head to relieve the stiffness in his neck.

Jeff was watching from the doorway. "What's the matter?"

"Oh, nothing much. Just a client who wants to be reassured that the ice isn't slippery."

Jeff laughed wryly. "Same old stuff."

"Yeah. This client's CEO would like to be on the cover of *Fortune* but without so much as granting an interview. He wants questions submitted that he can dictate the answers to. Can you believe it? I mean, here's a guy who knows there's no reward without risk, but when it comes to media relations he wants to change the rules."

"You set him straight?"

"I don't know. Maybe I should ask Mr. Burson to call him. I told his PR guy but I'm not sure he heard me – or wanted to hear me. I know he doesn't want to tell his CEO what I told him."

"Well, hey, come on. Let's pack it in for the day."

Ben glanced at his watch. It was nearly 5:30. "Yeah, I guess so. I'm ready to get home to Sarah anyway. More than ready. Then to the hospital to see Barb."

"Bus or subway?" Jeff asked as they stepped outside onto Third Avenue.

"You up for walking?"

"Sure."

It was an unseasonably warm early March evening as they started south. The walk would cover some 14 blocks. Jeff let Ben set the pace. Jeff was smiling inside; they were virtually crawling by the standards of New York's scurrying pedestrians. He glanced at Ben and saw that he was oblivious to the multitudes streaming by in both directions.

"I'm having a will drawn up."

"Uh-huh." Jeff nearly found himself responding with a mindless *That's smart because you never know.* But he thought of Barbara and bit his tongue.

"That's something, isn't it?" said Ben. "I'm only twenty-six and I'm having a will made."

"Lots of people have wills," Jeff said. Self-conscious now, Jeff was striving mightily to voice only the most neutral thoughts. He didn't want to say anything that would distress his friend.

"Well, it seems like the right thing to do," Ben said pensively. "Not knowing if Barb…In case something ever happens to me. You never know. It's not that I have much money to worry about. But if anything ever does happen to me, I want to be sure Sarah is cared for the way I want. I don't want to leave anything to chance."

"Don't blame you."

"Right. Well, uh, I have a favor to ask."

"Anything. Just name it."

"Well, in the will, would you and Suni be willing to be named as Sarah's guardians? And trustees? I'm having a trust included in the will."

"I'd be honored. And I know Suni would too."

"Thanks. I appreciate it."

"You sure you want us? I mean, we don't have any experience as parents yet."

"I'm not worried about that. You two are my best friends. I know you'd take the best possible care of Sarah. I trust your judgment."

"I've been thinking," Natalie said, sipping a Coca Cola.

"About what?" Kate responded, laboring over an ironing board.

"Going home."

"Mmm." Kate pushed a loose lock of hair away from her forehead. "Let me have a sip of that." She held out her hand and Natalie placed the chilled Coke bottle in it. She raised the bottle to her mouth and swallowed. "For a visit?"

"For good."

"Oh."

"It's not that I dislike New York. In fact, I like it." Vickie toddled by unsteadily, dragging a small wagon loaded with wooden alphabet blocks. "But California is home. It's where I want to be. It's where I want to raise Vickie."

"I see."

"This year has been good for me. It was just what I needed. And you and Jake have been great to us. I'll never be able to thank you."

"Oh, pooh. What are sisters for?"

"I know. But you went way beyond any sisterly duty. Sharing your apartment. Babysitting. Helping a zillion ways."

"We wanted to." Kate reached for a stack of Jake's handkerchiefs.

"I knew when I came here that I'd go back sooner or later."

"Right." Kate finished pressing the first of the handkerchiefs. Her movements with the hissing iron were swift and efficient. "Are you really ready to go back?"

"Meaning?"

"Well, are you going back because you want to or because you want to leave?"

"Maybe...maybe a little of both."

"That's understandable. Look, you know I'd never pry or say anything to hurt you on purpose."

"But?"

"Well, I know what happened to Ben's wife was a real shock. You've been, well, a little down since then."

"It's showed?"

"Like a slip two inches too long."

Natalie smiled, a bit forlornly. "When I heard about Barbara, it made me sick. Sick at heart. I never met her, but you did, and I know she must be very nice. I'd like to reach out and help Ben and his daughter, but I can't. I have no idea how he feels about me. If I ever did see him, I don't know what I'd say. It's been almost three years since I've seen him. So much has happened. So much has changed."

"When will you be going back?"

"Not until the end of the school year. I couldn't go before then. It wouldn't be fair to the school or my students."

"You might have some company."

"Huh?"

"Jake has a chance to do his residency in LA."

"You're kidding!" Natalie shrieked happily. "That's wonderful! Wow!"

"I think it's wow, too."

"Is he going to do it?"

"We're thinking about it. It would be nice to have the whole family together again."

"Oh, that would be terrific, absolutely terrific."

"Let's celebrate. For a possible homecoming. Just you and me. We deserve it. Jake can watch Vickie – he'd love that anyway – and we'll do the town. Dinner and a show."

"Terrif! When?"

"Just as soon as I check with Jake on his schedule."

"Let's go to an Italian restaurant and pig out on pasta," said Natalie.

"Okay," said Kate. "There's something else, too."

"What?"

"My period's late."

"Oh, my God! That's super fantastic."

"Jake and I are ready to have a baby. We wanted to get started a little earlier, but..." Kate shrugged. She knew Natalie was well aware of the pressures Jake faced as a medical student and an intern and how those pressures had worked on Kate.

"When will you know?"

"I have an appointment next week."

"I want to be the first to know. Well, second. I guess you *would* want to tell the daddy first."

Kate grinned. "You're right, but you'll be a close second."

CHAPTER 78

Since Barbara's accident and continuing hospitalization, Mrs. Stock had occupied a much larger place in Ben and Sarah's lives. It wasn't something she and Ben had worked out formally; it just happened. In some instances she offered assistance; in others she just stepped in and did. She cooked for Ben nearly every evening. At first he had to insist that she stay to join him. Now it was routine, save for those evenings when Mrs. Stock had other plans. And except for those evenings, she stayed on while Ben visited Barbara in the hospital.

Mrs. Stock was a delightful dinner companion, asking numerous, intelligent questions about Ben's work and voicing well-formed opinions on an impressive array of issues and events. She also shopped for groceries and diapers and helped with the laundry, ironing and cleaning.

Ben had long since ceased protesting. And he didn't take Mrs. Stock's attentiveness for granted. He bought her gifts whenever he sensed a need or desire. Mrs. Stock had become so integral a part of his life – and Sarah's – that he wondered often how he would have managed without her. The obvious answer: not nearly as well.

This evening – a fresh, warm Friday in late April – Ben helped Mrs. Stock clear the dinner table. She was thinking how nice a walk would be when she heard Ben saying, "Do you feel like getting out tonight, Mrs. Stock?"

"It *is* a lovely evening."

"Well," Ben said decisively, "let's take advantage of it. What do you say we forget the dishes and go for a walk? The three of us."

"You've been reading my mind," Mrs. Stock responded cheerfully. "Let's do it."

"Give me a few minutes to change out of my suit," said Ben.

"Okay, I'll go home and change into my walking shoes."

Ben held open the lobby door of the apartment building while Mrs. Stock pushed through the stroller carrying Sarah. Mild air scented with the newness of spring wafted gently from the west. Sarah was gurgling her contentment.

"I think she's telling her daddy this was a good idea," said Mrs. Stock. "I share her sentiments."

"It *must* have been a good idea for two women to agree with each other."

"Now, *that*," Mrs. Stock chided good-naturedly, "is the kind of comment that is making Betty Friedan and Gloria Steinem deservedly famous."

"Touché."

"I should think so."

The trio turned west on East 71st Street and crossed Second Avenue. East 71st was pleasantly residential. It was flanked on either side by a mix of high rises and older, more expensive and elegant four- and five-story brownstones and townhouses. Small trees lined both sidewalks, and near front doors and stairways were occasional clusters of shrubberies. Many first-floor windows sat above flower boxes ablaze with the petals of spring. Even to Ben, a product of a small town, East 71st seemed like a neighborhood.

Between Second and Third avenues, on the other side of the street was Marymount Manhattan College. Dominican Sisters administered the school. About a half block west of the college, on the same side of the street, Ben noticed a yellow cab pulling to the curb. He saw a young woman alight. She was medium height, with dark brown hair that hung below her shoulders. He couldn't see her face. Idly he watched as she reached through the open front passenger window to pay the cabbie. As she was putting change into her purse, the cab pulled away. She fished keys from her purse and turned and crossed the walk to the steps of a handsome townhouse. As she started to ascend, Ben saw a mustachioed man in a brown stocking cap and faded Army field jacket dart toward the woman from beside a beige rusting van.

He rushed up behind her and looped his left arm around her neck. The man started dragging the woman back toward the van. She was struggling, squirming and thrashing her arms but steadily losing ground.

Mrs. Stock had stopped the stroller and placed a hand on Ben's arm. Her eyes showed the horror that had chilled and stopped her. Ben looked around quickly. No one else could be seen on the street. He hesitated, and the pain of that hesitation was acute. His involvement would mean the threat of danger. He looked down at Sarah and pursed his lips. Was the man armed? Ben had seen no weapon. He glanced down at his daughter, cooingly oblivious to all but herself and these two trusted big people and the security of them and her stroller. Ben could see the flailing woman was desperate. Her assailant was winning the struggle, would win and she knew it. Ben heard no screams; the man must have had his hand over her mouth. Precious seconds were slipping by. Ben hated his indecision.

He removed Mrs. Stock's hand from his arm. With athletic quickness he raced across the street in front of the college. On the sidewalk he braked hard, pivoted and started running toward the attacker and his victim.

They couldn't have been more than 50 yards away. Yet, as Ben started sprinting toward them, the distance seemed to close with agonizing slowness, as though his flying feet were weighted with iron boots. The assailant had not yet seen him. He was wrenching the victim toward the van's open passenger door. Through a screened window in one of the townhouses, Ben heard an organ; incongruously, it was playing a happy tune. The attacker jerked the woman's head, and she saw Ben coming. Her eyes were bulging with the terror of the doomed. Then the attacker caught motion from the corner of his eye. He wheeled and his right arm rose toward Ben. From 20 feet Ben found himself staring down the muzzle of a .38 caliber automatic. As he rushed headlong, closing the remaining distance, fire erupted from the gun's ugly snout and searing lead tore through Ben's flesh.

The woman screamed as Ben's momentum sent him crashing into her and the attacker. The woman fell away from the two men. The combined force of their bodies slammed them into the open van door, springing its hinges. The enraged attacker bellowed. The gun fell from his right hand and bounced across the sidewalk toward the woman. She recoiled in horror. Both of Ben's hands flew for the assailant's throat, but strength had already begun to drain from his arms. Viciously, the attacker kneed Ben's groin. As Ben crumpled moaning, the assailant drove a fist squarely between Ben's eyes, knocking him backward to the pavement. The punch was doubly painful because it drove Ben's glasses into the bridge of his nose, splayed the earpieces and sent the wire-rimmed lenses skittering across the sidewalk. Blood from the gash began running into Ben's eyes and down both sides of his nose.

In reaction to the gunshot and the woman's screams, doors and windows were flying open along the street. Ben heard someone yell, "Police! Police!"

The assailant eyed the gun, hesitated, but left it on the sidewalk. He scrambled into the rusting van, twisted the ignition key and sped away. Ben squinted, trying to read the license number, but failed. He could feel blood dripping from his chin and then saw a patch of blood spreading on his jacket. His breath laboring, he rolled onto his side and craned his neck, looking with blurred vision for Mrs. Stock and Sarah.

On her hands and knees, the young woman edged toward Ben. At the sight of the spreading blood, she paled. She forced herself to cradle Ben's head, the blood from his cut nose dripping onto her hands, and whispered to him to be still.

CHAPTER 79

Saturday morning, Jeff, as was his habit, arose early. Quietly he slipped out of bed and put on his bathrobe. As he cinched it, Jeff looked at his wife. Suni was sleeping peacefully, her visage the essence of innocence. Jeff smiled. Suni had told him he looked that way when sleeping. Hard to believe, he reflected, that I could ever look innocent.

Briefly, Jeff thought of his mother, Alice. If she was harboring resentment toward Suni, she was masking it well. Which, Jeff smiled again, was to her benefit because he had been clearer than he had ever imagined he could be in articulating his expectations for his mother with regard to her relationship with Suni and any children they might have.

Jeff eased from the room and headed for the kitchen. He plugged in a coffeemaker he had filled last night.

Jeff walked across the living room to the apartment entrance. He opened the door, stooped and picked up *The New York Times*. He walked back to the kitchen and scanned the front page while waiting for the coffee to finish perking. He opened a cupboard and got a large brown mug that bore the words Morning Calm. It was a gift Suni had purchased for him soon after he brought her from Korea, The Land of the Morning Calm. The lettering was her touch.

He poured coffee and sat at the kitchen table. He savored the hearty brew. Leisurely, he was paging through the paper. Several minutes later a headline caught his attention:

Man shot rescuing woman
from would-be abductor

I'll be, Jeff mused. Someone must have decided to get involved. Jeff's eyes began moving down the column of copy. They stopped and blinked twice in disbelief. Feverishly Jeff finished reading the account.

"Visiting hours don't start till after lunch, but I wouldn't take no for an answer," Jeff said as Ben shifted gingerly in the hospital bed.

"You must have been pretty persuasive."

"Told them my dad is on their board of trustees – which happens to be true."

Ben laughed and winced.

"Hey, take it easy, " Jeff said worriedly.

"I'll try not to laugh."

"I'll try not to make you laugh."

"Nah, that's all right. In fact, after last night I can use a good laugh. How did you learn I was here? Mrs. Stock call you?"

"Read it in the paper. You know, I have to tell you, as far as news goes, you picked a piss poor time to be a hero. Who reads Saturday papers except us news junkies? And then *The Times* all but buried it. The city gets a genuine hero and they stick the story inside. And you didn't make TV last night."

"How do you know?"

"I did some checking."

"You what?" Ben said incredulously.

"Well, I was curious," Jeff said defensively. "Suni and I were out last night, so after I saw the paper this morning, I called a couple stations and asked if they ran the story. Nothing. I asked why. The guy on duty this morning didn't know but he probably guessed right. 'No good pictures, maybe.' That's what he said, 'no good pictures.' Dammit, this story deserves to be on TV. We hear so damn much about people not getting involved."

"Yeah, well," Ben said dryly, "if people saw this story, nobody might get involved again. Get involved and get shot," he said, mimicking an advertising announcer. "I don't think many will buy it."

"Maybe, but I still was tempted to tell them to get their butts over here and interview you."

Ben eyed his friend warily. "You didn't, did you?"

"No, but maybe they'll do a follow-up today anyhow. They got the guy, you know. Later last night."

"How do you know?"

"*The Times* story," said Jeff. "The guy had an arrest record as long as one of Fidel Castro's speeches. His specialties seem to be robberies and sex offenses."

"I guess that explains his motive last night. He sure doesn't have many smarts."

"The guy's a bubblebrain. He'd escaped from a mental hospital before Christmas. You remember the movie, *The Collector*?" Ben nodded. "Well, this guy's apparently like the whacko in the movie. He studied the comings and goings of his victims. Geez, it makes you shudder to know that crazies like that are on the streets."

"How'd they catch him so fast last night?"

"Luck. One of the neighbors on 71st heard the shot and looked outside. He gave the police a description of the van and a partial license number. Mrs. Stock gave them the full number. He didn't get very far."

"Oh, damn, I better give Mrs. Stock a call. See how she's doing. And Barb, I need to check on her."

"No need," said Jeff. "I checked on Barb, and Mrs. Stock is doing fine. I called her before I came over. You know," Jeff said blushing, "just to see if there was anything I could do."

"Uh-huh. Does she know you're here?"

"Yeah."

"No change in Barb?"

"No."

"How's Sarah?"

"Just fine," Jeff said reassuringly. "Mrs. Stock is bringing her around this afternoon. In fact, if you don't mind, Suni and I will bring them over."

"That's fine. I appreciate it."

"Is there anything I can do for you? Anything at all?"

"Keep checking on Barb. Other than that, no thanks. You heard how the woman is doing?"

"She's fine. A few bruises and scratches. Mrs. Stock talked with her after the ambulance took you away. She was pretty shaken up. Fortunately her husband was home. Mrs. Stock said they were both grateful beyond words."

"Did you catch her name?"

"Emery. Gloria Emery."

A nurse's aide pushed open the door. She was carrying a large bouquet of mixed flowers. She asked after Ben and left. Jeff handed Ben the card. It read: *Thank you seems so inadequate, but we do thank you from the bottom of our hearts. You are in our prayers. If you don't mind, we would like to visit you this afternoon. Very sincerely, Gloria and Andrew Emery."*

"Very thoughtful," said Ben.

"You know," Jeff said, trying to lighten the mood but obviously concerned, "I thought you might have learned your lesson about guns in Korea."

"Guess I'm a slow learner."

"Try something like this again and you might flunk out."

Ben smiled. "Who knows? Maybe this sort of thing was inevitable."

"Huh?"

"Well, my dad and both my brothers stopped bullets." Ben smiled wryly. "Maybe it's just a family trait."

"Not one worth passing on. Look, I better get going. You need some rest."

"I'm going home tonight," Ben said quietly but firmly.

"What?"

"I just decided. It's a clean wound. No complications. The shoulder will mend just as well at home as here."

"Man, oh, man, I've heard of stupidity, but that gets a blue ribbon. Besides, your doctor won't discharge you."

"Yes, he will. He won't like it but he will. And don't worry. I can rest at home, really. And I'll be a lot happier. Nothing beats high morale, right?"

"I suppose, but-"

"I can stop back here to have the wound checked. But I want to be with Sarah. I need to hold her, feel her life next to mine. Understand?"

Jeff nodded. "I hope you don't plan to come to work on Monday. Mr. Burson would have a fit."

Ben smiled indulgently. "No, I'll take a couple days off, just to keep you off my case."

"A week. At least a week."

"Okay. You know, my friend, it's funny. I mean the way things work out. Last night I almost didn't do anything. I saw what was happening and I froze. Just froze. I couldn't help thinking about Barb and Sarah. I didn't see his gun till he turned on me. If I'd seen it, I wonder what I'd've done. I think I might have settled for getting the license number and calling the cops. Except...except then maybe it would have been too late. Too late for Gloria Emery." Ben shook his head in self-reproach. "You know, I guess I was lucky, damned lucky."

"So," said Jeff, "was Gloria Emery."

CHAPTER 80

"You are very quiet tonight," Suni said to Jeff. "Is everything all right?"

"Umm, yeah, I guess so. Actually, I've been thinking."

"Do you want to tell me your thoughts?"

Jeff blew out a breath. "I don't know. It seems kind of foolish."

"Perhaps," said Suni, "but I have not known you to have many foolish thoughts."

Jeff decided to tell Suni what had been troubling him. She listened quietly, attentively. When he had finished, he looked at Suni. "Well, what do you think? Is it foolish?"

"I do not think it's foolish, but I am not sure how wise it is. I am not surprised that you have thought of this, because you are a kind man. But I do not know if enough time has passed. And there are complications."

"Yeah," said Jeff, "that bothers me too."

"I am afraid this must be your decision alone."

"Yeah." Jeff glanced at the telephone. Two weeks had passed since Ben had been shot. His recovery had been swift, thanks to his youth and fitness. He still wore a sling, but that would be off in a couple days. Barb's vital signs had strengthened but she hadn't regained consciousness. Jeff reached for the phone and dialed.

"Hello?"

"Hi, Mrs. Stock. This is Jeff. How are you?"

"Just fine, Jeff. And you?"

"Oh, fine."

"Would you like to speak to Ben?"

"Yes, please."

"Just a moment."

Ben came to the phone. "Hi, Jeff. How goes it?"

"Fine, fine. Say, Suni and I have been thinking. We'd like to celebrate your recuperation. You doing anything for dinner next Saturday?"

"Nothing special. I think my otherwise jammed social calendar must just be open that night. Unless Barb regains consciousness…"

"Right. I understand. Well, look, Suni will prepare something special. Can you be here about seven-thirty?"

"Can do."

Jeff then thumbed through his personal address and phone diary. He swallowed a measure of anxiety and dialed again.

"Hello." the voice on the other end answered.

"Natalie?"

"Yes."

"This is Jeff Zink. How are you?" Jeff could feel sweat forming in his armpits.

"Fine, Jeff. How are you and Suni?"

"Oh, fine. We're both just fine. Listen, Suni and I were talking and we'd like you to come over for dinner again."

"Wow, this is certainly a surprise. Actually, I owe you an invitation."

"Who's counting? We just were remembering how much we enjoyed our last get-together, and we'd like to do it again. Suni really likes you. And besides, she has some special dishes she'd like to try out. She-" Jeff caught a stern, reproving glance from Suni. "We'd really like you to join us."

"You make it very difficult to say no. Not that I want to. I enjoyed our visit very much."

"Then that settles it. How about next Saturday?"

"All right."

"Can you be here at seven?"

"Yes."

"Great!"

"Do you want me to bring Vickie again?"

"Uh, well, that's up to you. It might be kinda late when we finish."

"I understand. I'll leave her with Kate."

"Great. See you then."

They hung up. Jeff looked sheepishly at Suni, pursed his lips and rolled his eyes upward. "At least my intentions are honorable."

Nervously, Jeff was pacing the living room floor. He glanced at his watch. 7:05. Suni was busy in the kitchen. Jeff walked to the living room window and looked down. No cab. Of course, he thought, maybe she walked. It's not that far, only about a dozen blocks. 7:10. The buzzer sounded. Jeff whirled from the window and hurried across the room. He spoke into the speaker. "Natalie?"

"Yes."

"Come on up."

Jeff and Suni greeted Natalie at the door. She wore a simple yellow dress, white cardigan and brown pumps.

"You look terrific," Jeff gushed.

"Thank you. Hello, Suni. It's very nice to see you again."

"Thank you, Natalie. Please come in."

"Sit down," Jeff said, motioning toward the living room.

"Thanks, but, Suni, can I help you in the kitchen?"

"Oh, no. You sit down and be comfortable. I have everything in order."

Jeff asked about Vickie, and Natalie chatted happily about her, now just a year old and passing rapidly from infancy to toddlerhood. Natalie was animated and relaxed. Jeff was tense. He looked at his watch. 7:20. Sometimes, Jeff reflected, time just absolutely refuses to budge. The buzzer sounded and to Jeff it seemed like a cannon shot. He leaped up.

"Were you expecting someone else?" Natalie asked.

"Uh, yeah," Jeff answered, moving toward the speaker. "Another friend." His armpits were sweating again. Jeff spoke into the speaker, "Come on up." Nervously, he walked back toward the living room.

"You didn't mention a friend," Natalie said.

"Oh, well, a good friend. Suni and I thought it might be fun to have friends over." Jeff felt his throat tightening and was wondering whether his voice was betraying his anxiety. "It's something we wanted to do. I hope you don't mind." Every time Jeff said "we" he felt a pang of guilt; Suni had not opposed his idea, but she hadn't participated in or supported the decision. Jeff forced a nervous half smile.

"No," Natalie said, "it's fine with me. I like to meet new people."

At this moment Jeff was half-wishing he was somewhere else. Anywhere else. The idea still seemed like a good one; he was just wishing he could observe the implementation from afar. "I'll be back in a minute." He walked to the kitchen, out of Natalie's view, and sighed deeply. Suni was eyeing him. He shrugged.

A rap at the door. Jeff swallowed, squared his shoulders, and left the kitchen. Natalie was rising. "Just stay there," Jeff said. "I'll get it." He opened the door. "Hi."

"Hi." Ben stepped inside, shaking Jeff's hand.

Natalie went pale. A cold shiver worked its way down her spine. Oh, Jeff, she was thinking, how could you? How *could* you? I'm not ready for this, not at all.

Then Ben saw her. He looked at Jeff and then his head snapped back toward Natalie in an involuntary double take.

Jeff, pushing the door closed, saw all too clearly the looks of utter astonishment. "I know what you're both thinking," Jeff blurted. "What an absolutely puerile, unforgivable stunt. But I thought it was worth taking a chance of alienating two good friends of mine to bring two old friends back together. Knowing that you're both here in New York and considering everything else, I felt like I had to do it. I wouldn't blame either of you if you just walked out right now. I want you to know that. I wouldn't-"

"Shut up, Jeff," Ben ordered. He had started walking toward Natalie. He was silent, his face expressionless. He stopped in front of Natalie and without hesitating slipped his arms around her and hugged gently.

Natalie, eyes moistening, cautiously placed the palms of her hands against his sides.

Ben released her. "It's good to see you," he whispered.

Jeff was watching nervously but with the beginnings of relief. From the kitchen doorway, Suni was watching with concern.

In a choked voice she was barely able to control, Natalie murmured, "It's good to see you."

With no hint of a smile but with eyes that were twinkling merrily, Ben said, "Do you think we should take Jeff up on his apology and just walk out? That would be after drawing and quartering him."

Natalie brushed at her eyes. "He deserves it, but Suni doesn't. She's worked too hard in the kitchen."

"Agreed."

"But if he doesn't offer me a drink," Natalie said, her composure returning, "I may not make it till dinner."

"A drink," Jeff blurted, still wringing away anxiety with his hands, "of course, a drink. Ben, I know you'll take a scotch. Natalie?"

"Do you have vodka?"

"Yes, of course."

"Make it a double, straight."

"I'll be right there," said Jeff, hustling off to a small side table where he kept liquors and wines.

"I guess we should sit down," said Ben.

"Before my knees collapse," said Natalie, her smile still somewhat weak.

"This is awkward. And I'm not sure how to make it unawkward."

"I don't know either," said Natalie. "Maybe we shouldn't try. I mean, trying might make it worse."

"I think you're right," said Ben. "You know, I almost just said, 'How have you been?' Somehow it doesn't seem appropriate."

"I know what you mean. I'm very sorry about your wife. How is she?"

"Not much change. She's breathing on her own. But still not conscious. Still hoping." Ben paused and then added, "Did you know about this?" He pointed to his shoulder.

"About what?"

"Uh-huh. I see our friend Jeff hasn't been dispensing much information."

Jeff brought their drinks. To no one's surprise, the cocktail conversation and the dinner talk never did achieve a truly comfortable level. The initial awkwardness diminished, but an underlying tension precluded the kind of uninhibited discussion so beautiful to observe among old friends.

Eventually, toward the end of dinner, the conversation ventured timidly into the future. Careers were discussed, as was Suni's quest for U.S. citizenship. Senator Humphrey was willing to help expedite that. Natalie mentioned her imminent return to California and the strong possibility of Kate and Jake moving there as well.

Then, dessert and coffee finished, Suni rose to begin cleaning up.

"Let me help," Natalie offered.

"Oh, no, I cannot allow an honored guest to work in the kitchen."

"Please."

"No, no."

"Well, Suni," said Natalie, "you prepared a marvelous meal. You are a wonderful cook. Jeff is very lucky. In many respects."

"You can say that again," Jeff agreed self-deprecatingly.

"It's getting late," Natalie said. "I think I'd better be going. I want to pick up Vickie early in the morning."

"I'll take you home," Ben offered matter-of-factly.

Jeff was beginning to feel relieved. Maybe this wasn't disastrous after all. *I don't know what Ben might say when we're alone, but I can handle any dressing down.*

"Oh, that's not necessary," said Natalie. "Besides, it's out of your way; you live just up the street."

"To be honest," said Ben, and it seemed a moment suitable for complete honesty, "I don't think I could simply walk two blocks down the street, hit the sack and go to sleep. I'm a little too keyed up for that. If you're not too tired, let me walk you home. It'll do me good."

"All right."

In the elevator, they descended in a silence that seemed not atypically awkward, given the worldwide tendency of people to lose their wits and tongues in elevators.

Outside, they began walking. Natalie shivered.

"Would you like my jacket?" Ben asked.

"No, thanks. I'll be okay in a minute, as soon as my blood starts circulating."

They walked on at an unhurried pace.

"I can hardly believe what Jeff did," Natalie finally said. She looked at Ben and smiled tentatively. "Did you notice how nervous he was?"

Ben grinned warmly. "I'm sure he had mixed feelings all night. I'll bet right now he and Suni are discussing it."

"I'm glad he did it," Natalie said, looking straight ahead, just in front of her feet.

"Me too."

They again lapsed into silence. Both their minds were a welter of past memories, good ones, bad ones, happy ones, sad ones. None seemed the kind they could bring themselves to share with each other. A few minutes later Natalie said, "My building's just down the street."

Ben nodded.

The doorman greeted Natalie. "Goodnight, John," she replied. She and Ben walked through the lobby, harshly lighted and painted off-white, to the elevators.

"Well," said Natalie, smiling thinly, "it was a nice evening."

"Yes, it was. Memorable."

"Good night."

"Good night."

Ben turned and began walking. He had gone only a few steps.

"Ben, wait," Natalie said quietly.

He turned. She approached.

"Yes?" he said.

"Ben, I - there's something I have to ask you." The hurt of pain remembered dimmed her eyes. "Something I need to know."

"Sure. Go ahead."

"Why didn't you answer my telegram?"

"What telegram?"

"You know, the one I sent when you were in Korea."

"I never got a telegram from you."

"What? You remember. You sent me a telegram. You know, the one that-"

"I remember."

"I answered it with a telegram."

He shrugged. "I never got it. Honest."

"I...I don't understand. It never came back. It must have been delivered."

"Army," Ben muttered. "Anything could and did happen. Sorry, but I never got it."

Natalie felt her eyes beginning to mist. She fought back the encroaching tears. Ben sensed something had gone terribly amiss. He put his hands on her shoulders. "Do you want to tell me what it said?"

"Not now. Maybe sometime. But not now."

"All right."

"I think I'd better go up," she whispered, her eyes blinking. "Good night."

"Good night."

Natalie turned away.

"Oh, Nat," Ben said. "Wait." She turned. "You're planning to go back to California." She nodded. "It depends, but maybe I'll see you out there."

"I don't understand," she murmured, her eyes still glistening through wet film.

"I guess you haven't heard the big news."

CHAPTER 81

Three mornings later, on a Tuesday, the bedside alarm clock jolted Ben awake. It was six o'clock. As was his custom since Barbara's accident, he immediately went to check on Sarah. Then he padded to the bathroom.

A few minutes later his face was covered with lather, and the phone rang. It startled him. He put down the razor and half ran to the bedroom phone. It wasn't yet 6:15.

"Hello," he said, feeling a too familiar tightness in his chest.

The hospital nurse on the other end of the line could sense Ben's anxiety. By now, through his daily visits, she and the rest of the staff had gotten to know him. She also was very aware of the early hour, and she knew how phones ringing late at night or early in the morning frightened worried spouses to the point of panic. "Ben?' she said, wanting to be sure.

"Yes."

"This is Nurse Tortelli."

CHAPTER 82

On this July Saturday in 1971, the sky was a canopy of royal blue and the sun a brilliant orb. Together they intensified the festive, expectant attitude of the guests. All knew full well that this was a very special wedding.

The view from Wayfarer's Chapel was breathtaking. The chapel itself was inspiring. Redwood columns and beams supported an all-glass ceiling and walls. In siting and designing the chapel, famed architect Frank Lloyd Wright had blended man and his elements simply and harmoniously.

The chapel sat atop a high hill on the Palos Verdes Peninsula south of Los Angeles. Lush green trees and bushes shared the hilltop with the glass church. Far below, high cliffs dropped to the azure Pacific. Lazy swells were rolling against the rocky shoreline and foaming gently. From high above, they were silent.

Dick stood before the altar. He was wearing the most elegant and expensive suit he had ever owned. Never had he looked or felt more handsome. Never had he felt happier. He did not try in the least to suppress the mirthful grin. Proudly he looked at his bride-to-be.

Never did a bride look prettier or happier. She wore a simple yet elegant white dress. White gloves and shoes complemented the dress exquisitely and contrasted sharply with her dark hair. Maria Santiago had helped select everything. Lee Chong Hee peered raptly into Dick's green eyes.

Their hands touched lightly and clasped gently. Solemnly, a minister addressed the gathering and began the ceremony.

Beside Dick stood his best man, Ben, chosen because he had introduced the groom to the bride two and a half years earlier at an Army compound on the far side of the Pacific. Today, the two ships that seemed to have passed but once were anchored at last in the same port. The splendor of the occasion was reflected in the visages of all present.

Beside Lee Chong Hee stood Maria. As Chong had no family or friends in America, Dick had asked her whether it would be all right for Maria to serve as matron of honor. Chong had agreed enthusiastically. Maria was beaming, happy for Chong and ecstatic for Dick, her beloved friend for a quarter century.

Behind the couple stood John. Dick had asked him to give the bride away. Moments earlier, when John had escorted Chong down the aisle, he felt as proud as he had when he had accompanied Jeannie Marie, Ruth and Kate on their wedding days.

There was only one usher, Jeff. His selection was Ben's suggestion. Jeff was a friend of Chong, and Ben knew he would be pleased and proud to participate. Suni was similarly pleased. In the days before the wedding, she and Chong grew close.

Some of the guests were very special. Dick's stepmother Harriet and his half-sister Susie and her family were there from Shelby. Ben's daughter, little Sarah Lawrence, was in Harriet's arms. The Santiago sisters – all four of them – were there, Jeannie Marie and Ruth with their husbands and children, Kate pregnant, Jake, and Natalie with Vickie.

Also there was an elderly but still very erect former brigadier general. His once gray hair still was close cropped but now was white – as was the mustache he had sported for 35 years. Henry Briggs was 72. As the minister conducted the ceremony, Henry's memory began to wander. A small smile began to form under the mustache. Henry found himself thinking back to that June day in Tokyo in 1950, when he had all but forced Dick to roll out of bed in the predawn to join him on their ill-fated weekend jaunt to Korea. Henry found it incredible that that misadventure, in some ways tragic, had led to this joyful occasion. He offered a quick prayer of thanks that he was alive to witness what he regarded as the ironically perfect punctuation to that turbulent, memorable time.

Beside Henry sat a couple in their late sixties. Henry shifted slightly and gazed tenderly at the tiny woman at his elbow. When Dick had gone to Korea to ask Miss Lee to marry him, and after she had accepted, they had journeyed to a small farm north of Seoul. Mr. and Mrs. Yoon had been euphoric to see Dick and learn of his engagement to Miss Lee. When Dick invited them to attend the wedding, the Yoons were deeply honored but frightened by the prospect of such a long trip to a strange land. After all, they were old and never had been more than a few miles from their home. Besides, such a long journey would be entirely beyond their small means. Dick would pay; there would be no debating that. He had been very persuasive, all but insisting they come. Now, their decision thrilled them. The trip had been captivating beyond their dreams. They considered it a great blessing that would lift their spirits on the day they left this earth.

Next to the Yoons sat a man, bald and bespectacled but still trim at age 47. With him was his wife. When he had read the wedding invitation, memories came rushing to the surface. Sitting in a chair, he had leaned forward, held his head in his hands and shook it slowly back and forth. He didn't try to stem his tears. Warren Maxwell, Bill Lawrence's buddy and at his side on Omaha Beach, immediately had made plans to travel from San Francisco to Los Angeles.

To some of the guests, it no doubt seemed as though everyone important to Dick and Ben was there. Of course, they weren't. Not their father Edward, not Dick's mother Sarah, and brother Bill. Not Ben's friend Gerry Graham, wasted by cancer. Not Dan Cohen, his life extinguished in a freak but bloody incident that would scarcely be a footnote to history. Not Barbara Mason Lawrence. Not long before the wedding, in the New York hospital early in the morning, Barbara's eyes had opened. Several times. Upon seeing Ben, she had smiled weakly. Her future still was uncertain. But when Ben had mentioned Dick's pending wedding to Chong, Barbara had smiled. Then she spoke her first word since the attack. It was a whispered "Go."

The night before the wedding Ben had slept little. I've never missed Barbara more, he'd reflected. I'd love to touch her, hear her voice, feel her enthusiasm. It's so contagious. I so much want her here with me. Today Ben had awakened still blue, but his spirits had begun to rebound as the morning wore on and the ceremony neared.

Helen Wakefield Hoerner wasn't at the wedding. Last December, the day after Barbara's accident, Dick had visited Helen. She had voiced her feelings softly and tenderly but clearly. Yes, Roger was dead, but she wasn't free. Not yet, and she wasn't sure when that would be. "You will always be in my heart, Dick. Always. Your whole family."

The wedding ceremony was drawing to a close. The minister paused and looked first at Chong, then at Dick. "I now pronounce you husband and wife."

Dick needed no cue. He turned and kissed Chong. The guests broke into sustained applause. Then Dick and Chong turned and started toward the rear of the chapel. A few paces and Dick stopped. The applause subsided. He smiled at Chong, then stepped to the side of the aisle. Simultaneously he shook hands with and hugged Henry Briggs. Then he leaned farther into the pew and kissed Mrs. Yoon. Then, as he shook hands with Mr. Yoon, the chapel erupted again with exuberant applause. It grew even more exultant when Warren Maxwell leaned toward the aisle and he and Dick clasped hands.

The procession continued, with the guests clapping and dabbing at moistened eyes. The warmth and openness engendered by Dick's show of affection for his elderly guests had carried over outside. In the receiving line inhibition found little room. Hugs and kisses were shared with scarcely tempered joy. Chong had been told to expect warm congratulations, but she had never seen adult, sober Americans manifesting such barely restrained elation. She was surprised to find herself being swept up by the obvious affection and responding in kind.

It took a while, but eventually the assemblage began heading for their cars. All had been invited to a reception at Dick's Westwood home.

Natalie was carrying Vickie. As she started toward the parking lot, she saw Ben step away from the departing gathering. He walked to the point where the hilltop fell away down a steep slope toward the road below and the cliffs beyond. He stood, hands jammed into his trouser pockets, gazing out to sea.

"Kate," Natalie said, "would you take Vickie? I'll catch up in a minute."

"Sure, I'll see you at the car."

Natalie started walking toward Ben. If at that moment someone had asked her why she had decided to go to him, she would have been stumped. She knew only that an impulse was drawing her to him. She, too, looked toward the cliffs below and the blue horizon beyond. Natalie was silent a long moment, then spoke softly. "It was a lovely ceremony."

"Yes, it was." Ben was surprised to find Natalie at his side.

"I can't tell you how happy I am for Dick," said Natalie.

"Me, too. He deserves it."

"This is a lovely view, isn't it?"

"Yes, I've never seen one more beautiful."

"Well," she said, shifting her eyes toward Ben, "I guess we'd better head for the cars. Okay? They're waiting for us."

Ben still was looking straight ahead. "Nat?"

"Yes, Ben?"

"I guess you're set on staying in California."

"Yes, I think so."

"I don't blame you," he said. "It's beautiful here."

"When are you going back to New York?"

"Tomorrow."

"I understand."

"I wish I did. Everything, I mean."

In profile, Natalie could see puzzlement in his face. She also thought she might be seeing hurt. "What do you mean?"

"Well, I do have to go back to New York. That's for sure. But I'm wondering whether we should stay. There, I mean. Or whether we would even want to. That's if Barb makes it all the way back. It's a lot not to be sure about."

Natalie hesitated before saying anything more. She was far from certain what Ben was thinking and she feared hurting or upsetting him. "If you didn't stay," she said tentatively, "in New York, I mean, where would you go?"

"I'm not sure about that either," Ben said. "I guess a lot will depend on Barb and what she needs and wants. Like you said, this is a lovely view. It's hard to imagine a nicer one."

"Do you think," she said so softly he could barely hear her, "that you might like to try living here? In California? I mean, it would be so nice if we all could see each other now and then."

"I don't know. Maybe. Nat," he said, exhaling strongly, "I've got to ask you something. That telegram you sent, the one I never got, you never told me what was in it. I think I'd like to know. Actually, I think I need to know."

Her eyes held his, then lowered. "I said I was sorry for…everything. I…" She shook her head.

"Hey, that's okay." Ben put a hand on her shoulder. "That tells me plenty. We better head for the cars or they'll be sending a posse." His other hand raised her chin. "Maybe one day we can come back here and talk again."

Epilogue

2006

This year marked the 100th anniversary of Henry Lawrence's death when dragged and kicked by a team of horses.

Dick Lawrence, age 84, and Chong, 62, still live in his big house in Westwood. They have two daughters and a son. Dick no longer visits Shelby, but occasionally goes to Palisades Park and gazes at the pier and carousel where he and Ann Sheridan cavorted more than a half century ago.

Dick remains in touch with Warren Maxwell. They meet once a year on June 6 to toast Bill Lawrence.

Barbara Lawrence recovered, and she and Ben had a second daughter, Harriet. They still live in Manhattan's Upper East Side but in a townhouse. Ben heads his own public relations firm. In 1987, Ben flew to Cleveland where he visited Gerry Graham's grave. Looking down at the headstone, Ben murmured, "Gerry, this isn't doing you a damn bit of good, but it's doing a lot for me." Every Memorial Day, Ben places a wreath at Dan Cohen's grave in Queens. Each time, Ben murmurs the same words: "Loyalty matters." In 2008, Ben and Barbara are planning to return to Shelby for their class's 45-year reunion.

Mrs. Anne Stock babysat for the Lawrence daughters through their mid-teens and remained close to Ben and Barbara until her death in 2004 at age 94.

Won Kyong Pok continued working at the bank in Seoul. She married and gave birth to two daughters. By the mid-1990s, she was a senior executive. In 1999, while attending a conference of the World Bank in New York, she phoned Ben. They had lunch. It was a happy reunion.

Jeff Zink and Suni have two sons. The first joined the Peace Corps and worked in Korea. Later, he became a senior Peace Corps administrator in Washington, D.C. The second son became a fireman and died in the World Trade Center collapse on September 11, 2001. Alice Zink doted on both boys. She died in 2003.

In 1976 in Chicago, Casey McDermott's wife left him when she learned he was having an affair with his secretary. Casey married another woman, who left him when she learned he was having an affair with a neighbor. His two children no longer see him.

Henry Briggs died in 1977, and Dick attended his funeral in Phoenix.

Natalie Santiago never married. She still lives in a small house on Glenmont in Westwood, not far from the family home where Maria still lives. Her father, John, suffered a fatal heart attack in 1982. In 1996, Natalie invited Dick and Ben and Barbara to Vickie's wedding. All three attended. Vickie, now 37, lives in Westlake Village, northwest of LA. She is an English professor at Pepperdine University in Malibu and has published several articles, including one in *The Kenyon Review.* Vickie never met her father; Evan Sloane was presumed drowned when his sailboat was found drifting empty in 1973.

Mr. and Mrs.Yoon died barely a year apart, he in 1988 and she in 1989. Save for walks to the local market, they never again left their farm. On a wall they kept a framed photo of them with Dick and Henry taken at Dick and Suni's wedding.

Hubert Humphrey passed away on January 13, 1978, at age 67. He is buried in Lakewood Cemetery in Minneapolis, Minnesota. In attendance at his funeral were Jeff and Suni Zink.

ACKNOWLEDGEMENTS

I owe special debts of gratitude to Lynne Haley Johnson, my wife of 37 years, who was extremely encouraging in this endeavor, and to Laura Iskra, my friend of 27 years. Both Lynne and Laura were very helpful in preparing the *Fate of the Warriors* manuscript for publication.

As the book neared completion, I was considering the question of a title. There were several possibilities, and I decided to explore them with a diverse group of friends who enjoy reading and whom I know to be thoughtful. I presented them with several possible titles, and they replied with thoughtful opinions. I am very grateful for their thinking. They are: Linda Bayman, Wadsworth, Ohio; Ken Berger, Lexington, Ohio; Dick Berry, Columbus, Ohio; Peter Bloomfield, Petworth, England; Dave Bowes, Keedysville, Maryland; Jan Catherwood, Titusville, Florida; Deb Broka Coulson, Weatherford, Texas; Rod Covey, North Canton, Ohio; Sharon Dillon, Williamsburg, Virginia; Jon Elsasser, Zoar, Ohio; Sara Bliss Enders, Mooresville, North Carolina; Bob Gardner, Reston, Virginia; Lynda Blair Glover, Phenix City, Alabama; Mel Helitzer, Athens, Ohio; Bill Henson, Sierra Vista, Arizona; Jodi Hutchison, Madison, New Jersey; Trudy Cox Jacobs, Shelby, Ohio; Andrea Johnson, Columbus, Ohio; Lynne Haley Johnson, North Canton, Ohio; Jean Riley Lash, Shelby, Ohio; Jodi Seaton Lowery, San Mateo, California; Jeff McKinney, Jackson, Ohio; Heather Maurer, Springfield, Ohio; Dee Dee Milligan Oman, Aurora, Ohio; Dick Parrish, Shelby, Ohio; Russ Pfahler, Sun Lakes, Arizona; Elaine Russell-Reolfi, North Canton, Ohio; Jason Saragian, Perrysburg, Ohio; Anne Lafferty Stock, Vermilion, Ohio; Lorraine Straw, Grand Rapids, Michigan; John Travers, Gaffney, South Carolina; Bob Tull, Lincolnton, North Carolina; Marzena Witek, Sosnowiec, Poland; Xiaoli Yuan, Taipei, Taiwan.

Special note: the portrayal of supporting character Gerry Graham is based on the life of my friend, Andrew Donald Blank, 1945-1968. His life and an incident in the Korean DMZ inspired *Fate of the Warriors*.

ROSTER OF REAL-LIFE PEOPLE

- Al Bourgeois
- General Charles Bonesteel
- Commander Lloyd Bucher
- Harold Burson
- Professor Stanley Fisher
- Father Albert Fate
- Dave Gump
- Fireman Duane Hodges (his corpse)
- Lieutenant Commander George Hoffman
- Senator Hubert Humphrey
- Kim Il Sung
- Doctor Wilson Kingsboro
- Charlotte Lingo
- Father Michael McFadden
- Major General Pak Chun Kuk
- Ann Sheridan
- Lieutenant Colonel Brad Smith
- Harryet Snyder
- Jerry Wilson
- Major General Gilbert Woodward

SOURCES

- Academy Foundation (Ann Sheridan biographical information)
- Building Bridges of Understanding - Koreans. Brigham Young University Language Research Center
- The Building of a Parish – The History of Shelby's Catholic Community – Heinz Frankl - 1976
- Inchon - the movie
- Instructions for American Servicemen in Britain 1942 - War Department
- Korea - Contrast and Harmony. Korea Overseas Information Service, 1980
- Korea - Freedom's Frontier. United States Forces Korea, 1967
- Korea. Korea Overseas Information Service, 1977
- Letter of apology by the United States of America to the Democratic Peoples' Republic of Korea, December 23, 1968
- MacArthur's War – Korea and the Undoing of an American Hero. Stanley Weintraub.
- One Bugle No Drums – The Marines at Chosin Reservoir. William B. Hopkins
- Stars & Stripes stories.
- United Press International. "Disney Finds Missing Mouseketeers" by Vernon Scott
- USS Corry – on-line history
- Walt Disney Treasures: The Mickey Mouse Club. October 3 – October 7, 1955. DVD
- Walt, Mickey & Me - Paul Peterson

Printed in the United States
78519LV00005B/52-99